Tower Over Me

To all those who have ever felt caged in their own life.

DOMINIQUE SIMONA BINGGELI

TOWER OVER ME

Bibliographical Information of the Deutsche Nationalbibliothek:
This publication is listed in the Deutsche Nationalbibliographie of the Deutsche Nationalbibliothek; detailed bibliographical information can be accessed under http://dnb.dnb.de abrufbar.

The automated analysis of the work to extract information, particularly patterns, trends and correlations in accordance with § 44b UrhG („Text and Data Mining") is prohibited.

© 2024 Dominique Simona Binggeli

Publisher: BoD · Books on Demand GmbH, In de Tarpen 42, 22848 Norderstedt
Print: Libri Plureos GmbH, Friedensallee 273, 22763 Hamburg

ISBN: 978-3-7597-8766-8

THANK YOU

A big thank you goes out to my husband, René, who had to endure my constant daydreaming during our world trip and the fact that most of my attention was reserved for this book.

He also designed the cover according to my imagination – better even – and even managed to read *Tower Over Me*, despite not being a passionate reader.

Another big thank you goes to my mom – the first person who read my book. She finished it in three days, despite reading the word file on her phone.

I really appreciate her honest and constructive feedback.

PROLOGUE

The sky was a mixture of shades of gray and white. Little snowflakes were starting to fall. Slowly, dancing lazily through the air. All noise was muffled and seemed far away. Only his heavy breathing close to her ear and her own heartbeat were clearly audible.

Alice knew she had goose bumps on her bare arms, and she felt the icy touch of the flakes landing on her skin, immediately melted by the warmth of her body. Yet she didn't feel that cold.

Her breathing became slower.

With every step he took, he softly rocked her to sleep. Her eyelids got heavier. Her hands and feet felt numb. Was it because of the cold?

Her belly was warm though. There was a fire inside her, but the burning sensation seemed to disappear steadily, fading out like the flames of an unattended fire.

It wasn't hurting anymore.

He was whispering again. She could not understand him. He seemed so distant.

Her eyelids fell shut, but she forced them open quickly, scared of what might come in the darkness.

It was nice to be held by him, facing upward, toward the white sky. Even though the light blinded her, she enjoyed watching the snowflakes dance. They looked so joyful.

She couldn't remember the last time she had looked at snowflakes like that. She could not even remember the last time she had been outside.

The air was so fresh and rich with scents. She could smell trees and earth. Wet soil and fern. Even moss.

Eager, she tried to inhale deeply, but her lungs protested, and the cold air pierced her chest, like tiny icicles stabbing through the membrane of her organs.

Her eyes wandered to his face, and she realized he was looking at her. His eyes were shiny and wet, glistening in the faint winter light.

Little droplets of sweat covered his forehead. Strands of his hair stuck to it. His jaw was clenched in agony and anger, so hard it seemed as though it was about to crush.

He looked mad, yet vulnerable.

Desperate.

She felt him move his hand slightly. His thumb began to softly move along the naked skin of her left arm. His fingers were rough against her skin, but not in an unpleasant way.

His hand was warm, but the gun it carried felt cold as ice.

Suddenly, the light disappeared, and Alice couldn't see the sky anymore.

They had gotten deeper into the woods. Dark branches of evergreen trees blocked the snowflakes from falling to the ground. The air felt warmer here. Moister. The ground appeared to be softer too. It was probably still covered in fallen autumn leaves.

She couldn't see them though. She wasn't able to turn her head.

His steps weren't shaking her so hard anymore. The rocking had gotten softer, and the lack of light made her even more tired.

Again, she felt her eyelids close. Her mind protested but was too weak to resist the drowsiness.

The movement stopped suddenly, and she seemed to be falling.

It was only him kneeling on the ground. He shifted her a bit on his lap and began to tap her cheek softly.

"Don't go." His voice was barely more than a whisper. Flat. Toneless. Broken.

Did he mean her? Where would she be going? She could not even move her legs.

She forced her eyes open once again. It cost her more effort than she would have thought.

One of his tears dripped down on her cheek. It felt warm on her skin. He took her left hand, which had been resting on the cold ground, and placed it on her belly.

Her fingers touched something wet and warm.

The blood.

With every drop, her life was running out of her body.

There were voices in the distance. Shouts.

"They're coming," she breathed.

1

The muffled voices fighting their way through both the closed bedroom door and living room door were lower than before, when Danny and his friends had been talking about the last football game they had watched. It meant they were talking about their secret business again. They always lowered their voices when discussing their precious business, and they would immediately stop talking if Alice entered the room.

She didn't think about doing that now, though. Nothing could make her go into the sticky, newly proclaimed *mancave* and face her boyfriend and his friends.

She was done with them. Done with trying to remain a valuable part of Danny's life anymore. Done with trying to get to know his *buddies* and be anything to them but an intruder in an apartment that once used to belong to just her and Danny.

Now, the men spent about every single day here, literally marking their territory by not only leaving behind an atmosphere thick with testosterone and menace, but also little yellow dots on the toilet seat.

Alice longed for some privacy like she once had longed for Danny's company. Times had changed, apparently. It was evident that her boyfriend had stowed away their relationship in a dusty box in the depths of his mind somewhere, like Alice did with the pictures that decorated their bedroom walls no more.

Practically spoken, they were a broken-up couple still sharing a bed, but admitting so hurt too much.

Despite his obvious dislike of her, Danny had made no attempts to leave or kick her out, and Alice was beginning to believe that he was slowly trying to create an environment in which she could no longer possibly exist. And his new friends seemed all too eager to support that plan.

Danny had only met them a couple of months prior, but ever since they had replaced Alice in being the most important part of his life.

Alice regretted having bought him that member card for a nearby gym to make him leave the house occasionally. He'd really clung to her after losing his job, and when he had begun complaining about gaining some weight Alice had grasped the opportunity to get some distance. Now, there was nothing *but* distance between them and what was worse: he had met his stupid friends at that gym.

Actually, he had only run into the guy named 'Tee' there, who'd then introduced him to his gang, Paul, Jonas, and the old guy, Waldo.

Alice did not know what else to call them but *gang*. They were equally built and shaped—muscly, tall, with broad shoulders and an even broader ego. She knew that Tee and Jonas worked as security guards in a mall, and Waldo was a former cop. Paul's job had not yet been revealed to her, but judging by his aggressive appearance, she figured he must be in a similar business. He was the only short guy of the group—but he seemed to want to make up for that by gaining width.

What had gotten into Danny to make him even talk to people like them was still an unsolved riddle to Alice. Danny had been a geek before he had met them. Quite tall with his six foot four, but his slender and quirky figure had never made him look threatening in any way. That had changed too, with his gym-obsession of the previous months and his apparent need to impress his new friends.

Dating someone who looked like a male model had never been Alice's intention. She also didn't need a boyfriend to protect her, but neither did she want to need someone to protect her from her boyfriend. Not to mention from his *bodyguards*—or hairless gorillas, as she liked to call them. Only out of earshot, of course. She wasn't suicidal.

Her friends weren't very supportive. Too blinded were they by Danny's now not only tall but also ripped body. Apparently, it had slipped their mind that his beautiful deep blue eyes, broad grin, and freckles had always been there. Sadder than about her friends' newly discovered shallowness was Alice about the fact that Danny's broad smile had not been directed at her in a very long time. What she received now were threats, sexist remarks, and occasionally, drunken attempts to have sex with her.

The latter occurred a bit too often for her taste these days. Danny's craving for booze had increased with the growth of his ego and the value of his clothes.

Where once black t-shirts with the lettering of metal bands had covered a flat chest, there were now blindingly white dress shirts stretched over firm breasts that Alice couldn't help but suspect were bigger than her own.

Danny's friends were different. Looks weren't why they worked out. Fights were. Whether beating up people was for fun or business, Alice didn't know. But those guys were drawn to fights like moths to a light bulb. And so it had happened more than once that they'd interfered in an argument between her and Danny. Waldo had once even told Alice to mind her tone.

Alice hated yelling just as much as she hated arguing in general, but raising her voice was often the only way to get Danny's attention.

An explanation for his change of personality had not left his lips yet. Losing his job and having to let her provide for him for a while had hurt his pride a little, but was it enough to excuse him being gone for days sometimes without telling her where he was or when he would be back? Was it the reason for his increased consumption of alcohol and war movies? Why he kept his friends around at all times?

Or maybe it was the secret business, allowing him to buy a Rolex and new flat-screen TV. Maybe the new personality had come as complimentary addition to the black leather shoes. Maybe, if you dressed like a nineteen-fifties gentleman's club owner, you had to act like one too.

A *gentleman's club*. What if *that* was the secret business?

Alice snorted disdainfully as the inevitable images flashed through her mind. Was that why Danny still kept her around? Maybe he wanted to tie her to a pole.

Alice's eyes flicked to the clock on the wall of her bedroom. It was a boring Sunday evening. Still quite early. Normally, she'd be huddled in a blanket on the couch, watching some superhero-movie. Now, the living room and everything that came with it were occupied. The small flat, they shared, was way too crowded.

As much as Alice wished to avoid the gang tonight, staring at the clock reminded her of the plumber who was supposed to have a look at the bathroom pipes the next morning. Since she would be at work Danny would have to let the guy or girl in.

Sighing, Alice got up from the bed, on which she had been sitting for about an hour, going through the pictures of her and Danny. They had once added some color to the walls, but Alice had torn them down in one of the rages that came with having to live with Danny's new personality. Alice put the pictures back in the old shoe box, which served to contain them, and shoved them back under the bed—where they again became a lurking monster, waiting to creep up on her at night.

A glance in the mirror revealed a pale, sleep-deprived face with dark shadows underneath dark eyes. Alice rubbed her eyes to make them look less puffy. She didn't need the men to know she had been shedding tears over Danny again. Her long dark hair was uncombed and messy, but it would suffice for an audience in the *mancave*, which had once been a clean and comfortable living room.

Alice pushed the door handle down slowly and carefully, and opened the door of the bedroom just a crack to be able to glance into the corridor. As expected, nobody was in the kitchen to her left or the bathroom to her right. Both were dark and empty. Light found its way through the narrow gap underneath the living room door and into the hallway. Along with it came the obnoxious noise of shots being fired, which indicated that the guys were playing some stupid war game again.

Alice chewed her lower lip and wondered if a note pinned to the door would suffice to inform Danny about the plumber appointment. But the risk of him being too drunk to read it was a big one and the pipes really needed fixing.

Taking a deep breath, Alice crossed the narrow corridor and came to a halt in front of the living room. She lifted her right hand to the door and hesitated, listening to the disgusting sound of war and wondering what kind of hell was awaiting her on the other side of the thin wood.

While taking yet another deep breath she told herself to get a grip and managed to knock politely. To her surprise and despite the noise, the door was opened immediately, startling her. Jonas was standing in the frame, his massive arms crossed in front of his chest. Interestingly, he did not look very amused, rather agitated somehow. Alice let her right arm drop back down to her side and her eyes found Danny, who was sitting on the old thrift shop couch, furiously handling some weird-looking controller. His dark locks looked glossy and bounced up and down with every move he made. Alice was glad that he hadn't cut them yet to look more like his bully-friends.

Waldo was standing behind the couch, Tee next to him. Paul was sitting next to Danny. Everyone seemed to be concentrating hard on whatever was on screen.

Jonas's huge shoulders were blocking Alice's view of the TV screen, but the war noise was way too loud for her taste.

"Bad timing?" She forced a grin and tried to sound nice.

Jonas just stood there, staring at her without saying a word. Alice couldn't remember having ever heard him talk. She turned away from him and tried to get her boyfriend's attention. "Danny?"

"Busy," was Waldo's response.

"I can see that." Alice sighed. "Anyway, the plumber's coming tomorrow morning at around nine, and I need you to open the door for him or her." She was talking to the back of Danny's head, which was still faced toward the TV. He didn't seem to hear her.

"Make sure you set your alarm and let them in, please."

Again, no reaction.

Alice gritted her teeth, trying to stay calm. "And please leave the leftovers in the fridge. I'd like to have them for lunch tomorrow at the office."

Danny's back remained toward her. Tee was grinning stupidly at her now.

She turned back to Jonas. "Well, you heard me. Let him know, okay?" Stretching her neck, she tried to catch a glimpse of the screen, but Jonas slightly shifted to again block her view.

"I'll let him know," said Tee with a cocky grin that revealed his yellowish teeth. At least they went along well with his flaxen hair, which rested in a greasy mess on his head. He had a rather narrow face and watery, blue eyes.

Jonas grabbed a pack of cigarettes out of the back pocket of his jeans and lit one. He inhaled deeply and seemed to study Alice's face, still not talking.

Alice had to admit that he was kind of good-looking. He had Italian-looking features, and his skin was always tanned, which made her suspect that he did construction work next to his security guard job. His eyes were blue and his hair ash brown. He was a bit shorter than Danny, but still tall with his approximately six foot one. Jonas looked bigger though, broader.

Waldo was the oldest of the group. His receding hair had already turned gray and white. It matched his little, evil-looking, gray-blue eyes. Waldo was always perfectly shaven and wore his shirt unbuttoned at the top, to expose some of his white chest hair as well as the golden necklace around his throat. He wore flawless dress pants and ironed dress shirts, but never a coat.

Paul was the only one who didn't look like the cast of *the godfather* movie. His self-consciousness made him appear more humane than the others and Alice liked him best, though like Jonas, she had never heard him say a word. In addition, he also avoided her presence whenever possible, and if not, her eyes.

Unlike Jonas, whose eyes were still fixed on Alice's face while he casually blew out a big cloud of smoke. Alice wrinkled her nose but kept her mouth shut. She hated it when he smoked in the apartment, but she didn't dare to say so.

She wouldn't let him know that he intimidated her however, so she held his stare coldly and said, "Good night," before turning on her heels and leaving the room.

Even before she reached the bedroom, the door fell shut behind her.

At least there had been no argument like the last time she'd had to face Danny and his gang. Alice found it embarrassing to have to address their issues so openly before his friends—only there was no way around it.

The cheap plastic clock on the wall was ticking noisily. It was only 7:30 p.m. but Alice felt tired enough to go to bed already. As usual though, the noise coming from the living room was so loud that sleeping would be impossible, so she decided to watch a movie on her laptop instead. A glance at the desk in the corner of the bedroom revealed that the laptop wasn't where she had left it.

It wasn't in the kitchen either when she checked. The gang had gifted her with a huge mess instead. Empty beer bottles were lying around, dirty plates and plastic dishes from takeout covered every surface. Apparently, Jonas had even put out his cigarettes on the kitchen table.

Was he insane? Alice felt anger boiling up inside of her. The mess could be cleaned, but there were black holes burned into the table now. Biting her lip hard, she tried to swallow her anger. There was no way she would go back to the living room and start an argument. Instead, she took the wet rag from the sink and wiped the ash from the table to see how deep the holes were.

The table was ruined. Not that it had been expensive—everything in the apartment was secondhand anyway. But she found it incredibly rude of Jonas to destroy someone else's furniture.

Swallowing her anger felt like it clumped and went down into the pit of her stomach, along with all the other bottled-up emotions from the previous months. Sighing, she threw the wet cloth back into the sink and started to load the dirty plates into the dishwasher, knowing from experience that the men were not going to do it themselves. Chicken bones got crushed under the soles of her feet, but Alice had recently begun to wear her shoes inside the house as well.

Great. He's getting drunk and playing games while I clean up his mess.

And the laptop was gone as well. Danny had probably used it and taken it somewhere. Alice paused and pondered on whether watching a movie was worth going back into the living room, just as she heard a door being opened. Seconds later, Tee entered the kitchen, a wide grin on his face.

"Cleaning?"

Alice frowned at him. "Obviously."

"Sorry for the mess. We would've done it later."

Sure.

Alice kept her thoughts to herself and continued loading the dishwasher.

"Is there any more booze?" Tee's watery eyes scanned the room.

"I wouldn't know. Check the fridge."

Tee strolled over and did as she suggested. There was beer, apparently, and he loaded his long arms with large brown bottles, then he shut the fridge, and turned to look at her.

"You're very welcome to join us, you know."

"I'm not really into war games."

Confusion flashed over his face, then he mouthed an "oh" as he comprehended. "They're done playing, actually. Dan was trying out a new game."

Good for him.

Alice gave Tee a smile and tried to be friendly. "So ... was it fun?"

"Uh ..." he seemed to consider. "I'm not really into ... war games either, to be honest. Dan seemed to like it. I prefer race games."

At least they seemed to have something in common. "Need for speed?"

Tee nodded eagerly. "Yeah, love those. Opener?" He nodded toward the bottles in his hands.

"I really don't know where you guys put all the stuff. You were the last ones to use it. It's supposed to be in the top drawer though, next to the sink."

"Oh, I remember. We took it to the living room!"

Alice grimaced at him, not knowing what to say. Apparently, he really wanted to chat with her.

"Any other race games you play?" he asked.

"Only Mario-Kart, but it's been a while since I last played. Especially with the TV being occupied all the time." Alice knew she sounded very passive-aggressive, but Tee wasn't usually that nice to her.

Now he gave her an apologetic smile. "I could lend you some games that'll work on your laptop, if you like."

Alice shrugged. "Thanks, maybe sometime. Talking about my laptop, have you seen it somewhere? I can't find it."

"Yeah, I think Dan took it. The black one, right?"

"We only got one since he broke his."

By spilling whiskey on it.

"Right. Dan mentioned something 'bout buying a new one. I always tell him he should get a PC instead. Way more you can do on it, and it's got a longer lifespan."

There was a moment of awkward silence when Alice didn't reply. As soon as the dishwasher was full, she shut the door and pressed the start-button.

"Well ... the beer is getting warm." Tee laughed nervously. "I'd better get back to the others."

"Could you tell Danny to bring my laptop, please?"

He nodded. "Sure."

"And did you tell him what I said before, about the plumber?"

"Oops, totally forgot. I'll do it now though," he assured her.

"Thanks."

Tee hesitated for a moment, his tongue sticking out between his lips like a slug trying to wind its way out of his mouth. He seemed to be thinking about something else to say, but when he failed to do so he finally left the kitchen.

Alice let out a relieved sigh. She could fill a book with things she'd rather do than talk to one of the gang, but Tee was surprisingly nice when he was alone. Maybe he just tried to impress the others when he made all those sexist remarks about her.

Alice turned off the lights and went back to the bedroom. There, she took off her clothes and put on a pair of leggings and a large T-shirt to sleep in.

Just as she was walking toward the door to switch off the ceiling lamp, it flung inward and bounced back off the little rubber doorstop on the wall. Danny stood in the frame.

The stench of whiskey that accompanied him made Alice screw up her nose. He seemed to be in a good mood, however. That was surprising.

"Tee said to bring your laptop," Danny said, while leaning against the doorframe.

"And where is it then?" Alice wanted to know.

Danny looked down at his hands and seemed surprised to only find a half-empty whiskey bottle in one and no laptop in the other.

"Oops." He chuckled.

Alice crossed her arms in front of her chest. "Glad you're in a good mood for once, but I was just about to go to bed. And I'd like my laptop here, where it's safe."

"I wouldn't break it!"

"I'm not saying you would. I just don't like it lying around in the living room while you guys are having a party."

Danny took a gulp from his bottle, then wiped his mouth with the back of his right hand.

"You should join us. Tee said he already invited you."

"It's Sunday, Danny. I have work tomorrow."

Again, Danny laughed. "No, you don't."

"Yes, I do. Some of us have serious jobs."

He seemed hurt by that. "I earn money."

"I know."

"More than you, even."

Alice clenched her teeth. "I know that. And yet you're always home."

"I work from home."

"I only see you playing video games. How d'you make money like that?"

Danny's eyes flicked up to the ceiling while he seemed to ponder. "It's part of my job."

"So, staying up late, getting drunk with your friends, is you *working*?"

Grinning, he nodded. "My friends are my partners. We work together. That *is* fun."

"Well, I guess being able to drink alcohol while working must be fun indeed. You do your thing. If you earn money with it, why should I care?" Sighing, Alice began to pull back the blankets on the bed.

"That's what I've been saying, ain't it?" Danny slurred. "No problem there, right?"

Scowling, Alice turned to face him. "There *are* certain things we need to discuss, Danny."

A stupid look came over his face and his eyes appeared glazed by his drunkenness.

Alice sat down on the bed. "You do know what I'm talking about, don't you?"

He shook his head.

"Well, then I guess now's not the time to discuss those things. You're obviously too drunk and playing stupid."

She watched him take another big sip of whiskey.

"You know what? Keep the laptop tonight. I just want to go to sleep. Will you please turn off the light and close the door?"

Danny took a clumsy step into the room and shook his head. "No, wait. I wanted to tell you something!" It took him a moment to find his balance. "The reason we're celebrating."

Why should I care?

Grinning, Danny waited for a reply. Disappointed by her obvious disinterest, he eventually gave in. "I bought a house."

Alice felt her eyebrows climb up her forehead. "A house?"

"A house."

Suddenly, her throat went dry, and she swallowed. It had been clear that this day would come, the way Danny had been acting lately, but she had dreaded it. There was a reason why she hadn't left him yet, but now *he* was going to leave *her*. To her distaste, her eyes turned moist.

No, don't cry in front of him. Be glad he's leaving.

With an inappropriately excited expression Danny waited for her to say something.

Alice cleared her throat. "So ... you're moving?"

"We're moving, yes."

"You and the guys?"

"No, it'll be our place mostly, but if you don't mind, they'll be staying with us from time to time."

Confused, Alice could do nothing but stare at him.

"I mean, it's a huge place, you know. There's lots of space, so we'll both have our privacy. We both know that this—" he beckoned toward the corridor and living room, "—isn't working out."

"Danny, please, you're being confusing. Will you please explain to me what exactly it is you're saying?"

"I'm saying," Danny leaned forward and gave her a wide grin, "that I bought a house for us and we're going to move tomorrow! Isn't that awesome?"

A long, awkward silence followed his words. Alice's thoughts were spinning, making her mind feel like it was on a merry-go-round. Was he serious? After everything that had happened, he still wanted to live with her? How could he just buy a house without letting her know and how could he even afford that?

Again, Danny was expecting an answer, an excited look on his face.

"Is ... this a joke?"

He shook his head.

"From the start, please." With a sweaty hand Alice brushed through a strand of her hair nervously. "I mean ... when did you buy a house? And where? And why do you still want to live with me after all of this?"

The questions seemed too much for Danny. He looked dumbstruck.

"Well ..." he began. "Waldo knows a guy whose wife ... uh ... committed ... you know ... suicide."

Alice frowned.

"In the house, I mean. So, he wanted to get rid of the house. The guy, I mean. And so, it was a real bargain. And well, Waldo told me about it and made me sign the contract a couple of days ago."

"Made you?"

"I mean, he told me about it, and I just had to buy it."

"And tell me *now*?"

Danny shrugged apologetically. "I wanted to surprise you, but we never talked."

"You could have told me anytime!"

"There were some ... uh ... problems with the business and we were really busy—"

"Problems with playing video games?" she interrupted him.

"I'm a programmer."

"We've been together for over two years, Danny. I know you're a programmer."

Danny scratched his chin, looking uncomfortable. "I mean, I program these ... uh ... games, you know." He started fumbling on a pimple on his chin. "To sell. The games, I mean."

Alice's eyes narrowed. "Sounds like your dream job. Where's the problem?"

"It is! It's just that building a business is quite hard, you know."

"Why did you never tell me about this?"

Danny thought for a long moment before he answered, his eyes glued to the ceiling. When they locked with hers again, they were full of accusation. "I thought you'd laugh at me."

"Why would I laugh at you?"

"Because ... I was unemployed and you were earning all the money and doing everything and kept urging me to get a job ... But I had this idea, you know." He pointed at his temple. "I knew exactly what I wanted to do, but I knew you wouldn't approve."

"Why wouldn't I?"

"Because ... people usually fail when they try these things, and I knew you wouldn't believe in me. But I found the right ... partners with the right ... ideas ... you know."

Alice took a deep breath. "No. As a matter of fact, I don't. I don't see how any of these guys—" she nodded to the living room, "—are any good at programming games. They don't seem very smart."

A deep frown appeared on Danny's forehead.

"Sorry, I didn't mean to insult your friends. What I mean is that they look like people who work with their bodies, not their minds."

"You underse ... underes ... uh ... underestimate them." It took him three tries to pronounce the word correctly.

"Danny, please stop drinking from that bottle ... okay?"

"I'm not that drunk!"

"Whatever."

He's swaying like grass in the wind.

"Anyways, I'm glad your business is going so well, and I do understand that you were stressed out, but that doesn't mean your behavior toward me is justified."

"You always make everything about you, don't you?"

"What?"

"Every time I say something, you only talk about yourself! You're so fucking selfish!"

"Excuse me?"

"It's true!" Danny exclaimed. "I'm working my fucking ass off to buy the lady a house, and what do I get? Criticism!"

Stunned, Alice stared at him. "Are you joking right now, Danny? I've been going to work every single day just to come home and find you drunk. You completely ignored me, never talked to me, and your friends are always here and make a mess. Every day, I clean up after your lazy asses and now you're telling me *I'm* selfish?"

Danny's cheeks were turning red. "I was having a hard time! And all I got from you was criticism! Every time you came home, first thing you did was nag. You're a control freak!"

"You ... you're definitely too drunk to think straight. Having a hard time? Really? Well, I'm sorry, but it sure didn't look that way when I saw you drinking beer and playing games with your friends."

"Just because my job involves ... *video games*, doesn't mean it's just fun! We had a rough start, and a lot was going wrong, and maybe ... maybe I just needed the booze to relax." He said the last part of the sentence quietly, with sadness in his voice, and Alice immediately felt bad.

He's doing it again. Blaming me for everything. Don't give in.

"Every time you walked through that fucking door, first thing you did was tell me to clean up or turn the volume down! Not even a word of greeting or a kiss, no. Don't you see how annoying that is?"

Alice rubbed her temples with her knuckles. Danny's words didn't make any sense and yet, they were messing with her head. Was it the whiskey talking? Or did he need the booze to open up? She tried to think back to those moments he had mentioned.

Did I really? Is it true what he's saying?

"You never gave me the chance to spend some alone time with you. You're always gone for days without telling me where you are or what you're doing. And when I try to talk to you, you cut me off. Don't blame me now, Danny. It's not fair. I hate playing *mommy*, but I don't want to be worrying about you all the time either."

I shouldn't have said that ... that's his weak point.

She bit her lip, wondering if she had provoked him.

His face was still red, but it was hard to tell whether it had gotten redder.

"I did more than you'd think," he muttered through clenched teeth.

"Okay, okay ... let's talk about that house now, please. How's all of this supposed to work out?"

Danny was breathing heavily, but he tried to answer in a calm manner. "I wanted to surprise you, so I organized everything. There's really nothing for you to worry about."

Alice studied his face. He looked hurt and stubborn at the same time. It made her sad.

"What about our apartment?"

"What about it?" He took another deep gulp of whiskey.
"We'll need to quit it."
"Already done."
"When did you do all of this? And why am I only hearing about it now?"
"I wrote ... a letter."
"It doesn't work that way. I signed the rental agreement and there's a cancellation period, unless you find another—"
"I know all of this! Don't treat me like a fucking baby!"
"Danny, please be honest."
He made a sound that was a mixture between a sigh and a moan. "Okay! I screwed up, all right? Your idiotic mess of a boyfriend screwed up again. But I fixed it, so stop worrying about it."
"I have no idea what you're talking about," Alice said softly, careful not to provoke him.

Seeing him like this was both shocking and hurtful. Apparently, he wasn't as happy as she had thought he was. Had he hidden it well or had she really been too self-absorbed?

"We're getting kicked out. We have to be gone by tomorrow evening." Danny's shoulders sacked and he stared down at his feet.
"They can't just kick us out! Why would they?"
"Because of the noise ... neighbors complained."
"Yeah but ... what about a warning?"
"There were warnings. Several. I threw them out."
Alice stared at him in disbelief. "Why would you do such a thing?"
"I mean, I tried to keep the noise down. But we have to work at night. The guys have other jobs during the day. It just wasn't possible. I never thought they would actually go through with this."

He looked at her with puppy eyes, like a dog awaiting punishment. "I screwed up, okay. I told you so. But I fixed it! I mean, with what I earn now, this place is too crappy for us anyway. Also, I want you to be happy and I want ... us to be happy, too." He took a step toward her, drunkenly and clumsily, and took her hand. "It's a very nice house, you'll see. English, big garden, trees, lots of space ... It's old, but beautiful."

Alice's thoughts were still spinning. Everything was happening too fast for her to grasp.

"Jonas destroyed the kitchen table," she muttered.

Danny gave her a warm smile. "I know. It's fine, we don't need it anymore. It's too cheap for our new place."

Alice sighed. "I don't know what to say. It's just … too fast. And how do I know things will get better?"

"They will," Danny assured her. "Just give it a try."

"I can't just forget these last couple of months, Danny … I can't just pretend everything never happened."

Danny pulled his hand back and his expression darkened. "You're never satisfied."

Quickly, Alice hopped off the bed and put her hand on his arm. "That's not true, really … it's just happening so fast, and I need time to think … and I would really like to talk about this again when you're sober."

Danny's face turned red at her words and his eyes glistened angrily. "No matter what I do, it's never good enough for you!"

"No … I didn't mean to make you feel that way. But see … this is one of the things I can't just ignore. You're so angry lately. I don't even know you like that. The mood swings … the drinking …"

He shook her hand off.

Damn, everything I say is wrong.

"That wasn't meant as criticism, Danny. I'm just worried about you."

"Stop worrying then, it's annoying," he snapped.

Alice bit her lip and tried to think of something to say that would soothe him.

Now's just not a good time.

"I'm tired. I have to work tomorrow …. Let's talk about this some other time when you … when your friends aren't waiting for you next door." She looked up at him and smiled.

For some reason though his face had gotten darker, and he looked as if he were boiling on the inside.

"You never listen to me!"

Alice stared at him, taken aback by his reaction.

"I told you we're going to move *tomorrow!*"

"*Tomorrow*? Do you expect me to call in sick? Just why couldn't you tell me sooner? You know my boss, she—"

"You don't have to go to work anymore. I earn enough."

"I can't just not go. This is a serious job—"

"Which I quit."

"What?"

Danny inhaled impatiently as if he were trying to explain something to a very slow person. "I earn enough for the both of us and I know you hated that job—"

"I don't hate it!"

"Don't interrupt me!" He was almost yelling now, and Alice wondered whether his friends were eavesdropping. It wouldn't be the first time, but it always made her uncomfortable.

"You told me you're tired of being just an assistant, and your boss is a fucking pain in the ass, and you'd rather not have to face her again."

"What ... are you saying exactly?"

"I'm saying," he inhaled through clenched teeth, "that I made sure you'll never have to face her again."

A nervous laugh escaped Alice's throat. "That sounds like you killed her and buried her in the woods."

"No, I just quit your job for you."

Anger chased Alice's confusion away at once. "You can't just quit my job without my consent!"

"I can and I did." He took another drink from his bottle. "You were always complaining, but you never found the guts to go through with it, so I did it for you. You can thank me later."

"What ... how ... what did you do?"

"Emailed her. Told her you quit."

"You mean ... from my laptop?"

He nodded. "Her reply was really polite by the way. Seems like a nice old lady."

Is he provoking me on purpose?

Alice took a deep breath to calm herself. Whatever mess Danny had created, she could surely clean it up, like she always did.

Turning her back to him, she walked around the bed and grabbed her cell phone from the nightstand.

"What are you doing?" he wanted to know.

"I," Alice said, whilst scrolling through her contact list, "am calling my boss to apologize for my idiotic, alcoholic boyfriend and his pathetic attempt to be funny."

A sudden movement in the corner of her eye made her duck down just in time to avoid being hit by the flying whiskey bottle, which instead crashed against the wall behind her and shattered into pieces.

Shocked, she turned and stared at the stain on the wall and the shards of glass on the floor. Her heart seemed to want to break through her ribs, the way it was hammering against them. Slowly, she turned her head to face Danny.

He was shaking with anger.

Did he really just do that?

Alice opened her mouth to say something, but her thoughts were taking somersaults, so she closed it again. Danny looked frightening the way he was towering over her, his face burgundy, and his hands clenched into fists.

A moving shadow in the corridor made Alice's eyes flick away from Danny and to Jonas, who had just appeared in the doorframe, a worried expression on his usually blank face. He glanced from Danny to Alice and then to the remains of the whiskey bottle on the floor. His mouth remained shut though, and he stood silently behind his friend.

Alice took a deep breath to slow down her heartbeat.

"Put. The phone. Down." Danny pressed the words through his teeth between heavy breaths.

Paralyzed by the shock of seeing him snap like that, Alice just stared at him.

Will he freak out if I say something ... anything?

She glanced at Jonas again. Danny surely wouldn't lose it right in front of Jonas, and he didn't have another bottle to throw.

The tension in the room was palpable; the air felt thick and heavy.

Why was Jonas just standing there? Did he want to make sure she didn't insult his precious friend anymore?

It was one of those moments when silence seems louder than noise, but Alice suddenly heard a faint voice coming from her right hand.

"Hello? Alice?"

It took her a moment to realize that it was coming out of her phone.

Shit ... I already dialed.

Danny couldn't have heard it from where he was standing. Alice slowly moved her arm upward and put the phone to her ear, careful not to move too fast, as if it were movement that would provoke him.

"Hello? Alice, are you there?"

She could hear the voice clearly now.

"I- I'm sorry Liz, I was distracted..."

"No problem, Alice, what's going on?"

She glanced at Danny. His upper lip was drawn back a bit, baring his teeth, his breathing was heavier than before.

"I was just calling to say that—"

It took him one big step to reach her and knock the phone out of her hand so hard, it left a throbbing pain in her fingers.

Before she could react, he had already bent down to pick it up.

"I TOLD YOU NOT TO CALL HER!" He *did* yell this time, only inches away from her face.

Intimidated, she took a step back.

Jonas stepped into the room at once and put his hand on Danny's shoulder as if to calm him. Danny whirled around. "What?!"

Jonas just nodded toward the living room. Danny's face was purple as a plum. He turned his head back to look at Alice.

Now Jonas was pulling at his upper arm to get him out of the room.

"Okay, okay. I'm coming!" Reluctantly, Danny turned around and followed his friend toward the door.

"Give me my phone back!" Alice called after him.

He gave her a warning look.

"Give it back," she repeated.

Danny ignored her and continued walking.

Alice hurried after him and grabbed the sleeve of his shirt to stop him. "Danny, give it back to me, please!"

"Don't touch me!" he yelled.

"I won't let you leave with my phone!"

Danny shook her off, and when she tried to grab him again, he shoved her away so violently it made her fall backward and hit the floor. All air got knocked out of her lungs at the impact, and she stared at him in shock. Jonas grabbed Danny's arm again and pulled him out of the room, this time with force.

Alice's cheeks were burning with shame when she looked at Jonas. Quickly, she pushed herself back up and walked after Danny, but this time, she didn't dare to grab him again.

"Danny, please..."

That made him turn around, but he didn't say anything. Instead, he pulled the key out of the keyhole, stepped out of the room, and closed the door.

Alice heard the key rattling in the lock. It took her a moment to realize what had happened.

He locked me in.

At once, her heartbeat accelerated, and her hands and feet turned cold. Panicking, she pulled at the door handle.

"Danny?" Her voice broke. She cleared her throat and tried again. "Danny!"

Still no reaction from outside.

Blood throbbed loudly in her temples, and it was hard to hear anything but that and her violently beating heart.

He knows I'm claustrophobic... Why is he doing this?

Her breathing got faster, making her dizzy. Alice tried to calm herself.

The window...

They were on the fifth floor. There was no way of climbing out, but at least she could let some fresh air in.

It helped immediately. Alice's breathing slowed as soon as the cold wind touched her nostrils, and she was able to think straighter. Was she supposed to call for help? No, that would be embarrassing. After all, it was only Danny, and she knew him. He would calm down and let her out again.

And then what? Was she supposed to leave him? Go to a friend's house? Leah or Jill would surely take her in.

Alice stepped away from the window and the cold air, that was gushing in, and went back to the door. Again, she tried to open it, just to make sure she hadn't just imagined Danny locking it.

It didn't move.

Desperately, she began knocking against the wood.

"Danny? Please open!"

Silence.

Alice pressed her ear to the door and listened. The gang was talking in the living room, but judging by the volume of their voices the living room door must be closed as well.

There was no point. Screaming and kicking against the door would have surely gotten Danny's attention, but Alice felt humiliated enough as it was. She didn't want to make an even bigger scene in front of Danny's friends.

Leaning her forehead against the cool wall next to the door, she took a deep breath.

I'll just wait until he's sober. I can still leave tomorrow.

2

Danny didn't appear all night long, and the suspense of not knowing if he would, as well as the memories of their fight, kept Alice awake until dawn. For once, there weren't any war noise or drunken shouts coming from the living room, but the strange silence made her feel much more uncomfortable.

Only when the sound of a typical Monday morning traffic started coming through the still open window, weirdly comforting like the waves of an ocean, did Alice's eyelids droop.

Her dreams were wild and confusing, but they didn't last long. A loud banging sound combined with laughter awoke her after what seemed like a five-minute nap. Moaning, Alice stirred in her sweat-soaked bed, and when the cold of the day touched her damp skin she shivered. For a moment, pretending that everything was just a dream seemed reasonable, but the noise coming from the corridor proved that heavy stuff was being moved. Immediately, all the fragments of last night's events came together, and Alice pulled her blanket over her head and pressed her eyes shut.

A knock at the door made her flinch, and her heartbeat accelerated at once. Was it Danny?

Not answering seemed like a good idea, but the knocking persisted.

"WHAT?" Alice snapped at whomever was out there.

Slowly, the door opened and to her surprise, an unfamiliar guy stood in the frame, dressed in an overall, glancing shyly into the room. Alice couldn't remember having ever seen him before.

"Oops, sorry, miss. I didn't mean to disturb you." He gave her an apologetic smile.

Alice forced the corners of her lips upward. "No problem. What is it?"

The man stepped into the room and looked from the pile of clothes on the floor to the books spread on the desk next to the window.

"Well ... we're supposed to carry the furniture downstairs, but I can see that this room isn't ready yet."

Alice shook her head. She winced when a stabbing pain went through her skull. Apparently, Danny's drinking had left her with a hangover.

"Isn't it still early?"

The moving guy arched an eyebrow. "Actually miss, it was 11:00 a.m., last time I checked."

Alice's eyes widened and she groggily turned her head toward the clock on the wall. He was right. Feeling embarrassed, she tried to think of something to say, some kind of apology, but in that instant, Tee's grinning face appeared behind the overall guy.

"Morning, Alice," he sang cheerfully.

"Morning," she muttered back.

"I see you're all packed and ready," Tee remarked while scanning her room with his eyes.

Ha ha.

"Where's Danny?"

"He's at the new house. Told us to let you sleep."

"How is he today?"

"Well, I'll be downstairs, if you need me," said the moving guy, and disappeared out the door. Tee took his place and gave Alice a curious look. "He's fine, I guess. Why?"

"Because he had so much to drink last night."

Tee grinned. "Aah, that boy can drink, don't worry about him."

That only worries me more.

Alice sighed and pushed the blanket back to get up. Tee theatrically covered his eyes with his hands.

"Oh, come on! I'm wearing pants and a T-shirt."

"But no socks ... I have a foot fetish, ya know," he joked.

"Very funny." Alice stretched her back and went over to the window to close it.

"Now that's a good idea. It's freaking cold in here." Tee rubbed his hands together. "Were you trying to freeze yourself to death?"

"I needed fresh air."

"Are you hungry? I could get you some bacon and toast from the kitchen."

Alice shook her head. "No, thanks. I don't eat bacon."

With a shocked expression on his face, Tee fanned himself. "Who doesn't eat bacon?"

"Vegetarians, for example," said a deep voice behind him. It was Waldo. "Now get out and make yourself useful!"

"I was just trying to be nice," Tee protested. Pouting, he left the room under Waldo's warning stare. Waldo's eyes found Alice. "We thought you'd be up earlier. Daniel told us not to wake you."

"I know, Tee said so. I ... I couldn't sleep last night. I only fell asleep when it was already daylight outside."

Waldo didn't seem to care. "Daniel's waiting. You should hurry. The moving van won't be here all day."

Who said I want to move?

"I wanted to talk to Danny first. I haven't even been to the new house yet—"

"We'll drive you there. You'll see it soon enough."

"But ... there's some things I have to discuss with Danny first. I'm not ready to move—"

"You should have thought of that earlier then," Waldo cut her off.

Alice glared at him. "He only told me last night that we're moving at all."

Waldo folded his arms in front of his chest and looked at her coolly. "That's none of my business. All I know is that the moving van is waiting." He turned his head toward the corridor behind him and yelled, "JONAS!"

A few seconds later, Jonas appeared in the door.

"Help her pack."

Jonas frowned at him.

"Daniel said so." Waldo turned around and left.

Jonas remained standing in the doorframe with his hands stowed away in the pockets of his jeans. Alice's heart began to thump faster, and she felt herself blush.

Jonas had been there last night. He'd seen her land on her butt after Danny had pushed her. He'd also seen Danny lock her in the bedroom. It made her feel incredibly embarrassed.

He just stood there, his face an expressionless mask.

"Boxes?" she asked.

He nodded toward the corridor.

Alice sighed and walked over to him. "Uhm ... you're blocking the door," she told him.

He stepped aside.

There were empty boxes stacked against the wall next to the kitchen. Everything in the apartment had apparently already been packed or even moved. The walls were white, the rooms were empty.

Our first apartment. So much history. Everything gone while I was asleep.

An unexpected sadness rolled over her and paralyzed her. For a moment, Alice stared at the spot near the entrance door where once a framed picture of her and Danny had hung. She couldn't help but wonder whether Danny had taken it to the new house or thrown it in the dumpster.

Alice told herself to get a grip. There was no way she could stay in this apartment, her stuff had to be moved. Where, she would decide later.

Sighing, she took two boxes and carried them to her room. Jonas was still standing near the door, eyes on her. Alice put the boxes on her bed and wondered what she was supposed to put in them. Jonas's stare felt like laser rays, burning the skin off her body. It was impossible to grasp a clear thought while he kept staring at her like that.

Feeling uncomfortable, Alice looked up at him. "Could you leave, please?"

Jonas didn't answer. Instead, he pulled a pack of cigarettes out of the back pocket of his jeans, pulled one out, and lit it. Alice wrinkled her nose and went over to the door to close it, but Jonas blocked it with his foot.

"What are you doing?" Alice asked him, unnerved.

Jonas just shrugged.

What a prick. Is he teasing me on purpose?

"I have to get dressed," she told him.

Slowly, Jonas turned around until his back was facing her, and continued smoking.

Alice hesitated for a moment, feeling the urge to shove him out the door but knowing it would be like trying to move a mountain. When she was sure he wouldn't turn around again she went over to her dresser and pulled out some fresh clothes. Suspicious, she checked again if Jonas's back was still facing the room, then she quickly changed her clothes. The cold weather called for jeans and a thick hoodie.

Once fully dressed, Alice cleared her throat. "I'm done."

Jonas turned around, again in that slow, casual way, like he had all the time in the world. Still, his mouth remained closed. Alice studied his face. Poker face.

"Can you talk?" she asked him.

Jonas exhaled a big cloud of smoke and said, "Yes."
"Are you going to help me?"
He grinned. "No."

When all her stuff was packed in the cardboard boxes, he was at least nice enough to help her carry them downstairs to the moving van.

The apartment building had no elevator, but his face remained expressionless while he was carrying the heavy boxes down the stairs, from the fifth floor to the entrance. Alice couldn't deny that she was impressed. Her own back hurt badly, and she was completely out of breath when the last box was stowed safely in the back of the van. She sat down on the sidewalk to pause for a moment.

Why am I even doing this? I don't want to move.

There was nothing she could do though. They were being kicked out of the apartment, and thanks to Danny's stupidity she didn't have enough time to look for anything else.

And he's not even here.

She thought back to what had happened yesterday and tried to put some sense into it. But just like last night, when she'd lain awake in bed, she couldn't.

Danny's behavior didn't make any sense. He seemed to be going through immense changes, but it couldn't be a midlife-crisis at only twenty-nine years old.

Depression maybe?

But what had caused it?

Alice watched the guys load some more things onto the van and realized at once that Jonas's eyes were still on her.

What is wrong with this guy?

Was he following her? It was a creepy thought, but she had to find out.

Carefully avoiding his eyes, Alice got up from the sidewalk and hurried back into the house. Having to walk all the steps up again annoyed her, but she needed to be certain.

Back in the apartment and completely out of breath, she slipped into the bathroom and closed the door behind her. Curious, Alice began checking the drawers of the cupboard underneath the sink. As suspected, they had all been emptied while she'd been asleep. Even her tampons. Both embarrassment and anger over losing even the last piece of privacy she'd had made her blush.

Biting her lip, she stared at her pale reflection in the bathroom mirror, until a noise from the corridor caught her attention.

To disguise her true intentions, Alice flushed the toilet and took a deep breath before stepping out of the bathroom.

She found Jonas waiting in the hallway.

I was right. He's watching me.

She stared at him with wide eyes. He was smoking another cigarette.

The thought of having to walk toward him made her heartbeat accelerate, so instead, she turned right and stepped into the living room.

There was nothing left in here either, apart from a couple of black trash bags.

How were they able to do all of this while I was asleep?

Alice cursed herself for her comatose sleep and let her eyes wander over the plastic bags. Something caught her eye, something soft and purple, sticking out through the opening of one of the trash bags.

Oh no, he didn't!

Alice crossed the room quickly, dropped to her knees, and ripped the bag open. There it was—the big stuffed purple monkey with heart-shaped eyes. It was corny, but it had been a gift from her to Danny and it had served as a couch-pillow many a time.

Seeing it lying in the bag, stained by the waste, made her feel as if Danny had thrown a piece of her away instead.

She pulled the monkey out of the bag completely and plucked off pieces of trash that stuck to it.

A feeling of utter sadness began creeping up inside of her. It wasn't right to move in with Danny again after everything that had happened. Was she supposed to let him get away with what he had done? But what else was she supposed to do?

The white wall before her became a blur while she stared at it, trying to put some order into the mess that was her life. She had no job, no apartment, and was about to move to a place she had never seen before. With a man she didn't know anymore.

Exhausted from trying to find solutions her mind got blank, and Alice kept staring through the wall rather than at it, as if the resolution were waiting behind it.

Suddenly though, the feeling of being watched made the little hairs on her neck stand up. Alice whirled around and found Jonas standing in the door, a curious expression on his face.

Her eyes narrowed and she glared at him.

Jonas seemed amused at the sight of her kneeling on the floor, holding the monkey.

"We should carry these down," Alice said curtly, gesturing toward the trash bags.

He nodded and stepped into the room to pick two of the bags up. Carrying one in each hand, he kept a cigarette dangling from his lips.

They walked down the stairs in silence. Jonas threw the trash bags into the dumpster in front of the house. He held its lid open for Alice to toss the bag she'd been carrying in as well. Alice stared at the monkey in her arms.

"Do you know where Danny put my phone?" she asked Jonas.

He shook his head.

"Can I use yours?"

He frowned at her.

"Just quickly."

He put out his cigarette on the metal dumpster. "For what?"

"I just want to call a friend."

"Why?"

"To tell her I'm moving."

Jonas scratched his unshaven chin. "Don't think so."

Alice glared at him, surprised and angry. Her grip around the monkey tightened and in a sudden impulse, she threw the stuffed toy into the still open dumpster. Jonas gave her a meaningful look and closed the lid without saying a word.

Alice averted her eyes and stared at her feet to avoid having to look at him.

They stood in silence while the rest of Danny's friends and some moving guys arranged the furniture and boxes in the back of the van in a way that would keep them from falling during the drive.

Alice wished it would take them as long as possible. She wanted to see her friends and she desperately needed some time to think before she made what could possibly be one of the biggest mistakes of her life.

An elderly woman with a little terrier on a leash was approaching them, catching Alice's attention. Alice recognized the opportunity, that presented itself, before the thought had even clearly manifested in her mind. The woman was Mary, her neighbor, who inhabited one of the ground floor apartments.

"Good morning, Mary," Alice greeted her.

Mary pushed her glasses up her nose with a crooked index finger and stared at her. A few seconds passed before recognition flickered up in her eyes.

"Oh, hello ... Annie, right?"

"Alice."

Mary glanced to the moving van with rheumy eyes and back at her. "Are you moving out?"

"Apparently, yes."

"Where to, dear?"

"Uh ..." Alice's eyes flicked to Jonas, then to the van, and back to Mary. "Into ... an old English house ... with a big lawn."

It was as good an answer as she could give, but luckily, Mary didn't seem to care.

"Well, that sounds lovely, dear. All the best then."

"Actually," Alice blurted out to stop her neighbor from walking away, "I was wondering ... could I use your bathroom, maybe?"

The old lady's frown stood out amongst her other wrinkles.

"I ... uh ... we don't have anything left in the apartment ... no toilet paper ..."

Alice stole a glance at Jonas, who stared at her, a mixture of confusion and suspicion on his usually expressionless face. He said nothing though.

Mary didn't seem too pleased, but she was a nice old lady. "Sure, dear. You're very welcome."

Alice followed her into the building, feeling Jonas's stare heavily on her back. Her heart was pounding like a drum and her hands were sweaty. She had no idea what she was doing and neither did she know why she even felt like she was doing something forbidden, but the fear was there all the same.

Jonas surely wouldn't follow her into Mary's apartment, but Alice didn't dare to turn around and check.

The lady's flat opened onto a narrow strip of lawn on the other side of the building. All apartments on the ground floor did. Alice was pretty sure that Jonas wouldn't consider that.

Mary led her to the bathroom and again, she pretended to go and flushed to not raise any suspicion.

The old lady was waiting for her in the corridor.

"Thank you very much, Mary." Alice gave her a polite smile.

"No problem, dear."

"Would you mind if I went out the back?"

Again, a frown wrinkled Mary's forehead and she pushed her glasses up her nose. "Oh … Of course not. Go ahead, dear."

Alice hurried out through the glass door that led onto the lawn.

The grass was still a bit moist from the rain of the previous day. Only a low wooden fence separated the lawns from the road on the other side. If Jonas was smart, he would walk around the house to check if she was there. Or wouldn't he? Was he really following her?

Doubt made Alice hesitate for a second, but she shook it off and climbed over the fence. All she knew was that she had to get rid of Jonas.

Alice crossed the street and walked into an empty alley which lay between two big apartment buildings and led to the main road. She glanced back over her shoulder to see if anyone was watching her, then she started running.

It wasn't far to the town center, but the streets were crowded by people taking their lunch break. Some were sitting on benches, eating a sandwich. Others waited in queues in front of fast-food restaurants.

Alice hurried down the sidewalk, until she found a young woman typing on her cell phone.

"Excuse me," Alice addressed her, out of breath.

The woman looked up curiously.

Alice glanced back over her shoulder quickly to check if Jonas was anywhere to be seen.

I'm crazy. I'm paranoid. Why in the world would he follow me?

But she couldn't shake off that weird feeling though. After all, he *had* followed her back into the apartment, and he had been constantly watching her.

"Uh … I forgot my bag on the bus and my phone was in there … Could I use yours to make a call, please?"

To Alice's relief, the young woman smiled and nodded. "Sure, go ahead." She handed Alice her phone.

"Thank you so much!" Alice quickly started typing in Leah's number, but her sweaty fingers slipped on the screen and made her miss the buttons more than once. After the third try, she finally got it right. The woman waited patiently, though there was a hint of suspicion in her eyes.

Alice gave her an apologetic smile and put the phone to her ear. She could hear the signal, but it was taking too long. Nervously, she started tapping on the ground with her foot.

Come on, Leah, pick up the goddamned phone!

The unnerving *Peeep* of the answering machine made Alice's hopes crumble.

"I'm so sorry, no one's picking up. May I try another number?"

Still smiling, the young woman nodded.

Maybe Jill would pick up ... she always took her lunch break at this hour. At least Alice got the number right this time, but it was the last one she knew by heart. If Jill didn't pick up, there was no one she could call ... Apart from Danny, but that seemed a bit counterproductive.

Chewing her lip nervously, Alice waited while the call was connecting. Again, she glanced over her shoulder—and her heart sank.

There he was.

He was walking down the sidewalk, taking big steps, looking left and right.

Alice quickly turned away from him and clenched the phone tightly between her sweaty fingers.

Come on, Jill, please pick up!

Jonas hadn't seen her yet and maybe he wouldn't recognize her from behind, especially with all these people standing around her.

Finally, there was a *click* and Jill's voice appeared.

"*Hello?*"

"Jill, it's me, Alice! I—"

"*What are you doing?*"

Alice's heart stopped at once. She whirled around and found him standing right behind her. He looked annoyed.

Her mouth turned dry, and she almost dropped the phone. "I—" she cleared her throat. "I'm making a phone call. Since you wouldn't let me use your phone."

The young woman's eyes flicked from Alice to Jonas and back.

Jonas grabbed the phone out of Alice's hand and handed it back to its owner. "Let's go."

Alice quickly took a step away from him. "Why are you following me?"

"I said, let's go." He tried to get a hold of the sleeve of her hoodie, but Alice took another step back.

"Don't touch me!"

Now the woman with the phone looked worried.

"Thanks for your help," Alice said to her before turning on her heels and hurrying away from Jonas. He followed her and grabbed her arm to stop her. "What are you doing?"

"I told you; I want to talk to my friends. Since apparently, you're not letting me make a phone call, I have to find another way."

"Why did you run away?" His fingers locked around her wrist.

"Let go of me!"

"I asked you a question."

Alice gave him an angry glare. "You're constantly following me; it's freaking me out!"

"If you hadn't run away, I wouldn't have followed you."

"If you'd allowed me to use your phone, I wouldn't have had to run away!" Alice's heart was still hammering against her ribs. Why was Jonas acting like that?

His expression showed a mixture of impatience and annoyance, but no hint of an explanation.

"Why are you watching me all the time?" she asked him.

"Danny told me to."

What?

"Why ... why would he do that?"

Jonas just shrugged.

"First, he locks me in the bedroom, then he tells his friends to *guard* me?" Jonas pulled her closer. "You're making a scene."

Alice tried to pull free of his grip. "Not yet, but I will if you don't let go of me!"

They glared at each other for a moment, Alice's stare furious and Jonas's warning.

"Let's go. Now. Everybody's waiting." Jonas was carefully keeping his voice down.

"They don't have to wait for me."

Still, Jonas was holding her by the wrist. He didn't hurt her, but his grip was like iron. "What d'you mean?" he wanted to know.

"I mean ... I need time to think. I'm not sure I want to move right now."

"Your stuff's in the van."

"Yeah, well ... where else would it be? We had to leave the apartment today, thanks to Danny."

"He's waiting."

"I'll talk to him soon, but right now, I have to figure out what I want."

Jonas remained silent.

"I need some time to think!"

Why was she even explaining this to him? It was none of his business.

"Leaving him?" Jonas sure was a man of few words.

"What? I ... I don't know ... I don't want to, but ..."

Jonas kept staring at her, as if he were looking right into her mind. It made her nervous.

"It's none of your business!" Alice tried to pull her arm free once again. It was no use.

What did that look on his face mean? Was he expecting an answer?

"Look," she began, sighing. "I *will* talk to Danny and I would never just run away without telling him anything, but right now, I need distance and time to clear my head."

Jonas's expression didn't change.

"I couldn't talk to him last night ... obviously. And I only just learned that we have to move. And this morning, he wasn't even there the whole time!"

"He was," Jonas disagreed.

"Not when I was awake."

Silence.

"Jonas ... let me go, please ..." It sounded like a desperate plea and Alice immediately hated herself for it.

"Danny's waiting at the house. You can talk there."

"Who are you to tell me what to do?" Anger was starting to boil up in her again.

"I can't let you walk away."

Alice tried to unlock Jonas's fingers around her wrist with her left hand. They didn't even move a bit.

"Stop that," Jonas growled.

Alice ignored him. He grabbed her hand and pulled it off. Now, he had both her arms locked in his fists.

"Did Danny tell you that? Is he afraid I might leave him?"

The question seemed to make Jonas uncomfortable. "Just come with."

Alice shook her head. "Last night, he threw a bottle at me. You saw that.

Today, he told you to keep me from leaving! I'm not even allowed to call my friends ... for god's sake, Jonas, what the hell is going on?"

For the first time, Jonas's eyes wandered away from her face. He seemed to be thinking of something to say. It was clear that he would always take Danny's side though. After all, he was his friend.

Finally, he looked back at her and sighed. "He'll explain."

Unbelievable.

"Yeah sure. You know what? Stop sticking your nose where it doesn't belong! My relationship with Danny is none of your goddamned business and you don't have the right to keep me from going where I want!"

Now, Jonas was starting to get angry too. His stare hardened.

"You can't force me to go back to Danny!"

"We'll see about that."

Alice laughed dryly. "You want to carry me? Or drag me along?"

"Maybe."

"In front of all these people?"

Jonas's eyes moved to the left and then to the right. He could see that she was right.

"I'll tell you one more time: Let me go!"

"Don't make this difficult," he grumbled in a low voice.

"Let me go!" Alice pulled back with as much force as she could, but Jonas just tightened his grip.

In that instant though, she noticed a group of teenagers approaching them. They were four boys, probably around sixteen or seventeen, looking concerned.

"Is he bothering you?" the one in the front wanted to know. He had brown tousled hair and freckles on his nose, and he didn't look at all as if he could win a fight against Jonas. Nevertheless, Alice nodded desperately. The boy scanned Jonas from head to toe and seemed to realize what Alice was thinking. He shot a glance at his friends and then looked back at Jonas, a bold expression on his face.

"Ahem, sir, I think you should do what the lady says."

Jonas gave him a contemptuous look. "And why is that?"

"Well," the boy grinned defiantly and said, "You're harassing a woman in public. I'm sure the police would have something to say to that."

Jonas's eyes narrowed.

"Actually," the boy continued, "I just saw a police car right around that corner. It would take one of my friends ten seconds to get it over here."

His friends were nodding approvingly.

"I'm pretty sure you don't want to beat up a bunch of kids in broad daylight."

Alice glanced anxiously at Jonas. His grip around her wrists had tightened, and he looked really pissed now.

His eyes swiveled from the boy to her, and he glared at her so coldly, it evoked goose bumps on her back and arms.

Finally though, he slowly began to loosen his grip and Alice was able to pull her arms free.

Carefully, she backed away from him, expecting him to grab her again any moment, but he remained where he stood, though his eyes followed her. When she reached a safe distance where his arms couldn't reach her anymore, Alice turned on her heels and started running.

The boys called something after her, but she couldn't make out their words through the rush of adrenaline that went through her body.

Alice hoped Jonas wouldn't let out his anger on the boys, but then again, it *was* broad daylight. He surely wouldn't risk getting arrested.

The street was getting emptier; people were on their way back to work. Alice knew that Jill always ate lunch at the same café, but her break was soon to be over. She had to hurry up.

Normally, she would have taken a bus there, but since she hadn't brought any money, Alice didn't dare to. Else, Murphy's law would strike, like it always did in situations like this, and she would run into trouble.

Soon enough, her lungs and throat were burning and her legs felt like jelly. She had to slow down into a walk.

A quick look over her shoulder calmed her nerves a bit. Jonas was nowhere to be seen. Maybe he had finally given up on following her.

A pharmacy's green neon sign displayed the time and temperature, and Alice's hopes crumbled when she saw that it was almost 1:30 p.m.

Jill might already be back at work. Again, Alice broke into a run. Finally, she was able to make out Jill's favorite café in the distance. It lay on the other side of the main road, so after quickly checking for traffic, Alice stepped onto the road—and right in front of a police car, which was just pulling out of an alley.

And thus, Murphy's law had struck nonetheless. The sirens howled once, and the driver pulled over on the right side of the road.

Reluctantly, Alice plodded toward the driver, who had gotten out of the vehicle and was beckoning for her to approach him.

"Hello there," the police officer greeted her cheerfully, a wide grin on his face.

"Hi," Alice said shortly.

"Can I see some ID, please?"

Alice bit her lip. She had no idea where her wallet was. "Uh ... I'm not carrying any at the moment."

"Tell me your name, then."

"Alice Bouchart."

"Do you know why I stopped you, Miss Bouchart?"

Alice shook her head.

The officer's eyes were hidden behind sunglasses, despite the overcast sky. Still, she could see that he was scanning her from head to toe.

"There are stripes painted on the road, for pedestrians to walk on."

Alice forced a smile. "Thank you for telling me, sir. I'll remember next time."

"Actually," the officer said, "Crossing the road outside of the crosswalk is considered an offense."

He's not seriously going to charge me for that?

"Well ... what's the penalty?" she asked him defiantly.

The man's grin vanished at once. "We'll discuss that at the station."

"What? Why? Come on, you're exaggerating!"

"You're not carrying an ID, so I have to take you to the station, where we'll write down your details."

"But ..."

"I expect you to cooperate. Otherwise I'll have to handcuff you."

Alice tried to swallow her anger. Fighting with a cop wouldn't get her anywhere.

"No, that's not necessary ... *sir*."

The officer opened one of the back doors of the vehicle and waited for her to get in. Alice took a deep breath and shot a last, wistful glance at Jill's favorite café. She had been so close.

Trying to hide the frustration on her face, she obeyed and got into the car. The officer closed the door and took his seat behind the wheel. Alice had never sat in a police car before, and she would have never expected her first time to be due to jaywalking.

"Buckle up," the cop ordered.

She did. He pulled onto the main road and drove back the way Alice had come from. Feeling anxious, she stared at her hands, which she had folded in her lap.

Closing her eyes and taking slow, deep breaths, she tried to calm herself. The police surely would not lock her up over something so minor. All they needed were her details, so they could write her a ticket.

Alice felt the car slowing down and coming to a halt on the right side of the road. *Already?*

The officer turned his head and smiled at her through the mesh that separated the back seats from the front.

"We're just waiting for someone."

A couple of minutes passed, and then the right front door was opened. Alice kept staring at her hands, but she could see through the corners of her eyes that a man was getting into the car.

"That her?" the officer asked.

Curious, Alice looked up. The man on the other seat turned around and …

Jonas!

Her heart stopped at his sight. Jonas looked at her, and the triumph in his eyes was unmistakable. He nodded.

To Alice, the world had lost its sense.

Utterly confused, she could do nothing but stare at him.

"Wasn't hard to spot her," she heard the officer say. His voice seemed far away. "Just had to look for a crazy brunette running through the streets. Ain't that many of them here, are they?" He chuckled.

Jonas just gave him a curt nod.

Alice wished the seat underneath her would open up and swallow her whole, make her disappear forever. Her eyes teared up and she quickly looked down at her hands again.

This is humiliating.

Embarrassment and fear began nagging on her. Nothing made sense anymore. Was Danny even involved in this? What if his friends weren't really his friends? What if they'd killed him and decided to kidnap her? She didn't actually know

Jonas. Before this morning, she had never even heard him talk. Where the hell was Danny? And why were the police involved?

Or maybe it was just a prank. A stupid prank, indeed, but hadn't Danny been acting stupid all the time lately? Alice couldn't shake off the feeling that something was utterly wrong. After all, she was locked in a police car. For the second time in twenty-four hours, she was locked in.

Her breathing accelerated. Alice began inhaling through her mouth to get more air.

Jonas was observing her. She could feel his stare through the rearview mirror.

He opened the window on his side and cool air began filling the car. Alice inhaled eagerly. Jonas turned around to face her.

"Better?" he asked.

She nodded.

3

They drove for a while, never talking. Alice looked out the window curiously to see where they were going. To her surprise, they drove out of town. How far away *was* that house?

The window was still open and the air, which kept streaming into the cop car, got fresher. The car fumes were gone and replaced by scents of wet leaves and mud. Fields stretched on for miles on either side, a line of trees separating them from the road. It was a beautiful sight. The leaves on the trees had turned orange and red, and glowed whenever they got kissed by sunrays that fought their way through the clouds from time to time.

Jonas pulled out his pack of Marlboros and offered one to the cop. He took it. They both lit their cigarettes. Then he pulled a third one out of the pack and offered it to Alice. She shook her head.

They continued driving in silence until the cop suddenly turned the steering wheel to the left and maneuvered them onto a gravel road which led farther into the fields. Alice could see a forest in the distance, and she thought she could make out the shape of a house. It was the first one in that area, after the couple of farms they'd passed on the way.

A dreadful feeling began spreading through her bones. Sure, the view was beautiful, but they were out in no-man's-land. Why in the world would anybody younger than seventy want to live here? Plus, it would take her forever to drive to her friends. Not to mention, she didn't have a car and Danny was quite fussy when it came to his precious Audi.

At least it didn't look as if she was being driven into the woods to be tortured and killed.

They were getting closer to the house, which seemed to be quite big, but Alice couldn't see much from the backseat.

The car came to a halt in front of a big, massive iron gate, which was built into a high stonewall. Alice estimated that it was about ten feet high. Someone opened the gate from the inside, and they drove through. Gravel crunched underneath the tires of the police car. The officer killed the engine and the men both got out. Alice couldn't wait to get away from them. She waited for the cop to unlock the door for her, then practically jumped out of the vehicle.

Instead of storming away from them though, Alice was paralyzed by the sight of the house in front of her. It was beautiful. Not quite some Beverly Hills-mansion, but it did look like a brick villa and the property was huge. Even a small wood decorated the back yard and a bunch of big old birches grew along the stonewall on the left side of the house. The grass was high and looked like it hadn't been mown in a while—just the way she liked it. A short-cut lawn couldn't provide a home for insects and Alice loved watching them buzz around.

The house was built from dark bricks, like most typical English houses. Ivy climbed up its walls, though apparently, someone had tried hard to keep it from growing all over the place. A swing in the far-right corner of the yard caught Alice's eye and made her guess that the previous owners must have had children.

Danny had called it a real bargain. It definitely had to be; else she couldn't imagine how he could afford a place like this. Alice couldn't deny that she was impressed, but she didn't trust the whole thing yet. A suicide house ... how spooky.

Jonas's eyes were fixed on her again. She scowled at him. "Where's Danny?"

He nodded toward the house.

Alice started walking without knowing where she was going. Getting away from Jonas and the officer was her number one priority, and walking toward the house was the only thing that seemed reasonable. Just when she almost reached the stony steps that led onto a wide porch, Danny stepped through the front door, taking her eyes away from the beautifully ornamented oakwood doorframe.

Dark shadows framed his eyes and his skin looked weirdly pale. For once, his hair was untidy.

Their eyes met and Alice stopped in her tracks. Danny studied her cautiously, probably wondering how she might react. Alice eyed him suspiciously.

Without saying a word, they stared at each other for a while, until Alice decided to break the ice with a half-hearted smile.

Her anger for him hadn't vanished, but now wasn't the time for a fight, especially not in front of all the people in the yard. Moving guys were busy unloading the van, and both the cop and Jonas were watching them.

Danny brushed a strand of hair out of his face and smiled too, almost shyly.

"It's beautiful ... the house, I mean."

Danny nodded. "So ... you like it?"

"I like what I've seen so far..."

That seemed to make him relax a bit and he took a step toward her.

"Listen," he began carefully. "I'm sorry about this morning. I checked on you earlier, but you were sleeping so peacefully, and you didn't even hear me open the door, so I figured you needed some rest."

Is that all he has to say?

Danny's eyes wandered from her to Jonas and then to the police car. "I'm sorry about *that*."

"What the hell was that?" Alice wanted to know.

Nervously, Danny brushed another strand of hair behind his ear. "Uh ..." He sighed. "That was really unfortunate ... I ... told Jonas to make sure that you came here." He rubbed his temple with the knuckles of his right hand. "Guess he took it a bit too literally."

"So, you did *not* tell him to call the cops on me?"

Danny held his hands up defensively. "That? No, that's just a friend of Waldo's. He was only helping out. It's not like he arrested you or anything."

Alice's eyes narrowed. "That's about what he did, though."

Danny's mouth formed a silent 'oh'. "Well ... He has a stupid sense of humor ..."

"How about next time he tells me it's meant to be a joke, so I know I'm supposed to laugh," Alice suggested.

To her distaste, Jonas was walking toward them, another cigarette dangling from his lips.

"What happened?" Danny asked him.

Jonas just looked from him to Alice and back.

"We'll talk about it later," said Danny. "Come," he turned to Alice. "I'll show you the house."

Alice followed him up the steps and into their new home.

It was generous on the inside, with lots of space, and most of the furniture looked rather expensive and antique, and had probably already been there. The floors were made of stone, naturally shaped, and in soft red and orange tones, here and there covered by thick, soft carpets in dark colors.

Left to the entrance was a big kitchen. There was an arch which led from there to the dining room, where a long table of dark wood stood surrounded by also dark wooden chairs, whose legs all had the same scrollwork carved in. On the right side of the entrance was a big, open living room with three sofas arranged around a wooden couch table. There was also a fireplace with a pile of firewood next to it.

Danny led Alice through the living room and showed her the door to what was going to be his office.

"The previous owner left most of his furniture, so I'm not going to need my own desk. I'll be working from home, usually in this office, so I—or you—won't be disturbed."

Alice just nodded to show him that she was listening.

"There's also a big bathroom down here, with a bathtub. And next to it is a separate toilet." He gestured to two closed doors next to his office.

"Over there is the cellar door. We have a large basement with another door that opens to the garden. Do you want to see it?"

Alice shook her head. She hated basements.

Danny smiled. "I thought so."

He led her around a corner to the left, just after the dining room, where they encountered another closed door.

"This is one of the guestrooms. My friends might stay here from time to time."

Great. Well ... he said they would.

Danny led her to a wooden staircase and began walking upstairs.

The second floor wasn't as open as the one below. It had merely a long corridor with doors on either side of it, which made it look a bit like a hotel.

"Up here we also have a bathroom, which can be accessed from the corridor. It's meant for the guests mostly 'cause there's another two rooms up here, which we'll use as guestrooms—if that's okay for you."

Alice shrugged. "I guess . . ."

Danny pursued toward the end of the corridor, where the last two rooms were. He opened the one on the left and led her into a large bedroom.

"This is our bedroom. We also inherited the bed, which is king-size." He smiled at her warmly. "There's a bathroom that belongs to this bedroom and can only be entered from here."

It was a beautiful room, rather elegant but not exaggerated. The furniture was modest, dark wood but not too fancy.

"See, our covers are already on the bed. Aaand," Danny said theatrically, walking out of the room, "this one is yours." He opened the door opposite to their bedroom and led her in.

It was a nice room, a bit smaller than the bedroom, but it had a large window with purple curtains. There was also the dresser from their last apartment and a sofa.

"I thought I'd put these in here, but the rest you can decorate yourself. You also have your own bathroom."

She smiled at him. "Sounds good."

He looked relieved that she liked it.

Alice went over to the window and checked out the view. From there, she could overlook the whole yard and far beyond that. Danny's friends and some moving staff were still carrying stuff out of the moving van, which was parked on the gravel parking space.

"Nice view," she said. "Why are there bars in front of the window?"

"Uh … they're in front of every window of the house, even the doors have them, but the ones on the windows are fixed. I guess the previous owner was afraid someone might break in."

Alice turned back toward him. "But this is a safe county … and it's a rural area."

He laughed. "Well, we do have crime here, and as soon as you got money, people start taking a special interest in your belongings."

"Do we?" she asked.

"What?"

"Have money, I mean?"

Danny seemed to ponder. "I earn quite well, but I would probably not have installed these bars myself. The wall outside is high enough, and the gate can be locked. Plus, someone will always be here."

"So, you *are* worried that someone might get in."

Or out?

"Uh … I guess … We don't have much expensive stuff here or cash, but how's a thief supposed to know that? The house looks quite fancy after all."

Alice sat down on the large windowsill.

I'll be sitting here a lot; I can feel it.

"I still can't believe we can afford this … you, I mean."

Danny nodded. "Everything happened rather fast. I never thought we'd be so successful." He walked toward her and sat down on the windowsill next to her.

"We both grew up rather poor, and I think we will have to get used to this new lifestyle, you maybe more than I, but I hope you'll get to like and enjoy it." He took her hand in his. It felt good.

"Thanks, Danny..." She let her eyes wander across the room. "For this, I mean ... for all of this."

He smiled. "I just want you to be happy ... I want *us* to be happy."

Alice looked into his big blue eyes. They looked exhausted, and some of their brightness had gone.

"You already said that yesterday," she reminded him.

He looked surprised. "Did I?"

She nodded.

His expression suddenly changed. Thinking about last night seemed to make him uneasy.

"We should talk about ... last night," she said.

Danny rubbed his eyes. "Yeah, I guess. But not now, I still have so much to do."

"Did you even sleep?"

"Yeah, sure, I went to bed at ... uh ..."

"No, you didn't."

He frowned.

"I mean, you didn't come to bed ... Did you sleep on the couch?"

"Yes."

"And the others?"

"Waldo went home shortly after you uh ... went to bed, and he gave Tee and Paul a ride. Only Jonas stayed overnight."

Alice looked out the window again. She noticed that the police car had disappeared. "I couldn't sleep last night—at first I mean—but I didn't hear anything."

"The others didn't really feel like celebrating, I guess..." Danny sighed. "To be honest, Alice, I don't remember much of last night. I probably fell asleep shortly after our ... discussion."

Is that what he calls it?

"Are you hungover?"

53

Danny smiled a tired smile. "My head hurts. And I'm tired. And my stomach's not too happy either, but I was able to do some heavy lifting and I've been up all day."

Alice studied his tired face. He looked older, worn-out. And even a bit puffy. Was that the alcohol? It made her worry. She was way too familiar with what alcoholism looked like.

"Anyway," he got up from the sill, "there's still a lot to do today. We'll have dinner this evening, and then we can talk about everything ... okay?"

She nodded. Her stomach rumbled, and Danny frowned at her. "Have you even eaten today?"

She shook her head.

"Come with me. I have to introduce you to some people."

She followed him back downstairs and into the kitchen.

"Henry," Danny called.

An elderly man with gray hair, dark skin, and a wrinkled face appeared in the door, smiling friendly.

"This is Henry, our cook."

Alice looked at Danny with widened eyes. "Cook?"

"I told you there'd be staff."

Henry shook Alice's hand. "You must be Alice! I'm very happy to meet you."

Alice smiled politely. "Nice to meet you too."

"Henry worked for the previous owners, and he asked if he could keep his job," Danny explained.

Henry nodded enthusiastically. "I'm very glad I can stay."

To Alice, he said, "I will be cooking twice a day during the week, lunch and dinner. But you are always welcome to just tell me if you're hungry, so I can prepare something."

Alice thanked him.

"She's actually hungry now," Danny said.

"I can make my own food," Alice protested. Henry laughed and shook his head. "I already prepared something. It's a buffet since you are busy with moving, so everybody can just serve themselves whenever they like."

Alice looked at Danny.

"Just go, Henry's food is delicious," he encouraged her.

Henry's food *was* delicious. He'd brought Alice a plate and made her sit at the big table in the dining room. Having the long table all to herself felt weird, but Danny had disappeared again. Whether he'd gone back to the old apartment or was just outside with his friends Alice didn't know.

Everything still felt unreal. Confusion had chased her anger away. There was so much she needed to get off her chest, so much she wanted to explain to Danny, but it felt good to see him sober and in a more or less good mood for a change. Mentioning their fight from last night or the dispute with Jonas might change that, and Alice wasn't sure if that was a risk worth taking.

When her plate of vegetable tarts was empty, Henry introduced Alice to Anita, who apparently was responsible for the cleaning. She appeared to be in her forties and her long dark hair was bound into a knot. Her big dark-brown eyes were beaming when she shook Alice's hand.

A cook and a maid. Feels like a movie-set.

Alice wanted to look for Danny, but once out in the yard, she saw that the moving van was gone and so was Danny's Audi. Only a group of strange guys were standing a couple yards away, talking and minding their own business. There was just one familiar face: Jonas's. With his black leather jacket and ripped blue jeans he looked like he belonged to the group; yet he stood a bit apart from the other men. Like always, smoking a cigarette.

Something seemed to tighten around Alice's guts at his sight, and she felt the urge to turn on her heels and run, but it was too late. He had already spotted her. Alice did not want to talk to him, not after the stunt he'd pulled today. Somehow though, his stare seemed to be paralyzing her, as if her instincts were keeping her from moving. She wasn't a mouse and he wasn't a snake though, so staying still would not make her disappear.

Jonas's face looked expressionless as usual. Coolly, he exhaled a cloud of smoke and said, "They're cleaning. Old place."

Could he read her mind?

Without saying anything, Alice managed to turn around and walk back into the house.

It was a peculiar feeling, standing in a house that didn't feel like home. Alice wasn't sure if it ever would. The only place that made sense for her to go seemed to be her room, so she rushed up the carpeted stairs and to the end of the corridor. Right now, the house appeared to be empty, but Alice didn't want to risk running into anybody else. Jonas had been bad enough.

The door to her room stood ajar and apparently, somebody had carried all the boxes with her name on them upstairs and placed them on the floor. Danny, maybe?

Alice began ripping the boxes open and sorting her stuff. It all appeared to be there—except for her phone and laptop. On the right side of the room, behind the door, Alice noticed a small walk-in closet. With a pile of her shirts in her arms she opened its door—and found it occupied by strange clothes already. Curious, she took some of the hangers out and inspected the pieces. There were silken blouses and posh dresses among other elegant things. In general, they were things Alice would never wear. She liked comfortable stuff. Oversized sweaters and t-shirts, leggings, or baggies, mostly black.

Assuming that the fancy clothes must have belonged to the previous owner's wife or daughter, Alice left them in the closet for now. Danny would surely know what to do with them.

4

The afternoon dragged on quiet and boring. Without her laptop and phone, and no one to talk to, Alice didn't know how to entertain herself. The men in the house or yard all looked unfriendly and she had no idea who they were. Were they other friends of Danny's? Staff? Business partners? She had no answer to that, but they all had the same arrogant attitude and they didn't seem to be very interested in her.

Anita and Henry were around too, but Anita was busy cleaning the cupboards in the kitchen and Henry was already preparing dinner.

Eventually, Alice decided to fetch a book from her room, but when she rummaged in the box that contained them, she found her diaries instead.

Curious, she skimmed through the pages. The last notes were from when she and Danny had started dating.

Time to update this thing.

By the time she was done, Danny still hadn't returned. Not knowing what else to do, Alice went back outside to get some fresh air. Jonas was sitting on a bench in front of the house underneath a big oak. Still not talking to anybody, still smoking.

He looked up curiously when she walked down the steps of the porch, but this time, she ignored him and went straight to the swing she had discovered earlier. She sat down on it, fingers wrapped around the cool chains, feeling the urge to push herself off the ground. With Jonas's eyes still on her, a little sway was all she dared though.

When the sky was already turning pink in front of her and dark blue behind her, Alice could hear a car approaching on the gravel road at last. One of the men in the yard went to the gate and opened it. Danny's old dark blue Audi Sedan appeared, and behind it, some white Mercedes Alice didn't know.

Both parked in front of the house, and the doors opened. Danny got out of his car and Waldo out of the Mercedes.

Alice wanted to greet her boyfriend, but then she saw that Jonas was doing just that, so she remained sitting on the swing instead. She didn't want to get close to that guy—if possible, not ever again.

The men talked for a while, but their voices got swallowed by the wind. Jonas gestured to Alice, and Danny turned his head.

Jonas and Waldo then went into the house and Danny walked toward her. He looked even more exhausted than before, but his smile was warm and inviting while he crouched down beside her, putting a hand on her knee.

"How did the cleaning go?" Alice asked him.

"I hired a cleaning service, but we had to fix the walls and stuff."

"Why didn't you say something? I would've helped too."

Smiling, Danny shook his head slowly. "You didn't choose this, Alice. This house, this day ... it was my fault that everything had to happen so fast. I didn't want to put this on you."

Alice gave his hand a squeeze. "Thanks."

For a while, they were both quiet.

"Who are these guys?" Alice broke the silence, nodding toward the man who had opened the gate and was still standing beside it.

"They work for me."

"As what?"

"Well, the one by the gate is responsible for the security of the house, but you don't have to learn his name. It won't always be the same."

"The name?"

Danny chuckled. "No, the man. They'll take shifts. You don't have to get to know them."

Frowning, Alice let her eyes wander through the yard. "Walls, bars, gates ... and security guards? What are you afraid of, Danny?"

"It's just ... Most companies have security, right? This," he pointed at the house, "is our company. This is where we keep our business plan, where we do our bookkeeping, basically everything. And I must say, the business is going rather great so far. It's not that unlikely people might be interested in our secrets."

With a heavy feeling in her stomach, Alice looked up at the big old house.

His company, my home?

How was that going to work out?

Danny misinterpreted her mimics. "Don't be afraid," he said. "Nothing's going to happen."

Alice gave him a skeptical smile.

He sighed, stood up, and stretched his limbs. "Dinner will soon be ready. I need a shower. And you should probably get inside. It's getting cold and you're not wearing a jacket."

They showered separately—Danny in the bedroom's bathroom and Alice in her own. It was wonderful to have him back, but she didn't need to go all in on the first day of their truce.

Maybe it had only been the thing with the business and the apartment that had agitated him so much. Nonetheless, there was that unavoidable and dreadful talk awaiting her at dinner, and it made her nervous.

To stall a bit, Alice took a long, hot shower and allowed herself to truly indulge in the bathroom's luxury. It had a large bathtub with a wide edge that provided enough room for shampoo bottles and candles, the floor was made of white heated tiles, and above the generous sink hung a big cupboard mirror.

Danny was already sitting at the long table, which had been covered with a cream-colored tablecloth, when Alice entered the room. Both their plates were set on one end of the table, for which she was glad. Sitting at opposite ends each, far apart from each other, would have been awkward, like they were an old rich married couple who had nothing to say to each other anymore apart from "Pass the salt, Richard" and "Lamb's a bit dry today."

With a thoughtful expression, Danny was staring at his plate. He looked up though when Alice stepped into the room. She took her place and scrutinized her boyfriend.

Dressed in a clean white dress shirt, his heavy golden watch around his wrist, he looked like a younger version of Waldo. A younger, more handsome version, that was. But still, it was so unlike him. He had even combed back his hair and fixed it with mousse.

After flashing her a quick smile, he looked back down at his fork, with which he was playing nervously. Alice let her eyes wander across the table. Henry had done a nice job. He had even lit two red candles in golden holders. How romantic.

A bottle of champagne and two glasses were waiting between her and Danny.

"Champagne?" she asked.

Danny nodded and looked up. "To celebrate."

"Ah, you're both here, perfect! I'll open the bottle for you." Henry had just come in and he was beaming. As announced, he opened the bottle and filled their glasses with the sparkling golden liquid.

"I'll let you enjoy your drinks for a moment before I bring out the food."

Alice thanked him and took her glass. Danny followed her example, and they clinked their glasses despite the obvious lack of enthusiasm. Something was evidently bothering him, and the toasting seemed a bit staged.

He drank half of his glass in one go and inhaled deeply.

"So ..." he said.

"So ..." she said.

"I'd really like to just celebrate this day with you, but there's an elephant in the room and I know we need to address it."

Biting her lip, Alice nodded.

"I talked to Jonas."

An uneasy feeling began spreading in Alice's stomach.

"What happened today?" Danny asked. "He said you ran away and made a big scene in public." A deep line of worry appeared on his forehead while he awaited her response.

"I ... I just wanted to see my friends."

Danny's eyebrows climbed upward. "Today? Why?"

What Alice saw in his eyes made her feel very uncomfortable. Danny looked as if he had already made up his mind and put his guard up. Something hard in his eyes made clear he was hurt, but instead of vulnerable, he appeared stubborn and distant.

"I wanted to tell them ... that we're moving. That's all."

"And you couldn't do that on the phone?"

"You have my phone."

Danny took the bottle of champagne and refilled his glass. "Right. It broke when it fell on the floor. I'll get it fixed. But why did you just run away? Without telling anyone?"

Alice took a sip from her glass. The champagne sent a tingling sensation across her tongue. "I felt ... trapped. I mean, I needed some alone time, but Jonas was always there ..."

"I told him to help you with your stuff."

"But he didn't really ... he was just standing there, watching me! He wouldn't let me out of his sight for even a second!"

"Why should he?"

Surprised, Alice gaped at him. "Why he should? Because it's rude to stare at people and because I don't need anybody babysitting me, that's why!"

Danny reached out and put his hand on hers. "Relax, I'm just trying to understand what happened. That's all."

Alice frowned at him. "He was creeping me out. He followed me back upstairs when I went to pee. I ... I felt suffocated ..."

Still suspicious, Danny studied her face. "I still don't understand why you had to run away. You could've just come here with the others and Jonas would've left you alone. And I was here, too."

Alice knew exactly where he was going with this. "I just needed time, that's all."

He took another drink of his champagne. "Time?"

She stared at her plate. "Time to think ... everything happened so fast. I woke up and all the stuff was gone, and no one gave me a moment to figure out ..."

He raised one eyebrow. "Figure out? What?"

Feeling cornered, Alice looked up at him. The sadness in his eyes almost broke her heart. "What I want."

There. I said it.

Leaning back in his chair, Danny pulled his hand away from Alice's. It was obvious he was leaning away from her.

"Is this not what you want?" he asked after a pause. "Am *I* not what you want?"

"Of course, you are! I ... I just ..." Why was it so hard to find the right words? "I just wasn't prepared to move ... and we had that big fight last night and no time to talk about it ... It was just too much, I needed to clear my head ..."

Again, Danny had emptied his glass and was reaching for the bottle. Alice took his hand and held it down.

"Please don't ... Not now."

Irritated, he looked at her, but then his features softened, and he pulled his hand back. "I'm sorry." He put his empty glass back on the table and said nothing for a while, eyes fixed on her. Alice felt like she was shrinking under the look he gave her.

"Do you want to leave me, Alice?" he suddenly blurted out.

"No, of course not!" Alice tried to assure him, taken off guard by the sudden bluntness. "I don't want to leave you, Danny, I swear!"

It wasn't a lie. She didn't *want* to leave him.

He examined her carefully, with a wary expression.

Alice took his hand quickly and gave it a squeeze. "Danny, I swear, I wasn't going to leave you! I just needed time and I panicked, that's all. I promise."

"But you're not happy with me." It wasn't a question.

Desperately, Alice tightened her grip around his hand. "I haven't been happy with the way things have been lately ..."

She saw Danny's other hand jerk toward the bottle, but he pulled it back quickly.

"I told you last night ... but I'm not sure you remember ... the drinking, the way you kept pushing me away ... You always seemed to be mad at me. You weren't nice to me anymore ..."

Danny looked at her for a while, his expression unreadable. "I was stressed out. Under a lot of pressure. There were some problems with the business."

"That's about what you already told me last night."

He raised one eyebrow, the way he always did. "We already had this conversation?"

"I wanted to talk to you ... when you're sober."

That seemed to annoy him. His expression hardened. "I'm sorry you feel trapped, Alice. Or pressured. That wasn't my intention," he said coldly.

Alice started chewing her lower lip nervously. She didn't like his tone.

"After all the trouble I put you through when I was unemployed, I finally found a way to turn things around. Now I can take care of *you*. You don't have to worry about money anymore ... or cleaning an apartment."

He makes it sound ridiculous.

"Do you think ... I'm ungrateful?"

He said nothing and started playing with his fork again.

"Danny, I just need some time to settle down ... To let everything sink in ... It's just happened—"

"Too fast, I know," he cut her off.

Henry appeared in the archway, carrying a big wooden bowl. "Time for starters," he announced cheerfully. His smile disappeared at once when he saw their faces. "Sorry, I hope I'm not interrupting something."

Alice smiled at him. "No, don't worry. Thank you so much, Henry!"

The cook began loading their plates with a mouthwatering salad. "Daniel said you like Rapunzel salad, so there's lots of Rapunzel in there. I also added some tomatoes and herbs from the garden."

"We have a garden?" Alice asked, surprised.

Henry nodded enthusiastically. "For sure, haven't you been behind the house yet?"

She shook her head.

"Well, you should add it to your to-do list. Right now, most veggies are gone. It's been too wet and cold these days. There are still some herbs though and lettuces. Feel free to just take whatever you need."

Beaming, Alice thanked him.

"You're welcome." He bent down to put some bruschetta and garlic bread on their plates. "Enjoy!"

"Wow, these look amazing, thank you, Henry!"

After giving Alice another wide smile, the cook went back to the kitchen. For a moment, Alice almost forgot about her conversation with Danny. The food on her plate made her mouth water. She grabbed a piece of garlic bread and started chewing on it. Danny hadn't touched his food yet, but he gave his glass a champagne refill. Again, he emptied it at once, to her distaste. Was he trying to get drunk at dinner?

Not daring to say anything though, Alice focused on her plate and eventually, Danny began eating as well. They ate in silence for a while.

When her plate was almost empty, Alice looked up and met his eyes. She tried to read his expression. There was pain and sorrow on his face, a sadness in his eyes, yet he was trying hard to hide it. It made him appear a bit stubborn and irritated.

"Danny," she began, and put her fork down.

"What?"

Hearing the anger in his voice made her sad. "I just want you to know that I really am thankful for what you've done for me ... for us. I do appreciate it."

Doubt flickered in his eyes.

"I mean it. I can see that you've been under a lot of stress lately. I understand that you meant well. It just makes me sad that you didn't open up to me or ask for my help ..."

"Why? So you could be in control again?"

Why is he always attacking me?

"No ..." She shook her head sadly and felt her eyes tear up.

Don't cry. Henry's next-door.

Trying to blink back the tears, she watched Danny fill his glass anew and chug it. Wasn't it obvious that he didn't want her anymore? Could he not stand her presence without being drunk? But why had he made her move in with him again?

The tears now started running down her cheeks and Alice angrily wiped them away with the back of her hand.

Henry appeared again, to collect their plates, though this time, he remained quiet and left quickly.

Danny let out an irritated sigh. "What do you *want*, Alice?"

Avoiding his eyes, she stared at the spot where her plate had been. "What do *you* want, Danny?" she muttered quietly. "Why did you even bring me here? You don't want this."

"What don't I want?"

"Me."

He seemed surprised. "What are you talking about?"

"You're always mad at me. Admit it. You ... you didn't buy a big house to give me some privacy. You bought it so you can be away from me! Why can't you just be honest?"

Danny seemed taken aback. "You're the one who was always in a bad mood, Alice. My door was always open, but you never came in, did you? And now you're blaming me again?"

Alice forced a sob back down. "Your friends were always there! How can you not get that I don't feel comfortable with them around all the time? We were never alone together—"

"They are a part of my life now, Alice," Danny said coldly. "Get over it. And don't even think of making me choose between you and them."

"*What?*" Alice stared at him, shocked at how shamelessly Danny twisted her words. "That's not ... that's not what I'm saying!"

With a cold flicker in his eyes, Danny leaned back again, arms crossed. "Then what the fuck do you want, Alice?"

For a long moment, Alice could do nothing but stare at him. Every desperate attempt to avoid making him mad was a waste of time. If he despised her so much that no matter what she said was perceived by him as criticism or provocation, why in the world was he still with her?

Alice hid her face in her hands, unable to bear the look on his face anymore.

When she heard him get up from his chair and walk around the table, she expected him to leave the room. To her surprise though, he crouched down beside her.

"What do you want, Alice?" he repeated softly. All harshness had left his voice.

Carefully, Alice took her hands away from her face and looked at him. His expression had softened. Now, he looked mainly concerned.

"Just you," she breathed. "I miss you, that's all."

Something in Danny's eyes shifted, as if a veil were removed from them. Behind all the sadness, suspicion, and anger, Alice could finally see affection and love again. Slowly, Danny put his arms around her and pulled her head onto his chest. His grip was firm and comforting, like he wasn't planning on ever letting go of her again. It felt good.

They kept their fingers laced while eating the main course.

Having opened up was a great feeling and Alice couldn't remember the last time she'd been this happy. Henry had brought them white wine to go along with the risotto, but Alice was still sipping her champagne. Danny was already on his second glass of wine, and as much as Alice wanted to ignore it and focus on how good the warmth of his hand felt on hers, she couldn't extinguish the acidic feeling of apprehension in the pit of her stomach. If Danny only drank when he was stressed out or unhappy, that was one thing. But if he couldn't even withstand the temptation to get intoxicated on an evening like this, he was in much deeper trouble than Alice had assumed. Also, practically emptying the bottle of champagne plus two glasses of white wine did not seem to have an effect on him yet; and that was truly alarming.

When their plates were empty once again, Alice finished her glass of champagne and watched quietly, as Henry collected them.

"What is it?" Danny asked, having clearly noticed the look on her face. "Something is still bothering you."

Alice started chewing her lip again and watched her boyfriend reach for the wine bottle.

"That is," she muttered.

He raised one eyebrow.

"The drinking," Alice explained. "I know you don't like talking about it, but it really worries me."

"We're celebrating, aren't we?" he said defensively. "How come you drink so little?"

"I just want to ... keep a clear head."

"What for?"

Alice felt a knot build in her throat, leaving her unable to speak. How in the world was she supposed to address the fact that Danny had turned into a maniac the previous night? She didn't want to make a big deal out of a little yelling and bottle-throwing, but she couldn't deny that his behavior had really scared her. Having to tiptoe around him, think twice about everything she wanted to say, afraid something might make him snap, was exhausting.

Danny's frown got deeper the longer Alice remained quiet. Worried, he leaned forward and took both her hands in his.

"Tell me," he urged.

"It's nothing, really."

"You don't look like it's nothing."

Sighing, Alice tried to lean away from him, but he kept her hands in his. "It's really no big deal ... you just scared me a bit last night, that's all."

Danny's grip around her hands grew stronger and Alice looked up at him. The look on his face made her wince, but then she realized that the contempt in his eyes wasn't directed at her this time.

"Did I hurt you?" he wanted to know.

Alice wondered how much he remembered of their fight. Apparently, he did take the possibility that he might have hurt her into consideration, so he couldn't be completely oblivious to his outburst.

"No, of course not. You'd never. You just threw a bottle at me, that's all." She chuckled, but it sounded more like a cough.

Self-loathing made Danny's eyes glint dangerously and he seemed to be grinding his teeth.

"You do remember that, right?" she asked quietly.

Taking a deep breath, Danny took his hands off hers and wiped them on his pants. He eyed the wine bottle with a disgusted look.

"I wish I didn't," he muttered. "I suppressed it, but I found the shards today when I was back in the apartment, and it all came back."

"It's no big deal—"

"Yes, it is!" he cut her off. "I shouldn't have lost my temper like that. I should be in control."

Alice watched him clench his hands into fists until the knuckles turned white.

"You usually are ... it's just the alcohol. That's why I don't like it when you drink that much."

"That's why you want to keep a clear head," he concluded. "So you'd know how to react."

Alice said nothing, but when his eyes bored into hers with an intensity that made her heart race, she nodded.

"I'm sorry." Danny's voice was sincere and firm, yet a bit shaky as well. He put his hand back on hers and gave it a squeeze. "I feel awful."

"I know," Alice said softly. "Don't. It's fine."

"It's not, Alice. But I'll make it better, I promise. I'll make an effort." Now, his voice was truly shaking, and his eyes glistened wetly. Alice got off her chair to give him a hug. She wrapped her arms around him, feeling the ice between them melt at last.

5

Alice awoke to Danny kissing her forehead. She kept her eyes shut and smiled. There was nothing she wanted more than to stay in bed with him all day long, just cuddling.

But then she realized drowsily that there was no one on the mattress beside her. She blinked and opened her eyes to see Danny standing next to the bed, fully dressed, buttoning up his shirt.

"What you doin'?" she muttered, her tongue still half asleep.

"Gotta go. Already too late. They're waiting for me," he said quickly, taking his phone from the nightstand and shoving it in the back pocket of his jeans.

"Why?" Alice pushed herself up on her elbows.

"Got a business meeting and totally forgot to set the alarm last night," Danny explained while fumbling with his shoelaces.

Alice pouted at him, and he chuckled and brushed a strand of hair behind her ear.

"It's Tuesday, Allie, I have to work."

Hearing the nickname, he hadn't used on her in months, made her smile. "But ... what am I supposed to do?" she asked, watching him walk toward the bedroom door.

"Sleep until noon, and then eat lunch with me." Danny winked and blew her a kiss, and then he was out through the door, closing it behind him.

Sighing, Alice dropped back down onto the pillow. Sure, she usually liked to sleep in on her days off, but they had gone to bed quite early last night and now she didn't feel tired anymore.

A glance at the digital alarm clock on the nightstand revealed that it was 8:42 a.m.

Being unemployed made her feel uneasy, especially since Danny had quit her job for her. But she didn't want to be mad at him, not anymore, not with everything going so well at last.

Not knowing how many people were in the house at this time, Alice put on her clothes from before instead of walking out into the corridor in her underwear. She didn't like it that Danny wanted to provide for her, but right now there was nothing she could do about it.

After two hours of letting her skin turn wrinkled in the bathtub, Alice got dressed and went downstairs. Danny's office door was closed, and the living room was empty. Muffled voices were coming out of the office, but it was impossible to understand what was being said.

Sunlight fell through the windows. It seemed to be a nice autumn day for a change. A fresh breeze played with Alice's still wet hair when she stepped outside into the yard. Around the corner she found Henry working in the vegetable garden. The garden looked quite generous, as if you could live off it. There were overgrown cauliflower plants, tomato plants, and lots of herbs. The cook was busy cutting off a lettuce when Alice greeted him. He beamed at her and nodded to the lettuce in his hand. "I'm going to make that one for dinner."

Alice helped him prepare the vegetable garden for winter, even though he objected at first. Having been raised in a tiny house without yard, Alice didn't know much about gardening, but Henry had answers to all her questions. He was a nice person to have around and Alice enjoyed helping him. He wouldn't let her help in the kitchen, however, so she went to sit on the swing instead and blinked into the sunlight.

Soon enough, lunch was ready, and Alice found Danny sitting at the table in the dining room. His friends, or colleagues, or whatever he liked to call them, were eating in the living room.

He didn't look as happy as this morning, Alice noticed. He seemed tense, but he smiled weakly when he saw her entering the room. After planting a quick kiss on his lips, Alice sat down opposite him.

"Rough morning?"

He nodded and took a sip of his sparkling water.

"How did the meeting go?"

Danny sighed. "Waldo wasn't pleased with me being late and gave me attitude." He put down the glass again and started to wipe off the fog with his thumb. "And we're facing some unexpected problems."

"What kind of problems?"

"That's not important, just ... stuff."

Henry appeared with two plates and set them down in front of them, then he went back to the kitchen to fetch a bowl of salad.

Danny began cutting his steak, and Alice took a bite of her spinach polenta. It was delicious.

"What are you going to do this afternoon?" she asked him.

Danny chewed and swallowed. "More work, more meetings. Potential client's coming over. Hope we'll get him to sign a contract."

Alice was disappointed. But what had she expected? It was unlikely he'd have an afternoon off.

"What did you do this morning?" he asked while taking a mouthful of his mashed potatoes.

"I took a bath and read a book, and then I helped Henry in the garden."

"You don't have to do that."

"I know. I wanted to. He taught me about gardening. It was very interesting." She smiled and took his hand, the one that wasn't busy delivering food to his mouth.

He grimaced back at her. "Sounds good, then."

Alice drank from her glass of tap water and finished her dish quietly.

"Uh, Danny," she began after Henry had collected their plates. "I was wondering if there's something I could do for you, maybe?"

"I thought you'd be glad to have some time to relax."

"Of course, but I can't just sit around and do nothing for hours."

"Right, I forgot. The TV's gonna be delivered today. We'll put it in our bedroom. The guys have their own in the basement. The box with our DVDs is in the bedroom closet. We'll also have Netflix as soon as the Wi-Fi's installed." He chugged the rest of his water.

Alice stared at her glass. "Are you sure I can't help you with anything?"

Danny frowned at her.

"Some administrative work, maybe. Bookkeeping and stuff..."

He shook his head. "I really don't think so."

Frustrated, Alice sighed. "Fine, I'll find a new show to binge-watch then."

"You could finally catch up on *Game of Thrones*, so we can watch the rest together," Danny suggested.

Alice grimaced. "I read the books. Show's too bloody for my taste."

"Shame. Guess we'll have to find something else to watch together."

"Shame's that you're not into comedies. You miss out on the good stuff."

Danny took her hand in his. "Not really into it. I need blood and violence to be entertained."

"I know." Alice rolled her eyes. "Too bad, really. Funny, how you're a pacifist in real life but you love watching people slaughter each other on screen."

Danny raised an eyebrow. "Pacifist? Me? Nah, Alice, guess you don't know me as well as I thought."

"I thought you oppose war?"

"Of course. But if there was a war already going on and the wrong people were being killed, I'd gladly join the fight."

Alice sighed. "The white knight saving them all. You just want to be a hero, don't you?"

"Don't we all?" He grinned.

"Not me. I'd be the first one to get killed."

Shaking his head, Danny squeezed her hand. "I don't think so. You're smart enough to survive."

After checking his wristwatch, he sighed. "Gotta go back to work." He pushed his chair back and gave Alice a kiss before she had time to object.

"Are we gonna have dinner together again?" she asked him quickly, before he left the room.

"I hope so," he replied.

After brushing her teeth, Alice went to sit on the swing again. There were still people standing around in front of the house, men she didn't know. One guy was sitting on a plastic chair next to the gate. He seemed to guard it, or maybe he was there to open and close when people wanted to leave or enter by car.

It was weird living in that house. Especially because it didn't feel like hers. It wasn't, technically. Danny owned it and used it as a workplace, so there would always be people around. And not to forget Henry and Anita. As nice as it was, not having to do any cleaning or cooking, it felt strange to have them around.

Alice watched two men in leather jackets smoking and having a discussion.

If they had at least seemed nice, things would have felt different. But somehow, they made her uncomfortable the way Jonas and Danny's other friends did. They all looked mean and aggressive. Well, if they were there to guard the house, that wasn't surprising. Couldn't really use nice guys to scare intruders off, could you?

But what intruders? They were in the middle of nowhere. The only neighbors they had were farmers, and Alice couldn't quite understand why anyone would take a big interest in Danny's company. He developed video games, so what?

Noticing a movement in the corner of her eyes, she turned her head and saw Jonas stepping out of the house, lighting a cigarette. He glanced in her direction for a second, then continued walking toward the two men in leather jackets. Were they friends? They all looked similar, a bit like a gang of bikers, only without beards and bikes.

Later that afternoon, their TV was delivered, along with some other boxes whose content Alice didn't know. She watched the delivery people install the big flat screen in the bedroom. When they were done, she went through the box with DVDs and chose one to watch.

That evening, when Alice went downstairs for dinner, Danny's friends were sitting around the table. They were talking in loud voices but stopped immediately when she entered the room.

Feeling uncomfortable, she sat down hesitantly. Having to eat with the whole gang was not something she had expected. Plus, the sudden silence, for which she was obviously responsible, made her feel very uneasy and unwelcome.

Danny kissed her though and put his arm around her shoulder, which managed to make her feel a bit better.

"Hi, Alice," said Tee. "How're you today?"

"Fine, thanks," Alice answered.

Paul was staring at the air in front of him. Jonas was wearing his usual poker face; his eyes seemed to look right through her.

"And what did *you* do today?" Waldo wanted to know. It sounded somewhat accusing.

"Uh ... some reading, gardening ..." Alice didn't like talking to Waldo.

"Gardening, huh?" He nodded. "Sounds useful. That house is big enough to keep busy."

Danny shot Waldo an irritated look. "I don't want her to do anything. We have staff for that."

Waldo arranged his napkin on his lap. "Just saying. Must be boring to have nothing to do."

Danny ignored that and turned back to Alice to put a kiss on her cheek.

"Alice, you should come to the basement with me," Tee offered.

Danny frowned.

"I mean, to work out. Everything's arrived this afternoon."

Curious, Alice looked at Danny. "Do we have like a private gym?"

He opened his mouth to answer, but Tee was faster. "Oh yeah," he said eagerly. "There's weights, lots of 'em."

Alice grimaced. "I'm not really into weight-lifting."

"We could add some girl stuff, right, Dan?" Tee said.

"Girl stuff?" She scowled at him.

"You know, treadmills, home trainers, stuff like that."

"Girl stuff," Alice repeated, shaking her head scornfully. "Though a treadmill does sound nice."

Tee grinned. "Wouldn't mind watching you sweat on the treadmill while lifting weights."

Danny gave him a warning look.

Tee quickly took a sip of his beer to stop himself from talking.

"Would you like a drink?" Danny asked her, gesturing toward his own beer bottle.

Alice let her eyes wander over the table. Danny, Tee, and Paul were drinking beer, Waldo red wine, and Jonas water.

"No thanks."

He raised his eyebrow. "You like beer!"

The more he drinks, the less I feel like drinking.

"It's Tuesday," she pointed out.

"You don't have to work tomorrow."

Alice knew that all too well and she still hadn't figured out how to feel about it, so she just shrugged.

Henry brought their food, and the guys began eating noisily while emptying more beer bottles and talking heatedly about some game they'd watched.

Then they started talking about video games, which caught Alice's attention. "How are yours going?" she asked.

The men fell silent and stared at her.

"The games," she explained. "The ones you're developing."

Danny cleared his throat. "Good, actually."

"So ... how does it work?" she wanted to know.

"Well," he thought for a while. "I do the programming, Paul's really good at drawing. We ... discuss our ideas together and try to make something out of it. But it's not games, it's *game*. You know, it takes a hell lot of work, and we only just got started." He took a sip of his beer. No one else talked.

"Then ... how come you're already making so much money?"

Danny rubbed his chin with his thumb and index finger, and licked his lips. "Funds."

"Funds?"

He nodded. "Investors who already paid a generous sum because they know it's going to be a ... *blast*."

"But ... isn't the market full already?"

Danny shook his head. "Nah, there's always new ideas, and graphics keep getting better. Now with the whole virtual reality thing, things get more ... *realistic*."

For some reason, Tee almost choked on his food and had to take a drink of his beer to refrain from spraying the table with his spit.

"I read about it," Alice told him. "VR-porn ... sounds like something you would like, huh?"

He grinned at her. "For sure." He gulped down some more beer. "And what would *you* like, *Lizzy*?"

Alice frowned at the new nickname. "I'd like a female main character with clothes on."

Tee and Danny laughed. "You should play more, Alice. There's lots of them already," said Danny. "Even Lara Croft wears more clothes with every new version of *Tomb Raider* that comes out," he continued.

Tee donned a sad face. "Shame."

They laughed again.

"Why do people call you Tee?" Alice asked to change the subject.

"His name's Timothy," explained Danny.

"They used to call me Big T because I was fat, but then I lost fifty pounds and now I'm only Tee."

"Is that a good or a bad thing?"

"I haven't decided yet." He winked at her.

When they were all done eating and Henry had collected their plates, Danny was on his fourth beer already. The topics got more heated and more perverted, and it began to annoy her. Only Jonas and Paul hadn't said a word throughout the whole time, but that didn't help much.

When Danny opened his fifth beer bottle, Alice pushed back her chair and got up. "I'm going to watch TV. Are you coming too?"

Danny looked at her and then he looked at his friends. "I think I'll stay for a while, but I'll meet ya later, okay?"

Alice grimaced and said goodbye to the others though only Tee replied.

Back upstairs, she went to brush her teeth in her own bathroom and changed into her pajamas. She had to take them out of one of the moving boxes, which reminded her about the occupied closet.

I forgot to ask Danny about those clothes...
And she'd also forgotten to ask him about the status of her cell phone.

When she stepped out of her room, she saw Jonas coming out of one of the guest bathrooms, wearing only boxers. She quickly turned away and hid in the bedroom.

They'd placed the TV opposite of the bed, which allowed her to cuddle into her blankets while zapping through the channels.

Danny didn't show up throughout the whole movie, and when the alarm clock showed 12:30 a.m., Alice decided to sleep.

This time, it was only a light sleep, and she awoke immediately when the bedroom door was opened.

A large shadow moved into the room, then something hit the bed and she heard an "ouch."

The clock showed 1:38 a.m. Alice bit her tongue and pretended to sleep while Danny got undressed and fell into bed next to her, shaking the whole thing with his weight. He smelled of alcohol and sweat. "Alice?" she heard him whisper close to her ear. "You awake?"

She tried to ignore him, but he started fumbling with her T-shirt. "Stop that," she snapped and pushed his hand away. He sighed deeply and turned onto his back.

"Are you going to work tomorrow morning?" she asked.

Danny moaned. "Of course ... *someone* has to."

She ignored that remark. "It's late. You won't get enough sleep."

He moaned again.

"And then you'll get irritable and stressed out. Sleep is important."

"Yes, *Mommy*."

Alice sighed. "Whatever."

He started snoring.

Alice slept badly afterward. Danny seemed restless. He kept tossing and turning and mumbling things in his sleep.

Only when dawn came did she finally manage to drift off into a sleep so deep, she didn't even wake up when Danny got up to go to work.

It was almost noon when she awoke once more, so she took a quick shower and went directly downstairs to meet him for lunch.

He was sitting on the same chair as the day before. Dark shadows framed his eyes, but he seemed to be in a good mood.

"Morning Allie," he said cheerfully when he saw her.

Alice forced herself to smile and sat down opposite him.

"Don't I get a kiss?" he asked.

When she didn't reply, he stood up and bent over the table to kiss her. She kissed him back but not enthusiastically.

"God, I'm tired today." Danny rubbed his eyes with both of his hands.

"You came to bed quite late."

"Ugh, I should've just listened to you and come upstairs . . ."

"Hangover?"

He shook his head. "Didn't have *that* much to drink last night."

"How much *did* you have?"

He thought for a moment. "Some beer and then some whiskey but not much."

Whiskey ... him and his whiskey.

"How long did your friends stay?"

"They uh ... well, Waldo went home before midnight, taking Tee and Paul along. Jonas went to bed shortly after you."

"So only he stayed here?"

"Waldo has a wife and kids at home, you know."

Poor bastards.

"Tee has a cat to feed and Paul lives with his mother," Danny continued.

"So, what did you do when they were all gone?"

Danny grinned. "I shared a bottle of whiskey with the gate guard. Nice guy, by the way."

"So, all your friends decided to be responsible ... why not you?"

Henry came in and put their plates on the table.

"I got carried away ... It was such a great evening with my buddies, and it was great having you there as well. I didn't want the night to end." He loaded a big pile of rice onto his fork and put it in his mouth.

Alice said nothing. Danny's words evoked a queasy feeling in her stomach. He'd stayed up and gotten drunk with someone he didn't even know ... just to artificially prolong his happiness. Like he didn't want the next day to begin; didn't want sobriety to strike again. His sadness really seemed to have deep roots and Alice wondered where it came from and why she hadn't noticed it sooner.

They ate in silence for a while until she asked, "How was work this morning?"

Chewing, Danny rolled his eyes. "Was late again. The others didn't like it. Wasn't as bad as yesterday, though."

"I'll set your alarm for you next time, okay?"

Danny smiled. "Thanks ... and if I don't wake up, just kick me out of bed."

"With pleasure."

That evening they all ate together again. Tee made some stupid jokes, but Alice was glad. At least, *he* was talking to her. Everyone except her and Jonas drank some alcoholic beverages, but no one as many as Danny.

Jonas was the first one to go to bed and the others left at around 10:00 p.m.

Alice had sat through the whole dinner and the annoying conversations to make sure that Danny came to bed with her this time. By the time she got up from the table, he was already drunk.

"Why now? It's so early!" he protested when she pulled at his arm.

"Because if you don't come now, there'll be no one around to make sure you go to bed at all."

Pouting, he gave her a pleading look.

"Come now," she insisted.

He moaned but obeyed and followed her.

As promised, Alice set the alarm for him when they were lying underneath the sheets.

Danny started to fumble her T-shirt again.

"Why are you always so horny when you're drunk?" Alice sighed.

He kissed her. "It's you that's making me horny, ain't got nothing to do with alcohol." He kissed her again. "And I'm not that drunk."

Again, Alice found it hard to fall asleep next to a mumbling and sweating Danny, who appeared to be having very troubling dreams.

6

The rest of the week passed in a similar manner. Alice spent her days reading, watching TV, and helping Henry in the garden. Her lunches were spent with Danny, her dinners with the whole gang. She got used to being around them and continued to bring Danny to bed every evening, even though she hated mothering him.

When they were enjoying a delicious lunch that Friday, Danny announced that he had to go on a business trip that afternoon.

"A business trip?"

"Yeah, we have to sort some things out, meet some people … stuff like that."

Alice made a face. "But I was looking forward to the weekend! I thought we could do something … spend some time together."

Danny took a sip of his orange juice and raised one eyebrow. "We spend every day together."

"I know, but it's not the same. I want a whole day with you, without the guys …"

"I thought you got to like them?"

"It doesn't matter whether I like them or not. I'd just like to do something with you alone."

"Like what?"

Alice sighed. "Don't know … go somewhere?"

"Where?"

"I don't know, Danny. Just out of this house."

Wiping his mouth with a cotton napkin, he leaned back in his chair. "I thought you like the house?"

"Again, Danny, it doesn't matter whether I like the house or not. It would just be nice to see something else for a change."

He looked at her without saying anything.

"We could take a nice walk through that forest behind the house. Weather forecast looks good."

Danny took her hand. "We can do that sometime, but I really have to go on that trip."

Disappointed, Alice sighed again. "When will you be back?"

"Tuesday night. Have to get back to work on Wednesday."

"But your business trip *is* work, isn't it?"

"Yeah but still ..." He scratched his unshaven chin. "Some problems came up that need solving, and on Wednesday it's back to normal work." He checked his watch. "Oops, got to pack!"

Before he'd left the room, Alice suddenly remembered: "There's some strange clothes in my closet."

"They're yours," Danny said, and he was gone.

Mine?

Two hours later, Waldo was waiting in his car in front of the house, and Alice was saying goodbye to Danny on the doorstep. He hadn't packed much, only a small duffel bag, and he seemed a bit agitated.

"Are you nervous?" Alice asked him when he was checking his watch for the third time.

Danny inhaled deeply. "I just hope that everything will go smoothly, that's all."

Alice pouted and hugged him. "You're leaving me alone for such a long time."

He brushed a strand of hair behind her ear. "I'm sorry. But you won't be alone. Jonas stays here. He'll keep you company."

"Jonas? But why? He's ... he's not good company."

Danny seemed surprised. "Why would you say that?"

"He never talks."

Laughing, he shook his head. "Of course, he does!"

"I mean, I've heard him talk ... enough to notice his British accent, but you can't really have a conversation with him."

"I can."

Alice frowned.

Smiling warmly, Danny let his fingers run through her hair again. "You're right. He doesn't talk much. But that's one of the things I like about him."

"I don't like him."

"Why not?"

"Hmm, let's see ... It might have something to do with him chasing me through town, keeping me from going where I wanted, and then having me arrested?"

Danny sighed. "We talked about this. He's a security guard, he got carried away."

"That's your excuse? Danny, the guy physically kept me from walking away!"

"He would never hurt anybody."

"He wouldn't let go of me!"

"Did he hurt you?"

"No, but—"

"See. I told him to make sure you came here, and he took it a bit too literally."

Annoyed, Alice rolled her eyes. "No wonder. Doesn't seem to think much, does he."

"Alice don't be mean. He's a genius."

"Him?" she asked doubtfully. "He doesn't seem too smart."

"He's majoring two subjects at the same time."

"He's a student? I thought he's a security guard slash construction worker."

"He is, to pay for his courses." Danny checked his watch again. "I mean, he was. Now he works for me."

"*For* you?"

He nodded.

"So, you're the boss of this company?"

"Yeah, you could say so. I got the most skills needed, and I came up with the idea, but the others have their place too and they're not less important."

"What does he study?"

"Psychology and law."

"Interesting combination."

"It's quite useful for us. Every company needs a—"

"Psychologist?"

"Lawyer, Alice, Jesus!"

"It was a joke ..."

Waldo honked and Danny lifted his bag from the ground.

"But why does *he* have to stay?" Alice insisted. "Why not ... Tee for example?"

"Tee?" Danny made a disgusted face.

"Yeah, he's an idiot, but he's entertaining."

"I don't trust him. The way he always stares at you ..."

"Jonas stares at me more."

"Jonas isn't like that. He doesn't stare at you *that* way."

"True but—"

"Alice, Jonas stays. End of discussion. He's my best friend, and I trust him to guard the house and ... to look after you."

"I don't need a babysitter!"

Danny appeared to get irritated. "I won't leave you alone here, period. Plus, Jonas lives here anyway."

"He *what?!*"

"The upstairs bedroom next to the stairs is his."

Great, so I have to see that guy every day now?

"Why does he live here?"

"He was living in a motel before, and we have enough space."

"Didn't he have time to save up for his own place?"

"Why would he? He started studying right after high school."

"Why is he taking so long?"

Danny looked confused. "What do you mean? He's going to be finished in about two years."

"But ... isn't he older than you?"

Danny burst into laughter. "I know I don't look like twenty-nine, but seriously Alice, the guy's only twenty-three."

Alice's jaw dropped. Jonas definitely looked older than Danny. Maybe it was the chain-smoking ... but she had to admit that Danny *did* look young for his age. Except that lately, his alcoholism was beginning to make him look older, more worn-out.

He caressed her hair again. "He really is a nice guy, Alice. You'll get to like him."

"He's just ... weird."

"He went through a lot."

"You mean, that's the reason why he is the way he is?"

"There's always a reason why people are the way they are." Danny kissed her and started walking toward the waiting car.

Alice watched him get into the vehicle and drive through the gate. She felt lonely the second he was gone.

Being alone in the house with Jonas *was* weird.

Henry had set the table for the two of them. Alice considered taking her plate upstairs, but she didn't want to be rude.

He entered the dining room after she had already taken her seat. He gave her a nod and she said "Hi," then he took his place and stared at his water glass.

At least he wasn't staring at *her* for a change.

Henry brought their plates—a mushroom pie for her and a minced meat pie for Jonas. Alice thanked him.

"So," Henry said, while he was filling up her glass. "Tomorrow and Sunday I won't be here, but I prepared something for you. It's in the blue and the light green Tupperware container in the freezer."

Alice smiled. "Thank you, Henry, but you really didn't have to. I can cook myself..."

Henry nodded. "I know, but since Daniel is gone, I thought maybe you don't feel like cooking for yourself."

He filled Jonas's glass as well. "You of course are very welcome to have some too. There's enough for the both of you," he told him. "That is, if you don't mind eating the same as Alice."

"No prob," said Jonas. "Thanks."

Henry smiled at them, then he disappeared back into the kitchen and let them eat in silence. It was awkward.

When he was finished, Jonas pulled out his pack of cigarettes and lit one. Alice glared at him.

"Sorry," he muttered. He pushed back his chair and left the room, leaving a cloud of smoke behind.

Alice finished her dinner alone.

When Henry came back to get the plates, he wished her a good weekend.

"I'll take care of the garden," Alice assured him with a crooked smile that made him laugh.

With Henry gone, the loneliness came back. It was Friday night and Alice cursed Danny for having broken her phone. Her friends were surely out enjoying their lives, and she was alone in an empty house with a guy who didn't talk to her.

There was beer in the fridge, so she took one bottle out and opened it on the counter. With Danny gone, she could say good-bye to her abstinence.

Henry had lit the fireplace in the otherwise dark living-room, so Alice sat down on the couch beside it.

In the darkness, she hadn't spotted Jonas, so when he suddenly moved, she almost dropped her beer.

"God, you scared me!" Alice exclaimed, feeling her heart pounding against her ribs.

Jonas exhaled a big cloud of smoke. "Sorry."

Alice wondered if it would be rude to get up and leave the room. She didn't think that Jonas found her presence valuable, but she also didn't want to make it too obvious that she disliked him. But what was she supposed to do? Start a conversation with him?

She glanced over at him and noticed he was staring at her again, like he was trying to read her thoughts. Why did he do that?

"So," she began. "Psychology, huh?" She took a sip of her beer. "Do you sometimes analyze people for fun?"

Jonas gave her a look that made her feel incredibly stupid. "Danny told you." It wasn't a question.

She nodded.

He took another drag on his cigarette and formed rings with the smoke, he blew out. "Sometimes."

"Is it hard to read people?" Alice wanted to know.

He grinned; his face enlightened by the dancing flames of the fire. "Not you."

Frowning, she began scratching the label off her beer bottle. "What d'you mean?"

Jonas finished his cigarette and flicked the butt into the fire. "You're an open book." He took out another cigarette and lit it. Then he grabbed a second one from the pack and offered it to her.

"No thanks."

He shrugged and took a deep drag. "Everyone can read you."

"Why?"

"Too emotional."

She scowled at him again.

"Now you're mad, but you know I'm right."

"Is that why you act like a robot?"

Jonas didn't answer.

"You're scared people might get too close to you?"

Jonas's face remained blank. "Provoking me to distract from you won't work."

Alice blushed, but it was too dark for him to see it. She put her bottle to her lips, to not have to say anything. Jonas continued staring at her. The light was bad, but she felt it.

How long do I have to sit here until it's acceptable to leave?

When his cigarette was finished, Jonas pulled out another one.

"Why do you smoke so much?" Alice asked.

"Why do you ask so much?" he replied.

He was right. Who said two people always had to talk to each other?

Alice tried to drink her beer quickly, to not have to sit next to him for too long. He noticed. "You're uncomfortable." Again, not a question.

Alice bit her tongue and remained quiet.

As soon as her bottle was empty, she got up from the couch to get another one. To be polite, she asked, "Would you like a beer?"

He shook his head.

"Do you drink at all?"

Jonas finished his cigarette, flicked the butt into the fire and grabbed the pack for another one, but he found it empty. "I like to keep a clear head," he said.

He tossed the empty pack into the fire as well and leaned back, watching it get consumed by the flames.

Alice went into the kitchen to grab a second beer from the fridge. When she walked back through the living room, she wished Jonas a good night, but he remained quiet.

Once in her bedroom, she turned on the TV and sat down on the bed.

Staring at her beer, she wondered why she had even gotten a second one. Drinking alone in her room on a Friday night made her feel pathetic. But the bottle was already open, so she felt obliged to drink it.

What might Jill and Leah be doing? They usually spent their weekends clubbing, looking for a boyfriend for Jill.

Alice decided to look for a phone the next day. A house as big as this one surely must have one somewhere.

After watching TV until 2:00 a.m., she slept until noon. The first thing she heard before opening her eyes, was rain drumming against the window.

A light headache made climbing out of bed harder than usual. Alice shuffled through the hallway and into her own room in her pajamas.

When she went downstairs half an hour later, she felt even lonelier. The house looked bigger when it was empty. Danny's office door was closed, as always.

The kitchen smelled like bacon and an oily frying pan sat on the stove. Wrinkling her nose, she grabbed the pan, but then she hesitated. Why should she wash that? Back in her old apartment, she had felt responsible to keep it clean because the threat of drowning in a mess had been a real one; but here? It didn't feel like home and Anita would be back on Monday.

"That's mine," said a deep voice behind her. Startled, she whirled around, and saw Jonas coming in, shaking water out of his hair, his leather jacket wet from the rain.

Alice put the pan back down. "Where were you?"

Jonas pulled a pack of cigarettes out of his jeans. It was still wrapped in plastic. "Ah," she said.

He grinned and began to unwrap it while she opened the fridge, but realizing she didn't have any appetite, she closed it again.

Jonas lit a cigarette and studied her. He was standing in the doorframe, so Alice went through the dining room to get into the living room.

There, she sat down on the sofa, pulled her legs up, and rested her chin on her knees.

What a boring day this was going to be. She had been looking forward to taking a walk through the forest, but the weather forecast had been wrong.

The sound of water running came from the kitchen. Jonas seemed to be washing up. That was something, at least.

The raindrops continued to fall against the window. It sounded nice somehow, but it also made her sad.

Alice remained on the couch for a while, but when she saw Jonas leave the house, she got up.

I wanted to look for a phone.

There had to be one somewhere. She couldn't see one in the living room, so she walked back into the kitchen. And really, there it was. It was hanging on the wall next to the archway. Alice checked if it was working. She could see Jonas's shape in front of the kitchen window. His back was facing the house. Would he have a problem with her making a phone call? Why would he? But somehow, she couldn't shake off the strange feeling that she was doing something forbidden. What was wrong with her?

Nervous, she dialed Jill's number. No one answered.

The phone had a cable, so it wasn't possible to walk around with it. Leaning her back against the wall, Alice dialed again, then waited while reading the notes on the fridge in front of her. There were several pages ripped out of a gardening book. Henry must have put them there. Next to them was a picture of Henry and Anita and some other guy—maybe the previous owner of the house?

"Hello?"

Alice exhaled, relieved. "Hi, Jill, it's me, Alice!"

"Alice? Where have you been? I texted you!"

Alice smiled. It was so good to hear her friend's voice again. "I, uh ... broke my phone and haven't gotten a new one yet."

"You broke your phone?" Jill laughed. *"You just bought it!"*

"I know ... It happened while moving, I—"

"You moved? Where?"

"Uh, I don't know the address yet, but I'll tell you later."

Jill chuckled. *"How can you not know your own address? Do you still live with Danny? Just ask him."*

"He's not here at the moment."

"How are things? With him, I mean."

Allice thought for a moment. She didn't want to worry Jill with Danny's alcoholism.

"They're better, actually. We spend more time together, and he's usually in a good mood."

"That's awesome, Al! I'm really glad to hear that."

"What about you? Anything new?"

"Hmm ..." Jill seemed to be thinking. *"Not much, really. Working all day, looking for a boyfriend ..."*

Alice laughed. "Still? Why don't you just enjoy your single life?"

"Says the one with the happy relationship."

It's not that happy.

"*So did you and Danny have sex in every room of the new place yet? You know that's good luck.*" Typical Jill.

"No ... his friends are always here. One even lives with us."

"*Oh la la, are they hot, his friends?*"

"Danny's friends are assholes. I wouldn't hook up my worst enemy with any of them."

"I wouldn't want to be hooked up with your worst enemy," said a voice behind her.

Alice felt her heart drop down into her belly and whirled around.

Jonas was standing in the door, smoking.

Feeling her face heat up and her cheeks burn, Alice figured she must be red like a tomato.

"*Oh my god, Alice, don't tell me that's one of them!*" Jill burst into laughter. She must have heard him.

Alice was speechless. Jonas didn't look insulted. He was wearing his usual poker face.

"*Alice? You still there?*"

Grinning, Jonas walked away.

Alice waited until the sound of his footsteps had faded out before responding. "Holy shit, Jill, that was so embarrassing!"

Jill couldn't stop laughing. "*So, that really was one of them, huh?*"

"Yes, the one that lives with us. God, Jill, seriously that was horrible! That was so insulting!"

"*Oh, come on, he'll forgive you.*"

Alice sighed.

He's weird anyway ... does he even have feelings?

"*Anyway, should we meet up sometime?*" Jill asked. "*We could invite Leah and go—*"

Suddenly, all the lights in the house went out at once, and Jill's voice was gone.

"Jill?"

Nothing.

Shit. The electricity's gone.

Was there a storm outside? Alice hung up the phone and went to take a look out of the window. It was still raining, but there didn't seem to be any wind and there was no lightning either. Alice cursed herself for saying something so mean in front of Jonas. If things hadn't been awkward before, she'd definitely made them awkward now.

Not knowing what else to do, she decided to go back to her room.

Jonas wasn't in the corridor and the door to his room was closed, so she managed to slip into her room unseen.

About half an hour later, the lights flickered back on.

Should I try to call Jill again?

But what if she encountered Jonas? Alice decided that her fear of running into him was worse than her need to talk to Jill, and remained in her room.

At around 8:00 p.m., her hunger became unbearable. She hadn't eaten all day.

Jonas wasn't in the corridor when she checked. Slowly and quietly, Alice sneaked down the stairs and when she reached the bottom, she spied around the corner. No lights were on downstairs, so no one seemed to be there.

Alice didn't dare to turn on the lights. The porch light was on, like it was every night, its rays falling through the windows and illuminating parts of the living room and kitchen as well.

Alice found a pot sitting on the stove. When she removed its lid, she saw that it was the food Henry had prepared for them. Apparently, Jonas had heated it up for himself and left half of it for her. To not have to spend too much time in the kitchen Alice decided to eat it cold right out of the pot.

When she was done, she put the pot in the dishwasher and turned around to leave the room, but something caught her eye.

The phone was gone. Her jaw dropped at the sight. In disbelief, Alice rubbed her eyes. Still, no phone. The wall was a bit whiter where it had been attached, and parts of its cable still hung out of a small hole.

Jonas had removed the phone. Had he done that to punish her for what she'd said about him?

Alice spent the whole Sunday hiding in her bedroom, watching TV. She only went downstairs twice to eat, after having carefully checked that Jonas wasn't around.

There was no trace of him, all day long. Maybe he was in the basement, working out. Like the day before, he had already heated up the food and left in in the pot.

Still, it was raining outside, and Alice's mood was very bad, so she grabbed a few cans of beer from the fridge after having finished her dinner.

Again, she drank them in front of the TV, hating herself for it. After all, she criticized Danny's alcoholism, but here she was, getting drunk alone in her room for the third time that weekend.

A knock on the door woke her up the next day.

Please let that not be Jonas ...

Alice blinked the sleep out of her eyes.

"Alice? Lunch is ready." It was Henry's voice.

The digital clock on the nightstand showed 1:00 p.m. Feeling bad about having let Henry wait, Alice hurried out of the bedroom. Henry had already gone back downstairs.

She found him in the dining room. "Well, good morning to you!" He laughed at her appearance.

Alice quickly brushed her hair with her fingers and looked down at herself. She was still wearing the leggings and T-shirt she'd slept in, and she hadn't even looked in the mirror. At least Jonas was nowhere in sight.

"Jonas has already eaten. I thought I'd let you sleep for a while, but then I got worried ..."

"I am so sorry, Henry! I should have set an alarm. I never thought I would sleep so long."

Henry smiled. "It's fine, Alice. No worries. I already heated the food up again."

Alice ate her meal alone.

When she was done and Henry came back, she asked him, "Are there any phones in the house?"

Henry took her plate from the table. "There was one in the kitchen, but it seems to be gone."

"Any others?"

"Not that I know of."

Sullenly, Alice stared at the table.

"Do you need to make a phone call?"

She nodded.

"You could use my cell phone, if you like," Henry suggested.

"That would be great, thank you!"

Five minutes later, Alice was standing in the corner of the dining room, Henry's phone pressed against her ear, waiting for Jill to answer. She didn't pick up.

Of course, it was Monday. Jill must be at work.

Alice sighed, knowing that she'd have to wait and try again that evening.

In the living room she found Jonas sitting on the couch, reading some book. Other books and sheets of paper were spread out on the couch table before him. He didn't look up when she walked by, for which she was glad.

Henry had set the table as always, and Alice ate dinner quietly. Jonas didn't show up.

Again, she asked Henry if she could use his phone and called Jill. This time, Jill answered immediately.

"Can I come over?" Alice asked her.

"Yes, of course," Jill said happily.

Alice hung up and saw Jonas standing in the door, looking at her. It was hard to read his expression, but he didn't look so happy.

When she came back downstairs, wearing a jacket and carrying her bag, Jonas looked up from his books. Alice ignored him and went straight out of the house. To her disappointment, Henry's car was gone. She had planned to ask him for a ride.

It was still raining, but Alice had no umbrella. The gate guard had probably fled the rain. No one was standing by the wall. Alice opened the heavy gate and started walking. She had no idea how far it was to the main road, but she planned on walking there and then hitchhike. Hopefully, there'd be a car to pick her up.

The rain had already begun to soak through her clothes.

She hadn't gotten far when suddenly, she could hear footsteps behind her. Jonas was following her.

"Where are you going?" he wanted to know.

Alice ignored the question and kept walking.

Jonas hurried to catch up with her. "Alice," he called.

She didn't answer. He grabbed her arm and made her stop.

"Let me go!"

"Where?"

"To my friend."

Jonas grinned. "The one you don't wanna hook me up with?"

Alice felt herself blush. She dropped her gaze, ashamed. "Sorry..."

"Don't wanna be hooked up anyway."

"I mean ... about what I said."

He didn't say anything.

"I'm really sorry for calling you an asshole."

"Why?"

Why?

She looked up at him, confused. "Uh ... because it's an insult?"

"It's what you think."

"What?"

"You're sorry I heard it, not that you said it."

She felt caught. *He's right.* Chewing her lip nervously, she tried to start walking again, but he wouldn't let go of her arm.

"Jonas, let go of me!"

The rain had already soaked through her thin denim jacket, and she shivered.

"No."

"I'm meeting my friend!"

"It's dark."

"So what?"

"Raining."

"And?"

"You're on foot."

She laughed bitterly. "Yeah well, lend me your car then."

"No."

"I can hitchhike."

"Too dangerous."

Furious, she glared at him. "I'm not having this discussion, Jonas. Let me go!"

He stared at her.

"What d'you wanna do, huh? Call the police again?"

"No." He bent down and put his arm around her waist.

What the hell is he—

He lifted her up and put her over his shoulder.

"Put me down!" she shrieked. Her bag dropped into the mud.

Jonas picked it up and started walking.

"Put me down! PUT ME DOWN!"

He ignored her.

"JONAS!"

Alice began punching his back with her fists. First only lightly, but when he didn't react, she punched harder. "Let me go!"

She struggled and kicked, but he had her locked in his iron grip and carried her back through the gate. The gate guard was standing there, staring at them out of widened eyes.

"Where were you?" Jonas asked him.

"T-toilet."

"Keep the gate locked!"

The man nodded.

Once again, Alice felt deeply humiliated. Jonas put her down and handed her the stained bag.

"I take it back," she hissed.

"What?"

"My apology. You *are* an asshole!" She turned on her heel and hurried back into the house.

Back in her room she threw her bag into a corner. Shaking with anger, she couldn't even think straight. What in the world allowed him to treat her that way?

She paced up and down, kicking at everything in her way. Her anger made her want to scream but she didn't want him to hear her.

What an asshole, what a fucking asshole...

7

Again, Alice hid in her bedroom. She didn't even go downstairs to eat. This time, Henry didn't knock on her door. But when she sneaked out to get a book from her own room, she almost tripped over a tray on the floor. There was a plate on it, covered by a lid. She picked it up and carried it inside gratefully. Her stomach was rumbling. The food was already cold, but she didn't mind. It was late afternoon, so it must have been sitting in front of the door for at least three hours.

Her anger and depression persisted even with a full stomach. Jill must be worried sick, and Alice had no way to apologize to her and explain herself.

Another six hours went by with her hiding, until she heard loud voices and laughter coming from downstairs. Was Danny back? She didn't dare to go and check.

A few minutes later though, the door opened, and Danny stepped in. He looked horrible. Tired, pale, and wet to the bone.

Alice jumped off the bed and hugged him. "I'm so glad you're back!"

He patted her shoulder. "Slow down, you're crushing me."

Alice let go of him and stood on the tips of her toes to kiss him. She smelled beer on his breath.

"How was it?" she asked.

Danny sighed. "Stressful ... annoying. I'm glad it's over."

"Did you solve the problems?"

Danny took off his wet coat and dropped it on the floor. He undid his shoelaces and kicked the shoes in a corner. "No, not really. I'm afraid things got worse."

"What is—"

"I don't want to talk about it."

"Okay, okay ... won't ask." Alice sat down on the bed again and watched him undress.

"I'm going to take a shower," he said.

When he was done, he put on a fresh pair of jeans and another dress shirt.

"Are you not coming to bed?"

He shook his head. "It's too early, and I haven't eaten yet. What's that tray doing in front of the door, anyway?"

"Oh ... that must be my dinner. I completely forgot about it."

"You should take it away. I almost tripped over it when I came in."

Alice went to the door and picked it up. "Do you want it?"

"Nah, the guys are preparing something downstairs. We're going to eat together." He put on a pair of socks and a dry pair of shoes, then he went to the door. "You want to come too?"

She shook her head.

Danny didn't reappear for a long time. Alice ate her dinner and put the tray on the nightstand. Her boyfriend was probably getting drunk again, and she was too afraid of Jonas to go downstairs and stop him. At least the others were back though. Alice didn't want to be alone with Jonas.

It was almost 1:00 a.m. when Danny finally came to bed. Alice was still awake, waiting for him. As expected, he was drunk, and it took him several tries to open the door. When he finally managed, he stumbled into the room and pushed the door shut behind him, then he dropped down on the bed and kicked off his shoes.

Alice grabbed the remote and turned off the TV.

"Did the guys stay until now?" she asked him.

He grumbled. "No, they left at around ... eleven or somethin'."

"Did you share a bottle of whiskey with the gate guy again?" she asked jokingly.

He didn't get it. "I talked to Jonas."

"Okay ... he didn't quite strike me as a whiskey-fan."

He shook his head, slowly. "He stayed up to keep me company."

"That's ... nice, I guess."

"D'you know what he told me?" Danny asked while he got up from the bed to take off his shirt.

Alice bit her lip.

"He said that a certain someone tried to sneak out yesterday." He threw his shirt in a corner and unbuttoned his pants.

"Sneak out? I didn't *sneak* out. I just wanted to see Jill. She was expecting me."

"How so?" He pulled down his pants and began to take off his socks.

"I called her, and she said I could come over."

Danny glared at her. "Then you decided to *walk* there?"

"No, I was going to hitchhike or find a bus."

"Are you fucking insane?"

Alice looked at him in shock. "Why? It wasn't late and—"

"Damn, Alice, you're so unbelievably naïve!"

"What's your problem? This is a rural area—people are nice here."

He shook his head. "You think you can just walk a mile to the main road, and then some nice guy will pick you up and drive you around in the dark?"

"A mile? Is it that far?"

"See! You haven't got the slightest clue what you're doing! Sometimes you're just so stupid!"

"I just ... needed to see her."

"You're too emotional, Alice."

I've heard that before.

Danny raked his hair with his fingers. "Too emotional and too fucking impulsive!"

"Says the guy who's yelling at me in the middle of the night."

That made his head turn red, and he kicked at the bed.

"Stop that!" she shrieked.

"And you insult my best friend! What the fuck is wrong with you?!"

"Did he come crying to you?" Alice bit her tongue quickly, knowing that she shouldn't provoke him when he was drunk.

Shaking with anger, Danny stared at her. "DON'T INSULT MY FRIENDS!" he shouted.

His precious friends. He loved them more than he loved her.

"Why, Alice? Why the fuck do you have to make everything so complicated?"

She stared down at her hands.

"ANSWER ME!"

Danny walked around the bed and stood beside her; hands clenched into fists. It scared her.

"Stop yelling!" she pleaded, with tears running down her cheeks.

Somehow, seeing her cry made him calm down. Breathing heavily, he remained standing there for a while, but then his breathing slowed down, and the color of his face returned to normal. He sighed deeply and sat down on the bed beside her.

"I was worried about you." His voice sounded pained.

Alice avoided his eyes.

"I ordered Jonas to stay here, to look after you … and you run off, in the dark." He put one hand on her knee. Alice winced at his touch.

"Promise me you won't do anything like that again."

"But," she objected, "I want to go out!"

Danny's expression turned hard again. "It's too dangerous in the dark, especially when I'm not here."

"What are you afraid of?"

"Losing you."

Alice slept in his arms that night, but it didn't feel like an embrace, more as if Danny was trying to lock her in his tight grip. It made her feel suffocated.

The sour stench of alcohol was on his breath and again, his sleep was troubled, but Alice didn't dare to move out from underneath his arms.

This time, she was able to fall asleep before dawn though.

By the time she awoke, Danny had already left. It was nine o'clock. Alice tried to go back to sleep, but the memories of their argument made that impossible, so she turned on the TV instead.

At around ten past twelve, Danny came into the bedroom.

"I'm waiting for you, Alice. It's time for lunch."

"Is Jonas down there?"

Danny raised one eyebrow. "Why?"

"I don't want to see him."

Irritated, he sighed. "Because of what happened? Alice for god's sake, he did what I told him. He didn't do anything wrong."

Alice stared at the flickering screen and said nothing.

"Fine. Be a bitch about it." Danny left and pulled the door shut.

Fighting the tears that welled up in her eyes, Alice turned off the TV. The voices of the commercials sounded like fingernails scratching on a blackboard to her.

Why was everything so complicated?

Alice walked over to the window to look out. The day was cloudy, but it wasn't raining for a change. The last birds were getting ready for their long flight south and a soft wind was blowing the leaves from the trees. She opened the window to breathe some fresh air.

Suddenly, there was a knock on the door.

"Yes?" she called.

Anita opened hesitantly and glanced into the room. A shy smile on her lips, she said, "Hello, Miss Alice … I am here to clean."

"Oh, of course. I'm so sorry, I'll leave."

"Can I clean your room too?" Anita pointed at the door of Alice's room.

"Sure, thank you. Is it all right if I take a quick shower first?"

The maid smiled and stepped out of the bedroom, to let Alice pass. "Of course," she said.

After the shower, Alice put on warm clothes and grabbed the book, she was reading at the moment. She had hoped to hide in her room all day and it annoyed her to have to see Danny's friends after all.

Danny and his friends were sitting around the lit fireplace. Dirty dishes were piled up on the couch table. Alice didn't look at them and went straight to the door and out into the yard.

The air was colder though than she had expected and hit her like a wave of cold water.

Alice contemplated her options, but decided the cold was worth not having to go back inside that house. She went to sit on the swing, as usual. The book lay in her lap, but somehow, she couldn't get herself to read. Her mood was still dark. First the horrible weekend with Jonas, and now she was fighting with Danny again.

Alice stared at the clouds and tried to dream herself far away, but it only made her feel more depressed.

After a while, she noticed that the gate guard was looking at her. It appeared to be the one from the other night, when Jonas had carried her back to the house.

His stare made her blush and she quickly got off the swing. She walked around the house, but in the backyard she found Jonas standing next to the vegetable garden, smoking a cigarette and staring up into the sky. He saw her coming though and turned his head.

Alice quickly walked back the way she'd come and decided to sit on the grass on the side of the house where neither Jonas nor the guard could see her. The grass was wet, but Alice already felt cold anyway, and it didn't matter. Through the windows above her, she could hear Danny and the others talking. Their voices were muffled, and she couldn't understand what they were talking about.

When the voices died out, Alice figured that everybody must have gone back into the office. The cold already made her shiver and clatter her teeth, so she decided to go back inside. As expected, the living room was empty when she stepped through the entrance door. The voices of Danny and his friends now came through the closed office door.

Alice hurried up the stairs and almost bumped into Jonas, who was leaning against the wall next to his bedroom, brushing his teeth ... topless.

Alice felt the urge to run back downstairs, but something caught her attention. There were small bruises on Jonas's back, purple and yellow.

Was that me?

Jonas must have heard her. He turned his head and looked at her. Speechless, Alice could do nothing but stare at him, frozen in place.

Casually, Jonas continued brushing his teeth, his face expressionless as always. When he was done, he turned around and walked into the bathroom.

Alice still felt unable to move.

When he came back out though, she blurted out, "Sorry for hitting you!"

Jonas stopped. "Huh?"

"I hit you, the other night," Alice explained. "I- I'm really sorry for that."

"Didn't feel a thing."

Alice chewed her lip. "But you got ... bruises ... on your back ..."

He seemed surprised.

"Didn't you ...?"

He shook his head.

"Anyway, I'm really sorry ... I shouldn't have—"

Jonas cut her off with a wave of his hand. "Don't apologize."

Alice dropped her eyes and stared down at the floor while she walked past him and toward her room.

"You got a wet bum," he called after her.

Alice decided to make up with Danny and go downstairs for dinner. But when she arrived at the bottom of the stairs, she saw him sitting on the couch with his friends, eating chicken wings.

Her empty stomach made her go to the dining room nevertheless, and she found that the table had been set for her. It looked a bit sad, the long wooden table with only one plate on it.

Henry served her meal, but his mood wasn't as cheerful as usual. He looked at her almost pitifully when she sat down to eat. "How are you?" he asked, concern in his voice.

"I'm fine, thank you." Trying to seem normal, she smiled at him. "What about you?"

Henry filled up her glass with fresh tap water. "I'm good, thank you. I just don't really like the cold weather ... I'm not so young anymore, and I can feel the cold in my bones."

Henry went back to the kitchen afterward, and she ate alone, trying to do it quickly so that she could go back to her room as soon as possible. The voices and the laughter coming from the living room were too much for her to bear. Especially Danny's voice was louder than the others, sounding drunk.

When she was finished, she rushed back upstairs without looking at the others.

Back in the bedroom, she sat down on the bed and stared at the wall. Should she watch TV and wait for Danny, or was it better to go to sleep, so he wouldn't start fighting with her as soon as he got back?

He came to bed at around 2:00 a.m., with whiskey on his breath. Alice pretended to be asleep, her back facing toward him. This time, he left her alone. Still wearing his clothes, he just dropped down onto the bed and began snoring softly.

Alice cried herself to sleep silently, but she could as well have screamed, it probably wouldn't have woken him up anyway.

The next couple of days were the same. Danny didn't want to eat lunch with her anymore, although she went downstairs on time. He had told Henry to serve him and the guys in the living room because they found it more comfortable.

Alice's place was always set, but after eating alone three times, she told Henry that he didn't have to set the table anymore. She asked him to leave the food in the pots on the stove, and she would come downstairs to eat after the guys had gone back to work.

Henry seemed concerned about her, but he was also intimidated by Danny and his friends, who treated him like a servant.

It was obvious that he was disgusted by Danny's habit to get drunk every day, but he didn't dare to say anything.

One time, when Alice went to the vegetable garden to see if she could help Henry, he lowered his voice and said, "Do you know why the previous owner's wife killed herself?"

She shook her head.

"He was a drunk. Every single day, he would drink himself delirious. I don't know if he was depressed or something, but the drinking made him very ill-tempered. He was abusive to both his wife and son." Henry wiped a tear from his cheek and took a deep breath. "One day, he drove drunk and wrecked his car with both his wife and his son inside. The child, Lucas, died instantly. The parents were only mildly injured, but Laura, the mother, killed herself about a week later."

Speechless, Alice stared at him.

"She was such a nice lady," Henry said in a shaky voice. "I really miss her."

"I'm sorry," Alice whispered, not knowing what else to say.

Suddenly, Henry looked up at her, his eyes clear and piercing. "I am telling you this for a reason, Alice."

Alice swallowed dryly, feeling uncomfortable under the cook's intense stare. "W-what do you mean?" she asked.

Henry sighed deeply and put a soil-covered hand on her shoulder. "I want you to be careful," he warned her. "Daniel's drinking concerns me. I do not wish for history to repeat itself."

Danny had never truly hurt her, but there were times when his behavior scared her. Especially when his guard was up, and she couldn't predict his next move. These times occurred every day that week. At least she was able to avoid him during the day, but she could feel her brain cells die with every minute she spent in front of the TV. So, Alice decided to start drawing instead. She drew only sketches in her notebook with a regular pen, but it felt good to get her emotions on paper.

Danny tried to sleep with her a couple of times, after he'd come to bed drunk. Luckily, he wasn't too persistent and gave up after one or two attempts.

The weekend arrived and with it came a strong urge to get out of the house and get some exercise. Sitting around, watching TV all day long, was physically weakening.

Even the sun made an appearance on that Saturday and the temperatures climbed up a bit.

Danny was sitting in the living room, playing cards, and drinking beer with his friends when Alice came downstairs. Only Waldo wasn't there.

Alice wanted to smile at her boyfriend, to say something, but Danny didn't even look up.

The lawn was wet and muddy, and the big oaks and birches had lost most of their leaves already, even though it was only the end of October.

The day looked nice enough to go for a run—or at least a walk.

The guard looked up from his phone when she walked past him and toward the gate, which was secured by a big chain with an even bigger metal lock.

Alice pointed at it and said, "Could you open that, please?"

Frowning at her, the guard asked, "Why?"

"I'd like to go for a walk."

He slowly shook his head. "I'm not allowed to open the gate for you, miss. I can only let certain people pass."

"And that would be who?"

"Well, the cook, the maid, the other guards, and the men who own the place."

"But ... I'm Daniel's girlfriend, I *live* here!"

The bald man looked at her apologetically. "It's for safety reasons. No one ever goes out here on foot."

"But I don't have a car and I just want to take a walk!"

"I'm really sorry miss, but I can only do what the boss says. Why don't you just ask him?"

"I don't need his permission to go out!"

"But I need his permission to open the gate."

She didn't know what to say to that.

He sighed. "Listen, I'm really sorry, but I don't want to lose my job."

"It's fine." Alice turned around and walked toward the house ... slowly, hesitantly.

Why not just ask Danny about it? After all, he had told her that it was only too dangerous outside after dark or when he wasn't around ...

It felt like walking into a cage full of lions. Everyone except Paul looked up when Alice entered the room. Tee was the only one smiling at her. Danny's stare was cold and distant, and Jonas's unreadable as always.

"Danny . . ." she began carefully. "The guy outside won't open the gate for me ... Could you—?"

"Why?" His voice was even colder than his stare.

"I'd like to go for a walk. The weather's nice. And I'd like to explore the area a bit ..."

"What's there to explore?"

She shrugged. "I don't know, the forest looks inviting. I might even go for a run."

"Can't you do that in the yard?"

She frowned at him. "You want me to go jogging in the yard?"

Now *he* shrugged.

"You said it's no problem during the day!"

He raised his right eyebrow. "Did I?"

"Well, you said last time that it was too dangerous to go out in the dark ... Now it's daylight and you're here ... and I won't go far—"

"You can get fresh air and sun in the garden, and if you want to work out, there's the basement."

He looked back down at the cards in his hands, as if to indicate that the conversation was over.

"You can't just keep me from going out!"

"Watch me," he muttered.

Lost for words, Alice stared at him with wide eyes. Was he seriously not allowing her to go out? As if he had the right to deny her that?

Danny wanted to continue playing, but Tee, Paul, and even Jonas seemed to feel uncomfortable with Alice still standing there.

"There ain't no wolves in the woods, Dan," said Tee with a crooked grin.

"Mind your own business," Danny snapped at him.

"I'm just sayin', I could go with her 'n' keep her safe."

Danny looked at him with such fury in his eyes that Tee quickly fell quiet and looked down at his cards.

"Danny, I just want to take a short walk, you can't deny me that," Alice tried again.

"I can do whatever the hell I want."

Frozen, she stood there, staring at him. She felt as if he'd slapped her. Was this still the same Danny? The man she'd fallen in love with?

"What're you still doing here?" he grumbled.

Alice tried to keep her expression blank and turned around, slowly.

I'll just climb over the wall or something...

"Jonas," Danny said in a firm voice, "make sure she doesn't try anything."

Shocked, Alice looked back at him. Jonas's eyes flicked to her and back to Danny.

"We're playing!" he protested.

Danny threw his cards on the table. "Can't concentrate anyway."

Alice didn't want Jonas to follow her, so she went back to her room, and once the door was closed behind her, she couldn't keep the sobs down anymore. Crying, she sat down on the windowsill, gazing out beyond the wall, longing for freedom more than ever.

This must be just a bad dream ... a nightmare.

The rest of the day Alice stayed in her room, and that night, she even slept on her couch to avoid Danny altogether. Her stomach was killing her. She hadn't eaten anything for dinner because she hadn't dared to go downstairs.

On Sunday morning, her hunger became unbearable and woke her up early.

The house was still quiet, and Alice was able to get some food from the kitchen unseen. When she looked out the window, she could see that the grass was still covered in frost and a thin layer of fog hovered above the ground. Everyone was still asleep.

I could sneak out now.

Alice got dressed quickly and went outside. The air was cold and moist; the gate guard seemed to be dozing in his chair.

Alice quietly walked around the house, close to the stonewall, letting her hand glide over the cold bricks. Maybe there were holes in it where she could put her foot to climb up.

She passed the vegetable garden on her way, then a couple of trees, and the swimming pool. There was no water in it now and it wasn't huge, but it looked nice anyway. Alice hadn't looked at it before, because it had always been covered by a big green plastic sheet. Now, the cover was gone. Maybe the heavy rain had destroyed it and they'd had to take it away.

The pool was quite deep on one side and the tiled ground led upward on the other side, ending in steps. It was covered with muddy leaves.

Alice took her eyes from the pool and focused on the wall again.

She found another gate, hidden by bushes. But it was just a plain metal door, with no bars to climb up—and it was locked. The lock was rusty though ... maybe she could break it open.

"Up already?"

Alice almost tripped over her own feet when she whirled around.

Jonas was standing in the back door of the house, smoking.

Glaring at him, Alice stepped away from the gate. His eyes followed her every movement.

A sudden sadness rolled over her. This wasn't a game. This was not hide and seek or catch me if you can. This was her life, her freedom. Her broken relationship, her drunken boyfriend, and her friends she wasn't allowed to see.

It seemed to be a game for Jonas though. He had a triumphant expression on his face, and he had thought it was funny to carry her back to the house, like a stubborn child who wouldn't obey. But Alice wasn't a child and she hated being treated like one.

And apparently, there was nothing she could do about it. Even if she'd dared to go to the basement and lifted weights every single day, she would never be strong enough to win a fight against Danny or his friends. They were taking advantage of her physical weakness, of her being alone without anyone on her side.

Sitting in the house all the time only made her weaker. She could already feel it after those two weeks. She was pale and skinny, and her appetite was gone.

Danny was making her sick, literally. And she was sure that he wasn't actually worried about her. He was trying to demonstrate his power over her by not letting her go where she wanted.

Jonas's face became a blur through the tears that had built up in her eyes. Alice quickly turned her back toward him, and hurried back around the house without saying anything. Since he was standing in the backdoor, she had to get back into the house through the entrance.

Danny awoke a bit before noon that day, so Alice tried to talk to him while he was still sober. When she stepped into the bedroom, he was just coming out of the shower.

"Can we talk?" she asked him. Her voice was faintly trembling, she realized.

Danny rubbed his hair with a towel. He had another one wrapped around his waist. "About what?" he wanted to know.

"About you ... not letting me out of here." Alice sat down on the bed and looked up at him to watch his reaction. Her boyfriend seemed to be thinking about something, but then he made a face as if thinking too hard was giving him a headache.

"Does that have to be now?" he moaned, his expression pained.

"When else?"

"When I got no headache, maybe."

Alice studied his face. Danny's eyes seemed distant, a bit glazed, as if there were a glass wall before them. She wasn't able to see his soul behind them, like she used to.

"When d'you ever got no headache?"

"An ice-cold beer will do the trick," he answered as if it were a normal thing to say.

"How about an aspirin instead?" she suggested.

"Pain killers and beer? That's unhealthy."

"The way you drink is unhealthy."

Danny made a noise that sounded like a mixture of a sigh and an irritated moan, and sat down on the bed beside her, keeping his distance, however. "Don't start."

"We'll talk about it *now*, with you being sober and hopefully able to think straight," Alice insisted.

He tossed his towel on the floor and gave her an annoyed look. "What's there to discuss?"

Is he fucking kidding me?

"Danny, I have no idea what's happening with you; that self-destructive attitude you put on every day, I'm sick of it. Hear me? I'm sick of trying to help you or even understand you, but I will *not* let you drag me down with you! You have no right to lock me in here like a prisoner! I have friends whom I want to see, for fuck's sake!"

Danny started rubbing his temple with the knuckles of his left hand, squeezing his eyes shut. Then he opened them again and stared at her, his expression blank. "You wouldn't come back."

"What?"

"If I let you go, you wouldn't come back."

Speechless, Alice remained silent. Was he right? She definitely didn't enjoy living like this ... with him.

"See? You can't even lie ... You know I'm right." Danny's tone was bitter, as if he had poison on his tongue and were trying to spit it out.

"But this ... this doesn't feel like a relationship, Danny! Why am I even here? You enjoy spending time with your friends more than spending time with me!"

"They don't judge."

"The hell they don't! They might not say it out loud, but they sure as hell judge. Everybody does. Or maybe they just don't care enough to say something!"

Danny jumped off the bed at once and walked toward the closet to fetch some fresh clothes. But before he opened the closet door, he turned around to glare at her angrily. "Oh, *now* you know them so well all of a sudden, huh?"

Alice sighed deeply. It was impossible to have a civilized conversation with this guy.

"Danny, I'm just trying to help you, because I *care*! How can you not understand that?"

"I DON'T NEED YOUR HELP!" he yelled.

Exasperated, Alice jumped up from the bed as well. "You're fucking killing yourself for god's sake!"

Danny shook his head contemptuously. "Now you're being melodramatic."

"Am I? You're always drunk, you don't sleep, and when you do, you got nightmares; you're constantly working ... where's that gonna get you, huh?"

"It got me *here*, Alice! I got a big house, people workin' for me, I'm my own boss. I'M IN CHARGE NOW!" He punched his fist against his own chest. It looked ridiculous, yet sad.

"Is that what you want to be?" Alice asked in a toneless voice. "*In charge* of me? This ain't love, Danny. This is you, wanting to *possess* me!"

"Oh, don't act like you got nothing out of this! You're living here too, ain't you? You got a cook, a maid, your own room; you don't have to do *anything*, yet you're constantly giving me attitude! Fucking hell, Alice, you're so fucking ungrateful!"

"Danny, we had this conversation before," she said sadly. "How can you not remember that? The day we moved here. We talked about all of this! I told you then and I'm telling you now, it's *you* I want, nothing else."

Danny's eyes glistened, both hurt and anger lay within them. "I'm here, ain't I?"

"Not the version of you that I'd like ..."

"Why do women always want to change their men? Huh?"

"I don't want to change you; I want you *not* to change! I want the old Danny back!"

"The one without money? With a fat belly? Who'd let you command?"

"I never commanded."

"Sure, you didn't ..." Shaking his head, he opened the closet door and started rummaging through his clothes.

Alice stared at his back and waited for him to face her again.

When he did, she asked, "Will I get my phone back? And my laptop?"

"To contact your friends? Plot your escape from this *prison*?" There was pain in his voice.

Alice said nothing.

"You got your answer," he muttered.

8

After days of staring out the window and nights of crying herself to sleep, Alice found herself giving up every hope of leaving that house.

She'd noticed that Jonas was now constantly tailing her. At least he was kind enough to keep his distance. As long as she was inside the house, he left her alone. But once she got out into the yard, he was always there, watching her every step.

Alice hated it—hated *him*—so she often preferred to hide in her room.

It was easy to avoid Danny during the day when he was working. But it was impossible to get herself something to eat in the evenings without being noticed. He would always be sitting in the living room, playing cards with his friends, getting drunk in the process. So, Alice often ended up not eating dinner at all.

Helping Henry in the garden didn't manage to make her feel better anymore. With Jonas constantly watching her, she couldn't talk openly, and Henry seemed to feel uncomfortable under Jonas's stare as well. Occasionally, Henry would give her an intense and meaningful look, but his mouth remained shut.

Alice wondered if Jonas's only job was to babysit her, since even during the day, he was never in the office with the rest of the group.

Sometimes, Jonas would mock her by pretending that everything was ordinary. He would offer her a cigarette casually, as if they were old friends. She usually just ignored him completely, but one day she had enough and snapped, "I don't smoke!"

Jonas just grinned and said, "Good thing with smokin', you can always start."

Alice glared at him through narrowed eyes and chose not to reply.

It was bad enough having him watch her all the time. She didn't need him to talk to her or even communicate with her in any way. It was easier to pretend he wasn't there if he didn't.

Yet Alice had to admit that not having anybody to talk to was beginning to make her feel as if a vital part of life were missing, like air to breathe or water to drink. She craved it like a starving person craving food.

One afternoon when Danny was out on business, Tee came up to her, carrying two mugs with steaming Chai.

"Tee's made you some tea," he joked and sat down on the couch next to her.

Alice really appreciated his gesture. They talked for a while, though merely small talk. Tee made some offensive jokes, as always, but beggars can't be choosers and Alice was desperate for some kind of conversation. *Any* kind.

"You know, Lizzy, I would never treat you that way." He gave her a pitying look. "Dan doesn't appreciate you."

That wasn't as nice at it sounded, since Tee's eyes wandered up and down her body while he spoke.

His presence still made her feel more comfortable than any of Danny's other friends, though.

"Tell *him* that," Alice replied.

Tee shook his head. "Nah, the guy scares me. Besides, he writes my paychecks."

If Alice chose to sleep in the bedroom, she often had to endure Danny's drunken attempts to have sex with her. His whiskey-breath was repulsive, and he usually reeked of sweat as well.

In the old apartment Alice had already gotten used to this sort of behavior but now, Danny was more urging, more persistent. Sometimes, if he'd drunk way too much, his body couldn't function the way he wanted it to, for which she was glad. Other times, Alice would just let him get on with it. It was the only attention he bestowed her with, though she couldn't enjoy it much.

Afterward, when she would sit on the toilet, she would stare at the wall for minutes, wondering why she was putting up with this—with him. Not that she had much of a choice, it seemed.

The first week of November was coming to an end and the temperatures had dropped rapidly. Alice didn't fancy sitting on her swing anymore, despite it being her favorite spot. It was too cold outside, too windy, too wet.

On that Saturday afternoon, Alice sat on the windowsill in her room, skimming through the pages of her diary, when a sudden fear struck her.

The entries she'd written during these last couple of weeks were discouraging. Empty, shallow, they got shorter with every day. Her days in that house passed in an endless, unnervingly slow manner and didn't offer her much to write about. Was this really what her life had become? A continuous routine of watching TV and Danny drink himself into a rage?

This has to end.

The longer she waited, the smaller her chances of escaping got. Reasoning with Danny seemed to be impossible, so there was only one other way.

I didn't fight hard enough. Why did I let him go through with this?

Jonas couldn't watch her every minute of every day. He would have to sleep or shit occasionally, and Alice also knew he often spent hours working out in the basement.

Sighing, she put her diary down on her lap and gazed out the window. The barren fields in the distance evoked an unquenchable thirst for freedom, and she balled her hands into fists and felt her nails digging into her palms.

I have to at least try.

A queasy feeling made her tense, but she clenched her teeth and got up from the windowsill to put her diary back in its box underneath the dresser.

Alice put on her worn out Converse and old denim jacket, and opened the door of her room. A glance into the corridor revealed that it was empty. After slowly tiptoeing down the stairs, Alice spied around the corner. Danny and the guys were sitting around the couch table, bent over something that looked important. They were muttering and pointing at whatever lay under their noses. Alice noticed Jonas's head among them.

Good, they seemed to be busy, and they hadn't heard her come downstairs.

Never taking her eyes from them, she carefully sneaked toward the back door and opened it silently. None of the men looked up.

The wind, that greeted her, was icy and Alice quickly closed the door again. Last thing she needed was one of the men to notice a sudden temperature drop.

Once outside, Alice took a deep breath of the cold fresh air and walked straight toward the rusty gate she'd found the other day. Her way led her around the pool, which was still empty and uncovered.

Her plan was to break the lock, and if that didn't work, she would climb up a tree and over the wall.

The gate looked as if it hadn't been used in decades. Its metal seemed to already be synthesizing with the lock, rusted through and through. But would it be weak enough for her to break it?

Alice didn't have anything to crack it open with. She had no idea where Danny kept their tools—if he even had them anymore now that he had staff for everything. It didn't matter though; she couldn't make too much noise anyway.

Pulling at the lock didn't break it, but Alice noticed that the latch, where it was screwed to the wall, was very lose. The screws all looked rusted as well. Alice began to pull at the latch, and when it didn't move, she tried to pull out the screws instead which proved to be hard, with just her fingers as tools. She pulled, turned a bit, pulled again, and managed to get one out. Only three to go. The others were harder though, and Alice ripped off part of her fingernail when she tried to pull one of the screws out. There was a bit of blood which she wiped off on her pants. To not get rust particles in the wound she used her middle finger and thumb to pull on the screw.

The sudden sound of a door falling shut made her flinch. Alice froze in place, feeling her heart drumming furiously against her ribs. Her hands got sweaty and she held her breath, listening.

After a moment of silence, the sound of footsteps approaching her appeared.

Let me guess ... Jonas.

A glance back over her shoulder revealed that she was right. He looked at her accusingly, a cigarette dangling from his lips, his hands in the pockets of his jeans.

Nope, Jonas, not this time.

Without a second thought, Alice quickly jumped upward, grabbed the top of the rusty iron door with both of her hands, and pulled herself up. She put one foot on the latch for support.

Jonas dropped his cigarette as his mouth opened in surprise, but he darted forward at once and tried to grab her leg. With all the strength her skinny arms could manage, Alice pulled herself upward and was able to put both her arms over the gate.

Jonas got hold of her right ankle. He didn't pull, he just held her in place.

"Don't be stupid," he warned.

"Let go of me!"

"Even if you get over the wall, we'll find you anyway."

"Fuck you, Jonas! FUCK YOU!"

Alice tried to pull her leg up, but Jonas was holding on to it tightly.

"There's no point," he said. "You won't—"

She kicked him right in the face with her left foot. Blood gushed out of his nose. He cursed and covered his face with both of his hands, letting go of her ankle.

Hah! Take that, asshole!

Her feeling of victory didn't last long. Just when she managed to get most of her upper body over the gate, a second pair of hands grabbed her by the jacket and yanked her down. Alice landed hard on the ground beneath her. Shocked, she looked up and saw Danny towering over her.

If he had been angry the day he'd thrown the whiskey bottle at her, it was nothing compared to what he looked like now.

He was panting, his chest heaving and dropping under heavy breaths. His hands were balled into fists and shaking.

"Danny," Alice shrieked, scared to the bone of the way he was looking at her.

"What the fuck, Alice? WHAT THE FUCK?!"

Alice tried to crawl backward and away from him, but he seized her by the collar of her jacket and pulled her up to her feet.

"THE FUCK YOU THINK YOU'RE DOING?" Little droplets of spit flew from his mouth when he bellowed the words. He smelled of whiskey.

"Let go of her," Jonas mumbled through his hand, which he was still holding over his nose and mouth.

Danny dropped her, and she almost fell back on her butt. He shoved her aside and took a step toward Jonas, his eyes fixed on the blood on Jonas's face.

"She fucking punched you?!"

Jonas put a hand on Danny's shoulder. "C'mon. 's nothing."

"D'you think you can keep me here, Danny?" Alice asked him, her voice trembling with anger and adrenaline. "If you don't tell Jonas to stop following me, this won't be the last time I broke his nose!"

Danny whirled around so quickly; she didn't even see it coming.

The blow seemed to crack her skull open and almost made her knees give in. Hot pain erupted on the left side of her face and blinded her.

Alice clutched her hands to her face and stumbled backward, trying to keep her balance, but her foot only found thin air and she fell ... but instead of landing on the soft wet grass, she seemed to be falling into a hole.

Another kind of pain exploded all over her body, and then she drifted into blackness.

"What the fuck, man!"

"Tell me she's alive! Please tell me she's breathing!"

"She is, now calm the fuck down!"

The voices seemed to be far away, and it took Alice a moment to realize whom they belonged to. A thick fog seemed to surround her, and her head felt much heavier than usual. What was going on?

With her consciousness, the pain returned as well.

Her whole head was throbbing violently and the sound of her blood pumping in her ears began to drown out the voices around her.

Everything on the right side of her body seemed to be on fire. Alice realized she was lying on her back on something hard and cold.

Breathing was incredibly hard. With every breath she took the pain increased. She tried to open her eyes but couldn't see anything. Blackness enclosed her like a cage, she couldn't get out of. Was she blind?

Panicking, she tried to put her hands on her face to see what was wrong with her eyes, but only her left arm followed her brain's command, the right one remained on the ground, unmoving.

Her left hand found her face and she realized that it was wet and sticky. What had happened?

Dully, a voice managed to break through the throbbing in her ears. Somebody was calling her name.

How had she ended up on the ground? And why was it so hard? Why was she hurting so badly?

The image of the iron gate appeared before her eyes, blurred like a dream that was trying to escape her memory ... Jonas trying to hold her back. Then Danny towering over her and ... had he pushed her? But why would that hurt so much?

She thought harder, but the effort made the pain in her head even worse. Gasping, she tried instinctively to put her right hand on her face as well, but a new kind of pain—a stabbing one—exploded in her arm.

Her breathing accelerated. Why wouldn't her arm obey her? And her legs ... she couldn't even feel them.

It was Danny ... what did he do to me?

Alice felt the touch of a hand on her left shoulder and jerked away from it.

It's him. He wants to finish what he started; he's trying to kill me!

"Don't," she tried to shout, but her voice was faint and weak, not much more than a whisper. "Don't ... touch me!" She tried again, though the words cost her a lot of effort.

"Don't move," the voice above her said. It was Jonas's voice.

She could still hear Danny cursing, but farther away.

"Go away!" Alice tried to sound fiercer this time, but still, it came out as barely more than a whisper.

The hand on her shoulder was taken away, but now she could feel him shoving one hand carefully underneath her neck and the other under the back of her knees ... and then she was lifted up in the air.

The sudden movement multiplied her pain and made her lungs deflate like an empty balloon. She forgot to breathe, and little stars began dancing before her eyes.

He's carrying me somewhere, she realized in shock.

"Alice, I'm so sorry, fuck, I'm so sorry!" It was Danny, sobbing.

Her heart was thumping furiously in her chest now and she struggled for breath.

"Alice ..." Danny's voice sounded much closer now and the panic seemed to strangle her, making her gasp for air like a drowning person.

"Stay here," Jonas's voice commanded close to her ear.

"But I—"

"You're drunk. Sober up!"

Alice's body was rocking up and down when he walked. It felt as if he was walking upward, steps, maybe? Then a sudden ice-cold wind hit her. It felt revitalizing.

The motion continued. She moaned in pain. There were more voices in the distance, but the man carrying her—Jonas—didn't say anything.

He shifted her in his arms, and then she heard the metallic sound of keys on a ring and a car being unlocked, followed by the noise of a car door being opened.

Jonas put her down on a car seat, first upright, but then he pushed the lean down a bit and pulled the seat belt across her. It put pressure on her shoulder, and Alice let out a choked whimper.

"Sorry," he muttered.

This was Jonas's car, without a doubt. Never before had she been in a car that smelled so much like an ashtray.

She felt his fingers close around her wrist, pulling her hand away from her face.

"Don't, I can't see! I'm blind," she sobbed.

"You're not blind," Jonas said in a strained voice. The sound of it made her tremble. Suppressed anger had tinged his words.

"It's only blood," he added when Alice tried to cover her face once again. He held her hand down firmly and started to dab her face with some kind of soft cloth. When he was finished, he left the cloth on the right side of her forehead and placed her left hand on it.

"Hold this," he ordered.

Alice flinched when the door to her right was shut, shaking the whole car under the impact. It sent another wave of pain through her whole body.

She could hear the driver's door open and close. The car shook again under Jonas's weight. He muttered something that she couldn't understand, but he sounded angry. There was no doubt about it now.

Alice's heart started racing. Her body trembled uncontrollably, and salty tears stung in her sore eyes. Where was Jonas taking her? And why was he so angry?

Now, with the blood gone, she made another attempt to open her eyes, but the faint daylight sent bolts of pain through her skull, so she quickly shut her eyelids again.

When the engine started roaring and the car moved, she was on the verge of hyperventilating. There was a brief exchange of words, then the shrieking of metal hinges, and she was pushed into the seat as the car sped forward.

It shook hard on the gravel road. Alice could hear little stones hitting the sides of the car. It was like torture. Her head hurt so badly it made her nauseous.

She whimpered between suppressed sobs, but the sound was swallowed by the noise of the tires grating on the gravel road and the howling of the engine.

After what seemed like an eternity, the bumping stopped, and they moved more smoothly. They must have reached the tar road.

Jonas pushed the gas pedal down even further, and they sped on.

Alice couldn't stop herself from sobbing in pain and fear, but she hoped that Jonas couldn't hear it. She opened her eyes a little bit and turned her head slightly to look at him. Fury contorted his usually blank features. His eyes seemed to be spitting fire while they were glued to the road in front of him.

Why was everybody so angry? Why had Danny been so angry? And why would he hurt her?

The last question was the most important one. How could he do something like that to her? But what was it exactly, that he had done? *Had* he even done something?

Alice's mind was busy like an anthill, one thought chased the next, but none of them made sense. She doubted her own memories, barely had any anyway, but she clearly felt Jonas's anger and couldn't extinguish the fear of what he was going to do with her. Was he trying to get rid of her once and for all? Had Danny given the order?

There was a pain in her chest that had nothing to do with her injuries.

How can he hate me so much?

A flow of tears ran down her cheeks, mixed with blood. They burned on her raw skin as if liquid acid were running down her face.

Jonas didn't say a word throughout the drive and Alice's mind was too chaotic to realize where they were going.

The car came to a halt and Jonas quickly undid her seatbelt and lifted her out of the vehicle. Alice weakly tried to resist, but he had her locked in his strong arms and carried her into a building. The light was way too bright inside and she had to cover her eyes with her left hand.

The light, the noise, and the strong smells in the building made her dizzy, and her stomach convulsed painfully.

Jonas was saying something to someone—to her? But the throbbing in her temples, the ringing in her ears, and the thumping of her heart made it impossible for her to understand him. Panic overpowered her when she felt him letting go of her. Other hands were gripping her now, pulling at her, and pushing her down onto something.

Her heart was racing so fast now, it seemed about to explode. Hyperventilating, Alice squirmed in the grip of all these unknown hands, trying to free herself. Everything and everybody seemed like a threat. People without faces were tearing at her clothes and limbs, their voices melting together and creating some sort of loud humming noise, as if her head were stuck in a beehive.

Suddenly, there was a pinch in her arm—nothing compared to the pain in the rest of her body—and then her heartbeat slowed down, and everything became black again.

Alice awoke to the nerve-wracking beeping sound of a monitor next to her head.

Her head was still throbbing, but the pain seemed distant, weaker. She tried to open her eyes, but her lids felt heavy and swollen. Her left eye remained almost shut, but the right one opened.

Something heavy on her whole body seemed to be pinning her down, but when she glanced down at herself, there was nothing but a thin blanket which had been drawn up to her chest.

The bed, she was lying on, felt hard and uncomfortable.

Why am I so tired?

She let her eyes wander across the room, slowly, since even swiveling her eyes sent spasms of pain through her skull.

Hospital... that's where he brought me.

At least the pain wasn't so bad now. Her right arm was covered by a bandage. Was it broken? What the hell had happened?

Again, she tried to think back. Danny turning around, something—his fist?—hitting her ... No, he wouldn't do that.

Or would he?

The door to the room suddenly opened, and a nurse walked in. She asked Alice how she was doing, but it was impossible to answer that question.

"What happened?" Alice asked instead.

While checking the machines around her bed, the nurse said, "According to the man who brought you here, you fell into an empty swimming pool."

Of course ... that stupid pool. It sounded ridiculous, but it made sense. How embarrassing. Alice tried to picture herself falling into the pool. She wanted to ask the nurse how exactly it had happened, but the young woman had already left the room again.

Alice felt her eyelids get heavier and again she drifted off into a deep, dreamless sleep.

The next time she opened her eyes, she could see Jonas standing next to the bed. He was leaning against the wall, his hands in the pockets of his jeans.

Something jumped in her guts at the sight of him, and her heart skipped a beat.

Why was he still here? He looked angry—furious even—the way he had back in the car. Still, his eyes showed that dangerous glint.

Alice remembered how she had kicked him. She glanced at his nose, but it looked normal and the blood was gone.

Jonas wasn't looking at her for a change. He seemed to be staring at some spot on the other side of the room. Alice followed his eyes with her own, but all there was were a white wall and a window with closed curtains.

A sudden stabbing pain in her head made her inhale sharply and clutch her left hand to her face.

Jonas's eyes flicked to her at once. "How you feelin'?"

Despite the medications which were making her drowsy, she felt her heart beat faster and her hands got ice-cold. Trying to avoid his eyes, she said nothing.

Jonas's eyes rested heavily on her; she almost felt suffocated by his stare.

What does he want from me?

"Alice," he said sharply and took a step toward her.

"I'm sorry!" she cried.

He stopped. "For what?"

"Breaking your nose."

"It's not broken."

The throbbing in her skull increased. Alice closed her eyes and tried to take a deep breath, but that only made her right shoulder hurt.

Jonas sighed deeply. "Don't apologize."

Alice was confused. What was up with this guy? Was he angry at her or not?

"Aren't you ... mad?"

"At you? No."

Surprised, she opened her eyes to look at him, but another wave of hot pain went through her body. It made her feel incredibly nauseous. The sweet drowsiness was starting to wear off.

Danny had hit her.

No, he didn't ... he wouldn't ... why would he do that? He could never ...

Again, her thoughts spun madly, and her breathing got flat. Something appeared to be putting pressure on her lungs, and her throat was dry. Trying to swallow, Alice started coughing, which only doubled the pain.

Jonas made a gesture toward the half-open door, and a moment later a woman in white scrubs appeared.

"She's in pain." He nodded toward Alice.

The woman smiled warmly, and fumbled with the tube which connected some infusion with Alice's left hand.

Almost instantly, the pain disappeared, and Alice's eyes closed again.

When she awoke once more, she felt a bit better. Blinking, she looked around and found Jonas sleeping on a chair next to the bed. He was still wearing the same clothes and his chin was resting on his chest.

Why hadn't he just gone home?

Alice carefully began touching her face with her left hand, trying to find out what was wrong with her. The area around her left eye was swollen and she still couldn't open it completely. The right side of her forehead was covered by bandages.

Suddenly, the door was opened, and the woman in the white scrubs reappeared.

"Good, you're up." She smiled.

Jonas had jerked at the sound of the door, now he lifted his head and blinked.

"Well, you've got a faithful friend here." The woman grinned and nodded toward him.

Alice just grimaced.

"I'm your doctor," the lady explained. She had dark skin, beautiful big brown eyes and black hair brushed back into a tight bun. "My name is Keller, but you can call me Liza, if you want."

"Alice," Alice introduced herself quietly.

Dr. Keller smiled an amused smile. "I know ... So, what happened, Alice?"

Alice barely knew that herself, how was she supposed to answer?

"I, uh ... fell into an empty pool ... I think."

Jonas's eyes seemed to pierce right through her. It made her incredibly nervous.

"I told you what happened," he said to Dr. Keller.

The doctor raised her eyebrows but nodded. "The pool was in your own yard? Where you live?"

Alice nodded slowly.

"How deep is it? Where you fell?"

Alice tried to shrug but winced at the pain in her right shoulder.

"Bout ten feet," Jonas answered for her.

"You're lucky you didn't break anything. The bone in your right elbow is slightly fissured, but it's going to heal without complications. According to this gentleman, you landed head-first." She turned to Jonas. "So, you saw it happen?"

He nodded.

"No chance to intervene?"

The question seemed to make him uncomfortable, and he shook his head. "I was ... too far away."

Dr. Keller just nodded. "All right then. Well, Alice, you have no fractures, only bruises, a concussion, and a laceration on your forehead that needed stitches. And that elbow injury, which I already mentioned."

Alice stared at her blankly.

"We'll keep you here tonight to see if anything gets worse. Do you feel nauseous?"

"Yes."

"Probably the concussion ... or the shock. I definitely want to keep you under surveillance for a while."

Am I ever not under surveillance?

Well, being watched by a doctor was better than being watched by Jonas ... although, he too was still here.

"She can't stay here long," Jonas said.

"And why is that?" Liza wanted to know.

He ignored the question.

Alice stared down at her blanket, which became a blur before her eyes. The possibility of going back hadn't even occurred to her up until now. Ice-cold anxiety crept through her bones and again, her heartbeat accelerated. There was no way she could face Danny now—not after what happened.

"After an *accident* like that, it is essential to put the patient on bed rest," Dr. Keller urged.

"She has a bed at home," Jonas replied coldly.

"Fair enough." The doctor turned back toward Alice. "It's your decision, Alice. But I am definitely keeping you until tomorrow."

Not knowing what else to do, Alice nodded slowly, careful not to make her headache worse.

"Now ... I'd like to ask you some *private* questions." Liza gave Jonas a meaningful look. "Sir, will you please step out?"

Jonas got off his chair and crossed his arms in front of his chest. "Private questions?"

"Regarding her medical history ... As far as I'm concerned, you're not a family member ... are you?"

Scowling, Jonas shook his head.

"Would you like him to stay?" Dr. Keller asked Alice.

Alice shook her head.

Jonas gave her a warning look, then turned and walked out of the door.

Liza Keller sighed, pulled the chair closer to the bed, and sat down.

"So ..." she said. "Why don't you tell me what *really* happened?"

Alice's pulse started racing. Why was the doctor looking at her in a way that made her feel interrogated?

"I ... fell into that pool ..."

"I know. But why?"

Alice tried hard to think of something smart to say but failed. "I ... lost my balance. I was stupid."

"Why did you lose your balance?"

"I don't remember."

Dr. Keller raised one eyebrow, the way Danny always did.

Danny ... What had he done? Why couldn't she remember? All she could recall was that she'd said something provoking, and he turned around and ... shoved her? Hit her? Or did he just bump into her by mistake?

Surely, he would have never pushed her into the pool on purpose ...

I could have broken my neck.

No, impossible. He hadn't done it intentionally.

"You're withholding something," the doctor observed.

"I really don't remember!" Tears of desperation threatened to flood her eyes, but Alice quickly blinked them away.

Dr. Keller sighed. "All right, I'll tell you what I know. According to that man who brought you here, you landed on your right side. Would you agree?"

"I don't know ... I was lying on my back when I woke up ..."

"He turned you to see how badly you were injured. Not very wise, if you'll allow me to say that. Anyway, your fall explains the injuries on the right side of your body." The doctor's stare intensified, as she paused to let her words sink in.

Alice started chewing her lip nervously, wondering where Liza Keller was going with this.

"For some reason, however, you have a bad bruise next to your left eye."

Instinctively, Alice touched it with her left hand.

"Now I would like to know where that one came from."

Dropping her gaze, Alice tried to think of an excuse. But how was she supposed to come up with a believable story, if she didn't even know what the bruise looked like? And why was she even trying to make up an excuse, if she didn't even know what exactly she was supposed to hide?

The uncomfortable silence dragged on until Liza Keller chose to break it.

"Is he your boyfriend?"

Puzzled, Alice looked up. "Who?"

"The man who brought you here."

"Hell, no!"

"You don't like him?"

"What?"

"I thought he might be a friend."

"Not really."

"So, you don't like him?"

"Not ... really."

"Did he hit you?"

The sudden bluntness of the question took Alice by surprise. "What? Jonas? Hell, no!"

"Then who did?"

Speechless, Alice gaped at the doctor, wondering if she had heard her right.

"E-excuse me?" she managed to stutter.

"Somebody did, am I right?"

"W-what? Why would you—"

"Who is he? The man who brought you here?"

"No one. Just ... one of my boyfriend's friends."

"So, did your boyfriend hit you?"

Alice felt herself get angry.

"I'm just saying," the doctor continued, "It seems a bit odd that your boyfriend's friend takes you to the hospital and your boyfriend doesn't even come with."

He was drunk ... didn't Jonas tell him to stay?

Gritting her teeth, Alice said nothing.

"Unless ..."

"Unless what?"

"Unless it was him who did this."

"You are being quite presumptuous," Alice hissed angrily.

"I'm sorry you feel that way. I just care for my patients, that's all. Are you going to tell me what happened?"

"I ... I really don't know!"

Dr. Keller frowned. "You honestly don't remember?"

Alice stubbornly shook her head.

"Do you want to tell me *what* you remember?"

That Danny had been locking her up for weeks and freaked out when she tried to climb over the wall?

No, thank you.

Staring at her hands, Alice remained quiet.

Liza Keller sighed. "Listen, Alice. When you came here, we had to sedate you because you were having a panic attack. You wouldn't let anybody touch you."

"I don't like hospitals, that's all," Alice muttered.

Liza put a hand on Alice's bandaged arm. "Has he ever hurt you before?"

"No! He'd never ... He wouldn't ..."

"So, I assume it was the first time."

Alice looked up, taken aback. "No, I didn't ... I never said—"

"You didn't have to."

Feeling cornered, Alice dropped her gaze again.

"You'd be appalled if you knew how many women suffer domestic abuse," the doctor said softly. "And most of them just go back to their husbands or boyfriends. And then it happens again. I'm giving you the chance right now to be smarter than that and tell me the truth ... so I can call the police."

"What? No! I don't want that!"

"You've got serious injuries—"

"He didn't want me to fall into the pool!"

"No, but he wanted to hit you. And judging by that bruise, he hit you hard. Even if the pool had not been there, you could have hit your head somewhere and died."

"You're exaggerating!"

The doctor shook her head sadly. "No, I'm not."

Alice stared down at her hands stubbornly to avoid Liza's eyes. "Why do you even care?"

"Because most people don't. Especially the ones that could help you ... this world is still dominated by men—men, who don't care about domestic abuse—"

"There is no abuse," Alice objected. There was just Danny—*her* Danny, going through a self-destructive phase and dragging her down with him. But he loved her, and she knew that he was still a nice guy, somewhere deep down ... behind the angry façade.

"He's not ... he's a good person ..."

"Does he drink?"

"Yes, and that's the problem, not him!"

"So as long as he drinks, he'll be a threat to you," the doctor concluded.

"He'll stop ... eventually."

"You're lying to yourself, and you know it."

"No ... I- I know he'd never want to hurt me!"

"But he did. And he'll do it again."

Alice stared at the white wall opposite her. The doctor sighed again. "Trust me on this, Alice. Don't go back to him. You're still so young, don't make that mistake."

Suddenly, Alice felt incredibly ashamed of herself. Not only had she managed to provoke Danny until he had snapped, now she was also a disappointment to the one person who was trying to help her.

"I'm sorry," she muttered.

Dr. Keller pushed the chair back and stood up. "Don't apologize to me, Alice. Apologize to yourself."

9

That night, Alice awoke to a hand softly shaking her. Moaning, she blinked into the light. Someone was bending over the bed, waiting for her to wake up. It took her a few moments to realize it was Jonas.

"Wake up," he ordered.

"W-why?"

"We're leaving."

Alice still felt nauseous, and despite the infusion she was in pain. "No ... not yet."

Jonas shoved one arm underneath her back and slowly lifted her into a sitting position. He pulled her blanket back. "I'll fetch your clothes."

Sitting upright made her feel dizzy. "No, Jonas..." she protested weakly. The room began to spin around her. "I feel sick."

Sighing, Jonas walked over toward her and crouched down next to the bed. "Listen ... Danny called me about fifteen times last night, he's worried sick."

"I don't care! I don't want to go back to him."

"Where else d'you want to go?"

Alice was about to collapse back onto the bed, but Jonas quickly caught her uninjured elbow and held her steady.

Trying to keep the nausea down, she swallowed. "I can ... go to my friends."

"Danny hates himself for what he did ... he's going mental."

Since when did Jonas talk so much?

"I don't care!"

"Yes, you do."

"No ... I- I need time to think."

Jonas got up and started to collect her clothes from the small white cupboard next to the toilet.

"Get dressed," he commanded. He put the bundle of clothes in her lap.

"No."

"I'll carry you out of here with or without your clothes. Your choice. Just know that it's bloody freezing out there."

Tears started to run down Alice's cheeks. She was too weak to even support her own weight, how was she supposed to fight Jonas?

"Please don't make me go back there!" she begged.

"Get dressed." He took her shirt from her lap and held it under her nose. "Come on," he urged.

Sobbing, Alice desperately shook her head. "No, don't make me, I don't want to!"

For a second, Jonas looked as if he was about to get angry, but then he sighed and crouched down again, putting one hand on her left shoulder. Alice flinched under his touch.

"Don't be scared," he said. "He won't do it again."

"It's not just ... *that* ... I don't want to be back there! All alone in that house, every day ... I just can't ..."

Alice quickly bit her tongue. Why in the world was she crying in front of Jonas? Why was she even telling him this? He was an asshole, and it was clear he didn't care.

Did I hurt my brain when I fell? Or is it the painkillers?

Alice tried to wipe the tears away with her left hand, but more followed instantly.

"Alice ..." Jonas's voice sounded softer. "There's nowhere else you can go."

Was that supposed to be comforting?

"I can go anywhere *but* there," she protested.

"You don't understand." He looked directly into her eyes. His eyes were green, not blue, she noticed.

"They're green."

He looked puzzled. "What?"

"Your eyes."

Why had she just said that?

What the hell did the doctors give me?

Jonas looked speechless.

"I thought they were blue," Alice explained.

He gave her a look that was both wary and concerned.

"I ... I really think I should stay here. I think I hurt my brain ..."

For a moment, Jonas just stared at her blankly, but suddenly, something shifted in his eyes and his upper lip twitched. Was he trying not to laugh?

"Was that a smile?" Alice asked.

He looked caught. "What? Of course not."

"Shame." She sighed. "For one moment there I thought you had feelings."

Jonas stared at her as if he was trying to figure out whether that was an insult or a joke.

"Guess I'm emotional enough for the both of us, ain't I?"

There it was again, that twitch of his lip.

Suddenly, exhaustion hit her like a wave, and threatened to suck her into a deep sea of sleep. Alice's chin dropped onto her chest, and she collapsed backward.

Jonas caught her and pulled her up again, shaking her lightly.

"Don't sleep!"

"I'm so tired," she breathed.

"Come on, get dressed."

"No, Danny, let me sleep, please ... just five more minutes."

Jonas stared at her, then his eyes fell upon the infusion which was connected to the back of her hand. He started to rip off the tape carefully and pulled the needle out of her skin.

That woke her up. "What are you doing?"

"You can't think straight with this in your system."

"That's not true, it helps me ... the pain ..."

"You just called me Danny."

Alice's eyes widened.

Did I?

Danny ... she remembered. "No, no ... I don't want to see him! Don't make me!"

Jonas's expression turned hard. "Not again, Alice! Now get dressed."

Her eyes teared up again. "Why can't I just stay a bit longer? Please!"

He shook his head sternly.

"Please Jonas, just ... don't ..."

Why was she crying in front of him again?

Now the painkillers were wearing off. Alice's head started throbbing again. It made her dizzy and the nausea got worse.

Jonas brushed her hair aside and undid the knot on the back of her neck, which was holding the hospital shirt she was wearing together.

"I can't," she protested.

"I won't do *that* for you, Alice." He held up her shirt again. "Put it on, I'll turn around."

Alice took it hesitantly, and he stood up and turned his back toward her.

"It's broken," she sobbed.

Jonas turned around and took the shirt from her, frowning. "Looks like they cut it off you." He handed her the jacket instead. "Put this on."

Alice just stared at it. How was she supposed to get dressed? She couldn't move her right arm. She was dizzy, on the verge to fainting, and her stomach was churning.

"I can't!"

Sighing, Jonas approached her and took the jacket out of her hands. He helped her get into it—at least her left arm. When he tried to lift her right arm, hot pain shot through her elbow and shoulder, and made her gasp.

"Sorry," Jonas muttered while he laid the jacket loosely over her right shoulder instead. He then took her pants from her lap—at least they were still intact. He helped her get her feet through the holes, then pulled her up and held her steady, so she was able to pull up her pants with her left hand. Jonas made her sit back down on the bed and went to fetch her shoes and socks.

By the time Alice was dressed, her tears were still streaming down her face, though she tried hard to suppress the sobs.

"Stop crying," Jonas said harshly, as if he perceived her tears as downright irritating.

"Why are you doing this?" Alice asked quietly.

He didn't reply.

"Why do you help him?" she tried again.

"He's my friend."

Alice wiped the tears away with the sleeve of her jacket. "That's your reason? That's why you're helping him keeping me in that prison?"

"You don't know shit."

"Then explain it to me!"

Jonas glared at her. "Let's go."

Alice stared at him. What had she expected? For one moment, he had seemed almost human; she had even stopped hating him for a second or two, thinking that maybe he might be nicer than she'd thought. But he was still Danny's servant, her prison warder. The guy who'd had her brought to Danny in a police car, who'd carried her back to the house when she'd finally managed to get out the gate. *He* was the reason why she was in this mess. Without him, she would have already escaped long ago.

Alice felt her tears dry out at once and they left behind nothing but emptiness.

Jonas had to carry her down to the car. Her legs wouldn't support her weight. Being carried by him like that felt horrible. Jonas was cold, distant ... professional. He was always careful not to hurt her physically—not because he cared, but because it was his job to keep her both locked up *and* safe.

When he buckled her up in his car, the pungent smell of smoke doubled her nausea.

Jonas drove out of the underground parking lot and into the dark. The streets were deserted. He had kidnapped her from the hospital in the middle of the night ...

Out of town, when they were driving on the tar road flanked by fields, Jonas pulled a cigarette out of the front pocket of his jeans. He lit it. Smoke began to fill the car instantly. Alice felt her stomach turn.

"Stop the car," she choked.

He looked at her, then quickly stepped on the brake and brought the car to a halt on the side of the road. He helped her unbuckle and even had to open her door for her from the inside. Alice dropped out of the vehicle, coughing and gagging.

She hadn't eaten much these last couple of days, so her stomach was empty. Yet, it tried to get rid of even the last drop of water she'd drunk, cramping violently, sending spasms of pain through her chest. When it finally stopped, she was huddled on the cold ground, panting and whimpering like a starving street dog. She hadn't noticed Jonas getting out of the car, but now he heaved her back inside.

He didn't smoke anymore for the rest of the drive.

Jonas parked the car on the gravel in front of the house and got out. Panic made Alice's pulse race once again and tears ran down her cheeks anew. She did not want to see Danny, not even a bit. What was she even supposed to say to him? What if he was still mad at her?

When Jonas opened her door, her heart seemed to drop down into her belly.

"Please don't do this, don't make me go in there!" Sobbing, she tried to wind herself out of his grip.

Jonas said nothing and pulled her out of the car.

The blood seemed to freeze in her veins when she realized that Danny was already waiting for her on the porch. He looked like a ghost. Like a big, scary ghost. His face looked white in the pale light, and his eyes were red and bloodshot. Was he drunk? Or ... had he been crying? His usually tidy hair was a mess on his head.

When Jonas carried her up the steps, Alice could see tears glistening in Danny's eyes. He stretched out a hand toward her, and she began to struggle and wind herself in Jonas's arms so hard, he almost dropped her.

"Alice ..." Danny's voice sounded strange ... hollow.

"Not now," Jonas told him. "Leave her be."

He carried her up the stairs and into her own room, where he put her down on the sofa in front of the window. He helped her out of the jacket and shoes again and went to fetch a blanket from the bedroom. He covered her with it, then shut the blinds of the window.

Alice turned onto her left side, so her back was facing the door. She couldn't stand to look at Jonas for another second. She could hear him go into the bathroom and fill a glass with tap water. When he came back, he put the glass down on the floor next to her.

For a moment, he lingered, staring at her. Alice pressed her eyes shut and ignored him, silently begging for him to leave. Finally, she heard his footsteps disappear. The light was switched off and the door fell shut. She was alone again.

There were no sounds apart from her heartbeat and the ticking of the clock on the wall. The night was dead and silent. The door remained shut and Alice couldn't hear Danny or Jonas, so she figured they must both be either extremely quiet or already have gone to sleep.

Alice tried to sleep, but despite her being incredibly exhausted, the pain in her head and limbs kept her awake. Tears continued to silently run down her cheeks, though the sobbing had finally stopped. The tears felt hot on her skin. She couldn't tell whether she was crying because of Danny or because of the pain.

Why hadn't Jonas just left her in the hospital? With the painkillers and a real bed? Now she was lying on an uncomfortable couch, which was too short for her to stretch her legs. The taste of bile was still on her tongue from throwing up earlier. Even a sip of the water Jonas had left her didn't help.

Alice tried to remember what had happened by the pool, to make some sense out of it. Danny had snapped—in a way she had never expected him to. His mood swings had become common, but she would have never thought that he could willingly hurt her. Sure, he hadn't wanted to push her into the pool, but her face was swollen where his fist had collided with it, and that wasn't nothing either.

The man she'd known and loved seemed to have disappeared without leaving a trace.

The new Danny was keeping her locked up in that house, taking away her freedom and her free will ... and wasn't the reason why she hadn't tried to run away sooner the fear of his anger?

Alice had felt intimidated by him long before he had actually hurt her.

A stabbing pain appeared in her chest that had nothing to do with her injuries.

How could he do something like that?

The fact that she still loved him—despite everything—hurt the most.

Dawn came and faint rays of light found their way through the gaps in the blinds.

Alice had been drifting in and out of a light and troublesome sleep for hours. Her face felt hot and her mouth was dry. Her tongue felt furry. Still, her head kept throbbing, but the tears had finally dried out. She had no idea what time it was and didn't feel like turning around to look at the clock. Since the sun had risen though, some people must already be up.

Alice heard the sound of tires on gravel coming through the window. Was Henry coming to work? Or Anita? Or was it still the weekend?

Maybe it was just the gate security, changing shifts.

More moments passed—or were it hours? Until suddenly, the door to her room opened. Alice flinched at the sound. Her heart started racing. Was it Danny? She kept her eyes fixed on the sofa lean and tried not to move.

The door was shut again but the presence of a person was clearly palpable, and Alice could feel a pair of eyes on her.

"Allie?" It was Danny's voice.

Her eyes teared up at once.

I thought I had no tears left.

His voice sounded weak and hoarse. Alice could hear him taking a few steps closer, but then he stopped.

"I know you're awake." Was he crying? "I'm so sorry, Allie! I never meant to …" His voice broke.

Alice clenched her teeth as much as the pain in her head allowed it.

Just go away.

"I know … that you don't want to talk to me … and I understand."

He took a step closer and Alice squeezed her eyes shut.

Don't touch me, whatever you do— don't you dare touch me!

He didn't. He remained standing close to the couch; she could smell the faint odor of his cologne.

Another dry sob. "Just know," he spoke, "that I really, really am sorry and … I hate myself for what I did! I'm never going to drink again, I swear!"

Sure.

"I haven't had a drop since … it happened and …"

You mean last night? Congratulations.

Her heart felt like it was made from stone, while Danny was talking. She would not accept his apology, not this time. Instead, she kept her eyes closed stubbornly and ignored him.

"I'm an asshole, Allie … I know that."

I know that too.

"Believe me, no matter how much you hate me right now, it's nothing compared to how I feel about myself."

Why did it sound like he was reciting some Hollywood drama?

Danny sighed desperately. "You don't have to talk to me, but please, if there's anything you need, let me know …"

Pain killers …

The throbbing in her head was getting worse. It took Alice a lot of effort to listen and understand Danny's words, and she wished he would just disappear. He moved closer though—she could feel it—and then she felt a light touch on her right shoulder.

Alice jerked away from it—from him—but the sudden movement made her gasp in pain.

Danny took his hand away. "I'm sorry ..."

A moment of silence passed, and Alice kept her eyes shut tightly. She didn't want Danny to see her tears, but she was pretty sure that he already had.

"I'll send Jonas to check on you."

No, not him! Why always him?

"I'm sorry," Danny said again, and then he finally left the room.

As soon as the door had fallen shut, the tears started flowing uncontrollably, but she tried to swallow her sobs and bit her lip. Danny wasn't worth her tears. She wanted to feel cold and empty, the way she had when he had first entered the room. But somehow, against her will, his words had managed to touch her.

What if he truly wouldn't drink anymore? What if he really regretted hitting her?

It didn't take long until the door was opened again. Alice didn't have to guess twice who it was, the smell of smoke and leather said it all.

Jonas walked into the room and came over to the window to open the blinds just a little bit.

The light blinded her, and Alice shut her eyes again. Jonas pulled back the blanket and grabbed her left shoulder without saying a word. He pulled her up into a sitting position.

"Stop, don't," Alice protested, but he ignored that.

Sitting upright doubled the pain in her head. She put both hands to her face, as if that would help. Jonas took her left wrist and pulled it away from her face. She felt something drop into her palm.

Curious, Alice opened her eyes to look at it. It was a big white pill.

"What is that?"

"Pain killers," Jonas answered. He took the glass of water from the floor and held it up. "Take it," he ordered.

Alice did without hesitation. The big pill almost got stuck in her throat. Jonas took the glass out of her hand and went to the bathroom to fill it once more.

When he came back, he asked, "Need to go to the bathroom?"
Oh, hell no!
Alice would rather have peed her pants than let him escort her to the toilet. Glaring at him, she shook her head.

He just stared at her without letting show his thoughts, the way he always did. "I'll get you somethin' to eat later."

"I'm not hungry."

He pointed at the glass on the floor. "Keep drinking."

Then he left the room.

Alice remained sitting on the couch for a while, staring at the spot where Jonas had just been. Time lost its meaning, but the pain was slowly fading out and the throbbing was gone. Instead, her mind became foggy and she was beginning to feel incredibly tired.

The next time she woke up, it was dark again. No light fell through the blinds and all sounds had died out. Her mouth felt dry again and the throbbing in her head had returned, but it didn't seem as bad as before. How long had she slept?

Without thinking, Alice began rubbing her eyes, but quickly stopped when it hurt where her face was swollen.

The swelling still made it impossible for her to open her left eye completely. Moaning, Alice tried to sit up again to drink some water. Suddenly, a shadow moved in the darkness. Her heart stopped at once. She froze, staring into the corner, trying to adjust her eyes to the darkness.

"You awake?" It was Danny's voice.

Why couldn't he just leave her alone? She didn't answer.

There was a *click* and then the light went on, blinding her. Alice clutched her hand to her face to cover her eyes.

"Sorry, I just wanted to see … you." His voice still sounded thick with pain.

Alice could see him now, through the gaps between her fingers. Danny had brought a chair to her room and been sitting in it, but now he was standing up.

"You slept so long; I was worried."

Alice stared at his feet. He wasn't wearing shoes and his white socks looked gray and dirty. Was he still wearing the same clothes?

In that moment, she realized that the hospital dress, which was still open at the back, had slipped over her right shoulder. She quickly pulled it up again, as if a stranger were standing before her.

"If you want something else to wear ... I could get you something."

Alice definitely would have liked to wear something else, but she absolutely didn't want Danny to assist her when getting dressed. Changing clothes would have to wait until she was feeling better and could do it alone.

Still, she felt dizzy and when she grabbed the glass to drink some water, she almost dropped it and spilled some.

Danny darted forward to help her, but then he thought better of it and remained standing, keeping his distance.

"There's food for you." He nodded toward the dresser, where someone had put a tray with a covered plate on it. "It's cold now, but I can warm it up for you."

Alice's grip around the glass tightened while she thought, *you could just leave!*

Anger was building up inside of her, but she was too weak to say something. Besides, her silence was his punishment.

"I'm so sorry, Allie," he said again.

Alice ignored him.

"If there's something I can do ..."

Leave, just go already!

Almost as if he had heard her thoughts, Danny slowly turned around and walked out of the room.

When he was gone, her eyes teared up again. She wiped the tears away angrily, though doing so hurt.

Why did she even cry for him? Frustrated, she punched a cushion with her right fist, which sent a sharp, stabbing pain through her elbow. Alice wanted to scream, but instead, she buried her face in the cushion.

She knew that she couldn't ignore Danny forever. Sooner or later, she would have to face him. But right now, the pain didn't allow her to think straight. It was better to say nothing than say something wrong.

The door opened again, and when she smelled cigarette smoke, Alice looked up. Jonas was standing in the doorframe.

"Did he send you in?" she asked. Her voice was shaky and thick from crying.

He nodded. "You slept long."

Alice was about to tell him to fuck off, but then she had a better idea.

"The fuck did you give me?" she asked instead.
"Something obviously too strong for you." Jonas turned to leave the room.
"No, wait," she protested. "I want more of it!"
For a moment, he stared at her, but then he grinned a cocky grin. "Eat first," he told her, nodding toward the tray on the dresser.

Alice stared at it. Her stomach was still aching with nausea, but it might as well be the hunger.

Jonas went over to the dresser and took the plate, uncovered it, and brought it over to her. Alice took it from him and placed it on her lap. It contained pasta with tomato sauce.

"Who made this?"

It sure did not look as good as the food, Henry usually cooked.

"Danny," said Jonas.

Of course.

Cooking for her wasn't enough to earn her forgiveness. Quickly, she tried to suppress her feelings and started to eat. It didn't taste that bad, but it was clear that the sauce came from a can.

Alice ate slowly, careful not to overwhelm her stomach. She didn't want to throw up in front of Jonas ... *again.*

When only half of the food remained, she couldn't swallow one more bite and put the fork down. Jonas took the plate and put it back on the dresser, then he went to fill her water glass. He pulled another pill out of a transparent bag in his pocket, and grinned as if he were a drug dealer, trying to get her hooked.

"What is that?" Alice wanted to know.

"Something that'll make you sleep for another twelve hours."

Fine by me.

Alice put the pill on her tongue and gulped it down with a mouthful of water. She shot a glance at the clock on the wall. It was 11:00 p.m. So, she *had* slept for over twelve hours.

I can just drug myself so I don't have to face Danny.

Jonas turned off the light and left the room, closing the door behind him, and Alice let herself fall back onto her cushions and waited for the pill to kick in.

Noises coming from the corridor awoke her the next day. Sunlight was falling through the blinds.

Drowsy, Alice turned her head toward the door, just as it was opened. She winced when the ceiling lamp was switched on. Quickly, she covered her eyes with her hands but spied through the gaps between her fingers. Jonas's back was coming into the room. It looked like he was carrying something.

It was a bed. Danny appeared next, holding the other end of it.

Confused, she watched as they put it down in the middle of the room, with the headboard to the wall next to the bathroom door.

"Sorry for the noise," Danny said, panting. "I thought it would be better for you to sleep in a real bed. The couch doesn't look very comfortable and ... I guess you don't want to come to the bedroom."

He was right. The couch *was* uncomfortable and nothing could make her sleep in a bed with him.

Alice just stared at the bed blankly and said nothing.

"It's from one of the guestrooms," Danny explained. "We'll fetch the mattress."

He and Jonas left the room and appeared minutes later, carrying a mattress as promised.

When everything was installed, they put on some sheets and went to get some pillows.

It was quite amusing to watch the two muscly men making a bed. Not enough to lighten up Alice's mood though.

Jonas then helped her off the couch, and walked her to the bed while Danny kept his distance, watching.

Alice pulled up the blanket almost to her chin and stared at the wall.

"I thought about putting the TV in your room, but ... you're not supposed to watch TV right now." He hesitated, looking ashamed. "You know, with the ... head injury ..."

Great ... how was she supposed to distract herself now?

Danny walked over to her dresser and took the tray away. "I'll get you some new food. Just try to sleep some more."

Alice did. Jonas gave her one more of his wonder pills and it made her sleep for a long time.

A couple of days passed with Jonas making her eat what Danny had cooked, filling up her water glass, and giving her more pain killers, though after a while, he switched to regular aspirin.

Alice wasn't too happy about that, but it at least made the pain bearable. She managed to go to the bathroom without Danny's or Jonas's help, and when she awoke late on that Thursday evening, she realized it was time to take a shower.

She still felt weak when she got out of bed, but that was probably normal after being immobile for days. The bathroom mirror showed her the image of a ghost.

It was the first time since the accident that Alice dared to look into the mirror. She had avoided it every time she had used the bathroom. Now, she could see that her skin was pale, almost grayish, and her eyes looked sunken and were encircled by dark shadows. She looked tired despite having slept for half a week. Her left eye was still purple and yellow, and the bruise went down to her cheekbone.

So ... that's what he did.

Seeing herself like that was shocking, and it made her wonder how bad she had looked before, when even now—days later—the sight was unbearable. Even her hair had lost its gloss and was a greasy mess on her head.

Alice took off the bandage and was glad to see that they hadn't shaved off any of her hair. She then examined the stitches on her forehead. The threads would probably have to be removed some day, but no one had told her anything, with Jonas rushing her from the hospital and all.

Alice glanced down at the hospital shirt she was still wearing, and wondered if taking it with her had made her a thief.

She took it off and let it fall to the tiled floor, then pulled down her pants and underwear, and stared at herself in the mirror.

Lots of bruises covered the right side of her body, but they were fading out and turning yellow. The biggest hematomas were on her right knee, hip, and shoulder.

That pool is deep. I'm lucky I didn't break anything.

But what was lucky about Danny hitting her in the first place? Without him, none of this would have happened.

That thought sent a pang through her guts and Alice quickly took her eyes from the mirror and her reflection.

Taking a shower felt good and it was necessary with the smell of sweat, hospital, smoke, and despair clinging to her. Rubbing in the shampoo made her head hurt and she had to be careful not to soak the bandage on her arm with water.

Alice's eyes fell on the razor, which was lying in the soap tray. Why should she bother? She wasn't allowed outside anyway, and she would by no means shave for Danny.

She left the razor where it was.

It felt nice to finally be able to put on fresh clothes. Alice chose a big, comfortable T-shirt, and only realized that it was one of Danny's after she had already put it on. For a moment, she considered taking it off again, but then she reminded herself that a piece of clothing did not define or affect how she felt about him, so she kept it on.

After taking another aspirin from the pack Jonas had placed on her dresser she went back to bed.

Without the 'wonder' pills, her sleep was lighter and troubled.

She saw Danny towering over her, his face red and contorted by fury. He was spitting fire, trying to burn her to death. In panic, she tried to run away from him, but wherever she went, a big dark shadow blocked her way. When she looked closer, she realized that it had Jonas's face.

Alice awoke with her heart thumping almost painfully against her ribs. Her clothes were soaked in cold sweat and clinging to her skin. Faint light was fighting its way through the blinds, so it must be day.

There was a bitter taste in her mouth, so she went to the bathroom to brush her teeth. On her way back to the bed, the door was suddenly opened.

Danny stood in front of her.

Alice froze in place and stared at him. She wasn't ready to face him, especially not now, with no blanket to cover herself with. She swallowed dryly.

"You look better," Danny said, smiling weakly.

It took some effort to take her eyes away from him and walk back to her bed. There, she sat down and stared at the wall.

Danny hesitated for a moment, but then he approached her, and sat on the mattress beside her.

Alice felt her whole body tense.

"Allie," he began.

Don't you dare call me that.

She heard him sob and looked up, puzzled. Big tears were running out of his big blue eyes and down his cheeks, which looked like he hadn't shaved in a while.

Alice felt a stab of pain in her chest. Danny looked so sad, so vulnerable ... so sober.

She quickly looked away again.

Don't fall for that, don't fall for him.

"I don't even know... what to say to you ..." He muttered with a pained voice.

Then be quiet and leave.

"I just ... I never thought ..." He took a deep breath. "I never thought I could do something ... like that. Especially not to you! The last thing I ever wanted was to hurt you! But somehow, that seems to be the only thing I'm doing lately ..."

Alice felt her own eyes tear up and blinked. When had he ever spoken so genuinely before? He really seemed to be sorry.

More sobs. She bit her lip and told herself to stay hard.

"It scared me, Allie ... I was scared of myself ... I- I thought I'd killed you!"

The wall became a big white blur through the tears in her eyes, but Alice didn't dare to wipe them away. She didn't want Danny to know that he still had the power to make her cry.

"I know I've changed, but I'm not like *that*— not when I'm ... when I'm sober, I would never ..." He fell silent.

Alice tried to suppress the sobs which were building up in her throat.

"I'll never allow myself to be like that again ... *ever*! I won't drink anymore, Allie, I swear!"

Oh, how she wanted to believe him, but she clearly remembered what the doctor had said:

He'll do it again.

Her heart hardened again. Danny would have to prove it if he wanted her to believe him.

"I know, there's no apology in the world that can undo what is done, but I still have to try, hoping you might forgive me someday ... probably even before I forgive myself. 'cause you have a good heart, Allie, unlike me."

He sighed and stood up. Alice sank deeper into the mattress when his weight was lifted off it.

"I have a meeting now, but I'll tell Jonas to put the TV in your room ... so you're not too bored."

Alice remained silent.

"I love you, Allie ... and I'm sorry," he said sadly, then he left the room.

Alice just stared at the wall blankly, eyes glazed. Why could she not remain cold and emotionless toward him? After everything he had done to her, he still had that effect on her, still managed to move her ... How could she be in love with him still?

Alice got off the bed to open the blinds and looked out through the window.

People were in the yard— men wearing black jackets. They were standing around, hands in the pockets of their jeans, some smoking, some talking, some both. The gate was opened, and a silver Jaguar appeared and drove onto the gravel parking space.

Alice saw Danny coming out of the house to greet the driver, a man in a suit. They shook hands and the man patted Danny's shoulder, then they both went inside, accompanied by one of the strange guys.

Alice remained sitting on the windowsill for a while, watching the guards talk to each other, then she decided to fetch her diary and write down some updates, which proved to be incredibly hard and her hand would not stop trembling.

By the time she was done, the sun was already disappearing behind the hills in the west.

A sudden knock on the door made her flinch. Alice wasn't used to anybody knocking before entering her room. When she didn't reply, the knocking continued.

"Yes?" she asked carefully.

The door was opened and Jonas appeared— the big flat TV screen under his right arm.

"Where d'you want it?" he asked, a cigarette dangling from his lips.

Alice closed her diary and put it on the windowsill beside her. "Uh ... in front of the bed, I guess."

Jonas put the screen on the floor and started to shove the dresser aside. The flat cardboard box, where Alice kept her diaries, appeared, but Jonas paid it no mind. He went back to Danny's bedroom to fetch the small table on which the TV had been standing.

When he was done installing everything, he left the room without a word.

Jonas reappeared a bit later, with her dinner on a tray.

Alice ate in front of the TV. It was nice to get some distraction.

The TV kept her entertained for a week and the pain was as good as gone, so Alice stopped taking the painkillers.

Jonas kept bringing her food upstairs and one day, she asked him, "Is it true what Danny says?"

Jonas put the tray down on her bed. "What?"

"That he stopped drinking?"

He stared at her for a while, wearing a poker face as usual.

Alice felt her hopes crumble under his stare. Disappointed, she looked down at the food in front of her.

"So far," Jonas said suddenly.

Surprised, she looked up.

"So far ... it's true."

Alice's mood lightened up at once. So, Danny had been sober for about two weeks. That was huge, regarding how much he had used to drink.

At her reaction, Jonas's expression changed a bit. It got darker.

What's up with him?

He said nothing, however, and turned to walk out of the room.

Three days later, Alice still hadn't left her room. She kept avoiding Danny and whenever he paid her a visit, she ignored him completely. Even if it was true that he wasn't drinking anymore, it didn't mean he deserved her forgiveness ... Not yet, anyway.

It was at around noon when there was a knock on the door and Danny stepped in, without awaiting a reply. When she realized that it was him, Alice quickly looked back at her notebook, in which she had been drawing.

Sighing, he sat down on the bed next to her feet.

"Allie ... I know you're still not talking to me. Which is understandable, I guess." His voice still sounded pained when he talked to her, but at least he wasn't crying. "I just wanted to say goodbye."

Surprised, Alice looked up.

Danny gave her a weak smile. "I have to go on a business trip and I will be gone for fourteen days."

Alice took her eyes off him again. Finally, she wouldn't have to see him for a while. That sounded promising.

"I'll be back for your birthday though."

Puzzled, she looked up again.

With everything that had happened, she had completely forgotten about her upcoming birthday. It didn't seem important now anyway.

"I'll need a wish from you," Danny said, smiling halfheartedly.

Alice frowned at him.

"You don't have to come up with something right now. I'll leave you in peace for a while, and then I'll just call Jonas's phone and you can tell me what you want …"

Alice already knew what she wanted, and Danny was not going to give it to her.

He remained sitting on the bed, looking at her, studying her expression.

What was it, Jonas had said? That she was an open book? Alice tried to keep her face blank.

Danny sighed and got off the bed. "I'll be back soon … Jonas will be here to … *assist* you, and you'll have Henry and Anita around during the week."

Alice stared down at her drawing and said nothing.

"I love you, Allie … bye …" His sadness made his voice shake, but she ignored him anyway.

When he was gone, however, she went over to the window to watch him leave. He stepped out of the house shortly after he had said goodbye to her, carrying a big black duffel bag. Waldo and Tee were with him; Paul was probably already waiting in the car. Alice couldn't see him from her window.

She watched, as Danny said something to Jonas, and then he and the others got into the dark blue Audi. They drove out the gate and the guard closed it behind them.

Alice watched the car disappear behind a big cloud of dust and felt sad at once. Had she been too hard on Danny? What was the proper punishment for what he had done? Especially, since he had only hurt her once and he genuinely felt bad about it.

Alice wasn't ready to talk to him, not until she had made up her mind about what he had done, but somehow, that seemed to be extremely difficult.

At least with Danny gone, she could finally leave her room.

The house was almost empty, just the way it had been when Danny had gone on his first business trip, back when Alice had tried to visit Jill, and Jonas had carried her back to the house.

Everything looked clean though, so Anita must have already been here. Henry was in the kitchen, preparing lunch. Alice decided to greet him. She'd come to really like him and it would be good to talk to someone other than Jonas for a change.

"Hi Henry," she said while giving him a friendly smile.

Henry turned around, smiling, but then his eyes found the scar on her forehead, and his smile disappeared.

"Alice, hi, how are you?" He sounded concerned.

"I'm fine, thank you. What about you?"

Henry had a deep worry line on his forehead that stood out among his other wrinkles. "To be honest, I have been very worried about you."

"Oh ... I'm so sorry I never came downstairs to eat, thank you for preparing the meals anyway."

Slowly, Henry shook his head. "Don't worry about that, Alice. It's just ... I feel so bad about what happened."

Alice's heart skipped a beat at his words. What did Henry know? "Uh ... why would you feel bad?"

Henry sighed. "I took the pool cover away because it had holes in it, and I was planning on replacing it ... I never thought that someone could slip and fall in."

Alice swallowed dryly. Was that what Danny had told everybody? And now Henry—of all people—felt guilty?

"No, it's fine, Henry, really. It's not your fault! I was just—" Suddenly, the little hairs on Alice's neck arose. Someone was standing right behind her. She whirled around and spotted Jonas.

"—stupid," she finished.

Henry shook his head again. "The marble gets very slippery after the rain. I really should have covered that pool."

Anger for Danny boiled up in Alice anew. "Don't blame yourself, Henry. This is so completely and utterly not *your* fault!"

The cook smiled a sad smile and continued stirring in one of the pots on the stove, using a wooden spoon. "Lunch is almost ready. You may already sit down if you like."

Alice went over to the dining room and saw that the table had been set for two. Did she have to eat with Jonas? Her guts seemed to twist at the thought.

She did. Jonas took his place opposite her and started typing something on his cell phone. Alice stared at her empty plate and said nothing, until Henry came in and brought the food.

It looked delicious, as always. This time, he had made a spinach pie with rice for her and a rump steak for Jonas.

"Don't you want to sit down with us?" Alice asked him while he was loading the food on her plate.

"Thank you for inviting me, Alice, but I really have to clean in the kitchen, and then I need to go shopping for groceries."

"Oh ... okay." Alice realized that her voice sounded a bit too disappointed. Both Henry and Jonas had heard it too. Jonas looked up from his phone and stared at her, and Henry gave her another sad smile. "Some other time," he promised.

Jonas's eyes were still fixed on her while Alice ate, and it made her extremely uncomfortable. She even dropped food from her fork while she clumsily tried to ignore him.

"Stop that," she snapped.

"What?"

"Staring at me ... I can't eat like this!"

Grinning, Jonas looked down at his food.

What an annoying freak.

After Henry had collected their plates, Alice quickly got up and went outside. It had been way too long since she'd been able to breathe fresh air. She stood on the porch and inhaled deeply. The air was freezing. It was nearly the end of November now and it felt like winter.

Alice watched the gate guard for a while, who was walking up and down to keep warm.

The vegetable garden had been prepared for winter; Alice noticed when she walked around the house. Thin sheets covered the beds and the last lettuces had been harvested.

The pool had also been covered again, though this time by a modern and stable plastic roofing. Alice felt a queasy feeling in her stomach when she looked at it. But at least there was no way she could fall into it now.

Even from afar, she could see that the back gate had been replaced. There was a new, silver, shining iron door in the hinges, and even the wall had been fixed where old stones had already begun to crumble. Escaping through there must be a lot harder now. But Alice had no intentions of trying again. Not with her head still hurting and with the memory of Danny attacking her on her mind. She could also already feel Jonas's eyes on her back. He was not going to let her out of his sight again.

It made no sense to linger behind the house for too long. The cold was already starting to make her shiver, and Alice didn't want Jonas to think she was plotting to escape again. Instead, she completed her walk around the house and went back inside.

The fire in the living room had been lit, and its flames were dancing vividly and spreading warmth.

Alice sat down on one of the sofas and stared into the flames. Danny was gone and she had the house almost to herself, but what good was that? There was absolutely nothing to do around here.

It was quiet, apart from the crackling and spitting of the fire, and the ticking of the big old-fashioned grandfather clock near the wall next to the downstairs bathroom.

Tic toc, tic toc ...

Alice felt a cold shiver run down her spine. Was that the sound of her life running out?

Tic toc, tic toc ...

It was nerve-wracking. Suddenly, the huge, open living-room didn't seem so huge anymore. It was a prison, and it began to feel like one more and more, with every second that passed.

Nervously, Alice wiped her sweaty palms on her pants and tried to focus on the fire, but fear was already overpowering her and the only thing she could think of was to flee.

The only place she could go, however, was her room, and so she hurried back upstairs and spent her afternoon watching TV.

The following days were all the same.

Henry never had time to sit down and talk, and Alice got the impression that it was Jonas, who scared him away. He, on the other hand, was always there, sitting opposite her, eating quietly. She couldn't think of anyone worse to keep her company.

On the fourth day of Danny's absence, Alice took her book and the warmest jacket she owned and went outside to read. She sat down on the swing—her favorite outside spot—and tried to concentrate on her book. Jonas was nowhere to be seen. Maybe he finally trusted her enough to give her some privacy. It was cold, but Alice was deeply sunken into her book and didn't care about the temperatures. Spending time in the yard couldn't replace her lost freedom, but it was better than nothing. Especially now, because it was one of the rare moments, when absolutely no one seemed to be around. Even the gate guard was absent. It might have looked like an invitation to escape, but a thick chain with a big lock secured the gate, and Alice wasn't entirely sure if Jonas was maybe watching her through a window or something. At least with no one to be seen, Alice was able to pretend that this was just a normal house she lived in, without anybody watching her every step.

Only a couple of crows cawed somewhere in the distance. Apart from that, everything was quiet and peaceful.

Suddenly though, a faint banging sound ripped her out of her concentration. Alice looked up and saw a man standing by the gate. He was knocking on the metal bars, and when he saw that she was looking at him, he began to wave his hands.

Alice hesitated, but when the man gestured her to come over, she got off the swing, put her book down, and walked toward him.

The man looked friendly, his face was withered and his hair tousled from the soft November wind. He appeared to be in his mid-forties.

"Good afternoon," he greeted cheerfully when Alice was close enough.

"Hi," Alice replied, examining him curiously. "Can I help you?"

He rubbed his hands together as if to indicate that he was feeling cold. "Do you work here?" he wanted to know.

Alice shook her head. "I live here."

The man smiled widely and bared two rows of perfectly straight white teeth. "So, you know Daniel?"

"Uh, yes. I'm his ..."

Prisoner? Hostage?

"Girlfriend?" he finished for her.

Alice nodded.

"Then you must be Alice." He held one hand through the bars. She shook it. "Pleased to finally meet you!"

"And you are ...?"

"Martin, old friend of Daniel's."

Alice let her eyes wander across the area. There was no car to be seen.

"Did you walk here?"

Martin chuckled. "No, not really. There's another road behind the house. It leads through the forest. I parked back there."

"Oh, okay ..." Alice felt herself blush. As a resident of this house, she was surely supposed to know things like that. "Danny's not here," she said, to change the subject.

"I thought so." Martin's eyes scanned the house. "Where is he?"

"He's on a business trip."

Martin nodded; his eyes still fixed on the house. "How long will he be gone?"

Alice shrugged. "About ten more days, I think."

"ALICE!"

Alice looked over her shoulder and saw Jonas hurrying toward her.

"And who's that?" Martin asked her curiously.

"Oh... that's just Jonas, one of Danny's friends."

"Alice!" Jonas called again, "Step away from the gate!"

"Your bodyguard?" Martin winked at her. "Good to have one, these days..."

Somehow, the way he had said it made her feel uncomfortable. There had been a weird undertone in his voice, almost threatening.

Jonas reached her and grabbed her arm to pull her away from the gate.

"What are you doing?" she asked, irritated.

"What are *you* doing?!"

"I'm just talking to Danny's friend ... Am I not even allowed to talk to anybody now?" She shook Jonas's hand off and looked back at Martin, who was still grinning widely.

"Anyway, it was really nice meeting you, Alice. I've heard so much about you already." He nodded toward the house. "And good to finally know where Daniel lives ... very nice house, indeed!" Martin winked and strolled away.

Jonas seemed furious. "Go inside!" His tone left no room for arguments. Alice gritted her teeth and picked up her book from the swing, then went into the house. Back in her room, she glanced out of the window, and saw Jonas pacing back and forth in front of the gate, his phone at his ear.

The gate guard suddenly appeared as well, and Alice could hear Jonas yell something at him.

Why was he so angry?

Jonas seemed to be extremely agitated for the rest of the day. Alice watched him restlessly pacing in the living room while she enjoyed the warmth of the fireplace. When his phone rang, he quickly pulled it out of his pocket to answer it.

"Go upstairs!" he snapped at her.

Alice stayed where she was and glared at him.

"Please," he added.

Fine...

Sighing, she got off the couch and walked up to her room, where she stayed until dinner was ready. It was impossible to concentrate on her book, however. Jonas's queer behavior was unsettling.

When they were sitting at the table, in front of their steaming vegetable lasagna, Alice couldn't keep quiet anymore.

"Why did you freak out about that guy?" she asked him.

Jonas gave her a warning look.

"It was just some old friend of Danny's—"

"He's no friend of Danny's," Jonas interrupted her. "And I don't want you to talk to strangers."

"Don't treat me like a child!"

"Then don't act like one."

Alice felt her cheeks turn red with anger. "How am I ... I'm not acting like ... I was just talking to—"

"Don't talk to strangers," he repeated.

Alice glared at him, but arguing with Jonas was impossible.

They finished their meal silently.

Later, back in her room, she heard the sounds of several engines and tires on gravel outside. Curious, she went to the window to see what was happening.

It was dark and she couldn't see much, but judging by the headlights, three cars had arrived. The unfamiliar voices of men talking fought their way through the window. What was going on?

Alice's curiosity turned out to be stronger than her disdain of Jonas, so she went downstairs to check.

Several men she'd never seen before had just stepped into the living room, and Jonas was talking to them quietly.

When he saw Alice standing at the bottom of the stairs, he frowned.

"You should be upstairs," he grumbled.

"I just want to know what's going on."

Some of the men looked from her to Jonas and back.

"I live here. I have a right to know—"

"They're staying here tonight," he interrupted her.

"Why?"

"They'll guard the house."

Fear struck her at one. What in the world was going on?

"No need to worry, miss," one of the strangers said. "With us here, there'll be no intruders."

You're the intruders.

"Does Danny know …?" she asked Jonas.

"I called him." Jonas made a dismissive hand gesture, as if he were trying to shoo away an annoying fly.

Alice bit her tongue. She would have loved to tell him exactly what she thought of his disrespectful behavior, but the men were still looking at her. Swallowing her anger, she turned around to walk back upstairs.

Jonas's behavior was odd. He hadn't seemed like a paranoid guy so far, but now he was freaking out because of one friendly guy at the gate … Or was there something else going on?

10

The men were still around the next day. Alice had heard them talking outside even long after midnight, their torchlights moving around in the dark. Now, she could hear them talking loudly in the yard.

She didn't feel like going downstairs for lunch and face them, but Henry surely had prepared a meal for her and she didn't want to disappoint him.

Jonas was already sitting at the table when Alice came into the dining room. He was typing something on his phone and didn't look up.

Alice sat down without saying a word to him, but she thanked Henry when he brought her food. The cook didn't seem too happy about the unexpected guests. Jonas had probably told him to feed them too, and now the poor man looked quite worn-out.

Alice ate in silence while Jonas kept texting. He didn't even touch the food in front of him. Alice noticed that he looked tired and in a bad mood. He was wearing his usual poker face, but there were deep shadows underneath his eyes and the way he was smashing his fingers onto his phone looked as if he intended to break the screen.

His eyes remained on his phone when Alice got up and left the room.

It was strange. There were more people around than usual, but she felt lonelier than ever before.

On the days that followed, Jonas remained cold and distant—more than usually—and some of the men kept sticking around, though several left.

Henry seemed to be avoiding the house as much as he could, which made it impossible for Alice to chat with him.

She spent her days watching TV and even started to play some of Danny's video games out of boredom. Some of which even turned out to be quite fun.

One afternoon, Jonas offered her his phone while Danny was on the line, but Alice refused to speak to him.

Shouts and screams yanked her out of a troubled sleep that night. Her heart began to race at once, and she stared at the ceiling in the darkness, trying to understand what was being shouted. The voices had come from the yard, but the sound of the front door slamming announced that somebody or several people had come into the house. Frozen by fear, Alice didn't even dare to get up and spy through the window.

Long after the noise had died out, Alice lay awake in bed, wondering what was going on and contemplating possible ways to escape this madness.

The men seemed to be gone the next day—at least she didn't see them anywhere anymore. Everything appeared to be back to normal and even Jonas was back to his relaxed self.

The weekend came, and Alice's mind was deeply sucked into one of Danny's Fantasy games when Jonas opened the door to her room.

Alice flinched at the sudden movement and almost dropped the controller.

"What are you doing here?" she exclaimed breathlessly.

"I knocked."

She paused the game. "I didn't hear anything."

"Twice."

"What do you want?"

Jonas was smoking and he took a deep drag on his cigarette before he answered. "Dinner's ready."

"But ... it's Saturday."

"I warmed somethin' up." He turned around and left the room, leaving the door open. Alice sighed and turned off the TV, then followed him downstairs.

The table was set, though not as properly as Henry usually did it.

Jonas had warmed up some leftover potatoes and made some frozen spinach with it.

"Thanks," Alice said when she took her place opposite him.

They ate quietly for a moment, Jonas staring at his food instead of at Alice for a change.

"Did they all leave?" she asked when she was almost done eating.

He nodded.

"So, we're safe again?" She meant it as a joke, but Jonas didn't even look up.

Alice wondered why he had wanted her to join him for dinner when he was just ignoring her as always.

When she was done eating, she took both empty plates, put them in the dishwasher, and started it.

She gazed out the kitchen window for a moment, wondering if she would ever see her friends again. She missed them so much, it felt as if pieces of herself were missing, leaving empty and aching holes in her chest. Jill and Leah, her best friends. Were they worried about her? Were they wondering where she was? Had they ever tried to reach her on Danny's phone? After all, they had his number ... Or had he changed it?

Her loneliness seemed to grow like a big black hole in her guts, sucking away all hope and happiness, and leaving behind only sorrow and longing. Alice decided to fill the hole with some booze and took a bottle of white wine out of the fridge.

Jonas was still sitting at the table, smoking and staring at his phone. He looked up when Alice walked past him, but she said nothing and went straight upstairs.

Why should she bother talking to him or even wishing him a good night or something? He never replied anyway.

Back upstairs, Alice turned on the TV and emptied the bottle of wine while crying into her pillow.

Who would have thought that her Saturday nights could get even more pathetic?

The days in her prison remained long, boring, and sad; and December didn't change that.

Jonas was always eating opposite her, but he never talked. Henry avoided Jonas, and since Jonas was around Alice all the time, she didn't have a chance to talk to Henry either.

The days became shorter and colder, and the lonely nights almost unbearably long.

Alice was starting to feel more and more depressed. The idea of getting drunk every day was tempting, but she didn't want to become like Danny, and she also didn't want to be a hypocrite. Instead, she sat outside on her swing for hours and hours, staring into the dead gray sky. It hadn't snowed yet, but it was only the first week of December, so there was still plenty of time for that.

December ... so close to her twenty-first birthday. Normally, that thought would have excited her. She would have celebrated with Jill and Leah, maybe gone clubbing or treated herself to a nice trip somewhere. None of this was possible now. Danny had promised to be back by then, but what good was that? Alice wasn't speaking to him, and she wasn't sure if she preferred being alone with Jonas or having Danny around. Both seemed equally bad.

Birthdays had never meant much to her, but spending it in this hellhole was surely going to be a nightmare ... unless, she'd manage to escape after all.

Alice had never tried at night so far, but now with Danny gone, it seemed to be the perfect time. With the strange men having left as well, and Jonas trusting her enough to not constantly tail her anymore, the time seemed ripe. The night guard couldn't have his eyes everywhere at the same time, and Jonas needed sleep like a normal human being.

So far, Alice had been too scared to dare another attempt, but Danny's return was coming dangerously close.

The night before his arrival, Alice stayed awake until 3:00 a.m. but kept her room dark, so Jonas would think she was asleep. The night guard was dozing in his chair by the gate, covered by a thick woolen blanket. Alice could see him clearly through the window because he had forgotten to turn off his torchlight, which was lying in his lap, illuminating parts of his face.

The house had an alarm system which Jonas always turned on at night, and the night guard knew the code so he could use the bathroom without setting off the alarm. There was, however, that basement door in the back of the house. Danny had mentioned it when he had given her the tour of the house on the day of the move. Alice was pretty sure that it wasn't attached to the alarm, since it wasn't much more than a wooden trapdoor.

She hated basements, but she knew she would have to suck it up to win her freedom. Important things came with a price.

She put on a thick hoodie but not her winter jacket. In case she might run into Jonas she didn't want to make it too obvious that she was trying to run away.

The door of her room made no sound when she opened it, and the corridor was dark and deserted. Tiptoeing carefully, she approached the stairs, and passed Jonas's bedroom. No light was shining through the gap underneath his door.

The thick carpet on the stairs muffled the sound of her footsteps, and she reached the bottom without making any noise. The living room was also dark and there were no sounds to be heard.

To Alice's surprise, the cellar door stood wide open. It looked like a big dark mouth, ready to swallow her. Her heartbeat accelerated at the sight of it, and her palms got sweaty.

It's just a basement ... the gym's down there and some storage rooms ... not more, not less.

Alice took a deep breath and entered the pitch-black staircase that led down into the basement.

She didn't have a torchlight, so she closed the door behind her and switched on the light. Falling down the stairs wouldn't win her freedom back ... Unless she broke her neck, then she wouldn't have to face Danny anymore. But that was a bitter thought and she pushed it aside.

The basement seemed much bigger than she had expected. It was probably as wide as the rest of the house, stretching out underneath it like another story.

Turning on more lights revealed a long, narrow corridor with doors on either side. The walls were thick and made of gray concrete, and the doors were heavy and solid iron. It looked more like a bunker than a cellar.

Alice knew that the door to the yard was supposed to be somewhere on the left, since she had seen it outside, but there was only a wall with one of those metal doors in it. Alice tried to open it, and to her relief, it was unlocked. She pushed it open and it flung inward, its hinges shrieking silently, almost inaudibly. The room in front of her was dark, but she found a switch on the wall, left from the door, and flicked it. Dim, flickering light came from an old bulb that hung by a cable from the ceiling. It made a buzzing sound.

Alice almost peed herself when she saw the big black shape of a man sitting in the middle of the room. Clutching her hands in front of her mouth quickly, she managed to keep herself from crying out.

The man was sitting on an old leather fauteuil, his back facing her. He appeared to be sleeping.

Alice's eyes wandered through the small chamber that held no more than the fauteuil with the sleeping man in it, a wooden table near the wall to the right, and a metallic bucket on the floor to her left. Stony steps led up to the big wooden trapdoor she had already seen from outside.

Even the cellar door was guarded … Alice couldn't believe it.

Would she be able to sneak out without waking up the guard? Or was there another way?

She decided to check out the rest of the basement before taking any risks, and turned around quietly. This time, she couldn't keep herself from screaming when she saw the man standing in the door, but he quickly put his hand over her mouth and shoved her back into the chamber.

Alice could barely breathe with the man's hand over her mouth and nose, and she felt something hard and cold on her right temple.

"Don't move, don't scream." His husky voice was barely more than a whisper.

Struggling and winding herself in his grip, she tried to pull his hand away from her mouth, but he pulled her closer to his chest.

"That thing in my hand is a gun, and if you don't stop resisting, I'll pull the trigger!"

Alice froze at once and tried to steady her breathing. Who was he? She didn't recognize his voice. He smelled though, of sweat and iron, and somehow burned. Her heart was pounding so loudly, Alice was sure he could hear it too.

"Can you promise me not to scream?"

She nodded, as much as his grip allowed. The man let go of her and pushed the door shut behind him. Alice quickly turned around to look at him.

It was Martin, the friendly guy who had talked to her through the gate the other day. He looked different though—his hair was sticking in strands to his forehead, and there was dried blood all over his face as well as on his T-shirt.

"You!" she gasped.

He put his index finger to his lips and shushed her. Her eyes flicked to the guard in the armchair, but he hadn't woken up yet.

"Oh, don't worry about him, he's dead."

The blood seemed to freeze in Alice's veins and she felt all color drain from her face. It was true enough; blood was dripping from the guard's head—she could see that now. Panicking, she stumbled backward, away from the corpse, and almost fell over the metal bucket on the ground.

"Stand still, you're making too much noise!" Martin urged. "Besides, I pissed in that." He nodded toward the bucket.

Alice quickly took a step away from it.

"Of all the people in this house, I have the pleasure to stumble into you …

what a lucky guy I am." He grinned at her, baring his once perfect teeth; but now, several were missing.

"W-what are you doing here?" Alice whispered, her back pressed against the cold wall behind her. Her whole body was wide awake, pumping adrenaline through her. She forced herself not to look at the dead man to her left and instead kept her eyes on the weapon in Martin's hand. "How did you get in here?"

Martin chuckled quietly. "How I got in here? Your friends brought me here, Alice. You surely know that."

Alice shook her head, gazing at him blankly. What was he talking about?

"That bodyguard of yours," he said, scratching his chin with the tip of the gun, "Him and his guys, they paid me a visit at my place, and dragged me here."

"But ... why would they do that?" And why hadn't she noticed? The screams ... had that been Martin?

"Oh, don't act stupid, missy! Either you or Daniel gave the order, and he's not here, so ..." He pointed the gun back at her.

Alice tensed at the sight of the weapon aiming at her. Her eyes followed its every movement.

"Did they ... Jonas and ... did they do this to you?"

"Fucking bastards beat me up down here and wanted to keep me tied up until Daniel returns. But guess what, your guards suck. Wasn't hard to fight that poor fat guy over there." He nodded toward the dead guard on the chair.

Alice felt bile in her throat and swallowed it back down. Jonas and those other men hadn't looked harmless from the start, but knowing that they had kidnapped somebody and—by the sight of it—tortured him too, made them a whole new kind of dangerous.

And I ate dinner with that guy ...

Martin was staring at her, carefully examining her expression. "You really didn't know, huh?"

She shook her head. "But why did they—"

He gave her a warning look and she fell silent. "You're gonna get me out of here."

"How?"

Martin spat on the ground, a mixture of blood and saliva. "How? You're gonna open the door for me, simple as that."

Alice spied over to the wooden trapdoor. It was secured by a heavy chain and lock, similar to the one at the front gate.

"I checked our dead friend's pockets, but apparently, they didn't trust him enough with the keys." He shot a disdainful glance at the dead guard and shook his head contemptuously. "Understandable."

"You killed him," Alice muttered aghast, more to herself than to him.

"Wow, you're really fast at grasping things," Martin remarked sarcastically, then he shrugged. "Can you blame me? I just wanted to get out of here."

Like magnets, the dead guard and Martin's gun kept drawing Alice's stare toward them, and her eyes kept flicking back and forth between the corpse and the weapon. How long was it going to take until blood would be dripping out of her own head?

"Get me out of here," Martin commanded.

"I-I don't have any keys."

Anger flashed in his eyes and he glared at her, taking a step toward her to shorten the distance between her and his gun. Alice instinctively tried to back away, but the wall blocked her.

"Don't you fucking lie to me! Get those goddamned keys and get me out of here!"

"I don't have any keys, I swear!" Alice tried to duck away when he raised his hand, but he grabbed her hair and yanked her closer. Her eyes teared up in pain, but she didn't scream.

"I'm not gonna say it again!" he hissed. His foul breath felt hot on her ear.

"I'm not lying, I don't have the keys!"

"But you know where they are."

"No!"

Martin let go of her hair and pushed her against the wall, pressing the gun so hard against her temple, it felt like he was trying to stab her with it. "I'm giving you one more chance!" His eyes glistened dangerously, his jaw was clenched, and his upper lip slightly drawn upward to reveal some of his broken teeth. He looked mad ... and Alice couldn't help but wonder what Jonas had done to him. Why would Danny leave her alone with a torturer? The fear of both Jonas and Martin made her tremble. What the hell had Danny gotten her into?

"I don't know anything, I swear!"

"You're Daniel's girlfriend. You must have the keys to this house!"

"No ... I ... I'm not allowed to leave the house ... They didn't give me any keys!"

Martin's eyes seemed to pierce right through her, as if he was trying to read her thoughts. "Are you his girlfriend or prisoner? Of course, you have the keys!"

Tears of desperation flooded her eyes. Alice hadn't chosen any of this and now, she was most likely going to die without even knowing why.

"He doesn't let me out of here," she tried again, realizing how stupid it sounded.

"What do you mean?"

"Danny ... he's locking me in here ... I tried to run away, but he's keeping me watched at all times."

Martin let go of her to scratch his chin, and lowered the gun. "Why would he do that?"

"I'm not sure ... I think he's scared I might leave him."

To her horror, Martin burst out into laughter. "This is hilarious!"

Alice glared at him. "I don't find it that funny."

"No ... No, Alice, I think you're wrong."

Confusion chased away most of her fear. Martin paused, as if to increase the suspense.

"I think ... he's trying to keep you safe."

"From what?"

Martin chuckled again. "Here's what's funny ... from me!" He continued laughing—a dry, hollow laugh that seemed to echo off the walls. It sounded insane.

"Why would he—"

"He's scared I might hurt you ... But he's an idiot, your boyfriend, honestly." Taking a deep breath to calm himself, he wiped a tear from his eye with the back of his hand. "See, first he locks you up to keep you safe from me ... and then, he locks me in the house *with* you! What a fucking moron!"

Alice felt something ice-cold run down her spine. "Why? W-why would he ... What would you want from me?" Terrified, she tried again to increase the distance between them, but the cold hard wall was still behind her.

Martin grinned. "Nothing in particular. But you're Daniel's girlfriend and there are certain things I want from *him*."

"Like ... what?"

He shrugged. "Oh, you know ... Just some business ideas ... secrets of his success ..." Suddenly, he pointed the gun back at her. Alice winced.

"Actually," he said, as if he'd just had a bright idea, "What do *you* know about these things?"

"What things?" Alice asked, not taking her eyes from the gun.

"The business."

She hesitated, taking a deep breath. "Not much ... Just that he designs games ... online-games, I think."

Again, Martin burst into laughter. "Okay, okay, stop, I get it," he chuckled breathlessly.

Alice scowled at him. "What?"

"I'll just use you as bait." He grabbed her arm and dragged her out of the chamber, keeping her at gunpoint. Out in the corridor he made her walk to the left.

"Where are we going?" Alice wanted to know while he pushed her onward.

"See if there's more exits."

"I don't think so. Danny only mentioned one door in the basement."

"Well maybe he didn't mention the others. Or maybe there's a window or somethin'." Martin made her try to open every door they encountered, though many were locked. The others belonged to storage rooms without windows, until they reached a bigger area, where the men did their weightlifting. Surprisingly, it actually looked like a gym. They had even put up mirrors on the walls and carpets on the ground. But no home trainers or treadmills, like Tee had said.

There were windows along the walls, narrow ones, right below the ceiling. Alice could surely squeeze through there, but what about Martin? He seemed to have the same thought.

"Sit down," he told her and gestured toward a chair next to the wall. Alice obeyed, and watched him as he tried to push open one of the windows, without success. He tried the next one and then another one.

"They're all sealed, fucking shit!" Martin cursed. He turned around and aimed the gun back at her. "The house has an alarm system, doesn't it?"

Alice nodded.

"And you probably don't know the code?"

She shook her head.

He laughed his insane laugh, then sighed deeply. "Oh this is just too hilarious ... too fucking hilarious." His left hand brushed through his withered hair. "Any ideas?"

Alice shook her head.

"You know, missy, your life depends on this as much as mine."

Alice bit her lip. "Aren't you gonna shoot me anyway?"

"Not if Daniel cooperates."

Would he? Did she still mean enough to him?

"Who's in the house?" Martin wanted to know.

"I'm not sure ..."

"Don't fucking lie to me!" He almost yelled the words, but Alice was pretty sure that the gym was soundproof.

"I think ... only Jonas."

"Your bodyguard?"

"My ... guard."

Martin seemed to weigh his chances. Did he think he could overpower Jonas? The thought scared her.

"And of course, there's the night guard. Very competent guy," she quickly added.

"No problem, I'll just shoot him from afar. If he's the same quality as the other guy, it won't be a big hassle."

Alice's eyes widened in shock. "He ... he's very good at what he does!"

Martin shrugged. "I don't think I'll trust *your* judgement. Now get up. We'll go upstairs and wake up your friend. Tell him to hand over the keys."

Slowly, Alice got up from the chair. "Why would he do that?"

"I'll just point the gun at your head and tell him if he doesn't want to pluck your brain off the wall, he'll better do what I tell him." Martin pushed her toward the door.

"But ... he doesn't care about me, he won't do what you say, it's no use—"

"Don't try to talk me out of this! I can just kill him in his sleep, then shoot the guard and off we go."

"But—"

"Silence! I want you to keep your stupid mouth shut and walk as quietly as you can, d'you hear me?"

Alice nodded, feeling desperate. What could she do to keep Martin from causing a blood bath?

He made her walk back through the corridor, constantly stabbing her in the back with his gun.

Up the stairs they went, first into the living room, and then up to where the bedrooms were. Alice's heart was thumping up in her throat, and fear crept through her bones when she saw Jonas's door in front of her. Her mind was unable to grasp a clear thought, but she stopped and turned around, holding her hands up imploringly.

"Please," she whispered, "Don't make me—"

Martin's eyes glinted in the darkness. The anger in them was unmistakable. "Open the fucking door," he hissed. "Quietly!"

Alice's sweaty hand almost slipped off the door handle, but she managed to push it down and open the door silently. She stepped aside to let Martin go in first.

Slowly, Martin crept toward the bed whose outlines were faintly visible in the dark. Alice couldn't hear anything, but maybe that was because of the pounding of her heart.

Suddenly, she felt extremely ashamed of herself. What had she been thinking? She couldn't let Martin kill Jonas!

Without knowing what she was doing, Alice darted forward at once and grabbed Martin's arm. "Leave him alone!"

Martin shook her off so violently, she stumbled over something on the floor, and fell right onto the bed.

For a brief moment, she expected to land on Jonas, but the bed was empty.

"He's not here," she whispered.

"Get up."

Alice pushed herself off the bed and onto her feet, and Martin yanked her out of the room by her hair.

"Where the fuck is he?" he whispered angrily when they were back in the corridor.

Alice blinked away the tears of pain and shrugged. "No idea. He's supposed to be here, but obviously, he's not."

Martin looked like he was about to slap her, but then he changed his mind. It probably would have made too much noise. Instead, he shoved her toward the stairs.

"We'll check downstairs."

Carefully, Alice set one foot in front of the other, trying not to fall down the steps in the dark. Martin seemed to be able to see much better than her. Maybe they had kept him in total darkness for several days and his eyes had adjusted. He urged her forward impatiently.

At the bottom of the stairs, he looked around and listened, but the house was dead silent.

"Why don't you just go out despite the alarm? Jonas isn't here and I can distract the guard while you run away," Alice suggested in a desperate attempt to keep her life.

"You're coming with me, end of discussion. I need you. And I don't want to wake the whole neighborhood," he hissed, irritated. "One more stupid comment and I'll break your jaw!"

Alice bit her tongue.

"Follow me," Martin ordered. He opened the door to the guestroom, but that was empty as well. He moved toward Danny's office.

Nervous, Alice followed him. She had never been in Danny's office so far and she wondered what it looked like.

The door was locked. Of course. Danny was too protective of his secrets.

"D'you think he's locked himself in here?"

Alice shook her head. Hiding didn't seem like Jonas.

"Well, at least we know he's not in the house." She tried to sound positive. "We should just walk out. You don't have to shoot the guard. He'll let us pass if he sees the gun—"

Martin hit her right in the face with the grip of the pistol. Alice stumbled backward, holding her hand to her mouth. She tasted blood on her tongue.

"I told you to keep your fucking mouth shut!" He didn't whisper this time.

Alice glared at him and wiped her throbbing lip with the sleeve of her hoodie. *We could just check if his car's even here. But I won't say anything anymore.*

Martin seized her arm and pulled her into the living room, where he made her sit down on the couch while he spied through the windows. Was he doing what Alice had just thought? But he surely couldn't know what Jonas's car looked like.

"There has to be a way out of here," he muttered, more to himself than to her. "Any suggestions?"

"I'm still here, ain't I?"

"Watch your tongue," he hissed.

"How do we even know the alarm's on?" Alice asked.

Martin stared at her for a moment, scratching his chin. "You're right." He walked over to the door, and examined the system which was installed on the wall next to the entrance. Alice had no idea how it worked, but Martin looked at the little lights on the machine and said, "It's off."

Alice's heart stopped at once.

Something had just moved in the dining room.

Martin didn't seem to have noticed and beckoned her to come over to him. She hesitated. "What are you going to do with me?"

Martin nodded to the gun in his hand and then to her, still waving her over to the door. Alice stayed where she was.

"Nothing, if your boyfriend gives me what I want. Now come here!"

"And what if not?"

"Then I'll send you back to him ... in pieces, now get the fuck over here!" Martin reached her with two big steps and grabbed her hair again to pull her off the couch. Alice gasped in pain and tried to wind free from his grip.

He put the gun to her head. "D'you want to die?"

"Rather now than later," she pressed through clenched teeth.

Martin hit her again, this time harder. The blow made her stumble backward and right over the couch table. Moaning, she pushed herself up on her elbows, but Martin was already at her side.

"You stupid bitch!" he barked. He didn't seem to care about staying quiet anymore.

When he bent over her to pull her up from the floor, Alice kicked out with as much force as possible and hit him right between the legs.

Martin yelped like a dog, then groaned in pain. His gun hand dashed upward at once, aiming for her. Instinctively, Alice rolled aside and jumped to her feet, but no shot was fired. Before he could aim again, she darted around him and attacked him from behind, jumping onto his back, and pushing her fingers into his eyes.

Roaring and shaking himself to get her off, he staggered backward. Alice tried to avoid his left hand, which was blindly groping for her. Again, her long hair doomed her and Martin managed to get a handful of it, and yanked her off his back, down onto the floor. The soft carpet caught her fall, but the impact was painful nonetheless. It didn't look as if her fingers had done much damage to his eyes, yet Martin was momentarily blinded. Tears ran down his cheeks and he cursed. Alice took advantage of that and kicked at his legs until he collapsed onto his knees. She tried to push herself backward and away from him, but his left hand got a grip of her right ankle and he hauled her toward him. Despite only using one hand, he was surprisingly strong. Alice stood no chance against him. In a second, he was on top of her, pinning her down with his knees. His weight made her feel like her rib cage was about to crush. Gasping for air, she struggled underneath him, trying to push him off her. Then she felt his fingers close around her throat while the muzzle of the gun moved down her left temple, almost tenderly. She heard him laugh his insane laugh.

"And you thought you could fight me," he spat contemptuously. "That's what you get for almost scratching my eyes out." His grip around her throat tightened.

Panicking, Alice struggled even more. It wasn't a conscious try to free herself anymore—it was the manic urge to stay alive.

Martin moved the muzzle of the gun to her forehead, while loosening his grip a bit. Alice used the opportunity and desperately sucked in as much air as her lungs could take.

"I give you one more chance, you maniac." Martin's eyes were open again, though they were reddened, which made him look even crazier. He seemed to be struggling for breath as well. "I really need you to get what I want and I promise you, I'll let you go after I get it ... unharmed."

"Liar," Alice gasped, while trying to pull his fingers off her throat.

"You can't blame me for wanting to have my fair share of fun with you, missy. But I swear, I won't cut off your fingers or anything. I just want to send a message to your arrogant boyfriend, and for that I might have to rough you up a bit."

Martin lowered his face until it was only inches above hers. His breath smelled foul and Alice tried to turn her head to the side, but he tightened his grip again, holding her still.

"What a waste to put a bullet through that pretty head. But I can't drag you out of here acting like that. Stop fighting and walk out with me, and I'll let you live."

Alice glared at him through tears of pain. "Fuck you!"

Sighing, he straightened his back, taking his face away from hers. "As you wish."

Alice regretted her decision the moment, she saw his finger twitch.

A deafening *bang* seemed to tear the whole house apart, and Alice thought she felt her eardrums burst. She pressed her eyes shut, expecting an explosion of pain ... but it never came.

Dizzy from the blast, Alice slowly opened her eyes again. Her heart was still beating, she realized, seemingly trying to break out of her chest, the way it was hammering against her ribs.

Everything was a blur and the room was spinning around her, making her sick to her stomach. Had Martin only wounded her? There was pain all over her body, but she couldn't tell whether it had already been there before the shot or not.

Blinking, she tried to grasp her surroundings. Finally, Martin's face became clearer in the semi-darkness. His eyes were on her, filled with unspoken questions. His mouth was slightly opened in surprise. Confused, Alice stared at him, until she noticed something dark and glistening on the right side of his face. Like black ink, it dripped down his temple and off his chin … it was blood.

Alice felt his hand slip off her throat, and then he collapsed right onto her.

Warm and sticky blood dripped onto her cheek and into the collar of her sweater. Horrified, she screamed out and suddenly, bright, blinding light flooded the room.

Alice squirmed underneath Martin, trying to get him off of her, but when her eyes adjusted to the light, she felt all strength leave her body like blood was leaving Martin's limp corpse. No doubt, he was as dead as the guard down in the basement. She seemed to be drowning in the pool of blood that surrounded her.

Groaning, she tried to push him off, but he was too heavy.

In that instant, the entrance door flung inward, and the night guard stumbled into the room, a gun in his hands. Then Alice saw Jonas running toward her from the left. He too was armed.

Jonas pulled Martin off of her with one hand. Alice pushed herself backward, away from the body, without taking her eyes away from his dead pupils. They seemed to be glued to hers and full of accusation. It was the most horrible thing she had ever seen.

Jonas kicked at the body to get it out of the way, and walked toward her.

"W-what's going on? Where did that man come from?" The night guard asked, his voice shaking.

Alice couldn't grasp a clear thought. All she could see were Martin's reproachful stare and the blood. The voices around here were muffled and seemed distant. In one moment, she had expected to die, and now, she was sitting in a pool of blood that seconds ago, had belonged to a living, breathing human being.

Jonas seized her by the sleeve of her pullover and pulled her off the floor. He took one look at her, then dragged her toward the couch, where he made her sit down.

"I'll explain later," he told the night guard.

"I- I don't know how that happened! I'm so sorry! I thought I had everything under control..." The poor man seemed to be on the verge of a nervous breakdown.

"Not your fault. He was already in the house." Jonas patted the guard's shoulder. "Get a blanket. Cover it." He nodded to the body.

The guard walked to the guestroom to fetch some bedsheets. Jonas turned toward Alice, but her eyes were still on Martin. She couldn't see his face from where she was sitting, but his grotesquely sprawled body was no less horrifying.

Jonas said something, but her ears could not transmit his words to her brain. Her clammy hands were lying in her lap, trembling, but she didn't even notice it.

Jonas's blurry shape disappeared for a moment, then he was back, right in front of her. Alice felt something hard and cool on her lips, and when cold liquid flowed into her mouth, she almost choked on it. Her eyes finally managed to break free of Martin and flicked to Jonas instead.

Jonas put the glass of water to her lips anew. "Drink," he said.

Alice gulped down some more, and then watched as he put the glass of water, he'd been holding, down on the couch table. Then he crouched down in front of her.

"Alice," he said in a loud and clear voice, "Can you hear me?"

Confused, she nodded.

"Did you let him out?"

Alice stared at him blankly. "What?"

"Did you let him out?" he repeated, again in that loud and slow manner.

Finally, his words began to make sense ... though they absolutely did not. How in the world could he blame her for this mess?

"W-what? No! I ... I didn't even know he was here!" Alice's voice was high and shaky, and she dug her nails into her sweaty palms, telling herself to get a grip.

Jonas's piercing stare seemed to bore right through her. "What happened?"

"I ... I came downstairs and he ... he was just there, and he said that he killed the guard—and I saw him! The guard—he's dead, it's true, he killed him! I thought he was only sleeping, but there was blood and—"

Jonas gestured her to be quiet. "What were you doing in the basement?"

Was that all he cared about?

Alice dropped her eyes to avoid his accusing stare. "I heard a noise ... and the cellar door was open, so I wanted to see ..."

Why was she even explaining this to him? *He* was responsible for this mess.

Scowling, she looked back up at him. "Don't blame me, Jonas! Why was he even in the house? And where the fuck were *you*?"

Sighing, Jonas sat down on the couch opposite her, while the night guard began to wrap the body in a bedsheet. "Outside. Behind the house. Saw the light coming out the cellar windows."

"Why were you even up? Martin, he— he went up to your room and wanted to shoot you in your sleep! You could be dead!"

Grinning cockily, Jonas pulled his pack of cigarettes out of the pocket of his jeans, then he lit one. He hesitated, but then he grabbed a second one and offered it to her.

This time, she took it.

The smoke managed to calm her down a bit, and Alice was able to think more clearly. "Why are you laughing?"

Jonas exhaled a big cloud of smoke. "I'm not killed that easily."

Alice glared at him. "That's not funny! None of this is funny ... You just shot a guy!"

He shrugged.

Alice stared at him in disbelief. How could he be so cold about this? She glanced at the gun in his belt. Had he used it before ... to kill?

"Martin said you tortured him ..."

"He deserved it," Jonas said curtly while pulling his phone out of his other jeans pocket. He dialed a number, then put the phone to his ear and waited.

"Are you calling Danny?"

He nodded. No one seemed to pick up, so he put the phone down on the couch table.

"I saw you ... I think ... In the dining room."

"Came in through the back door."

"How long were you inside already?"

"A while." He sighed. "I was hoping to capture him alive, but you made that impossible."

Alice frowned at him.

"Just joking." He grinned again.

"What was I supposed to do?" she asked angrily.

Jonas shrugged. "I dunno. Expected you to walk out with him. Didn't think you'd fight."

"I would have ... but I was afraid of ... what he might do ... later." Alice took a drag on her cigarette and coughed.

"He would've tortured you," Jonas said casually.

Alice glared at him. "He said he needed something from Danny."

He nodded. "Danny would've given him everything to get you back."

"But—"

"He would've tortured you anyway." Jonas put out his cigarette on the couch table. "For fun, probably. Or revenge."

Alice stared at him. "Is this all just a joke to you?"

Poker face.

"How can you be so calm about this?"

"Why? D'you want me to get all emotional? Like you?" He looked at her defiantly.

"Do you even have emotions? I'm starting to think you don't."

Jonas just stared at her for a moment, then he shrugged, and got off the couch to help the guard carry Martin's corpse away.

Did I offend him?

Was it even possible to offend Jonas? Or did his poker face portray his true self?

Alice watched as the men carried the wrapped-up body down to the basement. When they disappeared behind the corner, she shivered. She could still see Martin before her; the blood, the surprise on his face, the accusation in his eyes ...

Suddenly, the living room seemed like a dangerous place to be ... dark shadows were lurking behind every corner, underneath every furniture. The walls became blurry and started to move. The air became too thick to breathe. Alice pulled at the collar of her hoodie to free her throat, but it didn't help. She jumped off the couch, ready to run away—and go where? She didn't want to be alone, but what other option was there? To join Jonas and the guard in the basement, where the two corpses were?

Alice began to pace up and down nervously, trying to get Martin's face out of her mind, but it kept creeping back, no matter where she looked.

Still pacing, she began rubbing her temples, as if she could erase the images from her memory.

An eternity seemed to have passed when finally, Jonas and the guard returned from the basement. Both looked exhausted and had blood on their hands. The guard nodded toward the big blood stain on the carpet. "Should we clean that?"

Jonas shook his head. "We take it out." He pulled a knife out of the inner pocket of his leather jacket and snapped it open, then began cutting out the stained piece of carpet. Alice watched him take the piece out and throw it into the fireplace.

"Shouldn't we call the police?" she suggested.

Jonas gave her a look that could mean everything and nothing. She guessed it was a no.

The men washed their hands in the kitchen sink, and the guard went back outside to do his job. Jonas frowned at Alice, who was still standing in the middle of the room.

"Alarm's back on," he warned her.

Alice just stared at him.

Yawning, Jonas stretched his back and turned toward the staircase. "What a night. I'm going to bed. You should do the same."

Alice's eyes widened at the notion. There was no way she could sleep that night.

Jonas stopped and looked at her, waiting for her to move. "Fun's over. There's nothing to worry about."

"But ... they're here ... in the house."

"What? The bodies?"

Alice nodded.

Jonas's eyebrows wandered upward. "They're dead. They couldn't be any more dead, trust me."

"I know, but ..."

"You think they'll come back as zombies?" He laughed out loudly.

Alice couldn't remember having ever heard him laugh before, but now was definitely not the right time. She crossed her arms stubbornly. "No ... but I still can't sleep with them here."

Jonas just shrugged. "I can." He started walking toward the stairs.

"No, wait! Please ..."

Sighing, Jonas stopped and turned around again.

"You could at least let me out of the house."

"What for?"

"So I can sit outside with the guard until the sun goes up."

"His name's Brad," Jonas said. "And no way."

Alice glared at him and sat back down on the couch. Jonas rubbed his forehead and moaned. "I suppose I have to burn this anyway." He nodded to the fireplace with the bloody piece of carpet in it. Alice watched him make a fire, then she kept staring at the flames while they devoured the bloody scrap of carpet. The fire crackled happily and its warmth began spreading across the room. Drowsiness made her pull her legs onto the sofa, and lean her head against a cushion while Jonas sat down opposite her and lit a cigarette. He offered one to her and again, she took it.

They smoked in silence and when his cigarette was burned down, he put it out and pulled his gun out from under his belt. He released the magazine, counted the bullets, and put it back into the weapon while she watched. Again, he took it out, then turned it over to let the bullets drop onto the couch table, where they landed with a noise that made her wince. She watched as he rolled each bullet between his index finger and thumb, examining it, then put them all upright on the table in a straight line.

"*What* are you doing?" Alice wanted to know.

"Tryin' to stay awake."

"It's annoying."

He shrugged.

"Why was he here? Martin?" she asked him.

Jonas ignored the question.

"He said Danny wanted to keep me safe from him ... Apparently, he expected me to end up as bait. Now that Martin's dead though, I can get out of here, right?"

Jonas looked up; his expression as always unreadable. He put the bullets back into his gun. "Ask *him* that." He placed the weapon on the table, its muzzle pointing toward Alice.

"Can't you just put that awful thing away?"

Jonas grinned tiredly. "Gonna need it for the zombies."

"How can you not feel bad about this?"

"About saving your life?"

Alice blushed at once. She hadn't even truly realized that. "Right ... thank you for that."

Jonas stifled a yawn. "My pleasure."

Alice sighed, coming to terms with the fact that Jonas was never going to be serious about what happened. Maybe it was just his way of coping. It was sure healthier than hers.

"You got something to say?"

Alice quickly averted her eyes and stared into the flames instead.

"No, nothing," she muttered.

The dancing flames managed to keep Martin's image out of her mind and soon, the memories of that messy night became a blur and changed into dreams ...

11

Slamming car doors ripped her out of a dreamless sleep. Alice opened her eyes slowly and blinked. Men were talking outside in the yard. The light in the living room was still on, but there was also daylight falling through the windows.

Jonas was still sitting opposite her, the gun in his lap and his chin resting on his chest. He was sleeping silently.

The fire had burned down, but its smell was still in the air. Alice's back hurt from sleeping on the uncomfortable couch ... or was it because of Martin? The memories began to creep back into her head, slowly, like worms eating their way through her brain. She didn't have much time to think about them though, because the front door was opened, and Danny stepped into the house.

Relief immediately washed away all memories of last night and beyond, and Alice jumped off the couch and rushed toward him. She buried her face in his soft coat, wrapping her arms around his waist.

Danny dropped his bag in surprise and stared at her, perplexed, but then he hugged her back. "What the ..." His eyes wandered from the hole in the carpet to Jonas, who had just woken up and was rubbing the sleep out of his eyes.

Softly, he pushed her away a bit, to be able to look at her. He gasped. "Allie, your face! What happened?"

Confused, she blinked at him. "What?"

"The blood! You're covered in blood!"

"Really?" She tried to wipe some off her cheek with the sleeve of her sweater. "It's fine, it's not mine."

Danny's big blue eyes were widened in shock and he pulled her closer again, into a protective embrace that came a little bit too late. He spotted the gun in Jonas's lap.

"What happened?" he asked again.

Waldo had also entered the house and he looked around, frowning.

"We got a problem," Jonas said, yawning. "In the basement."

Danny seemed to understand, but he was speechless. He looked back at Alice and stroked a strand of hair out of her eyes. "Are you okay?"

Instead of answering, she hugged him tighter.

Danny pressed a kiss on her head. "How urgent?" he asked Jonas.

"Doesn't stink yet."

"Why?"

"Tried to kill her."

Alice felt Danny tense. "How did he get out?"

"Stabbed Stephan."

"Fucking bastard," Danny cursed. To Alice, he said, "You should get some rest."

Alice kept her arms wrapped around him. "I don't want to be alone."

Hesitating, Danny looked from her to Jonas. "You look tired."

Jonas nodded.

"I want to hear everything from you, but I think we all need some sleep first."

Again, Jonas nodded. "Guy can rot a bit longer."

"Let's take this day off," Danny told Waldo.

Waldo gave him a curt nod. "I'll be back after lunch to help with the ... *mess*." He turned on his heels and left the house.

"Where's Henry?" Alice asked Danny.

"Not here yet. It's only eight o'clock." He tenderly ran his fingers through her hair.

"I tried calling you," Jonas said to Danny while lighting a cigarette.

"I forgot to turn my phone back on after the flight."

"The flight?" Alice asked. "Where were you?"

"Let's just go to bed now, okay?" he said softly.

Walking upstairs wasn't that easy. Alice realized that she was limping. The fight with Martin must have sprained her ankle, though she couldn't recall how exactly it had happened. Her somersault over the couch table had surely not been helpful. Danny noticed it too and supported her by holding her arm.

Alice followed him into his bedroom. Danny wanted to wait until she had taken a shower, but Alice pulled him into the tub with her. Their history didn't matter. All she knew was that she needed him more than she had ever needed him.

Carefully, Danny wiped the blood from her face with his thumb.

"Ow!"

He quickly pulled his hand away. "Your eye ... it's swollen ... still?"

It took her a moment to understand what he meant. "No, no ... it was Martin. He *roughed me up* a bit, as he would put it."

Danny looked like he was about to curse again, but then he seemed to remember that *he* had hit her too. Ashamed, he dropped his eyes. "I'm so sorry!"

Alice quickly hugged him. She didn't want to think about what happened, and talking about it would not help her forget. It was great to have him back. He was a living shield, her protector. Sober, Danny seemed to always be in control, without coming off as cold and heartless, like Jonas. He managed to make her feel safe and calm, despite everything, and that was the only thing that mattered. Besides, she had no one else but him.

After the shower, Alice put on one of Danny's T-shirts and a pair of his boxer shorts and they huddled underneath the blanket. She rested her head on his chest and he softly caressed her hair.

"Do you want to tell me what happened?" he asked quietly.

"Jonas shot that Martin guy," Alice muttered, half asleep already. "Martin killed the guard and then ..." She yawned. "He wanted me to help him escape the house ... He thought I have the keys or the code, but I don't, so he wanted to shoot Jonas and look for the keys."

Danny's body tensed and his hand on her head stopped moving.

"But Jonas wasn't in his room, so Martin got all paranoid and kept looking for him. And he planned on shooting the guard—uh ... Brad, too."

"What did he do to you?"

Alice cuddled closer to him. "He wanted to take me with him as a hostage, so he could blackmail you ..."

"Did he tell you why?"

"No ... he just said he needed something from you."

"What happened then?"

"I refused to go with him, because he said he would mail me to you in pieces."

Danny held her tightly. "He wouldn't have. I would've done everything to get you back."

"But you're glad you don't have to."

"Of course, but you are the most important thing for me, Allie. Nothing comes before you!"

Really? So far, business had always come before her.

"Anyway, he said he'd shoot the night g- I mean, Brad, and I didn't want him to, so I tried to fight him. He wanted to kill me, but Jonas shot him first."

"And where was he—Jonas?"

"Hiding around the corner ... wanted to surprise Martin, I guess."

"And Brad?"

"I don't think he knew what was going on ... He came inside when he heard the shot."

Danny inhaled audibly. "What a night. I'm so sorry you had to go through this."

"Why was he even here? Martin?"

Danny hesitated before he replied. "He ... he was a threat. I mean, he threatened us, threatened to hurt you."

"Why?"

"To get something from me. He wanted to collaborate with me, but I refused."

"Was that why you didn't want me to go out?"

Alice felt him nod.

"But now that he's dead, I can?"

"We'll see ..."

"Why didn't you just call the police when he threatened you?"

"I'm not a fan of the cops, you know that."

"I do ... but this was serious. They could've helped you."

Danny sighed again. "No police, period."

Danny's secretive behavior and the heavily protected living situation had already planted a seed of suspicion in Alice's mind, and the thing with Martin had nurtured it. Now, Danny's reaction made it grow even further. To refuse calling the police in a situation like this could not come from a simple dislike of their demeanor. Even if you downright hated them, you would still call them if your life was at stake ... unless you had something to hide.

Alice looked up at him and tried to read his expression. "Are you doing something illegal?"

He stared at the ceiling and said nothing.

"You can tell me, you know. You don't have to keep it a secret."

"Stop asking questions, Alice. Let's just sleep."

"Come on, Danny, you have to tell me! Is it—"

He pulled her head back onto his chest. "Sleep now."

Despite the exhaustion and shock, falling asleep was hard after the conversation with Danny. What he had said—or rather what he hadn't said—kept haunting Alice's mind. Why was he so secretive about his business?

Martin's dead face still seemed to be printed on the inside of her eyelids. Whenever she closed her eyes she saw him, saw the blood, saw his widened eyes and limp body.

So when the alarm went off a couple of hours later, Alice clung to Danny like a barnacle. He, on the other hand, was glad that she wasn't ignoring him anymore.

They went downstairs for lunch, and ate in the dining room with Jonas sitting at the table as well. Danny did not address last night's events though. He only focused on Alice, and Jonas remained quiet.

After lunch, Danny kissed her softly and told her that he needed to speak to Jonas in private. The two of them then disappeared into Danny's office, and closed the door while Alice watched Henry collect their plates. Through the archway that led to the living room she could see the entrance door opening, and Waldo stepping into the house, accompanied by Tee and Paul.

"Hi, Alice," Tee greeted her cheerfully when he passed the dining room.

"Hi," she replied sullenly.

Henry stared at her. His eyes lingered on her swollen cheek. "What happened?" he wanted to know, while stacking her plate on the others.

"Oh, uh, there was a—"

"Alice!" It was Waldo's voice.

Tee and Paul were walking toward the office, but Waldo remained standing next to the dining room entrance.

"Come here, please."

Alice frowned, wondering what Waldo could possibly want from her. She got off her chair and followed him into the living room.

"Listen," he said when they were out of earshot from the kitchen, "You can't tell the cook—or anyone else—*anything* about what happened. Do you understand?"

She nodded.

"I know you're not too *happy* with the situation here," he continued, "but if word gets out about last night, it will be a disaster for *all* of us, understood?"

She nodded again.

Waldo's eyes seemed to pierce through her like daggers.

"Yes," Alice said quickly. "I won't tell anyone."

"Good girl," he said, and left to join the others.

Asshole.

Alice returned to the dining room to finish her glass of water, but Henry had already put it away. She went into the kitchen to get a new one, and found him washing up the pans and pots he had used.

"I'm sorry for walking away," she apologized to him.

Henry looked worried. "No problem, Alice ..." He bit his lower lip and scrubbed the bottom of a pot hard with a metal sponge, almost furiously.

"Everything okay?"

Sighing, he put the pot upside down next to the sink to let it dry. "It's just ... everything seems to be happening again."

"What do you mean?"

"With you and ... Daniel."

Alice tried to make sense of his words, then she remembered what Henry had told her about the previous owners. "Oh."

Henry nodded.

"No, it's not like that, honestly." Alice instinctively touched her swollen cheek, and felt herself blush.

It's not even a lie.

"Daniel didn't do this, I swear!"

Henry shook his head slowly and gave her a meaningful look out of sad eyes.

"Henry, I promise you that Daniel didn't do this," Alice tried again.

"I see him get drunk every day, Alice. I'm not blind. And I know how he treats you."

"He hasn't had a drop of alcohol in almost a month ... He stopped drinking for good and his mood is much better."

Henry gestured toward the swelling. "Then where did you get that from?"

Alice felt her face heat up at once. "That was ... a very stupid accident ... I tried going to the bathroom last night without turning on the lights, and I fell over one of the cardboard boxes that I still haven't unpacked."

Henry examined her with a suspicious expression. "And one month ago, you slipped and fell into the pool. You should be more careful, Alice, or you'll end up with a broken neck." He gave her a warning look.

He doesn't believe a word I'm saying.

"Thank you for your concern, really. I'll be more careful, I promise."

The cook continued washing up, but then he stopped and looked at her again. "What happened to the carpet?"

Now, Alice's face was *really* turning red. "Oh ... that, uh ... that was my fault." She looked down at her shoes quickly and tried to come up with a plausible excuse. "I spilled something."

Frowning, Henry stared at her. "What did you spill that can't be washed out again?"

"Paint ... I was painting in the living room and wanted to wash the bowl in the kitchen ... but then I dropped it."

"Why did you cut it out?"

"Jonas did that," Alice said quickly.

Henry's frown deepened. "What was that boy thinking?"

"Oh, you know how he is ..."

To Alice's relief, Henry just sighed and turned back to the sink, to continue washing up.

I'm a better liar than I thought.

Yet, Alice wasn't sure whether Henry believed her or not, so she fled the kitchen to not have to answer any more questions.

Danny and the others spent the whole afternoon in the office, probably discussing the Martin-debacle.

Alice was restless. She kept moving from place to place constantly, or zapping through the channels of her TV without actually watching anything. The images of Martin dying kept flashing through her mind, chasing away every sane thought, and it was driving her crazy.

When dinner was served, everybody ate at the table, so at least she wasn't alone. As always, Danny didn't tell her anything of what the gang had been talking about, and the men would just discuss things that weren't interesting for her.

Alice tried to cling to Danny as much as possible, needing his affection as well as his attention. It had been hard enough to spend every day alone already without having the memory of last night on her mind ... now it was unbearable.

He treated her nicely, glad that she was talking to him again, though Alice couldn't shake off the feeling that she was just like a puppy on his lap, whom he would occasionally pet while talking to his friends.

After dinner the men went to the basement, and Danny told Alice that they had to try and fix things and that she should just watch a movie or something.

That she did, though she couldn't process what happened in it. Later, she could hear car engines outside, so she decided to go downstairs and see what was going on.

The house appeared to be empty, and for a second Alice was tempted to sneak out—now, with everybody gone. Somehow though, it felt wrong. Danny was being nice to her and she was afraid to be alone in the dark anyway. Besides, a glance through the window revealed that more men than usual were guarding the wall. Having Jonas hold her back was bad enough, she didn't feel like risking a dispute with men she didn't even know—and she was pretty sure that they would not allow her to leave.

Danny came back late after midnight. Alice was still lying awake in bed and when she heard his car driving through the gate, she got up and hurried downstairs.

The others had probably gone home, since only Danny and Jonas stepped through the front door. They didn't say anything. Jonas looked at her for a moment, but then he went straight up to his room. Danny had a weird look on his face, like he was expecting her to say something annoying or accusing, but when Alice simply hugged him, he relaxed and planted a kiss on top of her head.

The both of them went upstairs as well, and Alice waited while Danny took a shower and got ready for bed. When he sat on the mattress next to her, she knew that he would not answer any of her questions, so she didn't bother asking.

His eyes were closed already, and he was deeply breathing into the pillow while Alice stared at the wall in the darkness. Suddenly, she heard him mutter something.

"What did you say?" Alice brushed through his dark hair with her fingers.

"Wish ... still need a wish ... birthday, two days ..."

"Tomorrow, actually," she corrected him, "And we'll talk about it in the morning."

He started snoring.

There was no chance to talk since Danny went downstairs to work at around 9:00 a.m. It was impossible for Alice to go back to sleep afterward. Her heart refused to beat in its normal manner, and her hands were cold and sweaty. Not knowing where exactly that nervousness came from only made her more anxious. To calm her nerves, she decided to take a bath and read a book until lunch was ready.

Her skin was wrinkled and her hair still wet when she finally went to the dining room, and sat down next to Danny. The others were there too, but they were deeply sunken into a conversation which didn't appear to be very interesting for Danny. He kissed her softly and brushed a wet strand of hair from her cheek.

"So," he began, after Alice had taken her place and started eating her mashed potatoes and peas; "I only have one day left and you know how bad I am with these things ..." He smirked apologetically.

Alice shrugged. "And you know how little I care about birthdays—at least if they're my own."

"But still ..." Danny shoved a big fork load of potatoes in his mouth and swallowed. "Especially now, when I can finally afford to give you something nice ..." He put his fork down and looked at her expectantly.

Alice stared into his eyes, his big blue puppy eyes, and couldn't help feeling bad for him despite thinking about how there was only one thing she wanted, and he wasn't going to give it to her.

His left eyebrow began wandering up his forehead and suddenly, he seemed very uneasy, as if he could read her thoughts. Alice quickly looked down at her food.

Danny cleared his throat and stared at his plate as well. "Is there something ... *material* that you want, maybe?"

My cell phone and laptop?

She bit her tongue. Again, he seemed to be guessing her answer.

Sighing, he squashed his mashed potatoes with his fork. "Just ignore everything ... that's been for a moment, and please just give me the chance to ... make you happy in some other way."

Alice suddenly realized that she had been imitating him and playing with her food as well. She quickly placed her fork down on the table.

For a moment she remained silent, thinking about possible ways to react, but ultimately, she came to the conclusion that the best thing to do was to just give him what he wanted and say something ... anything. "Since I can't go jogging, like I used to ..."

Danny looked up, a worried expression on his face like he was dreading her answer.

"Something to work out with would be nice," Alice finished. "Like a treadmill or something."

Relieved, he gave her a smile. "Sure, you'll have one!" He continued eating, more enthusiastically this time.

Alice felt her appetite disappear. Again, she had resigned and just given him what he wanted, even though he was clearly in the wrong. But Danny was all she had, and she needed him to be nice to her.

When she said nothing, he looked up again. "You can have everything, you know ... just say it."

Alice stabbed some peas with her fork but didn't put them in her mouth.

"I mean," he smirked at her. "Everything apart from a yacht or a flight to the moon. We don't have *that* much money yet."

She ignored his attempt to be funny.

Suddenly, Alice noticed the silence surrounding them. Several pairs of eyes were fixed on her and Danny. Apparently, the others could feel the tension between them.

Alice quickly tried to don a relaxed expression and even managed a smile. "Thanks, Danny."

He seemed relieved, unable to see through her act.

After lunch, everyone disappeared into the office—except Jonas, who sat down in the living room, bent over a thick book while smoking a cigarette. He seemed to be studying.

To avoid him, Alice returned to her bedroom and spent her afternoon drawing in solitude.

At dinner, Danny's attention was mainly reserved for his friends while Alice kept her eyes on her plate. She felt incredibly lonely—more so than if she had just eaten all alone.

Danny insisted on putting on some romantic comedy that night, though the mere thought of it made Alice sick to her stomach.

She did enjoy cuddling with him in front of the TV, however, and tried to focus on that rather than on the rest of her life.

"What's up?" Danny asked her when he noticed that she wasn't paying much attention to the screen.

Taking a deep breath, Alice tried to find a way to put everything that was bothering her into one sentence, but failed. It was as though Danny didn't even realize what he was doing, like his perception of reality differed from that of ordinary people.

Or did he have a good reason for all of this and was just afraid to tell her the truth?

Her eyes flicked to the remote. Finding the right words was hard enough already; the music and voices coming from the TV didn't help. She leaned forward, took the remote from the mattress, and pressed pause.

Danny stared at her with a wary expression. He was clearly feeling uncomfortable. Alice's eyes locked with his, but then her gaze went right through him until his face was nothing but a blur.

"Tell me why ... we live like this," Alice finally managed to say, after letting him sweat for a moment. "I want answers."

His eyes wandered away from hers, down to his fingers which were laced with hers. She felt his grip loosen.

"So far, whenever I asked you, you got mad."

Danny pulled his hand free and scratched his nose nervously.

"I'm hoping that now, since you're not drinking anymore, I can maybe have a real conversation with you ...?"

Staring at the unmoving image on the TV screen, he grimaced.

Alice waited patiently, carefully studying his expression. Was he thinking of a lie to tell her? Or was she finally about to hear the truth?

He cleared his throat. "What ... what exactly do you want to know?" His voice was low and sounded nervous, though there was a hint of annoyance in it as well.

Inhaling deeply, Alice shifted herself into a more upright position. "Most of all ... why am I not allowed to leave this place?"

Danny's eyes swiveled to hers and then down to his hands, which were lying in his lap. "It's not ... safe."

She wasn't going to let him off the hook so easily. "Why? It was safe before."

He bit his lip.

Alice noticed his expression getting darker. She was pretty sure—or maybe just hoping—that he wouldn't get mad when he was sober, but the look on his face made her feel uncomfortable nevertheless.

"I know that things must be complicated. After all, Jonas shot a man in the living room, and I cannot help but wonder what you did with the body ... But you of all people should know what I'm capable of and that I support you, no matter what." Trying to be encouraging, she reached over to him and brushed a strand of hair out of his eyes. "We've always trusted each other, haven't we?"

Danny pushed himself up a bit, the way she had, and leaned his back against the wall. His face was above hers now. That way it was easier for him to avoid her eyes.

"Danny, you know me," she urged, "Well enough to know that I'm not shocked easily. And that I value certain things more than laws ... So whatever it is, just tell me." Why was it so hard for him to be honest?

"It's complicated," he finally spoke, breathing sharply through his nose.

"Do you think I won't approve?"

His lips were pressed shut tightly, forming a straight line above his chin. His silence made her nervous.

"Is it something so bad that you think I would disagree with? Danny, I know you! There is really nothing you could do that I wouldn't understand."

He frowned. "It's not ... like that." His eyes finally went back to her face. "It's just ... I want to protect you and the less you know, the safer you are."

"Protect me from what?" He was speaking in riddles and it was irritating.

"Well—guys like Martin, for example?" His tone was both mocking and condescending.

"He's dead, isn't he? And he surely won't come back to haunt me more than he already does."

Sighing, Danny closed his eyes for a moment. "There's more like him ... people who want what I have and are willing to do horrible things to get it."

"Get *what*?"

"Alice, I really don't want to tell you too much about it. It's safer that way." He looked into her eyes intensely, trying to convince her.

"So, it's definitely illegal," Alice concluded.

Danny rubbed his temple with the knuckles of his right fist and inhaled sharply. He opened his eyes and stared at the wall behind the TV, looking defeated. "If ever something goes wrong ... you'll be held accountable as well—unless you know nothing about it."

Now, the only thing she could see displayed on his face was genuine concern.

"But ..." Alice hesitated, still curious of what his big secret was, but now unsure if she wanted to know it or not. "Isn't that my decision?"

"No," he answered after a moment of silence, "Because it's my responsibility and once you know, there is no turning back."

Alice frowned. "Danny, this affects me too, maybe even more than you ... *you* are allowed to leave the house and do whatever you want. I, on the other hand, have been forced to stay here for two and a half months already, unable to see or even speak to my friends, or simply take a walk! I don't call this a home—I feel like a prisoner here!" Her breathing got faster, partly because she was starting to get angry, but also because she was desperate to make him understand her situation—and it was just frustrating how he seemed unable to see the obvious.

He looked sad now, guilty even. "I know ... and I'm so sorry. The whole ... *situation* is just complicated, and you get to feel most of the impact." He stroked her cheek softly with the back of his hand. "It was easier for me to adjust because I had nothing apart from you. My friends are my colleagues, and I got everything I need here. You, however, had to give up your whole life because I was so eager and desperate to change mine. Trust me, I get that. I just realized too late ... what a dangerous terrain I was entering."

Alice stared at him, taken aback by his honesty and self-criticism. "But ... it can't be *so bad* ... can it?" She shifted uncomfortably.

"There's tons of bad people out there, Allie, and I only learned that when I started doing business with some of them ... and refused others."

Alice bit her lip, seeing Martin's dead body clearly in her mind, his face grotesque, and his eyes cold as ice ... Slowly, she was beginning to understand the true impact of what had happened.

I could have died ... shot by a stranger who was angry at Danny.

Something cold seemed to run down her spine and made her shiver. This was her life now, hiding from hazards she had never known before—hazards she would have never encountered if it weren't for Danny.

Then again, what would her life be like without him? He had given her purpose and happiness ... Jill and Leah were just friends she would see occasionally. Sure, she missed them, but she had never spent as much time with them as she had with Danny. Were they really equally important? Alice had found her home in Danny; he was her only family. She would always choose him over them, though it broke her heart to even have to make that decision. And Danny's recent behavior wasn't exactly making it easier.

Her thoughts must have been clearly displayed on her face because Danny leaned over and kissed her forehead gently, in a comforting manner.

"I'm sorry," he said, and she knew that he meant it.

"But ... what about you? I don't want to be worrying about you all the time, wondering if you'll come home ... or ... or ..."

Smiling, he pulled her closer. "Don't worry about me, I got the guys. And I got myself into this mess. I know how to handle it."

Alice freed her head from underneath his arms and leaned back, frowning at him. "You sound like you don't want this!" She looked at him accusingly. "Can't you just change it? Stop this, whatever it is you're doing, and go back?"

Danny's smile disappeared and his expression got serious. "Alice ... the only thing I regret is that I made you unhappy."

Her eyes widened. "What do you mean ...?"

A weird flicker appeared in his eyes, a hunger for power and control, something that didn't befit him. He smiled again, but it wasn't a warm smile.

"I mean ... I'm exactly where I want to be."

For a long moment, neither of them said a word. They stared at each other, Alice desperately trying to figure out what that look on his face meant.

Her eyes teared up.

Danny's expression softened again, and he pulled her into an embrace. "I know this is hard on you ... and I hate that you're not as happy as I thought you'd be." His voice was low, almost a whisper next to her ear.

Alice felt a single tear run down her cheek. "Just tell me it won't be like this forever! Please, Danny, I need to know that it won't stay that way!" She felt him inhale deeply, his chest pressing her tighter into his arms.

"Say something," she begged.

"It's just ... we had a rough start. Things didn't go as smoothly as planned. People got involved who shouldn't have ..." He muttered the words into her hair. "But I don't want it to stay that way either—for you, I mean. I promise you that I'll make it better." He kissed her forehead.

"How?"

Danny's explanations were vague, his excuses hollow, and his promises sounded empty ... It was frustrating.

"We'll sort everything out, find our place in this ... *game,* and earn some more money, until we're able to move again. Get our own place on the beach somewhere, or on an old farm where you could have horses—"

"Horses, Danny, seriously?" she interrupted him, rolling her eyes.

"Or donkeys, I know you love donkeys! Or those cute, little goats ... the dwarf ones ... Or you could save animals from slaughter, isn't that what you always wanted? A kind of farm sanctuary?"

Alice sighed with frustration. "Of course, I love animals, Danny. More than most people, anyway. But I can't just replace Jill and Leah with donkeys and pigs!"

"What I mean is we'll be able to live however we want. And where we want. I know you hate the cold. We could move to Hawaii or Thailand or Indonesia ... or if you prefer milder temperatures, Spain, Italy ..."

"I get it."

Danny chuckled and mussed her hair.

"Danny," she protested weakly. "That sounds great, I guess, but not very realistic."

"Why not?" He sounded surprised. "Money can buy these things."

"It can't buy real friendship though."

He shook his head. "You'll make new friends and I definitely don't want to keep working that much. The whole point of being rich is to not have to work, isn't it?" He played with her hair, running his fingers through it. "I want to spend time with *you,* Allie, every minute of every day—if I can. But it's hard work to get there, you have to understand that."

"And what about our safety?" she asked, unconvinced. "There will still be bad people—if you like to call them that—so I won't be able to go where I want. My cage won't disappear, it'll just get bigger ..."

"Cage?" He laughed. "Don't call it that, Allie, it's not fair. Most people hide in their houses, don't they? They might go to work or take a walk once in a while, but all in all, they're in their safe little homes. We'll take our walks on our own territory and hang out on our own beach, bathe in our own pool ... and we'll still be able to go on vacation somewhere else. We'll have people protecting our property and us, and by then, we'll have so much space that you won't feel like they're disrespecting your privacy."

Alice grumbled.

"And until then," Danny continued, "we'll have my friends and some other guys I know protecting us."

Sighing, Alice pulled herself out of his hug and leaned away from him. "Like Jonas? I don't feel protected, I feel *watched*."

Danny raised his eyebrows. "He saved your life, have you already forgotten?"

How could I ever forget?

"Of course not! But it was weird ... the way he waited until the last second ... He told me he'd wanted to catch Martin alive and I'd made that impossible. He didn't sound too happy about it."

Danny gave her a serious look. "It sounded different when he told me. If he had walked in from a distance, Martin would've been able to use you as shield, and there would've been no chance of catching him. Also, the risk of you getting hurt was too big. Jonas wanted to wait until he was close enough to overpower him, but then Martin attacked you and he had to react."

Alice shrugged. "Yeah ... I guess. I mean, I am grateful ... but I was just shocked at how normal everything seemed to be for him. He shot a man and treated his body like a dead cockroach ... It was disturbing, that's all."

And he grinned and made jokes.

"He's ... special," Danny said, "But that's what I like about him. It's why I trust him with you. He knows what he's doing, and he never lets emotions get in the way."

Because he has none.

Danny scratched his chin. "You know, Waldo's too impulsive ... Paul's young and inexperienced, Tee's an idiot—and I'd never leave you alone with him—and the others do their job well, but I don't know them well enough."

Resigned, Alice sighed. "I'd just like someone to talk to. And well ... he's definitely not the best choice."

Chuckling warmly, Danny pulled her closer again and kissed her on the cheek. "I'm here to talk with you and I'll make sure I have more time for you, I promise."

Alice frowned. "Really?"

"Yes, really. Tomorrow's your big day and I won't be working at all. And in the future, I'll try to get as much work done in the mornings as possible, so you don't have to spend your afternoons watching TV ... Although, sometimes I'd like to trade places."

Smiling, Alice rested her head on his shoulder. "What about your business trips?"

"There's none planned for at least a month, so I'll be here all the time over Christmas and until January."

He kissed her lips and she closed her eyes, trying to enjoy it as much as she could.

"So ... did I give you enough answers?" he asked carefully.

Alice sighed deeply and stretched her legs. "I guess ... I mean, as long as you're with me, I'm fine." She grabbed the remote, and pressed the start button to continue the utterly cheesy romantic movie, Danny had chosen.

He put his arm around her and rested his chin on her head.

It felt good.

12

"Morning, sunshine!"

Alice moaned and buried her head underneath the warm body next to her.

"Come on, it's a beautiful day," Danny's way too enthusiastic voice sang next to her ear.

"How can a day in December be beautiful?" she grumbled.

He laughed. "First of all, it's *your* day, and second of all, there's even some sunrays coming through the blinds, so I'm guessing the weather's playing along."

Alice blinked into the light and turned onto her back. Danny kissed her on the brow and smiled. "Ready to get up?"

"What for?"

"You'll see." He grinned broadly.

True enough, there *was* sunlight falling through the gaps in the blinds, and Alice wondered if it really could be a nice day for a change. The last couple of weeks the sky had usually been overcast and even some rain had fallen from time to time.

"It's still going to be cold outside, though," she protested.

Danny pulled the blanket away from her body and jumped off the bed, clapping his hands together in an attempt to be encouraging. He received a scowl as response.

"Come on," he urged, "there'll be breakfast downstairs."

Sighing, Alice sat upright, wrapped her arms around her knees and checked the window again, just to be certain. "There's never breakfast unless I make it myself."

"It's never been your birthday here so far."

She turned her head to look at him. "Did you trouble poor Henry?"

Danny grabbed his jeans from the floor and began to get dressed. "Oh, you know him—he likes things like that ... it was actually his suggestion." He snapped the belt shut. "I told him that lunch is usually your breakfast, but he thought it'd be a nice idea to have a breakfast buffet."

Alice's clothes were spread on the floor as well, after a passionate night with Danny. She got up to collect them.

"That sounds nice ... but it's only 9:30, way too early to get up."

Danny laughed and pulled her into a hug, which almost made her fall since she had only put one leg through her pants so far.

"Danny!"

He kissed her forehead. "Don't worry, I'm holding you."

"Why are you so enthusiastic?"

"Someone has to be on your birthday."

"Stop mentioning it!"

"Why?" he asked, surprised.

"What good is there about getting older?" Alice put her other leg through the pants and pulled them up.

"Don't say that, Allie, you're only twenty-one for god's sake! You're making me feel like an old man."

"Men get better with age."

Danny helped her pull her black T-shirt over her head, then he pulled her hair out the collar. "Who says women don't?"

"Society."

Laughing, he patted her back. "Since when do you care about society?"

Grimacing, Alice put on a fresh pair of socks while he went over to the window to open the blinds. A surprisingly big amount of sunlight fell into the room and made her blink.

"It really *is* a nice day," he commented and grinned, flashing his perfectly white teeth.

Henry had prepared a nice breakfast buffet with freshly baked bread that smelled mouthwatering, a bowl of fruit salad, freshly pressed orange juice, beans with tomato sauce, and mushrooms.

Since she liked sleeping until noon, Alice couldn't remember the last time she had eaten breakfast. On the weekends, when Henry didn't have to work, she usually just ate a bowl of cornflakes.

Breakfast was utterly delicious, and she ended up having three servings. Afterward, she felt heavy and even more tired. To her relief, the others left her and Danny in peace.

Yesterday's conversation had not been entirely to her satisfaction— especially the question *what* Danny's secret illegal business was kept nagging on her— but Alice didn't want to bring it up with him being in such a good mood.

When they were done eating, Danny led her to the spare bedroom next to his office, and gestured to a big cardboard box which stood on the carpet next to the bed.

"There's your present—at least one of them."

Alice eyed it suspiciously, but then she smiled. "A treadmill!"

He nodded. "We'll set it up in your room later. I doubt you'd want to work out in the basement with the others."

Beaming, she shook her head. "Thank you, Danny."

About half an hour later, Alice found herself dressed in boots and her winter jacket, following Danny out through the back door. He was wearing his usual black coat and with it, a brown leather backpack that made him look like a hipster.

"Why are you wearing that backpack?" Alice asked him while the door fell shut behind her.

"You'll see," Danny replied.

To her surprise, he walked straight across the back yard and toward the small iron gate behind the pool.

"Wait ... when you said we're going outside, did you mean *outside*?" Alice hurried to keep up with him. Danny's long legs were coming to a halt next to the wall, which had kept Alice and her freedom apart for so long already. Instead of answering, he grinned broadly and pulled a small silver key out of the pocket of his jeans. He turned it in the thick padlock, which sprang open with a satisfying *click*. The recently replaced iron door almost made no sound at all when Danny pushed it open.

A soft cold wind blew Alice's hair away from her forehead. Closing her eyes, she inhaled deeply—the scent of wood and moss, of fallen leaves and winter.

But most importantly ... of freedom.

Eagerly trying to catch a glimpse of what awaited her on the other side of the wall she almost shoved Danny aside. The huge stonewall had marked the end of her world for way too long and now, stepping through the gate felt like walking through a portal and into another dimension.

Danny let her pass, then followed her onto the wide strip of grass that kept the trees of the nearby forest from growing onto the property and destroying the wall with their roots.

There wasn't much else—nothing, Alice hadn't already seen from the window of Danny's and her bedroom. Standing here though, outside, surrounded by all these trees, was an entirely different feeling.

The bitter taste of shame threatened to chase away her joy. Alice felt ashamed of even feeling that excited. To leave the property and take a walk should not have been anything special, but after more than two months of being unable to do so, it felt marvelous.

Instead of hating Danny for keeping her locked up in the first place, she was now grateful that he was letting her out for a bit.

I'm excited like a child ... how pathetic.

Swallowing dryly, Alice tried to push these thoughts away and kept a smile on her face; one, she didn't even have to fake. As pathetic as it made her feel, it *was* an incredible feeling to see the wall from the other side for a change.

Danny's expression reflected her own. Still beaming, he seemed excited to see her smile again.

"A perfect day for a little hike, don't you think?" He took her hand in his. It was warm despite the cold, and Alice squeezed it gladly. Nodding, she followed his steps as he led her deeper into the forest.

Sunlight fell through the trees; through the gaps, the fallen leaves had left behind. Only some brown ones remained on the lower branches. Lots of evergreen trees kept the forest lush.

Sparrows, blackbirds, and finches inhabited the trees. Spreading their wings happily to absorb as much sunlight as possible, they hopped from branch to branch, twittering noisily in what Alice assumed was outrage about the strange intruders who dared to disturb their peace.

She watched them while quietly walking behind Danny, who was moving rather quickly through the trees, walking on a beaten track that was almost overgrown by thorns.

The ground became steeper after a while, and the number of trees began to shrink.

Finally, they reached the edge of the forest and walked out onto a big pasture that was now empty, but during the summer probably inhabited by cows.

Danny stopped and turned around to give her a smile. "You can see our house from up here."

Curious, Alice stepped beside him and let her eyes wander over the surrounding area. It was phenomenal. They were standing on one of the many hills that surrounded the little valley with its farmhouses and fields. Large patches of forest made the landscape look wild and pristine. The mountains in the far distance were covered in snow and added to a postcard-like ambiance.

Alice had always considered hiking to be something for old people or loners, but now, she was beginning to understand exactly why people chose to engage in that kind of outdoor activity.

"Can you see it?" Danny broke the silence.

"Huh?"

"The house." He pulled her toward him and stretched out his left arm, pointing at a spot straight ahead.

Alice could barely make out the reddish-brown roof, as it camouflaged with the brown trees around it, but she clearly recognized the pool with its light-blue marble and white plastic roofing.

"Yes, I see it," she breathed, still in awe of the beautiful view. She couldn't help but wonder if having been locked up made it seem more stunning than it actually was.

"It's so small ..."

Danny nodded while wiping some sweat from his forehead. He pulled a bottle of water out of his backpack and drank some, then offered it to Alice.

"Quite some altitude we conquered already," he said while his eyes scanned the area.

Alice drank some water and gave the bottle back to him. "How far is it still?"

Laughing, Danny mussed her hair affectionately. "We're hiking, Allie. The journey's the reward. You wanted to explore the area, didn't you?"

Nodding, Alice looked back down at the house. It looked much better from up here.

"Well, then let's go."

Pieces of forest alternated with meadows, and by the time they reached the top of the big hill, Alice was completely out of breath. Danny stepped out of the woods and onto the grass, then led her to the middle of a large meadow. There, he took off his backpack and put it down on the ground. After taking some time to catch his breath, he started rummaging in the bag and pulled out a picnic rug, which he spread out on the ground. Thankful, Alice sat down on it and Danny laughed.

"Good thing I bought you that treadmill," he remarked, "You're completely out of shape."

Danny was right, of course, but whose fault was that? She scowled at him. "How's your foot though? Does it still hurt?"

"The swelling's gone and I can't feel anything with the pain killers I took."

He bit his lip. "Not sure if it was a good idea to go hiking already."

"I don't care. It's worth it."

Chuckling, he handed her a plastic cup and filled it with steaming hot tea from a thermos can.

Alice warmed her hands on the cup and enjoyed the view. The house wasn't visible anymore from up here, but she could see much farther than before. A gray spot in the distance even turned out to be the city.

If sitting up here, far away from the world and its problems, wasn't freedom—what was?

Noticing, Danny was watching her, she turned her head to look at him. He seemed a bit nervous, as if this were their first date or as if he had handed her a gift and wasn't sure she liked it.

"What do you think of the view?" he wanted to know.

"Could be worse."

He laughed. "It's not what we're used to, but the countryside offers many advantages."

"Like?" Alice asked, to keep him talking.

"Fresh air, nice people, safety ..."

"It looks safe," she agreed while taking a cautious sip of her tea.

Sighing, he stretched his legs and leaned back a bit, turning his head toward the sun. "And it's beautiful ... in my opinion."

"It is," she murmured and took another sip.

They sat in silence for a while until Alice dared to address a certain topic. "It looks really safe ..." she said again while scanning the area with her eyes once more.

Danny nodded, his eyes closed and his face relaxed.

"Then ... why can't I walk around here myself?"

His eyes flung open and he looked at her, sighing again—though it was a different sigh than before. "I'm just ... a bit paranoid when it comes to you," he said hesitantly, and stared into his cup as if he were trying to read the answer in the tealeaves. "It may be safe today, but it might not be tomorrow, and it most definitely isn't safe to let you walk around on your own."

Alice stared into her teacup as well and said nothing.

"I'm not scared of what's here, Alice," he continued. "I'm scared of what—or rather *who*—might come here or of you wandering off, trusting people who are not to be trusted—"

"Do you think I'm *that* naïve?"

He shook his head sadly. "It's not that easy. I pulled you into this ... situation, and you don't know how to handle it. I don't think you understand how dangerous people can be or how to recognize those who are."

Alice kept her eyes on her cup, thinking of Martin. "I think I know that well enough now."

Danny put his hand on her thigh. "The thing with Martin made me especially wary. It really scared me ... He wasn't supposed to know where we live."

Surprised, Alice looked up. "It's not a big secret that we live here, people come by all the time."

"Only people who work for me and whom I trust."

"But ... it can't be that hard to find out, right?"

He shrugged. "It's a remote neighborhood and the farmers don't really try to become friends with their neighbors. But yes, if somebody really wanted to find out, I guess they could." He brushed a strand of hair behind her ear. "Martin proved that."

She shivered at the thought. Danny noticed it and put his arm around her shoulders. "I take it you know why I'm worried for your safety."

Nodding, Alice took a big sip of her tea, which wasn't steaming anymore. "But it's fine when you're with me?"

Danny bit his lower lip and frowned. "It's just ... I like to know where you are and that you're safe, that's all."

Alice finished her cup of tea and put it down on the blanket next to her. "So, can we make this a frequent thing?"

Hesitating, he took a deep breath. "When something becomes routine, people tend to find out."

"But you can come to town with me or we can drive somewhere ... I'm not saying we should always do the same hike." Alice didn't feel like being accompanied by her boyfriend every time she wanted to leave the house, but if this was her only chance to leave it at all, there was no way around it.

Chewing his lower lip, Danny stared into the fields. "I usually don't have time for that ... but we'll see."

It wasn't what Alice wanted to hear, but she didn't say it aloud. There were still so many questions on her mind, but most of them would never be answered by him.

What was going on with him?

Why was she putting up with this?

And why did she still love him, after everything he had done?

If the thing with Martin had not happened, everything would be different. Alice knew that, though she couldn't explain what exactly it meant. All she knew was that she felt as if someone had pulled the rug out from under her feet. She knew she was supposed to be angry at Danny, but all she could feel was uncertainty and a completely misplaced desire to be held and comforted by him.

Maybe that was normal; after all, witnessing a man getting killed in your own home—especially after your boyfriend and his friends kept him locked up in the basement for days, apparently torturing him— was not an everyday event. Not to forget that she had almost lost her life in the process.

The life, as Alice had known it, was over, and she was too confused to decide what her next step ought to be. It would probably be best to just go along with what Danny wanted until she felt normal again. Being with him wasn't bad as long as he was in a good mood. Plus, he hadn't had a drop of alcohol in a while and he seemed to be back to his normal self.

Danny took her silence as a hint that their conversation was over, and started rummaging in his backpack again, this time taking out two sandwiches wrapped in foil.

"Thanks," she muttered, when he put one in her hand. Slowly, she started to unwrap it.

They ate silently while enjoying the view and the sun.

At least that seemed to be what *he* was doing ... Alice couldn't help but keep thinking about the *situation*, he had put her in.

When they were done eating and the sky was turning overcast, Alice began to shiver. "It's getting cold," she said.

"Would you like to go back?"

She shook her head.

Danny smiled and pulled her into a tight embrace, trying to warm her with his body. "I still have something for you," he muttered.

"If it's in your pants, it can wait until we're back."

Laughing, Danny kissed her forehead. "Typical Allie ... but no, that's not what it is. Though technically, it *is* in my pants." He leaned backward and started to feel his pockets. "Ah, here it is," he said cheerfully while pulling a small satin box out of his jeans.

Alice felt her heart take a somersault and she held her breath. Terrified, she eyed the box and wiped her sweaty hands on her pants. After everything that had happened, Danny was going to propose to her?

Her fear must have been clearly displayed on her face. Danny chuckled. "Don't worry, it's not what it looks like." He placed the box in her sweaty palm.

Hesitating, Alice took a deep breath and opened it. Inside was a delicate golden necklace, its chain very thin and soft. Alice took it out of the satin box and ran it through her fingers.

"I know you don't like jewelry, but I thought you might like this one," Danny said quietly.

Carefully, Alice examined the necklace and noticed that the thing hanging from the chain, which she had taken for a pearl, was actually a tiny turtle. Its shell was made of a simple mountain crystal, set into an oval gold frame with four legs, a tiny head and an even tinier tail.

"I love turtles ..."

"I know." Danny leaned closer and kissed her. "Do you want me to put it around your neck?"

Alice nodded.

Bending over, he took the necklace from her hands and laid it carefully around her throat, closed it and pulled her hair out from underneath it. He kissed her long and passionately.

"Thanks," she said breathlessly after he had pulled back.

He grinned. "You're welcome."

"For the turtle, not the kiss." She stuck her tongue out at him.

He chuckled and kissed her on the cheek. "You should have seen your face when I pulled out that box."

Alice grimaced and fingered the necklace around her throat.

"Would it be so bad ...?" Danny asked hesitantly.

Avoiding his eyes, Alice tried to hide her panic. "No need to rush, right? We got all the time in the world."

"It's definitely getting cold now," he said. "Should we go back?"

Alice nodded.

Time seemed to fly after her birthday, a blur of constant ups and downs. The ups consisted of Danny staying off work almost every afternoon, playing boardgames with her or even taking walks in the forest. It was an amazing feeling to have him back, and Alice got used to the daily routine in the old English house with its walls and bars. The downs, however, were her headaches, which occurred all the time since her fall into the pool, and the nightmares that haunted her through the nights ever since the thing with Martin had happened. Danny was very beaten up about both. He would bring her tea and aspirin when the headaches got so bad, Alice had to stay in bed with the blinds closed; and he would hold her tightly, whispering that everything was okay, whenever she woke up from a nightmare, covered in cold sweat.

Two weeks went by and Christmas was just around the corner, and Danny informed her that he was expecting guests on Christmas Eve.

"Christmas is coming!" he told her on a gray and cold December morning.

Alice shrugged. "So? Since when do you care about holidays?"

"I don't. But Julio does." He checked his reflection in Alice's bathroom mirror, his razor ready in his hand to remove the last bits of his facial hair.

"Is that some business partner?"

"Not yet. But he might be." He washed the razor in the sink and put it in the cup next to Alice's toothbrush.

"Why d'you always shave?" she asked him, leaning against the door with her arms crossed, watching him brush over his smooth cheeks with the tips of his fingers, examining the result of his work.

"Because I want to look good." He turned around and flashed her a smile.

"But you look good with facial hair," she protested.

He walked toward her and kissed her forehead. "I don't scratch you though."

"I miss your facial hair."

He laughed. "You love those words, don't you?"

"Well, I can't really call it a beard, can I?"

He shook his head. "Nope, it's definitely far from being a beard ... though I tried hard and you know that."

Alice let out a theatrical sigh. "Worst couple of months of my life."

"How so?"

"Your constant complaining drove me crazy!"

Danny frowned, but then he smiled. "Oh, come on, you're the same. You always complain."

"About what?"

He grabbed his white dress shirt from a chair and put his arms through the sleeves. "Hair, weight, pimples, clothes ..."

"I'm quite happy at the moment," Alice disagreed.

He began buttoning up his shirt. "You could eat more. You look thin."

Alice scowled at him. "Now that I'm happy, *you* complain."

He smiled apologetically. "I'm just worried, that's all."

Sighing, Alice sat down on the bed. "Back to that dinner ..."

"Yeah, right. So, Julio is going to bring his wife, Theresa. Waldo's bringing his wife as well—her name's Marion."

"Oh wow ... other women in the house. That's a new one."

Danny grinned. "You'll have someone to talk to."

"I can talk to men as well, you know. Just not your friends."

He shrugged and fumbled with his belt. "They'll be here too, of course."

"How come I'm invited to a business dinner? I thought that's none of my ... well, business?"

"We won't be discussing it at the table, obviously."

"So why go through all this trouble?"

He chuckled. "It's no trouble for me, you know. I like fancy dinners."

"Fancy dinners, fancy houses, fancy clothes ... *who* are you and what have you done with Danny?"

His expression changed for a second, sincerity flickered in his eyes. But then he laughed it off and nodded toward her closet. "Talking about fancy, have you ever opened your wardrobe?"

Right ... *that* discussion had not yet been held. Alice had totally forgotten about the strange clothes in her closet.

Grimacing, she said, "Just once, and I thought the previous owner had left them ... the clothes, I mean."

"No, I bought them for you."

"You *what?*"

"I mean, I sent Anita to buy them for you. She has good taste."

"Why would you buy clothes for me? I have enough to wear."

Danny walked over to the closet and opened the door. He ran his fingers along the line of coat hangers and took out a light blue silken blouse with long sleeves.

Alice wrinkled her nose.

"I thought it would be good for you to have something ... more *fitting*."

"To what?"

"The house ... me."

"We were a perfect match before *you* changed," Alice pointed out.

He sighed. "Everything's changed, Allie. I cannot just walk around however I want. I need people to respect me in order to be successful." He put the blouse back. "My work is here, and my colleagues are always around. You never went to the office in ripped jeans and a *Disturbed* shirt, did you?"

"*Disturbed* is more your taste, so no."

Danny frowned at her.

"But no," she said quickly, "I would always dress ... appropriately."

"See," he said. "And I have to do the same. People must see that I have money. I need to show them. They need to know that I'm successful, otherwise they won't do business with me."

"And you have to throw fancy dinner parties for them as well?"

"It makes them trust me. Inviting them into my home, introducing them to my girlfriend—I'm making myself vulnerable to show them that I'm trustworthy."

Vulnerable?

Alice shivered. "More Martins?"

"No, don't worry," he assured her. "Never men like him." He fingered the coat hangers and took another one out, this time a red satin dress with golden buttons on the front. "That looks Christmassy, doesn't it?"

She grimaced. "Eww, Danny! *What* have you bought for me? These are so not my colors!"

"No color's your color, Alice, since you never wear any. All your clothes are black."

Alice opened her mouth to protest, but he was faster. "Apart from the blue jeans, of course."

She closed it again.

"Listen," he said softly, "I would really appreciate it if you dressed up nicely for that dinner, that's all."

Resigned, she sighed. "Fine."

Danny put the red dress back and shut the closet door. "Oh, and maybe you should shave for that dress." He winked at her.

"Why? I can just wear tights and long sleeves if female body hair makes your guests uncomfortable. It's cold anyway."

He shrugged. "I'm pretty sure you'll feel quite hot after a couple of glasses of red wine and countless boring conversations, but it's up to you."

Great.

"I'll think about it. Do I have to wear the red dress? I hate red."

"No, you can wear whatever you like—as long as it's formal and elegant. My personal favorite's the light blue blouse I showed you earlier, but it's not very Christmassy."

Alice raised her eyebrows. "*Your* favorite's something light blue?"

"Well ... I figured it would suit you, with your dark hair and eyes ..."

"Since when do you have an eye for colors?"

He bent down to put on his shoes. "I've always had an eye for colors."

When he was done tying his laces, he straightened back up and checked his reflection once again, brushing back his dark curls.

"Please keep those, at least," Alice begged. "They're like the only thing about you that's still *Danny*."

His lips tightened. "I was actually thinking about cutting them." He turned around to look at her. "But I can keep them if it makes you happy."

Alice beamed. "That's only fair, since I'm keeping the bangs you like so much." She pointed at her forehead.

"They're cute ... and they suit you." He crossed the room to kiss her.

"I know. It's just a hassle to always cut them back. And they make me look like a doll."

He smiled pitifully. "Sorry you're going through so much trouble for my beloved fringe."

Alice stuck her tongue out at him.

Laughing, he blew her a kiss, then he left the room to go to his office.

The dreadful day arrived way too soon, and Alice hadn't yet found a solution to the clothes-problem. Over and over, she went through the closet without finding anything she liked. Even on the twenty-fourth of December, only thirty minutes before Julio and Theresa were supposed to arrive, she still had not made up her mind. Nothing Danny had bought for her was even remotely her taste. She kept staring at the dresses and blouses, most of them silken or satin, some velvet and cotton.

He should know that I'd never wear silk.

All Alice knew for sure by now, was that she absolutely would not put on a dress and especially not the red one. In the end, she had two long-sleeved blouses laid out on her bed. The light blue, Danny's favorite, and a dark blue one with black buttons. Dark blue was as close to black as it would get, but the other one was what Danny would probably prefer.

Sighing, she put the dark blouse back.

Alice chose a short black skirt over black nylon tights to go along with it.

A look in the bathroom mirror revealed that the blouse *did* go great with her eyes and hair. Since Danny hadn't bought her any fancy shoes, Alice put on a pair of simple black sneakers. She actually was glad that he hadn't. The last thing she wanted was to wear high-heels.

When the clock showed 5:00 p.m., she rushed into the bathroom once more, to put on some mascara and brush her hair back into a ponytail. More or less pleased with her reflection, she hurried downstairs and went to stand next to Danny, who was waiting by the entrance; just as the door was opened.

Danny looked at her and beamed—his grin as wide as it could get. Alice knew she had made the right choice with the blouse.

He quickly turned toward the door, just as Waldo entered. The former cop was wearing a gray suit with a white shirt underneath and a matching tie. His wife came in after him, her back straight and upright, her blond hair tightly pulled back into a knot. She seemed to be in her late forties, with high cheekbones, hollow cheeks, and thin lips. Her expression was hard and a bit cold. She was wearing a tight red satin dress with golden embroideries, and Alice felt relieved that she hadn't put on her red dress. It would have been embarrassing to be twinning with Waldo's wife.

Waldo appeared to be ignoring his wife completely. He shook Danny's hand formally, almost crushed Alice's fingers when he shook hers, and then he walked straight to the dining room while his wife, Marion, held her cheek to Danny so he could kiss it. Afterward, she shook Alice's hand while Danny introduced them. Marion didn't say a word throughout the whole procedure and quickly followed her husband to the other room when more guests stepped into the house.

Julio looked intimidating.

He wasn't very tall, though taller than Alice, and he wore a black suit that looked very, very expensive. A massive golden watch hung around his right wrist, and his black hair was brushed back and patted flatly to the sides of his head. His body was massive. He wasn't obese, but he had quite broad shoulders and thick arms and legs. There was no smile on his face when he shook Danny's hand, and his eyes didn't even meet Alice's when he shortly shook her hand as well.

His wife looked much friendlier than Marion. Theresa was short and curvy, with a round face, full lips, huge dark eyes, and black hair which fell in thick neat curls to her shoulders. She was wearing a golden cocktail dress and golden high-heels—and Alice felt underdressed at once. Theresa kissed her cheek and beamed, though she looked shy when she did so.

All in all, both women looked like their husband's lapdogs, and Alice wondered how she was supposed to fit into this freakshow.

She watched with narrowed eyes as Danny led Julio and Theresa to the dining room.

Danny had forgotten to tell her how to behave around his guests. Alice felt the urge to leave the house and get some fresh air, but she knew that as his girlfriend, she was expected to follow him and entertain the guests—as far as that was possible.

Danny had hired two cooks and waiters for the occasion since Henry wanted to spend the holidays with his family.

The staff had prepared the dining room nicely. The long table was covered by a thick white cotton cloth and a chandelier hung from the ceiling. The dishes looked elegant and expensive.

Everybody was holding a champagne glass when Alice entered the room, and Danny quickly handed her one as well. One of the waiters filled their glasses with ice-cold, sparkling, golden liquid, and Danny said something that managed to make Julio laugh, though it sounded more like a cough.

Alice's mind was already leaving the scene. She kept a smile on her face and clinked her glass with the others, though she had no idea what they were toasting to.

Get-togethers were dreadful to her, especially with people she didn't know. It was even more awkward because Julio seemed to be a sexist jerk, just like Waldo; but Danny had to kiss his ass and expected Alice to do the same. The good thing about sexist jerks was though: they didn't bother talking to women.

It was true, Julio didn't look at her once and Waldo ignored her as always. Theresa smiled at her shyly every now and then, but kept her distance, and Marion seemed to be in her own private world, her lips pressed together tightly. She put her glass to her lips from time to time, but apparently, she only wet them a bit, since her champagne never got less.

The sudden realization of what was going on hit Alice like a blow, ripping her out of her thoughts. She quickly glanced at Danny, who was just getting a champagne refill by one of the waiters.

He's drinking again!

Horrified, she stared at him while he put his glass to his lips. He sipped at it and then nodded toward the archway. "Should we sit down in the living room until dinner is ready?" he proposed to the guests.

Julio nodded.

"The fire is already lit, so we'll have it warm and comfortable," Danny added.

Julio left the room and Danny's eyes met Alice's. Confused by the look on her face he hesitated, then his gaze fell upon the glass in his hand, and he seemed to understand. He bit his lower lip and put the glass down on the table, then he gave her a quick smile, and followed Julio out of the dining room.

Waldo followed, but to Alice's horror, Marion and Theresa stayed behind. Were they not allowed to attend the conversation?

Alice felt her hands get sweaty. Both women were looking at her as if they expected something. Apparently, they thought of her as their hostess.

Alice blushed and her heart started racing. Theresa smiled at her warmly.

"Uh ..." she cleared her throat. "Just tell me if you need something, okay?" She smiled, but her smile died when she saw Marion's expression.

Awkward.

"You'll excuse me, I have to ... uh, check on something." The panic won and

Alice fled the dining room and hurried straight toward the entrance door. Danny, Julio, and Waldo were sitting on the sofas, talking about something, but it was neither business talk nor did it sound interesting.

No one looked up, so Alice sneaked out through the door and went to sit on a chair on the porch. It was freezing outside and dark; and she immediately started to shiver. A mouthful of her champagne didn't help.

A sudden movement in a dark corner of the porch made her jump.

"God, you scared me!"

Jonas grinned and exhaled a cloud of smoke. "Flattering, but you can call me Jonas."

Alice stuck her tongue out at him.

"Escaping?" he asked.

She nodded.

"Already?"

She shrugged. "I just ... don't really know what I'm supposed to do in there."

"Me neither." He took a drag on his cigarette.

The sound of a running engine announced a car approaching, and Alice watched as a silver Ford appeared in front of the gate. The guard opened it, and the car pulled onto the gravel square where Jonas's, Waldo's, Danny's, and Julio's cars were already parked next to a couple of other vehicles Alice didn't recognize. She assumed they belonged to the staff.

Paul and Tee got out of the Ford. Tee waved and smiled widely while Paul stared at the ground, avoiding Alice's eyes.

"Hi," she greeted them.

Tee walked over to hug her theatrically, then he and Paul went inside. They too had dressed up and were wearing suits, though cheap-looking ones.

"Did you dress up as well?" she asked Jonas, who was still standing in the shade.

Jonas stepped forward into the light and she eyed his outfit. He had replaced his ripped jeans with dress pants, but otherwise his outfit was the same as always, including the black leather jacket.

"I hate suits," he complained.

"And I hate skirts," Alice replied, before chugging her champagne.

Dinner was awkward, and Alice was glad there was a plate with food in front of her so she could keep busy. She ate extremely slowly, careful not to make too much noise and draw any attention to her. It proved to be an unnecessary effort since no one was talking to her anyway. She was relieved, though at the same time it made her feel worthless to be ignored like that.

Danny, Waldo, and Julio were having an intense conversation while Tee made a joke every now and then. Not his usual dirty jokes though—more polite ones—and Julio even managed to smile at some of them. Marion ate in silence, her stare glued to something in front of her, only she could see. Theresa ate quietly as well, her eyes fixed on her plate, though she looked up from time to time, as if she were pretending to be part of the conversation.

Paul and Jonas were both quiet too, but they followed the discussion with interest.

Everybody had a glass of red wine in front of them to flush down the Christmas goose, though Jonas never touched his and Marion only sipped at hers occasionally.

Alice ate a soy steak with her mashed potatoes, but she flushed it down with wine, nevertheless. Danny had been right—she was beginning to feel very warm. Her cheeks were flushed and sweat trickled down her back. She intensely hoped for no visible sweat stains on her blouse.

Danny's cheeks had also turned red, but Alice had forgotten to count the glasses of wine he had drunk. She could only hope it weren't too many already—at least he didn't look drunk yet.

"So, why did you say you moved away from the coast?" he was just asking Julio, while he put his glass to his lips.

"The weather was apparently too rough for my wife," Julio replied while wiping his sweaty forehead with his cotton napkin.

Theresa blushed and looked down at her plate.

"It is quite windy there," Danny agreed.

Julio shook his head. "Women are just sensitive."

Danny laughed awkwardly and nodded.

Alice glared at him, and when his eyes met hers, he mouthed the word "sorry", while Julio wasn't looking.

Shove your "sorry" up Julio's ass, your head's already in there anyway, Alice thought bitterly, and beckoned at the waiter to give her glass a wine refill.

"That was a success," Danny said later, when he lay in bed next to Alice, his arms crossed behind his head.

She frowned at him.

"Give them wine and they'll eat out of your hand," he continued, looking pleased with himself.

"So ... you're partners then?" she asked him without much interest.

He nodded. "Made him sign the contract right away, after dinner."

"Good for you." Alice rolled onto her side so her back was facing him and closed her eyes.

"You tired?" He brushed her arm with his fingers.

"It was a tiresome evening."

Laughing, he said, "Sorry babe, I warned you."

Alice bit her lip.

Guess he did.

"Are all the guys you work with such assholes?"

"That's *your* impression."

Turning onto her back, she looked at him from underneath. "Oh, come on, Danny! You must've noticed that Julio's a complete dick!"

"Oh, I have. But he's rich, and rich guys usually are assholes, aren't they?"

Alice stared at him. "You just told me recently that your main goal is to get rich."

"I'll be different, I promise." He grinned.

"That's not funny!"

Danny shrugged indifferently. "You're taking this all too serious, Alice, baby, let me just do my thing. It doesn't have to bother you at all."

"What bothered me is ... that I felt worthless the whole time. It was awkward."

Danny's eyebrow wandered upward. "'cause you're not part of the business?"

"Because I'm a *woman*, Danny, that's why!"

He looked puzzled. "Why would you think that?"

"It's not what I think, it's what *they* think," she explained impatiently.

He obviously had too many glasses of wine.

"Come on, Allie, you're exaggerating. Just because of the stupid comment about the coast?"

Alice sighed. "You just don't get it, Danny, 'cause you're a man."

"Then explain it to me." He sounded irritated.

Alice sat up and leaned her back against the wall. "How can you not even notice things like that?"

"Like *what*?"

"Like Marion and Theresa never saying a word, constantly doing what their husbands tell them, looking like they're servants rather than wives! They looked so ... *devote*."

Adding to Alice's frustration, Danny laughed. "You're being overdramatic, babe. They're just a bit old-fashioned."

Alice glared at him angrily, but she knew there was no point in arguing. Men weren't likely to understand these things and especially not when they were drunk.

"Whatever," she muttered, while rolling back onto her side. "Just never *ever* become like that, Danny, 'cause I sure as hell won't put up with it."

Chuckling, he switched off the lights. "Don't worry," he whispered while kissing her shoulder and softly caressing her arm.

"Good night, Danny," she said firmly.

"Aren't you forgetting something?"

"*What*?"

"Christmas sex?" He fumbled with her shirt.

"I'm not in the mood." She pushed his hand away.

"You will be," he insisted. "I promise."

13

No! Not again, please ...

"It won't be too fancy, but Julio and his wife will be attending again, and some other guys I'd like to have in my team." Danny leaned forward to kiss her. Alice quickly turned her head away to avoid his wine breath.

"A New Year's Eve dinner?" Alice stabbed her salad with her fork, more aggressively than necessary.

"More like a party." He took another sip of wine. "There'll be a buffet and we'll move the sofas to the wall to have more space in the living room."

Grimacing, Alice filled her mouth with lettuce. "To seal more contracts?" she asked, after having swallowed.

"No, rather to tend to already existing relationships."

He should tend to our relationship instead.

Sighing, she said, "Do I really have to attend?"

"You should show yourself and eat with us, but if you don't want to stay until midnight, it's your decision," he answered while cutting his steak. "Though it would be nice to start the new year with you by my side, like we've always done it." He looked at her with deep blue puppy eyes.

"We'll see."

Danny continued drinking every single day until New Year's Eve came. He didn't get wasted the way he had before the pool-thing had happened, but he always drank a glass of wine with his meals—white wine for lunch, red wine at dinner. And he always took a refill.

When Alice voiced her concerns, he laughed it off. "Do I look aggressive?" he asked her, pointing at his wide grin.

"No, you don't ... but you only stopped drinking for about six weeks and now you're back to drinking every single day. Danny, I like a glass of wine once in a while, or a beer, but not *every* day!"

He shrugged. "I'm not you."

"It's not about that. It's about you falling back into old patterns."
His expression turned hard at her words.
"I'm just worried," Alice admitted. "And scared …"
He had his arms crossed in front of his chest, signalizing his dislike of the conversation. "Of what?"
Alice remembered the day well enough, the fourth of November, her attempt to escape.
She had forgiven him because he never wanted to push her into the pool, and it was easy to pretend that the whole gravity of the situation was due to her fall—and not his fist.
Now, he seemed to be reading her thoughts, and his expression got softer. "I was trying to drown my sorrows in alcohol back then, honey, now I only drink when I'm in a good mood—that's entirely different." He kissed her.
Danny had never called her 'honey' or 'baby' or anything like that. His sole nickname for her had been 'Allie'. For some reason that had changed since last Christmas—much to her dislike. Despite finding it annoying, Alice chose to remain quiet about it.

New Year's Eve was tiring as well, though it was easier for Alice to avoid any interactions with people since there were quite a lot of them in the house.
No one noticed when she went to hide in her room from time to time to calm her nerves and charge her social batteries.
She wore a shiny blue satin dress this time, with skin-colored nylon tights. Since the tights were transparent, Alice had even bothered to shave for the occasion, which only added to her frustration. Danny had never cared about things like that before, but apparently, having a girlfriend who didn't fit society's idea of beauty was embarrassing to him.
Again, the house was dominated by men—dominant men, for that matter.
Julio and Theresa left before 10:00 p.m., and Marion drove off as well to go back to her children, leaving a drunken Waldo behind.
Danny had been drinking wine while the buffet had been open, but afterward, he had switched to scotch. Apparently, he'd found new friends with whom he stood by the lit fireplace, laughing and making jokes. Waiters were filling up empty glasses and cleaning away dirty dishes; the food had been prepared by two cooks again. Not knowing what else to do, Alice ended up drinking a little bit too much as well.

After Theresa and Marion had left, there were only two other women around, women who were older than Alice. They already knew each other, so they kept their distance to the rest of the guests. Alice didn't know whether they were girlfriends or maybe just escorts of two of the men in the room—maybe those who were busy talking and drinking with Danny.

The atmosphere was thick and heavy with testosterone, making Alice feel very uncomfortable. The later it got, the drunker the guests became, and some of them began to hit on her—probably due to the lack of other women.

When one of the men tried to grope her, Alice took it as a sign to go upstairs and hide in her room for good. There, she kicked off her shoes and was opening the zipper of her dress, when someone knocked on the door.

Without waiting for an answer, the door was opened, and Tee stood in the frame.

"You tired?" he asked her with a wide grin on his face.

"I was just about to change."

He shrugged, not understanding.

"Could you …?" she gestured to the door.

"Oh," he laughed. "Sorry, Lizzy, I'll let you get changed, of course … I was just wondering if you'd like to play some video game, 'cause I'm really not the party-type, and I'm looking for an excuse not to go down there again."

Alice considered the offer. She wasn't *that* tired, and it was only 11:20 p.m. "Okay."

Tee beamed. "So, are you still gonna put on your pajamas?"

She shook her head. "Nah, maybe Danny wants me downstairs for the countdown … I'll just keep the dress on." She started fumbling with the zipper. Getting it up was much harder than pulling it down.

"Should I?" Tee offered.

"Sure." Alice let him pull the zipper back up, then she turned on the console and TV screen. Tee let her choose a game while he went back downstairs to fetch a bottle of white wine.

When he came back, Alice had started *Need for Speed*.

They played for a while, while drinking wine and having a good time. Alice beat him three times in a row before he finally managed to win a round himself.

Time was completely forgotten when suddenly, they heard cheers and shouts from downstairs.

"Must be the countdown," Alice said.

Tee nodded and they toasted with their glasses of wine. "Happy New Year," he said cheerfully.

Danny never appeared and Alice tried not to think about him too much, since she suspected him to be utterly wasted.

At around 1:00 a.m., there was a knock on the door.

"Yeah?" Alice shouted over the noise of slithering tires on tar and howling engines.

The door opened slowly, and Jonas stepped into the room, looking from her to Tee and back to her again.

"Tired of the party as well?" she asked him.

Jonas said nothing.

Alice patted the mattress behind her with her hand. She and Tee were sitting on the floor while playing, their backs against the bed.

"Here, sit down," she offered.

Jonas stared at Tee.

"We could take turns," Tee proposed, a wide grin on his face.

Somehow, Jonas didn't look very amused by that notion.

"Isn't it possible to add one more player?" Alice asked, and crawled on all fours toward the TV, where more controllers were lying in a small cardboard box. Dizzy from the wine, she almost tripped over a cable.

Jonas cleared his throat.

Oops, my dress ...

Alice quickly tried to pull her short dress down with one hand, chuckling, but the movement made her loose her balance, and she fell to the floor and burst into laughter. Tee joined in and offered her some more wine.

"The bottle's almost empty," he noticed. "Should I get a new one?"

"Oh, yes," Alice gasped between laughter.

"You should go downstairs." Jonas's voice was ice-cold, and his arms were crossed in front of his chest.

"But ... I don't wanna go downstairs, Jonesy, I don't like it there," Alice protested, and rolled onto her stomach, to push herself up on her elbows. The room was spinning around her.

"I'm not talking to *you*," Jonas said, eyes on Tee.

Tee glared at him, though his lips were still smiling.

Alice watched the two men for a while, though there suddenly seemed to be four in the room.

"Are you having some kind of a beef?" she asked, then she giggled. "Funny word, *beef*..."

Tee turned his head toward her and laughed.

"Can vegetarians have a beef?" Alice wondered, her voice serious.

That made Tee burst into laughter and spill some of his wine. "And I haven't even taken out the weed yet!"

Alice's eyes widened. "You got weed?"

He nodded.

"I want some!"

"If Mister Bodyguard allows it." Tee nodded toward Jonas, whose expression remained hard.

"No, no, he's not a bodyguard," Alice explained. "He's just a guard, without the *body*."

Tears of laughter were running down Tee's cheeks now. "He looks quite solid to me."

Alice sat down on her butt and crossed her legs, which proved to be difficult with the tight dress.

"No ... I mean, he's just the guard-part, you know, he's *guarding*, not protecting."

Jonas was looking at her now, but she couldn't read his expression. It was hard enough when she was sober, but now it was impossible, especially because his face kept splitting up into two and then fusing back into one again.

"Danny's here anyway, so he doesn't have to neither guard nor protect, right Jonas?" She giggled again.

"I think you're making him mad, Alice," Tee warned her.

Quickly, Alice tried to stand up, holding on to the bed for support. She stumbled a few steps toward Jonas. "That wasn't my int ... my int ... tension, sorry, Joney."

The room spun like a merry-go-round.

"How much did we drink?" she asked Tee while holding a hand in front of her mouth. The alcohol in her stomach was revolting.

Tee shook the empty wine bottle, then grabbed a second one from behind his back. "We finished two up here, but I have no idea how much you already drank downstairs."

Alice tried to count the glasses she'd drunk on her fingers. "I didn't have that much ... I'm just not used to it."

"That's why you should go to sleep now," Jonas commented in a stern voice.

"No," Alice complained, "Not without the Mary Jane!"

"It's never a bad idea to smoke some, to calm things down," Tee explained, his eyes on Jonas.

"Stay," Alice told Jonas. "We need someone to watch us play. I feel like Tee's cheating."

"Tee *out*!" Jonas said in a voice that left no room for arguments.

Tee sighed theatrically and got to his feet, blowing a kiss toward Alice while he stepped out of the door. The atmosphere in the room changed immediately. Even drunk as she was, Alice could sense that Jonas wasn't in a good mood. Unable to keep her balance anymore, she quickly sat down on her bed.

"You should go to bed," he said.

"Don't patronize me!" she slurred.

"Someone has to, apparently."

Alice glared at him. "I can look after myself, thank you."

Jonas looked at her for a moment, without saying anything.

Irritated, she asked, "What?"

"You should be careful."

"Why?"

"Because drunken men can be dangerous ... *you* of all people should know that."

Shocked, Alice stared at him. Referring to what Danny had done to her, in such a cold and harsh way—it was extremely insensitive.

"Get out!" she snapped.

The room began to spin faster, and she took a deep breath, feeling her stomach convulse.

"Do yourself a favor and lock the room when you go to sleep," Jonas said.

Alice gaped at him, at his two faces which bounced up and down in front of her.

"Or maybe don't ... in case you choke on your vomit and need to be rescued," he added.

That guy was unbelievable. "You're an ass! Just leave!"

When he didn't move, she got up from the bed, and walked toward him to shove him out the door. "Maybe you should have some fun once in a while, that would loosen you up a bit."

Jonas sighed. "*Someone* has to stay responsible." He stepped out, but before Alice could slam the door shut, he said, "You should drink some water."

"I've been drunk before, Jonas, thank you very much."

She *should* have drunk some water, was the first thing Alice thought when she woke up the next morning.

She felt horrible, her head twice its size and throbbing violently, her stomach cramping. Daylight fell into the room since she had forgotten to shut the blinds the night before. It was faint, yet it blinded her. The sour taste of wine was still in her mouth and she felt dehydrated. Moaning, she rolled off the bed and crawled to the bathroom on all fours.

Grabbing the sink, she managed to pull herself up and fill a glass with water. Chugging it a little bit too quickly made her end up with her head bent over the toilet.

At least she was able to get the rest of the wine out of her system that way, and the nausea was gone afterward, though the headache remained.

This day would be spent in bed.

Danny joined her a little while later, looking about as bad as Alice was feeling. They shut the blinds, and opened the window to let some fresh air in.

After a couple more hours of sleep, they went downstairs to fetch some food, but Alice only threw it all up again. At least they were suffering together.

Alice was angry at Danny for having drunk so much, but now, she was definitely not in the right place to tell him so. It would have made her look like a hypocrite and she was sure Danny would just tell her the same.

Evening came and their stomachs were beginning to feel better, so they went downstairs again to cook something.

Jonas was sitting in the living room and looked up from his books when Danny and Alice walked by. He just stared at them but said nothing—even though Danny greeted him.

Danny's drinking habit remained the same even after New Year's Eve.

He didn't go back to drinking whiskey during the day, but he drank quite an amount of wine instead. Talking about it only annoyed him, so Alice tried to look the other way. She didn't want to provoke him, though his behavior really worried her.

The first week of January was almost over when Alice realized that her stack of the birth control pill had come to an end. With everything that had been on her mind there had been no room for things like that. When she wanted to start a new pack after her break, she noticed that none were left in the little box where she kept her personal meds.

It was Friday afternoon and Danny was downstairs in his office. Alice had never been in there and she had never disturbed him while he was at work before, but she absolutely did not want to risk not having any pills for the weekend, so she walked down the stairs and knocked on his office door.

Waldo opened and when he saw her, he called Danny, who looked a bit stressed out when he stepped into the living room and closed the office door behind him.

"What is it?" he asked in a concerned voice.

"Sorry for disturbing you, but I really need to go to the pharmacy today."

"What for?" Danny looked worried. "Are you sick?"

Alice quickly shook her head and lowered her voice when she realized that Jonas, who was studying in the living room as usual, was listening.

"I've run out of pills."

"Oh," Danny said.

"I just noticed now, and I have none left, so it's urgent."

Sighing, he scratched his chin. "Can't you just not take them?"

"No, it would mess up my cycle. I can't just skip a few days."

"What d'you want me to do then? I'm really busy right now." He didn't appear to be very interested in the matter, though Alice found it had to concern him as much as it did her.

"Well, I was hoping you could just quickly drive me to town."

Danny shook his head. "I'm really swamped right now ... ask Henry."

"Can't I just use your car? I don't want to bother Henry with this ... he's old and conservative."

Danny frowned at her. "I don't want you to go out here without me, you know that."

"I know, that's why I'm asking you to give me a ride."

Rubbing his forehead, he took a deep breath. "We're really busy today, I can't just leave."

"When will you be finished? Maybe the stores will still be open?"

He grimaced. "I doubt that. We've run into some problems ... it's urgent and it might take a while. Anyway, I really can't help you, just ask Henry. He hasn't done the shopping for the weekend supplies yet. Just tell him to stop at a pharmacy as well." Danny's eyes flicked to the closed office door, as if he couldn't wait to go back inside.

Resigned, she sighed. "Fine. I'll ask Henry."

Danny blew her a kiss and hurried back into his office.

For a few seconds, Alice remained standing there, staring at the closed door. She felt Jonas's stare on her. Should she ask him to drive her instead? He was younger and not religious like Henry, but Alice couldn't stand him and would prefer Henry's company over his at any time.

The cook was checking the fridge and writing the shopping list for today's dinner when Alice entered the kitchen.

"Good afternoon, Henry," she greeted him politely.

He looked up and beamed when he saw her. "Afternoon, Alice, how are you today?"

It had been a while since the two of them had last talked. When things with Danny had been tense, Henry had begun to keep his distance to avoid risking his job. Alice missed the talks they'd had before.

"How can I help you?" he asked her now, reading her expression.

"Well, uh ... I was wondering if you could give me a ride to the pharmacy, since you're going shopping anyway."

Henry finished his list and put it in the pocket of his corduroy pants. "Is uh ... Daniel okay with this?" he asked carefully. "I mean," he added quickly, "I would drive you wherever you want to go, Alice, but I don't want to risk—"

"Your job," Alice finished for him and nodded. "Of course, Henry, I would never ask you if things were still ... *complicated*, but they've gotten better."

"I have noticed that as well," Henry agreed.

"He actually told me to ask you."

"Oh well, in that case ..." He gave her a smile. "Meet me in the yard in five minutes?"

Alice hurried upstairs, where she quickly put on shoes and her winter jacket, and grabbed her wallet and pill prescription.

The prospect of going to town excited her; after all, she hadn't been there apart from that one time in the hospital and she would rather not think about that.

Driving through the gate, and by the farmhouses and fields filled her with a feeling of freedom. The day was cloudy, and it snowed from time to time, though it didn't stick.

After what felt like thirty minutes, they reached their destination. As soon as her feet touched the pavement, Alice felt the urge to run off and go see her friends, but she knew that she couldn't do that to Henry. Instead, she stepped into the pharmacy while Henry waited in the car.

"Hello, how can I help you?" the elderly woman behind the counter asked her.

Alice handed her the prescription. "I'd like another six months, please."

The pharmacist studied the piece of paper Alice had given her, and frowned. "I'm sorry, but you'll have to get your prescription renewed. This one is only valid until March."

Already?

"I can give you pills for three months instead," the lady offered.

"Sure, no problem. Thank you."

The more often Alice could go to town, the better. For a moment, she considered buying only a pack for a month, but pushed the thought aside. Better safe than sorry.

Shopping with Henry was fun. He let her choose what she wanted to eat on the weekend, and they talked about this and that while filling the shopping cart with supplies. Afterward, they stopped at a café to buy two coffees to go, which they drank in the car on their way back.

Henry parked his old beetle in front of the house, and heaved the shopping bags out of the trunk. Alice grabbed two of the bags herself, and lifted them up when she noticed someone walking toward them. It was Jonas ... and he didn't look happy at all.

"Henry," he called.

Henry looked up and closed the trunk.

"How about you finish early today?" Jonas suggested.

"Excuse me?" The cook looked puzzled.

Jonas took the bags out of his hands. "Take the evening off and come back on Monday morning."

Henry's expression was utterly bewildered. He looked at Alice, but she could only shrug.

"So, I will see you on Monday?" he asked carefully, looking from Alice to Jonas.

Jonas nodded.

"Okay then ..." Hesitantly, Henry got into his car and drove off, looking upset as he did so.

Alice opened her mouth to speak, but Jonas was faster. "Danny's pissed," he told her.

Alice felt her heart sink. "But ... why?"

"Just try to avoid him until he's calmed down," Jonas said, ignoring her question. He gestured her to hand over the two shopping bags she was carrying. She did. He carried them to the house and through the door while Alice followed him hesitantly.

Danny was waiting in the living room, pacing up and down and looking extremely angry.

"Where the fuck have you been?" he exclaimed when Alice stepped into the house.

"I was in town. I told you I was going."

"You think you can just sneak out of the house? How *dare* you?!" Danny approached her, but Jonas blocked his way.

"Calm down, mate," he said.

"Don't tell me to fucking calm down, Jonas! You had one job! ONE fucking job and you just sat there and watched her leave? What the fuck?"

Jonas put the shopping bags down on the floor, and held Danny back with both hands as he tried once more to reach Alice.

"It was a misunderstanding," he said calmly.

Danny tried to shove him aside. "Misunderstanding? What was there to misunderstand about me telling you not to fucking leave her out of your sight?!" He was shouting now, and Alice saw Waldo and Tee coming out of the office, observing the scene with interest.

"And what the fuck were *you* thinking?" Danny asked, his eyes fixed on Alice.

"It was a misunderstanding," Jonas said again.

221

Alice stared at Danny, horrified to see him snap like that again, and was glad that Jonas was standing in between them.

"You talk for her now?" Danny tried once more to push his friend out of the way.

"It really was a misunderstanding," Alice said quickly. "Danny, I thought you'd told me to go to town with Henry!"

"Bullshit! You know I would never let you leave without me!"

"You told me to ask Henry—"

"Ask him to get you what you need, not give you a lift!" They glared at each other for a moment. Alice was beginning to feel angry as well. "Why is this such a big deal for you? I'm back now, ain't I?"

Danny's eyes narrowed.

Jonas turned to face her. "Just go upstairs."

Alice bit her tongue. There were many things she would have liked to say to Danny as well as to Jonas, but she swallowed her anger instead and walked toward the stairs, carefully making a wide circle around her boyfriend, who was still being held back by Jonas.

During the rest of the afternoon, Alice stayed in her room and Danny never showed up—luckily.

At around 7:00 p.m., she heard a knock on her door and got nervous.

"Yes?" she asked, her voice higher than intended.

Jonas opened—of course. He was the only one who waited for a response after knocking. Danny would always just come in and other people usually didn't visit her—apart from Tee on New Year's Eve.

"Wanna come downstairs for dinner?" Jonas asked her.

"I thought Henry went home?"

Shrugging, he said, "You can still eat, right?"

The fumes finding their way out of the kitchen announced pasta and tomato sauce. It smelled too nice to have been cooked by Danny though.

Danny was already sitting at the table, drinking wine.

"You should've said something," Alice told Jonas. "I would've helped you cook."

He shrugged. "There's no point having too many people in the kitchen."

Well, he was right about that.

Danny didn't look up when she entered the dining room. Alice took her usual place beside him. Pots with food were set on the table and everyone served themselves—for which she was glad. The portions Henry gave her were usually too big for her appetite.

Danny's aura didn't feel very inviting. Alice could sense his anger clearly while sitting next to him. He ignored her and began eating as soon as he had filled his plate.

Tee and Waldo were having a conversation; the rest of the table, however, remained quiet. Alice watched her boyfriend empty one glass of red wine after another, never looking up from his plate. It made her feel very uneasy.

"I'm sorry," she told him quietly.

He put his fork down with a loud *clunk* that made her wince. "Don't pretend," he hissed.

"I'm not," she insisted. "I *am* sorry about the misunderstanding. I didn't want to worry you."

Danny still wasn't looking at her. "You're not sorry now, but you will be, if you ever pull anything like that again."

Shocked, Alice stared at him. "Are you *threatening* me?" Her voice was a bit too loud, and everyone at the table looked up at once.

"I'm *warning* you," Danny growled, his voice rising as well.

Now Alice threw down her fork. "I can live with you being *worried* about me—about my safety ... Fear for my life is what I can accept as a reason to not let me out of this house—but *threatening* me? I'm a human being for Christ's sake and I'll go wherever I want!"

Danny downed the rest of his wine and wiped his mouth with his napkin, then he finally turned his head to look at her. "Watch your mouth when you're talking to me in front of others!"

Is he fucking serious?

Alice pushed back her chair and got up from the table.

Danny placed his cotton napkin back down and got up as well. "How about an apology for destroying the mood?" he called after her while she was walking toward the archway, which led to the living room.

Whirling around, Alice shouted, "Fuck you, Danny!"

She turned back to the archway, and was about to storm out when he grabbed her arm and yanked her back violently; and before she knew what was happening, he'd slapped her.

It took her a moment to grasp what he just had done. Speechless, she stared at him with wide eyes. He had used his flat hand this time, but her cheek was burning, nevertheless. Her whole face was burning—though due to humiliation rather than pain.

Danny had slapped her in front of everybody.

Alice could clearly feel their eyes on her, though all she could see were Danny's angrily narrowed ones right in front of her. He was breathing heavily, and his fingers were painfully locked around her upper arm.

"Apologize," he hissed.

The humiliation finally made her avert her gaze and Danny let go of her arm, apparently taking it as submission. Alice grasped the opportunity and hurried out of the room.

Stumbling over her own feet, she almost ran toward the stairs, eager to get as much distance in between her and Danny as possible.

The tears came when Alice was back in her room, far from anyone's eyes.

It had happened again. He had turned into a monster.

Staring at the wall, she sat down on her bed, only too aware of her throbbing arm and burning cheek.

It wasn't the pain itself that was bothering her. But the pain was a constant reminder of what he had done, proving that she had not only imagined it.

How had she even been able to forgive him the thing with the pool? She hated herself for it now. Weakness had overpowered her; her loneliness had made her long for his affection. But the main reason for her to fall back into his arms had been the thing with Martin. It had made her insecure, emotional, and weak; and she had allowed Danny to take advantage of that.

Not this time, she promised herself. *I will not forgive him this time.*

14

Things began to feel way too familiar when Alice hid in her room throughout the weekend. Danny never showed up—neither to apologize nor to demand an apology from her. She could hear him walk through the corridor several times, passing her door to go to his bedroom.

At night, when she was sure that everybody in the house was asleep, she was able to sneak downstairs to fetch some food.

Otherwise, she kept her door locked at all times.

Danny's grip had left a bad bruise on her arm as expected, but nothing compared to the last time he'd hurt her.

Henry was back on Monday morning, and Alice felt safe enough with him around to go downstairs for lunch. Anita was in the house as well, so Danny would surely behave himself.

The table was set, and the men were already sitting around it. They looked up when Alice entered, but she avoided their eyes, still feeling embarrassed by what had happened. She left an empty chair in between her and Danny, and pulled her fork and glass toward her.

Henry looked surprised when he saw it, but he said nothing and casually laid down the plate in front of her. Danny ignored her, but Alice couldn't sense any anger coming from him, which was a good sign.

Nothing changed over the next two weeks.

Alice joined the others for lunch and dinner, ignoring Danny's drinking and the men's stares, eating quickly and quietly to return to her room as fast as possible.

She hated having to sit at the table with him, and the only reason why she did it was to show him that she would not put up with his behavior, and that she would eat at *her* table in *her* dining room whenever it pleased her and without having apologized to him. He didn't need to know that she only dared to do so with Henry around.

On the weekend, Alice hid once again in her room; though this time she was prepared, and had taken some cans with beans and some bread upstairs to keep her stomach satisfied.

Being locked in the house had been bad enough—not being able to leave her bedroom made Alice feel like a zoo animal in a way too small cage. It was driving her insane. Her longing for freedom grew so strong, she could barely breathe. Yet, she didn't dare to attempt an escape. The risk of it going wrong was too high.

On a late Tuesday evening, the twenty-third of January, Alice heard a knock on her door. Already having been half asleep, she opened her eyes, confused and worried. The clock showed 11:39 p.m.

Had she only imagined it? Clinging to her blanket, she remained lying on her back, staring into the darkness that filled her room. Holding her breath, she listened for any sounds that might come from the corridor. It was quiet.

Faint and almost hesitantly, the knocking appeared again. Was it Danny?

If it was, it meant he had stopped ignoring her. Was he willing to apologize? Even if he did, Alice had sworn to herself that she would not forgive him, not this time.

The best thing was surely to just pretend to be asleep. She closed her eyes, hoping for whomever was out there to go away. The knocking began a third time, softly, then she could hear the footsteps of somebody walking away.

With her eyes shut tightly, she tried to fall back asleep, and eventually managed.

That night however, she awoke with a loud scream in her head that seemed to echo in her skull. Covered in cold sweat, she opened her eyes, but Martin's dead face was still there, grinning at her viciously, blood dripping down his forehead.

Terrified, Alice jumped out of her bed and switched on the lights.

The face was gone.

Her heart was racing in her chest and her whole body was shaking. The images of Martin's death had been haunting her for more than six weeks now and she was used to the nightmares. But this was different—her head felt like it was about to explode.

A glass of tap water from the bathroom didn't help, and letting in some fresh air only made her shiver more. The walls of her room seemed to be moving in on her.

Am I still dreaming? She asked herself. Or had she just been spending too much time in her room? Maybe she really *was* going insane …

Quietly, Alice turned the key in the lock and pulled the door open, careful not to make a sound. The corridor was dark and scary but turning on the lights was not an option. The shadows of the furniture seemed to be monsters, waiting, lurking for her, ready to attack.

Alice told herself that she was being childish. After all, darkness was nothing but the absence of light and everything was still the same, even at night.

Swallowing her fear, she slowly found her way through the hallway, and down the stairs into the living room. She needed painkillers for her head and there were none left in her room, so she had to get some from the first aid kit which Danny kept in the kitchen.

The house was dark and empty, and everything about it was menacing. Only the porch light was on, shining weakly through the drawn curtains. At least it made the way to the kitchen visible.

Alice continued to move forward, and saw too late that the door to Danny's office was open.

"Alice …" The voice sounded strange, hoarse, and somehow distant.

Alice jumped, clutching her hands in front of her mouth to keep herself from screaming out. Her heart seemed to want to break its way through her ribs, thumping hard against them.

"Come in," the voice called, barely more than a whisper.

Trying to calm herself down, she stared in the direction from where it had come.

It's no ghost … Just somebody sitting in there.

"Danny?" she whispered breathlessly.

The person started laughing dryly, quietly. It sounded somewhat insane. "Who else?"

Frozen, Alice stayed where she was, hoping for her eyes to adjust to the darkness.

"Come in," Danny said, still quietly, almost whispering.

She heard him move, the squeaking of a chair and a soft *thump* on a hard surface. Was it a glass being put on a wooden table?

Taking a deep breath, Alice walked toward the office. "Why are you sitting in the dark?" she asked him in a low voice.

"That's where I belong," he answered, his voice husky.

Oh fuck it, I'll turn on the lights. He's up anyway.

Alice switched on the light in the living room and it was bright enough to enlighten some parts of the office as well.

Danny was sitting in a black leather chair with a high lean and armrests. His desk looked expensive, made from massive wood with thick legs that had a similar kind of scrollwork like the table and chairs in the dining room.

He had his long legs stretched out underneath the desk, and in front of him stood an almost empty bottle of whiskey and a glass.

He looked horrible.

His dark curls were sticking to his forehead in thick wet strands—or were they greasy? Alice couldn't tell. He was pale, apart from his nose and his eyelids, which looked swollen and red. His eyes were staring into his empty glass, as if he were hoping to find the solution to all his problems at the bottom.

"What are you doing?" Alice whispered, concerned—despite what he had done.

Danny didn't look up. His hand wandered to the whiskey and he drank the rest of it straight from the bottle. It was a heart-wrenching sight.

Forgetting her anger, she bit her lip, pitying him and wondering what she could do to help him. He looked lost and depressed ... broken.

She couldn't help herself and moved closer. He reeked of sweat and alcohol and the remains of a cologne, which he had probably put on days ago and never properly washed off. Had he even showered lately? He sure didn't look so.

"What do you want?" he asked in a voice that was thick with grief.

Hesitating, she stared at him. "I ... I just came downstairs to fetch some painkillers for my head."

"They're gone."

"What do you mean?" Alice spoke softly, not wanting to provoke him.

He closed his sad blue eyes and began breathing heavily, as if his lungs had troubles functioning.

Alice noticed that his face looked grayish and a layer of sweat glistened on his forehead. He looked like he was about to throw up.

"Danny ...?"

"They're gone," he repeated. It sounded like speaking cost him a lot of effort. "I ate them."

"You did *what*?" Alice took another step toward him and put a hand on his shoulder carefully, the way you would approach a dog that might bite you. He didn't even seem to feel it.

"Danny, talk to me," she urged. "What's going on?"

Moaning, he put down the bottle, which fell on its side with a loud *clunk* that made her flinch. Pill wrappings were spread all over his desk, between sheets of paper that looked important but had stains of whiskey on them.

"It's no use."

"What's no use?"

Danny opened his reddened eyes and gestured drunkenly at her. "This." A grin appeared on his face. "Everything. It's pointless."

Perplexed, she stared at him. There it was again, that insane laugh of his.

"You know, Alice, I've realized something." He scratched his unshaven chin and closed his eyes again.

"What?" What was he talking about?

"When you're down ..." He pointed at the floor. "Down there, on the carpet ... or no carpet, doesn't matter ..." He cleared his throat and started coughing. "When you're down there ... you can't get any lower ... Right, Alice?" His eyes opened for a second, looking at her, then he shut them again. "Can you, Alice? You can't ... fall any lower. You can't fall, when you're already down, you know ..."

He's crazy. He's completely insane.

"Down where, Danny? What the hell are you talking about?"

Again, he pointed at the floor. "There, Allie, down there ... hell, yes ... *hell*, that's what it is, it's where I am. I'm in hell, Allie."

"Why would you say that? I thought ... I thought you got everything you wanted?"

Sighing, he grabbed the bottle, put it to his mouth, but realizing that it was empty, he let it fall back on the desk loudly. "Oh, yes. I did ... I do, but everything comes at a price. Am I supposed to be happy when everything I ever wanted comes at a price? I fucked up, okay ... I fucking fucked it up." His voice was trembling, but it got louder. "I thought ... money, that's what I need—money and power and influence, influence to change things ... things need to change, Alice, they can't stay that way, they just can't!" Sobbing, he buried his face in his hands.

Alice patted his shoulder weakly, not knowing what else to do.

"But what if you could change things and make money with it? What if that was possible?" He looked up at her. His eyes glistened under a layer of tears. Alice had never seen them look so sad.

"What are you talking about?" she asked once more, her voice hollow.

"I wanted to be a hero, Alice, that's what I wanted ... Fame, success, people looking up to me ..." he trailed off, lost in thoughts. "Everyone wants to be a hero," he continued after a pause. "Everyone."

"Danny ... what the fuck did you do?"

Another dry chuckle came over his lips. They looked dry—his lips—and fissured. "I was a hero, Allie, I was the Dark Knight." He fell silent, staring into nothingness. A tear escaped his left eye and ran down his cheek.

"What happened?" she whispered, squeezing his shoulder.

"I thought I was the Dark Knight ..." His voice was barely audible. "But then ... I realized that I'm the Joker."

There was no doubt about it: He was nuts.

"Are you on drugs?" she asked him.

Slowly, he shook his head. "Just some painkillers, some whiskey ... that's all I need, Alice. I don't need no drugs."

For a while, they were both quiet, Danny with his eyes closed again, leaning back in his chair. Alice's gaze was glued to him and she felt paralyzed, unsure of what she was supposed to do.

"I'm a monster," he said suddenly.

It took her off guard. Was this about him hitting her?

"Why ... what do you mean by that?"

"I'm no hero, Alice, no hero ... Never was, never will be. I made a huge mistake, a huge, huge mistake ... I'm a monster!" He started sobbing again and his hand wandered to the top drawer of his desk. He pulled it open, and took a small silver object out of it.

It was a knife.

"Danny what—"

He snapped it open.

"Put that away!"

Laughing again, he stroked the sharp edge of the blade with his thumb until a drop of dark red blood appeared on his skin. "I should push that through my ribs ... yes, that's what I should do, push it through my ribs and be done with all of this."

Horrified, Alice followed the movement of his fingers with her eyes. "Put it away!" she urged.

He looked up at her. "Why? I'd do us both a favor."

Shaking her head, she put her hand around the knife, trying to wind it out of his grip. "No, you wouldn't. Don't be stupid for god's sake, Danny, just give me the knife!"

Alice felt the blade cut into her hand, but she refused to let go. A sharp pain flashed through her palm, then it started burning.

"I deserve it," Danny insisted, but his grip around the knife finally loosened, and she was able to take it away from him and snap it shut.

"What is *wrong* with you?" She wiped the blood off on her pants, but more followed instantly.

"Me, Alice, that's what's wrong with me ... I wanted to be a hero ... became a monster ..." He buried his face in his hands once again and sobbed.

"We ... we can work it out, I promise!" She crouched down next to him.

"No, we can't ... I wanted to see you earlier, but you ignored me, didn't you? You kept your door closed, trying to keep me away—don't you, Alice? Try to keep me away?" He looked at her accusingly, but then his head dropped back down into his hands. "Who could blame you ... I'm a horrible person ... Who would want to be with me? I can't blame you for hating me, how could anyone not hate me?"

Alice's heart broke at his sight. She had never seen him so vulnerable, so lost. "Danny, please ... don't be like that. We can work it out, I promise you! You ... You're not like that, it's not you, darling, it's not the way you are ... it's the situation, your business, the stress ... your drinking ... There's therapy for that, facilities ..." She tried to sound positive and brushed his sticky hair out of his face. "Danny, you can get better, I know it."

"What's the point?" he whimpered. "You hate me."

Alice swallowed dryly. "I'd forgive you," she managed to say. "If you stopped drinking—for good this time—if you gave up your business and went back to doing something legal, back to a normal life ... if you could do that for me, I would forget everything that's been."

His beautiful dark blue eyes were fixed on her face. "No," he whispered.

Surprised, she stared at him.

"No," he repeated. "I'm already lost and nothing I could ever do would make up for the things I've done ... *nothing* ..." His tears had dried out and his expression was now hard and cold ... and bitter.

"Don't say that, Danny ... There's still hope. I promise you; I'd forgive you."

He laughed a hollow laugh. "I don't need *your* forgiveness." He nodded to the dark corner of the office. "I need *theirs*."

Shocked, Alice whirled around at once, expecting to see someone standing there, but there was no one, only darkness. "What ... who are you talking about?"

"They're haunting me, Alice, every day and every night ... No matter if I'm asleep or awake, they're always here ..."

"Danny ... *who* are you talking about?"

Has he become paranoid?

She studied his expression, but mental illnesses were usually not visible on someone's face.

"I don't even know what they look like, Alice, but they're here, haunting me ..."

Again, she turned around, just to make sure, but still no one was there.

"Who, Danny? *Who* is haunting you?"

He looked at her, his expression dark, as if his true face were hidden behind a veil. "The people I killed."

Something ice-cold seemed to trickle down Alice's spine. She stared at him, her eyes wide, her mouth half open. Her thoughts were racing.

What had he just said? Had she heard him right?

It must all be a misunderstanding, or maybe he *had* taken drugs, LSD, probably—or something similar. He must be on a bad trip, thinking he had killed someone, talking about ghosts haunting him ...

A nervous laugh escaped her lips. "That's not funny, Danny. Don't say things like that." Her voice was shaking.

He shook his head sadly. "I knew it, Allie. Not even you could forgive me something like that. How could you? I can't even forgive myself ... I'm a monster!"

Slowly, Alice straightened up and took a step backward, carefully avoiding any quick movements. "You didn't ... I'm sure you'd never ..."

Silence. He said nothing, but the look on his face said it all.

She felt her stomach turn. "Danny, please, I know you didn't mean that ... I know it! Is this about Martin? Are you ... blaming yourself? He tried to kill me, there was no other way ... Danny, it's okay. He had to die. Don't blame yourself, you're not a killer!"

She knew it before he said it.

"It has nothing to do with Martin."

"But ... what is it then, why would you say that you ... *killed* somebody, why would you say that?"

He sighed. "Because it's true. I killed them."

"No, no ... You're talking nonsense ..."

It can't be true ... Or could it?

"Please, just tell me what happened. You can tell me, I'll understand!"

"No, you wouldn't."

It wasn't Danny's voice. The voice came from behind her.

Alice screamed and jumped, but Jonas quickly put his hand over her mouth and gestured her to be quiet. He pulled her away from Danny and out of the office, where he made her stand still.

Alice's heart was racing, and she was gasping for air by the time he removed his hand from her mouth. Terrified, she stared at him. Did she know too much? Was he going to kill her now?

His eyes wandered to the knife in her hand. Right ... the knife. She quickly snapped it open.

"Don't touch me!" she warned him, holding the knife out in front of her protectively.

Jonas grimaced and took it out of her hand without any effort. The metal slipped right through her bloody palm.

"I wasn't going to," he muttered.

Alice waited for her heart to slow down a bit. "What ... are you going to do with me?" she asked breathlessly.

Frowning, he said, "You should go to bed."

Is he serious? Danny just confessed he's a murderer!

"Are you not going to ...?"

"To what?"

Biting her lip, she stared at the knife in his hands. There was a gun tucked in his belt as well.

"Kill me?" she whispered.

Jonas looked puzzled. He closed the knife and let it slip into the pocket of his jeans. "Why would I wanna kill you?"

Danny was babbling in the office, she could hear him, but his words made no sense. It sounded like he was saying *monster, monster* over and over again.

"Because ... I heard things ..." She swallowed dryly. "Things that ... I probably shouldn't have heard ...?"

Jonas stared at her and Alice was under the impression that he was very tired somehow.

"There will be a time for explanations, but it's not now," he said firmly. "Just go to bed."

Her eyes flicked to the office, where Danny was still talking to himself.

"I'll take care of him," Jonas said. "And don't worry," he added, more friendly, "I most certainly won't kill you."

There was no way Alice could have slept that night. Danny's words kept haunting her and she kept brooding over them, trying to understand what he had said.

He killed someone ...

It made no sense. Danny would never do such a thing. But then again, was he still the same person? He hadn't acted like himself at all lately, and she had gotten the impression that this—his new self—was not just a phase.

He had said that he had killed *people*, as in more than one person. Danny had also said that he didn't know what they looked like. How could you kill somebody without knowing what they looked like?

Lying on her back, Alice stared at the ceiling. She had kept the light in her room on to keep Martin's face away.

Oh God ...

There *were* ways to kill people without having to look at them, and Danny had talked about wanting to be a hero. He wanted things to change. Only, what did that mean? Could he have committed an act of terrorism? Alice had thought she knew his view of the world well and that they agreed on most things—ethically, politically ... but if he was able to kill to reach his goals, their opinions differed more than she would have ever expected.

Her mouth and throat turned dry at that thought, and she had to get some water from the bathroom. Terrorism had many faces, but she couldn't imagine it looking like Danny.

No ... it had to be something else. If he had wanted to kill somebody, he would not be so beaten up about it. It must have been an accident. Maybe he'd just wanted to blow up an empty building and then something must have gone wrong.

Still, even if that assumption was true, it meant a giant act of violence. Could he really have done something like that?

Alice tried to think back to the beginning of their relationship ... had she been too blinded by love to see the red flags? Or had there been none?

The questions tormented her all night long, and it had been daylight for a while already when she heard car doors being slammed.

A glance out the window revealed that Waldo's car was parked in front of the house, its doors open. Tee was standing next to it, leaning casually against the vehicle. Jonas was also there, smoking and ... there was Danny. He was carrying his black duffel bag and a jacket under his arm. He and Tee shook hands, and then Alice saw Jonas patting Danny's back and exchange a few words with him.

After that, Danny and Tee got into the car and drove off, leaving Jonas standing alone on the gravel.

Alice quickly ran downstairs, taking two steps at once. She was only wearing her nightshirt and a pair of Danny's boxers in which she sometimes slept – but it didn't matter. Panting, she reached the living room just as Jonas stepped back into the house and closed the door behind him.

"Where did he go?" she exclaimed, before trying to catch her breath.

Jonas was still smoking. He didn't seem to care that Danny hated the smell inside the house. Slowly, he turned around to look at her, then shrugged. "He'll be back in a couple of days."

"That wasn't my question!"

"But it's my answer," Jonas replied curtly. He walked past her and toward the stairs.

"What was going on last night?" Alice called after him.

Jonas ignored her question.

"Jonas, please!" she begged. "I'm worried. I need to know what's going on!" Suddenly, she felt completely out of place, like a dice on a chess board. This wasn't her game. Nobody explained anything to her, and nobody gave a damn about *her* part in this story. It was almost as if she didn't even exist.

Jonas had stopped though, and sighing, he turned around to look at her. "I'm sorry," he said, and it sounded like he meant it.

Alice spent the whole morning crying into her pillow, hating her life, hating her room in that stupid house with the stupid alarm system and the stupid wall around the yard. Hating Jonas, who was always making sure that she couldn't run away.

Her visions of Martin's corpse got worse. They intruded her mind, eating their way through her brain like a disease, chasing away every sane thought, and playing in her head over and over again, like a never-ending horror movie. Sometimes, Martin's dead face changed into Danny's or Henry's—or even her mother's—with stares just as accusing as his had been. Alice began to feel claustrophobic in her own room, even though she had the key to the door.

Why couldn't she just forget that dreadful night with Martin? She had seen violence in movies—plenty of times. She had seen blood and guts and bones and people getting shot. Why was it so different when it happened in real life? And why was it only affecting *her* so badly? Jonas didn't even seem to feel the slightest amount of guilt and Danny hadn't mentioned the corpses once, and Alice was pretty sure that they had buried them somewhere—at least Martin's.

I'm too fucking emotional, just like Jonas said.

How was she supposed to survive in a world like this? With a boyfriend like Danny?

Her hunger was nonexistent, but at 1:00 p.m., there was a knock on the door and Alice knew that lunch must be ready.

"I'm coming," she called through the locked door, not knowing whether she was talking to Henry or Jonas.

The table had been set for two and Jonas was sitting there, typing on his phone. Alice took her place and gave Henry a weak smile when he brought her plate.

His cooking was surely fabulous as always, but somehow, the look and smell of the food on the plate before her made her nauseous. She picked at her food while Jonas ate in silence. Henry noticed of course and she saw him glance from her to Jonas when he collected Jonas's empty plate. His eyes seemed to be asking 'everything okay?' but his mouth remained closed.

"I'm sorry," she said to him, feeling bad about wasting the food he had cooked for her.

"No worries, Alice. Maybe you should stay in bed today. You look pale." He took her plate away. "I'll leave it in the fridge, and you can tell me if you're hungry later, so I can warm it up for you."

Alice thanked him and even managed to give him a smile.

The cook went back into the kitchen, and she quickly got off her chair and left the room to avoid having to endure Jonas's presence longer than necessary.

Time seemed to be creeping by slowly ... very slowly.

Alice kept staring at the clock in her room, only too aware of the annoying ticking sound it made. She stared at it as if that could make the hands move faster. What was she even waiting for? For the evening? For Danny's return? For her life to be over?

Alice avoided dinner altogether. There was no point in going downstairs to stare at her plate. She knew she couldn't stomach any food right now.

The sun disappeared on the horizon, and the darkness it left behind made her feel extremely uneasy. It felt suffocating, heavy, and persistent, as if it would never go away again. Even the light in her room didn't help. On the contrary—it was way too bright and made everything around her seem unreal, as if she were in a dream. Soon enough, Martin's image was back and turned the dream into a nightmare. Whenever she closed her eyes, she saw blood and accusing eyes staring at her. When the walls began to move and shadows seemed to dance around her, her heart started racing at once. Without knowing what she was doing, Alice stormed out of her room and ran downstairs, where she found Jonas studying by the lit fireplace.

Curious, he looked up, but she avoided his eyes and went to sit on the couch opposite him. The fire crackling and spitting had a calming effect, and she managed to slow down her breathing.

"You need help?"

Alice shook her head and closed her eyes. Jonas's eyes were fixed on her, she could feel it, but she didn't want to look at him.

They sat there in silence for a while, with only the sounds of the fire and the occasional rustling of pages being turned.

When she heard a book being closed, Alice looked up and saw him piling his study books on one another, preparing to leave. She stared at him with wide eyes.

"Night," he said.

Her thoughts were racing. There was nothing she wanted less than being alone right now. Already, she could feel Martin's face creeping back into her mind.

"You okay?" he asked when her breathing accelerated.

"I just ..." Her voice broke.

He kept staring at her. "Spit it out."

Her mouth was dry. Alice swallowed and tried to find the right words. "I ... I feel like ..." What was she supposed to say? That she was crazy? That she was terrified of memories in her head?

"How can you do this?" she asked instead.

"Do what?"

"Be so ... calm about everything ... Turn off your emotions." Avoiding his eyes, she stared into the flames.

"Is that what you want?"

Alice nodded. "He's driving me crazy," she confessed.

He sighed. "There's really nothing I can say to that." Grimacing, he rubbed his knuckles against his forehead. "Just give him time."

Confused, Alice looked at him. "What? Oh ... no, I'm not talking about Danny."

"Then who—"

"Martin."

Staring at her, he said nothing.

Great. Now he knows I'm insane.

"Still?" he asked her at last.

Nodding, she said, "It got worse."

"Well ..." Jonas glanced at the books in front of him, and Alice suddenly remembered that he majored in psychology. Feeling embarrassed, she blushed. She didn't want him to think she needed a private session. But then again, maybe he *could* help her.

Thinking, he looked at her with an unreadable expression, but then he took his pack of cigarettes out of his pocket, gave one to her, and took one for himself. He lit them both with a match.

Memories of the last time they had smoked together flashed through her mind. It had been the night he had shot Martin. Alice inhaled a bit too quickly and started coughing.

Since it didn't seem as if Jonas would talk, she decided to break the silence.

"How ... How can I get rid of it?"

Jonas exhaled a perfect ring of smoke. "Face it."

She frowned.

"Face it as what it is: a memory. An image of something that has passed and can't hurt you anymore."

"How?"

"Don't let it scare you. Don't try to fight the memories, but don't obsess about them either. Just let them come and go."

Alice stared into the fire and saw Martin's accusing stare in the flames. "It's his face," she explained. "I see him, covered in blood and his eyes ... they're staring at me ... like ... like he's blaming me or something."

"Perhaps you blame yourself."

Chewing her lower lip, Alice kept staring into the flames, wondering if he was right. "But ... I know he had to die."

"Your brain knows it. Your compassion tells you otherwise."

"I'm too weak," Alice muttered—more to herself than to him.

"It's not every day you see someone die. Give it time."

Sighing, she pulled her knees up to her chin and wrapped her arms around her legs. "So ... you think he'll disappear?"

"Next time you see him," Jonas flicked his cigarette butt into the fire. "Laugh at him."

Somehow, Alice felt a rush of affection for him. There he was, giving her honest advice on her seemingly pathetic problems. And she had hated him with all her heart for keeping her under his watch. She smiled weakly. "I'll tell him to fuck off."

Jonas nodded.

They remained sitting on the couch for a while, not talking.

The warmth of the fire began to make her drowsy and Alice closed her eyes.

Martin's face was there, in front of her, but somehow, the threat it had imposed was gone. It was just an image, a memory. Nothing dangerous about it.

Daylight woke her up and Alice blinked. It took her a moment to realize where she was. The fire had burned down but the room was still warm, and she noticed that she had been covered with a blanket.

There had been no nightmares, no scary images haunting her, no waking up covered in cold sweat. She glanced at the empty sofa opposite her. Jonas must have left after she had fallen asleep, which meant she had slept all alone in the living room. And she hadn't even felt scared.

Now, her stomach was rumbling. That made sense since she hadn't eaten anything the day before.

The two meals she had missed were still in the fridge, and Alice ate one of them cold, right out of the plastic container. Afterward, she went upstairs to take a shower and get dressed.

This time, she went downstairs for lunch and dinner, and managed to eat, though she couldn't finish her plate both times.

Her stomach still felt very sensitive, and the mere thought of Danny made her nauseous.

Jonas was back to his quiet self and Alice didn't know how to start a conversation with him, so she remained silent as well. She wanted to thank him, but the words were stuck in her throat and wouldn't come out.

The weather was nice on the days of Danny's absence. The sun was shining, and its rays reflected off the snow which covered the landscape like a thick white blanket. It glistened and sparkled in the sunlight, and it made everything appear peaceful and silent. It was a beautiful sight and it managed to have a soothing effect, though Alice still couldn't stop thinking about what Danny had told her.

The people I killed.

The thought made her shiver. She found herself drawing sketches of human corpses and felt like a psycho. Sighing, she put the drawing pad down and leaned her head against the rope of the swing. Her fingers felt stiff and frozen from drawing outside in the cold, and she rubbed them together to generate some heat.

Suddenly, the noise of an engine ripped her out of her thoughts, then the big iron gate was opened, screaming in the hinges, and Waldo's Mercedes appeared in the yard.

He's back.

Alice felt something cold run down her spine and shivered again. What would Danny be like?

It was Monday, the twenty-ninth of January, which meant he had been gone for almost a week. Alice watched the car pull onto the snow-covered gravel parking space. The engine was killed just as Jonas appeared on the porch. He walked toward the vehicle, whose doors were opened by Danny and Waldo.

Danny looked different. His walk was stiff and upright, and Alice noticed with disappointment that he had cut his hair.

He promised he wouldn't.

Instead of shaking hands or patting his back, Danny just gave Jonas a nod. The three men then disappeared inside the house and Alice remained on her swing, still shivering.

She didn't see him until dinner that day.

This time, she arrived in the dining room before him, and had already sat down when he entered. He took his place next to her and sat down stiffly, without a word of greeting. His skin looked pale and there were dark shadows underneath his eyes. His lips were shut into a thin line.

Alice's appetite was nonexistent again and she played with her food, not taking her eyes from her plate.

No one talked. The atmosphere in the room was tense. There were no conversations, no remarks, no jokes—not even coming from Tee.

Alice fled as soon as Henry had taken her plate away—this time without commenting on the food that was still on it.

Danny never showed up at her door, and the next two days were the same.

He was drinking as always, but somehow, he seemed calmer. His movements were stiff and slow, as if he was concentrating very hard on not making too much noise. Indeed, he was very quiet. Not only to her, but also toward his friends. He answered questions with a nod if possible, or else with only one or two words. His voice sounded cold and hollow.

There were not many questions to be answered anyway. His appearance seemed to not only make Alice feel uneasy; his friends looked intimidated as well.

On the third day after his return home, he came to her room at around 9:00 p.m. He simply walked in without knocking and closed the door behind him silently.

He looked scary the way he towered over her, his back straight, his cheeks shaved neatly, his white dress shirt ironed, and the heavy golden watch shining around his wrist. His now short hair made him look stern and imperious.

He was still handsome—to some people now probably even more than before—but his face had lost its softness and there was nothing cute about him anymore. The warmth had left his eyes as well.

Alice stared at him, looking up from underneath him and somehow, it felt as if she was realizing only now how tall he was.

"Are you ... feeling better?" she asked him in a toneless voice.

His expression didn't change, but he nodded.

"What you said ... you ... did you mean it?"

His lips remained shut.

"You gave me quite a scare that night ..." Alice laughed nervously, trying to fill the awkward silence.

Danny looked at her coldly; every sign of affection toward her seemed to be gone. Had he stopped loving her?

Biting her lip, she studied his expression. He looked like an entirely different person.

Alice's whole body tensed when he started walking toward her. She was sitting on her bed, her drawing pad next to her—after another session of drawing obscure corpses.

He came to a halt in front of her and she stared at his shirt, not daring to look up and meet his eyes. The smell of cologne on his clothes couldn't quite hide the whiskey on his breath, but he seemed to be in control of himself. His hand moved toward her face slowly and she flinched, but he only stroked her cheek.

There were no hints of anger or aggression in his features and yet, he looked threatening. Alice had no idea why she felt so scared. Her heart had started to race when he'd touched her.

"Are you scared of me?" he asked without any trace of emotion in his voice. He moved his fingers along the lines of her face and twisted a strand of her hair around his index finger, which he then brushed behind her ear.

"Look at me," he ordered.

Slowly, she looked up, chewing her lip nervously.

It felt like there was a stranger in the room, nothing about him was *Danny* ... He smiled, but there was no warmth in it.

"You look ... different," she said quietly.

"I feel different."

"You ... You were a mess ... that night, I mean."

He nodded.

"What ... what has changed?"

He shrugged. "I've been able to solve my problems." His eyes wandered across her room. "What a mess," he said. "You should put your things in order."

Alice said nothing.

He took her arm and pulled her off the bed to make her stand up. Her heartbeat accelerated. He pulled her head to his chest and started caressing her hair.

Even his embrace felt different. There was no love in it and Alice felt as if she were hugged by a man she had never met before. The intimacy made her feel uncomfortable, but she didn't dare to move.

"I'm sorry I slapped you," he said while running his fingers down her back.

Surprised by the sudden apology, she held her breath.

"I don't like being insulted." He sounded as if he were explaining something obvious to a young child. No one liked being insulted, that was explicit, but the way he said it made it clear that he meant it as a threat. His fingers moved down her spine and over her butt, which made her shiver.

When she didn't answer, he took his hand away from her thigh, and lifted her chin with one finger to make her look at him again.

"I think we can get along well if you respect my requests." Again, it sounded like a threat.

Alice felt all color drain from her face.

"Do you think you can do that?" His stare was piercing and evoked goosebumps on her skin.

Unable to argue, she nodded. Her feelings toward him had changed since the night he'd told her that he had killed ... Everything about him was intimidating ...dangerous.

She half expected him to pull out a knife without a warning and stab her to death.

"Good girl," he said.

Alice could have slapped him for that – if she hadn't been so terrified.

"I will be gone more often now," he said, still with no trace of emotion in his voice. He pressed her head back against his chest and continued playing with her hair. "I have more work outside of this house and I expect you to not give Jonas a hard time." He squeezed her, but there was nothing affectionate about it.

"I won't," she promised tonelessly.

"He told me about your nightmares."

Alice winced.

Danny bent his head down and kissed her forehead. "I'm sorry you had to go through that," he spoke, his lips resting against her skin. "I promise you, that as long as you do as I say, I will make sure you're safe. Always." There was nothing comforting about his words. "I'm sure you can see why letting you out of this house is too big of a risk. We don't want to risk another thing like that happening to you, do we?" He stopped caressing her hair and she knew he was expecting an answer.

She shook her head.

His fingers started to move through her hair again, and she knew he was satisfied.

They stood in silence for a while, him hugging her, breathing into her hair. Alice didn't dare to move, but she was beginning to feel calmer now. She was rather sure he would not just explode and hurt her, even though his threats had unsettled her.

"Danny," she began carefully.

"Hm?"

"What happened ... with these people ..." Trying to steady her voice, she took a deep breath. "The ones you said ... that you ..."

His hand stopped moving at once and she felt him tense. Dreading his reaction, she chewed her lip nervously.

"Mistakes were made," he answered after a moment of silence. "But it won't happen again."

Alice felt her stomach contract painfully.

He'd said it so casually, as if killing someone were just something that could happen occasionally. His answer wasn't of much use to her, but she knew it would be unwise to chew on the subject.

He moved his hand down her body again, this time in the front. It tickled and she shivered again, but it wasn't the good kind of tickling; it felt like the tickling of a fly or bug walking on her skin, and she felt the urge to shake his hand off.

His fingers found the edge of her shirt and moved underneath it, then upward. Alice closed her eyes, shutting them tightly, trying to focus on something else.

This is my boyfriend touching me, she tried to remind herself. *This is my boyfriend, Danny, the man I love. It is all right for him to touch me.*

Not even her thoughts sounded convincing.

"Will you sleep in my room tonight?" he asked her, and she felt something move in his pants. "We should sleep in the same room more often, Alice. After all, we're a couple, aren't we?"

She nodded hesitantly.

He loosened the embrace and pulled her toward the door, his grip firm. "Ready for bed?" he asked—meaning if she had brushed her teeth already, but there was another meaning to the question, and it made her stomach turn.

She had never been less ready.

"I'd like it if you wore your nice clothes more often," Danny told her while they were sitting over lunch. The atmosphere was still tense.

Her appetite nonexistent, Alice only managed to eat a few bites of her lasagna.

His eyes were wandering over her body, taking in what she was wearing, and he screwed up his nose at her black hoodie and ripped jeans.

"After all, I bought them for you, and I feel that effort was wasted if they just keep hanging in your closet, being eaten by moths." He took a sip of his white wine and put the glass back down, eyeing her intensely.

Again, his words had sounded like a threat.

I don't want to wear those ugly clothes.

"Do you think you can do that, Alice?" His eyes narrowed and she knew, the longer she didn't reply, the angrier he would get.

"I'll wear them." Her voice was barely more than a whisper.

He nodded approvingly and took another sip of his wine.

Alice had noticed that everything he did, he did differently. His movements were not only slow but also elegant and formal. There was never even one drop of wine spilled or a stain of sauce on the table after he had eaten. He carefully placed a cotton napkin on his lap before every meal and he dabbed his mouth with it after eating, barely touching his lips when he did so.

She also couldn't see the alcohol having any effect on him anymore. Drunk or sober, his behavior was always the same. Cold, distant, stern. Even the color of his eyes seemed different. They looked darker somehow, like deep, dangerous holes that could swallow a person whole.

Tee never made jokes at the table anymore, and there were no conversations about football or video games or even about the weather.

There were only *"Could you pass the salt?"* and *"Pass the wine bottle, please."*

Henry never said anything and quickly collected the plates after every meal, carefully avoiding coming too close to Danny. He gave Alice a worried glance from time to time, seeing that she hadn't eaten up, but he didn't dare to say anything with the boss around. His job was hanging by a thread, he knew that. After he had given Alice a lift to town, Jonas had kept Danny from firing him, but there would be no second chance.

The only sign of the alcohol affecting him, which Alice noticed over the next couple of days, was that Danny seemed to lose control of his strength, the more he drank.

His grip around her arm was way too tight when he pulled her toward him, trying to tell her something or just wanting to hug her, and he often left bruises on her skin—apparently unintentionally. When she told him, he would always apologize, but he never seemed to truly care about having hurt her.

At night, Alice would sleep in his room, and having his arms around her felt like being in a cage—and what always came before that was torture.

Although his touch was usually tender and he waited for her to get physically ready before entering her, she never enjoyed it, not even a bit. Out of fear, she would always endure it though and just wait for it to be over.

On the second weekend of February, Danny left for two days, together with Waldo and the others. Jonas remained home as always, his job being to watch her.

With Danny gone, Alice dared to put on her old clothes for a change to feel more comfortable, and when she ran into Jonas in the living room, he asked: "New look?"

"Old look," she replied. "Feels better."

"Looks better," he said, winking.

Hesitating, she stared at him. "You won't ... will you?"

He shook his head. "I won't tell him."

Danny came home earlier than expected on that Sunday evening, and when he stepped through the entrance door, accompanied by a stranger in a noble suit, his tired eyes fell upon Alice, who had been reading a book in front of the lit fireplace—wearing an oversized hoodie and old, holey leggings. Alice knew she was in trouble, by the look he gave her. Without saying a word to her, Danny led his guest to his office and came back into the living room alone, closing the office door behind him. Alice quickly got off the couch and waited tensely for him to approach her.

"You're early ... I wasn't expecting you yet," she muttered when he reached her.

Instead of an answer Danny gave her a slap that left her face burning as if he had lit it on fire.

"Go change," he commanded. "We are going to have dinner together when I'm done here."

Alice barely saw where she was going through the veil of her tears while she hurried upstairs to her room. With shaking hands, she grabbed Danny's favorite blouse from her closet as well as a skirt, hoping it might calm him down. Racing thoughts and trembling fingers made getting dressed harder than usual, and Alice fumbled with the belt of her skirt, fighting against the tears that threatened to run down her cheeks.

Why am I even doing what he says?

She had no answer to that question. All she knew was that ever since he had returned from his last trip, he had been radiating with danger. Everything about him was threatening. It was hard to read his expression, and therefore she could never be prepared for what he was about to do. It had been different before, when he had used to get drunk from time to time, trying to drown his sorrows in liquor. Back then, he had been aggressive and impulsive. He had still been Danny, however. Now, it was as if he were a different person altogether—cold, distant, merciless. He could have a smile on his lips and squeeze her arm so tightly it made her eyes tear up; then again, he could look angry and brush her hair softly out of her face. It was a constant gamble to try and keep him happy, and losing meant getting hurt.

Right now, Alice found herself shaking with fear, which only made her clumsier and made her take way too long to put on her clothes. When her sweaty fingers finally managed to close her belt, the door was opened, and Danny stepped into her room.

Horrified, Alice watched him approach her while the door fell shut behind him.

"Looks like I'm a bit late," he said casually.

What was he talking about? Frozen, she stared at him, like a deer staring into the eyes of a hunter.

"I was hoping you'd still be naked." He stretched his arm out toward her, and she jerked away from him, expecting him to hit her again. Instead, his fingers found her cheek and caressed it lightly.

"Sorry about that." There was no sign of guilt on his face. "I'm weary from the trip, and you embarrassed me in front of my client. He has left now though."

Alice closed her eyes and waited for him to take his hand away from her face.

"Are you hungry?" he asked.

"No," she managed to say, though her voice was thin and barely audible.

His lips tightened.

"But I'll sit at the table with you," she added quickly.

Her plate contained a small piece of bread and a bit of salad, which she ate slowly, chewing every bite way longer than necessary, hoping, Danny would be finished with his dinner before her. That way, she wouldn't have to eat up. Her stomach was fighting every bite she swallowed.

Danny's eating habits had gotten more sophisticated. He sat upright, elbows never on the table, eating slowly, flushing down his food with red wine from time to time. He managed to make it look as though he were only sipping the wine and yet, after only a couple of minutes, his glass would already be empty, and he would take a refill.

"I'm thinking about hiring another cook," he said after putting down his empty glass for the third time.

"What's wrong with Henry?"

"Nothing." He wiped his lips on his napkin. "I just don't like having to cook for myself on the weekends."

Alice said nothing. As much as she liked Henry's food, she was always glad for the weekends when she could eat as much—or rather as little—as she liked.

Sometimes, she just wanted to eat a bowl of cereal in front of the TV and not have to dress up for lunch and dinner.

"What do you think?" Expecting an answer, he looked at her.

"I ... I don't really care. I like Henry's food, but I don't mind having to cook either." Or not having to eat at all ... but she didn't need to say that. Danny had already noticed and criticized that she was getting thinner, but the constant nausea, she experienced, was caused by stress, and the biggest stress factor in her life was him.

He shrugged, signalizing that he didn't really care what she thought. Alice suspected that he only tried to make her talk because the two of them eating in silence was awkward.

"I'm expecting guests in a week," he said while giving himself another wine refill. "Next Sunday, February eighteenth." He took a sip from his glass. "You know them. It's Julio and Theresa."

"So ... tending to the relationship?"

He nodded. "Things have been going very well with Julio. He has a lot of experience and ... money."

Alice put her fork down on her plate and took a sip of her water. "Is he funding your company?" she asked, faking interest.

"He's funding certain projects of my company, yes." Looking full and happy, he sighed. "Should we go upstairs now?"

Alice felt the color drain from her face. They had spent the weekend apart, which meant he had certain needs.

He did. As soon as they had brushed their teeth, Danny peeled her out of her clothes quickly and started to kiss every inch of her body his lips could reach.

Alice quickly switched off the lights before he pulled her into bed. It was better with the lights out. That way, she could pretend he was still the long-haired, round-faced metal head with whom she had fallen in love.

Though his new cologne made it hard to imagine him like that.

The week passed by, and Danny spent most of the time in his office while Alice sat alone in her room.

Sometimes, she took walks through the snowy yard, though walking around the house made her feel like a prisoner walking rounds in the prison yard. The guard by the gate would always look up when she came around the corner, and then again when the next round was finished. The house was big, but it didn't take long to walk around it.

The security guards had recently gotten a small hut next to the gate, which was heated, and one of them would always open the window and wave at her when she passed him.

She felt like he was mocking her.

Jonas kept his distance when Danny was home, but he still took his job seriously and always kept an eye on her, especially when she was outside of the house.

Alice didn't mind him that much anymore, after all, he had been nice to her during Danny's absence. Tee was also nice, always smiling at her encouragingly—but only when his boss wasn't looking. Spending time with him on New Year's Eve had been fun, but so far, there had not been a chance to do it again.

On Sunday, February 18, Danny seemed very aggravated.

He yelled at the cooks, who were preparing the meals, at the staff, who was in charge of making the dining room look more elegant and inviting, and even at his friends or colleagues—or whatever he liked to call them now.

Alice still hadn't figured out the hierarchy of her boyfriend's company, though there was no doubt now that he was the boss.

Throughout the morning, she tried to avoid him and his anger, and during lunch, she felt as if she were sitting on hot coals, shifting uncomfortably in her chair, hoping to make it through the meal without somehow provoking his anger.

The table had already been prepared for the dinner. A white cotton tablecloth with golden embroideries on the edges covered the wooden surface. They ate using the less expensive dishes, however.

When her plate was almost empty at last, Alice put her fork down and got up to flee to her room. Danny grabbed her arm though and held her back.

"You're in a hurry," he noticed, his voice sounding irritated.

"I just ... need to pee," Alice lied.

Without letting go of her arm he took a sip of his wine. "It's impolite to leave the table before everybody else is finished," he lectured her in a low voice.

"I'm not the first one," Alice objected indignantly. Jonas and Waldo had already left as well. Only Tee, Paul, and Danny were still sitting around the long table.

"Doesn't matter. I'm still eating," Danny said curtly.

Alice tried to pull her arm out of his grip, but the sudden movement made him spill some of his wine on his white, perfectly ironed dress shirt. He stared down at the stain and Alice felt his anger boil up again.

"I'm sorry," she apologized quickly. "I'll fetch a cloth from the kitchen."

"You want to wipe off the stain with a dirty kitchen rag?" He looked at her with one eyebrow raised, but it didn't make him look cute anymore.

Alice blushed, realizing she had no idea how their new expensive clothes had to be handled. Good thing they had staff to do the laundry now.

"I'm sorry," she muttered again, not knowing what else to say.

He let go of her arm and got up from his chair to go and change his shirt. Hesitantly, Alice followed him out of the dining room. There was no point staying in there with just Tee and Paul.

At the bottom of the stairs, Danny stopped and turned around. "Do you have any idea how expensive this shirt was? Not to mention the tablecloth, which was meant to last through tonight's dinner."

"Well ... good thing you only drink white wine for lunch. Imagine if I had made you spill at dinner."

It was meant to be a joke, but it was naïve of her to think she could loosen the tension between them. Her sarcasm only made him snap and he did what he always did these days—he hit her in the face. This time, he used the back of his hand and his rings felt especially painful on her skin.

"How dare you mock me?" he hissed through gritted teeth.

Before he could strike her again, Alice rushed past him and ran up the stairs, taking two steps at a time. Once in the corridor, she slowed down into a walk and tried to fight back tears of pain and humiliation that burned in her eyes.

The sound of quick footsteps behind her made her whirl around. He was hurrying after her, apparently not being done with her yet.

Fear spread through her body, like ice-cold water running through her veins. Terrified, Alice stared at him, frozen in place. His eyes were on her and there was a fury in them that made her throat tighten. Before she was able to grasp a clear thought, her instincts made her break into a run. He darted after her, his footsteps muffled by the carpet but still clearly audible. The door to her room stood ajar and Alice fled into her seemingly safe chamber and tried to lock the door behind her.

He was faster. Before she could turn the key in the lock, he pushed down the handle and crashed into the door with what seemed to be the full weight of his body, making it fling inward. The impact blew her away and hot pain emerged in her shoulder where the door had hit her. She backed away quickly as he stormed into the room, his face contorted by anger, looking as if he were about to attack her like a wild animal.

Panicking, she backed away farther, but the bed blocked her way, and she stumbled over it and fell onto the mattress. Alice quickly pushed herself back up into a sitting position, clutching her burning cheek and watched helplessly, as he took a step toward her. Her eyes were widened in horror, and she felt like a weak and injured antelope about to be eaten by a lion.

The lion stopped though and stared at her, and she saw something flicker in his eyes, an emotion that didn't match his features. Was it regret? Guilt? His expression softened slightly and if she hadn't known better, she could have sworn that he looked ashamed. Almost as if seeing her tremble in fear of him had somehow evoked his compassion. The look on his face made her feel ashamed herself. What had she expected? That he would beat her bloody? That he would rip her throat open with his teeth? He was still her boyfriend and he loved her, didn't he? Her mouth felt dry, and Alice tried to swallow the knot that had built up in her throat. Her cheek was still burning, but now not only because of the pain.

I'm acting like he's a monster ...

Biting her lip, she averted her eyes and stared at the floor in front of her, ashamed of her fear of him. For a while, everything was quiet apart from his heavy breathing and her own panting, and the ticking of the clock on the wall next to the door. The tension in the room felt suffocating and when he finally spoke, she cringed.

"I'm going to take this," she heard him say.

Curious, Alice looked up and saw him holding her key in his hand. His features had hardened again.

"I don't even know why I haven't taken it away from you already." He put the key in his pocket. "Our guests arrive at five. Be dressed and ready in the living room by then." He turned and started to walk out of the door, but then he hesitated. "And put some makeup on, will you? You look pale these days."

Alice watched him close the door and took her hands away from her face. Her eyes seemed to be glued to the spot where Danny had just been standing seconds before, but when she finally looked down at her hands, she realized there was blood on them.

A look in the bathroom mirror revealed that Danny's obnoxious emerald ring had left an ugly cut on her cheek.

Dressed and with makeup on, Alice stood next to Danny and greeted Julio and his wife, Theresa, who had just stepped through the entrance door. They had both dressed up for the occasion—or at least Alice assumed so, but it was hard to say since she had no idea how rich people dress on a normal day.

Julio greeted her stiffly, but Theresa gave her a warm smile.

They drank champagne in the living room, Alice and Theresa staring down at their feet while Danny and Julio talked about things they had bought or planned to buy with their money. The main topic was cars, and it could not have been any more of a cliché.

It didn't matter what they were talking about though, since Alice had managed to drift off into her dream world where Danny had no place and her thoughts could roam free. Being alone most of the time had made her realize how easy it was to get lost in thoughts. Especially with having to deal with Danny's libido a place to escape to was most welcome.

Thanks to the men being so self-absorbed, no one cared as long as she was physically present.

Alice noticed though that Theresa had not gotten any champagne and at dinner, there was no wine glass in front of her either.

The news was brought to them during the meal. Proudly, Julio announced that his wife was pregnant. Everybody showered the pair with profuse congratulations, and Alice shut off her mind once more to escape the uncomfortable situation.

I just hope this doesn't give Danny any ideas.

Absentmindedly, she scratched her itching cheek, imagining herself raising a child in this prison called home with a man like Danny. The child would probably not survive long. He would lose his patience and hurt it, like he hurt her.

Feeling nauseated by that thought, Alice continued playing with her food when Julio suddenly said: "You're bleeding."

Only when all heads turned and all eyes were fixed on her, did Alice realize that he had been talking to her. "Excuse me?" she asked, feeling herself blush.

"I said you're bleeding."

Having been so deeply lost in her thoughts and imaginations, it now took her a moment to understand what he meant. Slowly, her hand moved up to her cheek and she could feel something warm and wet there. Her eyes widened at once.

I scratched it open, she realized, panicking.

"It's fine. It just looks like a scratch," Theresa said warmly while handing her a cotton napkin. Alice took it and pressed it on her bleeding cheek. She could feel Danny's eyes on her and wondered what he might be thinking. The way he had acted that day, he would probably kill her for destroying the evening.

Forcing her trembling lips to smile, she pushed back her chair. "I- I'll just go and wash it off, you'll excuse me."

The guest bathroom was the closest to reach and Alice quickly closed the door behind her, gasping for breath. She checked her reflection in the mirror and realized, horror-struck, that the blood had dripped onto her expensive cream-colored shirt. Unable to think clearly, she tried to wash it out with water, which only turned the small red stain into a big pink stain. Tears started running down her cheeks.

Now he'll definitely kill me.

Alice knew how important this dinner was to Danny and even the slightest mistake would be punished. Everyone had been so happy with Theresa's news. The mood had been good, but she had managed to destroy it all by simply scratching her stupid cut open.

Sobbing, she buried her face in her hands and tried to steady her breathing. The air in the bathroom seemed too thick to breathe and it began to make her feel dizzy. The light was too bright, reflecting off the white tiles, sending bolts of pain through her skull. It burned in her eyes and blinded her. Struggling for air, she looked back up and stared at the pale woman in the mirror. She looked like a ghost. Makeup was running in streams down her face, making it appear as if she were shedding black tears.

A sudden knock on the door made her wince.

When she didn't respond, the handle was pushed down, but Alice had locked the door.

"Alice, honey? Are you okay?" Danny's voice sounded loving and concerned.

Of course. There were guests in the other room, and he needed to put on a show. Not opening the door would only embarrass him.

Her fingers were damp and shaking when she turned the key in the hole and took a step back. Danny opened and to her surprise, he even *looked* concerned, despite no one being there to see it.

"Honey are you all right?" he asked again quietly. He closed the door behind him and took a step toward her. Feeling threatened, Alice backed away.

"What happened to your face?" His hand reached her, and he softly stroked her neck.

"I- I'm sorry, I ruined the shirt," she stammered in a shaky voice.

His thumb brushed over the cut on her cheek and he examined it. Suddenly, his expression changed, and he froze as comprehension flickered in his eyes.

"Did I do this?" He looked at his hand and at the rings on his fingers. "I'm so sorry," he whispered and started to dab her cheek lightly with a tissue.

"It's nothing," Alice said quickly, leaning away from him. "I just ... it started bleeding again and it went on the blouse ... it's really nothing."

"You don't look like it's nothing," Danny objected and a deep worry line appeared on his forehead.

Alice's eyes flicked back to her reflection and she wished for the floor to open and swallow her whole. Almost furiously, she tried to wash off the blurred mascara by rubbing her hand against her skin, but Danny took her wrist gently and held her hand. "I'm sorry, Allie, I should not have done that."

Avoiding his eyes, she stared at his shirt instead. Now, when there was a bit of blood, he genuinely apologized ... but what about the countless other times?

"Why are you crying? Does it hurt?"

Shaking her head, Alice tried to pull her arm free, but he held her firmly—though not in a hurtful way.

"I can't do this," she admitted in a shaky voice.

He seemed to misunderstand. "Maybe you should just lie down? Get some rest ... I know you hate events like this. Just go upstairs and I will find an excuse for you."

He seemed honestly worried, and Alice was rather sure he would not attack her when there were guests in the house.

Tell him! Tell him he's an asshole.

Her mouth was dry. "It's not that ..."

"What is it then? Talk to me."

No anger was visible in his features, but he seemed to be growing agitated with the guests waiting next door. Now was not the time for honesty.

"Never mind," she muttered instead. "I'll go upstairs."

Danny put a hand on her shoulder and led her out of the bathroom and toward the stairs.

"Will you be all right?"

She nodded, still avoiding his eyes.

He planted a kiss on her forehead and brushed her hair behind her ear—then something caught his eyes. Frowning, he looked up.

"What are you doing?" he asked Jonas, who was standing next to the kitchen door, leaning against the wall with his arms crossed in front of his chest.

"My job," Jonas answered coldly, in a tone that didn't befit him.

"And what would that be?" Danny asked, his eyes narrowing.

"Watching."

"You don't have to do that when I'm here."

Jonas shrugged. "You told me to protect her."

"Like I said, I'm here now."

Jonas's eyes narrowed as well. "I'm aware of that."

Alice's eyes flicked from her boyfriend to her *bodyguard*, following the silent battle they seemed to be having. It was hard to read Jonas's features as always, but she knew that what he had said had another meaning, something Danny didn't seem to like.

Had he implicated that he would protect her from Danny?

So far, he had never intervened when Danny had hurt her, but then again, it had not happened often before his eyes.

Confused, she stared at the two men in front of her until Danny broke the stare-battle with Jonas and turned his head back to her. "Just go upstairs and I will check on you later, okay?"

Alice turned and walked up the steps, listening carefully, but neither Danny nor Jonas said any more.

It was eleven when Danny came into her room that evening. Alice had already been asleep, but the sound of the door opening woke her up immediately.

"Theresa gets tired a lot these days," he said while undoing his shoelaces. "The pregnancy, you know."

Alice nodded, not caring.

"So, they went home already, but again I'd say it was a success." Exhaling happily, he sat down on the mattress beside her. "Are you feeling better?" He posed the question as if she had the flu or gotten sick. Staring at the ceiling, Alice remained silent.

"They are nice people, you know. You don't have to be nervous around them." He caressed her arm lightly with the tips of his fingers, evoking goose bumps on her skin.

"I'm not ... I mean, I wasn't ..."

"Hm?" He looked surprised. "You looked quite scared."

Alice took a deep breath and wondered if it was safe enough to tell him the truth. "I wasn't scared of ... *them*."

Danny bent forward to kiss her and she quickly turned her head away from him, her heart drumming against her ribs.

"I was ... I'm ..."

"What is it?" he urged.

"It's you ... You're scary," she whispered.

Taken aback, he stared at her. "I'm sorry for what I did today. I didn't intend to hurt you."

"Today?" Alice pushed herself up into a sitting position. "It wasn't just today it's ..."

Danny's whole body seemed to stiffen, and his features turned hard. There it was, the moment she had dreaded. The moment he got all cold and distant, and it was impossible for her to predict his next move. She fell silent and stared down at her blanket.

"You make me angry sometimes and I am not proud of what I did, but sometimes, I just don't see any other way."

Was that his explanation?

"*Sometimes*? Danny, my mere existence seems to make you angry."

He frowned at her. "We have good moments all the time, don't we?"

"Good moments? Please don't tell me you're talking about our ... *nights*."

Judging by the look on his face, it was exactly what he was thinking.

"You never complain," he said coldly.

"As if you would ever respect my wishes!" It was hurtful. His ignorance, his way of pretending everything was okay when she cried herself to sleep every night after he had finished with her. It was more than she could take.

"You never said anything," he insisted, his eyes darkened by the hardness that lay within them.

Alice inhaled sharply. "You want me to say something? Fine ... I don't want to have sex with you, not since last Christmas. I've never wanted it, and the only reason I let you do your thing was because ... because I was scared you ... you might ..." Her voice broke and she struggled to find the right words.

Aghast, he looked at her. "I would never!" he protested angrily. "Alice, I'd never ... I wouldn't *force* you!"

She wasn't convinced. "You *forced* me to move here with you. You've *forced* me to live here. You've *forced* me to wear the clothes you bought for me ..." Worried, she fell silent when she heard him grind his teeth.

"You're being ungrateful. If you had just accepted me being in control for a change, everything would be all right. You're always so determined to resist me, to resist everything that comes from me. You're always trying to be *different*." His voice had not risen. Apparently, his new manners kept him from yelling, though his anger was clearly audible and his eyes glistened dangerously in the semidarkness.

"*You* changed, Danny, not me. We were okay before—no, we were great—until *you* decided to turn my world upside down."

He glared at her, his hand twitching. He balled it into a fist. "You're a difficult girl, Alice. You're hard to handle."

"I'm a human being. I have a free will and wishes and ... *rights*. I've got faults as well. If you can't handle that, maybe you should just buy yourself a sex doll."

There it was. The switch had been flipped and Danny's sophisticated and well-mannered mask dropped. He bared his teeth and grabbed her wrist, pulling her toward him.

"You're provoking me on purpose!" he hissed, squeezing her arm in a painful manner.

"No ... Like I said, even my presence seems to make you angry." She grimaced as he tightened his grip around her wrist even more. "Why don't you just let me go? I don't want to be here! I never wanted to."

Pain flickered in Danny's eyes. Her words had hurt him.

Alice didn't care. "I'm not your girlfriend, I'm your prisoner."

He was breathing heavily now, flaring his nostrils, glaring at her with veins sticking out on his forehead.

"Let go of my wrist, you're hurting me!" She tried to pull back, but it made him snap. He pushed her back onto the bed, her wrist still tightly locked in his grip.

"Let me go!" Struggling, she tried to push him away and off her. When he didn't move, she kicked out from underneath him and managed to hit him in the stomach with her knee.

"Get off!"

Danny sat on top of her, pinning her down with his knees, and when she tried to pull him off by grabbing his shirt with her free hand, the buttons sprang off and the shirt ripped.

Growling madly, he grabbed her neck right underneath her chin, pushing her head sideways into the pillow. Alice was sure that her jaw was about to break, and tears of pain blinded her.

"My prisoner?" The look on his face was one of plain madness. "You ungrateful little cunt!" His voice was shaking with fury, but still, he kept it low.

Alice whimpered in pain when his grip around her jaw tightened, but speaking was impossible.

"I can treat you like a prisoner if that is your wish," he threatened.

Not daring to look at him, she shut her eyes tightly. His hot breath was on her face.

After what seemed like an eternity, his grip finally loosened and she gasped, desperate for air. He got off her, leaving her lying on the mattress, gasping for breath and not daring to move.

When he remained standing next to the bed, his breathing slowing down, Alice turned onto her side slowly, pulling her knees up to her chest, and buried her face in the pillow to hide the tears from him.

"I don't want to have to do this, Alice." The sound of his voice made her wince. "I really wish we could just get along, but you're making it impossible." He brushed through his hair with his fingers and tried to rearrange his ripped shirt. "Two shirts you destroyed today—no ... with yours, it's three." He sounded thoughtful. "Is this you acting out on me? Trying to protest my rules? If so, I'd say it's rather childish, don't you think?"

Alice lifted her head from the pillow and glared at him. "You're mad, Danny, you're fucking insane!"

He laughed, a bright cold laugh that seemed to rain down on her like drops of ice-cold water and made the little hairs on her neck arise.

His face got dead-serious when he said, "I'd be careful if I were you."

Alice quickly dropped her gaze, not wanting to provoke another physical attack. Her jaw hurt awfully, and she could barely open her mouth to speak.

Danny gave her one last warning look, then he turned and left the room, locking the door from the outside.

Again, she was locked in.

The darkness seemed to devour her, and the only way to prevent another panic attack was to let the fear get flushed out of her with the tears that she silently cried into her pillow.

The door remained locked the next day and Alice stayed in bed with the blanket up to her chin until shortly before noon, when she heard the key turning in the lock.

Danny's face appeared in the door. "You can come down to eat. Cell's now open," he said with cold sarcasm in his voice.

Alice felt nauseous and she absolutely did not want to sit next to him. When she didn't move however, he said, "That was not a request. I am leaving tomorrow morning for a longer business trip, and I expect you to come downstairs and have lunch with me."

Slowly, Alice pulled the blanket off her body and sat up. Danny wrinkled his nose at the black T-shirt she had slept in.

Hesitantly, she got off the bed, and carefully moved toward the closet while his stare weighed heavily on her shoulders.

When he shook his head at the dark blue blouse in her hands, she put it back and went through the hangers with her fingers, nervously checking what else she could wear.

"How about something happy for a change?" he suggested.

Alice froze and stared into the darkness of the closet.

"The pink dress would be nice, don't you think?" He moved closer and looked over her shoulder and into the closet, breathing down on her neck, making the little hairs there stand up. Her heart started racing when he reached across her and grabbed the hanger with the light pink cashmere dress. He held it to her breast, examining the appearance and nodded approvingly.

"Wear this," he ordered.

At least he was kind enough to let her change in peace, and Alice checked her reflection in the mirror afterward. Danny's hand had left a dark purple bruise on her neck and jaw.

Trying to hide it with a lot of makeup made her look like a doll and she shook her head in disdain. Frustrated, she washed it all off again. Why would it even matter? Danny's friends knew what was going on, and apart from Henry, no one in the house cared. Somehow though, Alice felt ashamed of the bruise, as if it was her fault Danny treated her like that. His friends would just think that she had done something to deserve it. Had Danny gotten 'how to treat your girlfriend'-tips from Waldo?

Everyone was already sitting around the table, and she kept her eyes down when she entered the room and took her place next to Danny. As soon as she felt his aura, she tensed.

The food was served, and Alice took a few small bites to soothe her rumbling stomach, but the nausea made her end up just playing with her food again.

"You should eat more," Danny told her quietly while the others were discussing something else. Biting her lip, Alice stared at the fried potatoes and vegetables on her plate.

"A little meat wouldn't hurt you." Was he talking about the food or about the meat on her ribs?

She said nothing. Sighing, he took a sip of his white wine. Then he filled a glass for her and held it under her nose. "Drink that, it has calories."

Alice frowned at him. Was he mocking her now? It made her wonder how many glasses he had already drunk before lunch.

When she didn't move, he leaned toward her.

"Drink," he muttered into her ear. "It will loosen up your tight ass." His breath smelled strongly of wine and she jerked away from him. Nevertheless, she took the glass and put it to her lips.

Satisfied, he smiled and toasted. "Cheers."

The smell of the wine made her almost-empty stomach tighten and she bit her tongue. Danny was staring at her, expecting her to drink. She took a deep breath and chugged the wine in one go, then put her empty glass back on the table with a loud *clunk*.

"Happy?" she hissed.

He nodded and gave her a refill. "Now I'd say if you don't want to get drunk, you better start eating."

Alice gave him a hateful look, but obeyed and put a heavily spiced potato in her mouth. Carefully, she chewed it. It felt dry and sticky on her tongue and almost made her gag, so she washed it down with more wine.

Maybe I should always just drink with him. It makes him more bearable.

Alice noticed that everyone at the table had fallen silent and Jonas and Tee were looking at her while Waldo was looking at Danny.

Danny lifted his glass up and made a toast to them as well. "Cheers my friends, to our trip tomorrow morning, our escape from this cold and ugly weather."

Tee and Waldo answered his toast hesitantly while Paul kept staring at his plate and Jonas frowned.

Surprised, Alice looked at Danny. "Where are you going? Somewhere warm?"

He ignored her.

"I thought ... Are your trips always abroad? I thought you weren't going far."

"They're trips, like the name says, and depending on whom we're meeting, they are in different places." Danny put his glass down and continued eating. "Now keep your mouth shut and let us eat."

Glaring at him, Alice downed her second glass of wine. "Oh, I'm just concerned you might actually be going on vacation somewhere, to drink Cuba Libre underneath palm trees, while I rot here, freezing my ass off."

"That would be a shame," Danny sneered. "I like your ass." He took another sip of his wine. "And it would be unfair to Jonas, since he's staying here with you." Half-smiling, he glanced at his friend, but Jonas ignored him.

Wow, things are tense between those two.

Alice looked from one to the other and wondered what was going on.

Tee laughed nervously. "He doesn't drink Cuba Libre anyway, so no big miss there." He winked at Alice and she grimaced in response.

"Where *are* you going?" she asked him.

Scratching his chin nervously, Tee looked at Danny, whose eyes narrowed. "I told you to shut up, didn't I?" Danny snapped at her.

Biting her lip, Alice stared down at her food.

"Damn I should not have given you any wine," he muttered.

Alice drank four glasses of red wine during dinner. It *did* make it easier to stand Danny and time seemed to pass by quicker. Her cheeks were flushed with heat and the wine was making her drowsy. At least she had managed to eat half of her meal this time and the nausea had become bearable.

Danny watched her drink and seemed amused by it, always eagerly refilling her glass as soon as she was done. Apparently, he had already forgotten what he had said at lunch, about not wanting to give her any more wine.

"Are you trying to make me drunk?" Alice asked when he was about to fill her fifth glass. Quickly, she put her hand over the wine glass, trying to stop him from filling it.

"It's our last evening together before I leave." He tried to take her hand away, but she kept it on the glass.

"Don't be overdramatic. You've gone on business trips before."

Irritated by her attempt to stay sober, he gave her a narrowed-eyed look. "Not so long," he said. "Not for a month."

A month? Alice almost smiled at the thought but quickly forced her lip back down, trying to look indifferent. A month without Danny ... it sounded like heaven. He seemed to feel her happiness and gave her a hurt look. "Don't be such a tight-ass." Again, he tried to pull her hand off the glass.

Tee and Waldo and even Paul were deeply sunken into a conversation, but Jonas was following their fight for the wine glass with his eyes.

Smiling, Danny lowered the top of the wine bottle above her hand, letting the wine run through her fingers and into the glass, though most of it spilled on the tablecloth. Alice quickly pulled her hand away and stared at him in disbelief. "What is *wrong* with you?" She used a napkin to wipe the red drops from her fingers.

Danny just laughed drunkenly. "That's what you get."

She scowled at him. "If you think I'm going to drink *that*, think again." She threw down her napkin and pushed back her chair, but before she could rise from it, he had his hand on her thigh.

"Oh, come on, don't be like that. We are having fun, aren't we?"

"I'm going to bed." Alice pushed his hand away and rose.

He did not hold her back, but at the door she turned, suddenly remembering something. "Can I get my iPod back?"

Danny arched an eyebrow and took a sip of his wine.

"My iPod, it was in the living room of our old apartment. Do you know where you put it?"

He frowned at her. "Why would you want that old thing back?"

"Because you're not giving me back my phone—where I kept all of my music. But I can't call anyone with an iPod, can I?"

He seemed to be considering it. "We'll see ... I'm not sure it's still around."

"You're leaving *tomorrow*!"

"You survived without it these last couple of months, you'll survive another."

Alice glared at him angrily, then turned on her heel and left the room.

Before she reached the stairs, she heard him shout: "Keep the bed warm for me, will you?"

Alice was lying on her back, staring at the ceiling, her blanket pulled up to her chin. It was impossible to fall asleep with the anticipation of Danny coming to her room later, demanding 'favors'. Her thoughts were racing and her hands were covered in cold sweat. Her eyes flicked to the clock from time to time, though it was barely visible in the semidarkness. It was only minutes before midnight.

Please let him be so drunk that he forgets about it.

As soon as she heard footsteps in the corridor, she knew her hope had been wasted.

When the door handle was pushed down and the door silently opened inward, she pressed her eyes shut and bit her lip, sensing his presence approaching until she felt him sit down on the mattress.

Two muffled *thumps* let her know that he had kicked off his shoes, then she heard his belt being opened. He climbed into bed next to her, naked, smelling strongly of wine and cologne.

He said he wouldn't force me ... that I only need to say no.

His face came close to hers and knowing he was about to kiss her lips, she rolled onto her side, turning her back toward him. He started kissing her neck instead.

"Stop it," she whispered.

Chuckling, he planted a kiss on her ear. "Come on, let's have some fun."

"I'm not in the mood."

"You will be." He put one hand underneath her shirt and started moving it up her side. Alice tried to push it away, scooting away from him, but she was already lying too close to the edge of the bed and couldn't move away any further.

"No, Danny, I said stop it!"

His hand froze on her and she could feel his disappointment, even in the darkness. "We're not going to see each other for a long time."

"I don't care."

She could hear him exhale, irritated, and his stare seemed to stab right through her. Then she felt his aura turn cold—icy, even—and fear started creeping through her bones. There it was again ... that sense of danger, like waves of threat coming from him. Nervously holding her breath, she waited for what he would do.

"You know, Alice," he said in a cool voice, "with everything I have done—and still do for you—you could show me a bit of gratitude from time to time."

Gratitude ... that's what he calls it.

Still dizzy from the wine, Alice felt bolder than usual. "I said no."

His breathing accelerated.

"Just go, I want to sleep." She tried to push him out of her bed, but he caught her hand and held it tightly, squeezing her fingers together painfully.

"Don't you talk to me like that," he pressed through clenched teeth.

"Please, just go!"

He had no intention of leaving, that was obvious. Instead, he rolled on top of her, pushing her into the mattress with the weight of his body. It was hard to breathe underneath him. Again, his hand went under her shirt, pushing it upward until her breast was uncovered. Feeling exposed, Alice shuddered and struggled to get him off her.

"Danny, you said you wouldn't—"

He pressed his lips on hers, muffling her voice. There was nothing gentle about the kiss. His mouth almost crushed her lips and his tongue tasted sour from the wine.

Without taking his weight from her, he pulled down her panties with one hand and tried to make her open her legs.

Panicking, Alice started hitting him and her fist found his nose.

"OW!" he exclaimed, clutching his nose with one hand while the other one locked around her neck. Infuriated by her attempt to fight him off, he tightened his grip around her throat. Gasping for air, Alice tried to rip his hand off, clawing at it. Sudden images of Martin flashed through her mind.

"Don't you ever do that again," he roared into her ear, squeezing her throat tighter.

A dizziness that had nothing to do with the wine came over her, and she felt her blood rush to her face. Frantic, she scratched at his hand with her nails, and he punished her by hitting her in the face with a balled fist. The pain was muffled by the lack of oxygen in her brain, but she could clearly feel his attempt to enter her, though he failed at first.

"Can't breathe," she gasped. "Please, you're suffocating me!"

Slowly, Danny loosened his grip and took his hand away from her throat. Alice started coughing between desperate attempts to inhale.

"You're making this a lot harder than it has to be," he said coldly.

Alice's heart was furiously pounding against her ribs and dry sobs escaped her throat. Never before had she been so afraid of him and never before had he hurt her like that.

He said he'd never force me ...

Danny waited for her to catch her breath. At least he was nice enough for that. Tears were streaming down her face now and she noticed the metallic taste of blood on her tongue.

"Please don't be like that," she pleaded, sobbing. "I won't struggle, I promise, just don't be so ... rough."

Again, he had won, simply by being physically stronger than her. She hated him in that moment, with all her heart.

With a triumphant smile on his face, he planted a kiss on her cheek. She could see his bleached teeth flash in the darkness.

He finished what he had started, but this time he was gentle.

Alice closed her eyes and sent her mind far away, to the world she had built for herself, where winter didn't exist and the sky was always blue, trees were always green, and Danny was just a name without a face ...

15

He stayed in her bed that night, snoring loudly while she soaked her pillow with her tears.

Only when daylight fell into the room, sleep finally managed to lull her in like a warm and comfortable blanket.

It seemed to be only minutes later when a knock on the door awoke both her and Danny. Moaning, Danny started to move. Alice kept her eyes shut tightly. She was still naked, huddled underneath her blanket, and she hadn't even been to the bathroom after he had finished with her—too afraid it might wake him up.

The knocking began again, and Danny sat up straight, stretching his limps and yawning. "Yes?" he called.

The door was opened hesitantly. "You're late," Alice heard Jonas's voice saying. "I went to your room but saw that it's empty."

She felt Danny's weight being lifted from the mattress and heard his footsteps moving around the bed to where he had left his clothes the night before.

"What time is it?" His voice was hoarse and sleepy.

"9:40. You were supposed to leave at 9:00 a.m."

"Why didn't you wake me sooner?"

Jonas said nothing to that, but Alice got the feeling that he was looking at her. She kept her eyes closed.

"You can go downstairs, I'm coming," Danny said, and Jonas left the room. "Alice," he said.

She ignored him.

"Alice!" he called again more loudly, and put a hand on her shoulder, shaking her.

Alice put both her hands to her face and covered her eyes.

"Don't I get a kiss?" he asked.

When she said nothing, he sighed and walked out of the room.

Alice stayed in bed until the voices in the yard had been replaced by the sounds of an engine running, and only when the noise of tires grating on gravel had faded out completely, did she dare to get up.

Her head was throbbing and she felt sick to the point of throwing up, but when she kneeled on the bathroom floor with her head bent over the toilet for about fifteen minutes, nothing came but bile, and she pulled herself back up and sat on the toilet seat instead, finally able to rid herself of Danny's sperm.

Afterward, she stepped into the bathtub and rubbed her skin with a sponge, first with scalding-hot water, but when it doubled her headache, she turned the handle until it came out ice-cold and refreshing. Her stomach was cramping, trying to get the nausea out of her, but it wasn't food that made her sick, so there was no point in trying to throw up.

Stomach acid was starting to burn in her throat, and she washed her mouth with water, spitting out the rest of the blood. Her lower lip had burst under Danny's fist and was swollen. Her jaw and throat were bruised as well. Her reflection showed her a specter, a ghost of a woman, and she punched her fist against the mirror, too weakly to break it though.

I'm ugly ... pale, hollow, ugly.

She hated herself, more than Danny even. Why had she even dated him in the first place? Or was it her fault he treated her like that?

Maybe he'd be nice to me if I did what he wants.

After all, wearing the clothes he had bought for her wasn't *that* bad as long as she didn't think about it too much, and if she had just let him take her the night before, he would not have hurt her.

Disgusted by herself, she took her eyes from the mirror.

At least he was gone now, giving her time to think.

Alice put on an oversized shirt, and opened the window to let the freezing February air blow into her room, against her face and through her clothes. She sat down on the windowsill with her drawing pad and diary in her lap, but there was an emptiness in both her heart and her mind, and she couldn't think of anything to draw or write down.

Goose bumps covered her whole body, but she didn't care. The wind felt good.

Her gaze went across the yard, over the wall, and out into the world. Snow-covered mountains aligned the horizon, behind hills with evergreen trees on them. A farmhouse or two in the distance ... freedom.

Alice watched two blackbirds fighting over something to eat until one of them dropped it. The other one dived down and caught it in midair, then flew away toward the mountains, beating its little wings furiously to escape its rival.

Wings were great. Alice wished she had a pair and could just fly out of her window. Sighing, she looked at the iron bars in front of her. Even with wings she would not be able to get away. Slowly, she reached out and touched one of the bars, but quickly pulled her hand back when she felt how cold it was.

A knock on the door ripped her out of her daydreams, and it took her a while to remember where she was and what had happened. The window was still open, and her body had turned stiff from the cold.

A second knock made her flinch.

"Alice?" It was Jonas's voice.

She stared at the door blankly, unable to grasp a clear thought.

Jonas knocked again. "Alice? It's time for lunch."

Alice's eyes flicked to the clock on the wall, but her vision was blurred and her brain could not remember how to read it.

Suddenly, the door opened, and Alice quickly turned her head back to the open window.

"Oh," Jonas said. "Sorry ... I was worried."

The fact that she was only wearing a T-shirt seemed to make him uncomfortable.

"Lunch is ready," he said again. "Just letting you know." He stepped backward out of the door and closed it.

Dressed in black pants and her dark blue blouse, her hair brushed, Alice sat at the table opposite Jonas, staring at her food while he was eating.

Hoping to regain her appetite, she had decided to go downstairs, but the sight and smell of the Thai-curry steaming in the bowl in front of her only made her stomach clench. Even a sip of water threatened to come right back out, so she put her glass down.

Henry appeared, a worried expression on his face. "Is the food not okay?" he asked her.

Feeling ashamed of herself, Alice quickly grabbed her spoon. "Yes, of course it is. It's more than okay ... it's delicious." She managed to smile at him, but when her eyes met his, an expression of shock contorted his features. Her smile died and she remembered the bruises.

Did I put on makeup today?

She lightly touched her cheek with her fingers and doubted it.

Henry's eyes flicked to Jonas, then back to Alice. "I've noticed you're not eating lately," he said quietly.

"I've just ... been feeling nauseous."

Henry's expression lightened up a bit as he misinterpreted her answer. "Oh," he said, "in that case I will be careful and cook light food for you, something not too spicy."

He thinks I'm pregnant.

Light food would probably be a good idea though.

"That would be nice, Henry, thank you," she said tonelessly.

The cook went back to the kitchen and Alice forced herself to at least eat some of the plain rice on her plate. She washed it down with water, but after maybe five spoons, she pushed the plate away.

The next days were the same.

Alice went down for lunch and dinner on time, to keep Jonas from having to come upstairs and get her. Henry had switched to preparing soups for her with bread, and her stomach was beginning to feel a bit better, even though her appetite did not return. The memories of her last night with Danny were too nauseating.

Eating with Jonas was awkward. He kept his eyes on either his plate or his phone, ignoring her completely, and she avoided looking at him as well ...

Until Thursday at noon when her loneliness was beginning to feel unbearable.

"Why don't you ever talk?" Alice asked quietly, after finishing her potato soup and piece of bread.

Surprised by the interruption, Jonas looked up from his phone. "Why does that matter to you?" he asked coldly.

"Never mind," she muttered. Without looking at him, she pushed back her chair and left the dining room to spend yet another afternoon hiding in her daydreams.

At dinner, however, Jonas seemed to be watching her, and when she was done eating, he asked, "Wanna play cards?"

Confused, Alice looked up, wondering if she had heard him right. "What?"

He pulled a deck of cards out of the pocket of his leather jacket and laid it on the table. "We could play poker," he offered.

"Uh ... I can't ... I've never ..."

"I'll teach you."

Playing cards with Jonas felt odd, since he did not talk much, but he managed to explain her the rules of the game, and they ended up playing several rounds on the table in the dining room.

Alice now understood where he had gotten his poker face from and she figured it was impossible to win against him. Of course, she wasn't good enough yet to win against anybody.

"You're showing too much emotion," he lectured her after just having won another round. "Try to keep your face blank. Don't let me know what your hand is."

Grimacing, she nodded and tried to do it better in the next game.

They played again the next evening, and it managed to make her feel a bit less lonely.

On Saturday noon, the twenty-fourth of February, Jonas said, "I'm taking you out tonight."

Puzzled, Alice looked up and stared at him. "What?"

"We're going to the Shipwreck."

She knew the Shipwreck. It was a concert location where parties were held frequently.

"Why?" she asked curiously.

"I'm meeting friends there."

Friends? Alice was surprised that he had friends next to Danny and the gang. "And I'm coming with you?" She couldn't believe it.

Jonas shrugged. "I don't feel like sitting in this bloody house all the time, wasting my life watching you."

Feeling ashamed, Alice bit her lip and stared down at her plate.

"It's not your fault," he said firmly.

"What d'you want to do there?" she asked, wondering what it would be like to go out with him and his friends ... the thought of it made her anxious.

"There's a concert you can listen to. I'll just hang out with the blokes."

"What kind of concert?" The Shipwreck usually hosted rock and metal bands.

Jonas shrugged. "Don't know." He pulled out his phone and started typing something. "I'll ask."

Alice waited patiently until the phone vibrated.

"A band called Anti-Flag," he said, after having read the message.

Her heartbeat accelerated at once. "Are you kidding me?"

"Why? D'you know them?"

"I *love* them!" She beamed at him. "But ... are there still tickets?"

"Not needed." Jonas gave her a cocky grin. "I used to work there."

After pacing through her room restlessly, Alice joined Jonas for an early dinner, which he had prepared. She had put on jeans, a studded belt, a hoodie and even some dark eye shadow; and Jonas gave her an amused smirk.

"Nice look," he commented.

"Yeah, well ... this used to be my everyday-look." Alice felt stomach acid rise up in her throat at the thought of how Danny had made her change her appearance to be 'more fitting' to his new life. Quickly, she repressed the memory. With the prospect of seeing her favorite band perform live, she didn't want to destroy her mood by thinking about him.

They ate quietly, but Alice could barely hide her excitement, which made Jonas smile.

When they were sitting in his old gray BMW, however, his expression got serious. "Don't tell Danny about this."

"Of course not!"

"And please, don't run away. He'll find you and kill us both." His tone made it sound like a joke, but Alice knew that it was not only an expression.

"I won't, I promise." She glanced at the guard by the gate. "What about him?"

"I bribed him."

The Shipwreck was crowded with a bunch of beautiful people. People wearing black and purple, people with their hair colored like rainbows, people with piercings and tattoos and army boots. Alice felt at home immediately.

Jonas walked straight to the entrance and greeted the bouncer—a tall bald guy with big ears—by hugging him and patting his back.

"Jay-Bee," the man exclaimed happily, "how nice to see your ass out here for a change."

Jonas grinned broadly. "Lex."

"Happy twenty-fourth!" Lex said with a wide grin. He nodded toward Alice. "New girlfriend?"

"Anna," Jonas said.

Alice frowned at him and he gave her a warning look.

"I can introduce myself, thank you." She shook Lex's hand. "Anna, nice to meet you."

"I'm Alex." He smiled. "Nice to meet ya too."

Alice was busy scanning the other guests with her eyes, wondering if she knew some of them, and she didn't mind that Lex thought she was Jonas's girlfriend.

"You finally decided to get off your high horse and visit us down here? I heard you're rich now."

Jonas shrugged. "My new job's better for my hearing."

Laughing, Lex shook his head. "Well, people who hate music usually don't work at concerts."

A group of teenagers was approaching, so Lex moved in front of the entrance door, ready to check their IDs. "Just go inside and I'll meet up with ya later," he said to Jonas and Alice.

Jonas bobbed his head once and gestured Alice to follow him. Once inside, he greeted two of the other security guys, receiving more congratulations and handshakes. Alice was again introduced as Anna, but she didn't care.

The hall was almost full, and people were already cheering and waiting for the band to appear.

"Let's go up to the balcony." Jonas nodded toward the stairs.

"No, please let's stay down here," Alice begged. "The fun's always downstairs!"

He looked at her pouting face and sighed. "Fine. I'll go up alone. Just don't do anything stupid." He pulled out his box of cigarettes and lit one, then offered one to her. She took it.

"Isn't smoking prohibited here?"

Grinning, Jonas took a deep drag on his Marlboro. "Who's gonna kick *me* out?"

Alice grinned back at him. "Happy birthday, by the way, *Jay-Bee*."

"Thanks." He gave her a tortured look.

When the band appeared, the crowd seemed to explode with cheers and Alice quickly hurried toward the stage, carefully winding her way through the crammed place like a snake. She caught a glimpse of Jonas following her for a moment, but then his worried face disappeared in the crowd.

When she spotted him again, she was already jumping up and down, shoving people around and singing along to "*Seems every station on the TV is selling something no one can be.*"

Jonas looked at her, clearly feeling uncomfortable in the jumping and dancing crowd.

"*We will not witness this anymore! This is the end for you my friend.*"

Someone handed Alice a half-empty beer cup and she chugged the rest.

"*I can't forgive, I won't forget.*"

Jonas grabbed her arm and pulled her out of the circle pit. "It's too noisy here!" he yelled.

"I won't go anywhere, I promise!" Alice yelled back.

Hesitating, he studied her expression, then he nodded. "I'll be outside."

Alice couldn't believe that he trusted her enough to leave her alone at a concert. Maybe he had just realized how much she loved the music and knew she wouldn't run away. An exhilarating feeling of utter joy took hold of her. After months of feeling miserable, she was not only out of her prison, but also at her favorite band's concert—and Jonas even trusted her and wasn't watching her for a change.

Feeling high, Alice continued dancing until she had to take a break, gasping for air, and covered in sweat that was mostly not her own. Apart from the couple of times she had managed to use her treadmill, she had not gotten much exercise lately. That and the fact she had also not eaten enough due to her nausea, were beginning to truly show their effect on her body.

A group of friends standing next to her offered her a beer and Alice took it gladly.

When *1 Trillion Dollars* was playing, Alice sang, "*Fuck the world, a lot of people gotta die tonight,*" and wondered whom Danny might be killing right now.

The people who had offered her a beer were very friendly and she ended up dancing with them to *Hymn for the Dead,* until one of them went to the bar to get another round of beers.

"I'll pay you back," Alice promised. "My friend's got the money. I have to get it."

The guy called Aaron shook his head though and said it was okay. He was hot, she realized. Just a little bit taller than her, slender, with black hair that fell down to his shoulders, an unshaven chin, and dark brown eyes, just like hers. Alice couldn't help but wonder if it was okay to flirt with him. After all, she didn't feel like she was Danny's girlfriend anymore—at least not by choice. If it weren't for Jonas, she would have left him months ago.

"The bright lights of America" started playing and somehow, she felt as if the song were about her. Her mood darkened at once and her thoughts wandered back to the house and to Danny, knowing that the concert was coming to an end and she would soon be back there.

Aaron smiled at her and put yet another beer in her hand, and together they yelled, *"You've gotta die, gotta die, gotta die for your government, die for your country, that's shit."*

The music stopped, the lights went back on, but there was no sign of Jonas. Alice let her eyes wander through the building, which was emptying steadily.

"Wanna come to the bar?" Aaron asked her.

"What about your friends?"

"Kayla can't drink 'cause she's on meds and Rusty and Mike are going home with her."

"Rusty?" Alice asked, amused.

"It's his street name." Aaron waved at his friends, who waved back and then walked toward the exit.

"I'm not sure how long I can stay," Alice admitted. "My friend might be waiting."

Aaron gave her an understanding smile. "No prob, we'll just sit at the bar right next to the entrance. She'll see you there."

"He," Alice corrected him.

Aaron was incredibly charming. His eyes emanated intelligence and honesty, and it turned out he knew a lot about music. Alice wondered if she enjoyed talking to him that much because of how nice he was, or because she hadn't been able to talk to anybody, who had nothing to do with Danny, in what seemed like forever. They kept drinking beer, and she laughed at his jokes and blushed at his compliments.

"I don't feel comfortable with you paying for everything," Alice told him after they had switched from beer to gin and tonic.

"No worries, I'll let you pay next time. I'm here almost every weekend." He grinned at her and his smile evoked butterflies in her stomach—though she wasn't entirely sure whether it was just an effect of the alcohol.

"I don't think I'll be here again anytime soon ..."

"No problem, we can exchange numbers."

Nervously chewing her lip, Alice wondered what she could say to that.

"Or we don't, if you don't want to," he said quickly, misreading her expression.

"Things are a bit ... complicated."

"Are you in a relationship? I'm fine with just being friends."

"No ... I'm not ... It's not that, it's just ..." Struggling to find the right words, Alice stared at the lines that had appeared on Aaron's forehead. "I don't have a phone, you know." The words came out much sadder than she had intended, and she cursed herself for it.

Aaron's eyes wandered from her face down her body, to the ripped jeans and worn-out Converse.

"Oh," he said. "I'm sorry, I hope I didn't hurt your feelings ... I don't have much money either. I've only recently found a job. I know the struggle." He smiled warmly.

He thinks I'm poor.

Shame flushed her cheeks with heat when she thought back to the mansion awaiting her. Although technically, everything she had was Danny's, and she had neither money nor a phone. Still, there were surely many people who would have gladly traded with her, and that made her feel ungrateful. Staring at the drink in her hand, she said nothing.

"Let me just give you my number," Aaron offered. He grabbed a napkin from the counter and wrote his cell phone number on it, then handed it to her. Alice took it, folded it, and put it in the pocket of her jeans. "Thanks," she muttered.

The Shipwreck was almost empty now and the lights got brighter while staff started wiping the floors. Alice turned her head to look for Jonas and finally spotted him. He was standing next to the entrance door, talking to Lex and one of his other friends.

Aaron followed her gaze. "Looks like it's just us and the security guys left ... They'll probably kick us out soon."

Feeling dizzy and warmed by the gin, Alice smiled and nodded.

"Another drink?" Aaron pulled some bills and coins out of his pocket, and counted them. "Last one, then I'm broke."

Alice quickly put her hand on his to stop him from spending his money. "I don't want you to be broke. You surely need money to get home."

He shrugged. "I'll walk, it's not far."

"But it's freezing outside," she protested.

"That's why we should drink something warming." He winked at her and ordered two whiskeys.

When the barkeeper placed the two glasses in front of them, the smell of whiskey made Alice's stomach clench. Images of Danny flashed through her mind, a memory of his reeking breath when he grabbed her and pushed her to the ground ... the empty whiskey bottle shattering to pieces when it hit the wall above her head ... At the same time, Alice did not want for the night to end. Soon, everything would be over, and she would be back in her prison. The euphoria she had felt during the concert had faded out completely and Alice desperately wanted it to come back.

Determined to silence her unpleasant thoughts, she took a deep breath and chugged the whiskey—though it made her stomach turn.

"Trying to drown your sorrows?" Aaron asked in a concerned voice.

"Kind of."

He took her hand and goose bumps appeared on her arm, but when he brushed back her sleeve with his thumb, the bruises became visible. Wincing, Alice quickly pulled her hand back.

"Sorry," he said, leaning away from her.

"No, it's fine ... I just sprained my wrist recently." She took his hand in hers, feeling incredibly drunk. Aaron was exactly what she needed, the type of man who could make her happy. Even if he ever got angry, he would never pose a threat like Danny.

"What are you doing?"

Alice whirled around and saw Jonas standing behind her. She quickly pulled her hand back, and left a startled Aaron to look from her to Jonas and back.

"We were just about to leave," Aaron told him, mistaking Jonas for a staff member.

Jonas's eyes narrowed. "Were you now?"

"Uh, Aaron, this is my friend," Alice said quickly.

Aaron laughed. "Oh, I'm so sorry! I could've sworn you were staff."

"He used to work here," she explained.

"That explains everything. I was sure I'd seen your face here before."

Jonas's expression remained hard. "We're leaving," he told Alice.

"Oh. Could you maybe ... lend me some money? Aaron here has paid for way too many drinks and I feel guilty."

Aaron was about to protest, but Alice gave him a warning look.

"I'm sure he would've preferred something else in return," Jonas said coldly.

"He's not like that!" she protested almost angrily. "The guys here are never like that. That's why I like this place."

Jonas frowned at her. Aaron's eyes were widened, and he seemed to shrink when he caught Jonas's stare. Jonas fished some money out of his pocket and handed it to him. He took it reluctantly.

"Damn you're naïve," Jonas told Alice. "Now come."

Alice quickly said goodbye to Aaron and missed him the instant, she walked out of the door; with Jonas behind her, watching her every step.

They were driving in silence. Jonas looked angry and Alice felt her depression return, now that her night in freedom was about to be over.

"I didn't take you out so you could talk to boys," Jonas said after a while, his voice harsh.

"Aaron was nice and ... I'm not Danny's girlfriend anymore."

"That's none of my business."

Alice glared at him. "You're right, it isn't!"

Jonas inhaled sharply. "He's still my boss and ..."

"Your friend."

He nodded.

"You'll always take his side," she muttered.

"No, I don't!" he snapped, giving her a piercing look.

"But ... then why do you—"

"We're not talking about this," he cut her off.

Alice felt tears well up in her eyes, and was glad that it was dark in the car and he couldn't see it. The night had been perfect, but now the mood had spiraled down, and the alcohol made her feel even more depressed. All she wanted was to grab the steering wheel and maneuver the car into a tree.

"Don't be mad," she said quietly. "I don't want you to be in a bad mood ... It was a great night and it's your birthday."

"It's almost four o'clock. My birthday's over." He kept staring at the road, still looking angry.

"That's not how we should end this, let's do something fun before going back, please."

Jonas didn't reply.

Leaning over, Alice grabbed the steering wheel. "There's ice on the road, let's drift!"

Jonas hit the brakes so hard, Alice fell forward, and all air got knocked out of her lungs when her seatbelt held her back. Jonas had made her wear it, luckily.

Shocked, she watched as he killed the engine and got out of the car. He walked around it toward her. When he opened the door on her side, Alice leaned away from him, hiding her face in her hands, expecting some kind of punishment.

"Get out," he said.

She didn't move.

"Come on," he urged. "Get out of the car."

"Why?" she asked in a voice much higher than intended.

"I want to show you something."

Alice stared at him through the gaps between her fingers. His expression was unreadable, and she couldn't tell if he was still angry.

"I don't want to see it."

"Yes, you do. Now get out."

"No, I'm pretty sure I don't."

Frowning, Jonas stared at her. "What?"

"You can keep it in your pants."

His jaw dropped slightly, and he looked at her with widened eyes.

"You just said it yourself; I'm not supposed to trust men."

He looked hurt somehow, but then he smiled. "We're in the middle of nowhere, it's freezing out here."

"Exactly."

He sighed. "What exactly d'you think I'd want to do, out here, in the snow, when there's a heated car here and a heated house awaiting us?"

Alice took her hands away from her face and studied his expression. He was right, of course. If he wanted to hurt her, he could do it in the car.

"Are you gonna leave me on the side of the road ... because I'm annoying you?"

He laughed at that. "If I were suicidal, maybe ... but no. I wouldn't do that to you." He offered her his hand and waited patiently.

Biting her lip, Alice hesitated, but then she decided that Jonas couldn't do anything to her that Danny had not already done. She undid her seatbelt and put her feet on the ground.

"Take my hand, there's ice."

Stubbornly, she shook her head and pushed his arm away. Only two steps from the car, however, she slipped, and Jonas caught her before she hit the ground.

"Told you," he said.

Jonas led her out onto a snow-covered field, and they walked for a while. Alice wondered what the hell he was about to show her. Curiosity had chased her sadness away and even her fear had decreased to a bit of nervousness.

Up they went, their feet breaking through the frozen snow, making satisfying crunching sounds. The hill was quite steep, and Alice was out of breath after a couple of minutes already. Jonas took her arm and helped her reach the top.

"Voilà." He pointed at something and she looked up.

"Wow," she gasped.

The whole town was visible from where they were standing, its lights shining brightly through the darkness, golden and warm. The surrounding hills were all covered in snow and sparkled in the city lights.

Jonas lit a cigarette and gave one to Alice as well. They smoked in silence, breathing in the cold air and inhaling the taste of freedom.

"It's beautiful," Alice muttered.

Jonas nodded. "And it didn't even come out of my trousers."

She stuck her tongue out at him.

Enjoying the postcard-like view, they stood in silence, lost in their own private thoughts, until Alice's teeth started to clatter.

"We should go," Jonas said.

"No, it's fine, I'm warm."

"That's the alcohol."

Grinning, Alice took a step back and let herself drop backward. "Ouch," she yelped when her head hit the solidly frozen snow.

"I would have warned you," Jonas said while he watched her clumsy attempt to make a snow angel despite the ice. "If I'd known you were planning on plunging into ice."

Panting, Alice gave up and stuck her tongue out at him again.

"I'm sure your bed at home is more comfortable than this," Jonas remarked when she did not get up.

"I'm trying to look at the stars."

"And?"

"They move too fast." Closing her eyes, Alice tried to make her head stop spinning, but it was no use. She felt as if she were lying on a merry-go-round that was going fifty miles per hour. Taking a deep breath, she put her hand on her mouth, trying to keep down the drinks which were threatening to come back out.

"You okay?" Jonas asked in a concerned voice.

"I feel sick," Alice managed to mumble through her hand, right before she knew her fight against the nausea was lost. Luckily, Jonas was there to help her get up on her knees, and he even held her hair back while she spilled everything she had drunk into—or rather onto—the snow.

Jonas waited patiently while she rinsed her mouth with snow and waited for the dizziness to go away. Her pants were completely soaked by then and she shivered. The taste in her mouth was disgusting, especially the penetrant flavor of whiskey.

"That last drink was one too many," Alice moaned weakly.

Chuckling, Jonas offered her his hand to help her up. "Don't you think it might have been the one before that?"

Alice let him pull her to her feet and swayed a little when he let go of her. "Maybe. I definitely didn't plan on throwing up in front of you ... *again*."

Grinning, he put a hand on her shoulder to lead her back to the road. "Don't worry about that. I've seen worse."

Jonas lit a fire in the living room and Alice watched him, lying on the couch. She had kicked off her shoes and was struggling to keep her eyes open. To avoid a hangover, she had drunk a whole bottle of water, which was now rebelling in her stomach.

When the fire was crackling happily, Jonas disappeared to go to the bathroom and Alice lost the fight against her drowsiness and drifted off into a deep troublesome sleep, her ears ringing from the loud music and Aaron's face dancing up and down in front of her.

Daylight had filled the room when she awoke, and the fire had burned down completely. Alice noticed that she'd been covered with a blanket.

Thanks to throwing up and drinking some water, her hangover wasn't that bad, and the nausea was comparable to what she felt everyday anyway. There was a throbbing in her head, however, and she moaned when she sat up. Sniffing, she realized she had caught a cold.

Even through her locked airways, she could smell that food was being prepared in the kitchen. Curious, she pushed herself off the couch and walked toward it.

Jonas was frying bacon in a pan and looked up when she stepped into the kitchen.

"Morning," he said, his lips twitching upward when he saw the look on her face. "Hangover?"

Alice shook her head. "A cold, I think."

"That's what lying in the snow gets you."

She frowned at him, then eyed the bacon. "Smells good," she lied.

He chuckled. "I'm making beans and toast as well. Want some?"

"Sounds good, thanks."

They ate at the table and despite her sore stomach, Alice felt incredibly hungry.

"Thank you for last night," she said after swallowing her last bite of beans on toast.

"Thank you for not running away."

"When Anti-Flag's playing? I would never."

Smiling, he said, "It was nice to do something fun for a change." There was a sad undertone in his voice, and Alice quickly averted her eyes, feeling a stab of pain in her guts.

"Let me grab the plates, you've already done the cooking."

He didn't protest, so she brought the dirty dishes to the kitchen and started the dishwasher.

It was a sunny Sunday and Alice took a walk in the yard after having spent two hours soaking in the bathtub to cure her cold. She also drank lots of tea and in the evening, she and Jonas played cards in front of the fireplace after Alice had cooked dinner for a change.

The next couple of days passed in a similar manner, and living with Jonas began to feel normal, almost as if he were just a regular roommate.

Henry still prepared light meals for her and after a while, Alice managed to regain her appetite and finish her portions, very much to his satisfaction. Henry seemed to notice that she was more relaxed, and he now spoke friendlier to Jonas as well.

One afternoon, Alice was drawing in the living room, staring into the flames of the crackling fire from time to time, when Jonas appeared behind her and eyed her drawing.

"Impressive," he commented.

Alice quickly turned the pad upside down.

"Really, you draw quite well." He sat down on the other couch. "What's the meaning of it?"

"It's private."

Jonas raised his brows.

"I mean, it's like writing a diary ... it's personal."

He nodded and lit a cigarette.

"Those things give you cancer, you know," she said jokingly.

"There's worse things than cancer." Jonas blew out a perfect ring, then exhaled the rest of the smoke. Alice watched him smoke quietly, until he asked, "You ever lost someone to cancer?"

She shook her head. "What about you?"

He stared into the flames for a while before answering, "There's worse things than cancer."

Alice studied his expression, trying to read it, but failed.

"Anyway." He flicked the butt of his cigarette into the fire and rummaged in his jeans pocket, then pulled out something small and black. Curious, Alice took it when he handed it to her. It turned out to be an MP3 player.

"You wanted your iPod back, right?"

She nodded.

"No idea if it's still around, but you can have this one instead."

Alice looked at it and realized that it was an older model. "What's on it?"

Shrugging, he said, "No idea."

"Isn't it yours?"

"No, I don't listen to music."

Alice stared at him in disbelief. "How can you *not* listen to music? It's the most beautiful thing in the world!"

"Not to me."

The MP3 player felt light in her hand and she turned it over between her fingers. It might have been an older model, but it looked quite new. Not a scratch was on it.

"Whose is it?"

Jonas lit another cigarette. "My sister's."

"You have a sister? Won't she mind …?"

"Nah, it's old. She doesn't need it anymore."

"What's her taste?"

Sighing, he exhaled a big cloud of smoke. "I really don't remember."

Alice turned on the small device and started scrolling through the artists' names. There was lots of rock 'n' roll on it, old songs, from the seventies.

Smiling, she said, "Looks good so far."

Jonas said nothing, still staring into the fire.

Over the next days, Alice spent a lot of time listening to the music on the player.

Even though she missed her favorite bands, she found great pleasure in just lying on her bed for hours, listening to music and drifting away into daydreams. After not having been able to do so for months, it felt like something special, like a real treat.

Jonas had to study most of the time during the week, so Alice was glad she had something else to keep her busy.

The dreadful day of Danny's return was coming closer, and Alice felt her mood spiral downward again.

At least the weather was getting better. Even a few spring-like days brought sunshine and warmth, and flowers began growing in the beds around the house.

On March 18, however—the day of Danny's return—temperatures dropped again, and snow began falling anew.

Alice looked out the window, feeling empty and lost. The weather fit her mood perfectly.

After four weeks of not having to wear her stupid blouses and skirts, four weeks of feeling less miserable and even close to happy from time to time, Danny's car was now pulling onto the gravel parking space.

16

"I missed you." He pushed the door shut behind him, and Alice could feel him walking toward her. Without taking her eyes from the window, she stood, arms crossed, her back toward him.

"Alice ..."

She felt his heavy cold hand on her shoulder. How was she supposed to react? He had left her in a horrible state, broken and empty, depressed and lonely. He'd taken everything from her, her freedom, her friends, her dignity. Most of all, he had taken it as if it were *his* to begin with, as if he thought he somehow had the right to it. He owned a lot, everything money could buy, and he seemed to think that he owned her as well.

That last night with him had been especially bad. She could still feel his grip around her throat, his body pinning her onto the mattress, his fist hitting her face. He had been cruel that night, cruel in a way he had never been before.

Alice couldn't just forget that; even now, almost a month later, it still hurt. Though the physical pain had faded out, there was a stabbing sensation in her guts. She had still been in love with him despite everything, up to that night, and he had hurt her emotionally as well.

Now, she was not sure if she still had feelings for him. All she could feel right now, with his hand on her shoulder, was emptiness.

Danny moved closer toward her, pressing his body against her back, hugging her from behind. At least he didn't reek of alcohol for a change. He put his chin on her head, inhaling her smell.

"I'm sorry," he whispered.

For what? Alice wanted to scream at him. *Tell me exactly what you're sorry about!* The words would not come over her lips though, so she remained silent.

"I've had a lot of time to think and ... I can't even find the right words to express how I feel about myself." His voice cracked and he sniffed.

He was crying on her shoulder, as if he expected *her* to comfort *him*. Alice kept her eyes on the dancing snowflakes outside her window. They were fat ones. Thick and heavy, beautifully patterned, they fell, dancing, turning and spinning, until they touched the soft grass below.

"Alice ..." His voice was higher than usual, desperate, almost a squeak. "I'm such an asshole." Sobbing, he buried his face in her hair. "I'm a monster, like I told you ... that night, when you found me in my office. I should have just used that knife and ended it all."

His tears were soaking through her blouse. She had put on the light blue one, expecting him to be in a bad mood, hoping to soothe his anger.

Now he was snotting all over it.

"Alice ..." He lifted his head and made her turn around, his touch on her shoulders soft. His eyes were big and blue and beautiful, the sadness and guilt in them genuine.

Alice noticed that his hair had grown a bit and he had not yet cut it back. His skin was also darker, tanned.

So he really was in a warm place.

Suddenly, she felt a horrible sensation in her guts that made her gasp.

No, please no ...

He still had that effect on her. Alice tried to look away, avoid his eyes, but hers seemed to be glued to them. And with every tear that came out of his eyes, she felt the wall she had built around her heart crumble; and when he bit his lower lip and looked at her pleadingly, the last bricks were turned to dust and she felt tears well up in her own eyes.

"I hate myself, Allie, I really do ... but I can see that you still love me." He brushed his fingers over her cheek, and she tried to turn her head away. Trying to swallow the sobs, that were building in her throat, she shook her head.

"Do you?" he asked. "Do you still love me, after everything I've done?"

Stop it, she wanted to scream, but her mouth was dry, and she could not say the words aloud.

"I ..." she started, but her voice broke.

He caressed her hair back softly. "I know, I don't deserve it."

No, you don't, she wanted to agree, but again, she remained silent. He hugged her, pulling her head onto his chest.

"Don't," she said weakly, pushing him away.

This time, he loosened his grip and let her regain her distance.

"I don't want to," she added, her voice shaking.

"I'm sorry, I won't touch you." He pulled his hands back, holding them up defensively.

"I mean ... I know that I love you, but I don't want to, not in any way, not even a bit!"

He seemed shocked at her words and hurt, but at the same time relieved that she had admitted her feelings to him. "What can I do to make it right?"

Die. Die or disappear, and get out of my life forever!

Again, she kept her thoughts to herself. "Leave me alone," she said instead.

Hurt and sad, he looked at her, not quite understanding what she'd said.

"I mean it, Danny, just leave me alone! I don't want this; I don't want to be here with you!"

Slowly, he retreated. "I'll give you space," he said quietly.

"No, just let me go, let me out of here!"

He reached the door, opened it, and stepped out. "I'll give you time to think, time and space."

"Danny!" Alice screamed before he pulled the door shut. "Don't do this, just let me go!"

He was gone, the door closed. Shaking violently, sobbing and crying, Alice wanted to hit something, to smash a mirror or the window, to squeeze something until it broke, but instead, she paced up and down, tearing at her own hair, breathing so fast she was almost hyperventilating.

How dared he play with her like that? Push her away and then pull her back, hit her one instant and kiss her the next ... It was cruel beyond words.

No one knocked on her door at seven, and Alice assumed Danny was trying to keep his promise of giving her space.

At around eight, however, she could hear a faint knock, but no one came in. She opened the door and found a tray with food on the floor.

So ... we're back to being fed.

Sighing, she took the tray and put it on her dresser. The plate contained pasta with tomato sauce—the only thing Danny could cook.

Somehow, looking at the plate in front of her made her tear up again. It wasn't a nice gesture; he was just feeding his prisoner.

Knowing, that the food came from him, she felt the urge to throw the plate against the wall. Instead, she took a few bites. Encountering Danny had made her sick though, literally, and her appetite was nonexistent.

During his absence, she had managed to gain some weight. But with him being back, she knew she would soon start to look famished again.

Danny kept his distance over the next couple of days, as promised—though he was probably just too afraid of having to respond to her demand for freedom. Knowing that he still loved her, she couldn't figure out how he was able to treat her like that. Locking her up had been mainly to prevent her from leaving him, but the way he treated her—hurting her physically—was it supposed to be her punishment? Was he trying to make her pay for her attempts to leave him? Or were his assaults merely uncontrollable emotional outbreaks?

The first couple of times, when he had been drunk, it had seemed to be the latter. But after his breakdown and his transformation into his cold, distant, and sophisticated self, his strikes had seemed thought through and calculated, and he had even been sober in some of the cases.

Most of the time, Alice stayed in her room, but she did go downstairs or out of the house during Danny's office hours from time to time.

Jonas was more distant since Danny's return. He merely gave her a nod as greeting, and quickly looked away again when she passed him. Somehow, Alice found his behavior hurtful. He had become like a friend to her, even in the short time they had spent together. She had appreciated his attention and he had made her feel less lonely.

At least Tee would give her a smile whenever he saw her and on a sunny Saturday, when Danny had left to visit Julio, he approached her when she was sitting outside on her swing.

"Hey Lizzy," he greeted cheerfully, baring his yellowish teeth in a wide grin.

Relieved to have someone to talk to, Alice smiled back.

"What are you up to these days?"

Shrugging, Alice put the book she had been reading down on her lap. "Not much."

"Not much you *can* do, huh?" It didn't sound like mockery, more as if he was actually feeling sorry for her. Alice stared down at the ground miserably and nodded.

"Need some company?"

"Wouldn't hurt."

He sat down on the grass beside her, inhaling the fresh spring air which was rich with the scent of snowdrops and primroses—even though it had snowed only recently.

"What are you doing here anyway on a Saturday?" she asked him curiously. "With Danny gone, I mean."

"I thought I'd come to see you," he confessed. "You're better company than my cat ... she hates me."

Alice laughed. "Who says I don't?"

He shrugged. "Just a feeling."

They sat in silence for a while, watching a bird nesting in a birch close by.

"You know, I really find his behavior awful," Tee admitted.

Her throat tightened at his words.

"I really don't like the way he treats you. You deserve better."

Feeling uncomfortable, Alice said nothing and kept staring at the birds.

"He's changed," Tee continued. "Sometimes I don't even recognize him anymore. I mean, what's with this new attitude of his? The ironed shirts, the chandelier, throwing fancy dinner parties ... next, he'll make all of us wear a suit to work." It was supposed to be a joke and he laughed, but Alice didn't consider it to be very amusing. After all, Danny *did* force her to wear clothes she disliked. Part of her wished Tee would just leave the topic alone, but then she realized that he might be her only chance to find out more about the *business*.

"Where were you?" she asked him. "You really were somewhere warm, right? Danny's all tanned."

Grimacing, Tee thought for a while, probably considering what to tell her. "Well ... we were in a warm place, yup, but no beaches and parties ... no hot girls in bikinis or old, fat, sunburned guys in speedos."

He grinned broadly. "Which was a relief," he added, winking.

"Hm," Alice said, not in the mood for his jokes. She knew that his answer was as much as she would get on that topic. He was still Danny's puppet.

"How ... how was he, Danny? How is he anyway when he's at work?"

Sighing, Tee leaned backward on his arms, which he had stretched out behind his back. "Well ... Let's just say he knows what he wants. What started as a group thing turned into his own obsession."

"You'd say he's obsessed?"

"He's ... well, what do you know about it? I really don't wanna say too much, he wouldn't be too happy about it."

"I don't know that much ... but Danny had that weird breakdown. He tried to drink himself to death, babbling about trying to be a hero but messing it up. And ... I don't know ... He said something about ... well, killing people?" She watched his reaction and he seemed surprised that she knew so much.

"Uh ..." He laughed nervously. "What exactly did he say?"

"Well, that he's being haunted by the images—or ghosts, or whatever— of the people he killed, and that he's a monster and feels guilty ..."

Tee's expression turned serious, and he locked eyes with her, his stare piercing. "I can assure you that Danny has never laid a hand on anybody—in a way that would kill them, I mean."

Alice let his answer sink in, noticing that the way he had said it was weird, though she could not figure out why. Danny had definitely laid his hands on her, but like Tee had said, not in a murderous way.

"When Jonas killed that guy ... Martin, it was like ... like it was a normal thing to do. He didn't even flinch."

"Danny's not Jonas."

"I know, but even he didn't seem to be shocked or appalled or anything. He seemed more concerned about getting some sleep than about two dead bodies in the basement. And lately he's all cold and seems to have lost his humanity, so I'm not sure what he's capable of anymore." Alice looked at him, a pleading look on her face, hoping for answers, but Tee just laughed.

"Lost his humanity? Did you watch *the Vampire Diaries* by any chance?"

Annoyed by his way of ignoring her questions, she frowned at him. "Yeah, as a matter of fact I did, and it really seems like he's just switched off his humanity. Not that that's possible, but he does seem that way, doesn't he?"

Tee inhaled and seemed to think of something good to say. "He has changed," he admitted.

"But *why*?"

"I have no answer to that."

Again, his odd way of wording things. He had no answer, but that didn't mean he didn't know anything.

"Back to his obsession."

"Well, he's very determined, but *obsession* might be a bit exaggerated."

"But you're not happy with it?"

"It's just … It's his company now, he's the boss. We didn't know it would turn out like that."

"What's your role in it anyway?"

"Dan's got the skills, no doubt about that. That's why he's got most of the responsibility. But without me, honestly, this whole thing would not exist."

Curious, Alice raised her eyebrows and looked at him. "Why?"

He cleared his throat. "I'm not gonna tell you anything you're not supposed to know, but starting this business was my idea. I mean, Dan had a thought, but it was just that—a thought. He never thought we could make it happen, until I convinced him otherwise. And it worked out quite well, didn't it?"

"I wouldn't know," Alice said coldly.

Tee gave her an apologetic look. "Anyway, he makes the decisions now, but he still relies on our advice and without us, he'd be nowhere." It sounded bitter when he said it. Alice sensed a chance to use his envy of Danny to learn more details.

"Tee, I would never tell Danny what you've told me, you know."

Frowning, he brushed a strand of dirty-blond hair out of his face. "He'd still find out, and I really think it's best if you don't know too much."

"Please?" she begged, pouting.

"I normally could never say no to that face …" He smiled at her flirtingly. "But it really ain't a good idea."

Alice sighed. "Fine … But what else can you tell me? Do you know why he keeps me here? He's always mad at me, but he won't let me leave …"

Opening up to Tee was awkward; Alice didn't know him at all. But she was locked in a house with only Danny and his friends to talk to, and normal was not a term that applied to her life anymore.

"Good question." Thinking, Tee scratched his chin. "He always says how much he loves you, but honestly … I think he just wants to possess you."

"That's what I thought … But why me? Why not somebody who would look good next to him? I'm so not the trophy-wife type."

"Too big of a hassle, I suppose. He's got you and he's happy with it."

"So …" Alice's mouth felt dry, and she swallowed. "D'you think he still loves me at all?"

"That's a tough one ... Let me put it this way: Do you think he'd treat you like that if he did?"

Alice felt a stabbing sensation in her guts at his words. No, she really didn't think anybody would treat a loved one like Danny treated her. And even though she hated him for it, it was hurtful to imagine that he had no feelings left for her.

Tee was looking at her, a faint smile on his lips. "There's other men in the world," he said.

"How is that of any use when I'm not able to leave this place?"

Sighing, he said, "What a dilemma. But you got *me*." He grinned at her broadly.

"Do I?" she asked doubtfully.

Straightening up, he pounded his own chest with his fist. "At your service."

Alice sighed and rolled her eyes. "I could use a friend in this place, but that's it."

His expression turned serious, and he nodded. "Like I said, at your service." His voice was sincere, but he gave her a warm smile, and she couldn't help but like him.

Other than Jonas, Tee was usually in the office with Danny, so having him as a friend was not that entertaining.

The next Wednesday evening however, Danny went to Julio's house again. Apparently, they had become close friends. Alice didn't mind, as long as it meant he would be gone more often.

It was at around 8:00 p.m., when Tee knocked on her door and Alice let him in, surprised by his visit.

Tee had a wide grin on his face and a bottle of vodka in his hand.

"Came to celebrate our friendship." He stepped into the room and put the bottle on her dresser. "Only if you want, that is."

Smiling, Alice nodded. "Should we play?" She pointed at the TV.

"Hell yeah!" Tee sat down in front of the bed and leaned his back against it.

"Choose a game," Alice said. "I'll go downstairs to fetch some orange juice. There's no way I'll drink *that* without mixing it." She glanced at the bottle of vodka and Tee laughed, shaking his head.

"Girls."

Alice frowned at that but chose to remain quiet.

Jonas was just stepping through the back door and looked at her when she walked across the room. Alice took two glasses out of the kitchen cupboard, filled them with ice from the freezer, then took a bottle of orange juice out of the fridge.

"Got a visitor?" Jonas asked when she walked past him again. He'd settled down on the couch with his study books.

"Yeah, Tee's upstairs. We're gonna play some video games."

Jonas eyed her suspiciously. "Think that's smart?"

"Don't see why not. Besides, I need a friend in this godforsaken hellhole."

"And you think he's the right choice?"

"I don't see anyone else," she said coldly, referring to the way Jonas had been treating her since Danny's return. His expression remained blank, but she knew he understood.

Alice poured only a little bit of vodka in her glass and filled it up with orange juice. She didn't feel like drinking, but she didn't tell Tee, who laughed at her and drank his vodka with only ice.

"Have you gone soft, Lizzy?"

"It's Wednesday."

"So?"

"I just don't want to be hungover tomorrow. I hate hangovers."

"You should drink more often. That way you won't get hangovers." He took a big gulp from his glass and placed it down on the carpet next to him.

Alice started the game and entered their player names, when Tee said, "You can write 'Timmy', not 'Tee'."

"I was actually wondering whether your nickname's just the letter 'T' or like the beverage."

"No, it's the way they always pronounce it. It's supposed to be mocking. Jonas with his stupid accent started calling me 'T' and the others mimicked him. Now everybody calls me that."

"So, not 'Tee' then."

"Honestly, no. I prefer Timmy, or Tim, or just Timothy."

"Sure," she said. "Timmy it is."

Timmy seemed eager to get himself drunk as fast as possible, always urging Alice to keep up with him. She never filled her glass with more than a sip of vodka though. Her lacking appetite had resulted in an empty stomach once again, and she didn't want to take her chances and end up even more nauseous the next day. Even now, she was already feeling drunk, but since Timmy was drunker, she won most of the races, and managed to crash his car a couple of times by pushing him off the road.

When the game was finished and they were too exhausted to play another round, he put the controller down, sighed and emptied his glass. "I think I'm done."

Laughing, Alice put her controller down as well. "You just hate to lose, don't you?"

"It's embarrassing to lose against a girl, especially in a car race."

"And why is that?" she asked him, feeling irritated by his sexist attitude.

He held his hands up defensively. "Just joking, don't take it as an insult."

"What else is it supposed to be?"

He shrugged. "A stupid joke, I guess … never mind." He scooted a bit closer toward her, stretching his legs in the process. "Ugh, I'm getting old. Sitting on the floor ain't good for my bones."

Alice turned off the PS4, feeling drowsy and a bit nauseous. "What d'you wanna do now? Watch TV?"

"Hmm, I don't know … There's a lot we could do, ain't there?" He moved closer, breathing on her face.

"I need water." Alice quickly got up and disappeared into the bathroom, where she drank directly from the tap and splashed some cold water onto her face. Alcohol was definitely not her friend. Why had she even agreed to drink that stupid vodka? She stood, bent over the sink, holding her weight on her elbows, feeling like she was about to throw up.

When she went back to her room, Timothy had already filled her glass up again.

"I'm not going to drink anymore," she protested.

"Why not? We're young and having fun." He held the glass up to her. Alice took it and put it down on the dresser. "You just said you're old," she pointed out. "Anyway, I feel sick, I can't stomach any more vodka."

He shrugged. "Fine, let's just watch a movie or something."

Alice took her place beside him on the carpet and turned on the TV, flipping through the channels.

"Too bad you got no Netflix."

"Yep," she agreed. "Thanks to Danny."

"Why?"

"He doesn't want me to have internet access. Scared I might contact the outer world, and spill some of the things I don't even know."

"What a prick," Timmy muttered, and Alice stared at him, surprised.

"What? It's true, ain't it? So, there's no Wi-Fi in this house?"

"No idea ... I got no phone nor laptop."

He rummaged in his pocket and pulled out his phone. "Let's see ..."

Curious, Alice watched him.

"Nope, no signal." Sighing, he put the phone away again.

"Don't you need it for work?"

"There's internet in the office. Guess old-fashioned style."

Wow. Danny really was paranoid. "Could I maybe send a text to my friends or call them from your phone? They haven't heard from me in ages." Alice looked at him hopefully, awaiting his answer nervously. Timothy seemed to consider it, then grimaced and shook his head. "Look, I'm really sorry, but I can't go behind Danny's back."

Disappointed, she leaned her back against the bed and stared at the TV, where some stupid toothpaste commercial was playing.

He put an arm around her shoulder. "Sorry."

"It's okay ... whatever."

Timothy kept staring at her, which made her feel uncomfortable. She quickly grabbed the remote and continued zapping through the channels. There was absolutely nothing she wanted to watch, and she felt him lean closer.

"What are you doing?"

Smiling, he said, "Just thought ... we could entertain each other."

Alice felt stomach acid burn in her throat. "Don't," she protested, pushing him away softly.

"Why not?"

"Friends, remember?"

He grinned. "With benefits?"

"Oh, stop it, you're drunk!"

And I thought I'd found a friend ... but they're all the same.

She pushed him away again as he leaned in to kiss her. His breath smelled like vodka and it made her nauseous.

"Come on, we're just having fun."

Alice frowned at him. "I'm not."

His eyebrows wandered up his forehead. "Oh really? I know you're into me."

Speechless, Alice stared at him.

"Don't deny it, I've read the signs."

"What? What signs?"

Timothy's eyes narrowed. "You know exactly what I'm talking about."

Confused and indignant at the same time, she opened her mouth to contradict him while her thoughts raced back to every encounter there had been with him. What signs was he talking about? Was he just being a jerk or had she behaved wrongly around him?

His fingers went to her chin and he gently pushed it upward to close her mouth. "Save that breath for me."

Disgusted, Alice turned her head away from him. "What about not going behind Danny's back?"

He grimaced, looking trapped.

A sudden firm knock on the door made her flinch and Timmy quickly pulled his arm back, to her relief.

"Yes?" Alice called.

Jonas opened the door, his expression unreadable as always. "Danny's about to come back."

Alice felt her throat tighten. "You should go," she told Timothy. She wanted to thank Jonas for informing them, but he had already left the room and closed the door again.

"I don't have anyone to give me a lift."

"I don't care, take the spare bedroom." She got to her feet and walked over to the door to open it for him.

"I could sleep here; you got a big bed." He grinned again in a repulsive way.

"Leave, please, Danny can't find you here."

"Oh, come on," he begged. "I'll keep you warm."

Alice could do nothing but shake her head in disgust at that stupid and childish remark.

"You're too drunk to think straight, Timmy. Danny really can't find you here!"

"Is that why you want me to go?"

Alice hesitated at the question, not sure what he meant. "Well … he's gonna be furious if he finds you here."

Grinning, Tee slowly stood up. He straightened his back while moaning theatrically, the almost empty bottle of vodka in his hand. Then he stepped toward her. "So ... We'll just try again when he's not here?" He winked at her.

She sighed, starting to feel really annoyed. "No, Timmy, not now, not ever. Just no. Got it?"

Feeling insulted, he frowned.

"It was nice playing with you, but please leave now." She stood in the doorway, arms crossed, nodding toward the corridor.

"Playing with my feelings you mean?" Timothy stayed where he was and took another gulp from the bottle. He dried his chin on his sleeve and gave her a stubborn look.

"I didn't. I never played with your feelings."

"I really think you should be nice to me," he complained drunkenly.

"I *am* nice to you."

"I bought the vodka." He shook the bottle in his hand to make her look at it.

Rolling her eyes, she answered, "And you think vodka buys my affection? Or did you just hope I'd get too drunk to think straight?"

He grinned stupidly. Apparently, this was exactly what he had thought.

"Well, I guess it didn't work out as planned. Just leave now, the guest room downstairs should be ready."

Again, he took a sip of the remaining liquor and refused to leave.

Alice saw Jonas coming up the stairs, as he was about to go to his room. She gave him a meaningful look.

It was hard to guess what Jonas was thinking, but she imagined him sighing on the inside as he walked toward her. Before stepping past her through the door, he looked at her, and whatever emotion he put in that look made her feel utterly ashamed.

"Out!" he ordered curtly, his eyes on Timothy.

"Oh, the *bodyguard*," the drunk joked, a crooked smile on his face—though his eyes remained untouched by it.

Alice stepped aside as Timothy followed Jonas's order without much of an objection, but he gave her a look that was both hurt and threatening. She met his eyes and gave him a smile, trying to keep things okay between them. Maybe there was still hope in keeping him as a friend—though she would never drink with him again.

Jonas waited, standing next to her, until Timothy had disappeared down the stairs, then he himself began to move, but Alice caught his arm, suddenly feeling the urge to talk to him.

He stopped and turned without saying a word.

Her mouth felt dry and her courage crumbled under his piercing stare, but she forced herself to speak. "I'm sorry."

"You wouldn't listen."

"No, I mean ... Of course, I'm sorry about *that* as well, but I wanted to apologize for ... well, for what I said ... earlier."

His eyebrows moved upward, only slightly, almost invisibly, but Alice had learned to focus on the little shifts in his expression.

"I was unfair to you, I think ..."

"'bout what?"

"Uh ... I really appreciate what you did for me when Danny was gone, and it was nice ... to have someone to talk to or, well, play cards and stuff ... and I really am grateful for that, you know ..." She trailed off, feeling stupid, but he waited for her to finish. "I somehow ... thought we might be friends. Maybe I was just lonely and mistook your being nice to me for friendship. I feel stupid about that now and ... well, sorry for being rude."

"Don't apologize," he said, but there was no kindness in his tone.

Alice stared at him for a moment, trying to find out what had changed between them. She had thought he'd maybe kept his distance because Danny had been around, but even now, with no Danny standing next to them, there was no warmth in his eyes, no emotion whatsoever.

"He told me to," Jonas finally said.

"What?"

"To be nice to you ... entertain you. He felt sorry after he left and called me."

Alice felt a sharp pain in her guts and couldn't take her eyes off his, slowly processing his words in her mind. It had been Danny's order. Jonas had only been doing his job.

"The concert—"

"He has no clue. Like I said, I didn't fancy staying here all day. You were lucky it was a band you like." His voice was cold as ice and like icicles, it seemed to stab through her, leaving a pain in her chest that made it hard to breathe.

How could she have ever thought he was her friend? Even though it had only been a couple of weeks of their imagined friendship she felt betrayed and hurt ... and confused. Had she been deceived by her own imagination or was Jonas just impossible to see through?

I'm stupid. I'm naïve. I should have known.

Her eyes turned moist, and she hated herself for her lack of self-control. Unable to hide the tears, she quickly stepped back into her room and shut the door on Jonas.

There she stood, leaning against the wood, feeling drunk and depressed. She had begun to like Jonas, to feel safe around him. She'd even believed he would protect her from Danny. How incredibly naïve. Never had she felt as lonely and vulnerable as in that moment. The two men, she'd put her hopes into, had revealed their true characters. Both within one hour.

The only person who truly was nice to her, was Henry, but he was too afraid to talk to her.

Alice stared into the darkness beyond the window, tears running silently down her cheeks. Wanting nothing more than to just dissolve into nothingness and disappear forever. Her mind was a blur, but there was one thought clearly echoing in her head—dark, heavy, and persistent.

I'm getting out of here. One way or another...

Eating her meals in her room gave Alice the chance to avoid everyone. She fled into her daydreams while listening to the music on the MP3 player.

Danny still kept his distance, for which she was glad—though she wondered where he got his self-control from. Timothy was probably right. He didn't love her anymore and maybe he had even found other women to satisfy his physical needs.

Not that she would complain about that, but it made her wonder why he kept her locked up. As emergency backup? Or maybe he really thought time would heal all wounds, and that she would come running back to him after some time on her own.

She was getting worse though.

The nightmares reappeared, but this time, it was not Martin's dead face anymore; it was Danny and Jonas and Timothy, haunting her dreams, between monstrous creatures from her own daydreams, who became vivid in her mind, dangerous and hungry and willing to eat her alive.

Often, Alice would wake up in the middle of the night, covered in cold sweat, her heart racing.

Food was brought to her twice a day and enough of it, but she didn't feel like eating at all, feeling nauseous all day long. She could feel herself getting weak but blamed it on the lack of exercise. The treadmill was there all right, but she had lost interest in it and preferred to only do things that would let her mind wander.

One night, Alice fell asleep quite early, feeling exhausted despite having done nothing. She felt dizzy and sick, her stomach cramping heavily, the taste of stomach acid constantly on her tongue.

Sleep rolled over her like a heavy black avalanche, swallowing everything it could find in her mind, turning it over and over, until her thoughts spun and turned into dreams, and the dreams became more vivid and loud and suffocating, until they were nightmares.

"Come here," Danny said, his voice echoing from the walls of her room, though they were plain and gray and there were no pictures or windows.

"I don't want to."

He held out his hand to her, inviting her to take a step forward. "Come here," he repeated. There was a smile on his face, but his eyes lay sunken in their sockets, encircled by dark shadows that made him look like a skull.

His hair was moving, but there was no wind.

Hesitantly, she took a step forward.

He was casually leaning against the wall near the door, one arm still outstretched, the other at his side, hand stowed in the pocket of his jeans. She hadn't seen him wear jeans in a long time.

"Good girl," he said, smiling.

He was wearing a black leather jacket as well, torn at the sleeves, several buttons missing.

"I don't want to be here," she protested, trying to stop, but something invisible was pushing her forward and toward him.

"You're mine." His voice was ice-cold and when he spoke, the temperature in the room seemed to drop below freezing point.

"I'm not!" Struggling, Alice tried to push herself backward, against the force in her back. Danny got hold of her hand and where he touched her, her skin turned black.

"Let me go," she begged, panicking at the sight of her crumbling flesh. "You're burning me!" Gasping, she pulled her arm out of his grip, but her skin and flesh stuck to his hand, and what remained were only the bones.

Danny laughed. A high-pitched, evil laugh that echoed back from the walls, as if hundreds of Dannies were laughing at once, laughing at her. She stared at her arm in disbelief.

"That's what you get," he said, still smiling. He leaned closer to her. "Now kiss me."

"No!"

The wall had moved and was suddenly right behind her back, making it impossible to escape him.

"Kiss me," he said again while hundreds of voices repeated: *kiss me, kiss me, kiss me, me, me me . . .*

His face came closer, his breath smelled of smoke and whiskey, and when his lips touched hers, his eyes turned green and his hair brown, and her lips burned as if he had thrown acid in her face.

Jonas leaned back, grinning widely, pointing at her. "You got something on your face."

Alice's fingers touched her lips and they felt hard.

She whirled around, found the bathroom, and stepped inside, staring into the mirror. She was pale, like a ghost underneath her long, dark hair. Her reflection was smiling, though she was not.

Her lips were burned, fissured and black. She started to scratch at the wound, her fingernails removing chunks of burned flesh. Blood ran down her chin, but she couldn't help herself, and continued until the sink was filled with blood and flesh and her face was no longer covered in skin.

Her skull was grinning at her grotesquely.

That's what you get.

It was her reflection talking.

Kiss me, it said.

"No!"

Alice grabbed the edges of the sink, but she felt herself being drawn closer to the mirror.

Kiss me, kiss me . . .

She screamed with all her heart, trying to fight off her own reflection, and the screaming woke her up, but the face was still there, floating in the darkness, grinning at her.

Kiss me ...

"Go away! Go away, go awaaaayyyyy!"

Whimpering, she covered her face with her hands and suddenly, Danny was back, his eyes blue and his hair dark again. He reached her in two big steps and wrapped his arms around her tightly.

"Go away!" Alice tried to fight him off, but his touch was not burning anymore. He pressed her face against his chest and stroked her hair and she could feel his jaw moving above her head, but there was no sound apart from white noise in her ears and a faint *kiss me ...*

Danny was only in underwear, his chest naked and warm. The white noise was beginning to fade out and Alice was able to hear his voice, faint at first, but then louder and clearer.

"What's wrong? Alice, please talk to me, what happened?"

Sobbing, she buried her face underneath his arm while he patted her back.

"Was it a nightmare? It's all right, calm down." His voice sounded warm and concerned, and it felt good to be held by him.

"It's not," she whispered.

"What?"

"It's not just a nightmare, it's real ... the faces ... they don't disappear anymore when I wake up!"

"Let me turn on the light," Danny offered and loosened his embrace.

"No!" She flung herself back at him. "Don't leave me alone!"

"Okay, okay." He kissed her forehead and held her close. "Let's get up together and turn on the light, okay?"

Danny's bedroom light was on, and it fell through the door, into the corridor, and illuminated part of her room as well, but not enough to fight the darkness.

Alice nodded weakly, and together, they rose from the bed and Danny was able to lean toward the door, stretching his long arm out to switch the ceiling lamp on without letting go of her.

Blinded by the sudden brightness, Alice blinked.

"Is it still there? The face?"

She shook her head. "No, but everything's weird ... Danny, I think I'm going crazy!" More sobs found their way out of her throat and he embraced her tightly.

"What have you been doing lately? Did you ever leave the room? Allie, it's not healthy to stay inside all day long with no one to talk to."

"There is no one to talk to."

"The food Henry cooked for you ... you barely touched it." Softly, he pushed her away and held her at arm's length to be able to look at her. His expression turned even more worried, almost scared of what he saw on her face. "You look terrible," he gasped.

Normally, Alice would have thanked him for the compliment, but now she just stared at him blankly, hoping for his skin to stop bobbling and for the room to stop spinning.

"How much have you been drinking?"

She froze, feeling trapped. Had he found out about Timothy and the vodka? But hadn't that been a couple of days ago?

"I haven't drunk in a long time."

Danny gave her a warm smile, though his forehead was still covered in deep worry lines. "I mean water, honey."

"Oh." She could not remember. The past days had passed in a blur. Alice knew that she had been lying on her bed a lot, daydreaming or staring out the window, but what else had she been doing?

Danny made her sit back down on the bed and went to the bathroom. Alice heard the tap run and a few seconds later, he reappeared with a glass of water.

"Drink it," he said, putting it to her lips. He watched her drink while carefully studying her expression.

When the glass was empty, he pulled her up and led her to the door. "Come on, let's get you something to eat."

"But I'm nauseous!"

"Allie, you're never eating, *that's* what's making you nauseous."

"No, I'm pretty sure it's stress."

He sighed. "I understand, but it's a vicious circle. The hunger makes you feel even more sick."

Resigned, she followed him downstairs, holding on to his arm for support.

Danny warmed up some leftover rice, and added beans in tomato sauce while Alice sat on the kitchen counter next to the stove, watching him cook.

It was impossible to grasp the situation. All she could do was watch him as if she were in a trance, unable to think clearly.

When he was done, he filled the rice and beans into a bowl, blew some steam away, and fetched a spoon with which he began feeding her. Alice obeyed weakly, knowing that he was right.

All she wanted was to feel normal again, and if dehydration and starvation were the reasons for her hallucinations, she would gladly eat and drink as much as she could.

Even though she could only eat very slowly, the warmth of the food in her stomach made her feel a bit better and she even began to enjoy watching Danny feed her, with him still only wearing boxers, his muscly body moving so tenderly for a change.

"You can be nice if you want to," she pointed out without thinking, feeling high somehow.

A weird look flickered over his face and he grimaced. "I'm sorry," he said quietly, his voice thick with sadness and regret. "Sometimes I feel like I'm not myself and I do horrible things, and when I try to make it up to you, I only make it worse ... Whatever I do, it's wrong."

Alice said nothing and opened her mouth for another spoonful of rice, thinking that the only thing Danny would have to do, was open the iron gate for her and let her walk. But that was never going to happen, she knew that now.

"I really, really hope the business will get better, so we can finally move somewhere else, where you'll have more space and more ways to entertain yourself ... and more freedom."

"What's wrong with it?" Alice asked curiously.

Grimacing, he stirred the rice and beans over to mix it and cool it down a bit at the same time. "It's complicated."

"Who would have guessed." She sighed, feeling light-headed. "Danny, where were you? You were somewhere warm, weren't you?"

Danny's eyes flicked to her face, widening as they did so. "Who told you that?"

"Your tan."

"Oh." He gave her a weak smile. "Yeah ... okay, okay. I was in Northern

Africa, meeting with some potential buyers." He shoved another load of food into her mouth gently.

Alice chewed and swallowed and asked, "Where?"

"Doesn't matter, Allie, really. I don't want you to know too much." He filled the spoon again, but she lifted a hand and pushed the bowl away. "I can't, I'm full."

Danny sighed, looking at the still half-full bowl, but considered it best not to argue. "Okay, it's probably best if we don't overwhelm your stomach." He put the bowl in the fridge and filled a glass with water from the tap. "Drink some more, okay? Or would you prefer tea? I could go for tea right now."

She nodded. "If you take some, I will too."

They drank their tea in front of the fireplace, which Danny had lit.

He was stretched out on the couch, Alice snuggled under his arm, resting her head on his chest. Despite the food and liquid, she still felt dizzy, unreal somehow. It was why she didn't push him away and demand distance. Right now, all she knew was that it was a wonderful feeling to be huddled against him, feeling the warmth of his bare chest on her body. It was comforting.

He, who had made her miserable, was comforting her through her misery. She knew how absurd this was, but she also knew damn well that he was the only one she had, the only one who cared about her, even though he hurt her.

With his hand stroking her hair softly, she soon drifted off into a deep, dreamless sleep.

They slept late the next day and Alice awoke to the sound of the entrance door slamming shut. Whoever had opened it had gone outside apparently.

Danny felt her lift her head and awoke as well, stretching his limbs and moaning. The sound of raindrops smashing against the windows predicted a dark and depressing day. Alice checked the old grandfather clock behind her and gasped. "Danny, you overslept, it's almost noon!"

Danny rubbed his eyes and turned his head to check the clock himself. He grinned. "Nope, I quit. I didn't feel like working anymore."

Alice stared at him, trying to make sense of his words.

"April Fool's." Grinning broadly, he gave her a kiss.

"What?"

"It's Sunday ... plus, it's April 1st."

"Since when is it Sunday?"

He laughed. "I'd say since midnight."

"So ... yesterday was Saturday?"

"Probably?"

"I lost track ..."

Concerned, he looked at her and brushed her cheek lightly with his index finger. "How long have you been having the nightmares?"

"Not sure ..." She gazed at him, letting his image sink in—the lightly tanned half-naked muscly body, the dark hair that was tousled, the big blue eyes that had lost their hardness, the chin, where a light beard stubble had grown ...

"I like you better that way."

He straightened his back to sit upright. "What way?"

"Without your ironed shirts and the watch. You look innocent like this."

He grimaced sadly. "I'm far from being innocent."

"I know ... But you're nice right now, like you used to be ... Back when we were still happy."

Again, he began to stroke her face softly. "Do you think we can be that way again?"

Never. Not after what he's done.

She shrugged. "Maybe ... if you stay like this, I might put everything behind me."

It was a lie. One, she had planned to tell him to make him trust her again. Maybe he would stop sending Jonas after her if he thought she was okay with the situation. She needed his trust in order to prepare her escape.

He sighed and looked very sad all of a sudden. "I promise you; I'll never treat you badly ever again."

Liar.

Smiling, she kissed him, hoping his good mood would remain until she had found a way to run away.

I may be confused, maybe even a bit crazy after weeks of solitariness ... but I'm not stupid.

Danny went to the kitchen to prepare breakfast, insisting Alice was not allowed to help, so she remained sitting on the couch, staring into the rain, listening to her boyfriend—or whatever the hell she was supposed to call him—whistle in the kitchen.

The door opened and Jonas stepped in, a cigarette dangling from his lips. He gave her a quick look and she quickly turned her head away from him to avoid his stare, knowing that he must have seen her and Danny sleeping on the couch, and made up his mind about it. Jonas proceeded toward the stairs without saying a word.

Alice still felt a light stabbing sensation in her guts when Jonas was present. It made her feel ashamed, but she had really begun to feel affection toward him. And his betrayal hurt, that was undeniable.

Danny had prepared a breakfast of fried toast with beans, added her leftovers from last night and some bacon for himself, and a pot of tea was steaming on the table as well.

They both ate quietly for a while, Danny loading his toast with a huge amount of beans and bacon, and swallowing it almost whole.

"You starving?" she asked him and took a bite of her own toast.

He nodded, his mouth too full to speak.

Alice gave him a smile and looked at him for a while, wondering if she could use his good mood to ask him for a favor.

"What is it?" he asked, sensing that she needed to get something off her chest.

"I'm running out of pills again ..."

"Oh." He put down his toast and took a sip of orange juice. "I guess I could go and buy them for you or ask Henry tomorrow."

She shook her head. "The thing is, my prescription isn't valid anymore, so I'll need a doctor's appointment."

"Oh," he said again.

"Mhm."

"Do you really have to take that crap? I mean, it's so unhealthy to take hormones and there's tons of side effects. Besides, you've been taking them for years, it would be a good idea to give your body a break."

Feeling annoyed, Alice gave him a cold look. "I agree, Danny, but do I *need* them?" It was not as if their last times had been consensual. She cringed at the thought.

Danny looked down at his plate, thinking of an answer. "We could not do it for a while ... or use condoms," he finally said, his voice toneless.

Alice said nothing.

17

Danny kept his promise and they stayed abstinent until Thursday, April 12, when he went on another business trip and she decided to let him "say goodbye" passionately, though she made him wear a condom.

It felt like she was betraying herself, but at least he had been nice to her since her nightmare on April 1, and she had even stopped hating him a little bit.

Things with Jonas were still weird, and Alice did not at all look forward to being alone with him. She still hadn't figured out what was going on with him or if she had done something wrong, but he chose to ignore her.

After watching him for a while, she knew at least that he usually went to the basement to work out at the same time every day, so that had to be her chance. Else, he was always either studying in the living room or smoking in the yard, and there was no way to sneak past him unnoticed.

They ate their lunches and dinners in silence, as always, Alice carefully avoided looking at him. Her appetite was again nonexistent, but she knew better now than to let herself almost starve and forced herself to eat at least half of the portions Henry prepared for her.

On the weekend, she even went downstairs to cook something for herself, and sat down at the table to eat while reading a book.

The smell of smoke announced him even before he stepped through the door. Alice felt his stare but refused to look up from her book.

"There's leftovers," she said coldly when he didn't go away. "You can have some if you want."

He did. He warmed up a plate in the microwave and sat down opposite her, but she didn't look up.

"Thanks," he muttered and began to eat. After a few bites, she could hear him put down his fork.

"I'm sorry for hurting your feelings." His voice was calm and low, and there was no hint of emotion in it—which made the apology sound less sincere.

When she didn't reply, he continued to speak. "I knew you were vulnerable and that you'd get attached, and I wanted to avoid that."

Alice felt her guts clench and she bit her tongue hard, not taking her eyes from her book. Why did he have to bring it up again? He could have just left the topic alone.

"I can't be your friend, Alice, it wouldn't work."

She noticed that she had not been moving throughout his speech, trapped and frozen by his stare. Quickly, she turned the page of her book, her eyes taking in the printed words one by one, but her brain could not process them.

"We can still play cards or talk when he's not here," Jonas added.

"Why, because he told you to?" she finally said without taking her eyes from the book.

"Does it matter?"

She left his question unanswered, thinking about it. Did it matter? She was lonely and needed someone to talk to or to at least notice her, and what was so bad about him just pretending to be her friend?

The problem was that she would get attached while Jonas would not, and he would just end up hurting her again.

Alice looked up from her book, meeting his gaze, looking into his bright green eyes. They were distant, able to hide his feelings and not show any emotion.

"I can't."

He looked at her, taking in her answer and it was obvious that he understood exactly what the problem was.

About to rise from her chair, Alice closed the book and grabbed her empty plate.

"Wait," he said, and she froze. "Danny told me to entertain you, to keep you happy. But when he realized that you had begun to trust me more than him, he got jealous."

Her eyes flicked back to his face and she saw that his expression had gotten softer.

"He then told me to keep my distance, which I did." Jonas looked down at his unfinished plate and then back at her, his stare piercing. "Now, he told me to keep you company again, scared you might have another breakdown."

Alice cringed at the word and dropped her gaze, feeling ashamed. "Why are you telling me this?" she asked in a toneless voice.

"Because I honestly don't know what to do." He even looked a bit desperate when he said that.

"Scared you might not get paid? Or get fired?" Alice put as much disdain in her words as possible.

"I think you're suffering enough, and I don't want to make it worse. But if I piss him off, he'll let it out on you." His words seemed to hang in the air for a moment, while she tried to process what he'd just said. It had sounded so sincere, so honest, so not like Jonas.

Again, it was unclear whether he actually cared about her or whether he just wanted to avoid hurting her more because it was his job, like a butcher stunning an animal before killing them—instead of just not killing them at all.

"But ... why would Danny be jealous? He trusts you."

"Yes. But it hurt him that we got along while you ignored him."

Alice felt anger flare up inside her. "After what he—I mean, it's no wonder I ... Of course, I wasn't talking to him! I would have rather talked to *anybody* else, simply for the fact they didn't do what he did!"

Jonas said nothing but gave her a meaningful look that said he knew and he pitied her, and she instantly blushed and averted her eyes, wishing she hadn't said anything.

"Never mind, it doesn't matter. You don't have to be anything to me, just do your job and ... be done with it." She took her book from the table and carried her plate to the kitchen. Hearing his footsteps behind her, she realized he had followed her.

"Did you forgive him?"

Without turning around, Alice sighed and began to rinse her plate. "No ... not really. I don't know."

"Be careful."

Somehow, that remark infuriated her, and she whirled around. "Oh, thank you for that precious advice! See, I would've never considered being careful! I really like the way he treats me, it's exactly what I want my relationship to be like!"

Jonas looked startled at her outburst and stood there, saying nothing.

"What the fuck am I supposed to do, huh? He's always there and I can't even lock my own door. He comes whenever he pleases, one moment he's in a good mood, the next he's pissed without telling me why ... Whatever I do, it's not good enough for him and all I want is to just walk away, but thanks to *you*, that's not gonna happen!"

Jonas took a few steps toward her, thinking of something to say, but failed.

"It's *your* fault! He might be the boss and the one giving me a hard time, but you are keeping me here, you are making it impossible for me to run away! Without you, I wouldn't even have moved here! I would've been able to leave him, and the thing with the pool and everything afterward would've never happened!" She had tears in her eyes now, but she didn't care. The words just came out of her without her even thinking them through, but she realized while she said them that they were true, that it *had* been Jonas who had always brought her back or not let her go in the first place, and she wondered how she hadn't been able to see that before. Why had she been so nice to him?

"That's not fair," he said tonelessly. "If I were not here, someone else would be."

"*That's* your excuse?" Alice couldn't believe it. "Don't even act like that, Jonas, don't act all saint, you're just like him!"

"I'm not like him," he protested, suddenly angry as well.

"Yes you are!" Alice threw the knife, she'd been holding in her hands, into the sink, where it shattered the plate. "He's sick, you know, he's a sick man and you're just the same ... You enjoy this, don't you? You're all the same, feeling strong when you got power over others, that's why you're a security guy, isn't it? The next best thing if you can't become a cop. It's power you want, and women don't mean shit to you. You know, before he met you guys, Danny wasn't sexist, he wasn't *old-fashioned*, as he prefers to call it. He was a decent human being and he treated me with respect!" She could see that Jonas's face had turned slightly red but was too busy dealing with her own anger. Breathing heavily, it took her a lot of effort not to throw the broken plate at him.

"I'm not like him," Jonas said again, louder this time. He'd balled his hands into fists.

"Oh no, surely *you* are different! You know who else was different? Timothy, before he tried to get me drunk to fuck me! I know, you're not like *that*, but you definitely want *something* ... is it the money? Do you get paid more for making my life hell than the others for doing real work?" Alice saw his eyes narrowing and glared at him, putting as much hatred in her stare as she could.

"Don't be like that, it's not fair," he said.

"Oh, am I hurting your feelings? I'm the one getting hurt here, not only emotionally! Before he met you, Danny knew that no means no. Now, he seems to think he possesses me, taking whatever he wants, when he wants it! Who taught him that? Was it you or Waldo? You never gave a shit about what I wanted, about my right to walk away from this—that's why you brought me here. You *are* just like him! You *made* him that way!"

"Stop it, Alice!"

"Why did you even shoot Martin? To make sure Danny gets to torture me longer?" She glared at him furiously.

"I did it to save your life."

"Did you? Well, you shouldn't have! You should've just let him shoot me 'cause I sure as hell don't want *this* life!" She saw that her words had hurt him. Dismay flickered over his face and he opened his mouth but closed it again without saying anything. He took another step closer, one arm slightly outstretched, trying to calm her down.

"Why am I even talking to you? It's not like you have feelings, right? You and Danny and Timothy and the others, you only care about yourselves, about power and money. You don't care how many people get hurt along the way!"

"You know nothing about me!" The blush on Jonas's cheeks had intensified and it seemed to take him a lot of self-control to keep his voice down. He was standing close to her now, breathing heavily.

"Oh really? I know you have a sister and I feel sorry for her, for having a brother like you! Did you lock her up as well? Keep her from meeting boys? Or let her get beat up by her boyfriend?"

Alice regretted the words as soon as they had left her mouth.

Jonas's fist flew past her head and collided with the kitchen cupboard. She tried to duck away, but his other arm was blocking her way.

"I'm—Not—Like—Him!"

With every word, he punched the cupboard behind her head and with every blow, she expected the next one to hit her. There was a sickening *crack* and Alice hoped it was only the wood.

By the time he stopped, she had covered her face with her hands, trembling. She was half leaning against his left arm, ducking away from his right hand and the punches it had thrown in her direction. She didn't dare to lift her hands and look at him, scared it might provoke him, so she stayed frozen, shaking, hearing him breathing heavily just above her face, feeling the warmth radiate from his body.

Why did I say those things?

She felt him move and winced, but he had only taken his arm away; and without looking up, she could feel him stepping back, hearing his breaths fading out.

Alice tried to calm her breathing and swallow the nervous sobs that were building up in her throat. She felt her eyes tear up underneath her hands.

Jonas's sudden outburst had taken her off guard. Somehow, she had always thought he would remain calm at all times, like a big rock that could not be moved by anything. Turned out she had been wrong.

After a while, Alice spied through the gaps between her fingers and saw him leaning against the kitchen counters opposite her. He was staring at her, a bewildered expression on his face, as if he didn't know what he had just done. His right fist was bloody, and his fingers looked grotesquely bent.

Very slowly, she lowered her hands from her face, her eyes still on his injured hand. She felt her stomach turn at the sight of his certainly broken bones.

"You're right, you're not like him," she muttered. "Danny would have *aimed*."

Alice hid in her room for the rest of the day, too scared of Jonas to go downstairs again.

It was only on Monday that she decided to go downstairs for lunch—for Henry's sake.

Jonas was sitting at the table when she entered the room, and she noticed that his right hand was covered by a thick bandage.

She took her place opposite him and waited for Henry to bring the food before she dared to look at him. He was staring at his plate, a sullen look on his face.

Alice felt her heart beat faster. His presence was making her uneasy ... now, that she knew even *he* could lose his temper.

Feeling nauseous, she picked at her food for a while, but then she put down her fork and sighed. "Jonas?" she finally managed to say, and he looked up, his expression pained.

"I'm sorry ... for what I said."

The words hung in the air for a moment; it seemed to take him a while to understand.

"Don't apologize." His voice sounded hoarse.

"No, really ... I shouldn't have said these things, it wasn't fair and—"

"*I* should apologize," he interrupted her sharply. "I've never before lost my temper like that."

Alice stared at him with widened eyes, feeling utterly ashamed. She had managed to do what apparently no one else had before. "No ... I ... If what I said was so horrible—"

"There's no excuse for what I did!" Jonas dropped his fork angrily.

"It's not ... you didn't even ..."

"But I could have!" He stared back down at his plate and picked his fork back up, having trouble handling it with his left hand. Exasperated, he gave up and threw it down on the table, then pushed back his chair and got up. "You were right. I *am* like him."

Alice watched him leave, confused and speechless and still feeling incredibly ashamed.

Jonas avoided her over the next two days and Danny was supposed to return on Friday, so Alice knew that if she wanted to run away with him gone, it had to be as soon as possible.

The weather was finally nice. The sun was shining, and flowers had blossomed all over the garden, so Alice sat outside, listening to the cheerful singing of the birds and drawing in her notebook. She also studied the stonewall, not too obviously though, since the guard was sitting on a plastic chair near the gate, sunbathing and looking at her from time to time.

The lower branches of the trees had been cut off. Whether it was because of her or simply because Danny considered it to look better, she didn't know. She had been hoping to climb up a tree and jump over the wall, but without branches to pull herself up on the task did not seem manageable.

The back of the house was too risky, since it was visible both from Jonas's bedroom and from the basement, where he did his workout. Without the guard near the gate, it would have been easy to run away, but he seemed to sense that she was up to something.

Alice was rather sure though that from where he was sitting, he couldn't see certain parts of the wall. Those were on the right side of the house, behind the swing.

Inhaling deeply, Alice closed her notebook and got off the porch to go back inside. The living room was empty. She went upstairs and put her notebook away, then spied out of her window, trying to picture herself climbing over the wall and running away.

It was a long way to the road, and she would have to run all the way and hope for a car to give her a lift. At least the country road had more traffic than one would expect, since it connected Alice's hometown with the next bigger city. Maybe reaching the house took so long because the dirt road was bumpy and not straight. If Alice ran straight over the pasture, however, she might reach the road before either Jonas or the guard would realize she was gone.

It was risky and not well planned out, but it was the only thing she could think of and she had to try it.

Wiping her sweaty hands on her pants, she gave her belongings a sad look. If she wanted to be able to run fast, she could not carry anything with her.

Her heart was racing when she walked down the stairs, trying to keep a casual pace, prepared to run into Jonas any second.

This time, she took the back door to avoid being seen by the security guard.

In the backyard, she walked slowly, careful to look normal. She let her eyes wander over the trees with the birds hopping from branch to branch, over the still empty pool that had almost cost her life, then stretched her arms over her head and inhaled deeply, as if she had just stepped out for the first time today. She wondered if Jonas was watching her through the basement windows. He too would not be able to see her where she planned to climb the wall. Only the living room and Danny's office and bedroom were facing this side—and Jonas wasn't in any of them right now.

Casually, she strolled through the backyard and around the corner, where she stopped, making sure to choose the right angle from which the guard couldn't see her.

With closed eyes, Alice took a deep breath to steady her breathing.

You can do this.

Her eyes wandered up and down the wall, taking in its edges and faults—here, a brick was set a little bit too much inward, giving her an inch to put her foot on; there, parts of a brick had crumbled and left a small dent. The wall appeared to be almost exactly seven feet high where Alice was standing, which meant it was a bit lower than on the other side of the house. That was manageable.

Alice took a deep breath and jumped upward, her fingers gripping the top edge of the wall. Her right foot found the uneven brick and she pushed and pulled herself upward, her hips and knees grating against the stone painfully, until her elbows were over the wall. Now, she was able to pull herself up completely.

Nervous, she glanced back at the house and froze at once when she saw the large shape in the living room. Jonas was standing with his back toward her, looking down at his phone. He must have returned from his workout-session prematurely.

Alice stared at him, afraid to move, when suddenly, he flinched and turned around—almost as if he had felt her eyes on his back.

Jonas seemed to be as shocked as she was. Frozen in place, they stared at each other for a moment, until Alice found back to reality and pushed herself off the wall, down onto the grass on the other side. The impact sent a stabbing pain through her knees and ankles.

Without wasting even a second, she started running, despite the pain in her joints.

He saw me ... he'll follow me.

Alice ran as fast as she could, out into the field, her sneakers splashing drops of mud up her black pants.

A mile, maybe a bit less. That was what she had to run until she would reach the road. But what if no one would pick her up? The road looked empty now.

She pushed the thought aside and forced herself to keep running despite her burning throat and aching lungs. The last couple of weeks had drained all strength from her. The nausea, the nightmares, the lack of exercise, it all came together and made her incredibly weak. Nonetheless, she kept running. All she could hear were the sound of her footsteps and her panting.

Was Jonas following her already?

She didn't dare to look back and check. Her assumption had been right. The gravel road must take longer because of its curves. There was no way the distance she was running right now was a mile. Or maybe Danny had exaggerated on purpose to keep her from trying to walk to the road.

It gave her hope. The tar road was growing bigger before her.

I'm almost there!

She could hear him for a split second before he tried to grab her arm.

Oh god, no.

Alice yanked her arm away, avoiding his grip, and tried to keep running, but he was faster, and his fingers got a grip of the light-purple, flower print blouse she was wearing. He tried to stop her by pulling at it, but the buttons sprang off and the blouse ripped, leaving her shoulders bare.

Panicking, Alice pushed forward, trying to wriggle out of the sleeves, but Jonas's left hand found her arm and he whirled her around.

Losing her balance, Alice tripped over her own feet and landed on the moist grass. Jonas, surprised by the sudden stop, tumbled right over her and fell down as well.

Gasping for air, she tried to roll away from him, but he caught her and sat on her legs. With balled fists, she punched every part of his body that she could reach. Jonas grimaced when her fist found his nose, but it didn't do much damage.

He quickly grabbed her wrists and pinned her arms down on either side of her head. Alice could see pain contort his features when he used his right hand despite the injury.

"Why?" His voice sounded desperate and breathless from running after her.

Alice had expected him to be angry, but he looked merely pained instead. Still gasping for breath, she was unable to say a word. Her throat was on fire and there was a stabbing pain in her lungs.

"Why did you do that?" he asked again.

She kicked her leg upward, but the weight of his body was too much, and her knee didn't even reach him. Tears of anger filled her eyes.

"You trying to kill yourself?" He shifted his weight a bit, making it even harder for her to move. "He'll be back any second!" His bright green eyes were widened and looked worried—almost anxious.

"What?" she finally managed to say.

"He just called. He's on his way back already!"

Horrified, Alice could do nothing but stare at him. She was speechless.

"If he found you on the road …" His grip around her wrists loosened a bit, but he still pinned her down. "We have to go back now!"

It was too late.

The sound of screeching tires appeared and grew louder, and then it changed and became barely audible, and Alice knew that a car had just left the road and driven onto the grass.

Her heart stopped and she stared at Jonas anxiously. He seemed to be frozen in place, unsure of what to do.

There was no time to do anything anyway.

The car came to an abrupt halt about five yards next to them, then all four doors were pushed open simultaneously, and Danny, Waldo, and two men she had never seen before jumped out.

Jonas had let go of her arms at last and Alice turned her head to look at them. Danny's expression made her feel as if someone had punched her right in the stomach, and she saw him pull a gun out of his jacket.

"Get off her!" His voice was torn by anger.

It took her a moment to understand that he was pointing the gun at Jonas, not at her. Jonas obeyed, but before he could say something, Danny's polished leather shoe had found his face, and the impact sent him backward onto the grass.

"You fucking traitor!" Spit was flying from Danny's mouth.

Alice was unable to move, still out of breath. She stared at him, frozen by fear. The two strangers—both equally tall and broad, though one was dark skinned and had a beard and the other was bald and pink—were holding guns as well, all aimed at Jonas.

Shocked by the sudden turn of events, Alice could only lie on her back and stare at the gun in Danny's hand.

"Alice." There was a voice coming from right beside her, and she noticed Waldo crouching down next to her. He helped her sit up and laid the jacket of his suit around her shoulders to cover her naked skin.

"How dare you?" Danny's cry seemed to echo from the hills, and she wondered if the neighbors would hear.

Waldo helped her stand up, and Alice quickly pulled his jacket tighter around her shoulders, suddenly realizing that she was in her bra, surrounded by men.

Her eyes flicked to Jonas and she saw him spit out blood. Danny made a gesture toward the two strange men, and they grabbed one of Jonas's arms each and dragged him to the car.

A second vehicle had left the road as well and was coming to a halt next to the first one. Timothy and Paul got out, looking confused from Jonas and the men to Danny and then to Alice.

Danny gave her a quick look, then turned to Waldo. "Take her to the house, take my car. I'll drive yours."

Waldo nodded and Danny hurried after the big guys, who had pushed Jonas into the white Mercedes.

The shock was deeply in her bones, and Alice couldn't speak or move. Waldo had to nudge her toward Danny's brand-new Audi, which Timothy had been driving.

She let herself get pushed into the dark blue convertible and sat in the backseat, sunken, her mind a blur. What in the world was happening?

Waldo sat beside her, not saying a word, while Timmy drove to the house and through the gate onto the gravel parking space, where the white Mercedes was already parked.

Alice felt like she was in a trance when Waldo led her into the living room. There were shouts coming from Danny's office.

"You should go upstairs," he told her, nodding toward the staircase.

That woke her up. "No, no ... what's happening? What is he doing to him?"

Without waiting for an answer, she hurried to the office and burst into the room, Waldo, Timothy, and Paul at her heels. She found Danny standing in front of his desk, and then she saw the strange men beating up Jonas. His face was already glistening under a layer of blood.

They stopped when they saw her, and Danny turned around.

"You shouldn't be here," he said, trying to drag her back to the door.

"What are you doing? Danny, stop that!" She shoved him aside and tried to get past him, but Waldo grabbed her shoulders and forced her to stand still.

Timothy and Paul had entered the room and closed the door behind them.

"Where's the cook?" Danny asked them and they shrugged.

"His car's not here, he's probably out on errands." It was Timothy, who replied.

"Good." Danny turned back to Jonas and aimed his gun at him.

Alice gasped and tried to shake Waldo's hands off, but they held her firmly.

"He thinks he can fuck my girlfriend while I'm away?" he sneered, an expression of insanity on his face.

So, that's what he thinks.

"Danny, no, it's not—"

"Shut up!" He screamed the words at her, and she froze, paralyzed by his anger. "And I thought you were the one I could trust!" His voice sounded hurt, and he aimed the gun at Jonas's head accusingly. "Any last words?"

Alice darted forward, finally able to shake Waldo's hands off. "Danny don't!" She stood in front of Jonas, so that the muzzle of the gun now pointed at her. "Please don't shoot him, don't do this, please!"

"Move aside!" He grabbed her arm, yanked her toward him and out of the way, and aimed the gun back at his target.

"No! Danny, please don't! Don't!" Alice frantically reached for his arm which was holding the gun and tried to push it downward to take the aim off Jonas.

"Why? Why, Alice?" He looked at her, infuriated, and something in her expression made him flinch. "Do you love him? Is that it? You both betrayed me?! Do you love him?"

"What?" she gasped, shocked.

"Admit it!"

"I don't! Danny, I swear it's not like that, it's not about him, but you can't kill him! You're not like that! Danny, please, you're not a murderer!"

He stared at her with black eyes, shaking with fury and hatred. His pupils were humongous, she noticed. Was he high?

"He attacked you, Alice, he tried to fucking rape you and you tell me I can't shoot him?"

Again, he aimed the gun at Jonas, who was kneeling on the carpet, staring at the floor without saying a word. His lips were slightly parted, and blood was dripping down onto his lap, but he made no attempt to wipe it off.

"No, Danny, it's nothing like that! He didn't attack me, please, put the gun down, please!"

Why was no one else stepping in? Jonas was their friend, wasn't he? She looked at them.

Timothy was watching the scene, his face relaxed and at ease.

He hates Jonas.

Paul looked horrified, his eyes flicking from Danny to Jonas and back, but it was obvious that he would never dare speak up.

Waldo was the only one who would tell Danny what to do, but right now, he was standing near the desk, his arms crossed in front of his chest, a look of disdain on his face. He was watching the scene as if he considered it to be beneath him.

"Danny, he never touched me, you have to believe me!" Her voice was calmer now, less shaky, and she put as much sincerity in each word as possible.

Danny had hesitated so far, his expression pained, and Alice was sure that he didn't want to kill his best friend. But why wasn't Jonas defending himself?

Danny looked at her, unsure, but then pain turned to hatred and he raised the weapon once again.

Alice jumped in front of the gun at once and grabbed the barrel with her right hand, trying to move it somewhere else. "Danny, don't! Please, I can explain!" She heard her voice get thick while tears welled up in her eyes. Her words had no effect on him ... Or had they?

Slowly, he turned his head to look at her and his stare was ice-cold. "Oh, the lady's got an explanation? Let's hear it."

Alice felt her heart start racing at once and her legs felt wobbly underneath her. Quickly, she pulled her hand away from the gun.

"I ran away." The words came out fast and breathless.

Danny's eyebrows wandered up his forehead and his eyes narrowed. "What?"

"I ran away, and he ran after me and grabbed my shirt to stop me, but it ripped and I fell ... I tried to kick him and hit him, so he pinned me down."

The last words were only a whisper, but Danny was listening, his eyes glinting dangerously and his breathing accelerating.

"It must have looked weird to you, but really, why would he attack me in the middle of the fields, far away from the house?"

The logic seemed to trickle in slowly and Danny lowered the gun.

Alice's eyes flicked to Jonas, but his expression hadn't changed. He hadn't even flinched at what was happening and was still staring at the floor before him. Was he even present? Maybe he could turn off his mind, the way she always did.

"You ran away," Danny repeated, his voice quiet and icy. It left goose bumps on her arms.

"I'm sorry."

He sneered. "Oh, you're sorry ... that changes *everything*."

Alice kept her eyes on him, prepared to react to however he was going to take it. He laughed an insane laugh, looking from her to Jonas and back. "I almost killed my friend because of you! Isn't that hilarious?"

Not really.

Alice took a step back, trying to bring some distance in between them.

"You really make my life hard, Alice, do you know that?" He wiped some sweat from his forehead with the sleeve of his white dress shirt, and only then seemed to remember that he was still holding the gun.

Again, his expression changed in less than a second. Insane amusement changed into anger, and he brought the grip of the weapon down on her temple, screaming as he did so.

The blow made her knees give in, but she managed to fight off the little stars which had begun to dance in front of her eyes. Kneeling to his feet made her feel like a convict, waiting to get her head chopped off. She held the throbbing side of her face with her left hand and kept her eyes on the floor—just like Jonas.

"Why the fuck did you run away?" Spit flew from Danny's mouth when he spat the words, and never had he looked less handsome.

"Because she doesn't want to be here?"

Alice winced at the voice, and Danny spun around to face Waldo, who had left his place near the desk.

"Excuse me?" Danny stared at him with plain shock displayed on his face.

"Daniel, aren't we all just tired of this?" He nodded toward Alice. "She never wanted to be here, and you made Jonas babysit her, as if we don't have more important things to worry about."

Alice felt her whole body tense and she stared at Waldo, feeling scared to the bone.

"All she's ever done was give us trouble," the older man continued.

Danny was breathing heavily and his stare wandered from Waldo to her. "And what is that supposed to mean?"

Waldo sighed. "She doesn't know anything yet. So, either let her walk or kill her, but get it over with."

Alice felt something cold run down her spine and she saw Danny aim the gun at her.

"Is it true?" His voice was hoarse. "You really don't want to be with me?"

With widened eyes she stared into the muzzle of the pistol so close to her, pointing right between her eyes.

What was she supposed to say? Her mouth was dry.

"Daniel, for god's sake, be responsible! You can't kill her *here*."

"Shut the fuck up!" Danny yelled at Waldo, who gave him a cold look in return. He turned back to Alice, awaiting her answer.

"We have a business to run and don't have time for your relationship drama," Waldo went on, ignoring Danny's words. He didn't seem to fear him at all.

"I can't just let her walk!" Danny's voice sounded torn and desperate, and he was looking at his older colleague as if asking for advice.

"Then kill her, what do I care? She doesn't love you, Daniel, now don't be such a child about it."

When Danny turned back to look down at her, he had tears in his eyes, but he kept the gun's aim at her, nevertheless.

"Is that true? You don't love me anymore?"

Alice's eyes wandered to Waldo, who looked impatient, then to Timothy, who was now following the scene with more interest, looking worried. Paul and Jonas were staring at the floor.

She looked back up at Danny and the gun. Was this her chance to walk away? He surely would not kill her ... or would he?

"Just let her walk, man." This time, it was Timothy's voice.

"There's other women." Waldo. "You can't afford to be so emotional. Let her go."

Alice felt hope flare up in her chest. Danny would certainly listen to his friends.

"Shut up, everyone, just shut up!"

She flinched at Danny's scream and looked at the gun again, worried he might pull the trigger.

"Open your fucking mouth, Alice, do you really want to leave me?" He pressed the words through clenched teeth.

It took all of her courage to nod and say, "Yes."

He looked as if she'd slapped him. Alice could not bear to look into his eyes and dropped her gaze. Not even Waldo dared to interrupt the silence which followed her answer.

"But ... you still love me?" He sounded pleading.

"No." It was barely more than a whisper. It was not even true, she still had feelings for him, but Alice knew that he would never let her leave if she told him that.

A wave of pain seemed to engulf him at her answer. He took a step closer until the cold metal of the gun touched her forehead.

Alice felt all hope drain from her at once and tears began to run down her cheeks. She shut her eyes tightly and held her breath, waiting for him to pull the trigger.

It's not so bad. I'll still leave this place. Like I said, one way or another.

Her heart seemed to want to break out of her ribcage, as if it could sense that it was about to stop beating for good. Alice wondered if it would hurt to be shot.

Make it quick.

Nothing happened.

She opened her eyes a bit and, through a veil of her tears, saw him standing there. His hand was shaking, and he had troubles keeping the gun steady. It looked like he was fighting his demons.

Finally, he lowered the gun and Alice dared to take a breath. Everyone in the room was quiet and watching Danny, wondering what he would do next.

He walked over to the desk, where a glass and a beautifully patterned glass bottle containing a brown liquid were standing, filled the glass, and chugged it in one go. Then he turned to Waldo.

"Take her to the bunker."

Waldo's jaw dropped. "Daniel be responsible! Just let her go."

Danny whirled around and pointed the gun at him. "Do what I fucking tell you, all right? I'm still the one with the gun, and I'm willing to shoot it at each and every one of you, if you think you can disobey me!"

Timothy and Paul stiffened at once; Timothy's eyes were narrowed and Paul's widened.

"Now get her to the fucking bunker!"

Waldo hesitated, but then he walked toward Alice, who was still on her knees, frozen by fear.

He grabbed her upper arm and pulled her to her feet, then led her to the door, and it took all her remaining strength to walk without tripping over her feet. Her legs felt wobbly and the pain in her head made her dizzy. Her mind was a blur and she vaguely noticed that Waldo was leading her to the basement.

All the way he was muttering and swearing to himself. "What an idiot, what an immature little child, fucking irresponsible ..."

They reached the cellar door and proceeded downstairs. He nudged her through the corridor until they reached a heavy metal door set into the thick concrete wall.

Waldo unlocked it by turning a wheel and then pulled the door open with much effort. It was about twelve inches thick.

Alice hadn't even known they had a bunker. The door didn't look much different from the others, apart from the wheel. The room inside was empty and gray, a single lightbulb hanging from the ceiling. Apart from a drain in the far-left corner there was nothing, not even a chair to sit on.

Waldo softly shoved her inside and hesitated, studying her. "He's an idiot," he said, shaking his head. "I feel sorry for you."

Then he pushed the door shut.

18

As soon as the door had been locked behind her, Alice felt all air go out of her lungs.

The bunker had nothing, no furniture whatsoever, and it was small, maybe twenty-five square yards.

Don't panic, whatever you do, don't panic!

Alice tried to keep her breathing steady, but she was already gasping for air, like a fish on land, sucking in breaths as if there weren't any oxygen in the bunker.

The walls seemed to spin around her until everything was a blur. Her heart was racing madly.

Trembling, she sat down in a corner, rested her head on her knees and closed her eyes, trying to send her mind far away, to an open space. Maybe a hill somewhere, from which she could overlook the landscape ... With trees and oxygen ... lots of oxygen.

She felt her feet tingle. They were ice-cold.

There's lots of air, lots of air ...

The air did feel sticky though, and there was no window to open. Alice quickly lifted her head from her knees and brushed her hair back, away from her throat. Was her necklace too tight? She pulled at it, but it was loose. Nothing was keeping her from breathing, only her own imagination.

The realization rolled over her like an avalanche. They had locked her in a room with a thick iron door and no windows, and it was underground as well. Even people who did not suffer from claustrophobia would have a hard time down here.

Her throat felt dry and her airways seemed to be tightening. She was suffocating, no doubt.

Never had she been in a situation like this with no way out, not even a window to open. She listened to the sound of her racing heart and began to feel dizzy.

The shrieking sound of the huge door opening woke her up, and, confused, Alice turned her head.

The taste of stomach acid was on her tongue and she felt drowsy and nauseous.

Waldo was standing in the door, holding a plastic bottle with water and something soft and light blue in his arms. He put the bottle on the ground beside the door and gestured her to come over.

Standing up was difficult, but Alice managed and stumbled toward him.

"You're still wearing my jacket." He pointed at the black blazer around her shoulders.

Alice gave it back to him, carefully closing her ripped blouse with her other hand.

Waldo handed her the light blue thing, which turned out to be a cashmere pullover.

"I found this in your closet, it's cold down here."

Alice had already noticed that it was, and nodded.

When he was gone, she put on the pullover over her blouse and drank some water, but it tasted weird on her tongue, sticky somehow.

Exhausted, she vaguely noticed the beating of her heart getting faster again. Her feet and fingers were tingling.

Feeling drained, she sat back down in her corner and buried her face in her arms, rocking herself back and forth like a crazy person in a straitjacket in some Hollywood-movie.

How long was she supposed to stay down here? How long had she even been down here? Was Danny trying to decide what to do with her?

Alice stared at the wall opposite her and tried to imagine what he might be doing right now.

He had been high; she had seen it in his eyes. That gave her hope. Maybe there was still something good in him, something *Danny* ... Maybe it was just the alcohol and drugs that turned him into this angry madman. How could he have locked her in here?

Why? She thought desperately while frantic sobs escaped her throat. Tears streamed down her face and the salty water stung on her raw skin and almost burned when it trickled down her cheeks.

Why is he doing this to me? Why does he hate me so much?

Alice tried to remember how she had been around him.
Was I really such a control freak? Did I order him around?
Hadn't she always supported him and tried to help him? Or had she interfered too much? Had she made him feel emasculated?

Somehow, everything seemed so far away, too far away for her to grasp. Maybe it really was her fault, but why couldn't she remember? And when exactly had Danny begun to change? Why had she only noticed it when it was already too late? Or had he always been like that? Had her love for him blinded her?

It was all a blur now.

Burying her head in her hands, she let the sobs take over. No one could hear her down here anyway.

The hours passed—or maybe it was only minutes? And nothing happened, until the door awoke her out of a light sleep and the bearded guy who had helped beat up Jonas appeared. He said nothing, didn't even look at her when he put down a bowl of food, an empty bucket, and a blanket. As quickly as he had come, he was gone again, and Alice kept staring at the door, wondering if she had only imagined him. But the blanket and the food were still there.

Glad to finally have something warm and soft to sit on, Alice wrapped herself tightly in the blanket. The food smelled nice and her mouth began to water, but then she noticed the bucket and frowned. What was it for? Something in her mind flickered—a memory.

She had seen that bucket before ... the night, Martin had killed that guard and managed to break out of the room with the stairs.

It had contained his piss.

Her jaw dropped. They could not seriously expect her to pee in a bucket? They had made Martin pee in it obviously, and now they treated her the same way. Scornfully, she eyed the bucket, then moved away from it and sat down in the far-right corner of the room, huddled in her blanket.

He's stolen everything from me. My freedom, my life, even parts of my dignity ... but he won't make me pee in that bucket.

Her mouth felt dry, but she ignored the bottle of water next to the food, and left the bowl untouched as well, ignoring her rumbling stomach. Her life was over anyway, she could as well die of thirst.

More time passed and more panic attacks came and went.

Alice's hands were cold and damp, her feet numb. The lightbulb flickered and went out. Her eyelids drooped and she drifted off.

The next time she awoke, she was shivering in her blanket and her cheek hurt and felt cold. It took her a while to realize that she was lying on the floor, her face on the naked concrete. Her ears were ringing, and her tongue was sticking to her palate, dry and furry.

Every movement took a lot of effort, but she managed to push herself off the floor into an upright position, and leaned her head against the cool wall.

Her temples were throbbing, and she knew it must be the lack of water. But she was stronger than that.

I'm not going to drink until they let me use a bathroom.

How long had it been since the last visit, she had gotten?

To Alice, it felt as if she had been down here for days, but they had only brought her food once, so she was sure not more than one day had passed—unless they were deliberately starving her.

She crawled on all fours to where she suspected the door to be, carefully feeling the ground in front of her with her hand before moving forward. Her fingers found something—a bowl. She let them wander along the ground and found the bucket, the bottle of water and ... another bottle of water and then a plate with something soft and slimy on it.

Quickly, she pulled her hand away in disgust, but then she inhaled and recognized the smell of pasta with tomato sauce.

They had brought her food and water again, and she hadn't even noticed.

I must've been out cold.

Had they noticed the broken lightbulb? How was she supposed to eat in the dark? Or were they torturing her on purpose?

Alice wondered who had been down here. Waldo? Timothy? One of the new guys? Or ... even Danny?

She felt a stinging sensation in her chest that had nothing to do with the panic attacks.

How could he do this to her?

Despite his change of personality and everything he had done to her, there were still parts of her that loved him, and it hurt to be treated like that.

He must really hate me ... but why can't he just let me go?

She crawled back into her corner where she had left the blanket, and pulled it over her shoulders, shivering. Was it night outside? It must surely be warmer during the day. Or did the warmth not reach the bunker?

So many questions and there was no one to answer them. Dry sobs built up in her throat, but no tears came.

Apparently, there were none left.

Dots of light began dancing before her eyes. Was she hallucinating?

Alice touched her left arm with her right hand, feeling her cold skin and cashmere pullover under her fingers. She was still solid, but her own touch felt distant, as if there were a thick, invisible layer of some cold material around her, covering every inch of her body.

She pinched herself and felt nothing. Panicking, she pinched herself again, this time harder.

Still, there was no pain. Her heart began to beat faster, but even the panic seemed far away, as if it were not her own fear but someone else's.

Again and again, she pinched herself, harder every time. She even scratched at her skin with her nails, until it started to burn. Even that pain was only a fracture of what it was supposed to be. Something wet trickled down her arm and she realized it must be blood.

Trembling, she wrapped the blanket tighter around her body and lay down with her head resting on her arm and her knees drawn up to her chin.

"*Alice!*"

Danny's face was there. Tanned, beautiful, his big blue eyes opened wide. He wasn't smiling.

Let me sleep.

He moved closer, eyes fixed on her, his hair wallowing lightly with every movement. He was breathtaking. "*Wake up! Wake up and open your eyes.*"

Alice moaned and tried to ignore him.

"*Alice!*"

She wasn't going to get fooled by him.

I'm not falling for this. You're a product of my imagination.

"*Alice...*"

"*Alice...*"

"Alice!"

She felt her head roll on the concrete floor. Someone was shaking her, though their touch felt distant. Could it be … ? Was Danny really there?

Blinking, she tried to open her eyes, but immediately shut them again. There was light—way too much light—and it was blinding her, even through closed eyelids.

"Alice!" the voice called again from far away, but it sounded nothing like Danny's. Big hands gripped her firmly and pulled her into a sitting position.

She clutched her hands to her eyes to shield herself from the light.

Go away, let me sleep.

Her mouth was too dry to speak and she felt incredibly weak. The wall in her back seemed to be made from cotton balls, even the ground below was soft, as if she were sitting on clouds. Everything was muffled—the sounds, the pain, even her own thoughts.

I must be dreaming. But why can't I wake up?

She tried again to open her eyes but failed. The light was too bright.

"Can you hear me?" the deep, scratchy voice in front of her asked.

Alice decided to ignore it and go back to sleep.

"You must eat," the voice urged. "You haven't even drunk any of your water, are you trying to kill yourself?"

She heard him mutter something else, something that wasn't directed at her.

Is this real? What if it's not a dream? But why does it feel so unreal?

She opened her eyes a little bit but shielded them with her hands, only spying through the gaps between her fingers. The face in front of her was stern and wrinkled and framed by white hair. His skin looked tanned, almost leathery.

It was Waldo. She saw his lips move but could not hear anything.

Suddenly, she felt incredibly tired, and her chin dropped down onto her chest. Holding her hands against her face felt like lifting weights, so she let them fall into her lap.

The hands shook her again, but she almost couldn't feel it.

"Alice! For god's sake, get a grip!"

Irritated by him shaking her, she opened her eyes a bit. His eyes were fixed on her, cold and blue—not like Danny's blue. It was a light blue, almost grayish and there was no softness in them. He seemed to be thinking about something.

"You've lost it, haven't you? You've lost your wits."

I've lost a lot lately. If I could at least get some privacy.

"You've gone nuts," he added, shaking his head slowly.

White clouds seemed to be hanging in the air around her, in front of his face and everywhere in the room, like a thick fog.

Waldo sighed and his sigh seemed to echo from the walls. He pulled his hands away, and the sudden removal of the weight on her shoulders made her sink onto the ground, where she rested her head gratefully on the soft concrete floor. It didn't even feel cold anymore, it was just the right temperature, and it felt like a pillow.

"Alice, I really need you to finish now."

"I'm sorry, Liz, the computer's not working. I'm really trying." Alice gave her boss an apologetic look.

Liz frowned and her hawk's eyes wandered to the computer, where several windows were flickering frozen on the screen. "Have you called IT?"

Alice nodded. "They just sent someone; they should be here any minute."

Liz sighed. "These things always happen when we're under a lot of stress. I'm telling you, Alice, it's modern technology, it has been a thorn in my flesh ever since." She turned and walked away.

Alice remained sitting at her desk, legs crossed, and waited.

Her desk was next to the window, so she let her eyes wander over the street below, the busy road that was still covered in black mud—remnants of the snow that had fallen last night.

It was February and winter was far from being over.

"Miss Bouchart?"

Alice turned and saw a young man standing in front of her. He was tall—very tall—and he was wearing a black T-shirt with a skull on it. His dark hair was long and uncombed, and his big blue eyes beamed.

Liz grimaced at his appearance and Alice quickly got off her chair to greet him.

"IT?" she asked and shook his hand.

He nodded. "And where's—oh, never mind. I see the problem." Laughing, he came closer. "May I?"

Alice stepped aside and let him sit on her chair.

He gestured toward the desk. "Please take a seat, it might take a while. Looks like you've caught a virus."

His beautiful eyes followed Alice's boss, who was walking back to her private office. Then he turned and looked at her, and she felt herself blush under his gaze. "Been surfing too much online? Forbidden websites?" He winked.

Alice bit her lip and shrugged.

He laughed again and his laugh was contagious. "Don't worry, it'll stay between us."

She relaxed and sat down on the desk next to the computer. "Yeah, I've been surfing a lot. My work is boring."

The IT guy pulled a pack of chewing gums from the pocket of his ripped jeans and offered her one. She took it and started chewing.

"My work's boring as well."

"Really? I thought IT's very interesting."

He shook his head. "Nah, you wouldn't believe the people who call us up ... Usually we have to tell them to restart their computers and then the problem is solved." He shook his head and grimaced.

Alice watched him work and when he was done, he grinned at her broadly. She thanked him and shook his hand.

"By the way," he gave her a smile. "I left my contact in your Outlook account. Feel free to text me whenever you're bored."

Blushing again, she smiled. "I will, thanks."

He shook her hand again, even though they already had. "I'm Danny by the way."

The air was moist and cold and burned in her throat when she breathed it. A red glow pierced its way through her eyelids and blinded her.

She still saw his warm smile in front of her, his wallowing hair, and his beautiful eyes. A cough went through her body and she flinched at the pain in her lungs.

The ground still felt soft beneath her, though there was a faint pain in her head, like a pressure on her forehead. Her body was aching, but the pain seemed far away.

I'm still dreaming ... but the other dream was better.

She tried to hold on to Danny's image, his smile, the moment of happiness ... but the harder she tried to grasp it, the faster it was fading.

Suddenly, there was a pressure on her shoulders and her head was lifted off the ground. Someone was pulling her into an upright position.

She felt something on her lips, something hard and cool ... a bottle?

"Drink," a voice ordered, and cool liquid began to flow into her mouth. Alice started coughing, but then she remembered how to swallow and gulped it down—though half of it dripped down her chin.

The person waited for her to swallow, then the bottle was lowered onto her lips once again.

She shook her head.

"Drink," the voice repeated. "It's only water, why won't you drink it?"

I'm not using the bucket.

"What?"

Had she said it aloud? Her eyes flickered open, and she stared at Waldo, who was crouching in front of her, the bottle in his hand. "What did you say about the bucket?"

Her head felt wobbly on her shoulders and it took her a lot of effort to keep her eyes open.

"Not ... using it." It was only a whisper.

Confused, Waldo stared at her, but then he seemed to understand and shook his head slowly. "You're just like him. Immature, childish, irresponsible. Seriously Alice, you and him, you are giving me a hard time." He put the bottle to her lips, ignoring her objection, and she had to swallow the water in order for it to go down the right pipe.

When she was done gulping it down, she cleared her throat, but her words still only came out as a whisper. "Where is he? What's he doing?"

Waldo put the lid on the bottle and put it on the ground. "He's still unsure what to do with you." He stared at her, thinking, and there was pity in his eyes. "You know Alice, I don't like you but this ..." He gestured at the room surrounding them. "I wouldn't do that to you. I told him to either kill you or let you go, and honestly, both are fine by me. But keeping you down here, rotting, it's just inhumane."

Alice had troubles processing his words; they still seemed to be coming through a thick layer of fog.

"Can't you do it?" she whispered.

"What? Let you walk?"

"Or kill me, both are fine by me."

He grimaced at her using his words, not sure if she was mocking him. "That would not be wise." Sighing, he stood, and again, without him holding her, she was too weak to sit upright and slowly sank back onto the floor. She felt his eyes on her for a moment, but then he left.

Alice remained staring at the blurry wall for a while, until her eyes closed again.

The walls were gray and cold and towering over her like big, monstrous creatures, depriving her of her freedom. Sobbing, she stared at them, as if her gaze could make them crumble.

"I've had it with you and your behavior!" the high-pitched voice cried through the wooden cellar door. "You're giving me nothing but a hard time, *tous les* fucking *jours*! What did I do to deserve you? What did I do wrong? *Tu me fais chier*!"

Alice covered her ears with her hands and began humming. She knew the tirade of hate, could recite each and every word of it.

Go away, you evil bat, just leave me in peace.

After a while, she put her hands down again, knowing, her mother had grown tired and had left.

It was cold in the basement. Alice shivered and hugged herself to keep warm. She let her eyes wander through the storage room and felt her stomach rumble.

Was there anything to eat?

The shelves were stacked with jars of jam and there were some with pickles as well.

Grimacing, she pushed the thought of food away.

Time passed and the hunger grew worse. Had her mother forgotten her?

Alice swallowed her pride and disgust, and walked over to the nearest shelf, took a jar of pickles and one with strawberry jam, and sat back down on the hard, cold concrete floor.

She opened the lids and began to stick pickles into the jam, then she ate the sour-sweet mixture and it made her gag.

She's forgotten me, definitely.

Panic built up inside her and she let her eyes wander across the room. The light flickered and for a moment, she thought it would go out, which made her heart skip a beat. But it went back on and she exhaled, relieved.

Apart from bottles filled with alcoholic beverages, there was nothing to drink and her thirst was beginning to feel unbearable.

Desperate, Alice started calling for her mother and hammering her fists against the solid wooden door. No response.

Several hours passed and Alice began to believe that her mother was never going to let her out again.

She never wanted me. Maybe she finally decided to get rid of me.

Crying, she curled into a ball between two shelves, until exhaustion took over and lulled her to sleep.

Sirens yanked her out of troubled dreams, and it took her a moment to remember where she was. Alice blinked into the dim cellar light and stretched her aching back. Her whole body was aching from sleeping on the hard floor.

The sirens grew louder and louder, until dancing blue light fell through the narrow window underneath the ceiling. The sirens were right next to the house when they stopped.

Holding her breath, she listened, and then she could hear unfamiliar voices coming from upstairs.

Without thinking, Alice hurried to the door and punched her fists against it, screaming, until the key rattled and the door flung open. A paramedic stared at her, shocked by her appearance. She shoved him aside and ran upstairs, where she found her mother lying on the carpet, covered in puke.

Frozen, Alice stood, staring at the grotesque figure on the floor, until the paramedic who had let her out put a hand on her shoulder and said, "Don't worry, she's alive. We're taking her to the hospital."

Alice remained frozen in the same place, until the paramedics and her mother had disappeared. Then she went to her room, filled a bag with clothes, stole some money from her mother's purse, and left the tiny house without looking back.

"Alice!"

Alice seemed to fly upward, and the house grew smaller beneath her. She could still see herself from above but now, everything dissolved into thin air.

Someone slapped her but the pain was mild and muffled and she barely felt it.

She was shaken roughly and when she finally managed to open her eyes, she saw the unfriendly face of Waldo in front of her, his wrinkles looking deeper than before.

"Alice," he called again, and she blinked at him, confused.

Hadn't he just left?

"Get up, I'm done with this idiocy." He pulled her upward firmly until she was standing, but her legs were too weak to support her weight, and he had to hold her to keep her from falling.

"Danny...?" she whispered.

"He seems to have forgotten about you." Waldo shook his head in disgust. "One bullet, that's all it would take. One bullet, or just open the goddamned gate, that's it. But no, he rather lets you rot down here, pretending you don't exist." He pulled her toward the door and Alice did her best to move her feet along.

"Why?" Her foot got entangled on the step that led to the corridor of the basement, and she had to lift it up, which was harder than expected.

"He's in the office right now. I'm taking you to your room."

Waldo heaved her over the step and out into the corridor, where he dragged her along until they reached the stairs that led to the living room. He half carried her up the steps.

The living-room seemed to be empty. Danny's office door was closed, but muffled voices were coming through it.

Waldo dragged her up the stairs to the second floor, and down the hallway to her bedroom. Sunlight was falling through the window and onto her bed. Everything looked entirely strange, as if Alice had never been here before.

Waldo made her sit on the bed and studied her for a moment. "You should drink some water and I'll have food brought to you later. And this time, eat it, you got your toilet back."

Slowly, she nodded, trying to make sense of what he was saying.

Everything still felt unreal, but the events were too weird for a dream, so Alice couldn't shake off the feeling that it was actually happening.

But why did it feel so strange? Why was every sound, every feeling muffled by what seemed to be some kind of white fog?

"Why did you do that?" she asked him in a thin voice.

His stare was piercing and cold, but there was also something fatherly in his expression when he said, "I have a daughter almost your age. I really don't approve of you and I wouldn't mind if he had just shot you. But locking you up like that... it's simply disgusting."

He turned and walked out, closing the door behind him.

Later that day, Timothy came to her room and he smiled at her, though he seemed more distant than usual. He brought her a tray with some food and a cup of tea, and Alice drank the tea thankfully.

"How long was I down there?" Her voice was thin and weak, but at least she managed more than a whisper.

"It's Saturday, the twenty-first." Timothy's eyes wandered over her face and he frowned.

Alice took a bite of the slice of bread on the tray, but it felt very dry on her tongue and she had to flush it down with tea.

Three days ... She had been down there for three days.

"What happened?"

Timothy sighed and seemed to think. "He was ... crazy. Waldo told him to decide what to do with you, but he just yelled and told us not to talk about you. No one dared to mention your name at all and when Dan didn't bring it up, Waldo thought it would be best to bring you some water and food ... I really don't know if Dan wanted to starve you down there."

It felt like he was talking to someone else. His voice was far away, and Alice had to focus hard to understand him.

"The guy ... with the beard ... he came to me once."

Timothy nodded. "They're Dan's new gorillas. His personal bodyguards or assistants or whatever." There was disdain in his voice when he said it, and Alice suspected that no one liked the newest addition to the group.

"What happened to Jonas?"

Timothy winced at the name and grimaced, his hatred of Jonas clearly visible in his expression. "Dan apologized and they seem to have put it behind them, but Jonas left. I doubt he'll be back."

Alice nodded and forced herself to take another bite of bread. "Pickles would be nice ... and jam."

Timothy stared at her as if she were crazy. "We're gonna tell him you're here, by the way. As soon as he's done with work. Can't keep it from him anyway since he sleeps right next door."

Alice felt nothing at his words. Her whole body was numb, and she couldn't even remember why she had to be afraid of Danny. He was *her* Danny, after all—wasn't he? The nice guy with the skull shirt and uncombed hair ...

Somehow though, his name had a dark ring to it. Was she forgetting something?

339

Timothy watched her closely, a wary expression on his face. "You look horrible," he said.

"Thanks, Timmy, I'm relieved. That way I don't have to worry about you hitting on me."

Hurt, he grimaced, but then his expression got softer. "I'm not saying you're not pretty anymore ... You just look ... like you've been through hell."

After Timothy had left, Alice checked her reflection in the bathroom mirror, and she did not recognize who was staring back at her through the glass.

The woman in the mirror looked older, worn-out. Her cheekbones were clearly visible underneath her papery skin, and her lips were dry and fissured. There were deep, dark shadows underneath her eyes, but the loss of weight made her dark eyes look even bigger, like those of a cartoon character.

Alice took off her clothes and stared at her naked body. Her collarbone stuck out, and she was able to count her ribs. Her breasts had shrunk. At least she didn't need to put on a bra anymore.

It was funny. All, Alice could feel while staring at the strange woman in the mirror, was curiosity. The fact that her attractiveness had disappeared along with her weight made her feel ... nothing. Nothing at all. She felt no connection to the person in the mirror, so why should any of it bother her?

She brushed her teeth to get rid of the disgusting taste in her mouth, then took a long and hot shower, hoping it might bring some life back into her. After the shower, she was dizzy and out of breath, as if she had run a marathon.

Not even the TV managed to break through her numbness. Nothing felt real anymore, not the voices coming from the TV, not the singing of the birds outside or the warmth of the sunrays that fell through the window, not the scratching sound of her pen on paper and least of all, herself.

I'm dead after all.

Danny came to see her that evening, probably right after the others had told him that she was back in her room.

Alice was sitting on her bed, staring at the TV without following the story of what was playing. When the door opened, she tensed, knowing who was standing there even without turning her head.

Danny looked different from how she remembered him.

His hair was short, his cheeks neatly shaven, his dress shirt ironed, and there was something about him that made her shiver.

Or had he been like that before? She couldn't remember.

Danny said nothing, and just stood in the door for what seemed like an eternity.

Then finally, he stepped forward, reached the bed, grabbed the remote from where it was lying, and turned off the TV.

Alice stared at the black screen blankly, waiting for him to say something. Would he hurt her? Would she even feel it if he did?

He sat down on the mattress next to her, his eyes wandering up and down her body—from her eyes to the hands she had folded in her lap. She avoided his stare.

He seemed to be thinking of something to say, but no words left his lips. He reached over and laid his hand on hers lightly, as if to check whether she was solid or not.

Still, Alice kept her eyes on the TV and his touch didn't even make her flinch. She barely felt it at all. She heard him breathe slowly, and with each breath he exhaled the room seemed to get colder.

"Are you really here?" she muttered, confused by his silence. She looked up at him and barely recognized his face. His features were hard, his lips pressed together tightly into a thin line, and his stare was cold and distant. There was nothing geeky about him, nothing warm. He smelled of cologne.

At her words however, a line appeared on his forehead.

"What's going on with you?" he asked, his voice as cold as his stare.

"I don't know," she whispered. "I feel like I'm in a dream ... I don't know what's real anymore."

The line on his forehead deepened and he squeezed her hand. "What happened down there?" His eyes narrowed and she had the impression that he was struggling to remain calm. There was disdain in his eyes and even hatred.

"I don't remember ... Only that I saw you but then you disappeared, and Waldo was there ... and then I was with you again, but we only just met. I really thought it was real. We were so happy ..."

Somehow, her words made Danny's angry mask break and his eyes turned shiny. "Why are you saying things like that when it's clear you don't love me anymore?"

Alice's eyes flicked back to his face in confusion. "Of course, I love you."

He flinched and pulled his hand back, leaving hers warm where he'd touched it. "You said you don't love me anymore, that you want to leave me." There was pain in his voice.

"Did I?" Alice tried hard to remember what had happened, and finally the fragments of the memory fell into their right place, and together they created an image of what had happened in Danny's office, with Jonas and the others.

"Oh," she said, understanding. "I lied ... I really want to leave this house and I remember wanting to leave you as well, because of what you did ... But I do love you, you know ..."

Danny stared at her and his features softened a bit. His lips were slightly parted, and he seemed to be touched by her words. "Why did you say it?"

"Because I thought you'd let me go." Her gaze dropped down to her hands and she felt tears in her eyes, tears of frustration. She wanted to feel what she had felt back then, to remember why she hated him, why she wanted to leave him, but now, everything was so far away, all feelings had been shut down and a blanket of numbness was covering her.

Danny misinterpreted her tears and shifted over to sit beside her, his back against the wall. "I'll never let you go."

What could have been a lovely promise, sounded like a threat coming from him.

Alice shivered and he put his arm around her, pulling her closer.

"Let's face it Alice, I'm a selfish asshole. I might as well take advantage of my reputation, don't you think?" He laughed coldly and it gave her goose bumps.

"You're keeping me locked up." Her voice was toneless, dead, just like her spirit.

"If I have to, yes. But it's up to you. You can do what I say and have a good life, or you can fight me and lose."

She swallowed dryly. "You can't keep me here forever."

Danny pulled her head onto his chest and started caressing her hair. "I'm sorry I had to lock you in the bunker, I really am. But be sure of one thing: If I have to, I'll do it again."

Alice tried to pull her head away from him, but he put his hands on her temples and held her face fixed in front of his, looking deeply into her eyes. His grip hurt on the swollen side of her face, but she barely felt it.

"Do you want to go back to the bunker?"

She tried to shake her head, but his grip was too tight. "N-no."

Smiling, he said, "See, that's what I thought." He pulled her back into his embrace and held her there, while she lay in his arms, unable to move.

Minutes passed and finally, he muttered, "It's time for dinner." He loosened his grip around her, and she pulled back from him.

"I do worry about you ... Maybe the bunker was a bit hard on you." He studied her face and frowned. "You look horrible."

"I know." She tried to avoid his hand, but he reached over and stroked her cheek.

"You'll stay here in your room. I'll lock the door. I will have food brought to you and you will eat it, do you understand?"

Alice stared at him blankly.

"You'll eat and drink and sleep and you'll get better. I can't even let you be seen like this; people would wonder." He got off the bed and stood there for a moment, towering over her, his head blocking the light of the ceiling lamp. It looked like he had a halo. How unfitting.

"I don't miss your attitude Alice, but I do hope you'll get back on your feet. You're really miserable right now. It breaks my heart to see you like this." He turned on his heels and left the room, and Alice remained sitting on the bed in the same position for who knows how long, until the drowsiness won and she fell asleep again.

The numbness remained and it began to truly scare her. Was she actually losing her mind? She ate the food that was brought to her—at least some of it—and spent most of her time just lying on her bed, staring at the wall, but no recovery was in sight.

Again and again, she would pinch herself or claw at her skin, until her left wrist was covered in scratch marks.

The person in the mirror seemed to become stranger every day and she barely recognized herself at all.

Danny visited her a couple of times, but he never touched her apart from hugging and caressing her. She was glad that he wasn't demanding 'favors', and yet, she could not shake off the feeling that he didn't find her attractive anymore.

It was a good thing he had lost interest in her body, but it was hurtful all the same.

Alice stared at her reflection and fought against hot tears that threatened to run down her cheeks. The bruise, the grip of the gun had left on her face, had almost faded out.

Still, she hated her reflection.

I'm ugly.

Distraught, she punched the bathroom mirror hard, but there was no pain.

I could break every bone in my body and not feel a thing.

Tempted by the idea, she hit her fist against the glass, once, twice, and it broke to her surprise.

Shards rained down into the sink and she picked one up. It was big and she could still see herself reflected in it, as if she herself had broken, leaving behind only fragments.

Disgusted, Alice stared at it, and was about to throw it back into the sink when her thumb brushed over the sharp edge of the glass.

Without thinking, she held it to her already damaged left wrist and pressed it into her skin, only lightly at first, but when there was no pain, she pushed harder and dragged it along the blue line of her vein.

Finally, there was pain, though it felt distant and not nearly as strong as it was supposed to.

Bright red blood had emerged from the wound and was running down her arm, dripping off her hand and into the sink.

Make me feel again!

She glared at the shard in her hand, as if it were its fault that she couldn't feel anything. Tears of anger blurred her vision and she pressed the glass onto her skin again, hard, cutting it open, until the skin parted wide and revealed the flesh underneath it. Way more blood than expected gushed out of the wound and Alice stared at it, feeling a weird sense of satisfaction, until a sudden dizziness made her drop the shard. She grabbed the edge of the sink with trembling hands, but her legs were not able to support her weight any longer. Feeling nauseous, Alice sank to her knees and then down onto the white tiles. The food she had forced herself to eat was revolting in her stomach, and she rolled into a fetal position in front of the toilet in case she would have to bend her head over it soon.

Sleep came suddenly and rolled over her, numbing the nausea and pain.

Alice awoke to hands pulling her up from the floor and when she opened her eyes, she saw Danny's big blue ones in front of her—and they looked worried.

"The fuck did you do?!"

Confused, she blinked at him and watched him press some toilet paper on her arm.

"Why did you do that Alice? Why did you try to kill yourself?"

Weakly, she tried to pull her arm out of his grip but failed. "I didn't ... Why would you say that?"

Danny's eyes widened and he gestured to the deep cuts on her left arm. "Uh, because of *that*, maybe?"

She sighed. "It's just a vein, not an artery. I'd probably have to cut my whole arm off if I wanted to kill myself."

Danny looked taken aback by her answer. "But why did you do it?"

Tears welled up in her eyes and his expression softened.

"I just want to feel something, get rid of the numbness ... I feel like I'm dead inside." Sobbing, she covered her face with her hands, feeling embarrassed.

"Don't move, I'll get my first aid kit from the bedroom." He stood and left the room, and reappeared a bit later, carrying a small metal box in his arm. He squatted down beside her and put some disinfection spray on the cut. Alice watched him dab the skin around the cuts dry and apply several butterfly bandages to close the wound. Afterward, he put a thick bandage around her arm.

A voice from the corridor interrupted him and he looked up. "Someone's calling me, wait a second."

Alice watched him leave and stared at her bandaged arm. It felt weird to be taken care of by the same man who was responsible for her suffering.

Her eyes wandered to the metal box by her feet and she pulled it closer. Next to the usual first-aid supplies there were packs of medications that caught her eye. She took out one of the packs and read the description.

Sleeping pills ... Since when does Danny take sleeping pills?

She eyed the pack suspiciously. There was a second one in the box and she took it out as well. Maybe they would come in handy in the fight against her nightmares.

Without knowing what she was doing, she hid the pills in the cabinet underneath the sink and closed the first aid kit.

Danny took the box back without checking its contents, and ordered her to go to bed and get some sleep. He later sent Anita in to clean the mess in the bathroom, but Alice barely noticed, having already been overpowered by her exhaustion.

Later that evening, a knock on the door woke her up and to Alice's surprise, a very familiar face appeared in the doorframe: Jonas's.

Confused and speechless, Alice stared at him as he hesitantly stepped into the room and closed the door behind him.

Unsure of what to do, he remained standing in front of the closed door awkwardly.

"You're still here?" she asked him, her tongue still half-asleep.

He nodded.

Alice pushed herself up from the mattress and leaned her back against the wall, feeling dazed. Curious, she studied him.

Jonas looked worn-out but also younger, somehow. How was that possible? Her gaze wandered over his face and she realized that, despite the bruises on his cheeks and the deep shadows underneath his eyes, he looked more boyish than before. Had he lost his confidence?

"I'm sorry for almost getting you killed ..." Alice remembered how the strangers had beaten him up and felt guilty.

"Don't apologize." He shifted uncomfortably. "Not your fault."

Alice waited for him to say more, but when he didn't, she asked, "Why are you here?"

Jonas's green eyes had lost some of their brightness and he looked very tired. "He asked me to keep an eye on you. Says you're crazy or somethin.'"

She frowned. "Charming."

Sighing, he pulled a cigarette from the pack in his pocket. "Mind?"

She shook her head.

Jonas lit the cigarette and inhaled deeply, then leaned his back against the wall.

"Why would he send you to check on me?"

He shrugged. "Isn't that what he's always done?"

"Yes, but ... after what happened ..."

"He still trusts me. And now he feels guilty."

"Did you forgive him?"

His gaze rested on her and he seemed to ponder. "What else am I supposed to do?"

"I don't know ..."

They looked at each other for a moment without saying a word. Jonas put the cigarette out on the door handle and put the stub into the pocket of his leather jacket. "How d'you feel?"

Puzzled, Alice stared at him, but then she decided to be honest. "I feel unreal ... numb, somehow. Why d'you ask?"

"He's worried you might be mental."

"And what's that got to do with you?"

"He thinks I know what to do 'cause I study psychology."

Jonas's words seemed to take a long time before they reached her, and her gaze remained blank. "So ... you're my shrink now?"

He shrugged and stared at his feet.

Again, they remained silent for a while until he finally spoke. "What happened?"

The memory of the bunker brought tears to her eyes. "No fucking idea, Jonas. All I know is that I'm claustrophobic and I hate basements and he knows it, but he put me down there anyway. I almost died of a heart attack and since then, I feel like this." Alice felt anger in her chest, and it was a good feeling, but still, it was faint and only a fracture of what she was supposed to feel.

"You want my shrink opinion?"

She nodded.

"Sounds like derealization."

"De-what?"

"You've suffered anxiety to such an extent, your mind didn't know how to handle it anymore and detached itself from reality."

Alice stared at him, trying to understand what he was saying.

"What you're experiencing is normal ... under the circumstances."

At least that was understandable. "So, you think I'm not crazy?"

He shook his head. "It will pass, don't worry."

Alice smiled at him. "You're a good shrink ... unless of course, I'm just dreaming all of this."

"I assure you, you're not."

"So you're saying ... it'll pass just like that?"

"If you eliminate your stress."

"You want me to kill Danny?"

Perplexed, Jonas looked at her, not understanding the joke. "I'll tell him to give you some space."

"That'd be nice."

Jonas kept his promise and Danny left her alone for the next couple of days.

The fog seemed to slowly evaporate, but with the return of her sense of reality, all the memories and emotions came back as well, and Alice found herself spiraling down into a depression.

The bunker was gone, but ever since her attempt to escape, Danny kept her locked in her bedroom and she wasn't even allowed to get some fresh air anymore—except through the window.

Danny sent his new 'gorillas' to feed her, but they never talked to her or even looked at her, and she felt lonelier with every solitary minute that passed. She tried to recall her fantasy refuge, but since her time in the bunker her ability to daydream had been damaged by her fear of losing reality.

The world was wonderful outside. The sun was shining, the birds were singing, the trees had blossomed, and the air was enriched with the scents of spring.

Alice kept her window open and sat on the windowsill, gazing out and breathing in the smell of freedom. She rested her head against the cool metal bars and felt like a bird in a golden cage.

A knock on the door startled her. The door was opened slowly, and Jonas appeared. He looked at her and his eyes wandered from her to the open window and the world beyond. Pity flickered over his face.

"What is it?" she asked impatiently.

"Danny said—"

"To keep an eye on me? In case I break the mirror again and cut my arteries?"

Jonas grimaced. Her honesty seemed to make him uncomfortable. "Something like that," he admitted.

"I'm not going to do such a thing. Reality has finally struck again and there's no need to cut my arm open to feel something, trust me, I feel enough as it is." She turned her head back to the window, waiting for him to leave, but he remained standing in the door.

"He told me to keep you company ... if that's what you want."

Alice bit her lip and wondered if it *was* what she wanted. Her mind wandered back to the day he'd brought her to the concert and their walk in the snow afterward. She had gotten to like him then; it had felt like real friendship. Until he had snapped and smashed the cupboard behind her head, probably imagining it to be her face.

"I doubt it's what *you* want."

He hesitated, but then he took a few steps forward and she felt his gaze on her. "I don't mind ... if you want to play cards or somethin'."

Alice sighed and kept her eyes on the birch in front of her window, watching a bird feeding its chicks.

"I think you do, actually. I think being here makes you uncomfortable."

Jonas pulled his pack of cigarettes out of his pocket and lit one.

Alice reached out and he gave her one as well and lit it.

"You seem different," she noted.

He exhaled a cloud of smoke and said nothing.

"Why did you let him get away with this? He almost killed you!"

"He almost killed you too."

"Yeah, but I *want* to leave! Hell, I've tried to leave several times ... But you are not locked up, you could just go."

Sighing, Jonas dropped his gaze, as if the answer were lying on the floor. "You want honesty?"

Alice nodded.

"I left. But then I felt responsible."

"For what?"

"You."

She frowned. "Why?"

"Because I brought you here. Least I can do is make sure you stay alive."

"What are you talking about?" She studied his expression, which was still hard to read despite the apparent loss of confidence.

"What I said ... you know, in the kitchen back then ... it was true. If I'm not here, someone else is."

"Like Danny's new gorillas?"

He nodded.

"So ... you *asked* him to get your job back?"

He nodded again.

"You don't have to do this, Jonas. I don't need you to pretend to like me. It's not fair. If I can't have a real friend, I'd rather have none."

Jonas looked at her, and she saw a warmth in his eyes she hadn't noticed before. "You remind me of my sister."

What was that supposed to mean? Frowning at him, she said nothing.

"That is ... why I feel responsible."

Alice scoffed. "Charming. You're just like Waldo, you know."

"Huh?"

"He told me he can't stand me, but apparently, I remind him of his daughter, so he wouldn't let me rot in the bunker."

Jonas looked taken aback. "That's not what I meant, I'm not—"

"It's okay, Jonas, you don't have to explain anything to me. I know you don't like to talk. And I know he's your friend and you'll always defend his actions ... and I just don't fit in. I'm not supposed to be here, and I feel like everybody's blaming me for being here, even though I never chose this." Alice rested her head on her knees and covered her face with her arms. Talking to Jonas was giving her a headache and she wished he would just leave.

He misinterpreted her posture though and thought she was crying, so he stepped closer and put a hand awkwardly on her shoulder. His touch felt nice somehow and even though Alice doubted he actually cared, she decided to pretend he did.

"He's been ... very good to me. Like a brother. I feel like I owe him, but I don't approve of his actions," he tried to explain.

"I know nothing about your history, but like I said, you don't owe me any explanations," Alice muttered without lifting her head.

"I think I do." His voice sounded affectionate and a deep sadness rolled over her.

It was a good thing her face was already hidden underneath her arms, so he couldn't see the tears in her eyes. It felt like everybody was playing with her feelings.

Timothy had been nice to her because he wanted to have sex with her, Waldo had been nice because of his own personal moral code, Danny was constantly changing between being her caring boyfriend and a monster, and now Jonas was acting like a friend again, after having made clear only recently that he was just doing his job.

The more confusing the people around her behaved, the less she trusted her own instincts.

It was tiring.

"Tell me about him," she muttered. "I didn't even know your friendship is so deep. I was a horrible girlfriend, wasn't I? Is that why he's so angry all the time? I feel like ... I paid too little attention to him and his life."

Jonas hesitated and pulled his hand back from her shoulder. "It's not your fault."

"Thanks, now I feel better."

He sighed. "He went through ... some stuff. He hated being unemployed and having to rely on you and your money. It made him feel guilty."

"Because he's the man?"

"No, because ... he's older than you and he said that, well ... after the childhood you had, he wanted to provide for you, so you could relax for a change."

Alice tried to imagine Danny saying these things, and it all fit just too well. It really did sound like him.

"And I didn't appreciate it." Guilt began to grow in the pit of her stomach, eating its way through her guts. If only she had been there for him sooner and kept him from getting pulled into that stupid business.

It's a fucking mafia, and I realized it too late.

"It hurt him, yes. But who could blame you for not wanting this?"

She looked up and stared at him. "Do *you* want it?"

Avoiding her eyes, he hesitated, but then he said, "Yes."

"What is it with you guys and money and power and all that crap? How can you not see that there's more important stuff?" Alice rubbed her forehead, feeling her headache increase.

Jonas shrugged. "Not to me."

"Are you serious? What about family? Or friends or ... simply enjoying the little things?"

He didn't answer.

Alice got off from the windowsill and walked toward the door, trying to get some distance from him.

"I can't believe it." She shook her head in disgust.

Jonas turned, worried, she might leave the room, but Alice stopped next to the door, leaning her back against the wall. "I just don't understand it."

"You don't have to."

"But I want to! I want—no, I *need* to understand how a smart and nice guy like Danny could get dragged into something like this."

"For the greater good?"

"What greater good? For fuck's sake, Jonas, why don't you just tell me what that stupid business is about? Maybe I'd even understand!"

"I can't."

"Why the hell not? Is it considered terrorism?"

He sighed. "It's about eliminating bad things."

"You mean bad people? Is that what you're doing, killing people you think are bad for the world?"

He said nothing and lit another cigarette.

Alice turned around and rested her throbbing forehead on the cool frame of the door. "This is fucked up, Jonas, it's sick!"

"That's *your* opinion."

"It changes people! It changed Danny!"

"He was too weak."

Alice turned back around to look at him, and suddenly felt intimidated by him and the way he remained calm about murdering people. She remembered the night he had shot Martin—he hadn't even flinched.

Jonas must have seen the fear and disgust on her face, and he quickly tried to explain. "Are there no people you'd like to see dead?"

"Wishing someone were dead and actually killing them is entirely different."

"If killing them saves others?"

"Who am I to decide?"

"You choose not to. We choose different." He took a step closer and she pressed her back against the wall.

"I'd never hurt you!"

"Yeah? Well, Danny said the same."

Hurt flickered over his face. "I'm not—"

"Like him," she finished. "You said that before and then you destroyed the kitchen furniture."

He shook his head sadly. "One of my darkest moments."

"It changes you as well ... even if you don't admit it." Alice grabbed the door handle and pulled the door open to step out, but Jonas caught her arm and held her back.

"You can't," he said.

"I just need some fresh air." She tried to shake his hand off.

Jonas pulled her back into the room and pushed the door shut, and she stood for a moment, fighting the tears in her eyes, and looking at him accusingly. He sighed and said, "I'm sorry"; and before she knew what she was doing, she was standing on the tips of her toes and kissing him.

An eternity seemed to pass before he realized what was happening and pulled back, a shocked expression on his face.

They stared at each other for a moment.

Alice's mind was blank, and she had no idea what she was doing. But for some reason, a deep desire for him had taken control over her, and she grabbed the collar of his leather jacket and tried to pull him toward her.

Jonas awoke out of his trance and grabbed her wrist to hold her back. "Don't," he said in a hoarse voice.

Alice gasped in pain when he gripped her bandaged arm, and he quickly let go and took a step back.

"Sorry," he stammered, "but we can't, we shouldn't—"

Suddenly, she remembered her reflection in the bathroom mirror.

Of course, he doesn't want me, how could anybody want me, the way I look?

"Sorry," she said tonelessly.

Jonas stood there like a trapped animal, unsure of what to do.

Alice quickly stepped aside to let him pass and he gladly took the opportunity and hurried out of the room. She heard the key turn in the hole.

Jonas did not come back after that and Alice cursed herself for having destroyed whatever had been between them. He had been nice to her at least, not like the others, and she had somehow enjoyed his company. Now, she had chased him away.

The new men still brought her food, but apart from that she was all alone and her longing for freedom grew so strong, it physically hurt.

After a couple more days, Danny finally decided to pay her a visit, but it was only to still his needs.

Alice tried to fight him off when he pinned her down on the mattress, the whole weight of his body on her. She had run out of pills and told him that, but he didn't care.

"What's so bad about a baby?"

He refused to wear a condom and when he pressed his lips on her mouth, the smell of whiskey made her gag.

When she struggled it only made him wilder and she soon realized that he was too strong for her.

It hurt like it never had before, and all the while, she wished she could just die or go back to her state of detachment from reality.

When he finally let go of her and walked out of the room, her body seemed to be on fire and she remained lying on her back, staring at the ceiling, unable to move.

Suddenly, a dark sense of calmness began to cover her like a thick blanket, and she felt at peace with herself. Everything made sense now and she knew what she had to do to end this once and for all.

Danny would be fast asleep, knocked out by the whiskey in his system, so a little music would not wake him up.

Alice plugged the MP3 player of Jonas's sister into the TV speakers and chose one of the playlists which had already been on it.

Afterward, she went into the bathroom and filled the tub with scalding-hot water to wash Danny's sweat off her.

She filled a glass with tap water and put it on the edge of the bathtub, then took Danny's pills from the cabinet, wondering how strong they might be.

Some deep, dreamless sleep was all she needed. Eternal sleep if it had to be.

Without taking off her clothes, she let her body glide into the water and gasped at the heat of it. It immediately put a layer of sweat on her forehead, but it felt wonderfully soothing.

She sighed. How depressing the music on that playlist was. It was almost as if the MP3 player knew what she was doing and deliberately played the saddest songs that were on it.

Suddenly, a strange urge to laugh took hold of her and her laughter echoed eerily from the walls. She took the remaining pills out of the pack which had already been opened, pushed them out of their sheet, and held them in her palm, studying them. Why had Danny taken sleeping pills, and more importantly, why had she never noticed? Apparently, he wasn't taking them anymore, or else he would have noticed their disappearance.

He has other drugs now ... cocaine in the morning, whiskey in the evening?

Was it cocaine? All she knew was that his pupils had been huge, and he had been very energetic. Indifferent, she shrugged, and put a handful of pills in her mouth, flushing them down with water. They tasted bitter and she shuddered and suppressed the urge to puke. A bottle of red wine would have probably served better to flush them down, but how was she supposed to get one if she couldn't even leave her room?

Alice sighed once more and swallowed the second load of pills, which left her coughing and choking. She had to press her hands over her mouth to force the pills to stay in her stomach.

Breathing deeply, she rested her head on the cool bathroom wall and felt a dizziness take hold of her. Her eyelids drooped and sleep threatened to take over.

No ... not yet.

Quickly, she forced her eyes open and took the rest of the pills out of the pack, holding them in her left hand, which already felt numb. Pushing the little tablets out of the sheet was much harder now and cost her a lot of effort.

She swallowed them, coughing as her stomach convulsed painfully, but it was nothing compared to the pain she had been feeling before.

By taking deep breaths, Alice tried to control the nausea and finally, her body began to feel numb all over and she allowed her mind to drift off, her head falling onto her shoulder, her body slipping downward into the tub, and water began to cover her face.

19

Alice had thought a lot about dying after having had a gun to her head twice.
But the light after the tunnel never came.
For her there was only darkness.
There was also pain. Darkness and pain.
A both stabbing and burning sensation went through her stomach, and she gasped for air, surprised by its intensity. Was death not supposed to be painless?
She was cold and shivered. The warmth of the bathwater was gone.
Her throat was on fire and her mouth felt dry and furry. There was no doubt about it: she was still solid.
Alice managed to open her eyes, but there was nothing but darkness. Had she been put in a coffin and buried alive?
Panicking, she tried to move her hand to feel the walls around her, but her body felt stiff and every movement cost her a lot of effort. By touching the ground beneath her, she could tell that it was soft.
Moaning, she rolled onto her side, but suddenly, the soft ground was gone, and she fell and landed on something hard and cold. There was a sharp stabbing pain in the back of her hand that made her cry out. She tried to pull her hand away from whatever was hurting her, but the hand seemed to be held back by something, and every movement made the pain worse.
Struggling, she tried to get rid of the thing that was holding her back and suddenly, there was light, and she had to close her eyes, blinded by it.
"What are you doing?" the worried voice of a woman asked.
Alice felt someone grab her hand and something was pulled out of her skin. Finally, her arm was free.
She covered her face with both hands, trying to shield herself from the light.
"Did you fall out of your bed?" the voice asked.
Hands grabbed her underneath her arms and pulled her upward, and Alice could feel the softness of a mattress in her back and sat down on it.

The hands pushed her down onto her back softly and pulled a blanket over her body.

Blinking, Alice tried to adjust her eyes to the brightness, and after a while she was able to make out her surroundings.

"What's happening? Why does my throat hurt?"

The woman standing in front of her was wearing gray scrubs and she had short black hair and a round, friendly face. "We had to pump your stomach."

The realization hit her like a blow.

It didn't work!

Alice buried her face in her hands once more. "No, no, no, why am I here? This is not right!"

"I'll get someone for you," the nurse said quickly and disappeared.

I took the fucking pills in the bathtub, so if they didn't manage to kill me, I'd still drown ...

For some reason though, she was still here. Sobbing, she turned onto her side and buried her face underneath the blanket. Why did everything have to go wrong?

She heard the door open and there were footsteps coming closer. Someone cleared their throat and Alice heard a female voice say, "Alice?"

Keeping her face hidden, she ignored it.

"I believe we've met before."

Curious, Alice pulled the blanket off her eyes and stared into a familiar looking face, but she could not recall where she had seen it before.

"I'm Liza Keller, I treated you the last time you were here."

Slowly, the memory of the last time those warm, dark brown eyes had looked at her began to sink in, and Alice remembered how after the pool-incident she had been cared for by the same woman who stood in front of her bed now.

She felt herself blush, recalling the last conversation they'd had.

Liza pulled a chair toward the bed and sat down.

Alice avoided her stare, feeling embarrassed and ashamed of herself. "I'm not supposed to be here."

Liza nodded. "I know. You had no intention to be here." She sighed, and Alice felt her intense gaze pierce through her. "That's the thing, Alice, that's what worries me." She laid her hand on Alice's left arm, which had apparently been wrapped in a new bandage. "*That* might be a call for help but trying to drown yourself in the bathtub is not."

"It wasn't!" Alice felt anger flare up inside of her and pulled her arm away. "It was nothing like that, I was just feeling ... *numb*."

Liza looked at her and her expression said everything.

"Don't look at me like that, I'm not stupid. I know that cutting a vein doesn't kill you, and I'd never try anything like that ... and I sure as hell wasn't calling for anyone's help." She glared at the doctor and immediately felt bad for being rude. "I'm sorry," she said quickly. "I'm just–"

"Don't apologize, I understand your anger. It must be hard to hope for everything to be over and then realize that it didn't work."

Alice bit her lip. "You know nothing."

"You are right, I don't, and that leads me to making my own assumptions ... and they might be wrong?"

"And what kind of assumptions would that be?"

"I remember the last time you were here; we spoke about issues with your boyfriend."

Alice scoffed at that. "You're making this sound like a teenage drama."

"That was not my intention. There is nothing harmless about what happened."

"You don't know what happened."

"Then tell me."

Alice bit her tongue and dropped her gaze, staring at her feet that were covered by a faded, green blanket.

"How did I get here?" she asked to change the subject.

"You were brought here by your friend ... or roommate, or whatever you said he was."

"Jonas?"

"Young man with brown hair and a black leather jacket."

Alice sighed. "Yeah, that's him. He's starting to really annoy me."

Liza frowned. "Because he saved your life?"

"There was nothing to save."

"But there might be. One day you might be glad."

"I doubt it."

They were quiet for a moment and suddenly, the door opened and Jonas appeared.

"Speaking of the devil," Alice muttered and gave him a hateful look. He looked tired and there was a deep sadness displayed on his face.

Liza sighed. "You should talk to someone."

"I really don't feel like it."

"It's hospital policy. I can't let you walk out of here before you've spoken to a psychiatrist."

"Oh great. Really. Just what I need."

"As a matter of fact, it *is* what you need." Dr. Keller stood, gave her a chiding, yet compassionate look, and walked out of the room.

Jonas remained standing near the door, staring at his feet.

"Why did you do that? Why couldn't you just leave me alone?" Alice hissed.

He said nothing.

Her anger disappeared as suddenly as it had come, and was replaced by sadness. The tears came again, and she buried her face in her hands. She could feel his eyes on her.

"I'm sorry," he muttered.

"For what, Jonas? Tell me exactly what you're sorry about!"

He cleared his throat. "I'm *not* sorry for pulling you out of that bathtub."

"And?"

"I didn't mean to ... hurt you."

Confused, she looked up. "When did you ever hurt me?"

He took a cigarette out of his pocket nervously, then seemed to remember that they were in a hospital and put it away again. "I ..." he swallowed, which made his Adam's apple move up and down. " ...rejected you?"

Alice's jaw dropped and she stared at him in blank disbelief. "You think *that's* why I did it? Wow, seriously, and I thought you'd lost your confidence."

"I'm not saying ... I thought perhaps it was the ... last straw."

"Danny was that straw, Jonas, as well as the rest of it."

His eyes wandered to hers, and he looked so sad she almost felt sorry for him.

"If you want to blame yourself, blame yourself for bringing me to that house and keeping me there and ... blame yourself for pulling me out of that fucking tub!"

Jonas came closer and sat down on the chair next to the bed, hiding his face in his hands. For a split second, Alice thought he was about to cry, but he only rubbed his forehead with his knuckles.

"My sister died like that. In the bathtub."

Speechless, she stared at him.

"She cut her wrists and bled out, and I found her. When I found you … it was like the same thing all over again. Even the same fucking song was playing." His voice sounded torn and thick with grief. "I thought … this time, I was not too late. But you're not her and I'm sorry for trying to clear my conscience by forcing you to live a life you don't want to live." He fell silent and kept his face hidden in his hands, and Alice could do nothing but stare at him, amazed by his honesty.

"Who knew you could be so … emotional."

He looked up and gave her a weak smile.

"I'm sorry … about what happened."

"Don't be. This is about you, not about me. I just thought … I should be honest. You deserve honesty."

Before Alice could answer, the door opened and a man, who appeared to be in his fifties, walked in. He was partly bald and wearing glasses, and he gestured for Jonas to leave the room.

They had wasted fifteen minutes staring at each other, the doctor awaiting her answers to his stupid generalized questions, and she ignoring him.

"No, I'm not depressed. My life's just depressing, that's all," Alice finally said, annoyed by his patience.

"I can't let you leave before you've told me what happened." He took off his glasses and wiped them with the sleeve of his shirt.

"Fine." She took a deep breath and saw the shrink look up, looking interested all of a sudden. He readied his notepad and waited.

"You want the truth?"

He nodded.

"Okay. So, my boyfriend became a mafia boss and he locks me in my room and has his bodyguards watch me, and recently, he let me rot in a bunker for three days to punish me for trying to run away. Oh, and he has a friend who controls the police. They all have that weird secret business going on, they kill people for the greater good, trying to save the world or something."

Speechless, the doctor stared at her.

"Yeah and he treats me like shit, so anyway, that's why my life's pretty depressing and I decided to swallow his sleeping pills and drown myself in the bathtub."

Sighing, he put the cap on his pen.

"And did I mention I was almost shot by one of his enemies? My bodyguard saved me by blowing the guy's face off. Left a huge mess and we had to burn the carpet."

The doctor arose from his chair and gave her an angry look. "You're free to leave. Though I suggest you go to therapy. Trying to commit suicide is no joke." He turned and walked away, and Alice couldn't help but laugh out loudly.

Jonas reentered the room and looked at her confusedly. "What did you tell him?"

She shrugged. "The truth."

"And?"

"He said I'm free to leave."

She was sitting in his car, looking out of the window, watching the trees and fields pass by in a blur.

He was smoking and his eyes flicked to her occasionally.

"Why?" she asked him.

He flinched and slowed down to be able to look at her. "What?"

"Why do you always take me back there?"

He was quiet for a while, thinking. "It's my job."

"So, it's all about the money? One moment, you're pretending to actually care and the next, you're thinking about the fat paycheck awaiting you."

"He'd find you."

"Would he? I could hide. Run away to another city, maybe even fly out of the country if I have to."

"He'd find you."

She turned her head to look at him. "Are you scared of him?"

"No, but you should be."

"I am, Jonas, he gives me the creeps. But he's not almighty, I'm sure I could hide."

He sighed. "You don't know what he's capable of."

"Oh, I'm sure I know it better than you," she hissed.

"I'm sorry."

"Stop finding stupid excuses, just tell me the truth. You don't give a shit about me; you're only talking to me because it's part of your job. You only care about the money and he'll always be your best friend, no matter what."

He pulled over and stopped the car on the side of the road.

"What are you doing?"

"Allowing you to get some fresh air before bringing you back."

"Oh, how incredibly generous of you." She opened the door and got out of the car, inhaling the fresh and crisp spring air. It was a sunny day and birds were singing in the trees while insects buzzed busily in the long grass on the side of the road.

He got out as well and walked around the car to sit on the hood next to her.

"You're poisoning my fresh air."

He put out the cigarette on the car and flicked the butt into the grass.

"Now you're littering."

"Sorry."

"Don't apologize to me, apologize to the environment."

He sighed and bent down to pick up the cigarette butt, and she stared at him, her eyes wide.

"Are you actually listening to me? Jesus, what is wrong with you? Who are you and what have you done with Jonas?"

He put the stub in his pocket and gave her a sad look. "I haven't been ... quite myself lately," he confessed quietly.

"I'm sorry for what they did to you ... but why didn't you defend yourself?"

"And blame everything on you?" His green eyes were hypnotizing, and she felt the sudden urge to kiss him again. This time though she knew better.

"It was the truth ... You only did your job."

"Thank you for telling him. That was kind of you."

"I couldn't let you die, for Christ's sake."

"Why not? I don't deserve any favors from you."

Bewildered, she looked at him. "I wouldn't let anyone die like that. I don't want him to shoot people and I don't want people to die and least of all you. I've come to like you, somehow."

"Somehow," he repeated thoughtfully. "That's a problem. You should not like me."

"I also shouldn't be in love with him, after everything he did. Yet I can't seem to let him go. I'm too fucking emotional, just like you said."

He looked confused. "You said you were over him?"

"I lied. I thought he'd let me go." She sighed. "Guess I was wrong."

"He's unpredictable."

She nodded. "And dangerous. So why don't you tell me what your plan is? To just let him do his thing? Destroy his own life and the lives of those around him?"

"He's still Danny, you know. I'm hoping to get him back. He listens to me."

She raised her eyebrows. "Does he still?"

He shrugged. "There have been certain changes. He doesn't respect me the way he used to."

"And that's what destroyed your confidence?"

"That and my outburst the other day."

"I shouldn't have provoked you …"

"Stop taking the blame Alice, you're driving me crazy!" He jumped off the hood and stomped a few steps into the field, inhaling in an unnerved manner.

"Sorry," she said without thinking.

He turned around. "Are you even listening?"

When he saw the confusion on her face his features softened, and he sighed.

"I'm not sure what to think about the new you." She eyed him carefully. "I mean, you used to be so calm … and you never talked. And now you talk so much."

"Too much."

"No, not too much. It's finally possible to have a conversation with you."

"We shouldn't."

"I'm glad to have someone to talk to."

"I know."

She bit her lip and watched him loosen a small rock in the ground with the tip of his shoe. "He really shattered you, didn't he? He does that."

He looked up. "I thought he's my friend."

"And I thought he's my boyfriend."

They looked at each other for a moment without saying anything.

A cool wind blew through her shirt and made her shiver. "Promise me something, Jonas. If he still listens to you, even a bit … please try to get him back. The old Danny, I mean."

"Would you forgive him?"

"No. But maybe he'd be nice enough to let me leave."

Goose bumps began to spread on her arms, and she hugged herself against the sudden cold.

"We should go back," he said.

"I really don't want to."

"I know." He gave her a meaningful look and walked back around the car to sit behind the wheel.

She hesitated and inhaled once more the cool, fresh spring air and let the sun touch her for a few seconds.

Who knew when she would get that chance again.

Danny stormed out of the house at the sound of the car, and hugged her as soon as she had gotten out. He buried his face in her hair and inhaled her smell, and she allowed herself to lean against him, enjoying the moment of kindness.

"What did you do Allie, what the fuck did you do," he muttered, and she said nothing. He led her upstairs where he made her sit on the bed. "You look so pale; I think you should rest."

"As you wish."

Grimacing, he sat down next to her. "Do you really hate me so much that you would take your own life to escape me?" His voice sounded hurt, yet cold.

A weird calmness took hold of her. She knew she had nothing to lose and she had already been more than honest with Jonas, so why not continue?

"You really hurt me, Danny," she muttered without looking at him.

"I'm sorry ... I shouldn't have ... I had promised to give you space. It was just too hard to stay away from you."

"I didn't want it. Not even a bit."

He said nothing.

"If you want me to forgive you, to ... be your girlfriend, you can't treat me like that." Her voice was toneless, she realized.

He took her cold hands in his and stared at them. "Would you? Try, I mean?"

"I still love you and I'm willing to follow your rules." There was no life in her voice, she noticed.

I'm dead inside. I killed myself after all.

"Just ... please don't hurt me like that."

He hugged her and the smell of his cologne made her battered stomach nauseous. It was better than whiskey though.

"I'll never do it again, I promise," he whispered and kissed her. He pulled back and looked at her. "Your lips are cold ... and blue."

"Well, I almost died. It's only normal I look like a corpse."

"I see you got your humor back." He stroked her overgrown bangs out of her eyes. "I'm glad."

"Guess I need to cut that back," Alice said.

"Or grow it out, whatever you like."

"You're giving me permission to look like I want?"

He frowned. "I'm not a monster, Alice. As long as you look decent, I don't care what you do with your hair."

"*Decent*," she repeated thoughtfully. "I'll remember that."

His eyes filled with tears. "You gave me such a fright Allie, I thought I'd lost you!"

"What happened anyway?"

Danny sniffed and hugged her once more. "Jonas found you and screamed for me to come, and he'd pulled you out of the tub, and you were pale and blue and didn't respond. You weren't breathing, so he gave you CPR and I just stood there, unable to move. I thought you were dead."

"He gave me CPR?"

So he kissed me back after all.

Danny nodded. "I was still drunk; I couldn't think straight. I'm so glad he found you."

"Why was he even in my room?"

Danny sighed. "The music was stuck, apparently. The same song kept playing over and over, and he began to worry because you never changed it."

"Creepy."

He nodded. "Almost as if some greater force had saved you."

Alice frowned at that. "Since when do you believe in that? Honestly, I think it was set on repeat, and I didn't notice when I put the player on."

"Where did you get that player anyway?"

"Jonas gave it to me. It was his sister's."

"She killed herself."

"I know, he told me this morning."

They sat in silence for a while, Danny stroking her hair and holding her tightly as if he were afraid she might suddenly dissolve.

Alice's throat and stomach were still hurting badly. "I'm sorry for stealing your pills," she finally said.

He sighed. "It's okay."

"Why did you even have them?"

"When ... when I stopped drinking last November, I couldn't sleep, so I got them."

"Prescribed?"

He nodded. "All legal."

"They were strong, huh."

"Yes. They would have killed you if Jonas hadn't found you."

"I would've probably drowned first."

Danny frowned. "Is that why you were in the bathtub?"

Alice closed her eyes and listened to his heartbeat. "Yes."

She heard him inhale sharply. "I can't believe you did this. Honestly, what's gotten into you?"

Apart from you?

She said nothing.

"Don't ever do that again, promise me."

"Why? What does it matter to you?"

Danny held her at arm's length and stared at her, a mixture of pain and anger on his face. "I love you, Allie, I fucking love you, okay? And okay, maybe I haven't been showing you lately, maybe I've been too hard on you ... Because sometimes, I'm a fucking asshole and I know it, but my feelings for you have never changed! Why do you think I'm keeping you here? For fun?" He lifted her chin with his fingers and forced her to look at him. "I couldn't live without you and I hated you for trying to leave me."

"I don't want to leave you," she whispered. "I just want to leave this house."

A tear rolled out of the corner of his eye, and he quickly brushed it away. "I'm sorry, Allie, I'm so fucking sorry."

Alice felt her own eyes turn moist. Where did those feelings come from? He didn't deserve them. And yet, she couldn't ignore them.

He kissed her, long and tenderly, and it reminded her of how things used to be. It felt too good.

Danny treated her like a porcelain doll. Alice still wasn't allowed to leave her room, but he had food brought to her three times a day and hot tea in between—chamomile, linden, vervain, lemon balm; all meant to soothe and relax her.

He stayed abstinent after his promise not to hurt her.

Alice wondered if that one time had been enough to get her pregnant. She had not gotten her period since she had stopped taking the pill, but maybe it was only because it had messed up her cycle.

She could only hope it was.

In the evenings, he would come to her room and sit on the bed next to her, leaning his back against the wall and wrapping his arms around her.

They would watch movies together, but only comedies and romances—Danny considered violent movies bad for her, and Alice didn't feel like arguing.

He would even sleep in her bed and though she found it hard at first to fall asleep with him next to her, it became normal routine after a while, just like it used to be.

Alice noticed that he barely ever smelled of Whiskey anymore and she wondered if he had stopped drinking again.

The riddle was solved one morning, after they had slept in his bed instead of hers.

Danny awoke and sat up, and thinking, Alice was still sleeping, he opened the top drawer of his nightstand. She was awake, however, and watched him through almost-closed eyelids.

She saw him take a small transparent tube with a white content out of the drawer. He unscrewed the lid and put a tiny spade, that was attached to it, to his nostril.

Alice shuddered when she heard him snort, and he quickly put the drugs away and turned around, but she kept her eyes closed and pretended to still be asleep.

Cocaine ... I was right.

Danny moaned and stretched, then bent down to kiss her.

Acting as if his kiss had awoken her, Alice opened her eyes and saw him smile at her. He brushed a strand of hair away from her forehead and she smiled back at him.

"Good morning sunshine." His expression was kind and loving, but the size of his pupils made his eyes look cold and dark.

Sighing, Alice buried her head in the pillow.

"You still tired?" His voice was soft and tender.

She nodded and he leaned in to kiss her again.

"What day is it?" she muttered.

"It's Wednesday. May second."

"Already?"

He nodded. "You're losing track of time, aren't you?"

"It doesn't really matter."

"I know ... Listen, I'm going away for a while again. Another business trip."

"Again? But ... you've only just been!" She frowned at him and he stroked her cheek.

"I know. I'm leaving on Friday. For three weeks, maybe a month ... who knows."

"What about your gorillas?"

Danny laughed. "You mean Viktor and Jean-Pierre?"

"I was never introduced to them, even though they're in my room every day."

"I'm sorry about that. They have strict instructions not to talk to anybody except me."

"Why?"

Danny sighed. "I know nothing happened with Jonas, but it has made me paranoid, I must admit. I trust Jonas—now even more than before—but I heard what Tee's been trying to do and even Waldo went behind my back when he let you out of the bunker. I just need someone who's on my side and does only what I tell him."

Alice just looked at him, unsure of what to say. How had he found out about Timothy? Jonas must have told him.

Danny seemed to be reading her mind. "Don't worry, Allie, I know you would never do anything with a guy like Tee. I trust your taste and your judgement."

"Are you mad that I let him into my room?"

"No ... No, honey, I'm not mad. I know you needed someone to talk to. I'm merely mad at myself for not properly warning you about him. I knew all along that he would try to get in your pants. I mean, who would not want to?"

Alice dropped her gaze, suddenly remembering the reflection she'd seen in the mirror before she had shattered it to pieces.

"Now? Probably everybody."

Danny raised one eyebrow, the way he always did. "What do you mean?"

"I'm ugly ... I'm too thin and my hair is dull, and I look pale and sick."

He laughed, but then he saw her expression and pulled her up into a hug. "Allie, babe, don't talk like that. Why would you say such a thing? Just because you look ... a bit sick doesn't mean you're not pretty anymore! You're still the most beautiful girl I've ever seen and that will never change."

Alice snuggled against his chest, enjoying his embrace.

What the fuck am I doing?

"You have been through some stuff and that is visible, but it doesn't make you less attractive. I mean it honey. Please believe me. And you'll be back to your old self soon, I'll make sure of that."

Alice nodded weakly and he kissed her forehead.

"All you need is rest and food and someone taking care of you," he added.

His kindness brought tears to her eyes and when he realized that she was crying, he pulled her closer.

"I'm sorry for hurting you," he muttered.

Alice let him comfort her as best as he could. She had grown accustomed to the paradox situation. It was her life. It was the way things were going. There was nothing she could do but enjoy the moments when he was nice to her, and try to forget the ones when he was not.

After a while, he pulled out of the embrace and smiled at her. "I really have to go downstairs to the office. I'll bring you back to your room, okay?"

He did and Alice heard the key turn in the hole as soon as he'd closed the door behind him. She sat down on her bed, feeling miserable.

Alice had grown attached to him again however, and when he left, she found herself missing his presence.

Danny had ordered Jonas to take care of her and instructed Jean-Pierre, the man with the beard, to stay and keep an eye on her as well.

He trusted Jonas, but after Alice had almost succeeded in running away, he felt like having two pairs of eyes on her was a good idea.

Alice had hoped Jonas would let her out of her room, but with Jean-Pierre around that was not going to happen.

The new bodyguard did not seem very interested in her though and kept his distance, so Jonas was able to visit her in her room and play cards with her or watch a movie.

"I'm so done with romantic comedies," Alice said while putting the second *Resident Evil* DVD into the player.

Jonas was sitting on the bed, his back against the wall, a cigarette dangling from his lips. "Romantic comedies?"

"Danny thought they'd be good for me. He seems to think I'm very fragile at the moment and shouldn't watch anything violent." She shook her head scornfully and took her place on the mattress next to him, carefully keeping her distance, however.

Alice knew that being with her still made him uncomfortable—especially after her attempt to kiss him.

Jonas shook his head as well and grinned. "You don't look so fragile."

Serious, she looked at him. "You think?"

He grimaced. "Okay, okay ... you do look fragile, but not as bad as you used to. I genuinely think some sun would do the trick."

"Yeah, well ..."

"You could at least open the window."

"I usually do, but not when you're here and we're talking. Jean-Pierre might be outside, listening."

The title melody began playing and Alice pressed Start.

They watched the movie in silence, smoking a cigarette from time to time. It was hot in the room. The sun had grown stronger and temperatures had climbed up to almost seventy-seven degrees. The bedroom got heated up by the strong rays that fell through the window.

Moaning, Alice wiped sweat from her forehead. "It's almost summer and we're inside, watching a fucking movie." She looked at Jonas, who had even taken off his jacket—something he didn't do often. He was wearing a gray T-shirt and his muscly upper body was clearly visible through the thin fabric.

Again, Alice felt a strong desire to kiss him. Feeling overwhelmed by the urge, she quickly got off the bed.

Jonas turned his head and watched her. "What you doing?"

"Uh, it's hot. I thought I should close the blinds, maybe." She turned to the window and looked out, amazed by the beautiful deep blue sky and the lush green of the leaves on the trees. Her gaze wandered over the wall and out into the bright green and yellow fields, up onto the hills in the distance.

The gate guard downstairs had taken off his jacket and was sitting on a plastic chair in the sun, tanning his bare arms.

Alice kept gazing outside, struck by the beauty of her surroundings, the birds in the birches, the pansies below in the beds. Henry had planted them, as well as some other flowers whose names she didn't know. She missed helping him in the garden.

Suddenly, she felt his breath on the back of her neck and tensed.

"What you looking at?" Jonas asked curiously.

Her breathing accelerated and she quickly tried to steady it. "It's just ... beautiful," she gasped.

"It's a nice day," he affirmed. He leaned against the frame of the window casually and followed her gaze with his own. "You okay?"

She nodded.

"Maybe I could talk to him, ask him to let you out of the house."

Alice cleared her throat. "That'd be nice." Her voice sounded hoarse.

Jonas misread her behavior and took a step closer. "I'm sorry. It's cruel to let you rot in here." He put a hand on her shoulder.

"Don't touch me!" she burst out without thinking, and quickly stepped away from him.

Taken aback, he stared at her. "Sorry ..."

Alice left her place by the window, and began pacing through the room restlessly while he watched her.

"You okay?" he asked again, sounding genuinely concerned. "Are you having a panic attack?"

Near the door, she stopped and pressed her forehead against its cool frame. *What is wrong with me? What the fuck is wrong with me?*

"It's too bloody hot in here, let me open the window," Jonas offered.

"No, don't open it." Alice covered her face with her hands and tried to breathe slowly.

"Want some water?" He sounded very worried when he approached her.

Keeping her face hidden, she said nothing.

"I'll let you out, I'll tell him you needed air." He was standing behind her now, she could feel it.

"Alice?" he asked, concerned. Hesitantly, he reached out to her, then softly turned her around so he could look at her. "Talk to me. What d'you need? Water? Air?"

Tears were running down her cheeks now.

"Alice," he spoke in a gentle voice and pulled her hands away from her face.

She tried to avoid his piercing stare, but felt his eyes on her, nevertheless. He wiped a tear from her cheek gently with his thumb and she flinched at his touch.

"What is it?" he asked, and his voice was full of affection and honest concern; and in that moment, she knew that he wasn't only pretending. He actually cared about her.

"It's you," she replied tonelessly, and he pulled his hand back, looking stunned.

"You ... need to be alone?" he asked, and when she didn't answer, he stepped toward the door and put his hand on the handle, but she caught his arm and stopped him.

Confused, he turned around and they looked at each other, and then she stood on her toes and kissed him.

Again, he pushed her away softly. "Don't," he said weakly.

Blushing, she dropped her gaze. "I'm sorry. I'm not your type ... you don't want this. How could you ...?" Embarrassed, she tried to turn away from him, but he held her back.

"That's not true, really ..." He seemed to struggle with the words, but then he added, "I do find you beautiful, but we can't—"

Alice put her hand on his cheek and kissed him again, and this time, he did not pull back.

He tasted of tobacco and she loved it.

They kissed and her hands wandered over his body, underneath his T-shirt and down to his pants.

He winced and pulled away, but when he saw her expression, he surrendered to her touch. Her hands found his belt and she opened it and pulled at his jeans.

His arms were hanging at his sides awkwardly and Alice got the impression that he must be very unexperienced.

His body however, was responding to her touch, and she saw his eyes turn glazed and knew that his blood had rushed out of his brain and that he wasn't able to think straight anymore.

She took advantage of that and put her hand down his pants, which made him gasp. His breathing got heavier, and she pulled down his pants and tried to take off his shirt, but he had to help her with it. At least he was taking some action now and when he stood there topless, she let her fingers glide over his chest and belly, and noticed that he did not have abs like Danny. Jonas worked out a lot, but he seemed to care mostly about his strength and not about his looks. She liked that about him as well.

After taking off her own shirt and letting it drop to the floor, she pulled him downward and his back glided down the wall until he was sitting on the floor. He kicked off his worn-out Converse and jeans completely and put his hands on her back, pulling her closer.

Alice got rid of her own pants and sat down on him, which made him gasp again.

Finally, she was in charge and it was an incredible feeling. She decided what to do and how to do it, and Jonas seemed to like it.

At some point though, he grimaced because of the uncomfortable position on the floor, and got up without removing her from his body. He carried her to the bed and Alice half expected him to take control, but to her surprise, he just sat down on the mattress and let her continue.

For way too long, Alice had not felt such passion and now, she enjoyed it deeply.

Danny had taken her dignity, but she was determined to make sure that she could still enjoy sex the way she used to. She was eager to prove to herself that it was still something beautiful, something good for her—not something that made her shut her eyes and hope for it to be over.

And with Jonas, it was definitely good.

His hand was still on her back, gliding downward slowly, and she opened her eyes to smile at him and realized that he was looking at her. She tried to read his expression. He looked worried somehow and his fingers moved down her skin very slowly, almost hesitantly. Could it be his first time?

She smiled again, but then it hit her like a blow.

Jonas was not unexperienced. He must have slept with many women—or people—already, probably incapable of keeping a long-lasting relationship.

Alice froze and stared at him in shock. He was not worried about having sex—he was worried about *her*.

He looked at her as if he expected her to break any second or in case he touched her wrongly. Was he only sleeping with her out of pity?

He had turned her down the last time, and shortly afterward she had tried to kill herself. Was that why he had surrendered this time? Because he didn't dare to say no?

Now, he was staring at her and his expression grew even more concerned.

"D'you want to stop?" he asked quietly, and it sounded almost hopeful. Or was she only imagining it?

Suddenly, all the passion was gone, vanished into thin air.

Alice sat on him awkwardly. Should she stop? But what if he wanted to continue?

Would he ...? He's not like Danny ... or is he?

She bit her lip.

I should continue. He thinks I'm fragile and if I stop now, I'll just prove him right. I should finish—or make him finish, rather.

"Alice?" His voice was barely more than a whisper.

She forced herself to smile and quickly bent down to kiss him, to keep him from staring at her. Still bent over him, her face against his, she continued to move and kissed his neck to distract him. His hand moved up her back until it was on her head, and he left it there, his fingers entangled in her hair.

He took longer than Danny and when he finally climaxed, Alice pretended to as well and rested her head on his shoulder, exhausted and out of breath.

He was breathing heavily and softly stroked her back, which gave her goose bumps.

Suddenly and unexpectedly, she felt tears well up in her eyes. She rolled off him and remained lying on the bed, her back facing him, her hair sticking in sweaty strands to her skin. She put her arm over her face to hide the tears.

Jonas turned onto his side as well and began to softly caress her shoulder, realizing that something was wrong. He said nothing though and Alice bit her tongue and let the tears flow silently.

What have I done ...? What the fuck have I done ...

For once, she had wanted to be in charge, to take advantage of somebody instead of having people take advantage of her. But she had ended up forcing herself to do something—finish something—she had not wanted to. It had been good at first, until he had stared at her all pitifully and worried. Why had he done that?

Again, she felt used—and it wasn't even his fault. Hadn't she practically forced him to sleep with her? Hadn't she inflicted emotional pressure on him—even if not intentionally?

Alice felt self-loathing burn in her stomach like acid. She had ruined everything ... and for what? For an urge—no, a *craving* to feel something, to feel happy or at least satisfied in some way. To feel *alive*.

Now, guilt was eating her up inside, devouring what little comfort spending time with Jonas had given her.

She didn't know what was worse—knowing that there was in fact no way for her to enjoy intimacy anymore, or the fact that she had hurt someone else in the process of trying to find something to relieve her own pain. Biting her lip, she tried hard to force down the sobs.

"I'm sorry," Jonas whispered. "I shouldn't have ..." He fell silent.

"It's not your fault," Alice replied quietly, her voice thick with tears. "I practically made you do it."

"What? No, you didn't—"

"Don't lie to me. You only did it because you didn't want to hurt me! You thought ... you thought I might not take a second rejection too well. That's why you did it."

He said nothing but his silence was enough affirmation. She felt him move and thought he was about to leave, but he merely pulled the blanket toward them and covered her with it. He then lay back down behind her and put his arm around her—now with the blanket in between them. He held her and his fingers softly caressed her arm as she cried silently.

"I only rejected you because of Danny," he explained quietly, and the sound of his voice next to her ear was comforting. "Had we met under different circumstances ... Alice, you *are* the kind of woman I like." His voice sounded sincere and she tried to believe him. It did not change anything though. She still felt empty.

He kept holding her as she cried, his arms wrapped around her, until exhaustion took over and her eyelids drooped shut.

When Alice awoke, the light had changed outside. The sun must have wandered, and her room was now in the shade.

Jonas's arm was still wrapped around her and she heard his slow and soft breaths close to her ear. Her eyes felt swollen, her throat dry, and she felt empty and numb.

Slowly, she moved out from underneath his arm without waking him up. Once standing, she watched him sleep for a while. He looked peaceful and innocent the way he was curled up on the bed, his arm entangled in the blanket that had covered her. She felt sorry for him and guilty, ashamed of having used him.

The bathroom mirror was still broken, but it was better like that. She didn't want to see her reflection. Sighing, Alice closed the bathroom door and sat on the toilet to pee. She then washed her face with cold water and rinsed her mouth to get the taste of bile out. Her eyes fell upon the long scar on her left arm and she felt an overwhelming urge to rip it open again. Exasperated, she sat back down on the toilet lid and stared at the tiled wall, hating herself.

Several minutes passed until she finally came to terms with the fact that she had to face Jonas eventually. Resigned, she wrapped her naked body in a towel and left the bathroom.

He was gone.

The bed was empty, and all of his clothes had vanished as well. It felt as if he had ripped out her heart and taken it with him.

Despite being glad that she didn't have to face him she felt abandoned and lonely, and when she sat down on the mattress, the tears came back. Alice remained sitting on the bed, crying silently, until the door was opened without a knock and Jean-Pierre appeared, a tray in his hand.

When he saw her crying, wearing only a towel, he put the tray on her dresser quickly and hurried back out of the room.

At once, Alice understood the seriousness of the situation. If Jonas had still been here ... She stared at the door and felt her heart drum against her ribs.

That was close ...

The title music of *Resident Evil* was still playing over and over again. Irritated by the sound, Alice grabbed the remote and turned off the TV.

The penetrating smell of the food on her dresser made her feel nauseous, and she walked over to the window to look out, and found Jonas standing in the yard, smoking and watching the sun go down.

20

The next couple of days were overshadowed by a dark and crushingly heavy loneliness that made it hard to breathe.

Jonas stayed away and Alice was still locked in her room, with only Jean-Pierre coming in three times a day, bringing her food and collecting the dishes from before.

She kept her window open to be able to get some fresh air and a little bit of sun. Her days consisted of sitting on the windowsill, watching Henry gardening or Jonas smoking or the guards talking to each other.

Jonas never turned his head to look up at her window and she found his behavior hurtful. He did not owe her anything and she knew she had destroyed what little friendship they'd had, so it was entirely her fault. Yet, she missed his company and found herself hoping every day that he might change his mind and come see her.

The loneliness began to physically hurt. At times, Alice could barely breathe, and her appetite was gone completely, having been replaced by a persistent nausea and stomachache. The plate was usually still full when Jean-Pierre picked it up, but he never said a word, for which Alice was glad.

She was at a point where she wanted nothing more than to die. No sleeping pills were available though and she could not get hold of a weapon either. The more her thoughts circled around the topic of how to end her life once and for all, the stronger the urge became, until she could barely think about anything else anymore.

The days seemed to creep by extremely slowly and Alice realized she was falling back into old patterns. Even without the thick walls of the bunker surrounding her, she found herself talking to people who were not there, just to fill the bone-crushing silence. Memories of better times became more vivid with every time she played them in her mind, until reality blurred into a dream.

When the fear came back, Alice knew she needed someone to talk to.

"Jean-Pierre," she said quickly after the huge bearded man had put the tray on her dresser. He turned around and looked at her coldly.

"I ... I know you're not allowed to talk to me, but could I please talk to Danny? Please? Could you contact him and tell him I need to talk to him?"

The guard grunted and left the room, leaving her wondering whether his grunt had been a yes or a no.

The next day however, he came into her room in the late afternoon, holding a cell phone in his hand. Alice felt her heart skip a beat and hurried toward him, her hand outstretched. Jean-Pierre handed her the phone and remained standing in the doorframe, arms crossed, watching her.

"*Alice?*" Danny's voice sounded through the speaker.

"Danny," she gasped, surprised by her own relief of hearing his voice.

"*What's wrong?*" He sounded concerned. "*Jean-Pierre said you really needed to talk to me.*"

"It's just—" She sobbed and immediately felt stupid.

"*Allie, what's wrong? Has something happened?*"

"No ... I'm just really lonely and I'm scared."

"*Of what?*"

"Of being alone."

She heard him pause.

"*But, Allie, you're not alone! You got people in the house, I made sure you'd never be alone. I told Jonas to keep you company.*"

"But he—" The image of Jonas's naked body on her bed flashed through her mind. "He's busy ... with his studies ... He doesn't have time for this."

"*I told him to keep you company, Allie, it's part of his job.*" Danny sounded irritated.

"No, really, it's fine. He's got exams ... I understand."

Danny sighed. "*If you say so ...*"

They were quiet for a moment.

"*Honey, you still there?*"

She nodded, then realizing he couldn't see her, quickly said, "Yes."

"*You okay?*"

"Not really ... Please come back soon."

"*Allie, it's still going to be at least three weeks ... can you do that? Can you wait another three weeks?*"

"What else can I do?"

"I'm so sorry, honey, I wish I could come back sooner ... I'll call you frequently, okay?"

"Okay."

"Please take care of yourself."

"Hm."

"I love you."

Alice said nothing, and after a few seconds, she heard him hang up.

Jean-Pierre held out his hand and she gave him the phone. He left without saying a word, leaving her sitting on her bed, feeling even lonelier than before.

The nausea became worse and Alice left her food completely untouched, feeling herself get weaker with every day that passed.

After a while, she stopped getting out of bed in the morning. What was the point anyway? There was nothing to do in her room and looking out through the window only doubled her loneliness, so she kept the blinds shut at all times. Sleep began to be her only way to escape her life, and it amazed her how long she was able to stay asleep.

Jean-Pierre still appeared three times a day, but Alice kept her blanket pulled up to her chin and her back toward the door, ignoring him.

Every time she got up to drink some water in the bathroom, it cost her more effort. Lying in bed all day long made her muscles decrease, but she was at a point where she didn't care anymore.

Maybe not eating was the answer. Maybe she could just starve herself until death brought relief.

Alice listened to Jean-Pierre closing the door behind him, after having brought her yet another plate of food that would go to waste. She wondered why he even bothered. People were starving all over the world and he kept wasting food on someone who did not want it. Did Henry know his efforts were wasted? What did he think about her disappearance anyway? Did he know that she was locked in her room?

Alice remembered his dark friendly eyes, the short gray hair, the wrinkled skin, and the huge smile he would always give her. The image made tears run down her cheeks and she wiped them away angrily. She had cried way too much these last couple of weeks. Sometimes even several times a day.

Even though she had more than enough reasons to be sad, Alice could not quite figure out why the tears came all the time. Shouldn't she be all dried up inside by now?

Voices fought their way through the closed window. Someone was laughing and making jokes outside, and without knowing what it was about, she envied them.

Alice closed her eyes and listened to the laughter for a while until sleep rolled over her once again and she drifted off into a deep, dreamless state of unconsciousness.

Someone shook her roughly and she flinched, startled, and tried to wind free of the two hands that were gripping her shoulders.

The light in her room was on and Alice put her hands to her face to shield her eyes from the brightness.

After a while, her eyes had adjusted enough for her to take her hands away again and see who had woken her up. She looked into green eyes that were studying her, looking concerned.

"Wow, thanks for honoring me with your presence," she muttered sarcastically. Her voice was weak and barely audible.

Jonas dropped his gaze and said nothing.

"You didn't have to shake me so hard, you know." Alice pushed herself up into a sitting position and was surprised by how much effort it cost her. Little stars began to dance before her eyes, and she rested her head against the wall.

"I called your name," he said quietly. "Then I shook you lightly. Several times. You didn't respond. I was worried."

"Oh ... I must've been deeply asleep then."

Jonas sighed and his eyes flicked back to her face. "What you doing, starving yourself?" There was accusation in his voice.

"Why would *you* care?"

"I do. Danny called me. Jean-Pierre told him you're not eating."

Irritated, Alice scoffed and glared at him. "Why does everybody think they have to tell me what to do? It's my fucking life and my fucking decision, okay?"

An expression of utter pain and sorrow appeared on his face, and Alice immediately felt sorry for snapping at him. "I'm not ... starving myself or whatever."

"Then why aren't you eating?"

"Because I'm not hungry, okay? I feel sick all the time."

Jonas sat down on the mattress next to where her feet were, and she pulled them back quickly. His presence was making her nervous and she looked down at her hands to avoid his accusing stare.

"We had this conversation already," he said sadly.

"I know ... Guess I wasn't able to *eliminate the stress*."

"Is that all it is?"

"What else would it be?"

"Don't know ... some illness? Perhaps you should get checked."

"It's psychosomatic, Jonas, I know it. It's always when ... things suck that I get sick, physically."

"Things do suck," he agreed in a toneless voice.

Alice felt her eyes turn wet again and sighed, feeling annoyed.

What the fuck is wrong with me? Do I have feelings for the guy or something?

She wiped the tears away with an edge of her blanket. "I'm sorry for ... making things awkward between us. I messed up everything." She still avoided his eyes when she said it.

Jonas turned his head to the door, as if to check that no one was standing there, then he put his hand on hers.

Alice winced under his touch and almost pulled her hand away, but then she changed her mind, realizing it felt good.

"*I'm* sorry," he objected.

"For what? For not saying no or pushing me off you? It would have been your right, you know."

"For staying away ... leaving you all alone up here."

"You don't have to keep me company if you don't want to."

Jonas took a deep breath. "That's the thing ... I *want* to."

Surprised, she looked up and the look in his eyes made her shiver. "You said ... I remind you of your sister."

He grimaced. "Not like *that*, you look nothing like her."

"Then how?"

He hesitated and his eyes wandered through her room as if he were trying to find the right answer. "The ... situation. You're in a similar situation as she was."

Alice frowned and wondered what he meant by that.

Jonas took his hand away from hers to rub his temple, and she immediately missed the warmth of his skin on hers.

"Are you going to say more?" she asked curiously.

He shook his head.

They sat in silence for a while, Jonas lost in thoughts and Alice watching him, wondering what his story was.

"We can never do it again," he muttered suddenly.

"I know," she whispered.

I wasn't planning on it anyway.

Again, they remained quiet for a moment. Alice stared at him and tried to understand her feelings toward him. It was not love; that she knew for certain. Jonas was attractive, but his quiet manner and the way he hid his emotions annoyed her. Because of the expressionless mask he wore every day, she didn't know him well enough to decide whether or not she liked his character. He had killed and he seemed to be okay with it. And yet, she felt the urge to be held by him, the way he had held her after they had slept together. He had held her to comfort her, and it had worked.

What if she was just deprived of human affection?

I might even want to be hugged by Jean-Pierre…

Her sense of judgement wasn't exactly great. Despite everything, she was still in love with Danny. Even after the countless times he had hurt her. Jonas had never hurt her.

"What you thinking?" he asked her now, and she blushed.

"Nothing … just … it was such a risk."

He nodded. "When I woke up, it was almost 8:00 p.m. Dinner was late."

"We were lucky." She dropped her gaze, ashamed of talking about what had been between them. Nervously, she cleared her throat. "Do you … think we can go back to normal?"

"Define normal."

Alice bit her lip and said nothing.

He gave her a weak smile. "I'm not gonna let you starve up here."

Again, she felt tears well up in her eyes and quickly wiped them away.

Stupid tears.

Jonas's expression got worried and she felt his piercing stare on her.

"I'm too fucking emotional ... Seriously, I hate myself for that." She forced herself to grin at him but he remained serious.

"Don't be so hard on yourself." He put his hand on her foot, which was covered by the blanket, and gave it an affectionate squeeze.

Alice laughed, but it came out as a sob.

"I'll tell Henry to prepare lighter food for you like last time."

She nodded. "What does he think anyway? About me, I mean."

Jonas sighed and it was obvious what he thought about the situation. "Danny told them all you're ill."

"Well, guess he's not entirely wrong."

Jonas did as he had promised and visited her from time to time, and Alice forced herself to eat at least a little bit—for him.

They watched movies and played on her console and she felt her mood get better. At least she was not looking for ways to kill herself anymore, though she was still far from being happy.

The nausea remained and Alice knew that even her friendship with Jonas could not change that. She needed to get out of the house or at least out of her room.

Danny called several times, worried about her well-being. It was ironic since he had put her in that situation, but Alice had accepted that nothing about Danny made sense anymore. His actions were driven either by the desire for power and money or by the drugs he took. He was impulsive and unpredictable and worst of all, madly in love with her.

Soon enough, his business trip was over and when Alice heard his car on the gravel outside of the house, her heart made a jump and her mouth turned dry. Would he be in a good mood?

She waited for him freshly showered and wearing the clothes he'd bought her, hoping he would not be too shocked by her appearance. Again, she had lost a significant amount of weight and the lack of sunlight had left her skin a grayish white.

Danny's expression said it all when he stepped into her room, and Alice looked down at the floor, feeling ashamed.

He hugged her, but only lightly and carefully, as if he thought he might actually break her. They sat down on the bed and he pulled her head onto his chest, stroking her hair.

"Sorry I was gone so long." He kissed her forehead. "I should not have left you alone. I should have taken care of you."

Alice said nothing and stared at his shirt—his perfectly white ironed dress shirt.

"Jean-Pierre said you've stopped eating. Why would you do such a thing?"

"I'm not ... I mean, I'm eating again. I was just ... sick."

"Did you have the flu?"

"No, it's just my stomach ..."

"Do you need a doctor?"

She shook her head. "It's nothing physical ... just stress, that's all."

Danny sighed and continued stroking her hair and cheek. "It's my fault. I was too hard on you with that bunker. I should have known it would be too much for you."

"And yet you'd do it again, wouldn't you?"

"I was ... furious about you running away and telling me you wanted to leave me. I was ... too impulsive. But you won't try to run away again, right?"

Alice shook her head slowly.

"See, then there's no problem and we can just put it behind us."

Sure, you can. You're not the one locked up in a bedroom.

When she said nothing, he lifted her chin with his hand and looked into her eyes. "Can you? Put it behind you?"

Intimidated by his stare, she felt her heart beat faster and her eyes teared up.

Danny's expression softened at once. "I'll give you time, honey. I know you're not doing well. Jonas said you might have had some kind of mental breakdown."

"Did he?"

He wiped a tear away from her cheek with his thumb, the way Jonas had before they'd had sex. Alice blushed at the memory.

"It's nothing to be ashamed of, darling." He kissed her forehead again. "We all have been going through some stuff. Our lives are not easy but it's worth the struggle."

For you, maybe.

More tears began to run down her cheeks and she cursed herself for it silently.

Danny kissed her cheek and her nose and then her lips, and dried her tears with the sleeve of his shirt. "You're so fragile ... I'll have to be extra careful with you."

Alice wondered if her 'mental breakdown' could be a good thing. Danny had been nice to her since her suicide attempt. He had not slapped her or hurt her in any other way since she had swallowed all those pills.

There was something Alice had noticed about Danny and even Jonas: whenever they saw her tears, they softened. And she definitely did not lack tears these days.

"Danny?" she asked him after a moment of silence.

"Yes?"

"Will you let me out of the room again?" She felt him tense and bit her lip, dreading his answer.

"Do you think that would be wise? Regarding your condition ..."

"I ... I actually think some sunlight and fresh air would help me."

He sighed and thought about it. "I've been doubting Jonas's competence since your last attempt to run away. I don't think I'll let you just walk around like that, but I'll allow you outside under my supervision."

"I told you I won't do it again."

"Allie, Allie, Allie," he said while shaking his head slowly. "I love you, darling, but I'm far from trusting you."

Danny was leaning back in his chair casually, allowing the sun to give him a tan. He looked incredibly handsome. His dark hair had grown back a bit and was for once not tidily styled, and he'd opened the buttons of his shirt and was stretching his chest toward the sun.

Alice had been eager to feel the sunrays on her skin, but she had grown extremely sensitive. The heat was already giving her a headache, so she had chosen a shady place on the porch instead, not too far away from Danny.

There was a wooden table in between them and Henry had prepared a delicious soda with herbs from the garden. Despite the shade, the heat was going in waves through Alice's body and it made her feel dizzy. She took a sip of soda to cool down.

Danny's deep blue eyes were watching her. "You okay?"

She nodded. "It's just ... hot."

"I knew it would not be good for you."

"It's hot in my room as well, you know. It's like a sauna ... I prefer to be outside."

He sighed and took a sip of his drink. "You worry me." It sounded like an accusation.

Jean-Pierre was leaning against the wall, wiping sweat from his forehead with a fabric tissue. Viktor, Timothy, Waldo, and Paul were sitting around a plastic table underneath a big oak, playing poker.

Henry was working in the vegetable garden and the gate guard was sitting in his plastic chair near the gate as always, tanning his face and arms. Everyone was out in the yard, except Jonas.

Alice had noticed that he had kept his distance since Danny's return, and she thought it was probably for the best.

"I'll buy you a fan." Danny put the glass down and watched his friends play poker.

"Thanks ... You can join them, you know. I won't go anywhere."

Danny turned his head to look at her. "I'm spending time with *you* now, honey. I can play poker some other time."

Alice gave him a weak smile and took another sip of her drink. The heat was unbearable. She had donned a light blue summer dress with tiny flowers on it—and yet it was hard to breathe.

"It's hot for the first of June, isn't it?" she asked breathlessly.

Danny shrugged. "It's only seventy-eight degrees. I wouldn't call that hot. Since when do you remember the date anyway?"

Alice grabbed a video game magazine, which was lying on the table, to fan herself with. "I'm trying to keep track, that's all."

"You okay?" he asked again.

She nodded. "Is there water in the pool now?"

"Not yet, but I'll have it filled up."

"Hm, yeah. A swim would be nice."

"In your condition? You might drown."

She ignored that.

"You should eat something. There's avocados."

Alice felt her stomach convulse and a wave of nausea overcame her. She stopped fanning herself and rested her head on the table.

"Honey? Should I tell Henry to prepare some guacamole toast?" Danny's face became a blur and his voice seemed to echo in her mind.

"Or maybe something even lighter, some fruits?"

Breathing was suddenly incredibly hard, and Alice pulled at her necklace. Her stomach rumbled dangerously.

"Darling, what's wrong?"

"Jean-Pierre, bucket!" Alice gasped, one hand on her mouth.

Jean-Pierre flinched and stared at her, then he dropped his tissue and quickly handed her the small copper spit bucket, which stood next to the entrance door. Jonas usually used it for his cigarette stubs.

Danny got off his chair and hurried around the table to hold her hair back, while she threw up into the bucket. It was already the second time that day, but he didn't need to know that.

Tears streamed down her cheeks as she coughed and gagged while her stomach turned over and over again, even though there was nothing in it.

"It's the sun, I knew it's not good for you." Danny wiped some pearls of sweat from her forehead and put the bucket back on the ground when she was finished.

"There's nothing to see here!" he shouted at his friends, who had stopped playing cards to watch the scene on the porch.

Moaning, Alice put her head back on the table. Shivers went through her whole body. Danny softly pulled her up from her chair.

"Let's get you inside." He heaved her up into his arms and brought her into the house. "Maybe you should rest in the guest room next to my office for a while. There's aircon."

Alice said nothing and let him carry her to the room, where he put her down on the bed before shutting the blinds and turning on the air-conditioning.

"Why's there aircon in this room?" Alice asked weakly.

He shrugged. "It's been here before. Maybe this was supposed to be the main bedroom."

It worked immediately and the temperature in the room dropped significantly.

Alice shivered. "Don't make it too cold, please."

"I put it on seventy degrees. Is that all right?" He sat down on the bed and held her hand.

"I guess ..." Suddenly realizing how tired she was, she closed her eyes.

Danny sighed. "If I only knew what's wrong with you."

"It's nothing, don't worry." Alice rolled onto her side and, noticing her goose bumps, Danny pulled the blanket over her.

"First, you're too hot, now you're too cold ... what am I going to do with you?" He bent down and kissed her forehead.

A couple of hours later, Alice awoke to Danny's gentle touch. He was stroking her cheek.

"Dinner's ready ... if you want to join us."

Confused, she blinked into the light and sat up. Being cared for by Danny felt wonderful, but she was afraid it wouldn't last long.

"I'm sorry for giving you so much trouble," she said quietly.

Smiling, Danny tried to kiss her, but she quickly turned her head away from him. "I haven't brushed my teeth yet ..."

He kissed her cheek instead. "Are you feeling better?"

"Better than before, yes. Thank you."

Danny brushed a sweaty strand of hair away from her forehead. "If it's too much with all the people around, I understand. You can eat here or in your room if you like."

"No, it's fine, really ... but I should brush my hair and ... try to look less horrible."

He laughed. "You look a bit sick, but you're far from looking horrible." He hooked the strap of her dress, which had glided down her shoulder, with his index finger and gently pulled it back up.

His words filled her with warmth.

If he stays like that, I might even forgive him.

Suddenly, she was a naïve eighteen-year-old again, blinded by love. And he was her knight in shining armor.

Since the story with the bunker, none of Danny's friends would talk to Alice or even look at her and she was glad for that. She wondered what Waldo thought about her still being in the house and about her surrender to Danny. Luckily, she owed none of them any explanations.

Except Jonas, maybe?

He kept his eyes on his plate when she entered the dining room and took her seat next to Danny. Danny kissed her gently and smiled, glad that she finally joined them for dinner again.

They were all eating steaks and Henry had prepared a vegetable broth for her to not overwhelm her stomach. Alice was glad. Despite the nausea, she felt hungry.

Jonas's every movement seemed stiff somehow and Alice wondered if he was feeling nervous. She was, in any case. If Danny knew what they had done, he would probably kill them both. She pushed that thought aside and ate her soup quietly.

Viktor and Jean-Pierre were eating as well, and the room certainly felt more crowded than usual.

Alice smiled at Henry, who was busy filling up their glasses, and he froze, his expression bewildered. He quickly got a grip, however, and smiled back. "Glad to see you're doing better, Alice."

She nodded.

Henry went back to the kitchen and Danny followed him with his eyes, a suspicious look in them. "I don't like that guy's tone," he muttered.

Confused, Alice looked at him. "What tone?"

"I don't know ... He's got that weird undertone in his voice. I'm not sure if it's supposed to be sarcasm."

"Hm." Alice looked down at her bowl and the rest of cold soup, she could not manage to eat.

Danny grabbed her upper arm to make her look up. "Don't you hear it?"

She shook her head. "I think he's very nice and polite."

Thinking, he scratched his chin. "He's nosy. But he's a good cook."

"I like him."

"Of course you do, you like everybody. Doesn't change anything. He should mind his own business." Danny took a sip of his red wine and brushed the glass with his thumb, pondering.

Since when was he so paranoid? Alice hoped he would not end up firing Henry. Sure, having staff to cook and clean in a house where illegal business was done was probably risky, but Danny should have thought of that before.

She pushed her bowl away and sipped her water, feeling hot again.

There're too many people in the room.

The voices of the men talking seemed to grow louder and began to give her a headache.

"What have you two been doing anyway?" Danny suddenly asked.

Alice flinched and heat rushed to her face. Confused, she blinked at him. "Me?"

Jonas had frozen in place and was still staring at his plate.

Danny took another sip of his wine and grinned. "I was just wondering how you kept busy."

Hot flushes now went through Alice's body and she felt her hands get sweaty. "Playing ... video games ..." Taking a deep breath, she pulled at her necklace. "Movies ... poker ..."

"He taught you to play poker?"

She nodded.

"Wow ... I thought you would hate it."

Danny's face became a blur.

"It's not ..." She cleared her throat. "Not my ... favorite game ... but keeps busy ..."

"Allie, you okay?"

"Need ... bathroom."

Danny quickly grabbed her and helped her get off her chair, then he brought her to the downstairs bathroom where she fell onto her knees, bent over the toilet, throwing up the soup she'd just eaten.

Danny held her hair back until she was finished. "I really am worried about you."

Alice wiped her mouth with some toilet paper. "I'm fine."

"No, you're not." He helped her get up and filled a glass with water.

She drank half of it, but it almost slipped through her trembling fingers.

"You're glowing," he pointed out. "We should check your temperature."

"Not necessary."

Danny eyed her suspiciously. "Allie, if you're sick, we have to do something about it."

"No, it's fine. It must be psychosomatic ... it'll pass."

"Do you ever keep any food in your stomach?"

She thought about it. So far, she had thrown up everything she had eaten. Even water was hard to keep down.

"Sure," she lied. "I eat more than I puke."

Sighing, Danny put an arm around her shoulders to lead her out of the bathroom. "I can only hope."

He brought her upstairs and she took off her uncomfortable clothes and put on one of Danny's oversized T-shirts.

"You still wear my old shirts?"

"They're comfy to sleep in." Exhausted, she sank onto her bed and he sat down next to her. He caressed her head with one hand while she fell asleep.

When Alice awoke again, he was still sitting next to her, but he had changed his position and was now leaning against the wall, his legs outstretched on the bed. He was talking to someone and Alice tried to understand what he was saying but failed.

Confused, she blinked into the light and finally realized that he was speaking Spanish.

It had been a while since she had last heard him speak that language and she loved the sound of it. Still drowsy, she listened until he hung up the phone.

"You're awake," he noted.

"Who was that?"

"Julio. He wants to come over for dinner."

Alice yawned. "When?"

"In a week, exactly. Next Friday night." Danny pulled her head onto his chest and kissed her forehead. "You're sweaty, mi amor."

"I'm hot."

He sighed. "We really should check your temperature."

"Why? Even if I got a fever, it will pass. Nothing to worry about."

"If you say so ..." He didn't sound convinced.

"Why are you so worried?"

"Because ..." He took a deep breath. "Because I made a mistake locking you in that stupid bunker and now I'm scared of what might be wrong with you. I really hope it's just the flu."

"Or like I said, just stress. It was the same last winter."

"Did you throw up then as well?"

"Sometimes."

That seemed to calm him down a bit. "Is it really so horrible for you to be here?" he asked quietly.

Tears welled up in her eyes and she blinked them away.

Not those stupid tears again!

"I'm just scared," she admitted in a thin voice.

He brushed over her cheek with his fingers. "Of what?"

"Of you ... becoming someone you're not supposed to be."

"What do you mean?"

"When Jonas shot Martin ... he was so calm about it. I thought you're different, that you'd never be able to kill someone."

"Is this about what happened a month ago?"

She nodded.

"I didn't kill anybody, Allie."

"But you almost shot your best friend."

"I was blinded by fury, thinking he'd hurt you. Everyone would freak out if they thought their girlfriend had been hurt."

Does that also apply to people who hurt their girlfriends themselves?

"You also told me you'd killed people, remember?"

He laughed. "You mean that breakdown I had? No, babe, don't worry. I didn't kill anybody."

"But you said—"

"I felt guilty about not being able to save some people. I ... I was supposed to help someone, but I failed, so I blamed myself."

Could he be telling the truth? It didn't change the fact that he had hurt her badly several times. He definitely was able to hurt people, even people he loved ... but was he able to kill?

Danny lifted her chin and kissed her, and then he smiled at her warmly. "I promise."

The weather stayed nice and Danny bought her a fan, as promised, so Alice spent her days lying on her bed, enjoying the cool air coming from the ceiling fan and fighting her nausea. She kept the blinds closed, but the hot flushes came nevertheless and no matter how hard she tried, she couldn't keep any food down.

The effects of malnourishment were already palpable, and Alice was barely able to get up and use the bathroom anymore.

Danny bought her some pills against nausea and after a while, they began to work.

Being sick had its advantages though since he finally treated her nicely and touched her carefully.

Since his return from the last business trip, he had slept with her several times, but not too often and he'd been incredibly tender and careful not to hurt her. Not that she enjoyed it, but at least it didn't hurt. It made it easier to accept her situation and she was able to focus on her own well-being rather than worry about Danny's drug problem. She realized that he was more in control of his actions when he was on cocaine. Plus, he drank less, which kept his anger issues down to a tolerable level.

The rain came suddenly, and it stayed for several weeks. Henry complained that all the water was destroying the vegetable garden and Danny's tan began to fade.

Alice was grateful for the mild temperatures and when Danny allowed it, she would sit on the porch and watch the rain fall while he and the guys stayed inside playing cards. They spent less time in the office, she noticed. At first, she thought they just wanted to enjoy the weather and lay off work, but even now, during the rainy days, they usually only worked in the mornings and took the afternoons off. It gave her more time with Danny, which wasn't always pleasant.

He still treated her with care though and for that she was glad.

On Wednesday, the twenty-seventh of June, the gang was working, and the pool had been cleaned recently, so Alice decided to try it out.

It was a hot day for a change and the hot flushes were making it hard for her to breathe. She donned her old bikini and realized that it didn't quite fit her anymore due to her weight loss.

Wrapped in a towel, Alice went downstairs on bare feet and ran right into Jonas. He stopped awkwardly and let her pass without saying a word.

His behavior was odd. One day, he appeared to be over the whole thing, and the next, he could barely look at her.

With him keeping his distance, Alice was glad Danny kept her company more often.

The pool looked clean and inviting, and Alice put her toes in first to feel the water temperature. It was cool but not too cold, so she dropped her towel on the ground and glided into the water.

Swimming would have required strength she didn't have, so instead, Alice put her arms on the warm marble surrounding the pool and rested her head on them, enjoying the refreshing coolness of the water and listening to the birds singing in the trees. Her eyes drooped shut and she began daydreaming, when suddenly, someone casting a shadow over her sent a shiver down her spine.

It was Henry. Looking up at him, Alice smiled.

The cook seemed nervous and unsettled, and kept glancing over his shoulders as if he felt watched. He crouched down to her. "I know something bad is going on here."

Alice opened her mouth to say something, but closed it again, unsure of how to respond.

"I know he treats you badly and that he's dangerous ... and I see the way he looks at me." Henry kept his voice down. Again, he glanced back over his shoulder.

"Do you think someone's watching you?" Alice asked him quietly.

He shook his head. "Not me. You." He wiped sweat from his forehead. "You're always being watched. I've noticed that, and I know you're not allowed to leave this place."

Alice felt her heartbeat accelerate. Henry was stepping onto dangerous terrain.

"Don't worry, Henry. Nothing shady's going on. I'm fine," she lied, trying to keep a smile on her face.

"I know they're doing something illegal. I've seen them carry guns and they don't look like the kind of people who should be armed," Henry added, ignoring her objection.

Wondering where he was going with this, Alice bit her lip and said nothing.

"There isn't much I can do about it, but I know you have nothing to do with it. I like you, Alice, and I'd like to help you." His big dark eyes were full of concern and determination at the same time.

Quickly, Alice averted her eyes, feeling ashamed and also scared for him. How dangerous *were* Danny and his friends? Would they kill someone to silence them? Or would they fire Henry and hire a cook who did not ask questions?

She cleared her throat. "I don't ... you shouldn't ... It's fine, really."

Henry sighed. "You're scared of them, aren't you? I am as well ... but I might be able to help you get away from here."

Alice looked up again, suddenly feeling hopeful. What if Henry really *was* able to help her? Maybe she could hide in his car and let him drive her far away, out of Danny's reach. But what if Jonas was right and he would always find her, no matter where she went? Was he really that powerful?

"It's not a good idea, Henry. I'm sorry, but I don't want you to get into trouble."

"If I can't get you out of here, Alice, I will find another way. Find out what it is they're doing and call the police, maybe ..." He looked sad and desperate when he said it, and Alice couldn't help but feel incredibly sorry for him.

"They treat you okay, don't they? And you got a good salary, so everything's fine ... Please, just leave it at that and forget about me. It's my life and my responsibility to find a solution."

Frowning, Henry stared at her for a moment. "I can't do that."

In the corner of her eye, Alice saw something move. Her eyes flicked to the house, where Viktor had just stepped through the back door. He shot them a glance and started walking toward the pool.

Henry stiffened and slowly stood up.

"What you talkin' 'bout?" Viktor eyed them both suspiciously.

"Plants," Alice quickly answered.

Viktor's tiny eyes narrowed. "Plants?"

She nodded. "Vegetables, to be precise. Henry's been explaining some gardening rules to me."

"Does he get paid for that?"

Henry gave Alice a meaningful look and turned around to walk back to the vegetable garden. Viktor remained standing at the edge of the pool, his massive arms crossed in front of his chest.

"This is my house as well, you know," she told him coldly. "If I want to talk to the staff, I have every right to do so."

Viktor sneered. "That so? I got a different impression."

"Since when are you allowed to talk to me anyway?"

Keeping his mouth shut, he shrugged. Slowly, he began marching around the pool toward the wall, where he remained standing in the shade of one of the tall birches, eyes again on her.

It was evident that he was not going to let her out of sight again. His stare felt heavy and threatening.

First, Alice tried to ignore him and enjoy the pool a bit longer, but she shivered under his stare. Resigned, she swam to the ladder and climbed out of the pool but had to walk back to where she had left her towel. All the way, his stare was on her and it felt as if he were undressing her with his eyes. She hastily wrapped herself in her towel and hurried back into the house.

Again, Alice almost collided with Jonas, who apparently was about to enjoy a smoke in the yard.

"That was a short swim," he noted.

"I'm being watched ... It's creepy." She rushed past him and upstairs to her room.

That night, dinner tasted different. Alice noticed that Henry was nowhere to be seen. Goose bumps arose on her arms and disgusted, she pushed her plate away.

"Are you feeling sick again?" Danny asked, concerned.

Her eyes wandered across the table and to Viktor, who was eating his roast beef noisily. He licked his greasy fingers and looked up. When he saw her expression, a vicious grin parted his oily lips.

Alice quickly averted her eyes.

"Alice?" Danny lightly brushed her arm.

She flinched and looked at him.

"You look pale."

"Where's Henry?"

At once, Danny's expression hardened, and he pulled his hand back and put it on his wine glass instead, ready to take a sip. "Why would you care?"

"Because he's a great guy and I like him."

Danny wiped his mouth on a napkin. "He's got the evening off. He has children he wants to see occasionally, you know."

Is he telling the truth?

"So ... he'll be back tomorrow?"

Nonchalant, he shrugged. "We'll see, won't we?"

Something in his eyes made her shiver and a new wave of nausea washed the last bits of her appetite away. "Is it okay if I go upstairs? I feel sick." Her voice sounded weak and higher than usual.

Knowing that her reaction had to do with their conversation, Danny eyed her coldly, but then he nodded.

Henry did not come to work the next day and neither the days that followed.

What did they do to him?

Alice was lying on her bed, cooled by the ceiling fan. She wiped a layer of sweat from her forehead and inhaled deeply. Worrying about Henry had made her worse and she had already thrown up three times that day. Now, she felt dizzy and was shaken by chills every now and then.

Loud voices and laughter were coming through the window. It was Saturday and Danny was having one of his parties.

They usually started at around noon and the yard soon got filled up with rich men and women in tight bikinis that left nothing to your imagination. It made Alice wonder whether Danny enjoyed the company of one of these women from time to time. She wasn't entirely sure if she would mind.

Right now, the noise was giving her a headache, and she decided to go downstairs and fetch some painkillers. When she pushed down the door handle, the door did not move. Surprised, she realized that she had been locked in. Didn't Danny know that she would never talk to his guests anyway? There was no need for his paranoia.

Angrily, she punched the door with her fist and walked over to the window to glance out. A group of people was sitting around the plastic table underneath the trees in the front yard, drinking and playing poker. Some others were standing around, talking. Most of the guests, however, were in the back yard by the pool.

Danny might be making out with escorts right now while I'm locked in my room.

Alice pushed the thought away. What did it matter anyway? The less attention he paid her, the better.

Hot air blew inside when she opened the window, and it sent a spasm of pain through her skull. Sitting on the sill, she let her eyes wander across the yard until she spotted Jonas, who was wearing a black T-shirt and smoking a cigarette all by himself, standing near the swing.

Alice watched him for a while.

He dislikes social events as well.

She ripped a piece of paper from her notepad, made a ball out of it, and threw it at him. It missed him but landed in the grass about an arm's length away from him. Confused, Jonas looked up.

"You're littering," he called up to her before picking up the paper ball.

Alice wildly gestured for him to come upstairs and he gave her a nod in response. About a minute later, she heard a knock on her door.

"Come in if you can … it's locked."

Apparently, he could, and the lock rattled before he stepped inside and closed the door behind him.

"Cold in here," he said, looking uncomfortable.

"I like it that way." Alice got off the windowsill and walked toward him, and he took a step back.

Annoyed, she came to a halt. "I'm not going to ... *do* anything, I just want to talk to you."

"About what?"

Alice lowered her voice. "About Henry."

"What about him?"

She took a deep breath and felt tears well up in her eyes. "He's gone, isn't he? Did they ... did they kill him?"

Puzzled, Jonas stared at her. "Why in the world would anybody kill Henry?"

"Because Danny doesn't like him ... He said he's too nosy and he knows too much."

Jonas brushed through his hair with his fingers and said nothing.

"Please, you have to tell me the truth. I need to know what happened to him!" Alice grabbed him by the shirt and shook him.

"Okay, okay." He pushed her hands away. "They fired him. Paid him a generous sum to keep his family fed and watered until he finds a new job."

"Dammit Jonas, that's not right! Even if they paid him; he loved this house!" Exasperated, Alice sat down on her bed and wiped the tears from her eyes.

"And you thought they'd killed him." Jonas grinned, amused.

"Fuck you! That's not funny."

"You think he's a monster?"

"Uh, yes? That's what he is, a fucking monster! You think he almost shot you 'cause he's a good person?"

Jonas's grin vanished. "Nah, 'cause he's in love with you. He was on drugs and he thought I'd molested you."

Aghast, Alice stared at him. "Why are you defending him?"

"You looked quite happy with him these last couple of weeks."

Alice looked into his eyes blankly, feeling a whirlwind of emotions inside of her. Jonas had sounded almost hurt when he'd said it.

"He's been nice to me," she muttered.

"So, you forgave him?"

"No! Of course not!"

"Looked like it."

Alice felt the urge to slap him for that, but her anger instantly turned into desperation and hot tears began running down her cheeks. How dared he make assumptions about her without knowing how she felt? He didn't seem to have the slightest idea of what life in this hellhole was for her.

Angrily, she wiped the tears off her cheeks and glared at him. "What am I supposed to do then, huh? Tell me!"

"I'm not saying anything."

"Yes, you are! You're accusing me of being too nice to Danny while you kiss his ass all the time and do everything he says. You're a fucking hypocrite!"

Jonas took a step closer and gestured her to keep her voice down. "Sorry," he said softly. "I'm just confused. One day you hate him, the next you don't."

Sobbing, Alice grabbed her blanket to dry her tears and hide her face behind it. Jonas sat down on the bed beside her.

"I'm confused too, you know. I don't know what to do ... But I have to live with him and it's easier if I don't hate him. It's easier if I just pretend everything's fine. As long as he's nice, it works."

"Sorry," he said again and put a hand on her shoulder. "I sometimes forget we're not in the same position."

Alice jerked away from his touch. "You're damn right we're not! I never chose this, I never wanted this ... I'm his prisoner and you can just walk in and out as you please."

Jonas said nothing to that, but he gave her a sad look. They sat in silence for a while, listening to the laughter coming from outside.

Slowly, Alice took the blanket away from her face and placed it on her lap instead. "What's up with *you*, by the way?"

"Hm?" He gave her an uncertain look.

"I know things are awkward between us ... but sometimes you ignore me completely and then suddenly you talk to me again. I make you uncomfortable, right?"

Jonas sighed. "I'm only uncomfortable around you when Danny's nearby. And I ignore you 'cause either Viktor or Jean-Pierre are constantly watching."

"They're so annoying ... I miss the time when only you were watching me."

He grinned. "Is that so?"

"You were more discreet about it. You didn't purposely invade my privacy and enjoy it."

"And they do?"

Alice nodded. "At least Viktor does. How am I supposed to enjoy a swim in the pool when he's there, staring at me like a pervert?"

"He did that?"

"Yeah ... He's like Timothy, only bigger and bald."

"Just don't invite him to your room, okay? Unlike Tee, Viktor isn't scared of me."

"I wouldn't think of it ... Timothy's scared of you? Why? I thought you were already friends before Danny met you?"

"I'm a scary guy." He grinned mischievously.

"You're an idiot." Alice punched his upper arm lightly.

"You should eat more, there was no juice in that punch."

She frowned at him.

"Sorry, stupid joke." He gave her an apologetic smile.

"Can I ask you something?"

Jonas nodded.

Nervously, Alice chewed her lip. "Does Danny ... does he ... well, have other women?"

For a moment, Jonas seemed surprised by that question, but then his expression changed back into its normal unreadable state. "Would you mind if he did?"

"I'm not sure ... I mean, it's not that I'm jealous or anything. But if he did fuck other women behind my back, it would make him an even bigger asshole." Her eyes met his and she noticed the uneasy look in them. "Sorry, that's too private. You don't want to hear this."

"He doesn't."

"What?"

"He might be a lot of things, but he's not unfaithful. At least I wouldn't know. But I honestly doubt he would do such a thing. It's you he wants and only you." A hateful look appeared in his eyes. "He's obsessed with you."

Alice felt goose bumps arise on her arms and shivered. "Maybe he *should* hook up with other women ... it might take his mind off me."

Again, Jonas gave her an uneasy look.

Sighing, Alice got off the bed and walked toward the window. The sun blinded her and sent yet another wave of pain through her skull. Grimacing, she shut the blinds a bit, then turned back to Jonas, who was still sitting on the bed.

"Could you do me a favor?"

"What?"

"Get me some painkillers?"

His eyes narrowed with suspicion.

"I'm not planning on swallowing them all at the same time," Alice said, irritated. "You can bring me one and then the next in a few hours, if you don't trust me."

He shook his head and got off the bed as well. "No, it's okay." His eyes wandered down her body and up again, resting on her face.

"What?" she asked, annoyed. "You've already seen me naked. No reason to look at me like that."

To her surprise, he blushed. "You look sick," he said in a serious voice.

"Thanks, Jonas. That's exactly what I needed to hear."

"I'm worried, that's all."

"Sure you are. Anything else?"

He gave her a sad look. "What's wrong?"

"Everything's wrong, but to be specific: It's a mental breakdown. You said it yourself."

"I told *him* that."

Alice walked past him to open the door for him and he stepped out hesitantly.

"You can keep telling him that, should he ever doubt it."

Jonas grimaced, looking pained. "I'll get you the pills."

"Thanks."

"If I knew what's wrong, I could get you the right pills, you know. Not just aspirin."

"It's a mental breakdown, okay? So unless you find a way to eliminate what caused it, there's really nothing you can do." Alice gave him an impatient look and shut the door in his face.

The morning sun reflected off his naked body and made him glow, and it looked almost as if he had a halo on his shiny dark hair.

Demons have no halos.

Alice's eyes wandered over Danny's sleeping body and she couldn't deny he was beautiful. She had never wanted a boyfriend who looked like a model though, and even less one who took cocaine as a morning ritual after a night of drinking whiskey until passing out.

The summer sun had given him a nice tan and she envied him for the time he spent out in the sun. Even if he allowed her to be outside occasionally, she could not stand the sun anymore. It seemed way too bright and too hot and usually gave her a headache or made her feel dizzy.

Now, it was still low, yet its rays that fell through Danny's bedroom window were already heating up the room.

Outside, everything was still peaceful. The water of the pool was smooth and sparkling, and birds were hopping around in the yard, picking up the leftovers of last night's party. Soon, they would be cleaned away by Anita or one of the other maids, who recently had begun working on weekends as well. That was definitely necessary with Danny's guests leaving empty bottles and cans lying around everywhere—even in the pool and Henry's vegetable garden. But Henry wasn't here anymore, and no one took care of the plants, so they were rotting away.

Alice felt a stabbing pain in her guts when she thought about Henry. He had been her only real friend in this place and now he was gone. The new cooks were friendly but distant, and they were careful not to step on Danny's toes. It turned out that was hard these days, with him being on edge all the time, paranoid about people being too nosy and risking his business secrets being revealed.

Still, Alice had no idea what it was that he did. She had her theories, but they never added up and they didn't explain why Danny and the others were always away on business trips in Northern Africa or the Middle East.

This much she had found out by going through Danny's trash and finding old plane tickets or snack wrappings with Arabic writing on them. When he was on whiskey and not on cocaine, he occasionally became more careless.

She watched him shift in his sleep, murmuring something through innocent-looking lips. He rolled onto his side, breathing deeply.

It must be something I would never approve of. Otherwise he would have let me in on it.

Did he sell drugs? Weapons were more like it, judging by the destination of his trips. But that didn't explain the video games and Danny was a programmer. How would his skills be of any use? And video games had never killed anyone, had they?

Alice rested her forehead against the cool glass of the window and watched two birds fighting over a slice of pizza, until one of the maids appeared, picked it up, and threw it into a big plastic bag she was carrying.

Poor girl ... I hope she gets a decent salary at least.

Anita came around the corner as well and the two maids began talking noisily, laughing from time to time.

"Allie?"

Alice winced and turned around.

Danny blinked at her and rolled onto his back, half covering his eyes with his arm. He moaned. "What're you doing up so early?" His voice was hoarse.

"Sorry if I woke you up."

"Nah ... those chattering chicks out there did. I've got to tell them to keep quiet in the morning." Rubbing his temples, he moaned again.

"Rough night?"

He nodded.

"I figured." Alice turned back to the window and watched the maids picking up trash.

"You look beautiful," Danny muttered. "The sunrays make you look like an angel."

Alice looked down at the white shirt she was wearing. It was almost blindingly white, like all of Danny's shirts. Due to its size, it covered her like a dress.

"I like it when you wear my shirts." Yawning, he stretched and then patted the mattress beside him. "Come back to bed."

Reluctantly, Alice took one last glance outside, and then walked toward him slowly to sit on the bed next to him. He rolled over and brushed her hair back to kiss her neck. It tickled and made goose bumps rise on her arms. Danny's fingers went down her spine and underneath the shirt, tracing along her hips and then forward to her belly.

"Sorry for waking you up last night," he whispered, and his breath still smelled of alcohol. "I was lonely and wanted to cuddle."

He had wanted more than just to cuddle, but Alice didn't correct him.

"I'd like us to sleep in the same bed more often. We're a couple after all, aren't we? It's so depressing to sleep alone."

She let his fingers wander upward and managed not to flinch when they reached her breasts.

403

"My bed or yours?"

He kissed her neck and then nibbled her ear softly. "Doesn't matter."

"You don't like it when I'm in here alone," she said quietly.

"It was supposed to be our bedroom, so it's yours as well ... but you're right, I don't see the point of you being here during the day. There's nothing to do anyway, with the TV being in your room."

Bullshit ... he doesn't want me to go through his drawers. What is he afraid of? That I might steal his drugs?

"You never bought another one."

Chuckling, he kissed her cheek from behind. "I don't have much time to watch TV lately."

"What about the video games? I thought they're your work."

"In the basement ... that's where we play. The living room looks better without a TV. More old-fashioned." He gently pushed her down onto the mattress and caressed her cheek while his deep blue eyes seemed to be swallowing her.

"You're so pale ... You look like Snow White." He kissed her lips and she held her breath to avoid inhaling the smell of whiskey. "It's beautiful."

"I'd rather be tanned like you."

Laughing, he kissed her again. "You'll never be if you don't go out in the sun."

"I can't stand it. It's too hot."

His expression changed to worry, and he put a hand on her forehead. "Alice Bouchart finding the sun too hot ... You really must be ill."

Grimacing, Alice turned her head away from his hand.

Danny kissed her neck again and started to unbutton her shirt.

"Aren't you hung over?"

He grinned and showed two rows of perfectly white, recently bleached teeth. "I don't easily get hangovers." His lips wandered down her body and Alice tried to remember what she'd ever found nice about his touch.

When he was done with her, she quickly fled to the bathroom and closed the door behind herself. Even through the closed door she could still hear him snort his daily dosage of cocaine. At least she hoped it was the daily dosage. Maybe he had already increased the amount with his steadily growing drug tolerance.

Her lower belly hurt, and she laid a hand on it, breathing slowly to make the nausea and pain go away. Her tongue felt furry and tasted of bile.

The nausea grew unbearable and Alice quickly wiped herself, and knelt in front of the toilet. The smell of urine made her gag and soon enough, she was puking out what seemed to be her soul. Her empty stomach turned and cramped, but nothing but stomach acid left her lips. By the time she was done, her whole body was shaking and her naked knees hurt from kneeling on the cold bathroom floor. Despite the smell, she rested her head on the toilet and closed her eyes, waiting for the dizziness to fade away.

She hadn't heard Danny enter and when he put a hand on her shoulder, she winced.

"I thought you were feeling better." He brushed her hair back and helped her get up, and when she shivered, he hugged her.

"I need water."

He took his arms away and Alice stumbled to the sink, where she splashed her face with cold water before drinking some out of her hand.

"I have never seen such extreme psychosomatic reactions, but if it really is just a mental thing, I think I can help you." He stepped aside to let her leave the bathroom.

Before being able to get dressed, Alice had to sit down on the bed and wait for the room to stop spinning.

Danny walked around the bed and opened the top drawer of his nightstand. "I know you know it, so I might as well let you have some." He sat down next to her and Alice lifted her head from her hands to see what he got.

It was one of those little glass tubes with a tiny spade in it. Alice already knew what it was for. Grimacing, she shook her head.

"Have some," Danny insisted and held it under her nose.

"I don't want to."

"Come on, don't be so boring! You need to loosen up. You're always in a bad mood and worrying about stuff—that's what makes you sick. I know how to handle stress, trust me."

"By getting high or drunk? No, thank you."

"Since when are you like that? Here's a real chance for you." Again, he held it under her nose.

"Weed can help with nausea, but cocaine? Seriously, Danny, I don't think it would do me any good."

Danny ignored her objection and put some powder on the spade. "You want to smoke a joint, go ahead. But first, try this." He held the spade under her nose.

Alice got up from the bed and walked over to lean against the wall instead. "I said no."

She saw him frown and felt his mood change, as if cold radiation were coming from his body. He got up as well and approached her. "Take it," he ordered firmly.

"Why is this so important to you?"

"Because I can't stand seeing you like this and I'm not going to watch you suffer any longer."

"Really? Seems to me you're only trying to drag me down with you."

Danny sneered. "Down? I'm trying to pull you up because that's where I am." He held the coke right under her nose. "Now take it."

Alice studied his expression and concluded that he was not going to let it go. His anger wasn't worth it. Looking at the powder, she swallowed dryly, but then she put her index finger on her nose, shutting one nostril, and snorted the powder through the other.

She felt it clump and slowly run down her throat, and it was bitter and disgusting. Her nose and airways burned, but a rush went through her body and took her by surprise. Gasping, she clutched her hands to her chest, feeling her heart racing. The room looked much brighter than before but instead of feeling euphoric, she felt a wave of panic go through her body. A stabbing pain went through her skull, blinding her.

Half gliding down the wall, she expected to faint, but the panic made her get back up. She rushed to the door, but then remembered that she was naked and there was nowhere for her to go. The thing that made her feel like this was inside of her and would follow her wherever she went.

Danny was laughing and his laughter seemed to echo from the walls. "See, now you're energized." His voice sounded louder and yet distant somehow.

Alice shook her head and gasped for air. "I'm having a heart attack!" Desperately hoping for him to help her, she looked at him pleadingly.

He just grinned and shook his head. "No, you're not. Calm down, you're going to be fine."

"No, no, no, you gave me way too much, Danny! Did you give me as much as you usually take? That's not right, it's my first time! You should have given me less!"

"Don't worry, it won't last long. You're just being paranoid." He held up his hands defensively and took a step toward her.

I'm dying right here, naked.

Something wet was on her lips and she licked it off. It tasted like iron. Alice clutched her hand to her nose and then looked at it, her heart sinking at once. It was blood.

Now, even Danny looked worried, but before he could say something, there was a knock on the door.

"No, no, Danny, don't let them in! I'm dying and I'm naked, don't let them in!"

Quickly, he grabbed the blanket from the bed and wrapped it around her shoulders. He then made her sit on the mattress and handed her a tissue to wipe the blood from her nose.

A second knock sounded through the door.

"Don't open it, Danny, don't, I'm begging you! You don't know who this is!"

"Calm down, Allie, it's not going to be a monster or anything."

"No, don't open it, please, it's not safe—"

Danny put a hand over her mouth to silence her and wiped a tear from her cheek with his thumb. "Calm down," he said again in a softer voice. "You're not going to die, and no monster is lurking behind that door. You're just being paranoid, but that's normal. It will pass ... okay?"

Alice nodded, though she didn't believe him. His voice however, had a calming effect and when he took his hand away, she kept quiet, biting her tongue nervously.

She watched him walk over to the door, but then he seemed to remember that he was naked as well. He quickly grabbed his boxers from the floor, put them on, and opened the door.

Alice had half expected it and when she saw Jonas's face, she wasn't surprised. His eyes seemed to examine her for a moment, but then they quickly flicked to Danny. "We got a problem."

Danny's head turned back to her and he bit his lip, hesitating. "Office?" he asked Jonas.

Jonas nodded and turned to leave, and Danny closed the door again and hurried to grab some clothes from the closet. "Can I leave you alone for a moment?"

Horrified, Alice stared at him. "You can't leave me here! What if I do have a heart attack? Or, or—"

"Nothing will happen." He planted a quick kiss on her head and buttoned his shirt, then tucked it underneath his belt. "Gotta go." He pulled the door open and stepped through, but then he hesitated and looked back at her. "Don't do anything stupid."

As soon as the door was closed, Alice jumped off the bed and began pacing through the room again, pressing the paper tissue against her nose to stop the bleeding.

She hated Danny with all her heart for forcing her to take cocaine, and it had done nothing to make her feel better—the nausea was even worse than before.

It was so bad that she ended up on the bathroom floor once again, gagging and choking into the toilet until all strength was drained from her body. Exhausted, she curled up on the floor, huddled in the blanket, and dozed off.

A high-pitched scream woke her up and Alice opened her eyes to see Anita standing over her, eyes wide open and one hand clutched to her mouth.

"Miss are you all right?" the maid asked, trembling from the shock of finding her on the floor. "I thought you are dead!"

Alice blinked at her and pushed herself up on her elbows, realizing the anxiety had passed and her heartbeat was back to normal. She must surely look horrible though, with dried blood on her face and eyes swollen from crying. "I'm fine, I just fell asleep," she muttered.

"On the floor? Did you slip?"

Alice wondered if slipping might be a good excuse for lying on the floor with a bloody face and decided to leave the question unanswered. "Sorry for startling you."

The maid gave her a hand and pulled her up, and Alice drank some water from the tap and wiped the rest of the blood from her face before stumbling back into the bedroom, feeling like she was having the worst hangover of her life.

"Miss ... can I clean this room?" Anita's eyes wandered over the pieces of clothing on the floor and the messy bed.

"Of course, sorry. I'll leave." Alice made sure she was properly covered by the blanket and stepped out into the corridor, which luckily was deserted.

The sun had risen higher and was now shining its light into her bedroom as well. A quick glance at the clock on her wall revealed that it was 10:00 a.m., still quite early for a Sunday.

Danny stayed gone for a long time and his office door remained closed. Whatever the problem was that Jonas had mentioned, it seemed to be hard to solve.

At least no one had locked her in her room, so Alice went down to the kitchen to fill her aching stomach, hoping she would be able to keep the food down this time.

The fridge was stocked with raw meat—leftovers from yesterday's barbeque. The sight and smell of it made her nauseous again, but she quickly caught herself and took the upper half of a pineapple from the vegetable drawer. She placed it on a plastic chopping board and took a big knife from its holder next to the bread case.

A noise coming from the kitchen door made her whirl around, knife in hand, and she almost stabbed Jonas in the stomach.

"Careful with that." He grinned.

"Maybe you should stop sneaking around like that."

"Maybe you should stop being so easily frightened."

Alice scowled at him and turned back to the pineapple.

"Need help?" Jonas offered.

"Cutting a fruit? I think I'm good, thank you."

"Just asking. Pineapples are hard."

"I'm pretty sure I can handle it."

He didn't seem convinced. "Should you be handling a knife right now?"

Was he referring to the cocaine? Had it been so obvious? Alice bit her lip and stabbed the knife into the pineapple with more force than necessary.

"I'm fine."

"Sure?"

"Pretty sure, yes." She drove the blade down and was surprised by its sharpness. It cut through the fruit as if it were butter. She could feel Jonas's anxious eyes on her back.

"Shouldn't you be in the office with the others?"

"Danny wanted me to check on you."

"Why? To make sure he hasn't killed me after all?" Alice wiped her hand, which was sticky from the juice, on a towel and chose a smaller knife to cut off the peel.

Jonas said nothing.

"Aren't your skills needed? Seems to me you're never working with the others."

"I'm not a big part of the company."

"But you were advocating for it, weren't you?"

"Hm?"

"Well, you seemed to be quite fond of whatever it is they're doing, last time I checked."

"I support it. But I'm not part of it, really."

"Why?"

He hesitated and Alice put the chunks of pineapple in a glass bowl and ate one, then offered it to him as well. He took one and began chewing.

"Well?" she urged.

"I need time to study. Every company needs a lawyer, but I'm not quite done yet."

"Don't you feel left out?"

He grinned cockily. "Nah, I earn as much babysitting you as the others doing real work."

"Well, I'm glad I can help," Alice said sarcastically, and ate the rest of the pineapple, surprised at how good it felt in her stomach.

"Back to eating?"

"I'm always eating, I just usually throw up afterward."

Jonas frowned.

"Not on purpose," she added quickly.

"What did he give you?"

"Coke."

"And did it help?"

"Does it look like it?"

He shook his head.

"Is there chocolate somewhere? I'm craving chocolate ... and pickles ... and jam, do we have strawberry jam?"

Jonas's eyes followed her as she went through the kitchen cupboards, collecting jars with different kinds of jam. She turned to look at him. "Well?"

"Uh ... no idea if there's chocolate, but I saw some Oreos earlier."

"They'll do."

Alice found them in a cupboard corner among other cookies and began dipping the cookies in jam before putting them in her mouth.

"You do know there's a breakfast buffet in the dining room, right?" Jonas asked.

"No ... is there?"

"Yeah, the cooks work on the weekends now as well."

Alice took another bite of cookie with jam and shook her head scornfully. "He's grown so lazy."

"Danny?"

She nodded.

Jonas shrugged and lit a cigarette. "Money does that to people."

"Can you not do that maybe?" she asked him, irritated.

"What?"

"Smoke. In the kitchen. While I'm eating. It stinks."

Looking taken aback, he put the cigarette out in the sink. "Sorry."

Alice strolled over to the dining room, where the long table had been set with pots and plates and jugs of juice and a plate of what appeared to be the first half of the pineapple.

Hungry, she loaded a plate with toast and beans in tomato sauce, fried mushrooms, and fruit, and sat down at the table, where she began digging into her food.

Jonas watched her curiously. "You sure the coke didn't help?"

Alice gave him a warning look. "Don't watch me eat." She wondered where the hunger was coming from. The effect of the cocaine must be over by now and it had only made her even more nauseous. Now though, she felt starved like never before. Did that mean she was finally recovering?

Jonas remained leaning against the wall and his fingers brushed nervously over the pack of cigarettes in his pocket.

"Why don't you just go out to smoke? You don't have to watch me. Actually, it would be nice if you didn't."

"I can leave ..." His eyes swiveled to the archway to his right and the living room behind it, and back to her. He lowered his voice. "Viktor's here. If I don't watch you, he will."

Alice frowned. Were they now watching her inside the house as well? "I prefer you, but it's still annoying."

Jonas smirked apologetically and she saw his hand twitch nervously.

"Go ahead. Smoke. I'm done."

With a look of utter relief on his face, he lit a cigarette and inhaled deeply. Alice chuckled and shook her head. "Junkie."

"Says the cokehead."

"I didn't want to."

"Then why did you?"

"Danny can be very ... *persuasive*." She took her plate off the table and Jonas stepped aside to let her pass to the kitchen, where she put her dishes in the dishwasher.

He sighed. "He should pick at people his own size."

"That might be hard. But he shouldn't pick at anybody," said Alice.

"True." He took another deep drag on his cigarette and filled the kitchen with smoke. "I reckon you don't want one?"

Alice shook her head. Even smoking passively was making her feel nauseous again, but she was determined to keep her food down this time.

"How long are they going to be in the office? It's Sunday."

Jonas shrugged.

"Did something bad happen?"

"Nothing I would tell you."

Angry, she glared at him, and left the kitchen. It was past noon already and the house was hot and smelled strongly of cleaning chemicals. Alice wrinkled her nose and wrinkled it even more when she saw Viktor sitting on the couch, playing some game on his phone. He looked up and gave her a slimy smile.

The smell of smoke announced that Jonas had left the kitchen as well and was now standing behind her. The three of them stared at each other for a moment in awkward silence, until Alice decided to fetch her drawing pad from her room and sit outside in the shade of a big chestnut tree to enjoy the weather, now that she was feeling a bit better.

Danny appeared sometime later. When he spotted her, he gave her a sharp look without smiling and Alice could tell he was in a bad mood.

Later that day, a police car appeared and drove through the gate and onto the lawn. Two officers got out. Curiously, Alice watched them.

Danny and Waldo stepped out of the house to greet them and they all went back inside, except Viktor, who stayed on the porch and watched her every movement. His poisonous stare broke her concentration and she decided to draw him instead and make it obvious that she was doing so.

It seemed to make him uncomfortable and finally, he took his eyes off her.

Alice finished her sketch by giving him horns and hooves, and then she put the pad away, closed her eyes, and listened to the birds in the trees.

It didn't take long until the men came back out of the house. Strangely, they were smiling and shaking hands with the policemen.

Looks like they got more allies.

One of the officers gave her a nod, probably expecting her to be on terms with what was going on. Alice ignored him but watched them get back into the car and drive off.

She noticed that the men's grins disappeared along with the police. Seemed like the problem had not been solved yet.

Danny and Waldo exchanged a few words and then Danny turned and walked toward her, and his way of walking made her nervous.

He squatted down beside her, the sun reflecting off his white shirt. He'd rolled the sleeves up to his elbows and the white of the shirt made his skin look even more tanned.

"Could you solve the problem?" Alice immediately felt ashamed of her shaky voice and tried to steady her breathing. Why was Danny looking at her as if she had done something wrong? His deep blue eyes seemed to pierce right through her. The pupils had gotten smaller again after his hit of coke in the morning.

"Henry called the police on us."

Blood rushed to Alice's cheeks and she cursed herself for it. "Why?"

"You don't know anything about it?"

She shook her head. "Why would I?"

"You talked. A lot." His eyes narrowed and his mistrust was obvious.

"Not that much, no ... not since long ago anyway." Danny's stare seemed to be melting her and she quickly looked down at her drawing.

His eyes followed her gaze and he raised one eyebrow when he saw the sketch of Viktor.

"Looks like you caught his sunny side." His voice was cold when he said it and Alice knew he was not in a good mood, despite the joke.

Biting her lip, she said nothing. His hand went underneath her chin and he lifted her head to make her look at him.

"Let's hear it."

"I really don't know anything, he never mentioned anything to me!"

"Viktor saw you talking the other day."

"We talked about gardening. I told him that." She turned her head away from his hand.

"It sure didn't look like that."

"How would Viktor know what it looks like when people talk about gardening?"

"Don't mock me Alice, I'm not in the mood for it." Danny seemed to be back to his cold and threatening state, and Alice felt torn toward telling him everything, just to avoid his anger. But Henry didn't deserve that and whatever Danny might do to her, she had been through worse. So, she swallowed the words that lay on her tongue and remained silent.

"I told you he was nosy ... I should've fired him long before." Disgust tinged his words.

"I don't know anything, Danny. I don't even know what it is you're doing," she said quietly. "So unless Henry knows more than me, I really can't figure out why he'd call the police."

Danny's eyes examined her, looking for signs that she was lying, but Alice saw doubt in them and felt relieved.

"What did they want anyway?" she asked curiously.

"Nothing a little money can't buy."

"So ... you bribed them?"

He shrugged. "Call it whatever you want. They know Waldo, so they're not too keen on investigating us." Sighing, he turned his head to look at the others, who were still standing on the porch, watching. "I'd prefer to spend my money on other things though, so I don't like having the police sticking their noses where they don't belong." There was a threatening undertone in his voice and when he turned back to her, his eyes seemed to pierce right through her. "Clear?"

Alice nodded. "Crystal clear." Automatically, her hand jerked to the necklace he'd given her, and his expression got warmer.

"Anyway," he stood up and flattened his pants. "I'm starving."

"The buffet is delicious."

Danny gave her a warm smile. "Glad you tried it."

Feeling her heart beat faster, Alice froze, but it had nothing to do with nervousness. Danny's smile seemed to go through her every bone and made her guts clench. How could he still have that effect on her, after everything that had happened? She had begun to believe that her love for him had finally gone away, but with the kindness he had shown her these last couple of months, it had become hard to hate him.

Her eyes followed him as he walked back to the house, and she wanted nothing more than to drive her pencil through her throat and end this stupidity once and for all.

I'm stupid. I'm incredibly stupid and dumb, and I should just end my pathetic existence.

But even her dark thoughts could not chase away the warmth she was feeling inside. Sure, Danny took coke now, but he seemed to be more in control of himself and less angry. Maybe it had just been some kind of winter depression, or like he had said, the start of the business had been rough on him.

But can I really forgive how he treated me?

Alice thought of the three days in the bunker, and hoped intensely that she wouldn't. But she knew right away that she couldn't control her emotions.

Like Jonas said, I'm too emotional.

She looked up and met his gaze. He was standing on the porch next to Viktor, smoking a cigarette and watching her.

Why does it always seem as if he can read my thoughts?

His stare made her feel ashamed of her feelings for Danny. Jonas had seen her in Danny's room several times and he surely also knew that Danny paid her late-night visits almost every day—his libido seemed to have grown during the warmer season ... or maybe it was the coke?

Did Jonas think she had no self-respect at all and slept with Danny despite everything he had done? Or did he know that she didn't want to?

Quickly, Alice dropped her gaze and watched a bug crawl through the grass.

Why in the world do I even care what he thinks? And why would he care anyway?

And now, she had two pairs of attentive eyes on her instead of one, and couldn't even talk to him. Viktor took his new job way too seriously, and Alice got the impression he was watching Jonas as well. Did Danny suspect something? Had he told Viktor to watch and report? Or was it true what he had told her—that he thought one pair of eyes was not enough to keep her inside these walls?

So many questions and no one to answer them.

A cool wind blew through her clothes and she looked up and saw a big dark-gray cloud approach in the distance.

Looks like summer's about to be over.

21

The following weeks were rainy and the house was shaken by occasional storms.

Alice loved it, but Danny's mood had gone darker along with the weather. Not only was the weather turbulent though, but business also seemed to be facing troubles, and the men were on edge. Everyone except Jonas looked agitated.

Police officers showed up on the doorstep from time to time, and Danny even invited them in for tea or whiskey, to stay on good terms with them.

Alice wondered how much money they had already received from him. They didn't seem interested in the business at all, but once they had smelled the money, they always came back for more, pretending to be looking for drugs or have been called by the neighbors for noise complaints. That was ridiculous since the neighbors lived far away—but it only showed that they didn't even bother to make up a reasonable excuse.

Alice was told to stay in her room whenever the police arrived. She suspected that Danny worried about her telling them of her involuntary stay in the house, and maybe about the violence and the bunker. She was not *that* naïve though. She knew the cops would not care a bit, and she didn't feel like risking her finally endurable relationship with Danny. He still treated her more or less nicely when she was sick but became rather cold and distant on the days she felt better.

The nausea never left completely but there were days when it was fainter and tolerable. Alice even managed to gain some weight. Still, she was underweighted and disliked her body, but at least she didn't look completely famished anymore.

Danny had bought her some vitamins to make up for the lack of sun and food, and she took them every day.

The sun returned by the end of July, but it did not manage to enlighten Danny's mood. He and his friends spent every day in the office, probably plotting over how to get rid of the police.

A new wave of nausea tortured Alice to an extent she could not bear the heat anymore. So, she hid in her room with the fan on and spent her days lying in bed and feeling miserable.

At least Danny didn't insist on giving her more cocaine.

The days passed in a blur until one morning, Alice was shaken awake softly. Blinking, she saw the blurred figure of Danny standing next to her bed.

"What's going on?" she asked weakly.

"It's almost noon, I thought I'd check on you."

"Oh ... already?"

He sat down on the mattress beside her and stroked her hair. "How are you feeling today?"

"I don't know yet ... I'll know when I get up."

Danny frowned and his eyes scanned her face. He looked worried. "There's going to be a party today and I'd like you to attend."

Slowly, Alice sat up and rubbed her throbbing forehead. "Why? You usually don't want me there."

"Yes, but since it's my thirtieth birthday, people will expect you to be there."

Frozen, Alice stared at him. "Oh."

"Did you forget?"

"No ... I'm so sorry Danny, is it already the fourth?"

He nodded.

"I'm sorry, I lost track of time, but I didn't forget when your birthday is, of course!"

Smiling, he leaned forward and kissed her forehead. "Don't worry about it. You've been ill ... I didn't expect you to remember."

"I don't even have anything for you."

Not that I could have gone anywhere to buy something anyway.

"I don't think you're in the right place to give me presents." With the tips of his fingers, he traced her cheekbones and Alice rested her head on his chest. He brushed some hair behind her ear and sighed. "Just put on something nice and show yourself from time to time, okay? But if you really feel too ill, just let me know and I'll tell the guests you caught the flu."

"I don't know them anyway, why would they ask?"

"Julio and Theresa will be here ... and people will surely want to know where my girlfriend is."

"Right ... sorry. I'm sorry for making things complicated ... I was feeling better for a while but now it's worse again."

"I know, it's all right. I'm just really worried, you know."

"Don't be."

"How could I not be worried, Allie? You've been feeling sick for months now. Jonas said it might be a mental thing, but you seem normal otherwise." Danny lifted her chin and examined her face again. "I mean, if it really is a mental issue, maybe I should get you some anti-anxiety medication or something."

"That's not necessary, really. I'm fine."

"You don't look fine."

"I think I have an inflamed stomach ... caused by stress. It's probably become chronic, but really nothing to worry about."

"Are you still taking your nausea pills?"

"I've taken them all ... I think I need something against heartburn."

"I'll get you something," Danny promised.

Alice gave him a smile. He was acting more like the Danny she had fallen in love with more than three years ago.

"I don't want to trouble you on your birthday."

"It's troubling for me when you're unwell. All I want is for you to get better. Besides, I'll just tell Viktor or Jean-Pierre to go to a pharmacy."

"Okay ... about Viktor ..."

"Yes?"

"Well ... did you tell him to watch me?"

"I told him to keep an eye on you, yes. I'm concerned, that's all. For all I know, you could faint and fall down the stairs or ... hurt yourself in some other way."

Is that really the reason?

"It's just that ... he's very indiscreet about it. He seems to enjoy it a bit too much." Chewing her lip, Alice anxiously waited for his response.

"Allie, you know I'm not ready to trust you yet."

"I'm not saying nobody should watch me ... just not Viktor, please. Anyone but Viktor."

"All right. I'll put Jean-Pierre on the task." It sounded weird when he said it like that, and Alice felt herself blush with shame.

"You know I'm not strong enough to go far, right?"

Danny smiled a smile that showed how little her words meant to him, and shook his head. "I'd rather be safe than sorry, Allie. I know you got along well with Jonas, but he seems to be a bit uncomfortable about having to watch you, especially after what happened last spring. I guess he needs time to study and doesn't have the capacity for much else." Pensive, he fell quiet for a moment. "You know, he seems a bit weird, lately. I'm not sure if he blames himself for what happened or if he's still angry at me for aiming the gun at him."

That's not all you did. You had your bodyguards beat him up first and then you threatened to kill him.

As if he had read her mind Danny said, "He's got every right to be mad at me, of course. But I apologized to him what seems like a thousand times. I just wish he'd talk to me at least. He's become very distant."

Alice was amazed at how Danny addressed her in this matter. He had never discussed his friendship with any of the guys with her before.

"I miss him, you know. He was like a brother to me."

Too bad you tried to kill him.

"Do you know anything about it? Did he mention something?"

Quickly, Alice shook her head. "Just because I've stopped hating him doesn't mean we're friends or anything."

"Really? Viktor said you seem to get along quite well."

Feeling caught, Alice's heart began to race at once. "I ... we do get along, but he doesn't ... confide in me or anything. He's still rather distant toward me and ... we never discuss personal stuff."

"Hm." Thinking, Danny scratched his perfectly shaven chin. "I guess I should just try to talk to him again." He smiled warmly and gave her a kiss, then got up from the bed and walked toward the door.

"Danny," she called after him, "Happy birthday!"

The yard became more crowded within the hours, and Alice knew that soon she was supposed to go downstairs and greet the guests. Even though she was the host's girlfriend and therefore considered the hostess, she felt anxious and like a stranger in her own house. The people downstairs were all rich and powerful or they were beautiful women in tight dresses, hoping to hook up with somebody who was rich and powerful. Where was she supposed to fit in?

For a while, Alice observed the guests through her window, eyeing their clothes and trying to decide what she was supposed to put on. To her, their clothes were either too posh or too scarce—and definitely not what she wanted to wear.

Danny was nowhere to be seen in the front yard, so she suspected he must be behind the house by the pool. Sighing, she got off the windowsill and walked to her closet.

The heat and her belly ache called for some light fabric, but Alice worried if she wore something with short sleeves, people might notice her scarred wrist. In the back of her closet though, she discovered a white long-sleeved dress. It was made of thin linen, and quite floaty with a bohemian touch. Not even too appalling for her taste. For a while she stared at it, wondering whether it would be nice enough for Danny. In the end, she concluded that if it weren't, he would not have bought it for her in the first place.

Her reflection in the bathroom mirror revealed a thin pale face with hollow cheeks and sunken eyes. Alice wondered if there was anything she could do about that. Luckily there was nothing, a little makeup couldn't fix and soon enough, she looked a bit less pale and a bit less sick. Trying to stall for time, she bound her long hair back into a French braid. Brushing her overgrown bangs away from her forehead revealed the scar from her fall into the pool.

Maybe I should keep the bangs nonetheless.

The sight of the scar made old memories flash through her mind. Danny's constant drinking, the anger issues, the first weeks of her captivity, the first time he'd hit her ... the first times he had forced himself on her ...

It came unexpected and violently, and Alice had barely time to fall onto her knees and bend over the toilet before her stomach seemed to explode.

She hadn't eaten yet and only water and acid came out. But her stomach would not stop cramping and turning over, and in the end, she was spitting out blood.

Gasping for air, she remained lying on the cold bathroom floor for a moment, with a burning pain in her stomach and throat, and a painful throbbing in her skull.

Whatever had caused her nausea in the first place, there was no doubt now that at least some of it was psychosomatic.

If this is not being too sick for the party, I don't know what is.

Alice waited for her breathing to calm down and then pulled herself up on the sink and flushed the toilet. Her hands were shaking, and chills went through her whole body. Tears of pain had messed up her mascara and she cursed her reflection angrily.

I can't go downstairs like this.

Annoyed by her own weakness, she threw her eyeliner against the wall and punched the mirror, but this time it remained whole. Her stomach wouldn't stop cramping, so she decided to lie down for a while. Sleep rolled over her immediately.

Alice awoke to a sharp pain in her belly and her head felt twice its size. Moaning, she rubbed her forehead.

It took her a moment to realize that she had fallen asleep on Danny's birthday.

Horrified, she jumped out of her bed at once, but had to sit back down and wait for the dizziness to wear off.

The clock on the wall showed that it was already after 6:00 p.m. Alice hurried to the bathroom to drink some water before refreshing her makeup and fixing her braid. Her dress was crinkled, but she kept it on anyway.

Laughter and muffled voices were coming in through the window and made her feel nervous. She hated big events that involved many people, and most of all on a day like this, just after puking out her guts. Taking a deep breath, she told herself that everything was going to be fine and managed to leave her room.

The corridor was empty, and it occurred to her that she could get a better view of the party from Danny's bedroom window before going downstairs.

The room wasn't locked for once, so she stepped inside and walked straight to the window. The backyard looked crowded. Staff had put up wooden tables and covered them with tablecloths. They offered a buffet with what seemed to be a wide variety of different fancy-looking meals and snacks. People were also barbecuing and the smell of burned meat found its way through the glass and into her nose, making her nauseous again. Or was she only imagining it?

Her eyes wandered over the guests, but apart from the usual men and Julio, there was no one she knew. Theresa must have already left—probably because of the pregnancy. There was no sign of Marion as well.

But where was Danny? Squinting, Alice took a closer look and spotted his wet dark hair between other heads in the pool. He was leaning backward casually, with his elbows on the marble edge of the swimming pool, his bare and muscly chest glistening wetly in the evening sun. He appeared to be enjoying himself. No wonder, with the two beautiful women at his sides. Frowning, Alice examined them. One of them was blonde and her curvy tanned body was stuffed into a tight red bikini. Even from up above, it was clearly visible that she was heavily flirting with Danny. The other woman appeared to be the blonde's friend. Her brown hair was pulled back into a ponytail and she was holding a glass of champagne in one hand, while listening to Danny and her friend talking.

Alice bit her lower lip and remained standing in the window, watching them.

The blonde put a hand on Danny's chest and bent forward in what seemed to be an attempt to kiss him, but instead, she said something into his ear, and he started laughing.

Well, he's enjoying himself... no need for me to go downstairs then.

Despite the bitter taste of jealousy on her tongue, Alice felt relieved for not having to attend the party.

Before she could step away from the window though, Danny cocked his head back in laughter and his eyes fell right on her. At once, his smile died.

Shocked, Alice stepped back from the window. Her heart was hammering against her ribs and she couldn't grasp a clear thought. Not knowing what else to do, she hurried back to her room and closed the door, cursing herself for watching him so carelessly.

What would he be thinking? Did he feel caught? Or was he angry at her for not showing up, yet watching him through the window?

Sitting on her bed, biting her nails nervously, Alice tried to ignore the queasy feeling in her stomach.

For about ten minutes, nothing happened, and almost convinced Danny didn't care about her, she calmed down. Suddenly though, there was a knock on the door.

Without waiting for a reply, Viktor stepped into her room.

"Daniel wants you downstairs," he proclaimed in a cold, dragging voice.

"I'm not feeling well."

"Don't care. He wants you to come downstairs and he won't be pleased if you don't."

Both anxious and angry, Alice stared at the bald, pink head of his. He really was a sadist; she could tell by the way he enjoyed the power that had been laid upon him.

"I really don't want to come downstairs."

"I got the order to bring you to him."

"Yeah? Well, you'll have to drag me down there then, 'cause I'm not coming."

Viktor's eyes narrowed, but his lips parted into an evil grin. "Whatever the lady wants. Just know that he won't be pleased. At all. He might even fall back into old habits and well ... lock you in the basement or something."

Alice's heart stopped for a second. She remembered the bunker only too well. Danny surely wouldn't put her down there over something so minor ... would he? Nervously, she chewed her lip and a triumphant expression appeared on Viktor's face.

"You don't want that, do you?" he asked, and Alice wanted nothing more than to smash his ugly, yellow teeth in.

"He wouldn't do that," she objected, but the doubt in her voice was clearly audible.

Viktor just shrugged and turned to walk out the door.

"Wait ..."

He stopped and turned, a wide grin on his face.

"I'm coming."

Danny's bodyguard was at least smart enough not to walk her through the crowd like an obvious escort. He stopped at the back door and remained standing there, arms crossed and eyes fixed on her.

Alice forced herself to smile at the guests and greeted some back that greeted her. Was it so obvious that she was Danny's girlfriend?

Maybe it's because I'm the only person here wearing normal clothes.

She eyed some of the guests scornfully and realized that many of them were eyeing her in the exact same way. Julio was standing near the grill, his face flushed by the heat of the fire and the alcohol he'd been drinking. Alice gave him a nod but he ignored her.

Taking a deep breath, she strolled over to the pool, carefully keeping her expression smooth and friendly.

Lots of glasses, either full or empty, were spread on the ground around the pool, and she had to mind her every step in order to avoid crushing them underneath her shoes.

Danny looked up and smiled when he saw her, but something in his eyes made her shiver.

The blonde leaned away from him at once when her eyes found Alice. "So, *that's* the woman of the house." Her voice sounded bored, somehow.

Alice gave her a smile and quickly looked at Danny again. Standing at the edge of the pool, she wondered what she was supposed to do.

"I'm Palina." The blonde made a greeting hand gesture and bared two rows of perfectly bleached teeth.

"Alice. Nice to meet you." Alice put as much sincerity in her voice as possible, but it still sounded like a lie.

"Oh, I figured," Palina said, still smiling. "Danny's mentioned you, you know. Great husband you got there."

"Boyfriend," Alice corrected.

The blonde looked at Danny and grinned. "So there's still a chance, huh?" To Alice, she said, "I'm just joking, of course. The good ones are always taken." She let out a theatrical sigh.

Danny remained quiet and took a sip from his glass with what seemed to be some sort of whiskey on ice. He looked pleased though.

"I can scoot over," Palina offered.

"Thank you ... but I don't feel like bathing." Alice looked at Danny, wondering why he had ordered her outside when he wasn't even going to talk to her.

"I'm Keira, by the way," the brunette with the ponytail said. She sounded much nicer than her friend.

Alice gave her a smile as well.

"I'm sorry for only coming outside now," she told Danny, hoping for him to say something.

"It's fine Allie, really," he spoke in a way too sweet voice. "I already told the guests that you're recovering from the flu. Are you feeling better now?"

"Yeah ... yes, I am," Alice lied, feeling her stomach rumble.

"Have a drink. There's cocktails and some champagne ... wine ..." He nodded toward the tables and the waiters with trays, loaded with glasses and bottles of all sorts and shapes.

"I'm fine, thank you. I might get myself something to eat though."

Smiling, he nodded. "Come back when you're done."

Alice filled a plate with different kinds of salad and some bread. Some of the guests—especially the male—tried to start a conversation with her. Others were visibly drunk and made lewd remarks about her, even with Danny only a short distance away.

Alice shook them off as politely as possible and scanned the yard, desperately looking for a place to eat in peace. She felt like a pig that had been thrown into a lion cage. Everyone seemed to be looking at her, men predatory and women disdainfully. Or was she only being paranoid?

Luckily, she spotted Jonas standing in the shade of an oak, leaning against the stonewall and smoking a cigarette.

Alice hurried toward him, plate in one hand, and he gave her a grin.

"Can I stand here?" she asked breathlessly.

"You can stand wherever you like."

Relieved, she leaned against the wall as well, and started eating despite the protests of her stomach. When she was done, a waiter appeared to take her plate away.

"Wow, they're attentive."

Jonas nodded.

"You're not socializing?" she asked him.

He shook his head.

"Sorry if I'm disturbing your peace. I just really needed to get away from these people."

"What people?"

"All of them ... They're weird ... and drunk."

"Some of them are more than drunk." He nodded toward a couple that was dancing lasciviously and almost eating each other's faces off.

"Wow," Alice said. "And it's only 7:00 p.m."

Jonas nodded again and lit a cigarette, then offered one to her.

"No thanks."

"Stopped smoking?"

"Never truly started."

He shrugged. "I must've misread the signs then."

"I should go back to Dan—" Alice's eyes fell on two men who appeared to be in their late thirties. They were standing near the house, each with a beer in their hand.

"Who are they? They look ... familiar."

Jonas followed her gaze with his eyes and grimaced. "They're coppers. Been here before."

"Right ... that day when Henry called the police."

He nodded.

"What are they doing here?"

"Eating. Drinking."

Alice scowled at him. "No, I mean really. What are they doing here?"

"Like I said ..." he exhaled a big cloud of smoke. "They're eating Danny's food, drinking Danny's alcohol, taking Danny's drugs. In other words, they're taking advantage of their power over him, knowing they're untouchable."

"Are they?"

"They're not gonna start an investigation on us. Not with Waldo's still existing influence at the station." He paused and exhaled more smoke. "But they got other ways of making one's life hard. Pretending to have to search the house for drugs, for example. Giving out fines for shit like playing music too loudly or somethin'. You name it." He gave them a disgusted look and took another drag on his cigarette.

"I still have no idea what it is you're doing," Alice admitted.

"Then I'm not going to say more."

"People are taking drugs here too though, aren't they? Won't that be a problem?"

"Nah, the coppers don't care as long as they get their fair share."

Alice grimaced when she saw Viktor walking toward her.

"Shouldn't you be with your boyfriend?" he sneered and gave Jonas a scornful look.

"Yeah, right. Sure. Whatever." Sighing, Alice gave Jonas a meaningful glance, which he returned.

Again, Viktor did not walk her to the pool, for which she was glad. But he watched her go there from a distance.

Alice found Danny sitting at the pool's edge, legs dangling into the water. He was drinking some kind of blue cocktail, which she found odd, until she saw him give it back to Palina. He turned around and smiled, and Palina looked up, obviously unpleased by Alice's return.

"You took a long time," Danny commented.

"I know, I'm sorry ... People were talking to me."

Danny raised one eyebrow and eyed her suspiciously. "Sit down," he said. "Take off your shoes and enjoy the water."

"Thanks, but ... I don't think that's a good idea ... since I'm recovering from the flu, you know."

He frowned when she said that, and she wondered if he felt mocked.

I should watch my tongue.

Danny heaved himself up from the ground and walked toward her. His naked chest was still wet and felt cold when he wrapped her in a tight hug.

"Danny! You're wetting my dress!" Alice laughed, hoping it sounded real to him and to the guests.

He pulled back and smirked. "I'm what? Sorry, I didn't hear you."

"I said you're wetting—"

Suddenly, she was up in the air and Danny had her locked in his arms; and before she knew what was happening, he jumped into the pool, taking her with him.

The water wasn't *that* cold, but the sudden temperature drop still shocked her and she almost choked. Kicking, she struggled to surface.

Danny was laughing and so were the guests who stood near the pool.

Alice could have slapped him, but she remembered to keep an amused expression and laughed with them. She punched his chest softly. "You idiot! Now my dress is transparent."

His eyes wandered down her body and his laughter grew louder. "You're wearing a bra, so no harm done." He lifted her up with both hands around her waist and kissed her.

Alice couldn't help it, but his suddenly good mood was contagious. For a moment, she forgot the laughing people surrounding her and focused solely on him and the grin on his face.

It was his birthday and all he wanted was to enjoy it with his girlfriend. Why should she deny him that? Her stomach was feeling a bit better, and she desperately wanted things between them to remain peaceful.

They ended up moving over to the other side of the pool, where they sat in the shallower parts where the steps were. Danny had his arm around her shoulder and a whiskey in his hand.

Palina gave her a disdainful look and Alice chuckled. "She has a thing for you."

"You jealous? Is that why you were watching us from the window?" He cocked his head to the side and grinned.

Alice blushed. "Nah, I was just worried about your taste ... She's such a cliché."

"Next time you want to watch someone, maybe don't wear white."

"Sorry ... I just wanted to see where you were, so I didn't have to look for you in the crowd."

Danny began rubbing the skin below her left eye with his thumb. "It's okay. Although you kind of spooked me, with your white dress and long dark hair."

"What are you doing?"

"You look like a panda bear."

"And whose fault is that?"

Laughing again, he continued wiping her mascara away. "I thought you'd join us this afternoon. Talk to Theresa and Marion." He sipped his drink thoughtfully.

"I wanted to ... I was already dressed and ready, but then I got really sick."

Danny put the drink down and brushed a strand of wet hair from her forehead. "You're going to puke out your own guts one day."

"I almost did."

Sighing, he pulled her closer. "It's a shame you can't even enjoy the summer. Being sick all the time ... are you sure you don't need to see a doctor?"

"It's not necessary."

"What if there's a tumor growing in your belly?"

"Not happening."

Something else was growing in her belly and it was worse than a tumor. But he didn't need to know that.

The sun disappeared behind the hills and shadows crept through the backyard, covering it like a blanket until everything was in the shade. It was perceptibly colder, and Alice shivered in her wet clothes. Danny didn't seem to feel anything, but she had lost track of how many glasses of whiskey he'd drunk. He seemed to have lost interest in her anyway, being wrapped up in business talk by some guy in a suit. They mainly talked about buying shares and it bored her.

"I'm going inside to change," she announced to him.

Confused by the sudden interruption, he turned to look at her. He said nothing though and Alice took that as an okay.

It was even colder outside of the water and a light breeze blew through her dress and made goose bumps arise on her arms. Her shoes had soaked up water like sponges and made a weird sound with every step she took. For a moment, Alice worried about dripping on the carpet in the house, but then she realized that she couldn't be the first wet person to go inside. Danny had gone inside to pee from time to time and he surely hadn't bothered drying off first.

Some of the guests looked at her as she passed by and laughed at her appearance, but Alice ignored them.

The house was almost empty with most of the guests enjoying the mild temperatures outside. Alice only encountered Jonas in the corridor upstairs, as he was coming out of the bathroom. He started laughing the instant he saw her, and she scowled at him.

"The hell happened to you?" he asked, breathless from laughing.

Alice stuck her tongue out at him. "Bikinis are overrated."

"Or you overdressed."

"I wasn't planning on taking a swim."

"I can see that." He grinned widely.

"What are you doing up here anyway?"

"Going to bed."

"Already?"

He nodded.

Alice sighed. "Lucky you."

"You got a bed as well."

"Yeah, but I don't think I should just sneak away ... He might get mad about it."

"He's got other people."

"What about you? You're his best friend but I barely even see you talking to him."

Jonas hesitated and seemed to think, though his expression was unreadable. "He asked about you ..."

"Hm?"

"He's worried about losing you as a friend ... or brother, or whatever."

Jonas said nothing.

"He must be very desperate, coming to me with something like that. As if I knew you better than he does."

"What did you say?"

"That letting his gorillas beat you up and aiming a gun at you was probably not beneficial for your friendship."

He grimaced.

"Actually I didn't say that aloud. I don't have a death wish."

Jonas raised his eyebrows.

"Don't look at me like that! I'm not suicidal anymore, I swear."

"Glad to hear." He smirked.

Alice tried to read his expression, but all she could see was discomfort in his eyes. She wondered if it was her presence that made him nervous or the things she'd said about Danny.

"You said you're hoping for him to change, you know ... that you haven't given up on him."

Jonas dropped his gaze and stared at his shoes. He looked like a schoolboy who's being scolded by a teacher.

"Looks like you have," Alice added, watching him shift uncomfortably.

"It's complicated," he muttered.

"No, it's not." For a moment, Alice held her breath, listening for any noises coming from downstairs. No one seemed to be around. Nevertheless, she lowered her voice. "It's about ... what we did, isn't it? You're scared to face him."

Jonas's eyes flicked back to her face and something in them made her feel a wave of affection for him. She felt herself blush.

"I'm sorry I put you in that position," she muttered, averting her eyes like he had.

"Don't apologize."

"It's true though, I'm sorry for what I did. I shouldn't have done it. Maybe it's easier for me because I have nothing to lose ... There's really nothing he can do to me that hasn't already been done ... Except killing me maybe, but I wouldn't mind if he did."

"Don't say that!"

Alice flinched at the sudden sharpness in his voice, and looked up to see anger on his face. Without saying anything, they stared at each other for a moment.

Does he really care? Or does he think I'm ungrateful?

She realized that she hadn't truly thanked him for saving her life ... twice.

"He would never do that," Jonas insisted.

"I'm not sure what he's capable of, really. It would be nice to have someone watch over him. Someone who's responsible and makes reasonable decisions."

He sighed and hesitated before saying, "And that would be me?"

Alice nodded. "You're his best friend, aren't you? And honestly, I think he's just really fucking lonely."

Closing his eyes, Jonas leaned his back against the wall, looking exhausted.

"Not sure I can pretend to enjoy his company," he muttered quietly.

"Then why are you here? Why don't you just leave if you don't like it here? *You* are not locked up. You can go wherever you want."

"I wouldn't do that."

"Why? Are you still in it for the money? I really thought Danny was important to you, I was hoping you'd help him."

"It's not that simple."

"You're not even trying."

"I *am* keeping an eye on him."

"And when will you step in, huh? What line does he have to cross for you to do something?"

Jonas gave her a tortured look and she almost felt sorry for him.

"You're scared of him, aren't you? You're terrified he might find out about us."

He didn't answer.

"He won't, Jonas. There's no way he could read your thoughts when no one can even read your face. You're too good at hiding things, so what are you afraid of?"

Again, Jonas remained quiet, and Alice knew there was no point in arguing with him.

"You know what? Just do what you want to do. I don't want to interfere in your ... friendship, or whatever the hell you wanna call it." Feeling both angry and resigned, Alice turned and started walking down the corridor toward her room.

"Wait," he called after her and she stopped. "I'm sorry."

Yeah? Well so am I.

Alice took a hot shower and got dressed again. This time, she put on pants and her dark blue blouse and left her hair down for it to dry faster. Once more, she applied some makeup and wondered why she even went through all that trouble. Danny had seemed happy without her company, but she'd told him she was only going to change clothes and she supposed he might be mad if she didn't return. At least she should tell him that she was going to bed. He didn't like being lied to.

It was dark now, but the staff had put up lights in the backyard and the buffet was still standing. The party looked even more uncivilized than before, and the waiters were busy balancing overloaded trays through the drunken crowd.

Alice found Danny still soaking in the pool, talking to Timothy and some guys she didn't know. All of them were drinking, and she couldn't help but wonder how much of the water had been replaced by urine by now.

Danny was visibly wasted and didn't see her until Timothy tapped his shoulder and made a gesture toward her.

"Oh, good, you're back! The other ladies have gotten too cold and left. We could use some estrogen in the pool."

"I just put on dry clothes; I'm not coming back into the water. Haven't you grown tired of bathing yet?"

Grinning, he shook his head. "With the climate in this country you gotta enjoy every bit of summer you can get, and a mild night like this is a treasure."

Alice crouched down near the pool beside him and gave him a smile. "I'm glad you're having fun."

"You were gone for a long time."

"Yeah, I showered and had to fix my messed-up makeup."

"I liked the panda look."

"Yeah. People found it hilarious," she replied dryly.

Laughing, Danny took a big gulp of his whiskey. "Where's Jonas? I haven't seen him around."

"I ran into him upstairs. He's gone to bed."

"Already?" He looked disappointed. "He's become boring, hasn't he?"

Alice shrugged. "I wouldn't know. He never quite struck me as a partygoer."

Danny frowned at the glass in his hand. "He's not. But he could at least stick around on my birthday."

Wow ... he's really hurt.

Alice looked at Timothy for help, and he grinned and patted Danny's shoulder. "Ey buddy, you got me and booze, so what else d'you need?"

Grimacing, Danny took another sip of his whiskey. "They're all boring. They're like rats, invading other people's houses, looking for free food and alcohol." His expression grim, he let his eyes wander over the guests. Disgust was clearly visible on his face.

"Aren't they friends of yours? Or business partners?" Alice asked, surprised by Danny's sudden mood swing.

"Not all of them ... and especially not those two."

Following his gaze, her eyes found the two cops, who were now flirting heavily with Palina and Keira.

"Dirty little fuckers ... What d'you do when your house is infested with rats? You get rid of them."

Timothy seemed to like the idea and grinned broadly. "You could poison them or shoot them ... or build a trap."

"I'd like to put a bullet in their heads. One through each eye." Danny's tone was threatening, and something cold seemed to run down Alice's spine at his words.

"That would be two bullets per head then," Timothy corrected him.

Nervously, Alice laughed. "Yeah ... funny, very funny. Anyway, let's change the subject, shall we?"

"They're infesting, Alice, that's worth talking about. Don't you think?" Danny gave her a sharp look.

"Well, yeah ... I guess. But maybe not now? There's people around and you're drunk. Let's just enjoy the party."

Danny didn't appear to like her suggestion. A dark shadow covered his face and his eyes glinted dangerously. "How am I supposed to enjoy my party when I'm not allowed to choose my guests? And those rats are harassing the girls."

"They don't look very harassed," Alice noted and caressed some wet hair away from Danny's forehead, trying to soothe him. He grumbled.

"He's jealous," Timothy joked, giving her a meaningful glance.

Alice ignored the remark.

"I just enjoyed talking to them," Danny defended himself. "Apparently, they enjoy other company more."

"Or like you said, they got cold and wanted to leave the water. Maybe you should do the same. Most of the guests are still at the buffet or dancing and I'm sure some of them would like to talk to their host."

He scowled at her. "You should keep me company ... as my girlfriend."

"I am."

"But you're not even drinking anything."

"You know why, Danny. I still feel sick and alcohol won't help."

"Maybe this will." Before Alice could react, Danny had grabbed her and yanked her into the pool.

Shrieking, Alice swallowed water. Coughing and gasping for air, she surfaced and glared at him.

"The fuck was that?!"

Timothy was laughing tears and Danny chuckled as well. "That was funny," he said.

"No, it wasn't! It was the first time, maybe, but now it was just immature and stupid! I just changed for god's sake!"

Danny's smile vanished. "You're bitchy today."

"I'm going to bed." Alice tried to storm away from him, but with the water surrounding her, all she managed was a slow-motion walk to the ladder.

Again, people laughed at her as she emerged from the pool, dripping and shivering.

Fuck you all, she thought angrily. *Danny's such a child.*

Careful not to slip on the grass with her wet shoes, Alice hurried toward the house.

"Wait," she heard Danny's voice behind her back. He appeared to be following her. Ignoring him, she continued walking. Before she reached the door though, he caught her arm and stopped her.

"You're tense," he noted. "You should loosen up a bit."

"I'm going to bed."

"It's still early, let's have some fun."

"I don't think we got the same perception of fun," Alice said coldly.

"Maybe that's because we're not on the same level." He opened his fist to her, showing her his palm and Alice saw the little glass tube she knew all too well.

"No, Danny, no way. You know what happened last time."

"You were right, it was too much. But I'm smarter now. I know you should take only about half of what I take." He began to unwind the tiny lid.

"I'm not taking any of it." Alice turned, but he caught her arm again.

"Come on, don't be so boring."

"I said no!" Lowering her voice, she said, "There's cops here and other people, what's *wrong* with you? Put it away!"

He sneered. "Oh, they think they own me and I can't do anything about it. But they're wrong. See, if I go down, they go down as well for what they've done. And they know it." He held the little tube up, now visible for everyone who was standing nearby. "They want drugs and money, and they got it. They'll keep quiet."

Slightly turning her head, Alice saw the cops staring at them and her heartbeat accelerated. "Don't make a scene, Danny, please."

"I'm not. I'm just enjoying some coke with my girlfriend." He lowered his voice as well. "Now take it."

"No."

"I said take it," he hissed, holding the tube under her nose.

Cocking her head back, Alice pushed his hand away, but Danny had not held on to it tightly and the little glass tube dropped to the ground, spreading its content onto the moist grass, where it dissolved immediately.

Shocked, she stared at him and felt her throat tighten.

For what felt like an eternity, Danny said nothing, but she clearly felt his anger. His grip around her arm had gotten tighter.

"Sorry," she whispered. Feeling him loosen his grip, she looked up ... and found him smiling.

"That was clumsy," he commented in a careless voice, loud enough for the people nearby to hear. Laughing, he bent down to pick the tube up. "Well, luckily I got more." He got back up and looked at her. Despite his smile, his cold stare seemed to stab her.

"I ... I'm going to bed," Alice muttered again and turned to walk away.

Danny reached her in two big steps and hugged her from behind, locking her in an embrace. He bent his head down to hers, as if to kiss her neck, but whispered, "You've humiliated me twice in one evening—in front of everybody." With his left hand, he stroked her cheek softly, carefully putting on a show for the bystanders.

"I'm sorry," she whispered again.

"Why don't we go inside and work it out?" he proposed.

Alice shuddered at the thought. His embrace was cold and hard, and she knew he was bottling his anger for later. "Or ... we could stay out here," she suggested quietly.

"Don't you want to change clothes?" His hand wandered down her wet blouse to her belly, and she shivered. Both from the cold *and* his touch. Her heart was beating furiously against her ribs and she tried to fight back tears.

It had been months, since she had last seen Danny like that—cold, menacing, angry. She didn't want him to fall into old habits.

"I don't want to be alone in a room with you right now, Danny," she admitted in a low voice.

"You will be, sooner or later." He loosened his hold of her, and she was able to wind free.

Frozen, she stood, staring at the back door and trying to think of something to do. Fear made it impossible for her to grasp a clear thought.

Still, Danny was standing behind her. His breath brought goose bumps to her skin. Slowly, he let his fingers glide over her shoulder and down her arm, clearly aware of how intimidated he was making her feel.

He's back to his sadist self.

Playing with her fear seemed to entertain him and he remained standing there for a while, waiting for her to react in some way.

When she didn't, however, he sighed. To her relief, he turned and walked back to the pool.

It felt as if her feet had grown roots. Her mind spinning, she was well aware of the policemen still watching her.

Should she go inside and risk an unpleasant encounter with Danny later? Chewing her lip, she looked back over her shoulder and saw him glide into the water, talking to Timothy. He would surely go back to drinking and if she was lucky, he would forget about her. Plus, she could not stay out here forever. The night air made her shiver in her wet clothes and she decided to fight her fear of him and go to bed.

A small group of sophisticated-looking men was sitting in the living room, drinking wine and talking, when Alice entered the house. Apart from them, it seemed to be empty.

Alice hurried up the stairs, all the way dripping onto the floor. When she reached her room, she suddenly heard footsteps behind her.

Shit ... Danny followed me after all.

She froze, one hand on the door handle, and slowly turned around. Surprisingly though, her eyes found one of the cops standing in the corridor.

His face was reddened from alcohol and he was panting from following her up the stairs.

"Can I help you?" she asked him, suspicious.

"I thought we might chat." His voice was high and a bit squeaky, and he wiped sweat from his large forehead with the sleeve of his shirt.

"Party's downstairs. I'm going to sleep." She gave him a warning look, but he proceeded to walk through the corridor until he was standing right beside her. Grinning, he showed two rows of yellowish teeth.

"What do you want?"

"I have some questions about your husband." Crossing his arms in front of his chest, he leaned against the wall.

"He's not my husband," Alice corrected him. "And I got no time for this." She pushed the handle down to open the door, but the cop put a hand on her arm.

"I'm sure you got five minutes."

"I'm not obliged to talk to you. As far as I'm concerned, you're not on duty."

He laughed dryly and pulled his hand back. "You're right, I'm not. Which gives me the chance to do whatever the hell I want. I advise you to answer my questions."

"And what would they be?" Alice asked coldly.

"Do you know why we're here?"

"To get drunk and fed for free?"

Chuckling, he shook his head. "Well, I won't deny we're enjoying ourselves, but that's not the main reason." His smile vanished and he looked serious all of a sudden. "We got a call from someone who used to work here." His eyes bored right into hers and he started to play with his mustache.

"So?"

"You know why they called us?"

Alice shook her head.

"They wanted to report domestic abuse. They were worried about *your* well-being."

Heat rushed to her cheeks and she swallowed dryly. "I know who called."

"Good. So I suppose you know what he told us?"

"No, I don't."

"Well ... let's just say it didn't sound like you and Daniel are in a happy relationship."

Alice glared at him. "How is this any of your business?"

"The thing is, when we did some research, we found out there might be a lot more to the story than some relationship-drama."

The cop took a step closer, and Alice instinctively backed away. "What d'you want?" she asked again.

"We know something big is going on here and we also know that you have connections at the station. Somehow, paperwork has disappeared, and no one seems to be interested in clearing that up."

"Well, that sucks for you then."

His eyes narrowed and he stopped playing with his mustache and placed his hand on his gun holder instead. "I haven't been long enough at the station to know Waldo personally, but everyone seems to think he's some kind of a god. Apart from the ones who're responsible for his sack, of course."

"He was sacked?"

"You don't know the story?"

She shook her head.

"He killed an unarmed pedophile."

"A child molester?"

"He hadn't actually committed a crime yet."

Alice frowned. "And that only got him sacked?"

"Perks of being a cop." He grinned.

"And the other cops applauded him?"

"Officers," he corrected her. "And yes. They said it's good to have one less of those fuckers on the planet."

Alice grimaced. "Wouldn't expect more."

"Anyway," he snarled impatiently, "I know there's something going on here and I'm sure you can tell me more about it." He took another step forward, and Alice backed away to escape his breath until her back was against the wall.

"Are you threatening me?" she asked coldly, noticing his hand was still on his gun.

"No, of course not. I'm merely asking." Smiling, he took his hand away from the gun.

"I don't have anything to tell you."

"I'm sure you do."

"No, I don't." Annoyed, she glared at him, keeping her stare steady, but he wasn't impressed.

"I want to know what he does and where he gets his money from," the cop continued.

"That makes two of us then."

He sneered. "Oh, don't act like you don't know anything! You're his girlfriend."

"Not voluntarily."

"That's the point. I'm sure you want to get rid of him, don't you?" He gave her a smile that almost looked friendly.

He's playing good cop ... what a pathetic little liar.

"It's none of your business what I want." Alice tried to walk past him, but he pushed her back against the wall firmly.

"We're not finished." The smile was gone.

"I'm not telling you shit."

"I'm trying to help you."

Alice scoffed. "Yeah sure."

"We want the same thing, right? To see him behind bars?"

Irritated, she tried to push him aside, but he blocked her way. "Let me go!"

He shook his head. "If you cooperate, everyone's happy."

"Are you seriously expecting me to believe that? You're not investigating, you're simply trying to get your share of whatever Danny's got."

At her words, his expression got dark and he gave her a cold look. "I'm a police officer."

"The kind that just spent hours getting drunk in the yard of the person he's supposed to arrest. Do you think I don't know what's going on here? You're getting bribes for not bringing the case to the station, but instead of just staying away, you keep coming back for more, pushing forward to a dangerous level."

He frowned. "Is that a threat?"

"No, it's an observation. I have no idea what the guys are doing, but if what you said about Waldo and the missing paperwork is true, it seems to me they got allies at the station. And I don't think it's smart to mess with them."

"I'm not afraid of my colleagues." He seemed amused.

"I don't know who you should be afraid of. All I know is you're messing up honest police work as well as the gang's business, and one of the two will put an end to it."

"What are you saying?" His face came dangerously close to hers and she smelled beer and meat on his breath.

"I'm saying you'll either lose your job or your life, if you continue what you're doing." Alice saw a vein pulsing on his temple and the color of his face turned from pink to deep red.

"So you *are* threatening me." He put a sweaty hand around her throat and pinned her against the wall. "I'd be careful if I were you!"

"You don't scare me." She held his stare.

"You're on *his* side after all, huh? He beats you up and yet you defend him."

"I'm not defending him. If you were actually doing your job, I would tell you everything I know, hoping you'd get me out of here. But you're just messing up everyone's life, including mine."

"The day you go down I'll tell them you were withholding information."

"And when was that? Right after you got drunk in the house of the guy you were supposed to be investigating? Will you tell them you snuck up on me drunk, threatening me because you're too scared to face Danny himself?" Her voice grew louder, and the cop's eyes narrowed while his jaw was clenched in anger.

Alice pulled his hand away from her neck. "You want drugs and money, and you got that, so fuck off!"

"Hey!" someone shouted from the other end of the corridor.

The cop whirled around, and Alice saw Jonas standing there, wearing only boxers, a gun in his hands and its muzzle aiming toward them.

"You better not point that thing at me!" the cop threatened.

"Oh, it's you." Jonas lowered the gun. "The fuck you think you're doing?"

"I was talking to the hostess." He took a step away from her and Alice watched him place his hand on his gun as well. "Got a problem with that?" His tone was defiant.

"If *she* does, yes." Jonas's eyes flicked to Alice and back to the cop.

In that instant, they heard footsteps on the stairs, and a moment later Danny and Timothy appeared. Danny was still only wearing his swim shorts. He looked at Jonas and the gun, and then to Alice and the cop.

"I'm pretty sure we had an agreement," he said coldly.

"I was just talking to your girlfriend."

"I'd rather you didn't." Danny's hands were clenched into fists and Alice saw his eyes swivel to the gun in Jonas's hand. She knew he wanted nothing more than to take it from him and use it.

"Get out of my house, Thomas, and take your friend with you." Danny's tone left no room for arguments.

Thomas turned and glared at Alice. "I'll see you again," he hissed, only for her to hear.

She watched him walk down the hallway and Danny stepped aside to let him pass.

"See them out," he told Timothy. Timothy obeyed and followed Thomas downstairs.

"What was that?" Danny asked Jonas.

"Just woke up and heard them talking. He was harassing her."

Danny's eyes wandered to Alice and she felt her throat tighten. Or was it only the cop's grip, she could still feel?

He walked toward her, and she found herself backing away again—only this time, she was truly scared.

Danny walked past her and opened the door to the bedroom. "Come," he said. "Let's talk."

She stared at him for a moment, heart pounding heavily in her chest, then she looked at Jonas, who was still standing in the corridor, gun in hand.

He gave her a nod and she had no idea what it meant but decided to follow Danny into the room. He closed the door behind her and went to the bathroom, where he grabbed a towel and began to rub himself dry.

"Why do you always get into trouble?" He pulled down his wet shorts and put on boxers instead.

"Whenever I get into trouble, it's got something to do with you." Her voice was shaking, and she warily watched him as he put on a pair of neat jeans and one of his white dress shirts.

"Is that so?" he asked coldly.

"Martin asked me questions about you ... and the cop—Thomas—he did the same."

Danny buttoned up his shirt and eyed her suspiciously. "And what kind of questions?"

"Nothing specific ... he ... he wanted to know what it is you're doing, but I don't even know that myself." Nervously, she wiped her sweaty hands on her pants, but her clothes were still wet, so it was useless.

"And you told him that?"

"He didn't believe me."

Danny sat down on the bed and put on socks and shoes. "What did he say?"

"He threatened me ... but I told him to leave me alone."

At once, Danny looked up. "He threatened you?" His eyes were almost entirely black, and Alice knew he was high.

"He ... choked me."

"That bastard ... Coming here, taking coke from me, filling his stomach at my cost just after I gave him a generous bribe ... and then harassing you ... He has to go." He finished knotting his shoelaces and got off the bed. "And you're sure you didn't tell him anything?"

Alice nodded quickly. "I don't know anything, what would I tell him?"

Taking three big steps, he crossed the room and when he reached her, she dropped her eyes, scared of what he might do next.

But getting high somehow seemed to have sharpened his senses. The uncontrollably angry Danny from before had disappeared. Nonetheless, his appearance was scary.

"About Martin, maybe?" He lifted her chin to look into her eyes.

"No, I would never! I promise!"

"So you weren't hoping he would get you out of here? Out of this ... *prison*?"

"He wouldn't, he's not investigating. He just wants money."

"Oh, I know that. But he might always change his mind. Maybe climbing up the career ladder suddenly seems more rewarding than getting paid off?"

"I don't know, but I didn't tell him anything!"

Danny's expression remained hard, and the tension brought tears to her eyes.

"Why are you crying?"

Because you scare me.

She wiped the tears away angrily. "I don't know."

Softly, he brushed her cheek with his thumb. "I believe you. I knew something was up when I saw him enter the house right after you, and when he didn't come back out, I followed." He sighed. "I should've just put a bullet through his head."

"You can't kill a cop, Danny! Hell, you can't kill *anybody*!" Her voice sounded incredibly desperate and Alice hated herself for her naivety. The way things were going, it was pretty obvious that Danny considered killing people normal.

"Well, he's got to go. That's all I know so far." He shrugged and grabbed his towel from the bed to wipe away some drops that were dripping off his hair and down his face. "That ugly little skunk ... I should have messed with his car brakes, so he'd get in an accident. He's drunk enough anyways."

"Stop talking like that, please ..."

He can't be seriously considering murdering a police officer.

Alice felt her blood rush to her face and her head began to throb while her stomach twisted.

"Things are serious, Alice. I don't want to go to such dramatic extents, but I don't see another option right now. Of all the cops Henry could have called, he found the one greenhorn whose confidence is bigger than his sense. And now he's fucking with us, thinking he's smart."

"But ... if he's only a greenhorn, there must be other ways to deal with him." Her voice was shaking, she noticed. She shivered in her wet clothes.

Danny put the towel around her shoulders. "It's complicated ... He doesn't have much on us, so there's nothing he can do, but he also thinks we wouldn't kill a cop. He thinks he's untouchable." He walked around the bed and to the nightstand, where he sat down and opened the top drawer. Alice heard him fumble with something and then he was snorting.

"Danny, please stop ... haven't you had enough already?"

"I'm only having fun."

"Five times a day?" Alice tried to fight her nausea by taking deep breaths, but the room seemed to be spinning around her.

Danny got back up and wiped his nose with a tissue. "Mind your own business."

The room spun faster, and Alice leaned her back against the door. Her hands were shaking and so were her knees.

"It is my business ..." she muttered weakly.

"It can be." He offered, holding the tube out toward her. "I really think it would loosen you up."

"Put it away, I'm not taking your stupid drugs."

This time, Danny did not insist, and he stowed the tube away in the pocket of his pants. Staring at him, Alice tried to picture him as a father. He was an addict and abusive as well. Would he hurt the baby too?

The thought sent a sharp spasm of pain through her belly and, whimpering, she clutched her hands to her stomach.

"You okay?" Danny asked.

"Just ... sick."

She felt him put a hand on her forehead. "You're hot."

"I'm cold."

"You should lie down."

"No ... I need a shower first."

He frowned at her. "You look pale."

"I'm fine. Just go back outside and enjoy your party."

Danny's expression hardened as his thoughts clearly went back to the two policemen. "Not sure the mood can be restored after what that fucker did."

The air in the room seemed thick and heavy, and Alice found it hard to breathe. "Just ... stop worrying ... about him."

Danny's cold hand moved to her neck and he lightly brushed over her throat with his fingers. "How could I? He fucking choked you."

Another chill went through her whole body at his touch and his face became a blur. He seemed to be growing taller and Alice wondered what was going on, until she realized that her back was gliding down the wall because her knees had given in. The white blur of Danny's shirt expanded until it looked like a thick white fog surrounding her and then she couldn't feel anything anymore.

Bright light blinded her through her eyelids and Alice blinked and tried to open her eyes. Her whole body felt hot and heavy, and she could barely move.

She didn't even flinch when a cold hand was placed on her forehead.

"How are you feeling?" Danny's voice asked close to her ear.

Moaning, Alice closed her eyes again.

"Can you hear me?" he wanted to know.

"Where am I?"

"In bed. You fainted and I carried you over here. You have a fever."

Alice moaned again.

"I had to strip you of your wet clothes."

"Sorry ... for keeping you away from your party. You can go back, you know. I'll be fine."

Danny's hand brushed over the side of her face gently. "The party's long over, Alice."

Surprised, she opened her eyes and found him scrutinizing her warily, concern in his eyes.

"It's afternoon, Allie. I slept next to you. Don't you remember?"

"No ..." Alice swallowed dryly, feeling thirsty. "When did you come to bed?"

"I never left."

Taken aback, she stared at him. "You didn't go back?"

Danny shook his head sadly. "I didn't want to leave you alone. I was worried you might stop breathing."

"Don't be overdramatic. I just have a fever."

"Overdramatic? You collapsed and remained out cold, even when I undressed you and put you to bed. I wasn't going to leave you like this and I sure as hell didn't want anybody else near you, defenseless as you were."

"Sorry ..." Alice muttered again. "I ruined your birthday. I'm ruining everything." Tears welled up in her eyes and began running down her hot cheeks. Danny looked even more worried now.

"It's okay, honey. I wasn't in the mood anymore anyway." He wiped some tears away from her face with his sleeve. "Why are you crying?"

"I don't know."

He sighed. "You always say that. I'm not doing this anymore, Alice. I want you to see my doctor."

"*Your* doctor?"

"I'm not going to send you to town. I have a doctor whom I can trust."

More tears streamed down her face and Alice cursed the fetus in her belly silently. It gave her nothing but problems. "You mean one who asks no questions? The one that gave you all these prescription pills?"

Danny can't know I'm pregnant ... No one can.

"He's competent and he keeps quiet, yes."

"No."

"No?"

"I don't want to see him."

"Alice, you're sick. You need help."

"You're being paranoid, Danny. I'm malnourished because of my inflamed stomach, and because of that, my immune system is weakened. So now I got the flu. Taking two baths in the pool surely didn't help either." She scowled at him, but Danny wasn't impressed.

"You're trying to blame this on me now?"

Alice heard suppressed anger in his voice and averted her eyes. Again, tears blurred her vision.

Sighing deeply, he once more dried her tears with his sleeve. "Why are you making this so difficult?" He sounded irritated.

"I don't like doctors and especially not male doctors ... Let's just wait for the flu to be over and then I'll take those acid reflux pills you got me. And I'll try to eat mild food only." Alice looked up at him and saw doubt and suspicion in his expression. "Please?" she begged.

Sighing again, he gave her hand a squeeze. "Fine. But don't you dare die on me."

"I won't."

The following night, Alice dreamed of Danny. He was laughing viciously, and his white shirt was covered with bloodstains. When she approached him, she saw that he was holding a dead baby in his arms.

Panting and covered in cold sweat, she awoke. She couldn't shake off the feeling that there was truth in her nightmare. Was it an omen? Would Danny lose his temper and kill the baby?

I never wanted this baby ... I should abort it.

But how? She wasn't able to see a doctor—apart from Danny's. But Danny wanted a baby, and he would never let her abort it. Trying to kill the fetus herself was bound to go wrong.

But Alice also knew that she could never raise a child in an environment like this.

I have to get out of here.

22

Another heat wave dominated the rest of August and gave Alice a hard time. Everyone else loved it though and they spent their evenings barbecuing and their weekends bathing in the pool.

Danny stopped urging her to see a doctor when the medication finally kicked in and she began to feel better. She chose her food carefully and avoided everything sour or spicy, and she also took her vitamins daily, hoping to make up for any possible damage done to the baby due to her malnourishment of the previous months.

Her belly was starting to bulge lightly, and she knew there was not much time left until Danny would find out about the pregnancy.

Alice knew she had to find a way out before he did. But Viktor or Jean-Pierre were watching her every day and Jonas kept an eye on her as well. Even if she found a way to shake them off, there was still the guard at the gate, and he was not going to let her leave. Alice wondered if he was in on what was going on or if they had simply told him that she was nuts and couldn't be on her own or something like that.

Danny's mood grew darker by the beginning of September and he spent more time in his office. The weather seemed to adjust to him, and rain kept falling for days while the temperatures remained below sixty-eight degrees. Even the other men's smiles disappeared, and it was clear that something bad had happened or was about to happen.

The two policemen returned several times, showing up unannounced, and Danny would tell Alice to stay in her room whenever they came. She did not protest. After all, she didn't want to have to see Thomas again. He had made it clear to her last time that he would not give up looking for answers.

With her feeling better, Danny stopped treating her like a porcelain doll and that was definitely a bad thing. Old habits returned and he began to treat her coldly, distantly, and more roughly than before. Therefore, she tried to avoid him and was careful not to talk back at him, though she hated acting like a submissive housewife. It was not like her and it was everything she'd never wanted to be. Right now though, she had to focus on the well-being of her unborn baby and it would not be beneficial to have Danny hurt her.

Jonas still avoided her whenever Danny or his bodyguards were around. Alice wondered how much Danny suspected. Did he actually think there was something going on between them or was he simply jealous because he assumed that she liked Jonas more than him? It was true that she trusted Jonas more, after all, he had never hurt her and apart from keeping her locked up, he had shown her kindness most of the time. Alice couldn't figure out her feelings toward him though. He wasn't really her type and she hated his way of hiding his emotions—it made him look hard and cold, like a rock. Yet she had seen his soft side before, only she wasn't sure if it was always there or not. Jonas had admitted he supported the business, he had killed a person in front of her, and Alice was rather sure that his reason to be in the business was to get rich and powerful—just like Danny. It could also not be forgotten that he was the main reason why she was in this house. She couldn't stay mad at him for that though, not with him being the only nice person around.

Now that she was feeling better, being locked up was even harder than before. During her sick days she had been in bed all the time anyway, so it had been easy to pretend that everything was normal. But now, the urge to take a walk or enjoy a day with friends in town grew almost unbearably strong and with it, the need to bring her baby to safety before it was too late.

The old house with its thick carpets and antique furniture made her feel suffocated, and Alice found herself taking every opportunity to go outside in the yard—even if it was raining. Danny noticed it too and it made him even more paranoid. He seemed to sense that she was up to something and had Viktor or Jean-Pierre tailing her at all times. Often, they would simply stand a couple of yards away from her and stare at her while she was reading a book or drawing sketches—and it was driving her crazy.

When the first week of September was coming to an end, Danny's mood got even worse. At dinner, they would all sit in the dining room, spread around the table, but he would just drink his five glasses of red wine silently and say nothing at all. Alice could see that it wasn't only worrying her. The men were stealing discreet glances at him from time to time, but no one dared to address him.

Even until late in the evenings, they would have meetings in Danny's office, and it was wearing him out. The drinking got worse, and Alice could only wonder what else he took to live through the day.

He left for another business trip on the twelfth of September, and with him went Timothy, Waldo, Paul, and Jean-Pierre. Alice felt a wave of anxiety go through her body when she watched the cars disappear through the gate, and was left standing on the porch with Jonas and Viktor. She had hoped to be left alone with Jonas and maybe get him to take her to town, or just sneak out without him noticing, but with Viktor here, it would be much more complicated.

Alice ended up spending hours thinking about possible ways of escaping, while the rain turned the yard into a mud pit and the gate guard remained in his hut. At least that was something positive. It would be easier to run away unseen while it was pouring like this and you couldn't see far.

Viktor was determined to make her life a living hell and he seemed to enjoy that Danny had put him in charge instead of Jonas. At night, he would even lock the door of Alice's room. Whether on his own terms or by Danny's order, she didn't know, but Viktor made sure to sneak up on them whenever she was talking to Jonas. He seemed to sense that something was between them and he wanted to find out what.

The house felt more like a prison than it had ever before, and her hope of escaping was drained from her with every unsuccessful day that passed, leaving her empty and depressed.

Jonas noticed it and she realized he was watching her often with a worried expression on his face.

Alice kept wearing her elegant clothes, knowing Viktor would report to Danny if she didn't.

The meals were sad and awkward. The cooks never talked, and Jonas's contempt of Viktor was palpable. Viktor's way of teasing Alice didn't help.

Apparently, he had told the cooks that no meatless meal was needed, and one evening at dinner, Alice was served a fat steak. Its smell made her instantly feel nauseous. Viktor said nothing and just smiled viciously while she ate her salad instead and shoved the plate with the meat far away from her. Lately, she had grown very sensitive to smells and a greasy piece of flesh was about the worst thing she could imagine.

"Not hungry?" Viktor asked, chewing loudly on a piece of his own steak while eyeing her mockingly.

Ignoring him, Alice continued eating her salad.

"Some meat would serve you well," he went on. "You look pale."

Still, she remained quiet.

"You are what you eat." Grinning, he cut another fat piece off his steak with his sharp knife.

"Is that why you look like a fat pig?" She glared at him. "Actually, I take that back. Pigs are cute ... and intelligent."

Viktor's face turned red at her words and she saw him clench his fists, but in that moment, Jonas walked into the room and took his seat, leaving one spare chair in between him and Viktor.

"You on a diet?" he asked her, eyes on her salad.

"Not on purpose, no," Alice replied coldly.

Jonas shrugged. "Cooks are still new. Sometimes they mix things up."

"No, they didn't." Irritated, she pushed back her chair and got up. "But it's fine. I'm not hungry anyway."

Jonas gave her a look that asked, "Did I say something wrong?"

Alice felt sorry for him, but her hatred of Viktor was too strong for her to spend one more minute in the same room with him.

More uneventful and long days passed, and Alice began to hide in her room again to avoid Viktor.

One afternoon, she noticed him talking to the gate guard out in the yard. Watching from her window, she assumed that it was going to be a longer conversation, so he would leave her in peace for a while. Quickly, Alice sneaked out of her room and closed the door behind her. She quietly hurried down the corridor until she reached Jonas's bedroom door. Jonas usually hid in his room as well these days, probably also wanting to stay away from Viktor.

Alice knocked once and he opened. When he saw her, he froze, standing in the doorframe, looking surprised.

"Can I come in?" she asked, but before he could answer, she walked past him. "Close the door."

Jonas hesitated.

"I'm not going to mount you or anything."

She saw his cheeks turn faintly red, and he pushed the door shut. Alice let her eyes wander through the room for a moment. She had only been in here once and it had been dark. Jonas didn't seem to possess much. He had a single bed and a desk, a dresser, and a bookshelf... and that was it. No pictures on the walls, no plants, and apart from an iron ashtray on his desk, no decorative items. The room was tidy, apart from the books that were spread out on the bed and sheets of paper, where he had scribbled down notes in an almost unreadable tiny handwriting.

He followed her gaze with his eyes and waited for her to say something.

"I thought maybe we could talk in here since Viktor's got his eyes everywhere."

Jonas just looked at her with a blank expression, the color in his cheeks already gone.

"He's driving me crazy," she confessed. "He's so nosy and suspicious, and he obviously seems to think something's going on."

Jonas grimaced in a way that said, 'and what should I do about it?'

Sighing, Alice sat down on the chair beside the desk. "I was hoping you could talk to Danny or something."

"And say what?"

"That Viktor isn't needed ... that you're better at babysitting me on your own ... I don't know. Just something. I'm sure he wouldn't like it if he knew that Viktor is mocking me on purpose." Nervously, Alice spun in his swivel chair from side to side.

Jonas rubbed his forehead with the knuckles of his right hand. "Stop that," he moaned.

"Sorry." She stopped swiveling but couldn't help wiggling her feet.

"I don't think that's a good idea," he said, sounding exhausted.

"Why not?"

"Because he clearly already suspects something, and what d'you reckon will happen if I tell him to take Viktor off the job?"

He was right. Alice hadn't thought about that. "He's not giving me any space though," she complained. "You were never like that."

Jonas sighed. "Pass me that." He nodded to the desk, where a pack of Marlboros was lying. Alice tossed it to him, and he lit a cigarette and offered one to her as well. She declined.

"Things are tense," he said after blowing out a cloud of smoke.

"I noticed."

"Really tense."

Alice began chewing her lip. "Like how tense?"

"We could go down."

"Is it because of the cops?"

He nodded.

"But ... I don't see how they can have such an effect on you. They're just greenhorns, aren't they?"

"They're stupid and stupid people are dangerous."

"How?"

Hesitating, Jonas took a drag on his cigarette. He seemed to be considering what to tell her. "We thought we had the police under control. There's one half supporting us and one half doing their job, and then there's those two idiots in between, fucking with both sides as well as with us." He finished his cigarette and stomped it out on the carpet. Alice noticed that there were already dozens of black holes burned into it.

"And how will you proceed?"

"The question is whether to bring them in or get rid of them."

Shocked, she stared at him. "You're not honestly considering murder, are you? When Danny said it, I thought he was just being drunk and stupid."

"I never said that."

"I'm not an idiot, I know what you guys mean when you say *get rid of someone*! Just like you got rid of Martin."

"I killed Martin 'cause he was going to kill you."

"Yeah, but the way you handled things—disposed of the two bodies and everything—it seemed like you've got experience." She studied his expression, trying to bring some sense into it, looking for hints that might reveal his true character. The odd thing about Jonas was the warmth in his eyes that stood in contrast to the cold and blank features of his face, but it was impossible to say whether he was of kind nature or not.

"Aren't you going to say something?" Alice asked him after a moment of silence.

"What d'you want me to say? You know I can't tell you stuff he doesn't want you to know."

"I was hoping you would." She said the words quietly, almost in a whisper, and realized how disappointed her voice sounded. Jonas lit another cigarette and avoided her eyes.

Absent-mindedly, Alice started playing with a pencil on his desk, turning it over between her thumb and index finger, until something on the wooden desk caught her eye. It was a picture of a girl, probably around sixteen, with brown, curly hair, and large, green eyes.

That must be his sister.

She stared at it and the resemblance was undeniable. Suddenly, she felt Jonas's eyes on her.

"Anything else?" he asked sharply.

Alice spun the chair around to look at him. Jonas looked impatient. She started chewing her lip again and they stared at each other for a while without saying a word.

He's a riddle I can't solve.

Resigned, she sighed and dropped her gaze. "I thought ... maybe you'd get me out of here ...? It's been over six months since I've last been outside of these walls—apart from that time in the hospital—and I'm really going crazy in here ..." Alice kept her gaze on his worn-out Converse, dreading his answer.

"You want me to let you out? You know I can't do that."

"No ... that's not what I mean. I know you wouldn't help me leave this place, or you would have done it before. You're still his friend and on his side, I get it. But I was hoping you might maybe drive me somewhere ... just for a couple of hours."

"Where?"

"Nowhere in particular ... just so I could see something else." Alice realized that her voice was shaking and wondered if Jonas could tell that she was lying.

He said I'm an open book ... he'll know I'm lying.

For what seemed like an eternity Jonas said nothing, and all the time she felt his eyes on her.

"What's wrong with you?" he finally asked.

Confused, she looked up, but when she saw his piercing stare, she quickly averted her eyes again. As if magically drawn toward it, her gaze wandered to the picture of Jonas's sister.

"Nothing's wrong. I just need to get away from here, but I know that's not going to happen ... so I was hoping you might at least give me the illusion of freedom ... the way you did before." Alice trailed off and tried to picture Jonas's sister in real life. Had she been quiet and sad and drawn inward, hating her life, hoping for someone to save her? Had there been a specific reason for her to end her life, or had she been mentally ill? Had her brother been there for her, or had he been too busy trying to start an illegal business?

"You're different," he said curtly.

"What? No, I'm not ... I'm feeling better, that's all."

"Bullshit."

Alice flinched at the sudden harshness in his voice and looked up to see him scanning her like an X-ray. His stare seemed to push her deeper into the chair and she felt her cheeks get hot.

"Why did your sister kill herself?" she blurted out—and her own words took her by surprise.

Why did I just say that?

Anxiously, she looked at him and saw him tense. A tortured look came over his face and he turned his head away from her. She watched him stand there, motionless, and only heard the rhythm of her own heartbeat and the throbbing of the blood in her ears. He remained that way for a very long time and Alice began to worry.

"Jonas?" she asked nervously.

He didn't move.

"Sorry, I shouldn't have asked that. It's too personal, I don't know why I even said it ..."

He fished another cigarette out of his jeans pocket and lit it, then he finally turned to face her.

"Tell me what's going on." His voice sounded hoarse.

"W-what do you mean? Nothing's going on ..."

"You've changed somehow."

He's a psychic.

"Like I said, I'm feeling better .... That's why sitting in this house all day long is driving me crazy."

"You're up to something."

"No, I'm not! Why are you accusing me?"

Jonas deeply inhaled the smoke of his cigarette and kept it down for a while before exhaling it again. "You're lying."

Alice felt her face turn red and her hands got sweaty. Again, her eyes wandered to the photo on Jonas's desk.

What kind of brother was he? Cold, concealed, distant? Or was it his sister's death that made him like that?

"Alice!"

His call made her look back up. "What?"

"I said you're lying. Why don't you just tell me the truth?"

"There is no ... truth ..." Her eyes flicked to the picture and back to him. "I ..." A hot flush went through her body and her heartbeat accelerated. "I'm not lying about anything ..." Her breathing got faster, and she looked back at the photo.

I can't be seriously having a panic attack right now. In his room. Without any reason.

Or was it the hormones?

"Then why are you so nervous?" Jonas had approached her and was now looking right down on her.

"I'm not nervous ... I'm just ... dizzy ..."

"So you're *not* feeling better."

"I usually am, yes. Just not ... right now." She closed her eyes, hiding her face in her palms and trying to steady her breathing.

Stupid pregnancy. Stupid Danny. Stupid hormones.

The image of a bloodstained Danny with a dead baby in his arms flashed through her mind and with it, a stabbing pain went through her skull. Alice winced and shivered.

"Alice—"

"Just get me out of here!" Shaking, she glared at him. "Is it so fucking hard? All I'm asking is for you to do me one tiny favor, that's it!"

A spasm of pain went through her belly and she gasped and clutched her hands back to her face.

"I can't do that," Jonas said, his voice strained.

"Please!"

"You don't trust me, Alice, but you expect me to trust you ... It doesn't work that way."

"Then how does it work?" she asked, exasperated. "What is this between us? 'cause I don't get it, Jonas! I can't seem to figure you out, not even a bit. I still don't know if you're my friend or if you're just nice to me because you have to ... or ... or if you're actually conspiring with Danny, trying to gain my trust to report to him later!"

He shook his head vigorously. "That's ridiculous."

"No, it's not! Why should I trust you? What have you done to earn it?"

"You want something from *me*, don't you?" he asked coldly.

"I'm just hoping ... you might help me ..." Her voice broke, and she looked back at the picture to avoid his eyes.

"And I might. All I'm asking is a little honesty from your part."

Alice said nothing and kept her eyes on the photo, her vision getting blurred by tears.

I can't tell him I'm pregnant ... he'd tell Danny.

She held her right hand next to her face, trying to shield herself from his gaze and hide her tears.

It's useless. He'll know I'm crying, he's a goddamned psychic. I hate you, baby, and I haven't even met you yet.

"You're not honest with me either," she muttered quietly, eyes on the photo.

"I am honest, I'm just not telling you any personal details."

He's such an idiot. Why did I put all my hope in him?

"Well then ... I guess that counts for me as well." More tears were running down her cheeks and she kept her eyes fixed on the picture, scared to face him.

He sighed. "Then I'm afraid I can't help you."

Again, they were quiet for a moment, Alice trying to fight back the tears until he asked, "Are we done?"

Alice got up from the chair and wiped her cheek with the back of her hand. "Yes, Jonas. We are done."

He stepped aside to let her pass and she kept her eyes on the floor and walked straight out of the door without looking back.

The corridor wasn't empty though and Alice bumped right into Viktor, who appeared to be coming from her room.

"Aha," he said. "And I was worried you'd run away."

Ignoring him, Alice tried to walk past him, but Viktor grabbed her arm and stopped her. He looked at the tears on her face and grinned. "I saw you coming out that door, you know. Was he mean to you?"

Alice shook his arm off and hurried to her room, where she quickly closed the door behind her. Frozen, she stood for a moment, staring at the door, trying to bring some order into her thoughts.

Jonas won't help me ... Viktor's always watching ... I'll never get out of here, ever.

Again, she saw the image of Danny holding the baby-corpse in her mind's eye. And even if the child survived—what kind of life would it live? Locked up in a house with its mother, with a father who took drugs and got drunk every day ... surrounded by bullies carrying guns ... Was it even a life worth living?

A feeling of utter hopelessness overcame her, and Alice buried her face in her hands, sobbing until she started hyperventilating. Gasping for air, she pulled at her necklace and watched the room spin around her while her back slid down the door. Raindrops were smashing against the window, making a rhythmic and soothing sound. Listening, she closed her eyes and took a deep breath.

Like I said, one way or another.

Alice ignored both Jonas and Viktor that evening at dinner. She stared at her food in silence, never touching it, and neither of the men spoke either. The only noises were the clattering sounds of the dishes.

That night, she lay awake in bed, plotting over possible ways to escape, but no matter how hard she tried, without Jonas's help there was no solution. Crying silently into her pillow, she promised her unborn child that she would do whatever it took to get it away from Danny.

Desperate, she tried to figure out whether she should tell Jonas about the pregnancy nevertheless. But the more she thought about him, the more she realized that she did not know him at all. What if his friendly demeanor in truth was nothing but an act and he would end up telling Danny everything?

The risk was too high, and Alice knew that if word got out that she was pregnant, Danny would keep her under extra watch. Maybe he would even tie her to the bed until the baby was born.

The night dragged on and her desperation grew with every passing minute.

As usual, sleep came after dawn and Alice slept through the morning, until a knock on the door woke her up at around noon. Without awaiting an answer, Viktor opened and stepped inside, carrying a tray in one hand. He placed it down on the dresser and turned, letting his eyes wander over her. A grin appeared on his lips.

"Feeding the lioness," he joked, and walked back out of the room. The door fell shut and Alice heard the key turn in the hole. It took her a moment to grasp what had happened.

"What are you—?" Panicking, she jumped out of her bed and rushed to the door, where she desperately pulled at the handle. It was locked. Alice began punching her fists against the wood.

"Viktor! Viktor!" Frantic, she put her ear to the door and listened for any sounds coming from the corridor. To her relief, she heard footsteps.

The key rattled in the lock and she took a step back to let him open the door.

"Something wrong with the food? It's no steak this time, though one would expect a lioness to like steak." He laughed at his own joke.

"Why did you lock the door?" Alice asked breathlessly.

"New rule. Ruled by Daniel."

She stared at him in disbelief. "What are you talking about?"

"Told him about your little get-together with *Lorenzo*. Wasn't pleased."

"We were talking, that's all! I'm allowed to talk to Jonas!"

"Not anymore. From now on, you'll stay in here, day and night, until your boyfriend gets back. Who knows, if you're nice to him, he might even let you out again." He winked at her and she felt the urge to squish his eyeballs in with her thumbs, but she knew he was only waiting for an excuse to tackle her. She watched him close the door again and the sound of the key in the lock sent a stabbing pain through her guts.

That's it ... now it's officially over.

"Aaaaaaaaaaaaaaaaaaaaaaaaaaaargh!" Screaming, Alice kicked the door, but all it did was crack her toe, and she blinked away the tears of pain and dug her nails into her palms.

I'm a loser. I can't even protect myself, how am I supposed to protect my child?

The days passed slowly, mercilessly. Not the dream-like blur it had been the last time, Alice had been damned to solitary confinement. Now, every second seemed to be mocking her, taking at least twice as long to be over as it was supposed to. Every minute was pure torture, and the urge to flee combined with the fear of not being able to do so snowballed into an avalanche of emotions, making her feel like she was about to implode. It took all of her effort not to take it out on herself. With nobody around to aim her anger at, it boomeranged right back at her, and the compulsion to punish herself for the situation she was in grew so strong, it was barely controllable. Alice did not know exactly how she got to where she was now, or what she could have done to avoid it, but she was certain there had been at least *something* she'd done to make matters worse. The bitter taste of self-loathing was constantly on her tongue these days and she ended up covering her bathroom mirror with a towel, not bearing to look at herself any longer. The only thing that kept her from physically hurting herself was the baby in her belly. Her body might be nothing but a prison to *her*, but she was determined to keep it whole for the child that was growing in it.

The trees out in the yard began to shine in gold, red and yellow, while temperatures dropped and left the grass covered in a white frosty blanket during the early morning hours.

Unable to sleep, Alice began to get up before dawn, sitting down on her windowsill huddled in a blanket, watching the faint sunrays cast their light onto the distant hills and forests, before being swallowed by thick, gray rainclouds. She kept writing in her diary, filling it with thoughts and dreams rather than with what actually happened—since there wasn't much happening at all.

Viktor brought her food three times a day and apart form a few insulting remarks, which she ignored, he said nothing. Jonas never showed up, but she saw him smoking down in the yard from time to time, never looking up at her window.

A police car turned up at the main gate once, but the officers were not let in—not with Danny being absent. Alice watched the dull figures, she knew all too well, emerge from the car and have a vivid discussion with the gate guard and Viktor, but after about five minutes, they gave up and left. From that day on however, Viktor and Jonas both carried their guns in a holster on their hips—every single day. It made her feel uneasy. Even though Alice knew that they would never use it on her, it was intimidating to be brought food by a man carrying a gun. Viktor noticed that, of course— the way he noticed everything that could be used against her.

"When will Danny be back?" Alice asked him one evening, after he had placed her meal on the dresser. The business trip seemed to be taking awfully long and she had been held in solitary confinement for three weeks already, with no one but her unborn baby to talk to.

Alice had begun to do that way too often and by now, it felt like she actually had a relationship with the baby.

Viktor snorted disdainfully and shrugged. "In about a week, probably."

"Why is he taking so long?"

He gave her a cold look and left the room, leaving her question unanswered. Alice kept staring at the door long after he had disappeared, fighting against her tears.

One week ...

Would it be easier to try to run away now or was it better to wait until Danny was back and let her out of her room again? But who said he was going to do that? What if he kept her locked in, just for the hell of it?

I have to try as soon as possible.

The sun slowly began to disappear behind the house and its fading light made the trees glow in bright orange, as if they were on fire. Ravens were cawing on the muddy grass below, fighting over food, while other birds in the distance were aligning in the shape of a *V*, practicing for their long flight south. It was mid-October already—a year after moving into the big English house with its barred windows and walled yard.

A year in prison ... in a golden cage. Alice couldn't believe she had already survived a year like this, locked in a house that not even remotely felt like home; constantly threatened by Danny's mood swings and anger issues.

A year of wondering when he would hurt her again or when another person would get shot before her eyes.

A year of longing for freedom and desperately trying to hold on to what little hope of ever seeing her friends again was left.

I gave up. I didn't try hard enough. But now it's not just about me anymore. Now I have a baby to care about.

Alice took a deep breath, trying to calm her racing heart, and waited for the dreadful but familiar sound of the keys rattling in the lock of her door, announcing dinnertime.

It came at 7.15 p.m., and Alice quickly wiped her sweaty palms on her black cotton dress, and then placed one hand on the floor next to her while leaving the other one on her stomach.

For more than ten minutes she had been lying on the floor now, waiting for Viktor, not sure when he would come. Sprawled on the carpet behind her bed as she was, he would not be able to see her face at first. Through almost closed eyelids, Alice was able to spy through the gap underneath her bed, and watched as the door was pushed open and Viktor's thick ankles in tight jeans appeared. Her heart hammered against her ribs and breathing was hard, but Alice forced her body to remain motionless.

The dishes on the tray clattered violently and she could only assume that Viktor had almost dropped it, probably spooked by the sight of her legs on the floor. His feet moved quickly now, hurrying toward the dresser, where he ungently set the tray down. Then they began walking right toward her and Alice quickly shut her eyes completely.

Viktor remained quiet, but the rustling of his clothes and the stomping of his feet announced him walking around the bed. Anxiously, Alice held her breath and wondered if he could see her heart racing through the layers of clothes, skin, and bones.

She almost shivered when she felt him crouch down beside her. His breathing was fast and heavy, making him sound like a panting ox. A grim sense of satisfaction took hold of her when she realized how much the sight of her on the ground unsettled him. Did he think she was dead? Was he already wondering how Danny would punish him for letting her die?

"Alice!" he barked her name, and the sound of his voice was further proof of his panic. It was utterly rewarding to hear him like this.

"Alice!" he called again. Somehow, even him just saying her name sounded like a command, but Alice remained motionless.

He shook her roughly, and she barely had time to relax her neck so that her head rolled from side to side. For a moment, she wondered how realistic her pretended unconsciousness was, but then it occurred to her that it probably didn't need much acting skills to fool a guy like Viktor.

True enough, his breathing accelerated even more at the sight of her head rolling lifelessly on the floor. Suddenly, his massive hand collided with her left cheek and the pain almost made her yelp. Luckily, a strand of hair had moved in front of her eyes by the impact of his slap, now covering the tears of pain in her eyes. Alice tensed, dreading another slap, not sure if she could manage to keep acting if he struck her again. Her left cheek burned like it was on fire and she could only imagine how much Viktor had enjoyed hitting her.

Nothing happened though and she kept her face blank, feeling his stare weigh heavily on her.

"Shit ..." she heard him whisper. "Shit, shit ..."

Then it seemed to occur to him that there were other ways to find out whether someone was alive or not. The sound of his breathing grew louder as he lowered his head down to her, and she almost flinched when she felt the weight of his skull on her chest. He held his breath, apparently listening for her heartbeat.

Now or never.

Her eyes flung open at once and fell on the gun at his hip. Fortunately, Viktor had put his left ear to her chest, his face looking down in the direction of her feet. He didn't see it when her hand shot to his hip, grabbed the weapon, and yanked it out of its holster. He felt it of course, but by the time he grasped what was going on, Alice had already rolled out from underneath him and jumped to her feet, now backing away to bring some distance in between them.

Perplexed, he remained kneeling on the carpet, eyes widened in surprise.

With shaking hands, Alice cocked the gun and aimed it right at his head.

It took him a moment to fully realize what had happened, but then he slowly stood up, arms tense at his sides, underneath his broad shoulders, ready to grab her. His face had turned dark red and his stare was warning.

"Don't move!" Alice said quickly, her voice as shaky as her hands. Never before had she held a gun with the purpose of actually using it on someone—even if only to frighten them—and her palms were sweaty, the weapon threatening to slide through her fingers. She squeezed it tightly, desperately trying to hold it steady.

"You stupid bitch," Viktor hissed through clenched teeth. "You don't even know what you're doing!"

"Back away," she told him. "Go to the bathroom—slowly—and close the door."

"You'd never shoot me." He sneered and his eyes narrowed into thin slits.

"Leave your phone here and go to the bathroom!"

For a moment he stared at her, his eyes flicking from her face to her shaking hands and back. And then he started laughing. An evil, twisted laugh, and Alice felt hot anger flare up inside of her like fire. It went through her body like a wave, filling her chest with heat and giving her a rush of confidence.

"I said leave the damned phone here and go to the bathroom!" Her voice was steadier now, firmer, but nonetheless, Viktor was not impressed.

"You don't even know how to shoot a gun, don't be ridiculous." He took a step toward her and Alice backed away.

"I'm warning you ..."

"You wouldn't shoot me. You don't have the guts." Grinning widely, he bared his yellowish teeth, and then he took another step forward.

I have to prove him wrong.

Alice slightly moved the gun to the side, aiming at the wall behind Viktor ... and pulled the trigger.

The recoil was stronger than anything she had anticipated, and a sharp stabbing pain went through her wrists and almost made her drop the gun.

The massive blast kept ringing in her ears, making her feel dizzy, but she steadied herself and looked at Viktor, who had fallen to his knees. He was bent over in what appeared to be fear.

Look at that pathetic asshole, all curled up and shaking.

"You bitch!" he screamed. "You stupid bitch!"

When he looked up, Alice saw that his face was contorted with pain. Shocked, she realized his arm was covered in dark, glistening blood.

I hit him!

Her heart was racing furiously now, and she could do nothing but stare at him, eyes wide, but then the door was flung open completely, hitting against the dresser and bouncing back from it. Looking up, Alice saw Jonas standing in the doorframe, his own weapon ready in his outstretched hand.

Jonas's eyes flicked from her to Viktor and back, taking in the scene before him, and then he lowered the gun.

"She shot me! She's fucking crazy!" Viktor yelled at Jonas, grabbing the bed with his good hand and trying to pull himself back onto his feet.

"Stay on the ground!" Alice aimed the gun back at him. "Don't you dare move!"

Viktor froze at once and glared at her. He turned his head around to look at Jonas, a pleading look on his face.

Jonas said nothing and just stood in the door, unmoving, slowly processing the strange scene before him.

"Tackle her! What are you waiting for?" Viktor's voice was torn with pain and rage. He looked pathetic, the way he was kneeling on the floor, his massive figure hunched forward in what looked like a big ball of pink flesh with clothes on. He had his good hand pressed on the wound to stop the bleeding, but the blood emerged from in between his fingers in a steady stream.

Jonas took a step forward, his hand with the gun hanging loosely at his side.

Quickly, Alice pointed Viktor's gun at him instead. "Don't move!"

"Alice, don't," he said in a tormented voice. "Be reasonable."

"I *am* reasonable, I'm getting out of here! I'm done with this place, once and for all!"

Viktor moved and Alice aimed the weapon back at him while taking a step toward him.

"Get out of my way," she told him, her voice hoarse.

Hesitating, Viktor looked at Jonas for support, but then he cursed and crawled around the bed, away from Alice. He remained leaning with his back against the mattress, breathing heavily. Her eyes followed his every movement, making sure he wasn't going to do anything stupid. Slowly, she turned back to Jonas.

"Let me pass." Fear and adrenaline made her voice tremble.

Jonas stayed where he was, his features blank, but his eyes held a sad look.

"Move aside!" Alice aimed the gun at his head, but to her surprise, he took a step toward her.

"I'll shoot, Jonas, I shot *him* already," she warned him, but her confidence was leaving her.

He took another step.

Alice fired the gun, but this time, she moved it aside far enough from him to hit the wall. Jonas flinched and froze, but kept his own weapon down.

"I'm warning you," she said breathlessly, shaken by the blast.

Another figure suddenly appeared in the doorframe, panting from running up the stairs—the gate guard. He held his own firearm in both hands, aiming at Alice, ready to shoot.

"Drop the weapon!" the guard bellowed.

"Put the gun down!" Jonas had whirled around and was shouting at him. He grabbed the man's arms and pushed them downward to aim the gun somewhere else.

Surprised, the guard asked, "What are you doing?"

"You can't shoot her, idiot!" Jonas gave him an angry look, then turned back to Alice. "Alice, please drop the gun, be smart."

"Don't move," she warned him again. "I'm getting out of here. Let me pass!"

"And where d'you want to go, huh? He'll find you."

"I'll take my chances." Furious, she glared at him. "Now put the damned gun down or I'll shoot you!"

"You won't," Jonas said calmly.

"Viktor said the same." She nodded toward Viktor, who was still sitting on the floor, breathing heavily and holding his injured arm.

"You won't shoot me." Jonas took another step forward and Alice felt her guts clench. Her breathing accelerated and she backed away, taken off guard by the effect he had on her.

He's right ... I could never kill him.

Trembling, Alice aimed at the gate guard instead. "I'll shoot, I swear!"

Jonas frowned and turned to the guard. "Get out."

The man's jaw dropped, and he looked at Jonas like he thought he was insane. "But—"

"Out, now!"

Reluctantly, the guard obeyed and stepped out of the room, leaving Alice alone with Jonas and Viktor.

"Just let me go, please!" she begged.

Jonas shook his head. "Calm down, Alice."

"Don't tell me to fucking calm down! I've been locked up in this shithole for a year, Jonas, a fucking year! I can't do this anymore!" Her voice cracked and her vision got blurred by tears. Quickly, she blinked them away, trying to keep a clear sight.

Jonas took another step forward. "I can't let you go like this."

"Drop the fucking gun!"

He stopped and hesitated, then slowly crouched down to place his weapon on the floor. He held his hands up defensively. "Please, Alice, you're not like that."

"Step aside! And don't act like you know me."

"You're letting your emotions take the upper hand."

"Yeah, Jonas, like you said, I'm too fucking emotional. At least I got a heart though, at least I *care* about people!"

A pained look came over his face. Hesitantly, he got back up and took another step toward her. He looked as if he were trying to help a wounded wolf; like he expected to get bitten any moment.

It was hurtful. It made her feel like Jonas solely saw her as a mentally instable person having a fit. She was not crazy; she was only trying to get her life back. How could he deny her that?

"Put the gun down, Alice," he said quietly.

"Step aside!" The gun in her hand now trembled violently and it took all of her effort to keep it aimed at his chest.

"You won't shoot me."

"I will!"

He came closer and Alice found herself backing away from him.

"Stop, I said stop!"

Jonas ignored her and continued walking toward her slowly while she backed away further. Despite her being the one with the weapon, he was the one in power, like he always was. With or without gun, Alice felt weak and defenseless—and he knew it. His eyes said it all.

He's ruining me, he's ruined my life ... but I can't shoot him.

His bright green eyes were fixed on her and next to determination, she saw something else in them ... affection. It was too much for her to bear. A sob escaped her throat.

"Don't, please ..." she said desperately, still walking backward.

Jonas took another step forward, forcing her back further, until the wall was right behind her. Alice flinched when the thick, purple curtains brushed her right shoulder. She was trapped in between him and the wall, frozen in fear, like a deer who's about to get hit by a car, and she knew that it would only take him one more step until he'd be able to rip the gun out of her hands.

Shoot him for God's sake, it's him or the baby!

But her body wouldn't obey her, and the gun almost slipped through her fingers, suddenly being too heavy for her to hold.

It's over. He's not going to stop.

"Stop," she sobbed. "Stop or I'll shoot!"

Jonas gave her a meaningful look and took the last step. Now, he was only an arm's length away from her.

"You won't shoot me," he said again.

Through a veil of tears, she stared at him. There were no sounds apart from the ticking of the clock on the wall and the furious beating of her heart.

"No," she finally affirmed, her voice thick. "I won't shoot *you*."

Quickly, she pulled her arm back and pointed the muzzle of the gun at her own temple, feeling its cold metal against her skin.

Jonas stood frozen, his eyes wide, and she whispered, "I'm sorry." But it was meant for the baby, not for him.

Alice squeezed the trigger and heard him yell "Don't!", and his voice seemed to echo in her mind while the room around her began to spin, faster and faster, until everything got blurred.

23

Instead of a blast, only a faint *click* broke the silence which had followed Jonas's shout. Right next to her ear, it sounded horribly loud and crushing.

When Alice opened her eyes, she was still in the room with Jonas towering over her, his lips slightly parted in shock and his eyes wide.

No ... it didn't work!

Again, she pulled the trigger and Jonas flinched, but another *click* echoed through the room, louder and more menacing than the first one. At least it sounded that way to Alice.

Jonas exhaled audibly and Alice stared at the gun, horror-struck. At once, all strength left her limbs and the weapon slid through her numb fingers and clattered to the floor.

It's over ... everything's over.

Her whole body felt numb and lifeless, and she let her back slide down the wall until she was on the floor, with both hands in front of her face to shield herself from Jonas's gaze. Tears ran down her cheeks and through her fingers, and her heart was pounding heavily against her ribs.

A noise coming from the other side of the room made her spy through the gaps between her fingers, and she saw that Viktor had stumbled onto his feet and was now walking toward her while Jonas still stood frozen in place.

He laughed viciously. "Too bad you wasted that bullet on me, ain't it?"

He tried to reach her, but Jonas managed to shake off his petrifaction and grabbed Viktor with both hands, shoving him away.

"Leave. You need medical care."

"Don't tell me what to do." Viktor's tiny eyes glistened dangerously.

"You want to sew yourself up or what? Just go!" Jonas glared at him and Viktor returned the stare defiantly.

"I'm not leaving you alone with her," he hissed.

Jonas's eyes narrowed. "You'll have to, unless you want to bleed to death."

Indeed, Viktor was looking rather pale by now and blood was running down the length of his arm, dripping off his fingertips and onto the floor. He was swaying a little too and seemed to realize that Jonas was right. Grimacing, he spat on the floor, but then he turned and stumbled out of the room. Jonas pushed the door shut behind him, then he turned back to Alice.

Her throat tightened at once and she felt as if her heart was about to break through her ribs at any moment. She tried to keep the sobs down, to suppress them, but they kept coming. When she saw Jonas approaching her, she held her breath, dreading his reaction.

But Jonas just crouched down in front of her, and Alice flinched when his arm moved toward her, but he only picked up the gun that was lying on the floor beside her. He checked the magazine to make certain that it was empty, then he sighed and tossed the weapon onto the bed, where it landed with a soft *thud*.

She felt his piercing gaze on her, but still, he said nothing.

After a long moment, he came closer and Alice tensed when she felt him sit down beside her, his back against the wall as well.

The smell of leather and smoke—*his* smell—filled her nose and his presence made her shiver. Tears continued to run down her cheeks and silent sobs kept emerging from her throat, though she tried hard to keep them down.

They sat next to each other and he remained quiet. After a while, he put his arm around her hesitantly, and even though she hated him for what he'd done, Alice couldn't resist the urge to lean her head against his shoulder. Jonas rested his chin on her head, and she inhaled his smell, feeling it calm her down.

Darkness fell and they remained sitting on the floor, until her sadness and shock were replaced by a cold and dead emptiness. The tears dried out, leaving her skin raw and burning. Jonas moved and she looked up, but the room was spinning, and it made her feel nauseous. Her skull seemed to be made out of lead and she could barely lift it from Jonas's shoulder. Her heart was beating irregularly and breathing was hard.

Softly, Jonas cupped her head with one hand and lifted it off his shoulder. He stood up slowly and Alice watched blankly, as he crossed the room and picked the two guns up.

"I'll be right back," he said quietly, before leaving the room and closing the door behind him.

Alice stared at the door, her mind empty and unable to grasp a clear thought, and she remained that way until he returned. Again, Jonas closed the door behind him and then he took a glass of water from the tray with her cold food. He crouched down beside her and opened his fist, showing her a big, white pill, he was holding.

"Take this ... please."

Alice looked at it and took it from him, placing it on her tongue. It didn't matter what it was or why he gave it to her. Nothing mattered anymore.

Jonas handed her the glass of water and she flushed the pill down, then gave the glass back to him. He put it back onto the tray on the dresser and returned to sit down on the floor again, beside her, and like before, he put his arm around her shoulder, and she didn't object.

They sat like that, quietly, until a heavy drowsiness overcame her and pulled her away from reality and into darkness.

Cold wind blew through her hair and over her cheek, and pulled her out of a heavy, dark sleep, which had not been accompanied by dreams. It tickled the little hairs on her upper lip and moved through her eyelashes, and then it went underneath her shirt and made her shiver.

Alice blinked and opened her eyes, but closed them again immediately, blinded by the faint autumn daylight. She put her hand over her eyes to shield them and tried to grasp her surroundings. The breeze was coming from her window and she was lying in bed on her left side, covered up to her chest by a blanket. Shivering, she grabbed it and pulled it up to her chin.

"Sorry," a voice sounded from where the wind came.

Alice flinched and blinked into the light, suddenly realizing that someone was sitting there, their large shape casting a shadow over her bed. She heard the window being shut and the breeze disappeared, leaving the room perceptibly warmer.

"I opened the window to smoke," Jonas explained, and she saw him put out a cigarette.

What is he doing here?

Alice tried to recall what had happened, why she was lying in bed fully dressed, feeling stiff and exhausted, accompanied by Jonas, who had taken her place on the windowsill.

The memories of last night's events began creeping back into her mind—Viktor's injured body huddled on the ground, Jonas's face in front of her, worried and yet stern, the heavy gun in her hands ... She shuddered and tasted bile on her tongue. A feeling of utter hopelessness overcame her and panic rolled over her like an avalanche. The realization hit her that she had done something bad—something very, very bad—and that sooner or later, she would have to pay for it. Alice stared at the ceiling blankly, horrified by what she had done and scared to death by what Danny would soon be doing to her. He would be furious ... no, *maniacal.*

Tears veiled her eyes, and she was amazed that there were still some left, after what she remembered of that dreadful evening. Her throat was dry, and she figured she must be quite dehydrated, yet the tears came. Motionless, she remained lying on the mattress, letting the tears run down her cheeks and drip onto the sheets. Why should she bother hiding them from Jonas? He already thought she was nuts. He had seen her at her worst several times already, and Alice was convinced there was nothing she could do that would shock him. Not anymore.

His eyes were fixed on her, and she rolled over onto her right side, turning her back toward him. The memory of him blocking her from leaving the room, keeping her locked up in this prison once and for all, was way too vivid on her mind and she knew that she could never forgive him.

He's my worst nightmare. Without him, I wouldn't be here.

"I'm sorry," she heard him say. His voice was low and sincere and sounded pained. "I don't intend to invade your privacy, I just wanted to make sure Viktor doesn't seek revenge."

Viktor ... Alice wondered how he was doing. Was it only his arm that was injured? Had the bullet gotten stuck in his bone, or had it just been a graze shot? He must be furious as well.

She let her eyes wander to the clock on the wall. It showed a quarter past ten and since it was light outside, she knew it was morning, though she had lost all sense of time.

Her wrists were aching, and she wondered if it was because of the recoil that had occurred when she had fired the weapon—twice. Two warning shots, one too many.

I should have kept that bullet for myself.

But how was she supposed to know there were only two bullets left? Had Viktor recently been shooting at something ... or somebody? Or was he just sloppy?

Why was it so hard for her to die? It seemed Jonas was always saving her life—even unintentionally.

Alice's head began to throb, and she squeezed her eyes shut and took a deep breath. Whatever pill Jonas had given her, it had left her with a bad hangover. She hoped it wasn't bad for the baby but pushed the thought away at once—it was too painful.

The baby, whom she had tried to save. The reason why she had done what she had done, to give her child a better future ... or a future at all. But it hadn't worked, as always, Jonas had made sure of that.

I should have shot him.

Hatred and anger began flaring up inside her and she cursed herself for not having been able to pull the trigger on him. He had been so sure she wouldn't do it—too sure.

I should've proved him wrong.

He was right after all: she was way too emotional.

Alice heard footsteps coming around the bed and saw his shape through the corner of her eyes but refused to look at him.

"You thirsty?" he asked, and she heard him fill a glass with water. "You slept quite long."

Alice *was* thirsty, but she would rather have died of thirst than taken water from him. She pushed herself up on the bed quickly, but slowed down when a spasm of pain went through her skull. Carefully, she placed her feet on the floor and got up to go to the bathroom, supporting her balance by letting her hand glide along the wall until she reached the bathroom door. She stepped onto the tiles and closed the door behind her, leaving Jonas alone in her room. There was no key for the bathroom—Danny had made sure of that—but she knew Jonas would not disturb her in here.

The cold water from the tap was most welcome, and she gulped it down eagerly until her stomach ached. Carefully avoiding looking in the mirror, she crossed the small room and sat down on the edge of the bathtub, staring at the wall and wondering what turns her life was about to take.

Again, her mind wandered back to yesterday's incident and she felt nauseous.

I fucked up. Badly.

It had been her only chance, but now she was doomed. Danny was never going to let her out of her room again, unless maybe in a body bag. But Alice knew she could not even hope for that much. Danny wouldn't have gone through all that trouble of keeping her locked in if he'd had any intentions of killing her. He loved her, and even though he didn't exactly show her as much, he didn't want to live without her and that was the problem. He would keep her here until the baby was born and then who knew what would happen.

He'll either kill it or damage it for life.

Alice dropped down to her knees and managed to push the toilet lid upward just in time before her stomach turned, and she gagged and spat out the water she'd just drunk along with stomach acid and blood.

Shaking and gasping for air, she closed the lid again and rested her head on its cool surface, feeling dizzy.

"Alice?" Jonas's voice came through the door, sounding concerned. "You okay?"

I would be if I had just shot him and run. I'd be in town now, probably with Jill and Leah.

"Alice?" he asked again.

"Go away," she tried to yell, but her voice was hoarse and weak. He heard her nevertheless and stopped calling.

After stubbornly lying on the cool floor for about thirty minutes, she decided to go back to her room despite Jonas's annoying presence.

He was there, leaning against the wall, a tortured look on his face. He watched her as she walked back to her bed and sat down, not knowing what else to do.

"You're still sick," he noted.

Alice stared at her hands in her lap and said nothing. Her throat was burning and her tongue felt furry, while a stabbing pain in her stomach made it hard to breathe.

"Alice ..." he said, sounding desperate.

"Just go, please." Her own voice was hollow and thin.

"I'm sorry, I know you're mad at me."

She kept her gaze on her hands and imagined them choking Jonas to death, his face turning red and his green traitor eyes bulging. It filled her with grim satisfaction.

"Alice, I'm really sorry."

"Stop that," she hissed without looking up.

"I mean it."

"No, you don't! Stop pretending you're anything but my prison warder! You're only doing your job, and as far as I'm concerned, apologizing to me and pretending to be nice is not part of your job. So stop it, once and for all!" Anger made her voice shake.

There was a moment of silence and Alice fought back tears, swearing to herself that she would never again cry because of him, not anymore—but it was harder than she'd anticipated.

"You're angry, I know, but—"

"No, Jonas, *angry* doesn't even begin to describe it! I hate you; I fucking despise you with all my heart, more than I could ever hate Danny! You are the worst thing that has ever happened to me and I wish ... I wish you hadn't shot Martin and pulled me out of that tub, I swear, I hate you for that!"

The words *I wish I had just shot you* had been on her tongue, but she couldn't get herself to say them. Despite everything he'd done, it was too hurtful.

He looked tormented enough as it was and she almost felt sorry for him, but then she remembered how he always manipulated her like that, looking at her with puppy eyes that made her melt and forgive him, made her believe, even, that *she* was at fault, that *she* had treated *him* wrongly somehow—just to betray her again a bit later.

I will never fall for that ever again.

Alice returned his stare and put as much hatred and contempt in hers as possible, and Jonas seemed to be shrinking under her glare.

"Just go, Jonas, get out of my room!"

He seemed to be frozen in place at first, but then he pushed himself off the wall, eyes still on her. Finally, he dropped his gaze and walked out into the corridor, closing the door behind him silently.

Alice remained staring at the door for a while, until she noticed the tray with food on her dresser. Her aching stomach made her walk toward it. To her surprise, it was not yesterday's dinner anymore. There was a plate with fruits and some toast with beans in tomato sauce, as well as fried mushrooms. Jonas must have brought her breakfast this morning. She felt another stabbing pain in her guts and cursed him for being so hard to hate.

The week went by way too fast, and the dreaded day of Danny's return approached inexorably.

Persistent and paralyzing fear made her feel numb and heavy. Even getting out of bed was hard, and Alice stopped trying after a while. Jonas kept bringing her food three times a day to keep her and Viktor apart, and she gave him the silent treatment. He gave up trying to talk to her after several failed attempts, for which she was grateful.

Her stomach rebelled against the food. At first, she tried to eat for the baby, but when she just threw it all up again, she gave up and left the tray untouched. By the end of the week, she was weak enough to fall asleep despite the panic attacks, which came and went like the autumn breeze outside, ripping the leaves off the trees.

When the dreadful day dawned, Alice woke up with an inextinguishable fear in her guts that spread through her body until every limb, even her fingers and toes, were tingling and ice-cold. She remained lying in bed that way, staring blankly at the ceiling and wondering what Danny would do to her.

He's already hurt me in every possible way, and I know he wouldn't kill me ... so what am I afraid of?

The thought persisted and she found no answer to it. It was true, there was nothing Danny could do to her that he had not already done—and yet the mere thought of him brought her to tears and made her heart race madly. She wasn't even scared of physical pain, but whenever Danny hurt her, he hurt her emotionally as well, for she had loved him once and seen a future with him.

Jonas seemed to sense her fear; she saw it in his eyes that morning when he brought her breakfast. He remained quiet though, knowing she didn't want to talk to him.

Even looking at the tray on the dresser managed to turn her stomach, and Alice ended up with her head over the toilet once again, as if her body were trying to get the fear out of her. It didn't work that way though, and she knew that if she couldn't get the nausea under control, she would end up damaging the baby.

Alice let her hand glide over her belly and wondered if Danny would already notice the bulge. Or maybe he was too self-absorbed for that. She hoped for the latter.

The sound of tires on gravel felt like a punch in the stomach. Alice's eyes flicked to the clock on the wall. It was 4:23 p.m. and the light outside was already fading after it hadn't been able to break through the clouds during the day. Thick and heavy dark clouds in the distance announced a rainy night, and the ravens had already fallen silent.

The car doors fell shut and Alice heard muffled voices. The cold, tingling sensation of another panic attack went through her limbs, and the adrenaline gave her the strength to get out of bed and hurry to the window to spy out.

Danny was standing next to his car, dressed in a long, black, woolen coat and a gray scarf that he had wrapped tightly around his neck. His hair was shorter again, but he hadn't shaved. The dark beard stubble made him look older and even more intimidating.

He was talking to Waldo and Timothy while Viktor and Jean-Pierre stood motionlessly, carrying the men's luggage. Paul was saying something to Jonas, who nodded and took a drag on his cigarette.

Alice was sure that Danny already knew what had happened. He had a phone after all. Would he come straight upstairs to bash her head in, or would he wait and bottle his anger for later?

Trembling, she sat down on the windowsill and started chewing her nails.

The terrifying rattling of the key appeared shortly after Alice had seen the men enter the house.

He's not wasting any time.

Paralyzed by fear, she stared at her trembling hands in her lap, seeing the door open through the corner of her eye.

He came in, tall and scary, still wearing his scarf but not his coat anymore. The door fell shut behind him and the tension in the room felt suffocating.

The ticking of the clock seemed to grow louder in the threatening silence that filled the room. It was nerve-racking. Alice's heart was racing so fast, it made her feel dizzy.

"I got a call from Viktor," Danny finally broke the silence, but to her surprise, his voice sounded pained and hoarse—not angry.

Too scared to look up, she remained quiet.

"He told me what you did," he continued, still standing by the door, his eyes resting on her heavily.

"I'm sorry," Alice burst out without thinking. "I didn't want to shoot him; you have to believe me! I didn't even aim at him, but ... it just happened!" Tears began clouding her vision and she stared at his blurry shirt instead of his face.

"And you taking the gun from him just happened as well?" Cold sarcasm tinged his voice.

Alice said nothing.

"I thought this was behind us ... that you'd accepted your life here." He crossed the room and stopped a few steps away from her, arms crossed in front of his chest.

She felt herself shrink under his stare. "I could never accept living here ... like this," she said tonelessly.

He inhaled sharply. "I've given you everything, Alice ... and you thank me by shooting one of my men?"

"I didn't want to shoot him!"

"But you did! You could have killed him for God's sake, Alice, what is *wrong* with you?" He glared at her and the sound of his heavy breathing filled the room, along with the annoying ticking of the clock. "You almost shot a man over what? A day in town? Is that it?"

Alice shook her head and stared at her hands. They looked blurry through the veil of tears.

"Then what? Huh? Were you trying to run away? To leave me?" His voice grew louder, and she knew that his anger had gotten hold of him after all.

Of course I was trying to leave you. Just as I have done for a year now.

The words remained unspoken, but the heavy silence had the same meaning. She felt his aura change as the comprehension trickled in.

"I just need more freedom," she said quickly. "That's all, I swear!" Desperate, she looked up at him and noticed the faint red color on his cheeks, even through the tan, which he had somehow kept during fall.

He must have been someplace warm again.

The cold rage in his eyes made her tear up again in fear and despair.

"I'm sorry!" Alice desperately tried to soothe his anger.

Danny kept staring at her quietly and it made her shiver uncomfortably.

"You're crazy," he muttered at last. "You're insane. I can't even trust you to make reasonable decisions anymore, it's like you've lost your mind."

Alice gazed at him, taken aback by his heartless conclusion.

"It's like the only place I know you can't do anything stupid is the bunker ..."

Something cold seemed to trickle down her spine at his words and she held her breath, feeling terrified.

"But I'm not going to put you down there again, even though I could use a break from looking after you. Hell knows I've got too many problems to deal with already." He rubbed his temples with his knuckles and when he looked back at her, his face was contorted by stress and pain and exhaustion.

"I know you can't handle the bunker," he continued. "I've realized that it was a mistake putting you down there in the first place. It caused your mental breakdown, didn't it? I can't have anything like that happening again." Sighing, he stowed his hands in the pockets of his black pants.

Alice was amazed and shocked by how coldly he described her mental status. As if she had been a nerve-rack from the beginning—and not only due to his treatment.

"We need to do something about it, though. Perhaps you should see a doctor and get some meds prescribed. Something to calm you down."

"I don't want that," she protested.

This wasn't about her well-being. It was just him trying to silence her, trying to make her easier to handle ... was that why Jonas had given her that pill? So she wouldn't bother him anymore?

"Honey, I think we're far from making decisions based on what you want," Danny said curtly, giving her a warning look. "It's about what you need and what I need, and most importantly, what's good for the business. I really have too many problems to deal with already and there's only so much I can handle."

He began walking closer toward the window and Alice cowered down, making herself as small as possible, but he merely looked out through the glass and let his eyes wander over the landscape.

"What happened to Viktor?" she asked nervously.

"The bullet went through his arm, but he's fine. He's angry though and who could blame him?" He glared at her and Alice felt a sharp pain in her guts, as if his gaze had actually stabbed her. She dropped her eyes and said nothing.

"Shooting him ... I mean seriously, Alice, a gun's not a toy. What were you thinking? *Were* you even thinking?"

"I need to leave this place, Danny, it's been a year and I just can't do this anymore!" Her voice was trembling, and she blinked away the tears, trying to hide them from him.

Sighing, he sat down on the sill beside her, putting a hand on her knee, which made her flinch.

"We *are* leaving this place, Alice. Soon."

Confused, she blinked at him. "What?"

"Thanks to our friends from the police, things have gotten too risky here and we have to move."

This can't be ... is he being serious?

Frozen, she stared at him.

"You'll have more space, like I promised. I keep my promises, Alice. I told you this was only temporary."

"But ... where are we going?"

"We don't know yet for sure, but it'll be warmer than here, like you wanted."

All I want is to be far away from him. I'd move to fucking Alaska if it meant I'd never have to see him again.

"When ... when are we moving?" She felt her throat constrict and swallowed dryly.

"Not yet. Probably in December. We still have to prepare everything." Again, he let his deep blue eyes wander over the landscape. "Already a year ... I can't believe it."

Me neither.

"Why are you crying?" He put his hand underneath her chin and made her look up at him. "You never wanted to live here. Aren't you glad we're going away?"

Alice tried to avoid his eyes but his grip around her jaw tightened and the tears of despair got replaced by tears of pain. She tried to push his hand away, but his grip was too firm.

"Talk to me," he commanded.

"I ... I just ..." Her eyes flicked to the window, as if the oak tree outside might tell her what to say. It remained silent though. "I just don't want to live like this anymore. It's not about the house ... it's the security and your business and not having friends around. I can't ... I can't do it anymore ..." The tears streamed down her face now and she kept her eyes on the window, too scared to face him.

Through the corner of her eyes, she saw him purse his lips while his eyes narrowed.

"I'm not giving up the business," he said coldly.

Alice forced herself to look at him instead of the tree outside. "But you could give up ... me." Her voice was toneless, and she saw something flicker in his eyes as he took his hand away from her.

"Please, Danny, consider it. This is not a relationship! You're living in the past, but you don't need me anymore, I'm only in your way."

Danny got up from the windowsill and wiped his pants flat, then he started walking toward the door.

"Danny," she called after him. "Wait!"

He ignored her and Alice followed him through the room and grabbed his arm.

"Please, just let me go, I don't want to be here!"

He turned and shoved her away from him, a disgusted look on his face. The impact almost made her lose her balance. Not daring to approach him again, she stared at him and he glared at her, his arm twitching as if he was trying hard not to hit her. Cautiously, she took a step back.

"There's only so much I can take," he said, breathing heavily. "You shot one of my men, but not enough, no. You think you can make demands? I can still change my mind about the bunker, Alice. Don't make me change my mind."

He loosened the scarf around his neck a bit, as if it were strangling him, and then he brushed his hair back and straightened up, which made him appear even taller.

"You'll remain in this room until we move," he said curtly, and left, locking the door behind him, leaving her frozen in place, paralyzed by the horrors that were awaiting her. A future with him, somewhere far away, in an even bigger house with even more security and no chance of ever seeing her friends again.

A state of utter hopelessness and despair got hold of her over the next few days and left her feeling as if she were sleepwalking. Every single day, she sat on the windowsill, looking out and dreaming about a life outside of these walls. Even the birds were lucky enough to fly over the wall and head south to a warmer place and a better life. Alice envied them and the people in the cars, which she could make out on the road in the distance. They drove wherever they wanted, whenever they wanted ... or so it appeared.

If she ate, it was only for the baby and not for herself. Food and even water were hard to keep down and she had run out of acid reflux pills but didn't dare ask for more.

Neither Viktor nor Jonas came to her room anymore and even Danny stayed away. The food was brought by Jean-Pierre, and he never talked. He also did not tease her or look at her in a scornful way—no, he was completely neutral and for that she was grateful.

She saw Viktor in the yard from time to time and noticed that he had his bandaged arm in a sling. Apart from that, he seemed to be all right though.

Jonas sometimes smoked in the front yard and seeing him made her sad. Alice regretted having yelled at him—even though he'd deserved it. She missed having him around and talking to him or watching movies with him. She even missed playing poker with him despite her dislike for the game.

I should have just been content with him being nice to me and not expected more.

After four days, Danny paid her a visit—but only to still his physical needs. Even though he hurt her, Alice didn't resist. She knew he would use force if she tried to get him off and she didn't want to take that risk.

Afterward however, her lower belly hurt badly, and she remained lying huddled underneath her blanket, crying silently and hoping the baby was still okay.

At least Danny had not noticed the bulge and she wondered how long she would be able to keep her secret from him.

November came and with it, memories of the pool incident—the first time Danny had ever hit her. It had been the start of a life much more miserable than she could have ever imagined.

Temperatures dropped massively, leaving Alice's window fogged up. When it froze, beautiful ice crystals covered the glass, and they managed to put a smile on her face, though it was a weak one.

The trees lost their leaves earlier than usual, and Alice watched them dance in the rough wind until they dropped onto the grayish grass, where they remained.

The yard was usually empty now, with the gate guard hiding in his hut and the men barely leaving the house anymore. Only Jonas did not seem to care about the cold and kept standing outside, smoking, and watching the sun set every day.

Alice tried to keep her window open as often as possible, to get some fresh air and feel the wind on her skin. She needed to know how cold it was to not completely lose track of time. She began to sit on the windowsill all day long, leaving the TV turned off and watching the outside life instead—even if there wasn't much life at all. She didn't even turn her head anymore when Jean-Pierre brought her food; it was easier to pretend he didn't exist.

Danny kept coming to her room late at night, usually drunk or high and horny. Alice could see that he was stressed out. He looked older and pale despite his tan, and he didn't shave anymore. Under different circumstances, she would have liked his unshaven and uncombed look, but knowing it was due to problems with the business and knowing he would use her to blow off steam made the whole thing tragically serious.

He hurt her and he didn't care anymore.

The nausea got worse until one rainy mid-November day, Alice threw up three times even before Jean-Pierre brought her breakfast. The beans and toast got cold and remained untouched on her dresser while she stayed curled up on the bathroom floor, keeping the toilet nearby as a precaution. Horrible belly cramps had joined the constant heartburn. Stomach acid had left her throat raw and bloody. Alice knew that she wasn't sick enough to die, but she felt like she was about to nonetheless.

When the nausea returned to a controllable state, it was already dark outside. Exhausted, Alice climbed back into bed and slept comatosely, until the alarming rattling of the key in the lock startled her awake. A beam of warm, orange light cut through the darkness like a knife, until the door was closed again, and the light vanished. Alice buried her face in her pillow and listened to Danny's heavy breathing approaching her. The smell of whiskey accompanied him like a shadow, and she held her breath when he dropped onto the mattress beside her. Trying to scoot away from him, Alice pulled the blanket tighter around her shoulders, but Danny put his arm around her waist. He pulled her closer toward him and his breath made the hairs on her neck stand up.

"Not tonight, Danny, please ... I'm not feeling well," she whispered, while trying to wind herself out of his grip.

Danny didn't seem to hear her—or maybe he ignored her on purpose. His hands wandered underneath her night shirt and he began fumbling with the button of his pants while breathing down on her neck.

"Danny, I said I'm not feeling well. I'm sick, please don't." She said it aloud this time and he hesitated, his hand still on her belly.

"You're in no position to reject me," he grumbled and continued pushing down his pants.

"Please, I've been nauseous all day and my stomach hurts," Alice tried again desperately.

"You're always nauseous, what difference does it make?" His hand wandered downward, past her bellybutton and lower. Alice shivered despite the warmth of his skin. Her breathing accelerated and so did his, though for different reasons.

"Please don't," she begged again.

"I gave you the chance to see a doctor. More than once. You refused. Don't expect me to be considerate now."

When he spoke, his hot breath reeked of whiskey, and Alice felt her stomach clench again. Hot pain burned in both her lower belly and upper thighs, and the thought of having Danny entering her made her tremble in fear. He felt it, but all it did was turn him on and a soft moan escaped his throat. It sounded unbearably loud right next to her ear.

Without thinking or knowing what she was doing, Alice pushed him off of her with force and rolled off the bed. Holding her aching belly, she retreated from the bed and bumped right into the treadmill, which still stood in the left corner near the window—despite not having been used in a very long time.

Even from a distance, she could feel anger flare up in him and his glare found her in the darkness.

"The fuck are you doing?" he growled as she changed direction and moved backward past the couch in front of the window. Slowly, her eyes adjusted to the darkness and the faint light falling through the blinds was enough for her to make out the shape of the TV and dresser.

"Danny, please, not now ... just go to sleep." Her voice was begging, and she hated herself for even having to beg for her own physical integrity. But hadn't she already lost it when Danny had first locked her up in that house? As far as *he* was concerned, she was his possession, and he could use her whenever he wanted. Alice could see how angry it made him that she had the nerve to reject him. It was an insult, a violation of his self-imposed rules, and it hurt his pride.

"Come to bed," he ordered through clenched teeth.

"No." Her voice was higher than usual and shaking, but her body was fully awake, ready to fight or run away if necessary. Adrenaline had chased her pain and nausea away, and Alice took her hand away from her belly while she retreaded farther away from him.

Had he even locked the door? She couldn't remember hearing the key rattle a second time. Danny pushed himself up into a sitting position and she felt his piercing stare on her. Her eyes flicked to the door.

There's a fifty-fifty chance the door is unlocked.

There was nowhere she could go, but at least she might get into the corridor. Danny surely wouldn't make a scene in front of the others, and maybe Jonas was still awake, and she was almost positive he would step in if Danny hurt her. Or wouldn't he? After what had happened and what she had said to him, would he still protect her from Danny? Alice remembered the time she had come back from her shopping tour with Henry, and Danny had been furious. He'd been close to hitting her in front of everybody, but Jonas had blocked his way and pushed him away from her. How had she never truly appreciated that before?

"Alice." Danny's voice was warning.

"I told you; I don't want to. Not today."

Or any other day, for that matter.

Her eyes flicked back to the door and she balled her hands into fists, digging her nails into her palms, and started running. Her hand found the door handle and she pushed it downward while pulling the door toward her. Again, warm light cut the darkness in half, but quicker than she would have ever expected, Danny was on his feet, and it took his long legs only two large steps to reach her. He grabbed her arm and it felt as if he were trying to rip her apart, the way his fingers dug into her skin. Drunk as he was, he underestimated the distance and collided with her with such force that he pushed her into the door. The door slammed shut, and Alice found herself pinned in between the wood and Danny's massive body. Instinctively, she tried to fight him off, but it only managed to make him furious. One of his arms was locked around her from behind while he tried to get a hold of both of her wrists with his right hand, again digging his fingers into her flesh.

Panicking, Alice cocked her head back and felt her skull crash against his nose. Yelping, he clutched his right hand to his face, freeing her wrist. His left arm was still locked around her though and he tightened his grip to hold her still, sending another stabbing pain through her belly.

Alice didn't even know what she was doing anymore. Panic made her instincts take over and all she wanted was to keep him out and away from her. Not realizing that she was only making him angrier, she clawed at his skin, trying to make him let go, horrified he might hurt the baby. Danny growled madly and grabbed her shoulders with both hands, turning her around so that her back was against the door.

"Stop that!" he barked while shaking her roughly.

Alice's head hit the door when he shook her as though he was trying to shake the resistance out of her. Feeling dizzy, she went limp in his grasp and he dragged her back to the bed. Despite the softness of the mattress, the air got knocked out of her lungs when he threw her onto the bed. He pinned her down and Alice started flailing frantically to get him off. Danny sat on her legs to stop her and driven by mad rage, he began hitting her until stars danced before her eyes and she tasted blood in her mouth. Only when she lay lifelessly on the sheets, did he stop punching her. She heard him panting right above her face, but the blood in her nose blocked the smell of whiskey coming from him.

Unable to grasp a clear thought, she remained lying on her back with the room spinning around her and her head throbbing violently, and only vaguely noticed he was pulling down her underwear.

She kicked at him weakly, but it only made him hit her again and her breathing got flat and rattled.

"Don't fight me, Alice," he growled, but his voice sounded distant, as if it were coming from another room. "That's what you get for fighting me." He lowered his body onto her, driving the air out of her lungs, and when he forced himself into her, it felt like he was ripping her apart from the inside. The pain made her cry out, and he put his hand over her mouth to silence her, leaving her unable to breathe.

Hot, stabbing pain flashed through her body with every move he made. It was not him anymore, not that body that had been able to move so tenderly once—it was a dagger slashing her insides apart and the pain was beyond anything she had ever experienced or imagined.

Terrified of suffocating, Alice tried to pull his hand off her face, but her weak attempt only made him press it down even harder. More stars began to dance around her in the darkness. Slowly, the dizziness eased the pain, and she stopped fighting and welcomed the blackness with open arms.

"Why didn't you tell me you got your period?"

Danny's voice seemed to be coming from far away, fighting its way through the fog surrounding her and echoing in her head, but she couldn't understand what he was saying.

"This is gross, Alice."

She turned her head weakly and saw him standing next to the bed, towering over her like a dark shadow. He was pulling up his pants, but the alcohol in his system made him clumsy and it took him several attempts to close the button.

Alice blinked into the darkness, but his shape remained a blur. Vaguely, she saw him put on his shirt, but he didn't even try to button it up.

Her whole body seemed to be on fire and her head was throbbing like it was about to burst. Her limbs felt stiff and paralyzed, and she could still feel his weight on her.

The door opened, sending a wave of light into the room, and Danny's shape disappeared into the light. When he was gone, nothing remained but darkness. Only the ticking of the clock and the sound of her blood pumping through her veins broke the silence.

She remained lying on her back, staring into the darkness, her mind blank, until her senses slowly began to return along with the pain. Whimpering, Alice rolled onto her side and pulled her knees up to her chest. Tears began flooding her eyes and running down her face, blurring her fuzzy sight even more.

Alice gasped and clutched her hands to her belly when a horrible stabbing pain went through it. The pain was worse than any stomach pain she'd had so far, and it left her unable to breathe.

The baby, she thought desperately, *what has he done to the baby?*

Something hot and wet was on her thighs and a wave of nausea almost made her stomach turn. She didn't want Danny's sperm on her as a reminder of what he had done.

Slowly and blinded by the pain, she pushed herself up and managed to move her legs over the edge of the bed, though every movement sent another spasm of pain through her whole body. Gasping for air, she froze and waited for the room to stop spinning, then she pulled herself up by grabbing the handle of the bathroom door and stumbled onto the slippery tiles. Her trembling hand found the switch next to the door. She flicked it, and white light flashed through the room and left her blinded for a moment. Another cramp made her bend over and whimper, but she caught herself quickly and waited for her eyes to adjust to the brightness. When they did, the horrible sight of dark red blood on her thighs almost made her knees give in. Grabbing the doorframe for support, Alice watched the blood run down her legs and drip onto the white bathroom tiles. She took the edge of her white night shirt and tried to wipe the blood off her skin with it. More blood followed instantly and panicking, she ripped a towel off its holder to clean herself, but it only left the towel stained and the blood kept flowing. Not knowing what else to do, Alice stumbled toward the bathtub and heaved herself over the edge by grabbing the metal towel holder for help. Her bloody fingers left stains on the shower tap when she turned it on. With shaking hands, she started washing off the blood. The heat of the water brought life back to her limbs, and she felt them ache where Danny had grabbed her and hit her. The worst pain of all though was the one in her lower belly, and when another stab of pain flashed through her, the metal showerhead slipped through her fingers and fell into the tub with a loud *clunk*. Alice cried out in pain and tried to turn off the water, but her feet slipped on the blood in the tub, and she fell, landing with her chest over the edge of the bathtub. A load of shampoo bottles and soaps fell down through the impact, and the noise was so loud, Alice feared it must have woken the whole house up. But Danny had been incredibly drunk and maybe his sleep was deep enough for him to hear nothing.

Moaning, she tried to pull herself up, but her legs would not obey and kept slipping on the blood and water in the tub. Hunched over the edge of the bathtub, she felt another sharp pain in her belly and her sight became fuzzy.

I'll bleed to death ... die right here in the bathtub. Isn't that what I wanted?

Suddenly, she heard a noise coming from her room and her senses sharpened. Was it the sound of a door being closed? Had Danny come back? She listened anxiously, but the drumming of her heart and the water gushing out the showerhead drowned out everything else.

For a moment, there was nothing, but then someone knocked on the bathroom door and the sudden noise made her wince. She tried to grab the towel from its holder on the wall, but the holder was empty. Vaguely, she remembered that she had already taken it down to wipe off the blood and now it was lying on the floor near the door—out of her reach. Alice tried to say something, to tell whomever was out there to stay out, but only a hoarse whisper came over her lips. It was already hard to breathe as it was, so she gave up and remained silent.

Another knock at the door made her flinch again, and she felt as if she had just awoken from a dream. A sudden exhaustion had overcome her, and her eyelids closed while the pain became fainter. She weakly noticed somebody calling her name, but the sound of the water and the throbbing in her skull made it impossible for her to recognize the voice. Alice felt her body go limp again, and desperately tightened her grip around the edge of the bathtub, but her hands kept slipping off the ceramic.

At last, the door was opened slowly, and a tall shape appeared, its dark clothes making it look like a shadow. It was blurry, but it was clearly approaching her. When the person crouched down in front of her and turned off the water, she finally recognized him.

"Don't look," she whispered weakly, and he grabbed the towel from the floor and put it around her waist.

"What happened?" he asked, and she felt him put a hand underneath her chin softly, to lift her head up a bit and look at her face. He inhaled sharply. "Did he do this to you?"

"H-hospital," she stammered, and he nodded and gently put his arms around her to pull her up, carefully leaving the towel in place.

When he lifted her up onto his arms, he saw the amount of blood in the bathtub, and she felt him tense. The pain increased when he moved her, and she gasped and put her hands over her face, as if she could block out the pain that way.

Jonas carried her to the bedroom and carefully put her down on the bed, where he wrapped the blanket tightly around her before lifting her back up.

Keeping her eyes closed, she focused on her breathing, trying to stop the cramps in her belly, but the pain persisted.

The air outside was shockingly cold and burned in her throat, so she held her breath until she heard a car door being opened, and Jonas placed her down on the front seat of his BMW. He buckled her up and it brought back memories of that afternoon one year ago, when he had first brought her to the hospital.

Jonas took his place in the driver's seat, started the car, and pushed the gas pedal down abruptly, sending gravel flying away in all directions.

They reached the gate and she heard him shout "Open!" to the guard, and then they were out on the gravel road, where he accelerated.

Jonas drove recklessly, and when they reached the hospital parking lot, he hit the brakes hard, making the car squeal.

He carried her into the overly illuminated building, and Alice kept her hands on her face to shield her eyes from the bright light. She felt hands on her and heard voices asking her questions, and she couldn't understand them, but kept whispering "I'm pregnant," and when Jonas heard her, he almost dropped her.

24

I should not have fought him.

The way too familiar and nerve-racking beeping sounds of the machines in the room kept reminding Alice of where she was, and the dull pain in her belly left no room for hope. A feeling of utter despair overcame her and made her feel as though she'd been buried alive, with a ton of cold, heavy earth pressing down on her, making it impossible to breathe. The guilt of having provoked Danny into hurting her like that was too much to bear.

I should have just let him do his thing... I should not have fought him.

Alice kept her eyes closed and fought against the tears that threatened to run down her cheeks. Every breath she took sent a sharp pain through her, and so she kept her breathing flat and short. Her face hurt as well, especially her nose and lips and the area around her left eye. She couldn't help but wonder what she must look like. Not that it mattered. Nothing mattered anyway, and Alice hoped intensely that the bed underneath her would open up like a big mouth with sharp teeth and swallow her whole, making her disappear forever.

Slowly and steadily, the drowsiness wore off and no matter how hard she fought it, her body and mind continued to wake up and the pain increased. Alice noticed a warmth around her right hand and pressure on her skin, and when she tried to move it, she realized someone was holding it tightly.

Her heart stopped for an instant. Was it Danny? The thought made her shiver.

Opening her eyes just a little bit, she saw that it was Jonas. Confused, she blinked at him, expecting him to disappear, but he remained solid. His eyes locked with hers and she could tell he was deeply worried by the look on his face and the dark shadows underneath his eyes.

A sharp pain flashed through her forehead and Alice closed her eyes again. There was way too much light in the room.

Jonas gave her hand a squeeze as if to see if she was still awake.

"I'm sorry," he muttered, and his voice was flat and toneless. She felt his thumb brush over the back of her hand and winced, taken aback by the sudden affection he was showing her.

"For what?" she whispered, too weak to use her voice. She forced her eyes open and tried to look at him again.

He returned her gaze and the sadness in his eyes was so piercing, it physically hurt. The realization hit her like a punch in the guts, even though she had somehow expected it. The baby must be lost, and Jonas knew about it.

"Is it dead?" she whispered.

He nodded. "I'm so sorry."

For a very long moment, they were both quiet, Alice keeping her eyes shut and fighting against her tears, and Jonas holding her hand and caressing it with his thumb. His presence was oddly comforting, and she almost forgot that she was supposed to be angry at him.

When the door suddenly opened, Jonas pulled his hand back almost too quickly and Alice's eyelids flung open. But it was only a doctor who stepped into the room. Her face seemed familiar and when she said, "Hello Alice," Alice remembered.

"Dr. Keller."

"Liza," the doctor corrected her. Her dark eyes found Jonas and she gave him a cold look. "I'd like to talk to her alone."

Without an objection, Jonas got off the chair and left the room. Liza took his place next to the bed and folded her hands in her lap. Alice stared at her blankly.

"Third time's a charm. When I heard you're back, I took over. Again."

Avoiding the doctor's eyes, Alice said nothing.

"What happened?"

"I lost the baby, didn't I?" Alice was surprised to hear how pained her voice sounded, despite her best efforts to act nonchalant.

"Yes, I'm afraid you did. But that's not the question."

Even without looking at her, Alice felt the doctor's eyes resting on her heavily like weights, pushing her deeper into the mattress.

"How far was it? The baby?" she muttered.

"You don't know when you conceived?"

She shook her head.

"I'd say about five months."

"What was it?"

The doctor hesitated. "Do you really want to know that?"

Alice nodded.

"It was a girl ... You can still see her if you like."

"No ... I'd rather not."

There was a moment of silence and Alice felt new tears building up in her eyes. She blinked them away, feeling uncomfortable under Liza's intense stare.

"So ... are you going to tell me what happened?"

Alice sighed quietly. "What do you want me to say? You've already made up your mind, haven't you?" Blinded by another flash of pain in her skull, she closed her eyes again.

"I have my theories, but I would like to hear it from you."

Why not tell her the truth? She might be my way out.

Alice opened her mouth to speak, but the words would not come. It felt as if her tongue were paralyzed. Not even in her mind did she manage to put what happened into a sentence. Instead, images flashed through her head, images of Danny's menacing shadow in the darkness, dark red blood dripping onto white tiles ... She gave up and closed her mouth again.

"Alice ... you look like somebody attacked you and I would like to know who."

I shouldn't be protecting him. But why is it so hard to say his name?

"Who did this?" the doctor asked again.

Alice took a deep breath and winced when another stabbing pain went through her belly.

"The baby's father." The words came out of her with the air, she exhaled.

"Did he rape you?"

Alice felt her throat tighten and her mouth got dry. The doctor's stare seemed to pierce right through her skin and into her very soul.

"Don't say that," she said weakly.

"Not saying it doesn't change what happened. I saw enough when we took that fetus out of you. You're bruised all over. I just need to hear it from you."

Like a hawk, she kept staring at her and Alice's heartbeat accelerated. She knew the doctor only wanted to help her, yet she felt interrogated, and Liza's persistency annoyed her and upset her at the same time.

Why is she making me so nervous?

"Yes ..."

"Yes?"

Keeping her eyes on her blanket, Alice nodded. There, she'd done it. Who knew what that would change—if it changed anything at all.

"He raped you?"

"Don't make me say that word."

"You don't have to." Liza paused. "I would like to call the police, since I doubt you'll do it yourself."

Alice said nothing.

"Is that all right with you?"

"I guess ..."

He'll get out again anyway, Waldo will get him out.

"Okay then. I'm going to call the police. They will want to speak with you." Liza Keller got off the chair and flattened her white coat. "It was right telling me the truth, Alice. I hope this will all be over soon."

Me too.

The doctor left and Jonas reappeared. He nervously ran his fingers through his hair and looked at Alice, then he hesitantly sat back down in the chair. His expression was still one of utter exhaustion.

"Did you call him?" Alice asked, her voice shaking.

He shook his head. "I'm not taking you back there, Alice ... not anymore."

Surprised, Alice stared at him blankly while her heartbeat accelerated.

"I'm going to take you away from here, as soon as possible. I don't know where yet, but he won't find you. I'll make sure of that."

Once more, he took her hand in his, and it was warm and comforting.

"So ... did he cross the line now?" she asked quietly.

To her utter surprise, Jonas teared up. Speechless, she watched him put a hand in front of his face. When he spoke, his voice was heavy with regret.

"I should have let you go ... I'm so sorry ..."

Tears began to cloud her own vision, and she turned her head away from him, overwhelmed by his display of emotions and by her own grief. She left her hand in his though, comforted by his touch.

After a long, dreamless sleep, which was probably caused by the intravenous painkillers, the nurse had given her, Alice awoke to find her room empty. The light coming from the window was faint and revealed that it must be late in the day already, and it made her worry. How long would it take for Danny and his men to notice that she was gone? Jean-Pierre must have surely noticed by now that her room was empty. Or had the gate guard informed Danny about opening the gate for her and Jonas? Was Danny waiting for Jonas to bring her back?

Alice tried to sit up in bed, but the pain in her lower body increased at the movement and made her gasp. The room began to spin around her, and so she laid her head back onto the pillow and took a deep breath.

A young nurse with dark brown curls opened the door and seeing that she was awake, she gave Alice a smile and approached the bed to check the machines and Alice's pulse.

"Where's the man who was in here?" Alice asked her.

"Oh, I don't know, dear. My shift has only just started."

"Is Dr. Keller still here?"

"I'm not sure, but I can check if you like," she offered.

"Yes, please."

Another ten minutes later, Dr. Keller appeared, wearing a long, purple winter coat.

"You asked for me, Alice? You're lucky, I was just about to leave." The doctor looked worried when she approached the bed.

"Thank you for coming," Alice muttered. "Do you know where Jonas—I mean the man who brought me here—is?"

A deep frown appeared on Dr. Keller's forehead, and she stared at Alice for a long moment without saying anything. Alice felt her heart beat faster under Liza's stare.

"We talked about this, Alice. Don't you remember?"

"About what?"

"I told you I was going to call the police."

Confused, Alice looked up at the doctor. Her mind felt foggy and was too slow to grasp a clear thought. "What does that have to do with Jonas?"

Dr. Keller sighed. "I know this might be hard to accept. Perhaps you did not expect me to go through with it." She took a step closer and put a hand comfortingly on Alice's shoulder.

"I ... I don't understand."

"Alice ... the police were here. They arrested him. They wanted to talk to you, but you were asleep, so they left. They'll be back once you feel a bit better."

Alice's eyes widened and she stared at Liza in disbelief. "But ... why Jonas? Why did they take him?"

"For what he did to you, of course." The doctor sounded like she was talking to a child.

"But no ... he didn't! He didn't do anything. He's just a friend!"

"Alice, you told me the baby's father did this to you and the police ordered a DNA test to have evidence."

Now, nothing made sense anymore. Speechless, Alice stared at the doctor, trying to process the words she'd just heard. "W-what are you saying?"

Dr. Keller shook her head sadly. "Why are you still protecting him, Alice? We have the evidence we need."

No ... that's impossible.

"But ... no ... it doesn't make any sense." Alice put her hands in front of her face and shook her head. She felt Liza's hands give her shoulder a squeeze.

"Are you sure you're talking about Jonas?"

"The man who brought you here and sat in this chair, yes. He was already here the last two times, wasn't he?"

Slowly, Alice took her hands away from her face and nodded.

It was his ... I can't believe it.

"I'm sorry, Alice. I know this is hard, but it's for the better." Liza sat down on the mattress beside her and took Alice's hands in between hers. "He won't hurt you anymore."

"No, Jonas never hurt me! You had the wrong man arrested!"

"But the test—"

"We ... we slept together once. Only once. It was consensual. I never thought he ... that he ..." Tears of despair clouded Alice's vision and she shook her head, hating herself. Jonas was in jail now and all just because she hadn't been able to say Danny's name.

Frowning, Liza was studying her expression, probably trying to decide whether or not to believe her. "If it isn't him, then who is it?"

Alice took a deep breath and considered her options, but the most important thing was to get Jonas out of jail. "Please, they have to let him out!"

"Alice," Liza said firmly, "I can tell the police, but you have to tell me who did it."

Again, merely thinking about Danny made Alice's throat tighten, but she forced herself to get a grip and managed to say his name, though it cost her a lot of effort.

"Where is he right now?"

"Home ... I think."

"You live together?"

She nodded.

"What's the address?"

"I ... I don't know." Alice felt herself blush.

Dr. Keller's eyes narrowed. "You don't know your own address?"

"I'm not really ... I'm not living there by choice."

Liza's expression darkened at her words and she nodded. "You can tell everything to the police. I will call them for you. I'm sure they'll be able to find him."

"Thank you."

"Don't worry." Dr. Keller gave her hands an encouraging squeeze. "It will be okay ... everything will be okay." She arose from the mattress and walked out of the room, and Alice remained lying on her bed, her heart racing. How long would it take Jonas to return to her? The hope of finally escaping Danny's claws drowned out everything else—even the grief over losing the baby.

When the door was opened anew about thirty minutes later, Alice's heart made a jump, but then it seemed to freeze. All hope drained from her at once, making her feel empty and petrified. Tears blurred the shapes of the two large figures entering the room and closing the door behind them.

No... please no.

Horrified to the bone, Alice could do nothing but stare at them with wide eyes.

"Hello, Alice," Viktor said, a contemptuous grin on his face. His injured arm was still in a sling.

Jean-Pierre was at his side, saying nothing.

"We're here to pick you up."

Alice quickly blinked away her tears, terrified of showing any weakness to Danny's bodyguards.

"I'm not coming with you," she said, her voice sounding hoarse.

"Yes, you are," Viktor insisted and took a step toward the bed.

"I'm not ready, I need to stay here."

"You can recover at home. Jean, go get a wheelchair."

Jean-Pierre nodded and left the room, leaving Alice alone with a viciously smiling Viktor.

"I'm not coming with you," she repeated, giving him a cold look.

"Oh, I assure you, you are."

"Jonas brought me here; he will take me back home."

He sneered. "Jonas doesn't seem to be here, does he? He also ain't picking up his phone. No one knows where he is ... right?" He eyed her suspiciously.

"He ... he just left, not too long ago. He'll be back."

Viktor crossed the room and came to a halt near the bed. Alice tried to swallow her fear, but she had never felt more defenseless and weak. Lying on the bed, injured, connected to tubes, she was completely trapped, and he knew that all too well. She could see on his face how much he enjoyed his position.

He wouldn't hurt me. Danny wouldn't allow it.

But Danny had hurt her himself, would he care what Viktor did? Alice knew how much Danny's bodyguard craved revenge. His eyes and his clenched fist did not lie.

"We're not waiting. And I don't think you have a say in this. What d'you want to do about it anyway?" Grinning, he took another step forward and Alice sank deeper into the mattress, unable to return his stare any longer. Her heart was hammering against her ribs and she could already feel Viktor's good hand closing around her throat, even though it was still motionless at his side, hanging from his thick, tree trunk-like arm. The tension made her tear up and she flinched when the door was suddenly opened again. Jean-Pierre returned, pushing a wheelchair. He paused to close the door behind him, then brought the wheelchair to a halt in front of the bed.

"Get in," Viktor ordered.

"No."

With narrowed eyes, he bent down over the bed, until his face was right above hers. She smelled onions on his breath.

"Get in the chair," he repeated. His voice was threatening.

"You can't force me," Alice said stubbornly.

"Oh yes, we can."

"If you drag me out of here, I'll scream."

Viktor straightened up and exchanged a look with Jean-Pierre, then he walked around the bed and examined Alice's IV.

"Is that painkillers?" His hand wandered to the tube and he let his fingers glide over it until they reached the regulator on top, right below the IV bag.

"What are you doing?" Alice asked, alarmed.

"I bet this'll make you sleep." He grinned broadly while adjusting the regulator. "Problem solved."

Quickly, Alice tried to pull the needle out of her hand, but Viktor was faster. He grabbed her wrist and held it still. Desperate, she lifted her other hand to her mouth, attempting to rip the tape that held the needle in place off with her teeth.

"Lil help here," Viktor barked, and Jean-Pierre slowly stepped toward the bed as well, a mixture of annoyance and boredom on his face. Alice stopped gnawing at the tape at once; Jean-Pierre's mere presence was enough to scare her to the bone. She'd never heard him talk nor had he seemed to register her at all since his arrival at the house. Even though she doubted anybody could be more sadistic and evil than Viktor, an unknown enemy was still a lot scarier than a known one. With now both Danny's bodyguards towering over her, one on either side of the bed, Alice felt smaller and more insignificant than she'd ever felt before. She wasn't human—at least not in their eyes. They treated her like a wild animal. If one person wasn't enough to keep her still, two would be. It didn't matter what she wanted or needed, Danny's wish was their command and that was it. The shock of realizing just how far Danny was willing to go to make her his was crippling. He already silenced her with drugs. If she kept resisting, would he end up tying her to the bed and feeding her through a tube? Where would he draw the line?

Alice felt the resistance leave her body along with the last bits of hope she'd still had. Staring at the ceiling, she allowed her body to go limp even before the medication kicked in. Jean-Pierre noticed it and saw no need to pin her down. With crossed arms, he remained standing next to the bed, his eyes on Viktor, who was still grinning viciously and holding her wrist in place.

At last, Alice's eyelids felt too heavy to keep them open any longer and she let the blackness swallow everything surrounding her, including Viktor's ugly grin.

When she awoke, she was in her own room, lying on her back in her bed, covered by a blanket. It took a while until the white fog had left her head and she was able to feel herself again. Still, her body ached and now she also felt incredibly thirsty.

It was dark outside, but the blinds weren't closed, so the light from the gate and the porch found its way through the window and made it possible for Alice to make out the shapes of her surroundings.

She could hear voices coming from downstairs, so she assumed it must not be too late yet. Her hand found the switch of the bathroom lamp on the wall behind her, though lifting her arm felt like lifting a weight. The bathroom light illuminated half of the bedroom when she switched it on, blinding her, and she waited for her eyes to adjust.

Someone had placed a glass and a jug of water next to her bed and she poured herself some and drank it thankfully. Afterward, she fell back onto the pillows and stared at the wall, feeling both angry and saddened by her unwanted return to her prison. But the emotions were muffled, buried somewhere deep down underneath a strange emptiness that reigned inside of her. For a moment, it had seemed as if everything were about to change. Jonas had promised her to take her to some safe place, away from Danny, and she had allowed herself to believe him and to hope. How could she have been so naïve?

When will I ever learn that there is no hope?

There was no way out—that should have been clear by now. Alice hated herself for having believed that Jonas or the police would save her from Danny. After all, Jonas had always been the one making sure she couldn't leave her prison. Now, Danny had apparently finally crossed the line for him to see, but it was too late. The baby was dead, and it had been her main motivation to attempt an escape. What was there now, with the baby gone and Jill and Leah having probably already forgotten about her, with no family out there waiting for her? What reason was there to escape now? And would Jonas even come back for her or was he finally done with the whole story? Would he just pack his bags as soon as they'd let him out of jail and leave? And why in the world did she even care about him? A few days ago, she had told him she hated him more than she could ever hate Danny. That had been an exaggeration of course, a lie in the heat of the moment. But still, Jonas taking her to the hospital and promising to help her hide from Danny, was it reason enough to justify her feelings toward him? Why did it feel like he was the only good thing in her life and like his presence would solve all of her problems—even though he had caused many of them?

I wish he were here now, but I also wish I'd never met him.

Alice tried to put her feelings in order, to understand them, but now, with the grief over losing the baby, everything appeared even more complicated. She was convinced she didn't love Jonas, but she couldn't deny that he made her nervous and she felt drawn to him like a magnet. At the same time though, she despised him for what he had done.

Can I really blame him for what Danny did?

Maybe Jonas had just been oblivious to what Danny did to her behind closed doors. Maybe he simply hadn't grasped the full extent of what was going on. Or did he just not care? The latter seemed impossible though, especially after witnessing his demeanor in the hospital ...

All in all, Alice knew she had to be careful not to blame Jonas for everything. Danny's actions were Danny's actions, and even though Jonas could have prevented them and didn't, it did not make him fully responsible for what happened.

The sudden movement of the door handle being pushed downward made Alice flinch, and her heart seemed to almost jump out of her throat and kept racing, even when she realized it was only Viktor coming into her room. She quickly took her eyes off him and stared down at her blanket.

"Good to see you're awake." He stepped into the room and placed a tray with food on her dresser. "I was almost scared I gave you too much of that IV."

Even without looking at him, she knew he was giving her his ugly grin. Why couldn't he just leave her alone? Her life was miserable enough without him.

"I'll tell the boss you're up."

"No," Alice said quickly. "I don't want to see him."

Viktor shrugged indifferently. "I'm pretty sure he wants to see *you*." He walked out of her room and closed the door behind him.

Still, Alice's heart kept racing, and her hands felt ice-cold and tingly.

Not Danny, not now ... not after what he's done ...

Thinking of the baby made her tear up and she let the drops of salty water drip down onto the hospital shirt she was still wearing.

I'm doomed to spend the rest of my life with him.

Perhaps she could at least affect how long that was going to be.

Alice took a deep breath and tried to ignore the pain when she pulled herself up on the wall and staggered out of bed, keeping her blanket wrapped around her shoulders. Despite the hospital shirt she felt incredibly naked, and the thought of Viktor and Jean-Pierre carrying her out of the hospital made her shiver. Had they even put her to bed or had that been Danny? At least she knew that with his injured arm, Viktor could not have carried her—but Jean-Pierre wasn't much better. After being intimate with Jonas, she had grown accustomed to being touched by him, even when wearing nothing more than a shirt, but with Jean-Pierre and Viktor—especially Viktor—this was a whole different story. It was an intrusion into her privacy right after Danny had intruded her body. What was there left to fight for with her dignity having been taken from her more than once?

Huddled in her blanket, she stumbled toward the window and sat down on the sill. The left side of her face was swollen, and she could barely see through her eye. To ease the pain, she leaned her head against the cold glass of the window, cooling the wounds Danny had yet again given her.

The continuously flowing tears made her raw skin burn, and Alice inhaled sharply and tried to fight them.

The outside air was misty, and parts of the window were clouded up by frost. The orange light coming from the guard's hut brought warmth to the scenery and gave it and almost Christmas-like look. But it was only November and no snow had fallen so far. Nevertheless, a peaceful silence covered the yard, and it seemed as if the world had stopped rotating and time had come to a halt. Alice's grief made room for a weird kind of calmness, which began spreading through her veins until every part of her body felt numb and her mind was completely empty.

She knew it would not take long until Danny would come to see her, but the thought of it seemed distant and strange, almost as if someone else were thinking it.

When the door finally opened, she barely heard it and though his presence brought a cold with it that seemed to freeze the air around her, she didn't even shiver. She kept her head leaned against the glass and her eyes on the yard, and watched a car appear in the distance and approach the house. Its headlights enlightened the gravel road before it and grew bigger, until the vehicle reached the gate.

When he spoke, his words sounded hollow and distant, and the thick fog in her mind made it impossible for her to understand what he was saying. She heard the words "sorry" and "forgive me" and the nickname he always used on her, "Allie".

The guard opened the big iron gate, and the car drove through it and onto the gravel space next to the other cars, where it came to a halt. Its dark gray varnish made it almost invisible in the darkness.

"Allie?" his voice called, louder this time.

The thick fog evaporated slowly and made his words boom like thunder in her head. A stabbing pain flashed through her skull, and she winced and squeezed her eyes shut, just as a tall, dark shape emerged from the car down in the yard.

She breathed out through her mouth to make the pain go away, and her breath clouded up the glass.

"Allie, I'm so sorry ... I didn't know ... the baby ..." His voice was husky, and she heard him sob.

"You killed it," she whispered, more to herself than to him.

"What? Allie, I can't hear you ..."

"You killed her," she repeated, louder this time.

He inhaled sharply and another sob escaped his throat. "I didn't ... I didn't know ... You never told me ..."

"And if I had told you, if you had known I was pregnant, you wouldn't have done what you did? Is that what you're saying?" The words came out slowly, dragging. Speaking was hard, especially to him. Alice kept her eyes on the now empty yard below. The shape had disappeared into the house.

"No ... I ... I shouldn't have ... not at all ..."

"But you did and now she's gone. You killed her; you killed our baby ... our daughter."

That made him break down. A dull *thump* revealed that he had dropped to his knees and by the sounds coming from him, she supposed he was shaken by sobs.

He really is sorry about what he's done ... until he's drunk or high again.

"I'm a monster," he sobbed.

"I agree."

"Allie, I'm so sorry! I wasn't myself; I wasn't thinking clearly ... I was drunk and stupid and—"

"And you'll be drunk and stupid again. Nothing has changed and I doubt it ever will."

The light coming from the guard's hut flickered. It sent another wave of pain through her forehead, but she kept her head turned away from Danny and closed her eyes. Danny said nothing and she heard him sob, but then a sudden thought made her turn to face him.

"How do you know about the baby?"

His face was pale and the area around his eyes was red and swollen from crying. He cringed at the sight of her swollen face, and she saw a mixture of guilt and regret flicker over his features.

"I ... I got a call from ... from a friend of Waldo's. At the station ... He said they had an arrest warrant for me and ... well, he told me why." He sniffed and wiped his eyes with the back of his hand.

"But you didn't get arrested."

He shook his head. "He made the warrant ... well, he made it disappear."

"How good for you." Alice turned her head back to the window. Looking at him made her feel nauseous. She heard him get back to his feet and flatten his pants.

"Did you call the police?" He sounded hurt, despite everything.

Alice chose not to answer and kept her eyes on the scenery outside, until a knock on the door startled her and made her turn her head. Both she and Danny stared at the door in silence until it was opened slowly.

Jonas stepped into the room hesitantly, and Alice felt herself blush and quickly averted her eyes.

"Where were you? I called you like a hundred times," Danny asked.

Jonas hesitated and she felt his gaze on her, but then he cleared his throat and answered, "In jail."

An awkward silence followed his words and Alice felt Danny's eyes on her, but she refused to look up.

"You brought her to the hospital, didn't you?"

Jonas said nothing, but Alice imagined him nodding.

"Thank you," Danny said, his voice firmer than when he had talked to her.

Another moment of silence passed, and then Danny cleared his throat. "We were talking."

Alice looked up and saw Jonas turn around, understanding Danny's remark as an order to leave.

"No," she said quickly. "I'm done talking to you. Why don't you just leave me alone?"

A desperate look in his eyes, Danny stared at her. His expression was pained and pleading, but then he shoved Jonas aside and left the room.

Jonas remained standing with his back toward her, his hand on the door handle, like he was thinking about leaving as well.

"Stay ... please," Alice muttered.

He pushed the door shut with almost no sound at all, and slowly turned, eyes on the floor.

Looking at him made her tear up anew, and she felt the urge to bury her face underneath his jacket and lean her head against his chest.

"Jonas?" Her voice was shaking when she called his name, and when he looked up, she saw that his eyes were glazed and he looked very worn-out and exhausted. Still, his stare was piercing as always, and Alice blinked away her tears and dropped her gaze, suddenly feeling nervous.

"It ... she was yours; you know ..."

"I know." His voice was higher than usual and thinner. "They told me ... after sticking a cotton bud in my mouth."

Alice hid her face behind her arms and rested her chin on her knees. It was still hard to believe she had been pregnant with Jonas's child, and she tried to imagine what would have happened if the pregnancy had proceeded. Somehow, having carried his child made her feel more affectionate toward him.

"Sorry they arrested you," she said quietly, without lifting her head from her knees. "I didn't want that to happen. I ... I told the doctor that the baby's father had ... and I never thought—"

"I know," he interrupted her softly. "Don't apologize."

She heard him cross the room, his steps soft and quiet, and then he was by her side and she smelled leather and smoke. He put a hand on her shoulder and his touch made more tears run down her face and soak into the blanket she had wrapped around herself.

"I wanted to save her from him, that's why I tried to run away." The words came out in between sobs, and she felt him squeeze her shoulder softly.

"I wanted her to have a life outside of these walls and now ... now she doesn't have a life at all. I ruined everything."

"No ... don't say that, don't take any blame." Jonas bent down to hug her, and Alice leaned her head against his shoulder gratefully. He held her carefully, afraid of hurting her and yet, his embrace was firm.

"I'm sorry, Alice. I'm the one who kept you here. It's my fault." His voice was full of contempt and regret. "I'm so sorry," he said again, and she looked up and saw tears in his eyes.

Seeing him like that was overwhelming. To see the big strong guy, who had always seemed like a steady rock, dissolved in tears. The man who had shot a person without hesitating and had made jokes afterward was now shedding tears on her shoulder, and it seemed she was comforting him as much as he was comforting her. Pulling him closer, she nestled up to him.

"It's *his* fault, Jonas. Not yours."

He said nothing, and she knew he wouldn't stop blaming himself. Ever. Alice didn't even know if she had stopped blaming him. All she knew was that she didn't want to be angry at him right now.

"I'm sorry for what I said the other day," she muttered into the collar of his jacket.

"Hm?"

She pulled out of the embrace; suddenly afraid someone might see them through the window. A quick glance through the glass revealed that the yard was still empty, and the guard would probably not see them through the fogged-up window of his hut.

"About hating you more than him … or hating you in general." Alice began wiping the glass with an edge of the blanket and let her eyes wander through the yard. It was hard to see much with the room being illuminated.

"Oh, come on," he said softly. "You love to hate me."

Shaking her head, Alice watched the guard leave his hut, probably on his way to the toilet.

"No," she replied, eyes still on the guard. "It's the other way around."

Jonas said nothing and she froze, suddenly aware of what she had said.

That came out wrong.

She felt his intense stare on her and was afraid to turn back around to face him. "I … I didn't mean … I mean, I don't …" she stammered, still avoiding his eyes. Then she sighed and leaned her forehead back against the glass. "I don't know what I mean."

"I know," he said quietly.

"You do?"

"No. I mean I know that you don't know."

Alice squeezed her eyes shut once more, trying to calm her racing thoughts and thinking of something to say.

"I'm confused," she finally admitted.

"I know," he said again.

For a while, they said nothing, Alice keeping her eyes closed but feeling him watching her. Her head kept throbbing where Danny had hit her and cramps kept going through her lower belly, but they were weaker than before.

"Why did you come back?" she broke the silence, at last looking at him again. "Is this still what you want? Is he still your friend, even after what he's done?"

Jonas bit his lip and gave her an intense look, hesitating and thinking of an answer. "I came back for you," he finally answered.

"Did you go back to the hospital?"

He nodded. "But that's not what I mean, Alice. I've been fed up with Danny since last spring when he almost killed me."

"You thought about leaving, didn't you?"

"Yes. And I did. But then I thought of you and what he had said, and I was worried he might kill you." Sighing, he sat down on the couch beside the windowsill.

"I didn't want to leave you alone with him." Again, his stare seemed to pierce right into her and made her belly tingle, despite the pain.

"He ... he was nicer during the summer," Alice muttered.

"Yes ... I noticed and I thought he had changed." Jonas put a hand on her foot and grimaced. "I didn't talk to him like you told me to. I should have known nothing had changed."

"He was only nice to me because I was sick. He treated me like a porcelain doll, but that was actually a good thing." She watched his thumb trace the line of her naked foot down to the toes and flinched when it tickled.

"You were pregnant," he muttered, more to himself than to her.

Alice nodded. "I didn't want him to know .... I doubt he would've let me out of his sight again. I did consider telling *you* though."

His hand twitched and he froze, eyes still on her foot.

"But I wasn't sure if I could trust you ... and then Viktor locked my room and I couldn't talk to you anyway," she added.

His expression darkened, and she knew he was thinking back to the day she had shot Viktor. The day, he had kept her from running away and proved once again that he could not be trusted. She wondered what her life would be like now if he had let her go. The baby would still be alive, and she would have surely found shelter somewhere Danny couldn't find her. A sudden rush of anger toward him went through her, and she quickly tried to suppress it.

I don't want to be mad at him, he's the only one who's nice to me.

Jonas seemed to perceive her change of mood and pulled his hand back, leaving a warm spot on her skin where he had touched her.

"I'm sorry," he muttered.

Alice said nothing and turned her head back to the window. The guard was back in his hut and judging by the blue, flickering light coming through his window, he was watching TV.

"What's your plan?" Jonas asked after a moment of silence.

She shrugged. "There is no plan. I'm done making plans ... it's not worth it."

He shifted uncomfortably.

"Just do whatever you want to do, Jonas, and stop worrying about me."

"Sounds like you've given up." His voice was tinged with sadness.

"Yeah well ... maybe I have."

"You shouldn't."

Sighing, she turned to look at him. His bright, intense eyes made her guts tingle, but Alice fought the warm feeling that threatened to spread through her.

"If you want to leave, leave. Please. Don't stay here because of me."

He stared down at his hands and said nothing.

"However," she continued, "*If* you decide to stay ... please don't leave me alone. I'm going crazy when I can't talk to anybody."

Jonas looked up and took her hand, squeezing it firmly. "I won't. I promise."

Danny gave up trying to make up with her after several failed attempts, and decided to give her space instead, hoping time might heal her emotional wounds as well as the physical. He even pulled Viktor from the job, like she had requested, and now only Jean-Pierre brought the food to her room. Alice was still not allowed to leave it and tried to distract herself from thinking about the baby by leaving the TV on at all times. Still, her thoughts kept spinning around the same old, depressing topic of how to end her life once and for all, but the courage she had felt when she had pulled the trigger on herself had left her completely. Somehow, though she didn't know why, she felt as if she owed it to Jonas to stay alive.

He kept his distance while Danny was around, but when Danny and the others went on another trip to prepare everything for the move to who knew where, Jonas began visiting her in her room every day.

It was comforting to have him around, although after that emotional evening of her return from the hospital they acted strangely distant toward one another and refrained from touching. It was still nice to have him there and watch movies with him or simply talk about stuff. Jean-Pierre, who was still home to keep an eye on them, didn't appear to be too interested in what they were doing. Other than Viktor, he didn't feel the need to make Alice's life more miserable and report to Danny about Jonas and her spending time together, so they felt safe enough to do so.

25

November made room for December and temperatures stayed at freezing point. But still, no snow was in sight, and Danny called, saying that he would not be back for Alice's birthday—for which she was glad.

Not that her twenty-second birthday meant more than her twenty-first had—it only made her more depressed because it reminded her of how much time she had already lived in that house. Time would not stop flying by, no matter what happened.

On the morning of her birthday however, Jonas knocked on her door and the sound of it yanked her out of a troubled sleep. Confused, she blinked at him as he closed the door behind him and sat on the edge of her bed.

"Why did you wake me?" she moaned, shielding her eyes with her arm.

"I thought we could go to town."

Frowning, Alice studied his expression, trying to decide if he was joking. "You for real?"

He nodded.

She pushed herself up on her elbows and stared at him. He was dressed as always: gray T-shirt, black leather jacket, and ripped jeans, and his brown hair was tousled. He scratched his unshaven chin nervously, still feeling uncomfortable in her presence, even after all that time they'd spent together.

"I thought we can't leave? Jean-Pierre—"

"Needs money," Jonas finished the sentence.

"You bribed him?"

He shrugged. "We gotta be back before dusk."

Alice sat in his car, showered and dressed in a thick black hoodie and winter coat; her long hair bound back into a braid. Her face was almost back to normal. The swelling had gone down but there were still purple-yellowish areas around her left eye. She glanced out the window nervously, watching the guard unlock the gate on Jonas's order. Somehow, realizing how easy it was to leave the house with Jonas's help made her sad.

When he stepped on the gas pedal and rushed the car out onto the gravel road, she turned around to watch the house grow smaller behind her. Excitement arose in her, mixed with fear.

The naked trees rushed by in a blur, and the empty fields were covered with swarms of crows, picking at the frozen dirt, looking for food.

Jonas lit a cigarette and Alice reached for the pack and took one for herself.

"I thought you'd stopped?" he asked her while handing her the lighter.

"I had to ... but I don't anymore." She inhaled the smoke deeply, eagerly as if it were oxygen. It burned in her throat and made her cough.

"Oh ... right." Jonas frowned.

When the fields were replaced by houses and traffic got dense, he stopped the car in front of a gas station and turned to look at her.

"Where d'you like to go?"

"Um ..." Alice stared at the big Shell sign above her. "I thought you'd decide."

"It's *your* birthday."

"Is it?"

He nodded.

"Oh ... I forgot about that."

"How about lunch?" he suggested.

"That would be brunch, but yeah, why not."

"Brunch, lunch ... as long as it involves food, I'm good." He gave her a crooked smile. "So, where d'you like to eat?"

She shrugged indifferently. "A place with food?"

"Sounds like a plan." Jonas started the car and pulled off the parking space and back onto the road. He drove down the busy main road, past its shops and restaurants and toward the mall, where he parked the car in the underground Parkhouse.

They took the escalator up, and Alice found herself being drowned in a flood of people, noise, and Christmas decorations. She grimaced and automatically shifted closer to Jonas.

"What's wrong?" he asked her.

"I hate premature Christmas decorating."

"It's December seventh, it's not that premature."

"Anything before the twenty-fourth is premature."

He grinned. "Good to see you still got your humor."

"There's nothing humorous about people putting their children on the lap of a fat old man in a red suit and taking pictures of their crying faces."

Jonas gave her a meaningful look but left the statement unanswered. "Wanna go to McDonald's?" he suggested.

"I'd prefer eating something with more nutritional benefits than the cardboard box it's served in."

Smirking, Jonas gestured toward a Thai restaurant and Alice nodded affirmatively. "That looks good."

They sat down at a table in the corner, which was shielded by a bunch of plants. An aquarium was bubbling between two potted palm trees, its fish colorful and exotic looking. They were swimming around vividly, looking to escape their glass cage.

Alice watched them for a while, feeling sad for them, while Jonas was busy reading the menu and deciding what he wanted to eat.

"How 'bout we share some vegetable spring rolls as starter?" he proposed.

"Yeah ... sounds good."

"It's a very lunchy brunch, but you don't mind, right?"

Eyes still on the fish, she shook her head. "I usually eat lunch for breakfast."

"I noticed. One might think you've got narcolepsy."

"I just like to sleep." She took her eyes from the fish tank and looked at him. "You don't sleep much, do you?"

He grimaced. "I'll sleep when I'm dead."

"I consider sleep to be a very valuable part of life. I'd sleep even if I didn't have to."

"No nightmares anymore?"

"Sometimes ... but I wake up from them if they get too extreme." She sighed. "Life doesn't work that way."

Jonas said nothing and just stared at her, and something in his eyes made her look down at the menu. She wasn't sure if he was just compassionate or if he pitied her or worried about her, but his gaze made her feel uncomfortable.

A waiter came by to take their order and Alice quickly let her eyes wander over the card in her hands. Nothing seemed very appealing, even though she usually loved Thai food.

"Vegetable spring rolls to share and seafood fried rice, please," Jonas told the waiter. Then his eyes flicked to Alice. "Or ... do you mind? I can get something vegetarian instead."

Alice rolled her eyes at him. "You may eat whatever you like, I don't mind. Although *they* might." She pointed at the fish in the tank right next to them.

For a moment, Jonas stared at the fish, his expression unreadable, then he turned back to the waiter. "Make that tofu fried rice instead, please."

Despite the tension inside of her, Alice chuckled, and Jonas smiled as well. The waiter scribbled down his order and turned to look at her.

"Uh ... for me the small tofu-noodle-soup, please ... and a beer."

Nodding, the waiter jotted that down as well and walked away.

"Back to drinking?" Jonas asked.

"Don't judge."

"I'm not."

"Just saying. I don't usually get the chance." She started fingering a paper napkin, which was stuffed into a cheap plastic container on the table.

A group of teenage girls at the table next to them was chattering in a nerve-racking manner and Alice felt her headache return. She rubbed her temples with her knuckles.

"You're moody," Jonas pointed out.

"I know ... sorry," she muttered.

"I thought you'd be more euphoric about leaving the house."

Sighing, Alice pushed the napkin holder away from her. "Yeah, me too."

"What's wrong?"

"Everything's wrong ... For more than a year, all I wanted was to leave that house. Now I'm here and I don't see the point anymore."

"Of what?"

"Of being outside ... with people ... they're annoying and loud, and there's so many of them. And I just don't feel like I belong here anymore. There's so much noise ... and colors and ads and screens ... you must think I'm crazy."

The waiter reappeared and placed a big plate with spring rolls in between them as well as Alice's beer. Jonas thanked him and put some hot sauce on the plate to dip the rolls in.

"Hasn't it always been like that?" he asked.

Alice stared at the spring rolls. They were oily and shiny and crispy brownish, and they did not look the least bit appealing to her. She took one and turned it over in her hand, burning her fingertips on the hot grease.

"Yeah, it has ..." she admitted hesitantly. "But it never bothered me before."

"Look," Jonas said and put the spring roll he'd been about to eat back down on the plate. "You've been locked in a house for months with no one around but the same five or six faces every day. You're not used to this anymore and it will take time to adjust ... There's nothing wrong with you."

"That was a long sentence for you."

He grinned. "Right. Don't make me say it again."

They ate quietly for a while, but Alice didn't feel much like eating and only managed two rolls. Jonas finished the plate for her, and the waiter came to collect their dirty dishes.

The group of girls was still talking in a way that the whole restaurant could hear them, and an elderly couple sitting near the entrance gave them an irritated scowl once in a while.

"Teenagers are annoying," Alice grumbled.

"We were all teenagers once."

"I was never like that."

"Sure." He grinned.

"No, really. I was very mature."

"Tell me about it."

"You too?"

"No. I mean, tell me about it."

Alice hesitated. "There's not much to tell, really ... I just had more important things to worry about than the newest smartphones or makeup, or what bikini to wear at the public pool."

"I bet you were busy smashing windows." He winked at her.

"Why?"

"I heard you were a punk."

Alice took a sip of her beer and grimaced. "Still am in some ways. But that's stereotyping. I was busy looking for a job and when I found one, I was busy working."

"Are we talking about your teenage years now?"

"Yeah, why?"

"What about school?"

She shrugged. "I needed money. Got my first full-time job at fourteen, waiting tables. Was definitely faster than *that* guy." She glanced at their waiter, who was busy flirting with a coworker.

"How's the beer?" Jonas asked.

"Good."

"Why did you work so early?"

"I had to. Needed to pay the rent, didn't I?"

"Didn't you live at home?"

"You're asking a lot of questions today."

"Wanna get to know you."

Alice took another sip of her beer and kept it in her mouth for a moment to truly savor its taste.

"Never knew my dad. Mom was a drunken skank."

"Sounds like you like her."

"I hated her."

"She dead?"

"She's dead to me."

Jonas hesitated and again, he looked at her in a way that made her feel uncomfortable.

"So ... you left home early?" he finally asked.

"Yeah, at fourteen."

"Never saw her again?"

Alice shook her head and chugged the rest of her beer.

"That's tough."

"Nope, it was actually a very good time in my life." She waved at the waiter.

"Trying to make him bring the food faster?" Jonas asked.

"Nope. I want another beer."

They watched the waiter come over and Alice gave her order.

"Don't you want to drink something?" she asked Jonas.

"Right ... a water please, sparkling," he told the waiter.

"Oooh," Alice teased him. "Sparkling, is it? Somebody's feeling adventurous today."

The waiter brought their beverages and returned to the kitchen to fetch the main course. Alice took a big gulp of her second beer.

"Back to your old self?" Jonas asked.

"I doubt I'll ever be." Her eyes wandered back to the fish tank and another wave of sadness went through her. "What's my old self anyway, according to you? We haven't known each other that long."

Jonas took a sip of his water and wiped the fog off his glass with his index finger. "Well ... you were more ... sarcastic. And you seemed more confident ..." He fell silent.

Alice noticed that he was avoiding her eyes. "I *was* confident. I knew what I wanted. Beer was only a very small part of my life, you know. And I never drank as much as ... *him*."

"Sorry."

"Don't be. He changed me. He made me fucking weak and I hate him for that." She let out a sigh and drank some more beer. "But the thing is, I can't even truly hate him because that's so exhausting and I'm too damn weak to hold a grudge."

The waiter returned with their dishes, but Jonas didn't touch his fork. He was busy staring at her the way he did so often, as if he were reading a book.

Alice dove her spoon into her soup and stirred it to make it cool down faster.

"Do you regret meeting him?" Jonas wanted to know.

Biting her lip, she thought about it. "I don't know. No ... not really. I mean, we had almost two great years together, you know. He made me really happy."

"He seemed like a good guy," Jonas agreed.

"He seemed perfect. I found my home in him after never truly having had one. He was, well, older and he had that calm way of looking at things, like he believed everything was manageable. He always made me feel safe, made me feel like nothing bad would ever happen again. I guess I was just too blinded to see the red flags ... if there were any."

Jonas picked up his fork and started picking at his rice.

Alice sighed and took a sip of her beer. "And then he changed."

She took a spoonful of soup and blew the steam away, then put it in her mouth. It burned her tongue nonetheless.

Jonas was still staring at his food and said nothing.

"How was your friendship?" she asked him curiously.

He looked up at her and seemed to think for a moment before he answered. "Uncomplicated. I liked hanging out with him."

Alice grimaced. "A lot has changed."

He nodded. "It's the business. It was too much pressure from the start."

"Only for him? What about you?"

"We're different."

"I know ... but how?"

Jonas sighed. "He was too sensitive. He had two options, either give up or adjust."

"He adjusted," Alice concluded tonelessly.

"Yeah. Started drinking to suppress his emotions."

"And you?"

"I don't drink."

"No, I mean ... how do you handle it?"

"I was never a good person like him. I never cared. I've always been ... an asshole."

"Don't say that."

"It's true," he insisted, then grinned. "You said it yourself."

Blushing, Alice looked down at her soup, which was still steaming. "Maybe I changed my mind," she said quietly.

"You shouldn't."

"Why? I like spending time with you."

"Only because you got no alternatives. I'm not a good guy just because I'm nice to you, Alice." His voice was suddenly very firm, and she looked up, taken aback.

"You're ... very influenceable and vulnerable at the moment, and I don't want to take advantage of that," he added.

"But you're not," Alice protested.

"I don't want you to like me just because I treat you nicer than the others do."

"That's an understatement. You're really helping me."

"If I were helping you, I would have let you go the first time you attempted to leave Danny."

Alice bit her tongue hard and stared at the table. It was true, of course, there was so much more he could have done for her, but did that really matter? He was the only one who was nice to her and it was only natural she liked him for that, wasn't it? But somehow, she could understand what he meant and why he didn't want her to. She *was* easily influenced, all right, and she was reaching for the thinnest thread to pull herself out of her misery, even if chances were high it might tear.

"You're not taking advantage of me," she said stubbornly. "I'm taking advantage of *you*."

Jonas sighed and his expression got softer. "I just don't want to hurt you. There's already enough people doing that."

Alice felt her heartbeat accelerate at once and something cold trickled down her spine. Jonas's words were salt in her still fresh wounds.

"Right. The damage is already done. Nothing you can do to make it worse. Unless ... everything I thought about you is wrong and you're only pretending to care." She took a deep breath. "Like what you said that day I got drunk with Timothy ... *That* was hurtful."

"I'm sorry for that," Jonas said. "You were ... getting too attached—according to *him*—so I tried to push you away."

"Yeah, I noticed. Your rice is getting cold by the way."

Jonas started eating, but he didn't seem to be very hungry all of a sudden. He merely picked at his food.

"I don't care enough about people," he muttered.

"How nice."

"It's not ... beneficial to care about others if you want to be successful. I just don't feel much for other people."

"That's a lie," Alice objected. "I'm sure you loved your sister."

He winced at that remark. "Of course I did. I mean afterward."

"But you liked Danny."

"Okay, let me put it this way: I don't care about people I don't know."

"Is that why it was so easy for you to shoot Martin?"

"I suppose so ..."

"So you don't care when people you don't know get killed?" Alice looked at him with wide eyes, somehow dreading his answer.

"Of course not," he said quickly. "Unless they deserve it."

"And who deserves it?"

"People who hurt *you*, for example." He looked at her in a way that made her blush and she quickly dropped her gaze.

"So ... would you kill *him*?" she asked quietly.

He frowned. "Is that what you want?"

"No, of course not! I don't want him to die ... despite what he's done."

"You still love him?"

Alice felt herself blush even more and quickly drank some more beer, hoping for it to cool her down. "No ... I'm not sure. But no, I think I'm finally over him.

I mean, all this time I was still in love with his old self. But it's gone. It doesn't exist anymore. I just need to remember that." She sighed. "But I still don't want him to die."

"Of course, you don't. You're a good person."

"Don't say that. There is no good or bad, and just because I don't want people to die doesn't mean I'm a saint or something."

"Nope." He took a sip of his water. "But it shows you have a good heart."

"I almost shot you when you were in my way."

"But you didn't."

"But I shot Viktor."

"He deserved it. And he's still alive."

"Yeah ... I should have aimed at his heart."

"You wanted to warn him and shot his arm. If you had aimed at his heart, you might have actually hit the wall." He winked at her mockingly.

"I hit the wall when I wanted to warn *you*."

"I suppose I was lucky." A wide grin parted his lips.

Alice stared at her soup and hesitated before asking, "How did you know I couldn't shoot you?"

"It was a wild assumption." Jonas loaded some rice and tofu onto his fork and put it in his mouth. Alice watched him chew and noticed he was avoiding her eyes again.

"That's not a serious answer."

"No," he affirmed, then he paused. "I ... I thought you liked me, for whatever reason."

"Because I'm too emotional and you were too nice to me and I'm an open book."

He looked up. "Are you reciting what I said?"

"Yup."

"Sorry for that." He smirked apologetically.

"Why? You're right ... about everything." Alice started to wind some noodles onto her fork.

"No." He shook his head sadly. "You're not too emotional, you just have a good heart."

"So that's why I like you?"

"No. You like me because you're naïve."

"Thanks."

"It's not meant to be an insult. You just have that ... innocent way of looking at the world, like you expect to find something good in everybody."

"Isn't there something good in everybody?" Alice put the fork load of noodles into her mouth and started chewing.

Jonas shrugged. "Wouldn't count on it. Not everybody deserves a second chance."

Alice swallowed and studied his expression. "You mean ... *him?*"

He said nothing.

"Are you accusing me of being too nice to him?" Taken over by a sudden rush of anger, she glared at him.

"I'm not accusing you of anything."

"Yes, you are! You think I'm naïve for falling for his act over and over again."

Jonas returned her gaze and his eyes looked big and sad and knowing, somehow.

"You have no idea," she said in a trembling voice, and rammed her fork back into her bowl to stab a piece of broccoli.

"No," he agreed. "I'm sorry."

"All I wanted, from day one, was to get out of that house. But I couldn't. It was bad enough as it was. If I had held a grudge against him, it would have been unbearable! He was the only one there, the only one to ever talk to me! What the hell was I supposed to do?"

"You don't have to explain yourself to me."

"Yes, I do!" She glared at him, and then looked down at the broccoli on her fork and sighed. "Somehow, I feel like I do."

Jonas leaned forward, and to her surprise, he put his hand on hers.

"I'm an idiot," he said quietly.

"Yes, you are ... but you're not an asshole."

He smiled warmly and then pulled his hand back and continued eating.

They finished their meals, and when the waiter came to collect the dishes, Alice got up to go to the bathroom. The beer was showing its effect—in her bladder as well as in her mind—and she even felt a bit dizzy. No wonder, after months of not drinking at all.

When she returned to the table, Jonas was just paying the bill. Alice sat back down opposite him and grimaced. "Sorry."

Confused, he looked up. "What for?"

"For letting you pay ... again. I still owe you money."

"Why?"

"You know, when Aaron paid for my drinks and you had to pay him back because I had no cash."

Jonas frowned. "Who?"

"The guy I was talking to in the Shipwreck."

"Ah, that kid."

"He was no kid; he was about your age."

"Really?"

"Yeah, Jonas. You may look a bit older—must be the smoking by the way—but you shouldn't forget you're quite young yourself."

He grimaced. "But that kid was small."

Alice rolled her eyes at him. "He was a bit taller than me, even. Not everyone's blessed with yours or *his* height."

"No one's blessed with Danny's height except Danny, and I doubt that's a blessing at all." He grinned.

"Well aren't you funny," she said coolly. "Anyway, I'm sorry for not being able to pay you back."

"Don't be ridiculous, you got no money. Besides, I'm paid by Danny, so it's practically yours."

Alice winced, like every time she heard Danny's name. Hearing it sent a stabbing pain through her guts. "We're not married."

"Nah, but he put you in that situation. Least he can do is pay for you." Jonas got up from his chair. "Plus, it's your birthday."

Alice got up as well and grabbed her coat from the empty chair next to hers. "Don't mention it," she grumbled.

"Why not? It's a nice age."

"Yeah, twenty-two has a nice ring to it, but I was twenty when I moved into that damned house, and I can't believe nothing's changed." She felt her mood get darker again and glanced back at the aquarium with its sad and caged fish.

They're just like me. Swimming against the glass, desperately trying to get out, but all they do is bash their heads.

Jonas put a hand on her shoulder and led her to the door of the restaurant, past the group of still noisily chattering teenage girls.

They stopped in front of the escalators and watched the other people for a moment. Most of them looked like desperate parents, hurrying from shop to shop to find the right Christmas presents for their spoiled brats.

"How can I lighten up your mood?" Jonas asked.

Alice shrugged. "Get me another drink, maybe."

His hand was still on her shoulder and he gave it a squeeze. "I'll get you coffee."

"Lots of caramel! And soy milk, please," she called after him as he strolled over to a nearby coffee-place.

Alice sat down on a yellow metal bench next to a small fountain and listened to the soft sounds of the water gurgling behind her, once in a while only disturbed by the high-pitched giggles of a small child who was playing with it, when suddenly, something caught her eye, and her heart skipped a beat.

It can't be ...

Jill and Leah were standing on one of the escalators, on their way down from the upper floor. They looked different from what Alice remembered. Jill had cut her reddish-brown hair at her shoulders and Leah had straightened her light blond curls so that her hair was now flat and shiny.

They were dressed in winter coats and thick scarfs and carrying loads of shopping bags.

Shocked and unable to move, Alice stared at them until Jill spotted her and tapped Leah's shoulder in excitement.

It's been more than a year ... what am I supposed to say to them?

What if they were mad at her?

She watched in horror, as they reached the bottom of the escalator and Jill hurried toward her, dragging Leah along. Slowly and feeling stiff, Alice got off the bench and, realizing Jill was beaming, she managed to smile half-heartedly. Jill flung her arms around her and knocked all air out of her lungs. Squeaking enthusiastically, she pulled back, still beaming, and her hazelnut eyes scanned Alice from head to toe.

"Oh my freaking Goodness, I cannot believe it! What are you doing here? It's been so long, jeez, Alice, where have you been? Have you lost weight? Gosh you're skinny, what did you do? I'm trying to lose some pounds, but it's just so hard—especially this time of the year. But here you are, making it look easy!"

"I ... uh," Alice stammered and looked at Leah, who appeared to be a bit more suspicious.

"We tried calling you, you know," she complained in a cold voice.

"I know ... I'm so sorry—"

"Gosh, Alice, you missed out on so much!" Jill blurted out. "Leah's got a boyfriend now; can you believe it? A boyfriend! And here I thought she'd die a virgin, but let's be honest, a girl with her hair and her killer blue eyes—we all knew that day would come. Who could resist her? Though I admit I'm a bit jealous 'cause you know, since Chris broke up, I've been looking for guys *everywhere*, but they always turn out to be assholes on the second date. Oh, her boyfriend's name is Jared by the way, and she calls him Jar-Jar." Jill burst out laughing.

"Uh ..." Alice tried to process what her friend was saying, but her brain was working too slowly for the flow of words that rolled over her like an avalanche. Jill let go of Alice's shoulders and touched her overgrown bangs instead, which reached down to her chin by now.

"New hairstyle? I always told you to outgrow that stupid fringe. Bangs are so outdated, and without the red tips it looked way too nice for you, not punky at all. You know, you should definitely go back to some special color—what about blue for a change? Though I envy you for your natural hair color. I was actually considering going a bit darker myself." She let her fingers wander down Alice's braid and gasped. "Lord, look at how long your hair is! When's the last time you've seen a hairdresser?"

Alice smiled weakly. "I like it long." She noticed Leah was still eyeing her with suspicion in her icy blue eyes, and it made her feel uncomfortable.

"And who is *that*?" Jill asked, eyes on Jonas, who had just reappeared with two big cups of coffee and seemed to be puzzled by the scene before him. He handed one cup to Alice and his eyes swiveled from her to her friends and back.

"You got a new boyfriend? And I thought you'd end up being buried next to Danny. I mean, I know you guys were having problems, but still, you were so perfect for each other ... and who would break up with a guy like him? Unless ..." Her eyes scanned Jonas from head to toe. "Who could blame you?" Grinning, she held out a hand to Jonas.

He shook it hesitantly.

"I'm Jill," she said, beaming.

"Jonas," Alice said quickly. "He's just a friend."

"Oh, so you *are* still with Danny?"

Alice felt herself blush. "Sort of."

"Ah, needn't say more, girl, I understand." She winked. "Everybody needs a little variety once in a while." She patted Jonas's arm, who appeared to be speechless.

"No," Alice objected. "It's not like that."

"So, he's single?" Jill chuckled and winked at Jonas. "Just kidding, of course." Leah put a hand on her shoulder and Jill fell silent at once.

"What happened to your eye?" Leah asked with a mixture of concern and suspicion in her voice.

Alice's hand jerked to her face and it took her a moment until she understood that Leah must have noticed her purple eye. After not having done so for months now, Alice hadn't even considered putting on makeup. Now, she blushed even more.

"Oh, that's nothing. Just hit my head."

"On a fist?" Leah asked coldly.

Alice let out a nervous laugh. "No ... I uh, was drunk. At a party ... and tripped."

"Still the partygoer I remember?" Jill asked, grinning widely. "I missed you. Leah's just not really the outgoing type and I'm in desperate need of a man. And where to find them if not in bars or clubs?"

Alice took a sip of her coffee to avoid having to answer but burned her lips on the still steaming hot liquid.

"Where have you been?" Leah asked, still in that cool tone. Her cold blue eyes were slightly narrowed, and Alice felt her throat tighten under her stare. A thousand thoughts flashed through her mind at once. After giving up all hopes of ever seeing her friends again, here they were now, standing right in front of her, and as expected, they had questions.

Nervously, she glanced at Jonas, who just stood there and stared at the coffee cup in his hands.

Six months ago, Alice would have looked for an opportunity to tell her friends the truth, to maybe ask them for help. She would have wanted nothing more than walk away with them and never ever return to Danny. Now though, there was so much to consider. Danny was dangerous and Jill and Leah were the first people he would turn to, to look for her. How far would he go to get her back? He was not per se a bad person, but would he hurt her friends to blackmail her into coming back to him?

Her situation had changed as well. Jonas did not agree with Danny anymore and he would probably not hold her back if she tried to leave now. But somehow, Alice felt like her friends lived in a different world, as if she were looking at them through a portal or something. Even if she got out now and walked away with them, nothing would ever be the same anymore. She would not laugh at the things they found funny, would not enjoy doing what they liked doing. She couldn't tell what exactly had changed, but her life was different now, she could feel it, and realizing that felt like losing something precious; it felt like being robbed of her soul.

Her eyes had gotten glazed by now, but Jill's words interrupted her flow of thoughts and pulled her back to reality. "We texted Danny, you know."

"You did?" Alice almost whispered.

He said they didn't. What an asshole.

"Of course, we did. We thought something had happened, you know, after that night when you called me and said you'd come over, but you never came. I was worried you'd had an accident on the way or something."

"And ... what did he reply?" Her voice was hoarse, and she quickly cleared her throat.

"He said you were really busy and that you needed some time with him to work on your problems and that friends didn't quite fit in your life at the moment."

Feeling a rush of hatred for Danny arise in her, Alice stared at her feet.

Jill put a hand on her shoulder and tapped it. "It's fine, really. We totally understand. Though it would've been nice to receive a text or some sign of life whatsoever, you know. We were really worried. It's not nice to be ghosted."

"I'm sorry," Alice muttered.

"You're forgiven. That year just rushed by in a blur anyways and I'm totally fine with continuing where we last were. I really need someone to go out with!" Beaming, she bared her perfectly white teeth. Had she gotten them bleached?

"Uh ..." Alice glanced at Jonas again and noticed he was staring at her, his expression unreadable as always. He remained quiet though.

"Maybe she doesn't want to hang out with us anymore," Leah pointed out.

Feeling utterly ashamed of herself, Alice swallowed dryly and looked at her friend, whose silvery blond hair glistened in the bright light of the mall. Desperately trying to make things okay between them, she put the biggest apology she could muster into her stare, but Leah's lips remained pursed.

"Oh, don't be ridiculous!" Jill objected. "Of course she wants to go out with me! Who in their right state of mind would not want to go out with me?" Her eyes flicked to Jonas and she gave him a wide smile.

A faint blush appeared on Jonas's cheeks, and he sipped his coffee nervously, still not saying anything.

"I mean, I know you usually go to the Shipwreck, but I'm sure I can put some brighter makeup on your face and get you to go to a *real* club for a change, right?"

"Uh ... sure."

"See?" Jill told Leah

"Didn't sound very convincing," Leah said in an icy tone.

"Oh, don't be such a bitch about it, Leah, for heaven's sake, give the girl a break! Now that you got a boyfriend, you should know how important relationships are. I barely see *you* anymore since you got Jared. She needed time to work things out with Danny and we're *real* friends, so we're not going anywhere, right? At least I know I'm not." Again, she put her hand on Alice's arm and squeezed it affectionately. "As long as you're back now, that is."

"Uh ... yeah. Thanks," Alice said hesitantly.

"I do want to hear the whole story though, hun, no way around it. I want to know *everything*, 'cause last thing I remember, Danny was acting like a jerk and you were thinking about leaving him—then *bam*, suddenly you've disappeared, moved away without saying anything and not answering your phone—"

"It's broken."

"Well ... you surely got a new one, right? Anyway, are Danny's friends still living in that house of yours? Are they still assholes?"

Alice froze and gave Jill a meaningful look, and Jill started giggling when Jonas held up one hand and grinned. "That would be me."

"Oh, you know ... inner values are so overrated," Jill commented.

"What are you doing here anyway?" Alice asked her. "Don't you have work or school?"

"Nah, we took the afternoon off to do some Christmas shopping 'cause the mall's so overcrowded on the weekends, you know. Leah found that stunning dress. It's red velvet, quite classy if you ask me. She's going to wear it on Christmas Eve when she's dining with her new lover and his parents. Isn't that adorable?"

Leah grimaced and rolled her eyes.

"And what are you doing here? I thought you hate malls," said Jill to Alice.

Alice noticed Jonas's eyebrows wander slightly upward and shrugged in response.

"Jill, it's her birthday," Leah informed her.

With an exaggeratedly shocked expression, Jill clutched her hands to her mouth. "Oh my gosh, I'm so sorry! How could I forget that?"

Exuberantly, she wrapped her arms around Alice and almost choked her with a tight embrace that made her spill some of her coffee.

"Happy birthday, hun! You're twenty-two now, finally as old as us! We missed your last birthday but that just means we can double the celebrations this time!" Beaming, she pulled back and grinned. "And it's Friday, so we could go out tonight, right?" Her big brown eyes glistened with excitement.

Alice felt her stomach clench at the sight of her friend, who seemed to have missed her more than she would have expected.

"I can't," she said sadly. "I have to be home …"

Disappointed, Jill pouted.

"She's going to be celebrating with Danny, *obviously*," Leah remarked in that cold tone of hers. "Happy birthday, by the way."

"Thanks," Alice muttered.

"You're welcome."

Unable to look at Leah any longer, Alice quickly dropped her eyes. Her friend was clearly very upset with her and that was understandable. She felt a stab of pain in her guts at the thought of how Danny had not only hurt her, but her friends as well.

Jonas seemed to read her thoughts and stared at her, which only made her feel more uncomfortable.

"Leah don't be so bitchy, it's her birthday! You can be mad at her on any other day, but not now." Jill patted Alice's back and gave her an encouraging smile. "She'll get over it."

"No, she's right," Alice objected. "I really am sorry."

"Don't be. But I'd really love to see that house of yours—seriously, a house? I mean, come on, that's wonderful! Not everybody's got a wealthy boyfriend … or a boyfriend at all." She sighed and made a face. "Is Danny still as hot as when I saw him last time? That guy really made progress in the gym."

Alice bit her lip, not knowing what to say. Sure, Danny was handsome, but she didn't feel like saying anything positive about him—or talking about him at all.

"I'm sorry, Al, I should stop talking about other people's boyfriends like that, I know. It's awkward. You're just so lucky, you know?"

Alice felt bile in the back of her throat. Too bad she couldn't tell Jill how she'd rather be homeless than live in a mansion with Danny.

"Really lucky," she muttered.

"Any plans to get married yet?" Jill wanted to know.

"She's only twenty-two," Lea threw in.

"So? You can get married at eighteen and the sooner, the better. You wanna look young and fresh in your wedding photos, don't you?"

"Well ... I hope not," Alice answered.

"What?"

"I hope there aren't any plans ... There's none on my part at least." Alice shifted nervously, feeling Jonas's eyes on her, and took a sip of her coffee to distract herself.

Looking impatient, Leah tapped her wrist with her index and middle finger. "We ought to go if we want to make it to the movie in time."

Jill grimaced. "Right, I totally forgot. I mean, come on, we just ran into Alice!" Grinning broadly, she turned back to look at Alice. "It's like you've been resurrected from the dead." She nudged Leah's arm. "Hey, I think she should come to the theater as well, shouldn't she?"

Leah shrugged indifferently.

"I ... don't really have time."

"Oh, come on. You can bring your friend, it'll be fun!" Jill insisted.

Alice tried to picture herself in a movie theater with Jill, Leah, and Jonas. The image looked odd in her head. "I can't, really. Some other time, but not today."

Jill made a disappointed face. "Oh, okay ... You want to be alone with your date, I get it." She shook Jonas's hand firmly. "It was a pleasure meeting you."

Jonas smirked and said nothing.

"Doesn't talk much, does he?" Jill asked Alice. "Anyway, give me your new number." She fished her phone out of her purse and placed it in Alice's hand.

Unsure of what to do, Alice stared at the huge smartphone in its glittery pink case.

"Come on, type in your number," Jill urged.

"Uh ... I don't have one."

"You what?"

"I don't have a phone ..."

"Everybody's got a phone!" Jill stared at her like she thought Alice was completely insane.

The way Leah was looking at her, Alice felt speared by her stare. "Jeez, Jill, she obviously doesn't want to give you her number."

"That's not true," Alice assured her. "I really don't have a phone."

Sighing, Jill took her phone back and stowed it away. "I still got the same number, so just call me from Danny's phone or whatever, okay?"

Alice nodded hesitantly.

"Fine then." Jill hugged her tightly, almost crushing her. "I missed you! Enjoy the rest of your birthday and give my regards to Danny, will ya?"

Alice nodded again.

"Bye," Jill said before she reluctantly followed Leah, who had already started walking away.

Their voices were still audible until they disappeared around a corner, and Alice remained standing frozen in place, staring at the spot where her two former best friends had just been. Had she just dreamed seeing them? It sure felt this way.

When reality finally kicked in again, it left her feeling incredibly lonely and depressed.

Jonas said nothing for a while, then he put his hand on her shoulder, but Alice didn't look up.

"Want to stay here?" he asked.

She shook her head. "Too many people."

"You could have told me you don't like malls. We could've gone somewhere else."

"It's fine, really."

Keeping his hand on her shoulder, Jonas led her to the escalator that went down to the Parkhouse.

Back in the car, he turned to look at her and studied her face while she stared at her now half empty coffee cup.

"So ... these were your friends, huh?"

She nodded.

"The one you didn't want to hook me up with?"

She nodded again.

"Shame. She's hot."

Surprised, Alice looked up at him. "Jill?"

"The brunette. I'm not into blondes and the blonde looked like an ice princess."

"Leah can be a bit ... cold. But you heard it, Jill's in *desperate* need of a man. I can still hook you up."

Jonas shook his head. "Nah, thanks. She talks too much."

Alice stared at him for a moment and to her utter surprise and despite everything that had happened in the months before, she burst out laughing and couldn't stop until tears were running down her cheeks and she had to gasp for air.

First, Jonas stared at her like he worried she might be having another mental breakdown, but then he started laughing himself.

When Alice had finally calmed down, he smiled at her and his bright green eyes were smiling as well.

"I don't think I've ever heard you laugh before," he said, and his voice was full of affection.

"Didn't have a reason to. You've been quite serious too, lately." Alice wiped a tear away from her cheek with the back of her hand and smiled back at him.

"There hasn't been much to laugh about," he muttered, his expression suddenly serious again.

"Right." She took a sip of her coffee.

Sighing, Jonas let his eyes wander through the Parkhouse. Two women were loading bags into the trunk of their vehicle, but apart from them, no one was around.

"So ... do you want to go back?"

Alice looked up and stared at the plain brick wall in front of which they had parked the car. "Do I have a choice?"

"I'm not forcing you to do anything anymore."

Her eyes flicked to his and she saw sincerity on his face. "What do you mean?"

He took his pack of Marlboros out the front pocket of his jeans and lit one, then offered one to her. She took it.

"I mean ..." He leaned over to light her cigarette, then put the lighter back into the cigarette pack. "He'll find you. Especially if you go to your friends or hide in some motel. He'll be looking for you."

Alice inhaled some smoke and then rolled her window down a bit to blow it out of the car. She kept her eyes on a bright green exit sign a few yards to her right and avoided looking at him.

"If you decided to go," Jonas continued, "I'd have to help you, and we'd have to go far away from here."

"I envy them," Alice muttered.

"Hm?"

"Jill and Leah. They ... they live their lives the way they want. I would have loved to just go with them and watch that movie."

Jonas sighed and blew out a cloud of smoke. "I'm afraid you can't."

"I know." She remained looking out through the car window and thought of her best friends, the way they had enjoyed their afternoon off, worrying about nothing but what movie to watch and what clothes to buy. She knew that for her, a life like that was out of reach and even if she got away now, she would never have a normal life again—at least not while Danny was out there.

"So?" Jonas asked.

She shrugged. "There's really no point then. I'll live in constant fear of him no matter if I'm in the house or not."

"I'm not saying it's impossible. I could come up with a plan."

"You said you'd hide me ... in the hospital."

He nodded. "That was a spontaneous idea. I had no clue what to do." He finished his cigarette and flicked the butt through the window. "I just think it would be best if I helped you, but that might not be what you want."

Alice rolled her cigarette between her thumb and index finger and stared at the ash that dropped from its tip. "I just want a normal life."

Jonas lit another cigarette and said nothing.

They sat in silence for a while, smoking, until Alice finished her cigarette and threw the stub out the window as well.

"Actually," she said, "I don't care anymore. I'll just spend my days reading and watching TV and pretending I'm somewhere else. He can be nice as long as he's not provoked."

Jonas frowned at her. "Don't say that, you won't have to stay there forever. I'll make sure of that."

"You said you have no clue what to do." Alice emptied her coffee cup and put it down on the car floor to throw it away later.

"Not yet," he admitted. "But I won't let you rot in there forever."

"Is that a promise?"

"I can't change what I've done, but I can do better now." He turned the key in the ignition and started the engine. "So ... back?"

Alice shook her head. "We still have some time. Let's take a walk in the forest, okay?"

"It's cold."

"I don't care. Let's take a walk, please." Alice put on her seat belt and when she turned to look at him again, she saw that he was smiling.

"Forest it is," he said, before backing out of the parking space.

The trees were naked and looked grayish underneath the thick layer of low-hanging clouds, and the ground was frozen solid. Crows were the only animals to be seen and no people had found their way into the forest at this time of the year. It was too cold to go jogging and since no snow had fallen so far, no winter lovers wanted to stroll through the bald landscape either.

The air was dry and burned in Alice's throat, and when she exhaled, it fogged up but immediately dissolved again. It was not a nice day to be outside, but any day that she could spend outside was a nice day.

They had walked for about ten minutes, Jonas smoking one cigarette after another, and Alice's legs had already begun to itch from the blood that seemed to have frozen in her veins. She ignored the uncomfortable feeling of a thousand needles on her skin and continued walking, hands stuffed deeply into the pockets of her coat.

Neither of them talked and the only sounds to be heard on that dead winter afternoon were their footsteps on the frozen soil, their breathing, and the cawing of the crows.

After a while, the path began to steepen and the trees got denser. Alice felt the strength leave her limbs after a couple of steps already. She paused to catch her breath, and Jonas stopped as well and turned around to look at her.

"You okay?" he asked.

She nodded.

"You look pale."

"I'm always pale."

"Yeah, but now you look especially pale." He took a step toward her and dropped his almost finished cigarette to the ground, where he stomped it out.

"You're littering."

"I did that in the Parkhouse also."

"Me too, but that's different. You shouldn't litter in a forest."

Grimacing, he bent down to pick the cigarette stub up, then put it in the pocket of his leather jacket.

"Thanks," Alice muttered.

"You sure, you're okay?"

Her lower belly was cramping badly. She had gotten used to the pain since the miscarriage, but now, due to walking, it was getting worse.

"Yes, I'm fine," she lied and nodded toward the path in front of them. It was quite steep, and steps were carved into the soil to make it easier to walk up the hill. "I want to go up there."

"Why?" Jonas stared at the path and then back at her.

"I know this place. There's a meadow up there with a bench and it's got a nice view."

He smiled. "As you wish."

The climb was harder than Alice remembered it, and after a couple of steps, the pain made her eyes tear up and she had to stop to pause again.

"You look horrible," Jonas commented.

"Thanks, Casanova." She grimaced and tried to breathe the pain away, but the stinging cold air burned in her lungs. "How can you even smoke when the air's freezing?"

"Makes it better … want one?" He fished the pack of cigarettes out of his pocket.

"No, not now."

Jonas shrugged and put it away again. "Perhaps we should go back."

Alice looked up and glared at him. "I want to see the view!"

"Okay, okay. Just saying." He kept his eyes fixed on her while she waited for the pain to decrease. "I'm ready when you're ready."

Frustrated, Alice sat down on the cold ground and stared at the dead leaves, gravel, and mud that surrounded her. She had hoped to be able to take her mind off the baby she'd lost, but with the pain in her belly as a constant reminder that was impossible.

The urge to scream and tear out her own hair threatened to overcome her, but she kept it under control, feeling Jonas's gaze upon her. He crouched down beside her and studied her, and even without looking up, she could tell he was worried.

"Need painkillers?"

"You're like a moving pharmacy. How come you've always got an arsenal of pills with you?"

"I don't carry them at all times ... and I never take any myself." He let his fingers run through his hair and it kind of looked like the question had made him uneasy.

"But?"

He sighed. "It's Danny's arsenal ... and I brought them for you."

"Right."

"Not that I want to drug you," he explained. "But I can't let you suffer like that."

Alice felt quite tempted to just let herself suffer. After all, she had provoked Danny by fighting him and it was her fault the baby was gone. She deserved the pain. But at the same time, the temptation to just swallow a bunch of pills and flush them down with a bottle of wine was also very strong, and she wondered which urge would end up winning. With Jonas around though, trying anything like that was inefficient. He would just save her life again.

"Alice?"

"Let's just keep walking."

He got back up and held his hand out toward her. "Let me help you."

"I don't need your help," she hissed, and took his hand.

Jonas looked puzzled. "I thought—"

"Maybe I just want to hold your hand ... it's surprisingly warm." She let him help her get back on her feet and he smiled.

"May I warm your hand for the rest of the way then? And maybe prevent you from tripping over your own feet, while I'm at it?"

Alice couldn't help but feel some of the grief and anger drain from her at his words. "You may."

By the time they reached the top of the hill, her lungs were on fire and she was completely out of breath—which made her feel embarrassed. Jonas did not seem to have taken any damage by the climb at all, despite his heavy smoking habit.

She knew she wasn't to blame. Who would still be in good shape after being locked in a room for months, lacking sunlight and exercise? Sure, Danny had given her the treadmill upon request, but with everything that had been going on, she had barely used it. Plus, with the pregnancy and feeling sick all the time, burning more calories hadn't seemed like a good idea. Now, after the miscarriage, it was probably normal she could barely move.

And yet, she felt embarrassed with Jonas eyeing her closely, a worried expression on his face. It was nice to be getting along well with him, but his constant concern was annoying and his way of always trying to protect her and help her made her feel patronized.

One man to order me around is enough.

Jonas had promised not to tell her what to do anymore, but she doubted he would keep that promise.

The bench was still there, and Alice began to wonder why she had insisted on coming up here. It was a place where she had spent many romantic hours with Danny, sitting cuddling on the old wooden bench with its fading yellow color, looking down over the trees and hills to the distant city lights. It had been either spring or summer though; they had never come up here when it was cold. Now, the place looked just like her life. Sad, gray, empty.

The yellow paint had faded even more, and the wood looked splintered and even a bit rotten in some areas, but still stable enough to sit on.

There was barely any grass left, and Alice suspected that farmers had let their cows or sheep graze up here and their hooves had made the pasture muddy and uneven.

She took a deep breath and sat down on the cool wood, letting her eyes wander over the landscape and wondering what she had ever found beautiful about it.

Everything seemed beautiful back then. Love makes you blind, it's true.

Jonas hesitated and looked around himself, but then he sat down beside her and lit another cigarette. Alice listened to the sound of his breathing while he inhaled and then exhaled the smoke, and somehow, it was comforting.

They were too far away from the road and town to hear any noise, and the crows and ravens had fallen silent. The only sounds were the ones coming from themselves, and it was creepy in a way. Everything seemed unreal.

"Can I ask you something?" she muttered after they had been sitting in silence for a while.

"Ask."

Not daring to look at him, Alice kept her eyes on the hills in the distance. "How ..." She cleared her throat. "How, uh ... has it made you feel ... knowing ... well, that the baby was yours and that he killed her?" She could hear him holding his breath and temperatures seemed to drop even more. He tensed, and she almost regretted having asked, but then he finally answered.

"I wanted to put a bullet through his head."

Alice frowned. "Is that all? Are you only capable of feeling anger?"

He sighed and she felt his gaze on her. "No ... of course not. It's just easier to be angry than ... sad."

"That's true ... Anger makes you stronger."

"Not really," Jonas disagreed. "At first, maybe. But you need to deal with grief in order to overcome it."

Alice thought about how feeling sad had always just drained her of energy and made her weak. It was easier to hate Danny for what he had done than to think about the actual loss and deal with the pain of it.

As always, it seemed as if Jonas could read her mind. "I'm not saying you shouldn't be angry at him. He should pay for what he's done."

"But he never will."

"He will, one way or another."

"Why would you say that? D'you think some god will smite him?"

Jonas shook his head and put his cigarette out on the bench before putting the stub into the pocket of his jacket. "I don't believe in that crap."

"I figured."

"But he's not only harming the people around him, he's harming himself. And one day he'll realize that and deal with the guilt, or he'll die."

Alice's eyes teared up at his words and she angrily blinked the tears away. "I wish I could hope for him to die," she said contemptuously. "But I can't ... I mean, he's a monster ... but it still doesn't seem like him. I still hope his real self might be buried somewhere underneath all that anger and that he might come back one day. What if it's only the drugs that made him like this? I just can't believe a person can change like that."

Jonas gave her a sad look and she saw pity in his eyes, and instantly hated herself for what she'd said.

"I've thought about that too," he said to her surprise.

"And? You're the expert."

He grimaced. "I'm not. And I'm afraid people *can* change, especially when money and power are involved ... and the drugs make it worse."

"He's gone to the dark side." Alice laughed bitterly. "I just don't understand why he still clings to me. Why can't he just be like other rich men and take one of the models who throw themselves at him because of his money?" Biting her lip, she watched Jonas light another cigarette. "I'm not special," she continued. "And I'm not the kind of woman he wants me to be, so why doesn't he just let me go?"

Again, Jonas gave her a sad look, and she quickly averted her eyes, feeling uncomfortable.

"You *are* special," he objected. "But honestly, I doubt it's about that. He knows he's changing, and I got the impression he's scared of losing himself." Pausing, he took a drag on his cigarette. "You're the only real thing left in his life, and I suppose he's terrified that losing you might mean losing himself completely."

"But ... he wanted all of this! The house, the money, the power ... it's exactly what he wanted, isn't it?"

Jonas sighed and shook his head. "Something happened that changed him."

"What?"

"Remember the time you found him in his office? Drunk and drugged?"

Alice nodded.

"Something very bad had happened."

She scowled at him. "I think we're past the whole secrecy thing, Jonas. Spit it out."

Taking a deep breath, he stared at the cigarette between his fingers. "He killed several people. But he didn't want to."

Alice felt her heart skip a beat. So it was true after all. "He said something like that ... But then Timothy swore it isn't true."

"Of course, he did ... Danny was a good guy, you know. He'd never hurt innocent people."

"*Innocent* people?"

"He wanted to kill someone bad to save someone else but ended up killing the ones he wanted to protect."

"But ... killing ...? How?"

"I can't tell you this. All you need to know is that he felt extremely guilty and he knew he couldn't live with what he had done. So at some point, I suppose, he just decided to extinguish his feelings with drugs and accept who he's become. It must be easier like that."

Alice felt her throat tighten and tried to swallow, but her mouth was dry. *So he is a killer.*

Jonas was trying to sugarcoat it, but that didn't change a thing.

"Tell me what happened," she said hoarsely.

Jonas shook his head slowly.

"I have a right to know!"

"It would make everything worse."

"But ... you're telling me he killed someone—several people, in fact—but you won't tell me how or why ... I need to know this!" Her voice grew louder, and she realized how desperate she sounded, which made her feel ashamed. But here she was again, being told she was not allowed to know what was going on in her life. After all, it *was* her life. It was what made Danny act the way he did and treat her the way he did, and if anyone was truly affected—apart from the people he'd killed—it was her, wasn't it? But Jonas just sat there, giving her an apologetic look and it was obvious that he had no idea how he was making her feel. Powerless. Controlled. Left out.

Jonas always acted nice, but the truth was, he did not respect her or the choices she made.

Feeling that she was about to cry, she quickly turned her head away from him and fought back tears.

"Look," Jonas said and sighed. "Things are going to change soon. We're going to move, and I want you to stay here. I'll work on a plan. As soon as everyone's left the country, the cops will have questions and they'll ask you. That's why you can't know anything."

"I don't want to protect your stupid business! He deserves prison," Alice hissed angrily. Still avoiding his eyes, she kept staring at the fir trees to her right.

"It's not about him. It's about you. They'll arrest you and question you."

"But I don't have anything to do with it! Even if I knew—"

"They won't care. They'll accuse you of withholding important information at the very least."

"How am I supposed to tell anybody anything? It's not like I can just grab a phone and make a call. Plus, they were informed about ... *other* things, but chose not to arrest him."

"They're on his side."

"Then why d'you think they'll arrest me?"

He sighed again. "Because once he's left the country, they won't get bribed anymore and they'll actually start doing their job."

Alice turned around to frown at him.

He shrugged. "That's how this works, I'm afraid."

"That's fucked up."

"I agree." He put out his cigarette on the bench, exactly where the last one had left a spot of black ash, and put the stub in the pocket of his black leather jacket. Then his eyes wandered back to hers. "So ... do you understand now why I can't tell you?"

Alice nodded and stared down at her feet. They were stiff and frozen, and she couldn't feel her toes anymore.

Jonas did have a point; the police would probably make her pay for Danny's crimes. But all of that seemed so far away still ... so unreal. Right now, she was still in Danny's claws and nothing had changed so far. Jonas had said he would be working on a plan. It was not enough to get her hopes up yet.

"You said ... I won't move?" she muttered after a pause.

"Yeah."

"So, you'll get me out of here before the move?"

"I hope so." He pulled his pack of Marlboros out of the pocket of his jeans and opened it, only to find it empty. He put it back.

"When?"

"Can't say until I know when the move is planned."

"The sooner the better."

"I think it's best to wait. He might choose to stay if you disappear too soon. If I get you out right before the move, he won't have time to look for you."

Again, Jonas's words made her feel extremely powerless, but she knew she had to trust his instincts. What he said made sense. Danny would probably stay behind to look for her, and she doubted any place would hide her well enough from him. And what if he was evil enough to threaten to hurt her friends to lure her out of her hiding place?

Alice nodded and said nothing.

"Alice ..." Jonas said after a moment of silence. "I can't promise you that things will go smoothly, but I promise you I'll do my best."

26

Alice sat in her room on the windowsill and tried to draw the yard below her, with its oak and birch trees, the bushes, the flower beds, and the swing to her left. It had been her favorite place outside of the house, but she knew that she would never again get the chance to sit down there and stare into the clouds. That was supposed to make her happy—after all, Jonas had finally decided to help her escape before the move and Danny had said they would move in December.

December only had twenty days left, but somehow, she couldn't get herself to feel excited. Oddly, she had grown accustomed to this kind of life and having to leave it seemed surreal—impossible even. Truth was, she had no idea what to expect of her future. Freedom was all she had wanted at first and she had tried to leave Danny several times, but the consequences had been dire and so she had eventually given up. Still unable to accept her situation, her only hope had been to die. But several attempts to do so had failed. The baby had been another motivator to dare trying to escape, but again, Alice had failed and now it was gone.

Staying with Danny was not what she wanted, but she also could not see the point in getting out anymore. What was she supposed to do out there? Get a job, an apartment, try to get back in touch with her former friends? What was she supposed to tell them about what had happened? Would they even understand? Would they even *want* her back? She was undoubtedly not the same person anymore, and maybe they wouldn't like her new self. They were happy now, living their lives the way they wanted. Why would they want to hang out with someone as broken as her? They didn't deserve that. They deserved better than her.

The truth was, there was *nothing* out there for her.

At least Danny loves me.

The big house with its barred windows and fenced yard was a horrible place to be, but at least it felt familiar. Horrified, Alice noticed that she was scared to leave it.

I've survived in here. Who says I'll survive out there?

There was so much evil in the world, so many hazards beyond her imagination. But what was she even scared of?

Alice put the pencil and drawing pad down and rested her chin on her knees, arms wrapped around her legs. A soft wind moved the naked branches of the trees outside and rustled through the fallen leaves on the ground. The gate guard was sitting in his hut, warmed by an electric heater. Only his shape was visible through the fogged-up glass of his window.

December 10 and still no snow in sight.

A knock on the door pulled her out of her dark thoughts and she looked up, just as the door was opened.

Jonas stood in the frame, a phone in one hand and a troubled expression on his face. Seeing him like that was unsettling.

"Danny just called," he said in a grim tone. "They're coming back today."

Alice felt her blood freeze in her veins. She had expected Danny to be back on the twentieth—which would have given her nine more days to prepare herself and get her feelings in order. Her throat tightened and she just stared at Jonas without saying a word.

He met her gaze with his beautiful green eyes and despite their warmth they made her shiver.

"He said nothing about the move," he told her.

Alice put her chin back on her knees and stared at the purple curtain hanging in front of her. It had never been closed, she noticed. She had the blinds, so she didn't need to. The curtain was nothing but decoration. Danny had purchased it for her because purple was the only color she could stand.

Her silence seemed to make Jonas uneasy. She didn't look up, but she could feel it.

I know him that well already. Almost like a real friend.

"So ... I don't know the date yet, but I'll tell you as soon as I do," he continued.

Still, she said nothing.

"Will you ... be okay?" he asked, sounding concerned.

What a stupid thing to ask ... but how cute of him to bother.

Alice knew she was supposed to answer him, say something, anything to make him stop worrying, but she felt too petrified to even open her mouth.

What would Danny be like? Would he still be feeling guilty and try to apologize? Or had the trip changed him again and the stress of it made him angry?

He was usually angry after his business trips—irritated due to a lack of sleep at the very least. Either way, she was sure he would force his way back into her life. He had given her space for a long time, longer than she had thought he would. He had really tried to stay away from her this time, but she doubted he would stay away any longer.

What terrified her the most was one particular thought: Would he want to sleep with her again? It would be the first time since the miscarriage, and she didn't know how she would cope with that. The thought made all color drain from her face and her heartbeat accelerated. Trembling, she wiped her sweaty hands on her leggings and tried to stop her thoughts from racing.

"Alice?" she heard Jonas's voice as if it were coming from far away.

Looking up, she tried to focus on him, but his face kept getting blurred by the white fog evoked by her anxiety. She tried to blink it away, but it only grew thicker. The walls began to move and seemed to be closing in on her, and the white noise in her ears grew louder until it was hard to hear anything else.

It's just a panic attack ... Danny's given me yet another panic attack.

She bit her lower lip hard and tried to concentrate on her breathing.

This is so embarrassing. Another breakdown in front of Jonas.

There he was, overwhelmed by the situation and not sure what he was supposed to do. Alice forced herself to get a grip and managed to slow down her breathing.

"I'm—" she began, but her voice broke. She cleared her throat. "I'm fine."

Jonas frowned. "You can ask me for help, you know."

Grimacing, she said, "It's just a panic attack. I can handle it."

"No, I mean about him. In case he snaps."

There was a moment of silence while Alice thought of an answer, and then she decided sarcasm was the best way to respond. "Yeah, why don't you install a button on my wall, like the ones they have in the hospital, and whenever he bothers me, I'll push it and you'll get a message."

Hurt flickered in Jonas's eyes and Alice regretted her answer. He only meant well, she knew that, but the whole situation was too complicated for her to see how he could help her. What did he expect from her? That she'd holler the next time, Danny tried to rape her?

A bitter taste appeared on her tongue at that thought, and the memory of Danny assaulting her made her nauseous. Jonas knew that Danny abused her, he'd brought her to the hospital more than once already, but Alice doubted he knew the whole extent of what was going on and she didn't feel like talking to him about it. Most men didn't understand these kinds of things and especially not men like Jonas.

He was still looking at her with a helpless expression.

"Thank you, Jonas," Alice said quickly. "But I really don't see how you could help me. You can't keep him away from me. The best thing you can do is get me out of here."

He grimaced and Alice knew how torn he felt, but then he nodded.

"Maybe you can keep him from getting too drunk ... that might help."

"I'll try," he said.

Alice's fear of Danny made her restless during the rest of the afternoon. She showered and shaved and went through her closet, trying to find something to wear that would please him, some color that would soothe him, maybe. She felt stupid while doing so, knowing her attempts were futile. Danny's mood was unpredictable and wearing a certain color would not have any influence. Nonetheless, she chose a dark lilac knitted dress and black tights to wear underneath it. It was one of the few things, Danny had bought for her, she actually liked.

Sighing, Alice checked her reflection in the bathroom mirror. Her skin was an unhealthy-looking shade of grayish white and grief and desperation had left their marks on her features and made her look ten years older. The scar from Danny's first violent outburst was now clearly visible since her bangs had grown out and weren't hiding it anymore. The scar brought back painful memories and they made her eyes tear up.

I should cut them back and hide the stupid thing.

Determined to do something about her unpleasant appearance, she went through some of her still not unpacked boxes, which she'd hidden in the back of her closet, and found a pair of scissors among other stuff she'd used for office work. Her eyes wandered over the shiny metal blades and she frowned.

Why did I never use this to kill myself?

Her index finger traced the edge of the blade and she found her answer. It wasn't sharp enough. It would be sharp enough to cut through hair though.

Back in the bathroom, Alice brushed her chin-long bangs down over her forehead and began cutting them back. The result was not too bad. The effect it had, however, was not outstanding. The fringe did not magically make her look good again, but it hid a third of her face and the more of her face was hidden, the better.

Getting ready had given her something to do, but now that she was done, she felt the fear creep back up inside her, leaving a cold sensation on her back. The last traces of color disappeared from her cheeks, making her reflection look like a ghost.

This is me waiting for my boyfriend, she thought bitterly. *Two years ago I would have been excited to see him.*

The evening dragged on and Alice sat back on the windowsill, trying to focus on drawing, but her eyes kept flicking to the window every two seconds, checking if Danny's or Waldo's car was already in sight. The nasty ticking of the clock was giving her a headache. The food on the dresser had gone cold by now. She had almost suffered a heart attack when Jean-Pierre had brought her dinner without knocking on the door first.

A movement in the distance caught her attention, and she flinched when she saw the two lights growing bigger on the gravel road outside. When they came closer, they split up into four—two pairs of headlights, two cars. Waldo's and Danny's.

Horrified, she watched the guard open the heavy iron gate and Danny's dark Audi drove through, followed by Waldo's white Mercedes. They both stopped in their usual parking spots, and seconds later, the driver's doors were opened almost simultaneously, and Viktor and Waldo got out. Danny came out the passenger's door of his car. There was no sign of Timothy and Paul, so Alice guessed they must have been dropped off along the way.

Danny looked handsome as always. He was wearing his usual long black winter coat and his hair shimmered in the light of the porch. Viktor grabbed Danny's bags from the trunk, and Danny turned around to say something to him, and when he did, his head cocked upward, and he saw her sitting in the window. Alice winced when his eyes locked with hers and she tried to read his expression, looking for hints of anger, but he merely looked exhausted. She saw Jonas appear in the yard and Danny turned to greet him. The four men then walked into the house and left her staring at the now empty yard. Her heart was racing madly. How long would it take for Danny to come upstairs? Would he want to see her right away? Would he eat first, or did he have business to attend to? Was she supposed to wait for him, or could she already go to sleep?

Alice's thoughts kept racing and doubled her headache. She began pacing through the room restlessly until she heard the key turn in the lock of her door. Horrified, she froze in place. Only a couple of minutes had passed.

He can't wait to see me.

The door opened and Alice automatically backed away until she almost tripped over the couch underneath her window. With the couch in the back of her knees, she watched Danny's feet step into the room and the door close behind him. Her heart seemed as if it were trying to jump right out of her chest, and she could not get herself to look up and meet his eyes, no matter how hard she tried.

"Allie," he said, and his voice sounded hoarse and worn-out, as if he'd had a rough couple of weeks. He appeared to be sober and no anger was veiling him the way it did so often. And yet, Alice felt trapped like a rabbit about to be eaten by a fox. Her anger and hatred for Danny had been entirely devoured by fear, and panic was all she could feel now.

Danny seemed to feel it too and remained standing near the door. He'd taken off his coat and she could see that he was wearing gray pants for a change and his white dress shirt was for once neither ironed nor tucked in his belt. It made him look less cold somehow, less sophisticated. But it was also a sign of exhaustion and when he was tired, he was easily irritated.

"I missed you," he muttered and took a step toward her.

Alice jerked backward, but the couch still blocked her way.

"I wanted to talk to you," he continued in a sad voice, "but Jonas said you didn't want to, so I stopped calling."

Alice felt her throat tighten. Jonas had never told her that Danny had called.

He must have known that I would have refused anyway ... that's the only explanation.

Why else would he keep something like that from her? To spare her? To keep her from falling for Danny's lies and apologies again?

"I understand," Danny said now, his tone tormented. "I'd hate myself too if I were you. Hell, I do hate myself for what I did, and I know I can't make it right." He took another step toward her and she saw him wipe his hands on his pants, as if he were nervous. Was he? Could the guy he had become still feel nervous?

He's never messed up like this before.

She felt his gaze on her like a weight resting heavily on her shoulders, but still she did not dare look up at him.

"But I miss you and I want you back in my life."

Don't we all want things we can't have? I want my life back, you selfish bastard!

Alice cursed herself for not being able to say these words aloud. It would make him incredibly angry, but there was nothing he could do to her that he hadn't already done. What was a bit of pain? She could deal with pain, she knew that now, but still, something held her back. Why was she so afraid of him?

I should provoke him so badly that he kills me, and this would all be over.

She watched anxiously as he stepped closer, and she smelled the cold from outside on him as well as cologne when they were only about six feet apart. Her hands were shaking, and she clenched them into fists and tried to hold them steady.

"I don't expect you to forgive me right away ... or ever, for that matter," he continued in the same tormented voice, but now there was also sincerity in it. "I just hope you can accept me back in your life and give me the chance to prove that I still love you ... and I'll never hurt you like that again, ever."

Like that, Alice thought bitterly. He'd said he'd never hurt her *like that* again. That was an easy promise to keep since she would never be pregnant again.

She tensed when he took the last two steps toward her, and her eyes teared up in fear of him. He held out one hand and she squeezed her eyelids shut while his fingers moved through the strands of hair on her forehead.

"You look cute," he commented while he traced her temple with the back of his hand. "You cut your hair ... looks nice."

His fingers wandered to her chin and he lifted it up to make her look at him, but she stared at his lips instead.

"Look at me," he said, but it sounded more like a plea than an order.

Alice kept her eyes fixed on his mouth, still too afraid to look into his eyes.

"Please don't look at me like that," he pleaded, his voice torn. "I don't want you to be afraid of me."

That was surprising. After all, he had put quite a lot of effort into making her fear him. Alice swallowed, trying to make her throat feel less tight, but her mouth remained dry.

"Why didn't you tell me you were pregnant?" Danny asked, his hand still holding her chin.

Alice winced at the question.

"Tell me," he urged.

"I ... was scared," she breathed.

His lips tightened and he shook his head sadly. "Why were you scared? You knew I wanted a baby! That's why I didn't want you to get that pill prescription." He sighed. "I know this must have been overwhelming for you, but I would have supported you. You should know that. We were doing so great last summer; I had the feeling you were happy with me. Didn't I care for you well every day? I always looked after you, didn't I?" He sounded hurt.

It was true, he had been nice to her throughout the summer, but that was only because she had been so sick and fragile that he'd probably thought he might actually break her if he hit her.

"I should have known it ... your *sickness* ... a mental breakdown, that's ridiculous! I should have known you were pregnant."

Alice still didn't know where he was headed with this. Sure, if he had known that she had been pregnant, he would not have attacked her that way and the baby might still be alive. But it didn't sound as if he was sorry for attacking her at all.

"Did you even want the baby?" he asked in an accusing tone.

Alice swallowed again and kept her eyes on his lips. "I ... didn't want to get pregnant ... but once I was ..." Tears clouded up her vision. It felt like Danny was interrogating her even though it was he who had messed everything up. Was he blaming her for what had happened just because she hadn't told him the truth?

"I loved the baby," she blurted out defensively. "I even had a name for her."

She felt the strength drain from him at her words, and he finally took his hand away from her chin.

"I'm so sorry," he whispered, and she saw a tear drip from his cheek. "I'm sorry for putting you through all of this—the miscarriage, I mean." He put his arms around her and pulled her closer until her head was on his chest and the smell of cologne made her nauseous. She could hear his heartbeat.

"We can always try again, Allie," he whispered. "We can still be a family one day."

Alice was glad for not having eaten anything that day, for her stomach turned at his words. Danny seemed to feel her breathing get faster and loosened the embrace to look at her.

"Wouldn't that be nice?" he asked.

She felt her whole body beginning to tremble and apparently, he noticed it too. "What's wrong?"

"We ... we can't," she said quietly, still avoiding his eyes. She tried to turn her head away from him, looking for a way to escape him and his questions, but his left hand was gripping her right arm and holding her in place. His right hand found her chin again and he turned her head back to make her look at him.

"Allie," he urged, "what's wrong?"

Alice felt like she was about to have another panic attack right there, with Danny towering over her, his fingers locked around her arm. Would he punish her for not being able to have children? It was his fault; he'd injured her badly— but would he take the blame?

"I can't get pregnant anymore." She said the words quickly and squeezed her eyes shut, expecting him to snap and punish her in some way.

Danny seemed frozen for a moment, but then he wiped a tear from her cheek with his thumb and to her astonishment, he bent down to kiss her forehead. He rested his lips on her skin for a while and somehow, they felt warm and comforting.

"I'm so sorry," he whispered again as tears ran down his face.

Alice watched them drip down onto his shirt. "You're not mad?" she breathed, surprised.

"At myself, yes. But this isn't your fault."

Of course, it wasn't. But still, his words managed to touch her. She hadn't expected him to react that way.

"I'll stick with you no matter what," he added.

"But .... You always wanted a family!"

"I have a family. You are my family."

"But you always wanted children!" Desperate, she looked up at him.

He shrugged. "Guess that's my punishment now, isn't it?"

Alice chewed her lower lip nervously. "You ... you could still have it though ..."

Frowning, he said, "What do you mean?"

"You don't have to stick with me. You could have any woman you might want ... I saw it at your birthday party ... They're older than me and beautiful and ... they would give you what you want."

Danny's hand found her jaw again and he made her look up to gaze deeply into her eyes. "It's *you* I want," he insisted. His eyes were still big and blue and beautiful, but despite his words, there was no warmth in them.

"But ...you could do better ..."

His fingers dug into her jaw at once and brought tears of pain to her eyes.

"Stop this nonsense," he hissed, and she could see cold anger on his face. "I don't want to hear it," he threatened. "Why would you even say something like that, huh? Are you hoping to get away from me?" His eyes narrowed and he examined her warily. "Do you want me to fuck other women so you can fuck other men?" Insanity glistened in his eyes. He looked both mad and frightening.

Just when Alice thought her jawbone was about to break, he finally loosened his grip and pulled his hand back. "Answer me," he ordered.

Stubbornly, she blinked away the tears and tried to hold his stare. "How am I supposed to fuck other men when I'm locked in here?" She regretted the words as soon as she had said them, but Danny just glared at her without losing control this time.

The defiance left her as suddenly as it had come and she crumbled under his stare, feeling something break inside of her as the desperation overwhelmed her. It had not even taken him ten minutes until he had hurt her again after returning from his trip. Keeping him happy seemed to be an impossible task.

Feeling weak and drained, Alice could do nothing to stop hot tears from streaming down her face. "I can't make you happy ..." she whispered. "I just don't understand what you see in me."

To her surprise, his features softened. Would she ever get used to his mood swings?

"I *love* you, Alice," he said sincerely. "I know a lot has changed, but *that* hasn't." His hand went back to tracing the lines of her face down to her chin and she winced when he reached the spot where his fingers had bored into her skin.

"I know you still haven't accepted your life here," he muttered. "I wonder what it is you seek out there. There's nothing out there for you, Allie. You should know that. You have no one but me." His words were as painful as a dagger stabbing right into her chest.

"I ... I have my friends," she objected weakly.

He smirked in a pitiful way. "They haven't heard from you in over a year, and I made sure they would not be looking for you."

Alice bit her lip, remembering her birthday and the encounter with Leah and

Jill at the mall. Danny could never know about that. But he was right. She didn't have her friends anymore and trying to get back in touch was not a good idea.

"You have no one," he repeated in a low voice, close to her ear.

"I had no one before I met you."

"Yeah ... and you were so happy, right?"

Alice fought against a new flow of tears. She didn't want to let him know how much impact his words had on her, but he surely already knew exactly how much he hurt her.

"I was happier than I am now," she answered quietly, without looking at him.

His eyes narrowed. "Are you sure? The way I remember it, you were a depressed little punk with no family."

"That's not true ... I had a good job and my friends."

"Maybe. But now you have neither of those, do you?"

She said nothing and Danny smiled triumphantly.

"That's what I thought," he muttered. He let go of her arm and took a step back. "I'll take a shower now." His eyes wandered to the tray on her dresser. "You should eat. You're way too thin." He turned and started to walk to the door.

No longer able to support her own weight, Alice sank onto the couch behind her and watched him open the door through a veil of tears.

He hesitated though and turned around to look at her. "It was never supposed to be like this," he said with sadness in his voice.

"Just tell me what you want," she pleaded desperately.

He raised one eyebrow, the way he always did.

"I don't want to live like this, I can't ..." Her voice cracked. "Tell me what you want, and I'll do it, I just don't want you to always be mad at me!"

His expression was unreadable. He studied her for a moment while thinking of something to say.

"Let's start over please," she begged him. His face was fuzzy through the tears that veiled her vision. She saw him hesitate, but then he walked back toward her. Unsure of his reaction, she dropped her eyes and sank deeper into the couch, but he just crouched down in front of her and took both her hands in his.

"I want you to stop questioning my decisions," he said after a moment of silence.

Alice looked at him, realizing it was easier when he was crouching like this and for once not towering over her.

"I want you to appreciate what you have here and to stop fighting against everything." He fell silent but Alice kept her mouth shut, knowing he wasn't finished yet.

He sighed. "But most of all ... I want you to love me. I want you to be happy with me."

She swallowed dryly.

"Can you do that?" he asked, but it sounded almost rhetorical, as if he didn't expect her to say yes.

"I want to," she admitted. "I really do ..."

"But?"

"You scare me."

He grimaced, struck by her words. "I know ... I scare myself sometimes."

"You're very ... angry."

He frowned. "It's my job. It requires me to be tough and shut off my feelings and well ... sometimes I forget how to turn them back on."

"Will that ever change?"

Danny's eyes turned glazed as if he were looking right through her. He said nothing.

Jonas was right. He looks like he's scared of losing himself.

"Danny?"

Blinking, he cleared his throat. "I ... I hope so."

His deep blue eyes looked incredibly sad, and Alice felt an unwanted rush of affection toward him.

He took his hands off of hers and slowly got up, then he walked out of the room without saying another word.

That night, Alice awoke to the frightening sound of the key rattling in the lock of the door. Startled, she froze and then pulled the blanket up over her head, terrified of what was about to happen.

Danny was drunk as always, and he stumbled toward the bed and dropped down onto the mattress, making the whole bed shake from the impact. Even before he crawled upward, toward her, Alice could smell the whiskey on his breath. He rested his head on the pillow next to hers and put his arms around her, pressing his body against hers.

Surprisingly though, he did not start to undress her and he himself remained fully dressed as well. Alice turned around to look at him, but in the darkness only his shape was visible. He leaned his cheek against hers and she noticed it was wet. It took her a moment to realize that he was crying.

"Danny," she whispered. "What is it?"

Sobbing, he tightened his grip around her, though not in a painful way. "I'm a horrible person," he whimpered.

Alice didn't know what to say. Any objection would have been a lie. "Talk to me," she said instead.

"What is there to talk about?" He sniffed. "I killed our baby and I can't stop hurting you, no matter how hard I try ..." His voice broke.

Alice freed one arm out of his embrace and hesitantly reached out for him. Her fingers found his face in the darkness. She wiped some strands of hair out of his eyes and let her thumb run over his wet cheek, not knowing what else to do.

"You shouldn't even be nice to me," he complained. "I don't deserve it ... and I know you only do it because you're scared of me."

Ignoring his words, she continued stroking his cheek.

Another sob shook him. "I'm in too deep ... I don't even know who I am anymore!"

That makes two of us.

"Danny," she whispered hesitantly, "let me ... help you, okay?"

"You can't help me. No one can."

"I want the old Danny back too ... I'll help you find him."

He laughed dryly. "I don't even remember how I used to be."

"But I do," she insisted. "I know you're not a bad person." Even before the last word had left her lips, she suddenly remembered what Jonas had told her about Danny being a killer, and she doubted her own words.

"Yes I am," he sobbed. "And that's all I can be, apparently."

Alice let her fingers wander down to his jawbone and over his unshaven chin, trying to soothe him. "Don't say that. Just because you made one mistake doesn't mean you can't—"

"One mistake?" His voice grew louder. "One mistake? Alice, I can't even count them anymore!"

Was he talking about the business now? Had he killed more than once?

"But you can still go back ... leave all of this behind you."

"No."

"Please, just try!"

"You don't know the things I've done."

"Then tell me!"

He turned his head away from her hand. "No, Allie. That's the only mistake I haven't made yet. And I want to keep it that way."

"But—"

"It's better you don't know. I don't want to pull you into this."

"I'm already in it, Danny. How can you not see that? It would help to at least know *what* I'm in, exactly."

"No, it wouldn't!" He grabbed her hand and pulled it off his face.

"Ow!"

Quickly, he let go of her. "See? I'm hurting you again, even without wanting it! I can't even control myself for a second." More sobs followed his words.

Alice stared into the darkness, trying to make out his eyes. "You're just drunk and ... impulsive, that's all."

"Stop making excuses for me!" he snapped. Then he sighed. "I don't deserve your forgiveness."

"I never said I forgive you."

He said nothing.

"But I still want to help you."

"You can't," he muttered.

"Then why did you come here?"

He sniffed again and let out a deep sigh. "To cuddle ... that's all. I can't be alone right now."

Glad, he had calmed down again, Alice continued running her fingers over his cheek. It was less to comfort him and more to know where he was exactly and be prepared for any sudden movement he might make. "You sure?" she asked. "You know I can't ..."

He tensed. "Of course, I know ... I just wanted to sleep in the same bed with my girlfriend. Like normal couples do."

"We're far from being normal."

"I know."

"Danny ..." she began carefully.

He twitched, as if he had just awakened from a few seconds of sleep. "Hm?"

Feeling nervous, she hesitated, but the question kept haunting her and she needed an answer. "Why ..." She swallowed. "Why are you always so mad at me?"

His breathing next to her ear stopped at once and he seemed to consider what to reply.

"I mean ... you say you love me, but ... it doesn't look that way."

Slowly, he rolled onto his back and took a deep breath. "You're right," he finally confessed. "You make me angry. Sometimes I just feel that mad rage ..."

Alice's mouth turned dry, and she found herself scooting away from him, her eyes pinned to the darkness to where she knew his face must be.

"But why ..." Her voice broke and she cleared her throat. "Why do you keep me here if you hate me so much?"

Danny sighed—a rattled sound—and put a hand on the side of her face, running his fingers through her hair. His hand was warm and heavy. Like a bear's paw that might rip you apart any second. She didn't dare move.

"I don't hate you, Allie. How many times do I need to tell you that? It's just ... you stopped loving me and I can see it in your eyes. All I can see now is fear. Like I'm some kind of monster—after everything I've done for us! This house, the business ... it was all meant to secure our future. But you turned against it—against *me*— before I even had the chance to prove to you how good wealth can feel. I wanted to give you everything you never had. I thought taking some of the responsibility off you would be like lifting a weight off your shoulders, but you never appreciated it." He paused and Alice bit her lip, feeling guilty and ashamed because of his words.

Was he right? Had she overreacted? Could she have prevented all of this by simply supporting him more? Somehow, the memories of her previous life were blurred or nonexistent.

"I knew I had lost you even before we moved here," he continued. "But I wasn't going to give up on us, so I decided that I won't let you go."

The sudden silence rang in her ears and his words kept echoing in her mind.

"But I would have stayed," she protested feebly. "If you had just let me see my friends ..."

"The first time you ran away, and Jonas brought you back—"

"I wanted to see Jill," she interrupted him.

"Is that so? Alice be honest with me. Would you have come back?" His voice was tinged with sadness.

Alice chewed her lip nervously. She hadn't thought of that. Not even on that day. All she had wanted was to see her friend ... But if truth be told, it would have been unlikely for her to return to this house—especially with Danny being absent.

"I thought so," he muttered, understanding her silence.

Alice felt tears well up in her eyes and she realized that she felt sorry for him. "But ... before Christmas ... you'd stopped drinking ... things were going well ..."

"Until I did something, and it ruined everything." His voice was so heavy with contempt and disgust, it sounded like the words were slimy slugs that he tried to spit out.

"You killed someone," she whispered. "No ... more than one person. But you didn't mean to."

Danny stiffened. "How do you—?"

"You told me. That night. You denied it later, but I'd heard enough." She didn't need to tell him that she *had* believed his and Timothy's lies, and that only Jonas had told her the truth after all.

"Right," he spat, still in that disgusted tone.

"You never wanted to kill anybody ..."

"That's not true. I just didn't want to kill *those* people. They didn't deserve it."

"But what—"

"Stop it now, Alice. I told you that you can't know any of this!" The harshness in his voice made her bite her tongue.

He exhaled noisily. "I already said too much."

"I'm glad you did ... it's good to hear your side of the story."

Although it would probably not change anything. What was done was done. Even if she had wronged him, the way he claimed, she couldn't take it back.

"If this were just some story, I'd be the villain."

"But you never intended to—"

"It's our actions that count, not our intentions." He took a deep breath and sniffed. "Let's just sleep now."

Alice hesitated, but then she leaned over and kissed his lips lightly but tenderly, which left him puzzled. She didn't know why she did it, but she desperately wanted his anger to go away, and if she had to pretend to love him, she would do it.

27

After the genuine talk with Danny, Alice felt safer around him and the general atmosphere was better. The room remained locked though and Jean-Pierre was still not allowed to talk to her. It was clear Danny didn't trust her yet and he was right. She only played the loving girlfriend to keep him from lashing out, and she knew Jonas must be preparing everything for her escape by now. That notion still made her anxious. The outside world scared her to the bone, and she felt torn trying to decide whether running away was really what she wanted. The answer had been so clear not long ago. Back, when she had been pregnant. She had played everything out in her mind, from breaking out of her prison to where she would stay afterward. But the baby was gone. Who would help her now? It would be wrong to take up space that other people needed and deserved more. Guilt weighed heavily on her heart after hearing Danny's side of the story. It was her fault he treated her like that. If she had only accepted his ways from the start instead of resisting and fighting him, he would have never hurt her.

I was disrespectful toward him in front of his friends.

And they were not only his friends—they were his employees, and he needed their respect. Danny had never been a macho like Waldo but contradicting him in front of his clique had hurt his pride.

Alice often wondered how things would be if she and Danny were equal in size and strength. Would he just tell his bodyguards to beat her up instead? Viktor would surely enjoy that. Jean-Pierre needed money and was likely to do whatever it took to earn it. Jonas … he surely would have never hurt her no matter what. Even when blinded by rage, he had still managed to hit the furniture rather than her.

Thinking back to that day still made her stomach convulse painfully. She had provoked him horribly, let out her anger and hatred on him instead of Danny. Her words had made him crack—as well as the bones in his hand. And there hadn't even been any time to talk about it afterward, with Alice's attempt to run away and everything that had followed.

I almost got him killed.

A fresh wave of guilt went through her at the memory of Jonas kneeling to Viktor and Jean-Pierre's feet, blood dripping from his lips.

Since Danny's return from his last business trip, Jonas was staying away from her—the way he always did when Danny was around. Only Jean-Pierre brought her food and Danny didn't talk about Jonas anymore, like he'd used to, back when their friendship had still been intact.

Alice found herself missing Jonas's presence. There was something comforting about him, and she longed for him and his smell of smoke and leather. His absence nourished the seed of doubt which was relentlessly growing in the pit of her stomach. Was he truly working on a plan to get her out? What if he had forgotten about her already? Danny had visited her every night in her room for the last week—to cuddle and talk—and Jonas surely knew this.

Maybe he thinks I'm happy with Danny again.

She couldn't deny that she wasn't quite unhappy with the current situation, and her fear did make her doubt whether escaping was the right choice ... but there was the ever-present and consuming loneliness. The solitariness was driving her mad.

Sometimes, Danny would keep her company during lunch, and they would sit on her bed and eat before he had to go back to his office. Alice wasn't sure if he just wanted to spend time with her or if he wanted to control her eating habits, but she didn't mind him either way.

However, those hours between lunch and bedtime seemed to drag on endlessly, and Alice would often sit on her bed and stare at the clock as if that might make the hands move faster.

On Wednesday, December 19, Danny was sitting on her bed, legs outstretched, his back against the wall. He had a tray with food on his lap and was spooling spaghetti onto his fork while complaining about Timothy's and Paul's behavior at work.

"They're unreliable," he growled while he aggressively forced the spaghetti onto the fork with his spoon after they had fallen off. He cursed and shoved the load of pasta Bolognese in his mouth. Alice watched him chew while she listlessly disentangled her own spaghetti with her fork. She discovered a single meatball which had somehow found its way into her sauce and stabbed it with her fork to put it on Danny's plate instead. He grimaced and swallowed.

"I should not have promoted their asses. Since I've started to pay them more, they've become arrogant and don't work properly anymore. Showing up late in the mornings, sometimes hung over and in no state to work. They forget to reply to emails and to call back clients, and on top of it all, they dare to talk back at me! I want them to keep their traps shut and remember who they work for." He looked at her. "Can you believe that?"

"Timothy? Definitely ... Paul? Well, I've never even heard him say a word, so it's kinda hard to imagine."

Danny grimaced. "Paul's uncomfortable around women. He's like that guy from *the Big Bang Theory*. What's his name again?"

"Raj."

"Right."

"How's business going apart from that?"

"Great, honestly. We're making good money. You'll see it when we've moved. This house is nothing compared to the new one. It's a real mansion, with a fountain in the entrance hall and a home cinema and the property is huge. The pool is also way bigger than the one we have now."

Alice felt her throat tighten at the notion of moving. She still hadn't decided how to feel about it. Maybe Jonas *had* forgotten about her. That would decide the matter for her. Somehow, she found herself hoping for that—but it made her feel utterly ashamed.

"Where is it? The house?" she asked.

Danny finished chewing another load of spaghetti and swallowed before he answered. "I can't tell you that now."

"Why?"

"Because it would only unsettle you." He gave her a piercing look that made clear that there would be no argument about the matter.

"*Now* you've unsettled me," she muttered.

He sighed. "It's just ... you hear things about places ... and they make you think badly about them. But there's beauty everywhere, and you need to ignore the prejudices and make your own experiences. I have and I know you'll love the place, trust me on this."

"You said it'll be warm ..."

"Yeah. We're not going to Hawaii or anything and it won't be hot all year long. But it never gets below fifty degrees during the day and the summers are long and hot and dry ... You'll love it."

Alice bit her lip and nodded, hoping she would.

He's so secretive about it. That can't be good.

"When are we going to move?"

He shrugged and stabbed a meatball with his fork. "Can't say yet. Later than planned. Mid-January, probably."

At least that gave her more time to figure out what she wanted. Pleased, Alice took a bite of her food. "It's far though, isn't it? Are we going to fly?"

Danny nodded.

"You know I don't have a passport, right?"

His eyes widened at once. "I completely forgot! I'm so glad you brought that up." He frowned. "We need to get you one as soon as possible, so you can get the visa."

Feeling excited, Alice lowered her fork. "Are you taking me to town?"

"What for?"

"The passport! I'll need to get my picture taken ..."

Danny chuckled. "You're too adorable, Allie. Really. We're not getting you the passport the legal way. That would take way too long, and I got no nerves for the procedure."

"So ... I'll get a fake passport?"

"No, not a fake one. Just a fake procedure."

Confused, Alice stared at him. "Why? What's the point?"

"The point is that I don't feel like taking you out of here, and bringing you to a federal institution to have your passport made while the cops already got their snouts in our business and their eyes on us. What d'you reckon they'll think you need the passport for?"

She shrugged. "For traveling? Like most people?"

"No. Not after everything that's happened with those two fuckers who invaded our privacy. They're watching us and they're waiting for something like that. They'll know we're fleeing the country."

Alice felt her pulse quicken at once. "Are we?"

He sighed. "I'm afraid so. We're not in a rush or anything. They're still satisfied with the bribes I'm shoving up their asses, but there's commotion at the station. People have been fired for fraud and it will only be a matter of time until our allies spill the truth in order to save their jobs. When the time comes, no amount of money will be able to buy their silence anymore and I want to be gone before that."

Something cold seemed to trickle down her spine at his words. The way he was talking about his dark deeds, as if they were the most normal thing in the world, made her feel uneasy.

It is normal for him, she realized. *He's grown accustomed to this kind of life.*

What about her? Would she too?

Danny put the fork down on his tray and stretched his hand out toward her to stroke her cheek. "Don't worry, darling, everything will be fine. We'll be long gone before things escalate and you'll be living a splendid life and finally enjoy some freedom again."

"What kind of freedom?" she asked suspiciously.

"Well, the house is near a small town. You'll be able to go where you want, as long as your bodyguard's with you."

Alice grimaced, a sour taste on her tongue. "I'll be *followed*?"

Danny gave her a warm smile. "Honey, most wealthy people are. It's for your own protection. You'll get used to it. You can make friends in town and take yoga classes and get massages—"

"Yoga classes?"

He laughed. "Or boxing, whatever you like. Though you definitely should get a pedicure once in a while, it's relaxing."

Alice frowned, not sure if he was joking or not. He burst into laughter at the look on her face and mussed her hair affectionately.

"I'm serious, Allie. That's the good thing about having money. Not everyone loves material things, but I'm sure everyone loves a good massage or a day at the spa. Even you."

"I don't like being spoiled."

Danny put the tray with the now empty plate aside and leaned over to kiss her forehead. His lips were soft and warm and for once, they didn't taste of wine and even his pupils were their normal size. He was making progress.

And all it took was for me to pretend I still love him and be a good girlfriend.

"Honey," he said softly. "I know what your problem is. You think you don't deserve this. You're used to living with nothing, and now you're overwhelmed by even a little bit of wealth." He let his fingers glide over her cheek and his touch made goose bumps arise on her back. "You know what I think? If anyone deserves prosperity, it's people like you. People who grew up with nothing. They're the only ones who can truly appreciate it."

"You grew up poor too. Do you still appreciate it? It seems like you've adjusted quickly to your new lifestyle."

"I worked hard for it and my business helps people in need, so I think I deserve it."

"See, that's the thing." She sighed. "I haven't worked for it."

"But you did before. You worked while I was unemployed. You worked extra hours while I was at home, sulking in self-pity. Now's your turn to lean back and enjoy what you're given."

Alice still didn't feel convinced. Not only because she truly didn't like being spoiled, but also because it didn't feel like being spoiled at all, being locked up and under watch with Danny's mood swings posing a constant threat. They were like a thick, dark cloud hovering above her, raining down on her when she least expected it. She wondered if now, things were finally going to get better. Maybe the prospect of moving had lifted Danny's mood up and restored his happiness; maybe with business going great, he was at last feeling more relaxed and therefore less angry. Maybe he did not need alcohol and other drugs to calm him down anymore and maybe, just maybe, he would keep treating her nicely once and for all. Maybe she would even manage to love him again.

Danny pushed himself into an upright position and gestured to her plate. "Are you done?"

Alice nodded. He stacked the plates on one another and leaned in to kiss her lips. It was a passionate kiss, still tender, but his hand was on her neck and his fingers were buried in her hair. His lips moved quickly, and she instinctively went with it. When he pulled back, she was breathless.

"What was that for?" she gasped.

He smiled and the corners of his mouth wandered up almost to his ears. "I'm looking forward to the future—*our* future … Living in that beautiful house with you by my side. Might be one day we'll even adopt a child, a refugee, maybe … We'll do good things and I'll make up for the bad things I've done."

He climbed off the bed and took the tray in one hand. "I'll take that to the kitchen."

At the door, he turned around once again to smile at her. "I'm feeling positive."

Nevertheless, he locked the door behind him.

Another two days passed, and Christmas was getting dangerously close. Still, Jonas had not shown up or given her a message. Sure, he had said it would be right before the move and the move was not before Mid-January. Still, his absence was hurtful and confusing. Danny was the only one who spent time with her and talked to her, and Alice felt herself growing attached to him again. She knew what game Danny was playing and that he knew exactly how to wrap her around his finger.

Deprive me of anyone to talk to and I'll always run back to him.

Alice hated herself for that, but she couldn't help it. She watched Jonas from time to time as he stood outside in the yard, smoking, with his back facing the house. He would stand there motionlessly, sometimes even for an hour, gazing through the iron gate at the distant hills and mountains. Alice often wondered if he was longing for something. Maybe his freedom? After all, he was only staying here because of her. At least that was what he had told her. Maybe he had just tried to make her like him, maybe he was in truth still in it for the money. Maybe he had even schemed with Danny, won her trust, offered her a taste of freedom to make her want to run away, just so he could report to Danny and give him a reason to lock her up.

No, that was ridiculous ... Or wasn't it?

I'm losing my mind. This seclusion isn't good for me.

When Danny sneaked into her room shortly before midnight, with whiskey on his breath and a dick as hard as steel, Alice cursed herself for being so naïve as to think he would stay abstinent. She was convinced that he *blew off steam* himself occasionally, but he was still a man and a man had his needs. Those were *his* words, obviously. Alice was rather sure that Jonas had not slept with anybody in a while, and he didn't look like he was about to burst. Maybe he'd had occasional dates before, but lately, she had not seen him leave the property much. With Danny though, it had only been a matter of time until he considered his *needs* were more important than hers; so when he started to pull down his pants underneath the blanket she wasn't even surprised. Panting, he disentangled his feet from his pants and boxers, and turned toward her.

"Don't," she told him firmly, pushing him away in an attempt to escape his reeking breath.

"I can't wait longer," he complained, sounding like a stubborn little boy. "I'm so horny."

"We can't. It still hurts."

He kissed her neck and her ear and sighed. "It has been so long though; it surely must be healed."

"It hasn't been much longer than a month and it still hurts. I get cramps and there are days when I can barely move."

"I'll be really gentle," he promised. His hand wandered underneath her nightshirt and up to her breasts. His hand was warm and soft, and the touch wasn't even *that* unpleasant, but Alice was far from enjoying it.

"We really can't, Danny. It could cause bleeding and then I'd have to see a doctor again." She tried to push his hand away from her chest, but he resisted and stubbornly kept it there.

"Danny, *please*," she said, growing both impatient and desperate.

Ignoring her words, he rolled on top of her. His weight was on his elbow, so he was not actually *on* her, but seeing his shadow in the darkness above her triggered unpleasant memories, and Alice's heart began to race at once while she felt like she couldn't breathe. Panicking, she tried to push him off, but he lowered his head toward hers and his lips brushed her forehead, then her temple, then her cheek and chin, and lastly her lips.

He really is gentle, she noticed, but the prospect of having him *enter* her was still terrifying. His kisses continued and they moved down to her throat and up again, until he tenderly nibbled her ear while his hot breath evoked goose bumps on her neck.

I used to like his touch once.

But those days were over. Paralyzed, she lay on her back while he pulled her shirt upward and began kissing her breasts and belly.

I have to do something, Alice thought desperately, but fighting him off would only provoke his anger. When he began to clumsily fumble her underwear, she awoke from her trance and quickly closed her fingers around his member. She did it a bit too quickly and he gasped, surprised, but then she heard him chuckle and his fingers caressed her temple while he kissed her lips. His lips were soft, but the kiss was passionate. The only thing bad about his kiss was the alcohol on his breath, Alice had to admit; otherwise, kissing him revived old memories—good ones—and she was able to forget her surroundings for a moment. Her hand moved up and down until his breathing got faster, and when his kisses stopped and his hand rested immobile on her cheek, she knew she had him where she wanted. She pushed him off of her and onto his back, and continued stroking him until he flinched and exhaled deeply. Alice wiped her hand on the blanket and stared into the darkness.

That was easy, she thought. *Why did I never try this before?*

It might have spared her a lot of pain ... Not all of it though, she had to admit to herself. Some of his assaults had been driven by rage, not by lust, and touching him surely would not have changed anything.

Like when he killed the baby ... it was my punishment for shooting Viktor.

The thought of that night immediately darkened her mood and she tried to shake it off. Danny was happy now and most importantly, *satisfied*. He began to snore softly, and Alice found it was safe to go to the bathroom and wash her hands. When she looked in the mirror, she barely recognized herself. Her eyes were dull and lifeless; dead, somehow. Danny had stolen her dignity more than once already, but this was the first time she had offered it to him on a silver tray.

I had no choice, she thought desperately, but she couldn't help feeling like she had betrayed herself.

Her mood was still dark the next day when he came to her room for lunch. Though *he* was especially cheerful.

"Morning, sunshine," he warbled joyfully while he pushed the door open with his hip, balancing two trays with food, one in each hand. Alice forced a smile and flattened the blanket on her bed, so he could sit down beside her. He leaned over and kissed her.

"Asian food today," he sang, while he took the lids from both plates. The food smelled delicious, but Alice's appetite was nonexistent.

She stared at the chunks of tofu floating between crispy-looking broccoli and peppers, red and yellow.

"Smells good," Alice said to keep the conversation going. She didn't want to think of last night and she didn't want him to know how she felt.

Danny did not seem to have anything to say though and they ate in silence for a while, Alice merely picking at her food like most times.

"How's work?" she asked him when she couldn't bear the silence anymore.

"Good." He smiled broadly. "Tee was late again, so I sent him right back home. That'll teach him a lesson."

"Doesn't that ... make you angry?"

"No, it was my pleasure. You should've seen the look on his face! He came into the office and I just sent him right back out, telling him the day will be deducted from his salary. He was pissed, I'm telling you." Grinning, he took a mouthful of his food.

"Are you not getting along anymore?"

He shrugged. "Don't care. He's never been much help. Things are better with Jonas again, that's all that counts."

Alice flinched and almost dropped her spoon. Danny's eyes were on his plate though and he didn't notice.

"So ... did you have a talk? About ... what happened?" she asked cautiously.

"It's hard to talk to Jonas if you know what I mean ... I've apologized about a thousand times since last spring, but he held a grudge and when he holds a grudge, he talks even less than what's normal. He approached *me* now, actually. Said he wanted to put everything behind him before the move. Wants to be on good terms for a fresh start."

"Sounds ... good."

Is Jonas playing him? Or does he really want his friend back?

The thought sent a pang through her guts. What if Jonas was just like her? Falling for Danny's act? But it couldn't be ... Jonas wasn't that impressionable. Or was he?

Danny nodded. "I'm glad he's back. I really hope we can be friends again, like we used to. He was like the younger brother I never had. I know, he's sometimes much more mature and wiser than I am, but I can't help feeling responsible for him."

Alice nodded, not knowing what to say.

"Even you have come to like him, haven't you?"

Again, she winced and felt herself blush. Luckily, Danny didn't seem to notice.

"I ... I don't despise him anymore," she said carefully.

He laughed and gave her a smile. "That's a start."

"So ... do you trust him again?"

He thought for a moment. "I always have ... Just that day ... I don't know." Frowning, he played with his food, his mood suddenly darkened by the memory of what had happened on that day in spring. "I just came home from a very wearying business trip and well ... I must admit I wasn't entirely sober."

You were on coke ... Your eyes were pitch-black.

The image was deeply etched in her mind.

"I just ... Something snapped when I saw him on you. I should've known it was nothing like that—it was plain obvious, actually. But still, I completely snapped and almost made what would've been the biggest mistake of my life."

And what would that be? Killing him or killing me?

She wondered whom Danny loved more—her or Jonas. At least it was clear whom he *respected*. Danny sighed and continued eating, and Alice too went back to picking at her food.

When he was finished, he eyed her plate suspiciously. "You've barely eaten ... Is it not good?"

She shook her head. "It's delicious ... I'm just not very hungry."

"You really could do with eating a bit more, you know."

"Thanks, Danny, I know that."

His eyes rested on her face, studying her features. "You're in a bad mood."

Alice stared at her hands sullenly.

"Why?"

"I don't know ... maybe I'm just tired of sitting in my room all day long, waiting for you to come and keep me company." She saw a flash of guilt in his eyes and quickly shoved another chunk of tofu into her mouth, worried she might have said too much.

"I'm sorry," he said softly. "I didn't think it would be so hard on you. I mean, it's freezing outside and there's not much to do in the house anyway, so I figured you'd be all right until we move."

"It's boring," Alice complained. "There's nothing on TV. You promised we'd get Netflix when we moved in, but we don't even have Wi-Fi ... right?"

"There's cable in the office. That's all we need."

"Don't lie to me, I know you wanted to install it. You only didn't because you were scared I might somehow contact the outside world." She saw him chew his lip and knew she was right.

I should watch my mouth, though. Better not provoke him.

"Yes, I was worried you might do something stupid. But it wasn't just about you getting out of here, it was about the business. We have secrets and I didn't want you to spill something."

"Spill what? I don't know anything."

"You know enough to get me arrested. Plus, there's hackers. All the devices we use for business are secured and everyone who's involved knows the Do's and Don'ts." He let his fingers run through his dark hair that fell down to his brow. "Why don't you just read a book?"

"I read a lot. In fact, I've read every single book I own and most of them more than once. And I draw, but there's only so much I can think of. I've even played every video game we own."

Danny gave her a tortured look and sighed. "Why didn't you just say something? You can get more books and games and also more DVDs. Just tell me whatever you want, and I'll get it for you."

"We're leaving soon. There's no point in buying more stuff now, is there?"

He shrugged. "If you think you'll still need it in the new place, why not? We'll move some furniture and lots of other stuff anyway. Couple more books or DVDs won't hurt."

Unsure of what to say, Alice just stared at him.

I want out of this room; I don't want books or DVDs.

"What's wrong?" he asked.

"Nothing..." She swallowed dryly. "It's just ... It's being in here all the time. It's driving me crazy! Why can't I just leave my room?"

Danny's expression hardened at once. "I'm not having this discussion with you. It's less than a month until we move and I'm not taking any risks."

Alice dropped her eyes to avoid his stare and looked at her food, which had gotten cold by now. The absurdity of the situation made her want to cry, but she didn't want to show him any weakness. Here she was, locked in her room by her boyfriend, and he seemed to think everything was normal. It surprised her how quickly Danny had grown accustomed to his mafia-lifestyle.

It's easy to adjust to change when you're the one benefitting from it.

Danny's expression softened again. "Christmas is around the corner. We'll be hosting a dinner again with Julio and maybe Theresa, if she finds the time. Who knows, maybe she'll even bring the baby."

Alice felt a sour taste on her tongue and swallowed. Danny's words pierced through her like needles. She felt her eyes tear up and blinked to fight the tears away. Danny immediately realized what he'd said, and an uncomfortable silence spread between them. But then he cleared his throat and spoke.

"Anyway, you're going to attend, so you'll be allowed to leave the room."

I'd rather rot in the bunker than attend that dinner.

"Do I have to?" she muttered.

His eyes narrowed. "I thought you *wanted* to. But fine, if you'll have it that way: yes, I want you to be part of it." His eyes flicked to her plate. "Are you done?"

She nodded. He stacked the dishes on one another and put his feet on the floor, ready to get up, but then he sighed and leaned over to her, putting a hand on her shoulder. "I want you to be happy, you know."

I doubt that.

Danny's fingers traced her neck and went through her hair, caressing her softly, and then he kissed her forehead. "Don't forget to tell me what books you want," he reminded her and lifted her chin to kiss her lips. She endured his touch without objection. She had gotten used to being his puppet and being kissed was better than being beaten.

Danny left on the twenty-fourth for a Christmas-Eve dinner at one of his business partners' house. He took Viktor along but told Jean-Pierre to keep an eye on things.

The day was as cold and gray as the ones before. A thick fog covered the yard and gave the whole landscape a mystical if not creepy look. No crows cawed today, and no wind rustled through the dry, brown leaves that still hung on some of the branches. Still, no snow was in sight, but the fog made up for it and covered the fields like a white blanket.

Alice didn't know why, but today she was feeling especially depressed. Whether it was because Christmas Eve made her think of all the happy families huddled together in front of a fireplace, or the prospect of the dreaded Christmas dinner the next day, or maybe just because her loneliness was really wearing her out, she couldn't tell. Lying in bed with the blanket pulled up over her head seemed to be the best thing to do after a glance out the window had revealed the sad ambiance of the day. She didn't even look up when Jean-Pierre brought her dinner and after placing it on the dresser as usual, he left the room without saying a word.

There was one good thing about being locked in a room with nothing to do though: sleep came whenever she wanted it to. Apart from the nightmares, which still woke her every now and then, she was able to sleep for sixteen hours straight if she wasn't disturbed. Alice found more and more that being asleep was better than being awake.

Beep ... beep ... beep ...

Pain flashed through her skull with every *beep* that found its way through her ears, and Alice felt her consciousness return, despite her best efforts to stay asleep. Reality was unpleasant, and she was determined to stay clear of it for as long as possible.

Beep ... beep ... beep ...

It was not the sound of an alarm. It was longer, less penetrating, and yet it gnawed at her nerves and evoked a queasy feeling in her stomach. Where had she heard it before?

Her eyelids felt heavy and opening them was an effort that left her breathless. Bright light burned her irises, and when she tried to put her hand to her face to shield herself, her arm would not move.

Blinking, she stared at it, and when finally her eyes had adjusted, she noticed that her wrist was bound to the mattress with a padded restraint. Immediately, she tried to lift her other arm—but it was bound as well. Even her legs had been tied to the mattress.

Her heart racing, she began pulling at the restraints, but it was useless.

"Don't fight it, Alice."

Her eyes flicked at once to where the voice had come from, and found Danny standing near the hospital bed, dressed in a white coat. He was wearing latex gloves, and they were stained with dark red blood. He held something in his arms, a bundle or blanket of some sort. There was blood on his coat as well.

"Don't worry, Allie. It's all good now. You can go back to sleep."

Horrified, she saw the bundle move in his arms.

"I've got what I wanted."

Gasping for air, Alice frantically pulled at her restraints.

"You can see her if you like." Danny quietly moved toward the bed, and she froze, staring at the tiny, pink hand, which had appeared from underneath the blanket.

"She's beautiful," he said softly. "Just like her mother."

Slowly, he held out his hands toward her, showing her the baby he was holding. Her eyes were surprisingly awake and locked with Alice's at once. They were green, she noticed.

"You can go back to sleep now, darling." Danny repeated. "I won't bother you anymore."

Something grabbed her shoulders and shook her while she watched him cradling the baby tenderly. The room crumbled around her, the beeping faded out, and Danny and the baby dissolved like smoke in the wind.

Alice realized that she was lying on her stomach, face buried underneath her arm. Her shirt clung to her body, wet and cold, and the pillow underneath her was moist as well. Was it sweat or tears? Something shook her again and she stirred, sucking in air as she did so. The room was dark, but she was able to make out a big shadow towering over her. Her heart was racing, and when the shadow beside her lifted an arm, she thrashed and kicked at it, and her foot found its target. To her surprise, it was solid, and the shadow groaned. Suddenly, light filled the room, so bright it left her blinded. Clutching her hands to her face, she waited for the fog to leave her head, and when it slowly evaporated, the memory of Danny holding the baby blurred and made room for reality.

It was only a nightmare, she realized.

Blinking, she spied through her fingers carefully, suddenly scared of finding Danny in his solid form next to her.

I kicked him ...

Her eyes adjusted and she saw that the person sitting on the edge of her bed was Jonas.

I kicked him!

"Sorry," he moaned, one hand on his nose. "Didn't mean to scare you."

It took her a moment to steady her breathing and she took her hands away from her face. "I kicked you!"

He shrugged it off. "Nightmare?"

Alice nodded.

"Sorry for waking you up, but with Danny gone, now seems to be the only time we can talk." His eyes wandered across her face and Alice became painfully aware of what she must look like. Quickly, she combed her tousled hair with her fingers, trying to flatten it.

"I thought you'd forgotten me," she complained.

Grinning at her lousy attempts to bring her hair in order, he said, "How could I?"

Alice gave up and let her hands drop onto her lap, sighing. "You've ignored me."

His smile vanished. "Danny was always around. He's become suspicious."

"He said he trusts you and that you're trying to restore your friendship ... I thought ..." She trailed off, realizing what she was about to say was stupid.

"That I'm on his side?" Jonas finished for her.

"*Back* on his side."

"Never."

"I know ... I guess. It's just ... he's the only one who talks to me."

Jonas gave her a meaningful look. "Why d'you reckon that is?"

"He's manipulating me ... he always is." Feeling ashamed, she paused. "I make it easy for him."

"Don't blame yourself. What else are you s'posed to do? It's best not to provoke him."

Not knowing what to say, she chewed her lip.

"Did he hurt you?" Jonas asked.

She shook her head. "He's in a good mood at the moment, it seems ... Looking forward to moving, I guess." Something flickered in Jonas's eyes at her words and Alice felt fear arise in her, making her heart race again.

The move ... what should I do?

Jonas studied her expression and his eyes seemed to pierce right through her. *He's reading me like a book,* she noticed, and quickly tried to don a blank face.

"Mid-January's the plan," he said.

"I know ... he told me."

"He did?" Jonas looked surprised.

"Yeah ... we talked about it."

"How much did he tell you?"

"Not that much ... Just that the new house is bigger ... and that I'll be allowed to go wherever I want."

Jonas's stare deepened even though his expression remained unreadable. "Does that sound tempting to you?"

Damn you and your X-ray stare.

"No, of course not!"

"You sure?"

Alice chewed her lip nervously. She hated it when he asked things whose answer he already knew, sometimes even better than she did.

"It doesn't tempt me." She put as much certainty in the words as she could.

He wasn't fooled. "But?"

"Nothing."

He sighed. "As soon as I know the exact date of the move, I'll plan everything through. Best to get you out of here when everyone's ready to leave, so he won't have time to look for you."

"And you think he'll leave without me?"

"I don't know. But if he doesn't, I'll make sure he gets arrested."

Fear crept through Alice's bones like ice-cold water at the thought of being hunted down by Danny.

Will he hurt my friends to get to me?

"Don't worry," Jonas said softly. "Everything will happen quickly. He won't have time to find you."

"Where will I go?"

"I'll have a friend pick you up and help you hide until he's out of the country—or behind bars, for that matter."

"Where will you be?"

"I'll stay with Danny. To keep an eye on him. That is, should he choose to stay behind and look for you."

Alice shivered. It sounded as if only a thousand things could go wrong. She wrapped the blanket tighter around herself and pulled it up over her shoulders.

"I'll be alone then," she said tonelessly.

"It's safer if we're not disappearing together. But my friend will be there, and I'll meet up with you once Danny's gone." He gave her a meaningful look. "That is ... if you want me to."

Not knowing what to say, Alice chewed her lower lip.

What is that between us?

"And then?" she asked instead.

"You'll have your life back. Your freedom ... your friends."

"And you?"

"I don't know yet."

Alice stared at her hands in her lap sullenly. "I can't go back to them."

"Why not? They looked nice. They said they miss you."

And I miss them.

"I don't want to ... inflict my drama on them. They won't understand."

"I'm sure they will," he objected.

"I'll drag them down with me."

"What if they lift you up?"

She shook her head sadly. "They're happy now. I want to keep it that way."

"You underestimate them."

"No," Alice snapped, feeling irritated. "I'm bad for them, I know it. They won't like the new version of me."

Jonas sighed. "I know how you feel, trust me. But they're your friends and they love you and you deserve to be with them."

"No, I don't!" Tears welled up in her eyes and she furiously blinked them away.

Jonas hesitated and remained quiet for a while before he spoke in a defeated voice. "I promised you that I won't tell you what to do anymore ... But please, don't punish yourself. None of this is your fault."

He doesn't get it.

"It's not about me, it's about them ... They're better off without me."

He gave her a sad look. "Whatever you say."

Alice kept staring at her hands, feeling a pressure in her chest that made it hard to breathe. There was tension in the air between them, words yet unspoken. Jonas knew something was off, but she couldn't get the words out. He would not have understood. Hell, even she didn't understand it. For over a year, all she had wanted was to get out of this place, and now that she finally had the chance, she was backing away from the opportunity of freedom because the mere thought of it scared her to death. Danny might put walls and bars around her, but what truly kept her imprisoned was her fear.

I'm a coward. A stupid, little coward.

She loathed herself for it. Jonas was putting his own life in danger to help her and she was failing him.

"Alice ..." he began carefully.

Alice turned her head away from him as tears veiled her vision anew. She didn't want to cry in front of him, especially not now.

"What's wrong?" he asked.

Everything's wrong. I'm wrong. Everything about me is wrong.

He placed a hand on her arm, and she winced under his touch.

"I don't know what I want," she finally confessed.

He squeezed her hand softly. "You'll have time to figure everything out. I'll get you money to support you."

"I don't want your money."

"It's not *my* money. It's Danny's. He deprived you of your income, you deserve to get something back. You earned it."

Trying to think of something to say, Alice stared at Jonas's hand on hers.

"I can get you enough," he offered. "You don't have to get a job. Not before you're ready."

He doesn't get it.

"I don't have anything out there ... I'm *nothing* out there." Her voice was shaking.

Jonas's expression hardened at once. "Those are *his* words," he said in a disgusted tone.

Alice nervously chewed her lip. "They're true though."

"No, they're not!" His tone made her flinch. "Don't you *dare* believe this crap, Alice! He's trying to manipulate you!"

"It's not just him," she protested. "I'm ... scared ... there's nothing for me out there!"

"There's nothing for you in here."

"But I'm used to this ... I don't have to think of anything here. World War III could happen out there, and I wouldn't even know of it."

Jonas's features softened. "I know you're scared, but the real threat is in here. How many times have you almost died, huh?"

"It's not death I fear."

"Then what?"

"I don't even know! People ... everything ... There's lots of things I'm scared of."

"You can't just hide underneath your blanket for the rest of your life."

"If I stay here ... I can."

Jonas appeared to be speechless. He studied her with a mixture of hurt, irritation, and helplessness in his eyes. Alice hated herself more than ever before. A single tear ran down her cheek and she wiped it away with the back of her hand.

"Please," he begged. "Don't give up like that. There's a future out there for you ... You can do whatever you want with it. Every door's open for you."

"No." She shook her head slowly. "Not this one."

Jonas's grip around her hand got tighter, but not in a hurtful way. He looked desperate now. "Don't give up," he said again. "You've fought your way up before. You had a job ... you had your friends—"

"Emphasis on *had*," she muttered bitterly.

"It's still your choice. They would want you back. You could have everything back."

"Not everything." Not her dignity, not her baby or her fertility, not her past ... and the memories ... they would haunt her forever.

"You're a fighter, Alice. Don't be like that."

Resigned, she sighed. "I'm done fighting. It's tiring ... and I'm tired."

"I'll help you."

"I don't want your help ... not anymore."

He looked as if she had slapped him. "What's your plan then? Stay here with *him*?"

She shrugged indifferently. "He's not so bad when he's not provoked."

Anger flared up in Jonas's eyes like fire, and he pulled his hand away from hers. "Does that sound like a life to you?"

"No ... but maybe life's not for everyone. It sure isn't for me. Not here, nor outside. At least he loves me."

Again, Jonas looked as if he'd been slapped. Alice felt sorry for him, but it was true. Was she supposed to ride into the sunset with Jonas, her white knight? She didn't know anything about him, and she definitely didn't want to impose herself on him. Danny was already lost, but Jonas could still do better.

I'm not going to be a burden for anyone. Not anymore.

Danny loved her. Jonas ... well, she had no idea what it was that he wanted.

"So that's what you want? A future with *him*?" He sounded hurt and the disdain in his voice was unmistakable.

Why don't you just tell me what you want, for a change?

"I can pretend to love him. Maybe I can even fool myself," she said instead.

The expression on Jonas's face made goose bumps rise on her arms. She wasn't sure if he was about to break something in rage or burst into tears, but he did neither. He just rose from the bed without saying another word and went to the door.

"I'm sorry!" she called after him, her voice heavy with guilt.

He hesitated at the door, one hand on the handle. "Don't apologize to me. Apologize to yourself."

28

Alice could not sleep that night. The memory of Jonas's face haunted her worse than any nightmare ever had. The pain in his eyes, the way he had looked at her as if he was about to break into tears. He had never been very talkative, but could he not see that *now* was the time to talk? To tell her how he felt? What it was that he wanted?

Poker face.

His specialty. It was impossible to read him, to understand him. The hurt in his eyes was as much as he would show her; his eyes had even turned shiny, but that was it.

Alice kept brooding over whether or not she had made the right decision, until dawn began creeping over the landscape and its fingers even found their way through the small gaps in her blinds, sending their faint rays of cold winter light through her room. It was about eight o'clock and the sound of tires on gravel announced that the night guard was being replaced with the day guard.

The realization of what day it was made her heart skip a beat. Christmas.

Her clothes still felt damp after the sweat-inducing nightmare of last night. There was no way she would be able to fall asleep again, so she took a deep breath, sat up, and stretched her stiff limbs. Determined to get out of her damp clothes, she went to the bathroom and took a long and hot shower, scrubbing herself madly as if she could get rid of the memories that way. Guilt clung to her heavily, making every movement twice as hard.

I'm the biggest idiot to ever set foot on this earth.

Jonas had been her only friend and she had pushed him away. She tried to tell herself that it was for the best, that he was better off without her, but her heart disagreed.

After disentangling her hair and drying it with the blow-dryer, she donned clean clothes—another oversized shirt and a pair of sweatpants. When she sat back in bed, she noticed that the sheets were still damp as well. Almost furiously, she ripped them off and threw them in a corner, and then she opened the window wide to let the freezing fresh winter air fill her room. It immediately brought goose bumps to her bare arms, but she didn't care.

It still had not snowed, but the grayish grass was covered in frost and it made the landscape look just as beautiful. A white Christmas after all. The sky was gray and covered by a thick layer of clouds. Alice couldn't remember the last time she had seen the sun. Its absence was depressing.

When Jonas appeared in the yard, dressed as usual in ripped jeans and his worn-out leather jacket, a cigarette in between his fingers, a pang went through her guts. She watched him walk toward the gate guard. The two of them talked, the guard widely gesticulating and Jonas smoking and nodding from time to time. Then Jonas went back into the house. She watched him sadly as he approached her before disappearing underneath the roof of the porch. He did not look up, but she was sure that he knew she was watching him. After all, he was psychic.

At around 10:00 a.m., Alice heard the key turn in the lock and the door opened. She looked up and saw Jean-Pierre standing in the frame, dressed for once in a black and white suit, freshly ironed and decorated with a bow tie. He didn't even look at her. He went straight to the dresser, shoved the book she had put there aside, and placed a tray on it.

"Nice look," Alice commented, hoping to provoke him into replying to her for once. Her loneliness made her want to communicate with someone—even if it was Jean-Pierre.

Instead of talking, he gave her a sharp look and walked back to the door.

"Wait," she called.

He stopped and turned, looking annoyed.

"I need new bedsheets."

Jean-Pierre gave her a curt nod and left the room, locking the door behind him. Alice sighed and lay down on her naked mattress, legs and arms outstretched, and stared at the ceiling.

Later, the rattling of the key in the lock ripped her once again out of her daydreams. Danny stepped into the room, dressed elegantly in an expensive-looking dark gray suit with a matching tie. He'd shaved his beard into a goatee and his hair was combed back. Alice had grown accustomed to his sophisticated look, though the memory of what he had looked like before, when he'd still been a long-haired metalhead and someone you could have fun with, was still vivid on her mind and filled her heart with longing. Now, he looked strict and cold ar boring. He appeared a bit stressed out as well this morning, but he gave her smile as he entered the room and closed the door behind him.

"Morning, sunshine," he greeted cheerfully.

"Morning," Alice said while quickly sitting up in her bed.

"Your room's a mess," Danny commented, his eyes scanning his surroundin

"I need new bedsheets ... that's all."

"It should be cleaned. When's the last time Anita or Helena were here?"

Alice had no idea who Helena was, but she guessed it must be the other ma

"Not since I came back from the hospital... Guess they don't have a key."

Danny's eyes widened. "It hasn't been cleaned all this time?"

She shrugged. "I did a little bit myself. Asked Jean-Pierre to bring me fr bedsheets for example."

"The maids have a master-key. They could have come in."

"Maybe they think I'm contagious."

Danny frowned at that remark, then he sighed and ran his fingers through hair. "I'll tell them to clean it. Why are you not dressed?"

"I *am* dressed. And it's only eleven."

"Oh, right. I forgot to tell you." He walked over to the dresser and eyed breakfast. "You haven't eaten," he muttered.

"What did you forget to tell me?"

He turned to face her. "Plan's changed. Some more guests will arrive at n and we're going to have appetizers and drinks until the dinner starts."

Alice felt her throat tighten. Two hours of dinner would have been one th Now, she had a whole day of feeling miserable and out of place ahead of h

Danny appeared to be reading her thoughts. "It will be fun, you'll see."

"Who's coming?"

"Some business partners, Marion and the kids, the guys obviously ..."

"The kids?"

"Yeah, Waldo has children ... I think I told you."

Poor bastards.

"What about Theresa and her husband?"

Danny shrugged. "Don't know yet. Julio will be there for the dinner, don't know if Theresa wants to leave the baby with the nanny. He tells m really clings to it."

At the mention of the baby, Alice felt a stab in her chest and tried to avoid his gaze. "I'll have to get dressed."

"Right, I bought you a dress."

She frowned at him. "A dress? You bought me another dress?"

"Yes. For the occasion. People will be dressed nicely, and I'd like you to do the same."

"Well, good thing I didn't get dressed already, then. Where is it?"

"In my room. I'll go and fetch it for you." He disappeared out of the door and Alice remembered the time when his room had still been *their* room.

That's the only good thing about being locked in here. He's forced to give me space.

Danny reappeared about a minute later with something purple wrapped in transparent plastic. He carefully laid it on her bed.

"Purple?" Alice asked, perplexed.

"I wanted to buy you a red dress because it's Christmas, but then I remembered that you hate red. You like purple though," he explained. "It'll go great with your hair."

It *did* go great with her hair, Alice had to admit when she checked her reflection in the bathroom mirror later. The dress was satin and went down to her knees. It was figure-enhancing, but not too tight. It left the shoulders bare, but the neckline was not too low, therefore not too revealing. What it covered in the front, it left bare in the back. Fine silver threads embroidered the bottom and the top of the dress in the shape of an endless mistletoe pattern, with tiny pearls sewn in between them. The dress was so soft and delicate, Alice was afraid to make a wrong move and tear it apart. It was probably more expensive than the rest of her wardrobe combined.

Her shoulders were bony, like the rest of her body, and she eyed her reflection scornfully. Sighing, she began to brush back her hair, when the sound of yet another knock on her door startled her. Curious, she stepped out of the bathroom and when the door remained closed, she called, "Yes?"

Slowly, the door was opened, and a nervous-looking Anita appeared in the frame. For a moment, she just looked at Alice with widened eyes, then she stepped into the room and closed the door behind her.

"Uh ... Mister Ortega told me to help you get ready," the maid spoke in a shaky voice.

She looks like she's scared of me. Maybe she does think I'm contagious.

"You mean the room?" Alice asked.

"No." Anita nodded to a small toilet case underneath her arm. "With hair and makeup."

Blood rushed to Alice's face at once and she dropped her eyes in shame. Having a maid to clean up her mess was bad enough, now Danny even wanted the maid to clean up the mess that was her face.

"That's okay, really," she mumbled.

"Uh ... Mister Ortega told me to," Anita repeated in a desperate voice.

"He insists?" Alice knew the answer before the maid nodded. Resigned, she sighed and sat down on the bed.

Anita hastily put the toilet case on the mattress, and began sorting its content and getting ready what she needed. Feeling uncomfortable, Alice stared at the wall while the maid started brushing her hair and pinning it up into what felt like a complicated hairstyle. Anita never looked into her eyes or spoke a word, and so Alice kept her mouth shut as well, silently hoping for the torture to be over soon. Under different circumstances, she would have been grateful to spend time with the staff, like she had with Henry, but Danny had obviously frightened poor Anita enough to keep her from talking to her. Or maybe, for some reason, she truly was scared of her.

When the hair was done, Anita began applying stuff to her face, Alice had never even seen before. She endured that too, without saying a word, and all the while, the maid appeared to be looking through her, rather than at her.

"Finished," she squeaked after putting her utensils away as quickly as she had taken them out.

"Thank you," Alice muttered.

Anita's eyes wandered up and down her body, but her face remained expressionless and did not reveal her thoughts.

"Shoes," she said suddenly when her eyes fell on Alice's feet that were only covered by nylon tights.

"I don't have—"

The maid was out of the room before Alice had finished her sentence. She was back in an instant though, with a pair of silver ankle-tie heels in her hands. Alice stared at them, pursing her lips.

"They belong to the dress. They were in Mister Ortega's room," Anita swiftly explained. To Alice's horror, she dropped to her knees in front of her and reached out for her foot.

At once, Alice pulled back her feet and shook her head. "I can put them on myself, thank you. Just leave them."

The maid obeyed and neatly set the shoes down in front of her. Relieved, Alice noticed that their heels were not too high. Still, she hated shoes that looked like they were designed for the sole purpose of torturing women. Reluctantly, she strapped them around her feet while Anita watched.

"Ready?" the maid asked out of breath, apparently eager to leave the room.

Alice nodded.

"You can go now, he is waiting."

Feeling awkward, Alice slowly got off the bed and stumbled toward the door. After a couple of steps though, she got the hang of it and managed to walk more or less normally. Anita opened the door for her and let her pass, and to Alice's surprise, Danny was already waiting in the hallway.

His jaw dropped when he saw her. "Beautiful," he exclaimed.

"How long have you been standing here?"

Danny held out his arm to her, and Alice put her hand on it and let him guide her toward the stairs. "A while. I didn't want to disturb her. She's really good at this." In awe, he kept staring at her and Alice felt herself blush.

"I wouldn't know. She didn't even let me look in the mirror. But the dress is beautiful, thank you."

He laughed brightly. "You don't need a mirror. Isn't my expression enough?"

Alice couldn't help but smile too. "I guess it is," she admitted.

Almost tripping over her feet, she followed him down the stairs. Not only were the heels uncomfortable to walk in, but the tension she felt added to her clumsiness. The prospect of having to meet Danny's guests made her heart race, and to be out of her room, after months of never being allowed to do so, was overwhelming. Her eyes widened when they reached the bottom of the stairs and she saw what had been done to the living room. The furniture was still in its usual place, but the surface of every table had been covered with a white, embroidered tablecloth and on top of each sat a marvelous poinsettia in a golden pot.

In the open space between Danny's office and the couches was now a long table, also covered by a white tablecloth, and on it balanced highly stacked silver plates with beautifully arranged bites. They looked mouth-watering, but in a way more like decoration than food.

Danny led her to the table and gestured at the plates. "Cooks did well, don't you think?"

Speechless, Alice nodded. Everything was too elegant, too perfectly arranged, and eating from it would have been a shame. There were sushi rolls—fish and plant-based—sweet and salty pastries, cheese and meat platters—the pieces cut into perfect shapes and carefully arranged on big silver trays—vegetables with complicated patterns carved into them, and bowls with different dips to dunk them in.

"There is another buffet in the dining room and the waiters will serve more on command."

Alice's eyes wandered to three men standing upright along the wall to her right, all dressed in white—even their bow ties were white. Timidly, she smiled at them and to her relief, they smiled back. Somehow, she had expected them to be expressionless like robots, the way they were patiently waiting to serve.

Faint noises were coming from the kitchen, the clattering of dishes and the spitting sound of something being fried.

"Food looks delicious ... and the room looks splendid," she told Danny. He grinned widely and planted a kiss on her cheek.

The sound of footsteps behind them made them both turn around, and Alice's heart stopped when she saw Jonas walking down the stairs. Even he had dressed up, she noticed, but for him, it meant black dress pants and a dark blue, long-sleeved shirt without tie or bow. His eyes were on Danny now and he pretended not to see her while he approached them.

"Jonas," Danny called. "Oh, how I love seeing you in a suit ... although you forgot the tie."

Jonas smirked and Danny patted his back in a brotherly way. "You should don a less tortured-looking expression. People might wonder."

"You *are* torturing me," Jonas grumbled.

Danny laughed at that. "Sorry, mate, but honestly, I feel honored that you'd go through all that trouble for me."

Alice continued staring at the food on the table to avoid having to look at Jonas. Her cheeks were burning with shame and she intensely hoped Danny would not notice.

The sound of the doorbell ringing made her flinch, and Jonas quickly left them standing to go and open the entrance door.

"The maids can do that," Danny called after him, just as a short, pale woman with blond hair tightly bound back into a bun appeared in the living room. She was wearing the maid's uniform. Danny gestured her to come over. "Helena," he said when the woman was close enough. "This is Alice. I think you have not met yet."

Helena shook her head and gave Alice a timid smile, which she returned.

"I forgot to tell you, but I'd like you to clean her room too. It's the one opposite my bedroom."

Helena nodded, but her lips remained closed.

"You can do it right now, actually. Anita already started but you can tell her to come downstairs instead. She's used to handling the guests."

Alice blushed and dropped her eyes, feeling ashamed. She hated the fact that maids had to clean the mess she made, and she also hated listening to Danny give orders—even if he did it in a friendly manner. Helena nodded again and hurried upstairs. Danny turned toward the entrance door, which Jonas had opened, and Alice followed his gaze with her eyes. Waldo was standing there, dressed in a light blue suit, and accompanied by his family. Marion had bound her hair back into a tight bun, similar to Helena's, only she was wearing expensive-looking golden earrings, a necklace, and bracelets that all appeared to belong to the same set. Her dress was red and fell down to her ankles, revealing pale feet in golden high heels. Curious, Alice looked at the children. The girl was a teenager, probably already eighteen. She had the sharp face of her mother, although she seemed to be rather shy and showed none of her parents' arrogance. Her dress was modest and pale lilac, and she was wearing flat silver shoes. The boy was younger, twelve or thirteen, and he already looked like a young version of Waldo, with his pale blond hair combed back and fixed with styling gel, his white ironed shirt, and the golden chain around his neck. His suit was dark blue and he was wearing black, polished leather shoes.

Danny tugged at Alice's arm lightly and she followed him to greet the guests. Jonas remained standing next to the door, still ignoring her, and Waldo gave her a look that seemed to say *And who let you out of your cage?* Again, Alice blushed, and she knew it would not be the last time that day. She greeted the guests with as much politeness as she could muster. Waldo introduced his children as Isabelle and Arthur. The name clearly fit, with Arthur being Waldo's little prince. It was plain obvious that Waldo was fonder of his son than of his daughter. The girl appeared to be intimidated by him, just like her mother, whereas Arthur showed as much self-confidence as only a rich spoiled boy could have. He did have manners though and generously complimented Alice on her looks, making her blush once again. She thanked him while silently hating herself for letting a little boy's words make her nervous. To her relief, he then darted off to the buffet.

"Don't make a mess," Waldo called after him, sounding amused.

Danny smiled and watched the boy stuff sushi rolls into his mouth. "Don't worry," he told Waldo. "There's enough food in the kitchen and the waiters will clean up the crumbs."

Alice suddenly noticed that Isabelle was watching her, and it made the little hairs on her arms stand up. Pretending not to notice, she kept her eyes on the carpet underneath her feet.

More guests arrived and the doorbell seemed to be ringing almost constantly. Soon enough, the wooden coat hangers on the right side of the entrance were covered by coats and jackets. Alice did not know any of the other guests. They were all rich men in suits, accompanied by beautifully dressed women. None of them brought any more children though. Danny introduced everyone to her, but Alice forgot the names as soon as she had heard them. Some exchanged some words with her and complimented her, making her turn red over and over again, but all of them lost interest when they realized that she was not very talkative. Before long, Danny was wrapped up in boring business talk and Alice let her eyes wander through the now crowded living-room, desperately looking for a place to escape to. Every single spot appeared to be occupied though, so she left Danny standing near the buffet, sipping on champagne while eagerly listening to his opponent. The dining room turned out to be crowded as well, so Alice slipped through the double door into the kitchen.

The cooks all looked up from their work and gave her curious glances, but when she smiled at them, they smiled back. Despite the opened window it was hot and stuffy in the kitchen. The air was thick and heavy with the fumes of the food that was being prepared on the stoves. Alice walked to the far end of the room and sat down on a counter in the corner. The cooks were very busy and she watched them as they handled hot pans and sharp knives with a casualness as if they were toys. From time to time, the waiters came in to collect the food and distribute it to the guests.

After a while, one of the cooks appeared to have finished his task and put a dirty pan into the sink before approaching Alice. He was younger than Henry, in his late thirties probably. Grinning, he wiped his hands on a towel. "Observing our work?" he asked in a heavy accent.

Alice smiled at him. "Oh, I'm sure you're handling things just fine. I'm Alice, by the way."

The cook used a towel to wipe some pearls of sweat from his forehead, then threw it onto the counter behind him.

"I know who you are," he said. "I'm Rahul, nice to meet you. The smell will cling to your clothes," he warned her.

Alice shrugged. "I doubt anyone will notice."

Rahul grinned again, baring two rows of grayish-looking teeth. "Don't you like parties?" he asked her.

"I don't like people."

He arched an eyebrow. "I'd better leave you alone then."

"No, no," she said quickly. "I mean, I don't like crowds ... I needed a place to hide."

"Aah, I see," Rahul remarked. "A drink will help."

"I don't really like champagne ..."

"What about wine?"

She shook her head. "Not really."

"Beer?"

"In the summer, yes. But not now."

"Aah," he said again and winked at her. "I know exactly what you need." Rahul strolled over to one of the cupboards and took a transparent glass bottle from it. He fetched two glasses and returned to her.

"Cherry schnapps," he announced while he poured. "We use it for cooking. It will warm your belly." Smiling, he handed her one of the glasses. Alice almost gagged at the smell of the liquor, but she took a sip nevertheless. It felt strangely good, and the burning in her throat quickly turned to warmth and spread through her belly and then her whole body, until every limb felt comfortably warm.

"Well, that brings some color to your cheeks," Rahul said cheerfully.

"That and misplaced compliments."

He laughed and took a gulp of his drink.

"Are you on a break?" Alice asked.

"My shift just finished." He downed the rest of the schnapps and gave himself a refill. "I've been here since 7:00 a.m. I'm going home to my family now."

"Christmas celebrations?"

He shook his head. "We don't celebrate Christmas. We're not Christians."

Alice nodded and took another sip from her glass.

"What about you?" Rahul wanted to know.

"Not religious. Neither is Danny. This is all just a farce to please the business partners, and also an opportunity to get people drunk and make them sign contracts."

Rahul appeared to be following her words with interest and Alice quickly bit her tongue. The alcohol was already loosening it and she worried she might have said too much.

"Never mind," she added.

Laughing, he gave her glass a refill. "Oh, don't worry. There are certain strings attached to this job, you know. I took a vow of silence. Don't want to end up like my predecessor."

Alice felt her guts convulse painfully at that remark. "What do you mean?"

Rahul shrugged. "Well, he was fired, wasn't he? For sticking his nose into the boss's business."

Trying to help me.

She remembered it only too well. But where was Henry now?

"Do you know him?" she asked the cook.

He shook his head. "No, I just heard what happened. It was a warning." He took a sip of his cherry schnapps. "We're not stupid, you know. We know what's going on here, but most of us came here illegally and need the money. Better not to ask any questions."

How much do they know? More than I do?

It made sense to hire illegal immigrants, Alice had to admit. Danny was protecting their secret while they protected his, knowing they were dependent on him.

"How long have you been here?" she asked.

"Me? A while ... I said most of us, not all of us."

Alice blushed. "Oh ... sorry."

"Don't worry." He gave her a friendly smile. "I could legally apply for any job now, but I like the work I'm doing. No restaurant pays as well as your husband."

"He's not my husband."

"Fiancé? Boyfriend?"

She shrugged.

The double door opened inward, and a younger man stepped into the kitchen, dressed in white with an apron tied around his waist. Rahul waved at him.

"My replacement," he announced happily. "It was nice chatting with you. Maybe again, sometime." He nodded to the bottle of schnapps. "Feel free to empty that one if you like. There's enough."

When he was gone, Alice watched the younger cook work while continuing to sip her drink. Rahul's absence made her sad. If only she weren't locked in her room all the time, she might hang out with the staff more. That seemed to be one of the main reasons for Danny to keep her locked up in her room though. He wanted to prevent her from making friends. He wanted to prevent another *Henry-situation.*

Something small and blond caught her attention, and she looked up to see Arthur sneaking through the door and into the kitchen. He walked around the cooks without so much as looking at them and began opening cupboards left and right, obviously looking for something. Amused, Alice watched him, until he spotted her and flinched, looking startled.

"*You're* here," he commented.

She nodded.

"What are you doing here?"

Alice took a sip of her drink. "Don't you think I should be the one to ask that question? What are you looking for?"

Arthur blushed. "Nothing," he lied.

"Booze?" She nodded to the bottle standing next to her.

The boy dropped his eyes, but immediately looked up again cheekily. "What if?"

"Aren't you a bit young for that?"

"What do *you* care?" he asked in a defiant tone.

"I don't." She pushed the bottle toward him. "Have some."

Arthur looked like he wasn't sure whether she was being serious or not, but then he approached her boldly and grabbed the bottle. When he opened it to sniff it though, he wrinkled his nose.

"Take a sip," Alice told him.

He obeyed and immediately started coughing. "This is gross!" he complained. "Can I have a beer instead?"

"If you can't handle schnapps, you can't handle alcohol." She eyed him suspiciously. "How old are you anyway?"

"Thirteen."

"Why don't you wait a couple of years to let your taste buds mature?"

Arthur gave her a stubborn look and took another sip of the schnapps, which made him screw up his face as if he had eaten a lemon.

"I'm sure *you* waited until it was legal," he remarked.

Alice sipped her drink. "Not at all."

"See."

"But I didn't have a father like Waldo."

Arthur's eyes widened for a second, but then he donned a neutral expression. "He's cool."

"I bet he is, as long as you behave."

That seemed to hit a nerve. The boy gave her a stubborn look and then eyed the bottle in his hand. "You gave it to me!"

"He can't hate me more than he already does." Alice shrugged and took another big gulp of her schnapps.

"Yeah, I don't think he likes you," the boy affirmed.

"Did he say that?"

"He mentioned you ... once or twice." He gave her an apologetic look that made her chuckle.

"I can live with that, you know."

"My sister talks about you too," Arthur proclaimed.

"Does she now?"

He nodded and bravely took another sip from the bottle. "I think she's jealous."

"Of what?"

"The glamor. She says life must be easy with a husband like Daniel."

Alice gave him an ice-cold look. "He's not my husband. Tell your sister that having a boyfriend like Danny is about as great as having a father like Waldo."

Arthur's voice reached an outraged pitch when he said, "He's a great dad!"

"I bet he is to *you*."

As if she had waited for a sign to come in, Isabelle appeared in the door in that instant, and when she spotted her brother with a bottle of schnapps in his hand, she shrieked and rushed toward him.

"What are you doing?" she exclaimed indignantly, before taking the bottle from him. "He's *underage*," she told Alice in a scolding tone.

Alice shrugged indifferently and continued sipping her drink. It had been so peaceful in the kitchen before Waldo's kids had intruded. They were really beginning to annoy her.

Isabelle put the bottle back on the counter and gave Alice another scowl, but to her relief, she then urged her brother out of the kitchen.

"If Daddy saw you ..." Alice heard her scold Arthur on their way out.

When her glass was empty, she put it in the sink with the other dirty dishes and stowed the bottle away in its cupboard. Drinking more did not seem like a good idea, since the two glasses had already made her drowsy. Feeling hot, she walked over to the open kitchen window to gaze out into the darkness and breathe in the piercing cold air. A voice calling from behind her made her turn around though.

"Miss Alice?" One of the waiters was approaching her. "Mr. Ortega has been looking for you," he told her politely.

Back to duty.

Alice took a deep breath and followed the waiter out into the living room, where the crowd of noisily chattering people made her feel suffocated at once. Right next to the kitchen door, she almost collided with Jonas, who was leaning against the wall, a glass of juice in his hand. Immediately, he turned his head away, refusing to look at her. Alice knew she had brought this on herself and he had every right to be mad at her, but it hurt nonetheless.

Danny was sipping white wine now and he looked up and smiled at her when she approached him.

"Where were you?" He put one of his heavy arms around her shoulders.

"I was talking to Rahul."

He frowned. "Who?"

Doesn't even know the names of his employees.

"One of the cooks," she explained while shaking her head rebukingly.

Danny's eyes narrowed. "What were you doing with the cook?"

"Rahul," she corrected him, feeling bold with the schnapps in her system. "We were talking."

"You do too much talking with the staff."

"If you did more, you might find out their names."

Danny opened his mouth to argue, but then he noticed that the couple standing beside them—a short round man with a bald head and his escort, a tall blonde woman who looked like a model—were watching them curiously. Laughing, he patted Alice's back and pulled her into a one-armed embrace, squeezing her tightly.

"Alice and her jokes," he told the guests. "Isn't she funny?"

The couple started laughing too, but it sounded forced. Alice forced a smile as well.

"And what were *Rahul* and you talking about?" Danny wanted to know.

"Religion. Though we did more drinking than talking."

Danny gave the couple an apologetic smile and led Alice a few steps away from them. "Are you *drunk*?"

"Only a little bit. From cherry schnapps."

"You were drinking cherry schnapps in the kitchen while I'm handling the guests out here? What are you, *sixteen*?" It sounded like a rant, but he had a wide grin on his face.

Alice wasn't sure whether it was real or just a mask for the guests. She stared at him, not sure how to respond.

"Why does the cook drink at work anyway?" he wanted to know.

"His shift was just over ... He's left now."

Frowning, Danny sipped his wine.

"What? Are you going to fire him like Henry? Are you going to fire everybody who talks to me?"

To her surprise, Danny's expression softened, and he chuckled. "Honestly? I'm rather amused right now, Allie. Seriously, stealing away like that, hiding out in the kitchen and getting drunk on schnapps ... It reminds me of how we used to be." He drank the rest of his wine and a waiter with a tray immediately appeared to fill up his glass anew.

"You know," he added, "whenever we were invited to a boring wedding or funeral. We would snatch a bottle of wine and hide somewhere."

The memories managed to put a smile on Alice's lips. "Yeah, I remember. We did the same thing at the office's Christmas party."

Danny burst into laughter and pulled her into a hug. "We were so *broken*."

She nodded. *We still are.*

When Danny freed her of his embrace, her eyes fell on Jonas, who was still standing next to the kitchen door. His eyes locked with hers for a split second, but then he quickly turned his head and walked away.

One after another, most of the guests left and only a few stuck around for dinner. Julio arrived at around 6:00 p.m. and to Alice's relief, neither Theresa nor the baby were with him. He brought his driver though and made him wait in the living room while everybody else assembled around the long table, which had now been set for dinner. Three small poinsettias were standing in the middle of the table and between them, two golden candleholders with five claret candles in each.

Alice took her seat next to Danny and stared at the table. There were so many different forks and spoons next to her plate, she didn't even know what they were for. But someone had once told her that you were supposed to start from the outside and work your way toward the plate.

The waiters waited until everybody was seated, then they began to pour the drinks. Alice watched the blood-red wine fill her glass. She tried hard not to look up, since Jonas was sitting opposite her as usual. Once or twice though, her eyes flicked to his face and she found him staring at his empty plate sullenly. A waiter filled one of Jonas's glasses with water and took the other one away.

Alice let her eyes wander across the table to see who else had stuck around for dinner. Marion was there, seated next to Waldo, but their children were not in sight. Julio was sitting next to Jonas and opposite of Danny, his thick belly squeezed in between table and chair. His suit was black, but faintly patterned, which made it shimmer in the orange candlelight.

Julio and Danny immediately began to chat, switching from Spanish to English and back, while Waldo was busy talking to some man Alice didn't know, and Timothy was having a conversation with Paul. The couple from before was seated to Alice's right. The little bald man was just telling his companion how much he loved the wine while he held his glass under her nose for her to smell it. She had a pointed little nose, which she wrinkled now since apparently, the wine displeased her.

When the first course—pumpkin soup with coconut cream—was served, Alice dove her spoon into her bowl and listlessly stirred it to make it cool down. She couldn't help it, her eyes kept wandering back to Jonas every now and then, and she noticed that he didn't seem to have much appetite either. The way he was staring at his soup, it appeared as though he were trying to read the future in its depths.

Alice picked a lush piece of parsley off her soup and put it in her mouth. Apparently, Danny had said something funny and Julio roared with laughter, splashing droplets of soup from his mustache. He picked up his napkin and wiped his mouth.

It was an odd feeling to be out of her room and surrounded by people—especially people like *that*. Alice sincerely hoped for the time to go by quickly, but it seemed to drag, and soon, she zoned out completely and nearly forgot where she was.

After everyone had finished their soup, salad was brought in and placed before them. Alice snapped out of her thoughts and turned to Danny, who was busy stabbing lettuce with his fork.

"How many courses does this dinner have?" she asked him quietly.

"Seven," he replied before taking a mouthful of salad.

"*Seven?*" she gasped. "Consisting of what?"

"Next is fish, then a cheese platter, then Christmas goose, then two desserts." He smiled and stabbed another fork load of salad.

"And what will I eat?"

He laughed and blew her a kiss. "The cooks know what they're doing, trust me." With that, he left her picking at her salad and went back to entertaining Julio.

The cooks *did* know what they were doing, Alice had to admit. When everyone was served a salmon filet, Alice got plant-based sushi rolls. The sight of them made her regain her appetite and Danny patted her shoulder approvingly.

The booze flowed en masse and soon enough, Julio's cheeks were as red as the wine and most of the other guests had blushed as well. The voices grew louder and the jokes dirtier, and Alice chugged her wine, trying to make the evening bearable. The noise was beginning to give her a headache.

Jonas was still ignoring her, but she was sure that he knew she was watching him from time to time. He looked tired and worn-out, and the people around him seemed to annoy him just as much as they did her.

The cheese platter brought the conversations to cheese, and Danny and the bald man to Alice's right started arguing vividly whether Swiss or French cheese was better. Sitting between them put her at the risk of having chunks of cheese spat at her and it made her extremely uncomfortable. She endured the discussion quietly though and gestured to one of the waiters to fill her wineglass anew.

When finally, the cheese platters were taken away, the bald man disappeared to go to the bathroom and Alice sighed, relieved.

Danny gave her a mocking grin.

"Seriously, Danny? Arguing about *cheese*?"

Still smiling, he took a sip of his wine. "I believe I haven't introduced you two yet. That's Harold and he despises everything French. His rants are hilarious, don't you think?"

"Maybe if you're not the one sitting next to him."

He chuckled. "I had them pour him French wine and told him it was Italian."

"Does he know I'm half French?" Alice asked.

"No ... and trust me, you don't want to tell him."

A break allowed the guests to go to the bathroom or to the living room to smoke. Jonas left the table as well, still without looking at her. It was saddening to see him like that.

I hurt him and he was only trying to help me.

Later, the goose was served and many of the guests gaped at it in admiration and complimented the cooks. The goose was immense and its skin was brown and crispy, its oily surface shining in the warm light of the candles. Slices of lime decorated the golden tray on which it lay.

Alice leaned backward when the waiters removed the flowers and moved the candleholders aside to place the goose in the middle of the table. As tasty as it smelled, it still looked a lot like the animal it had once been, and Alice stared down at her plate to keep her stomach from turning. When Harold spotted the marinated soy steak on her plate, he tried to wrap her up in an annoying discussion about vegetarianism, but luckily Danny saved her from it by telling him he had been drinking French wine throughout the evening. Fortunately, the following rant was over quickly and afterward, he let her eat in peace.

Another break followed the goose and half of the guests were becoming drowsy from the load of food and the booze and fell silent while the other half began talking even louder.

The first dessert was ice-cream and Alice waved it away, feeling too stuffed to eat another bite. She watched as a waiter refilled her wine glass.

To her horror, Julio suddenly began boasting about his sturdy little son and Alice kept staring at her wineglass, intensely trying to ignore him, but his voice roared through the room, drowning out everybody else's. Knowing the topic made her feel uncomfortable, Danny gave her a meaningful look. He did not want to be impolite though and who would interrupt a proud father?

Alice turned her head away from Danny to avoid his eyes. After all, it had been him who had caused the miscarriage, and that was hard to forget. Feeling her heartbeat accelerate, she quickly took a mouthful of wine, but the glass almost slipped through her sweaty fingers and she noticed that her hands were shaking. Taking a deep breath, she put them in her lap to hide them under the table.

Just let him talk, why should I even care?

But somehow, Julio's words were enough to make her heart race. The wine made her tongue feel furry and the sour taste in her mouth was beginning to make her nauseous.

"What about you two?" Julio asked loudly, after having finished talking about his son's magnificence. "Any baby plans?"

Alice bit her tongue hard and continued staring at her wineglass. All eyes seemed to be on her and the urge to get up and flee the room was overwhelming.

I'm imagining things. Nobody's looking at me.

Her cheeks burned though, and she imagined she must be at least as red as Julio.

"No. Now is not the best time," Danny replied in a low voice.

Julio gulped down the rest of his wine and put his glass back down on the table. "You're not getting any younger, amigo. They say the younger, the better."

"Actually," Timothy threw in, "they say if the father is young, the baby will be pretty and if he's old, it'll be smart." He laughed. "Which one would you prefer, Dan?"

Julio roared with laughter. "Judging by the parents, it'll get the looks anyway. Come to think of it: better wait a bit, amigo, to ensure the brains."

Danny chuckled and Timothy burst out laughing. All the other talk at the table had died out and Alice realized that everybody was following the conversation with interest. Nervously, she fumbled with the tablecloth while trying to keep a blank face. Her heart was racing madly, and the panic almost made her break into tears.

Julio waved at a waiter to refill his glass. "No, but seriously," he continued. "Children are a gift of God. They're a blessing. You should not wait too long. It's not only you who'll get older. Your woman will age too and for women, the best time is as soon as possible."

Anger flared up in her and chased some of the panic away, and Alice quickly took another sip of her wine.

"You may think you have your whole life ahead of you," Julio told her now, while looking at her for the first time ever. "But trust me, your man may be at the peak of his business right now, so don't waste any time."

It was not clear whether Julio meant Danny's actual business or if there was a double meaning to his words.

"Oh, I hope not," Danny exclaimed. "We're only just getting started."

Timothy laughed at that and Danny blushed, only just realizing how it had sounded.

"Trying, huh?" Julio winked and gulped down more wine.

"Not enough nuts on the tree?" Timothy asked, chuckling.

Alice's mouth was dry and her tongue was sticking to her palate, and she warily stole a glance at Danny, who was beginning to turn really red. He was not smiling anymore.

"How 'bout we change the subject?" he grumbled.

"Careful now, Julio. Dan's pride is hurt," Timothy joked, still chuckling. Danny gave him a warning look and he fell silent.

"I'm just saying," Julio continued, "you will love being parents. It's the best thing in the world."

Even though she tried hard to fight them, tears began to blur Alice's vision and she blinked them away. Not able to withstand the panic anymore, she pushed back her chair to flee the room. Danny quickly caught her arm though and held her back before she managed to rise from her chair.

"Stay!" he hissed through clenched teeth.

Now, there was no doubt anymore that every single pair of eyes was on them. Julio frowned. "What's wrong?"

Danny sucked in air noisily. "She had a miscarriage."

Alice felt all color drain from her face at once and she wished for the floor beneath her to open up and swallow her. The stares felt heavy and made it hard for her to breathe. The mix of grief, panic, and humiliation were too much for her to bear, and she tried her best to fight her tears.

No one spoke until Julio said, "Oh."

The tension was suffocating, and it was clear that everybody at the table felt awkward.

"That can happen," Julio finally said. "In the first two or three months, I heard. No reason to despair."

"It was almost the sixth month and I already had a name for her," Alice snapped, finally losing her temper.

Danny's grip around her wrist tightened painfully and he gave her a warning stare. Trying to avoid his glare, she turned her head and her eyes flicked to Jonas. To her surprise, he was looking at her and his eyes blazed with anger. His cheeks were faintly blushed.

Taken aback, she could do nothing but stare at him. Jonas's lips tightened and he looked down at his plate, but Alice could not take her eyes off him.

"That's very ... tragic," Julio said. "But you can always try again."

"Nope ... that ship's sailed," Alice muttered.

Danny's hand twitched as if he wanted to slap her, but he knew better than to hit her in front of the guests. Julio's eyes widened and he mouthed an 'oh', having understood.

The tension in the room grew almost unbearable and Danny's grip around her wrist brought tears of pain to her eyes.

"It's a tragedy," he growled impatiently. "Accidents happen."

Crack.

The sound of glass breaking followed Danny's words, and Alice looked up to find the source of it.

The red of Jonas's cheeks had intensified and his right hand was clenched around the shards of what used to be his water glass. His eyes were on Danny and they were full of hatred.

When Danny looked at him though, Jonas quickly dropped his stare. Blood was trickling through his fingers and Alice watched, horrified, as it dripped onto the white tablecloth.

A waiter hurried toward the table, carrying a towel, but Jonas pushed his chair back and stormed out of the room before the man could reach him.

Awkward silence filled the dining room, and Alice felt Danny's piercing stare on her. Her heart was racing violently, and she tried to look as if she had no idea what just had happened.

He doesn't know anything, she tried to convince herself.

After what felt like an eternity, Timothy finally broke the silence and managed to wrap Danny up in a conversation about a new video game, which had recently been launched, and Danny let go of Alice's wrist at last. People went back to their conversations and she remained staring at Jonas's empty chair, wondering what was going through his head right now. She wanted nothing more than to leave the table and hide in her room, but disappearing right after Jonas would have looked suspicious, and Danny wasn't trusting her as it was. The only thing she could therefore do, was sit through the rest of the dinner and endure the conversations and jokes silently.

The last dessert was chocolate mousse and she stared at it, devouring it with her eyes rather than her mouth.

After the waiters had removed the rest of the dirty dishes, only the booze remained, and it looked like it was going to be a very long and tiring night, until to Alice's relief, Julio wanted to talk about business and Danny told her to go to her room.

When she passed Jonas's room, the temptation to find out how he was doing almost made her knock on his door, but she knew it was a foolish idea and restrained from it. Danny or one of the others could likely come upstairs at any moment and if they found her with Jonas ... Alice sighed and continued walking toward her room.

The bed had been made, she noticed, and the room was exceptionally tidy. It even smelled nice. After kicking off her shoes, she dropped onto her mattress, fully dressed. Exhaustion overwhelmed her and made her sink into a sleep spiked with wild and confusing dreams and images of the horrible dinner.

Danny shook her awake after what felt like only a couple minutes of sleep. Confused, Alice blinked at him and pushed herself up into a sitting position.

"I need to talk to you." His tone was harsh, matching the dangerous glint in his eyes.

Puzzled, she asked, "How long did I sleep?"

He shrugged. "About two hours maybe. The guests are gone."

"What is it?" She eyed him carefully. He looked both angry and agitated.

"What was that at dinner?"

Alice felt her throat tighten at once. "What do you mean?" She knew exactly what he meant.

"There's something going on between you and Jonas. I want to know what it is." His stare was ice-cold and piercing, making her shiver on the inside.

I don't even know that myself. He never told me.

"I- I don't know—"

"Cut the crap!" he snapped. His cheeks had turned red.

Alice winced at his tone and felt her body tense in fear of him. She tried to think of something to say, but her brain was still half asleep and intoxicated by wine and schnapps. Looking for a smart answer felt like rummaging in an empty drawer. Her heartbeat accelerated when she felt Danny's impatience increase.

He grabbed her upper arms and shook her roughly. "Answer me!"

"Nothing's going on," she said hastily, feeling dizzy.

He tightened his grip until tears of pain flooded her eyes.

"Nothing's going on, I swear!"

"You swear?" He scoffed. "And what's that supposed to mean to me, huh? I want the truth!"

"There's nothing going on," Alice insisted. "Let go of me, you're hurting me!"

"I saw the way he ignored you today, and later at dinner, you kept staring at him. And when the miscarriage came up, he broke his glass! Do you think I'm blind?" He was breathing heavily now, hands still clenched around her upper arms.

"I don't know what happened ... and he always ignores me, what's new about that?"

"You were getting along quite well before." Anger and mad jealousy flickered in his deep blue eyes.

"Yes, until you told him to stay away from me!" Alice held his stare stubbornly. "Since then he's been ignoring me."

"Bullshit," Danny spat. He shook her again. "Tell me the truth!"

"There's nothing to it!"

"Why did he break that glass?"

"Why don't you ask *him* that?"

Danny was shaking with anger. "I'm asking *you* now. So answer!"

"Maybe it's because he went to jail for you and he's still mad about that," Alice suggested desperately.

He hesitated, then frowned. "You know, if it weren't for the look on your face, I might actually believe that ... but I know you well enough to tell when you're lying, and the scared look on your face says it all."

"I'm scared because you're drunk and acting out again."

"How convenient for you to blame everything on my drinking. You drank about as much as I did, the way I remember it."

"Yeah, but I'm not the one making a scene." Alice tried to keep her voice steady. "You're freaking out over nothing again and you're forgetting your strength."

"I'm not forgetting my strength; I remember it well enough ... and you should too."

It was a threat, she knew, and she froze in his grip.

"I'm giving you one more chance," he menaced.

Tears of desperation began running down her cheeks. She had known the day would come when Danny wasn't fooled anymore. He would kill her and Jonas both if he found out about their secret, but he already knew something was up. There had to be *something* she could tell him.

Her tears left him cold.

"We were getting along well once and now we're not anymore. That's all there is to it," she muttered, but even before the last word had left her lips, she knew she could as well have said nothing at all. The stare he gave her felt as if he were shrinking her.

To her surprise, he finally took his hands off her. His jaw remained clenched, and the sound of his teeth grinding together made goose bumps appear on her arms. He seemed to be boiling on the inside.

Alice took advantage of him not grabbing her anymore and quickly got off the bed, then backed a few steps away from him. He remained motionless, but his eyes followed her like those of a lion ready to attack his prey.

"You're a liar and a whore," he hissed.

Alice took another step back, until she was standing in the frame of the bathroom door. "If you don't believe me, why don't you just ask Jonas?" Her eyes flicked to the door and she thought about locking herself in the bathroom, but then she remembered that she had no key for it either.

Danny's eyes were still on her, unblinking. "What are you doing?" he growled.

Slowly, she turned toward the sink and reached for her toothbrush. "I'm brushing my teeth and then we're going to bed. Tomorrow, when we're both sober, we can talk."

Her trembling fingers closed around the toothbrush, but in that instant, she saw Danny's reflection in the mirror rise from the bed and approach her. Unmoving, she watched him come closer and tensed when she felt his hot breath on the back of her neck.

"We're talking *now*," he snarled.

"Now is not a good time," she insisted. "You're not thinking straight."

She flinched when he put a hand on her bare back and let his fingers wander up her spine to her neck. Where they touched her, goose bumps appeared. His thumb traced the line of her neck gently and Alice's breathing accelerated. His demeanor was confusing.

"I'm thinking straighter than ever," he said softly, then his fingers closed around her neck, and he smashed her head down onto the sink.

The impact took her completely by surprise, and she vaguely felt her lower lip burst. Blood filled her mouth. Numbed by the pain, her legs gave in, but Danny's hand was still clenched around her neck and he pulled her back up. His mouth came close to her ear and she felt his hot breath on her skin.

"I warned you," he breathed. "I will not endure your insolence anymore."

Alice's lip was throbbing. She stared at Danny's reflection, at the hatred in his beautiful blue eyes, and her mind was completely blank, unable to grasp a clear thought.

His lips brushed her ear and nibbled at it, then they moved down her cheek and to her throat. For a moment, she half expected him to rip her throat out after all, but then his kisses wandered to her neck and down her bare shoulders. His right hand was still holding her neck tightly, but his left went to her chest and he let his fingers glide over the smooth purple satin. Alice squeezed her eyes shut when they reached her breasts and slid down to her belly.

"You really look beautiful today," he commented while he pulled her dress up over her hips and fumbled with her tights and underwear. She heard a metallic *click* when he opened his belt, and her throat tightened, leaving her unable to breathe. She wanted to beg him to stop, but her tongue would not move, and her mouth was filled with blood.

"Open your eyes," he ordered.

When she didn't, he let go of her neck and grabbed her hair instead, yanking at it to make her look up, making the pins come undone. "Open your eyes!"

This time, she obeyed. A feeling of nausea overcame her at the sight of her reflection and she quickly looked at his lips instead. They parted into an evil smile, revealing two rows of perfectly white teeth.

"Do you see that?" he asked, nodding toward the mirror. "You're mine ... don't you ever forget that."

He thrust himself inside her and little stars began to dance before her eyes. To her horror, her eyes seemed to be glued to her reflection, and she couldn't help but watch as he claimed what he considered to be his.

As she watched, her face remained completely blank and her eyes dull. It wasn't her face at all ... the woman in the mirror looked like a stranger, like a lifeless doll with smeared makeup and blood running down her chin.

Alice kept staring at the mirror as if it were a TV, and the longer she watched, the more disconnected she became, until reality blurred into a dream.

When he was done, he slowly closed his belt, tucked his shirt back into his pants as if he had all the time in the world, and then left without saying another word.

Alice had sunken to her knees the moment he had taken his hands off of her and she didn't know how long she remained on the floor, but when the fog in her mind had dissolved slightly, she felt something small and hard on her tongue, so she pulled herself up on her feet, opened her mouth and spat blood into the sink. Motionless, she watched as the tooth slid toward the drain, leaving a trail of blood behind.

29

The following days passed in a blur.

The sun rose and set and then rose again, but its light was always hidden by a thick layer of gray clouds. The world outside seemed to be standing still. There were no crows cawing, no wind rustling through the last leaves on the trees, no talking or laughing in the yard, and due to the fog, which covered the land, it was impossible to see the cars in the distance. There was no rain, no hail, and still, no snow. Everything was gray and cold and silent.

Alice sat on her bed with glazed eyes, staring at nothing in particular, barely acknowledging Jean-Pierre bringing her food twice a day. He said nothing, as always, and the food went cold untouched until he came back to take the tray away.

Helena and Anita appeared every day as well, stealing glances at her while they rushed through the room, cleaning it in a hurry. Once or twice, they asked timidly to change the bedsheets, so Alice got off the bed and moved over to the windowsill instead, swaying like a sleepwalker as she did so.

Danny visited her as well. He came sober and cried, begging for forgiveness. He came drunk and shook her, shouting at her to tell him the truth. He came high on coke and horny and left her bruised. But nothing he did woke her up, and nothing he said made her reply. Her apathy made him angrier when he was angry and sadder when he was sad, but nothing he did pulled her out of her emptiness. She was lost somewhere deep inside herself, deeply shattered and scattered in pieces.

It had finally seemed as if life with him would remain tolerable. Alice had not anticipated Jonas's outburst and Danny's ability to put two and two together.

There was nothing for her now, she knew. Nowhere to go once outside of the house and no future inside of it either. All she could wish for was a quick and painless death if Danny found out the truth. Else, he would torture her until she blurted something out.

But for now, she endured his daily visits quietly and without even looking at him. Everything felt unreal anyway, so it was easy to pretend it wasn't actually happening.

At night, either the nightmares or Danny would shake her awake, and when Danny did, the nightmare only began.

The blanket was wrapped around her tightly, like a straitjacket. Cold and damp and sticky. Her breaths were short and quick, the heaving of her chest hindered by the tightly entangled blanket. Alice pulled one arm free and ripped the moist fabric away from her throat, panting heavily. It was cold in the room and she felt as if she had been thrown into a tub filled with ice-cold water, the nightshirt clinging to her skin, soaked by the cold sweat which had been evoked by one of her nightmares. Danny had been in it, as always, and when her eyes flung open, he was still there, eyeing her coldly from his seat by the window. His face was half illuminated by the orange light of a small camping lantern, which he had placed on the floor next to his feet. He was sitting on the couch, leaning back against the windowsill, his right arm resting casually on the armrest of the sofa. He was wearing a white dress shirt as usual, and it made him glow in the darkness.

Alice blinked and sat upright, rubbing her eyes with her damp palms; but when she looked back up, he was still there.

A chill went through her bones and made her shiver. How long had he been sitting there already, staring at her? How much of her nightmare had actually been a nightmare, how much of it true? Her head was throbbing, and her mouth was dry. All the sweating must have dehydrated her, she knew. She licked her lips and tasted salt on them.

The sudden movement of Danny leaning forward made her flinch. He rested his elbows on his knees, hands folded in the middle, and continued staring at her.

"The sleeping beauty has awoken," he muttered, and a cold smile parted his lips. "And I didn't even have to kiss you."

My lips would taste of sulfur, not salt, if you had, Alice thought and pulled the blanket back over her chest as if it were a shield.

"Another nightmare?" Danny's voice was low, as if he wanted to make sure that nobody except her would hear him. Alice's eyes flicked to the clock on the wall to her right. It was 3:22 a.m.

"I feel sorry for you," he continued. "Life must be a nightmare for you already ... if only sleep brought relief." There was hurt in his voice and a bitterness that made him almost spit out the words rather than speak them.

Alice dropped her gaze and stared into the darkness in front of her, away from the faint orange light and Danny's face.

"Right ... you're not talking to me anymore. How could I forget? I don't even know if you're listening ... if you're even *present*." He paused and the nerve-racking sound of his teeth grinding together filled the room, sending a tingling sensation through her spine. Goose bumps rose on her arms and she wrapped the blanket tighter around herself, but due to its dampness, it brought no warmth.

Coke today, she knew.

"I apologized to you a hundred times, but you weren't even listening, were you? You're just so fucking stubborn, do you know that? I wouldn't even have had to do the things I did if you had just told me the truth and answered my questions. But no, you'd rather just bite your tongue until you bite it off, rather than tell me anything." His voice was still low, but through the silence of the night, it sounded like thunder.

"Are you conspiring against me? Is that it? I didn't like Jonas's attitude from the start, the way he would stick his nose where it doesn't belong."

Among other things ...

"He criticized me for being too hard on you and I thought he was right, until I realized that this is the only way to deal with you and your insolence." He blew a strand of hair out of his eyes. His stare was still on her; she could feel it.

"Relationships are about sharing, missy, but you never wanted to share anything. You had to be in control all the time, and I let you, but when I took my fair share of power, you fought me from the start. Have I not given you *everything*?"

Alice let his words wash over her like waves of cold water, not even trying to grasp what he was saying. They kept echoing hollowly in her head until they were drowned out by new ones.

"I'm done apologizing," Danny said with venom in his voice. "You don't want what I've given you. You don't want any of it. You'd rather die than live with me, ain't that right?" He laughed dryly. "Hell, you even tried to kill yourself, and when that didn't work, you began starving yourself. I won't tie you to a bed and force-feed you, Alice, I get the hint, trust me. You'll never love me again and I'm tired of having to force you into being with me. I'm tired of it, once and for all."

His words rang in her ears long after he had spoken them, and when they finally faded out, all she could hear was her own heart pounding in her chest and the ticking of the clock on the wall. The silence around her was heavy and thick, and threatened to suffocate her. The menace in his voice had been unmistakable, and she wondered what he was implying.

When suddenly he spoke again, she almost choked on her own breath and did all she could to suppress a cough.

"You know why I came here tonight?" he asked, sounding sad all of a sudden. He sighed when she didn't answer. "I came here to bring you relief."

His right hand moved slowly, and he grabbed something that was lying in between his thigh and the armrest of the couch. Alice felt her heart pound faster and she turned her head slightly to look at him. There was a gun in his hand, she saw, but in the semi-darkness, it seemed twice its normal size. She swallowed dryly and couldn't help but stare at the weapon while he turned it over in his hand.

"*Now* I have your attention," he muttered. He lifted the gun and aimed it at her. "Tell me ... how come you're scared of guns when all you want is to die?"

Alice had no answer to that. He was right, she had attempted suicide and she had fantasized about dying almost every day since she had lost the baby, but still, the sheer sight of a gun made her tremble.

It's better than taking pills, she told herself, *it will be quick and painless.*

"You ... want to kill me?" she asked tonelessly. Her voice was hoarse.

Danny lowered the gun and laid it in his lap. "A miracle," he gasped sarcastically. "It even manages to make you talk."

Alice dropped her eyes and turned her head away from him, feeling humiliated by his mockery.

"I did come here to kill you, as a matter of fact," he admitted. "I wanted to end your life quickly and silently, that's how *merciful* I am." He lifted the weapon again and pointed at its lengthened muzzle. "See, I even put a suppressor on it."

Alice stared into the darkness on the other side of the room, avoiding his eyes. "Why didn't you do it already?" she asked quietly.

"You were having a nightmare ... It felt wrong. I wanted you to die peacefully."

"Oh, how very thoughtful of you," she muttered under her breath.

"What?" He leaned closer to understand her better. When she didn't answer, he sighed. "I should've just pulled the trigger and been done with it. I didn't want you to wake up."

"You were probably the cause of my nightmare." Alice felt bold suddenly, knowing that everything was lost anyway.

"Yeah, I know that much already. I'm everything that's wrong in your life, ain't I?"

She bit her lip. "You weren't always."

Silence followed her words. They had had this conversation before, many times, it seemed. There was nothing left to say.

"Things have changed. And they will never go back. It's time we both accept that," Danny said at last, his voice sad. He tapped the fingers of his left hand against the metal of the gun and the sound made her hold her breath. "It's almost New Year's Eve. Time for a change."

Alice tensed when she heard him rise from the couch. She clenched her fists so hard, her nails dug into her palms, but it managed to keep her hands from shaking. Danny walked around the bed and toward the door, and Alice half expected—half hoped for him to leave. But all he did was lock the door from the inside and put the key in the back pocket of his pants. Then he came back to where she was sitting and sat down beside her. He smelled clean, as if he had showered and donned fresh clothes. There was also a faint hint of cologne on him.

Did you dress for my funeral already?

She wanted to say the words aloud, but they got stuck in her throat. She closed her mouth again and bit her tongue.

Danny played with the weapon in his hands, turning it over and over while he looked at it as if it contained the secret of eternal youth.

"This is harder than I thought it would be," he murmured tonelessly.

Alice's eyes seemed to be glued to the shining gun in his hands. "If you're ready to live without me ... why can't you just let me go?" she whispered.

Danny put a hand on hers and to her surprise, it was ice-cold, even colder than her own. She winced and tried to pull free, but he held her hand tightly. When he spoke, his voice was thick with grief.

"You got me all wrong, Allie," he said quietly while his thumb caressed the back of her hand. "I could never live without you."

Her eyes flicked to his and she saw tears in them and couldn't help but stare at him, puzzled by his words.

"First you ... then me." He lifted the gun and pointed it at her, making her flinch.

"You want to kill *yourself*?"

Danny met her gaze with his big blue eyes and nodded.

"But ... why?"

"What do I have?" He looked desperate at once.

"You have everything you wanted ... don't you? Money, power, influence ..."

He sighed and shook his head. "Money was never the reason why I started this whole thing. I wanted to make the world a better place."

"By doing *what*?"

"You don't need to know that."

"You could at least tell me the truth if you're about to kill me. You owe me that much."

Danny's expression hardened at once. "I owe you nothing." His voice was cold as ice.

"What about your plans? The new house? What about your friends?"

"I have no friends. I have colleagues who don't follow my lead anyway. *Their* goal has always been the money. They made me do things I'm not proud of. They're turning against me, one by one, because I refuse to do business with a certain kind of people."

"Who knew you had morals," Alice said sarcastically.

He frowned and pursed his lips. "I've made mistakes. And maybe I've changed in certain ways, but I'm still me. I still have the same values. I won't support killing innocent people, not ever. But it seems my friends, as you call them, have different conceptions about what our business is supposed to achieve. Honestly, things are falling apart anyway. I might as well end them here and now."

He looked at the gun and then back at her, his face contorted with regret. He cocked the gun and raised it, and a sudden calmness settled down around her. It filled her heart and with every heartbeat, it spread further through her body and left her mind completely blank. She looked at him, right into his beautiful blue eyes, and remembered the good times they'd had.

This is not so bad, she realized. *I'm not even afraid anymore.*

Danny's finger was on the trigger and his hand began to tremble. Pearls of sweat glistened on his forehead.

The ticking of the clock echoed from the walls. Every second seemed to take twice as long to pass.

"Just get it over with," she whispered.

His breathing accelerated and his grip around her hand tightened. He moved the gun closer to her chest until the cold metal touched her ribs. She could feel him shaking now. He groaned and gritted his teeth, as if his inner struggle was actually physically painful.

A tear rolled down his cheek and he leaned forward, releasing her hand out of his grip and stroking her cheek instead without moving the gun away from her chest. He brushed the sweaty strands of hair from her forehead and kissed her skin gently. Even his lips were cold, Alice noticed.

Again, he tensed as if he were ready to pull the trigger. But he did not.

He gave her a tortured look and lowered the gun.

Alice dared not speak. She felt as if she were standing on thin ice and every movement, even saying a word, might break it.

He wiped sweat from his forehead with the sleeve of his shirt and muttered curses under his breath.

"I can't do it," he finally confessed.

Alice said nothing and they stared at each other in silence. The tension was bone-crushing, and her head began throbbing anew while she waited for Danny to make a decision. He sighed—a desperate sound—and then his face hardened.

To her surprise, he turned the gun around and placed it in her hands instead, its muzzle pointed at himself. Alice tried to wind her hands free and push the weapon away, but his fist was locked around her hand, pressing her sweaty fingers against the cold, hard metal of the gun in a painful manner. Tears filled her eyes and she tried once again to pull free.

"Shoot it," he ordered, his voice low yet firm.

"No," she said weakly, her throat dry and tight.

"Do it," he insisted. "I am giving you a chance here, Alice. The only one you might ever get. I can't kill you, no matter how much I want to, but I'm allowing you to put an end to this."

He tried to force her finger on the trigger, twisting it painfully, making her gasp.

"Ow, stop it!"

"Do it," he urged again.

"Why don't you just do it yourself if you want to die so badly?"

He glared at her and the corner of his mouth twitched. "That would be so convenient for you, wouldn't it? No, Alice. You told me you don't love me anymore. Prove it."

"Prove it?" Her voice grew higher and she tried once again to pull free of his grip, but it only made him grab her harder. "What is there to prove? I'm not a killer! I don't have to love somebody to not want to shoot them!"

"You shot Viktor."

"I didn't want to! It was supposed to be a warning shot! I never wanted to hit him, I swear, I could never kill anybody!"

"How desperate you get at once," he said coldly. "Minutes ago, I had the gun aimed at you, ready to kill you, and you just sat there ... Now that you're the one with the gun, you're suddenly not so calm anymore. This isn't even about me, is it? It's about you not wanting to get your hands dirty. You'd love it if I shot myself, wouldn't you? Best not even in front of you, right? Should I go to my room and close the door behind me, so you don't have to see it?"

"I don't want you to die," Alice said tonelessly.

"The hell you don't. You want to rid yourself of me, but you're too big of a coward to pull that trigger."

Tears welled up in her eyes at his words. It was not true, not even a bit. She had enough reasons to hate him, but she didn't, and she had never wanted him dead.

"It's not true," she whispered. "I don't want you to die."

"But you don't want to be with me."

"There's not only this or death, Danny! We're two grown-up people; we can live without each other."

He shook his head slowly. "If I can't have you, no one can. Or at least I don't want to be around to see it. You don't deserve an easy way out of this, Alice. I am giving you an opportunity here, right now. Take it or leave it."

He pressed her fingers around the gun even harder, and it felt like he was about to crush her bones.

"Danny, please," she begged, weakly attempting to wind free. "I don't want to do this!"

"I don't care what you want."

"I can't! Okay? I can't do it! I can't shoot you, is that what you want to hear? That you still mean something to me? Fine, I'll admit it. I can't hate you, no matter how much I want to ..." Tears ran down her cheeks now and her voice cracked. Danny's eyes were on her, unblinking.

"Please," she sobbed. "Don't make me do this! I don't want you to die and I could never live with myself if I killed you!"

"This is your only chance."

"I don't want it! Please put the gun away, please!"

His eyes were still on her, piercing and cold. He seemed to be trying to decide what to do. They wandered to the tears on her cheeks and lingered on her trembling lips.

"Does this mean you still have feelings for me?" he asked quietly, almost in a whisper.

Speechless, Alice stared at him. A pain in her chest made it hard to breathe. Did she? She had thought that she didn't, that her love for him was finally over. Now she wasn't so sure anymore.

She opened her mouth, but no words came, so she closed it again.

He said nothing and remained staring at her for what seemed like an eternity, until he released her hand at last.

"You made your decision," he said quietly while he tucked the gun underneath his belt and flattened his shirt. He leaned closer and planted another kiss on her forehead, then he caught one of her tears with his finger and crushed it in between his index finger and thumb.

Alice kept staring at the spot where he had just been sitting, long after he had gotten up from the bed. She felt incredibly torn inside.

Danny unlocked the door, his lantern in one hand, but he hesitated and turned around once again. "You're going to wish you had pulled that trigger," he muttered, before stepping out of the room and leaving her sitting in complete darkness.

On Monday, December 31 at around noon, Danny came to her room to announce that he was about to leave for a New Year's Eve party at Julio's house.

"I was planning to take you along, you know," he said, standing near the door, arms crossed in front of his chest. "I thought leaving the house would be good for you. You would have enjoyed it." He sighed and scratched his chin. "Things have changed, obviously. I won't let you out of this room until the day we move."

Alice's eyes remained on the white wall in front of her. Still, she felt as if she were wrapped in cotton balls. Danny's voice seemed far away and had no effect on her. It didn't matter what he had to say anyway.

After he had shut the door behind him, she remained where she was, unmoving, trying to send her mind somewhere else. Images of Jonas kept pulling her back to reality though, haunting her. An uneasy feeling in her chest made her fingers and toes tingle, breaking through the layers of imagined cotton, sharpening her senses against her will.

She had not seen him since Christmas—except through the window when he had been smoking in the front yard. He had never looked up at her window. It made her sad that he still held a grudge. She had never meant for him to get hurt or angry. She did not really understand it either. Sure, he had gone through the trouble of planning an escape for her and she had declined it, but was that reason enough to be mad at her? He had not let her run away throughout the whole year. Every single time, he had brought her back to her *prison*—brought her back to Danny. Was it even his right to be angry at her now? Alice wondered if there were other reasons involved, things he would not tell her.

Her thoughts were disrupted by the key rattling in the lock at around 1 p.m. The door flung inward, and Jean-Pierre appeared, carrying a tray in one hand. As usual, he placed it on the dresser, but this time, he turned around and looked at her—something he had never done before. His face was grim as always. "I've brought you enough food for the whole day."

Alice flinched at his words. She could not remember having ever heard his voice before. It was deep and a bit husky, as if he were a smoker, but she had never seen him smoke.

"You talk," she gasped, genuinely surprised.

He ignored her remark. "I'm out tonight. That's why I brought you enough to eat. You won't eat it anyway, but don't ever say I let you starve." It took him only two steps with his long legs to reach the door again.

"You're going out?"

He paid her no mind.

"You're leaving me all alone?" she asked before he could close the door behind him.

He stopped and looked at her. "There's guards outside."

With that, he pulled the door shut and Alice heard the key turn in the lock.

The day seemed to drag after Jean-Pierre had left. Alice remained on her bed, staring at nothing in particular, her mind empty.

The sudden rattling of the key in the lock made her flinch, and her eyes flicked to the door. The house was supposed to be empty. Her heartbeat accelerated and she stared at the door with wide eyes. When a frightened Anita appeared in the frame, Alice exhaled the breath she'd been holding.

"You're still here?" Alice asked her.

The maid nodded and stepped into the room hesitantly. "It is a normal workday, Ms. Alice. I finish at 6:00 p.m." Her beautiful dark eyes never looked directly at Alice. "I clean, okay?" she asked while nervously brushing a loose strand of black hair behind her ear.

Alice nodded. "If you must."

Anita seemed to almost hover through the room as she rushed around and about, wiping dust from surfaces, putting books back in their right place, and cleaning the bathroom. Alice followed her with her eyes, feeling awkward and out of place.

When Anita was done, a sudden thought ripped her out of her numbness, and Alice quickly got off the bed right before the maid was about to leave the room.

"Wait," she called, and Anita stopped, looking puzzled.

Alice approached her and before the poor woman could do anything about it, she snatched the key from her hand. All color drained from the maid's face and she stared at Alice with widened eyes. The fear in them was unmistakable. Alice felt bad at once, but she had no other choice.

"I'm keeping that for now," she explained to her. "Don't tell anyone, please."

The maid's cheeks turned pink and her lips began to tremble.

"I promise you, I won't tell Mr. Ortega anything. I just want to take a walk."

Anita's lips tightened and she seemed to consider for a moment.

Why was she so afraid of her? Had Danny told her she was crazy and dangerous? Sure, Anita was shorter than her, but Alice was only skin and bones.

"When is your next shift?"

"T-tomorrow."

"On New Year's Day?"

Anita nodded.

Danny really is a dick.

"I will leave the key in the lock and tomorrow morning, before Mr. Ortega gets up, you can lock the door, and no one will ever know."

The maid said nothing.

"Can I trust you to be silent?" Alice urged.

Anita nodded, looking like she was about to cry.

"You won't lose your job, I promise," Alice said softly to calm the poor woman. Again, Anita nodded and then she was off, hurrying through the corridor and away from her. Alice watched her until she disappeared down the stairs and seconds later, an engine was started in the yard below and the sound of tires grinding on gravel told her that the maid had driven off.

Alice was surprised at how easy obtaining the key had been. Now, all she needed to do was sneak out of the house and climb over the wall in the backyard, where the gate guard could not see her. It was very cold, she knew, but at least there was no snow. Alice hurried to her closet, her heart pounding like a drum in her chest. Her hands were cold and sweaty. She had no idea what she was doing, but she knew that an opportunity like this was unlikely to present itself twice. Her hands glided along the coat hangers. Her jacket was hanging near the entrance door in the living room, along with Danny's coats. With the big windows on either side of the entrance, fetching it would be too big of a risk. She could at least put on a warm pullover though.

There were probably not many cars on the road at this time of the year, and Alice wanted to be prepared in case she'd have to take a long walk. She chose the thickest sweater she owned. Then she wrapped a black scarf around her neck and put on a hairband, under which she hid her bangs. They had grown again and annoyingly fell into her eyes all the time. Plus, she could use the hairband to cover her ears in case they got too cold.

After having tied the laces of the warmest shoes she possessed, she walked over to the door, but when her hand touched the handle, she hesitated. For a moment, fear paralyzed her and made her thoughts race. She had no money, no phone, and nowhere to go. It was freezing outside. What if she couldn't find a place to sleep?

Freezing to death was still better than being tortured by Danny, so there was no way around it. After taking a deep breath, she pushed down the door handle and stepped out into the dark corridor.

Her heart stopped the instant, she saw the faint yellow light at the end of the hallway. She wasn't alone after all.

But it couldn't be true, Danny would never leave her alone with him—not after what had happened.

Her feet carried her toward his door, like a moth automatically drawn toward a light. Her steps were silent on the carpet, and when she reached the end of the corridor, she hesitated and stared at his door. If she left now, he would never know.

But she desperately needed things with him to be okay, she *needed* to talk to him. Swallowing her fear, she hesitantly lifted one hand and knocked on the door softly. Her heart threatened to jump out of her throat and her mouth felt extremely dry.

An eternity seemed to have passed when finally, the door handle moved downward, and the door was pulled open.

There he was, wearing old blue jeans and a gray T-shirt. He wore a black zip-up hoodie over it, unzipped. Her eyes were on a level with the collar of his shirt and she dared not move them away from it, too scared to look into his eyes.

Jonas said nothing, but he did not slam the door shut either, which was a good sign. Alice's thoughts were spinning in her head and she was unable to think of something to say. They stood, unmoving, an awkward silence between them, until suddenly and unexpectedly, she burst into tears and buried her face in his hoodie, wrapping her arms around his waist. Surprised by her own emotions, she wondered if Jonas was as perplexed as she was.

Some moments passed, but finally, he put his arms around her and responded to her embrace. He pulled her into his room and closed the door.

When the tears stopped coming at last, Alice felt incredibly embarrassed. She pulled out of the embrace and stepped away from him, still without looking at his face.

"Sorry," she muttered.

To her astonishment, he chuckled. "For what? Hugging me?"

Puzzled, she looked up and found his expression relaxed and his green eyes beaming—but only for a second. His stare suddenly hardened, and he frowned.

"You're ... mad at me ... aren't you?" she asked quietly, confused by his demeanor.

He said nothing and kept staring at her, a weird look in his eyes. Her hand automatically moved to her face, to see if there was something on it maybe that made him look at her like that. Her fingers found her mouth and she realized that her lower lip was still swollen.

Quickly, she turned away from him and walked to the other side of the room, eyes on the fogged-up glass of his balcony door. She fumbled with her scarf and pulled it halfway up over her mouth to cover her lip as well as the missing tooth.

"The fuck did he do to you?" Jonas growled behind her, and the anger in his voice made her wince.

"Nothing," she lied. "It's nothing."

Alice could hear his clothes rustling as he approached her. His breath was hot on her neck and she smelled tobacco. Jonas put his hands on her shoulders and turned her around. His eyes scanned her intensely, making her feel uncomfortable.

"You're bruised all over," he noticed. "Is that why you're wearing this?" He grabbed her wrist and pulled back the sleeve of her pullover to reveal more bruises on her arm.

Alice glared at him and yanked her arm out of his grip. "Stop that!"

"I should not have waited. I should've just taken you away from here," he muttered, regret in his voice.

"Or you could have left that glass of yours whole," she suggested coldly.

He flinched and hurt flickered over his face.

Alice immediately felt sorry. "I didn't mean … This isn't your fault! I just—"

"No, you're right," he cut her off. "I fucked up everything. It's just … he made me so fucking angry." He clenched his fists, looking like was about to punch the furniture again. Alice quickly backed away from him.

His expression softened. "Sorry."

"Do you think he knows?" she asked him.

He shook his head. "No, not really. He suspects something, but if he knew, we'd both be dead by now."

"Did he talk to you?"

He nodded.

"What did he say? What did *you* say?"

"I told him that I don't approve of how he treats you." He sighed and ran his fingers through his hair, then his eyes fell back on her lips. "The fuck did he do to you?"

Alice quickly pulled her scarf up once again. "It's nothing. It's just my canine, I have no use for it anyway." It was meant to be a joke, but Jonas didn't laugh.

"I didn't think ... It didn't occur to me—"

"It's fine."

"No, it's not."

"I'll survive."

"For how long?" he asked, his voice tinged with sadness.

Alice sighed and sat down on the swivel chair next to his desk. Her eyes flicked to the picture of his sister, and it evoked memories of the last time she had been in his room. A bitter taste filled her mouth when she thought of that day she had come to him, pregnant and desperate, begging him to help her. He had refused her coldly. Would her baby still be alive if he hadn't? Then she remembered that it had been *his* baby, too. Jonas hadn't known about the pregnancy though, so was he truly to blame?

"What are you thinking?" he asked.

"The last time I was here."

"Oh." Jonas dropped his gaze. He shoved some of his law books aside to make room on the bed so he could sit down. Then his eyes were back on her. "I didn't know—"

"I know," Alice said curtly. "I don't want to talk about this."

They were silent for a while, Jonas's sad eyes lingering on her face. She looked at the picture on his desk instead.

The awkward silence dragged on until he asked, "Would you reconsider?"

Alice knew what he meant, and she swiveled the chair around to face him. "I already have. Why d'you think I'm wearing a scarf? I was about to leave."

"How did you get out of the room?"

Alice grinned without parting her lips to hide her missing tooth. "I can be quite persuasive."

Jonas did not smile back.

"Anita's scared of me. I snatched the key from her."

He frowned. "What about Jean-Pierre?"

She shrugged. "Out. Partying."

"Danny would never leave you alone with me."

"I know." Alice bit her lip, thinking. "D'you reckon Jean-Pierre left without his consent?"

Jonas nodded. "Probably."

"Can we use that against him?"

"Probably." He scratched his unshaven chin and studied her.

"Don't look at me like that."

He averted his gaze at once. "Sorry," he muttered. "I just can't believe I let him do this to you."

You don't even know what he does to me.

"And what would you have done against it, huh?"

"I don't know," he admitted. "Something. Put a bullet through his brain, perhaps."

That was enough to make her eyes tear up anew and she looked away quickly.

Jonas got off the bed and put a hand on her shoulder. "What is it? Don't tell me you still don't think he deserves to die."

"He came to my room the other night ... with a gun."

Jonas's hand on her shoulder tensed.

"He wanted to kill me ... and then himself." She looked up at him and saw a mixture of anger and disbelief in his eyes.

"If the bastard wants to kill himself, he can go ahead. But why take you with him?"

"Maybe he thinks death wouldn't part us." She sighed. "He couldn't go through with it though. It was ... too hard for him, or whatever. He then put the gun in my hand and told me to kill him instead."

Jonas's eyes narrowed. "Why would he do that?"

"He wanted to give me a way out, but his terms were that I had to earn it."

Jonas shook his head contemptuously. "Bloody coward ... Why didn't you?"

Alice bit her lip and stared at her hands in her lap. "I couldn't. I could never ..." She did not know why, but somehow, she felt ashamed and weak for not having been able to kill Danny. It was absurd. A normal person would never think badly of her for *not* being able to kill ... but Jonas? He said nothing, but she felt his stare on her, pushing her deeper into the chair as if it weighed a hundred pounds. Even his hand on her shoulder seemed to have become heavier.

"You think I should have done it, don't you?" Alice muttered.

He hesitated. "I don't see why not."

Annoyance flared up in her at his words and she looked up at him with a frown. "You're just like him, you know. Thinking I'm in love with him, just because I wouldn't kill him. Don't you see how fucked up that is? I wouldn't kill *anybody*, I'm not a murderer. Killing is wrong. Most people think that, by the way."

"I know," Jonas said. "You have a kind heart."

"You're saying it as if it's a bad thing."

"No." He gave her a look full of sincerity. "It's not a bad thing. Don't ever think that."

"I don't," she replied coolly. "But you do."

Jonas sighed and took his hand away from her shoulder to run his fingers through his messy hair once more. "I wish I could feel as ... *compassionate* about others as you do ... but I can't."

"Then why didn't *you* kill him?" she asked sarcastically.

"Because you asked me not to."

Jonas's words hit her like a fist. A nervous laugh built up in her throat, but she quickly swallowed it down. The way he had said it made goose bumps rise on her arms. Sure, she had seen him kill before, but it had been to save her life. But cold-blooded murder? Speechless, she stared at him. Could he really mean that? After all, Danny had been his best friend, hadn't he?

"You think I'm a monster." It wasn't a question.

Alice quickly shook her head. "No, of course not."

"You saw me kill."

"Yes ... but you had to. You did it to save my life."

"And how would killing Danny be any different?"

Again, he left her speechless. Her mouth opened for an objection, but she closed it again, unable to think of an answer.

"You know I'm right," he said softly.

"He was your friend ..." Her voice was thin and barely more than a whisper.

"*Was*."

Alice bit her lip. His words trickled down her spine like cold water, making the little hairs on her neck rise. The way Jonas talked about murdering someone was both frightening and in a very disturbing way ... *attractive*. Alice felt herself blush.

"I scare you," he concluded.

"Sometimes," she admitted.
"I would never hurt you."
Alice looked up at him with narrowed eyes. "Why?"
Now it was he who was speechless.
"Why?" she repeated.
"*Why?*"
"You said it yourself; you don't feel compassion. You don't care about others, that's what you said. That's why killing people is so easy for you."
"I ... I care about *you*," he stammered.
"Why?"
His lips tightened and his eyes were on her, expressionless and unblinking. She held his stare coolly. *Say it. Just say it for god's sake.*
The silence stretched on awkwardly until the tension was palpable.
Jonas said nothing.
Damn, he's stubborn.
Irritated, Alice sighed and got off the swivel chair. His eyes followed her as she approached the door. Before she could push down the handle though, he called after her. "Where you going?"
"Out."
"Out?"
She turned to give him a cold look. "This might be the only chance I get. Everyone's gone."
"You decided to go to your friends after all?"
"No."
He frowned. "D'you even have a plan?"
"No."
"You'll freeze to death."
"There's worse ways to die."
He sighed. "Alice ..."
"What? You got something to say?" She crossed her arms in front of her chest and eyed him coldly.
Jonas opened his mouth and closed it again.
"It was nice knowing you." Alice opened the door and was already halfway out in the corridor, when she felt his hand on her shoulder, holding her back.
"Wait."

"For what? Better days?"

He pulled her back into the room and pushed the door shut. "Don't be silly."

"I'm not. I'm dead serious."

Sighing again, he shoved her toward the bed. "Sit down ... please?"

Alice glared at him, but then she sat down nevertheless. Jonas picked up his study books, which were still spread out on the mattress, piled them on one another, and placed them on his desk. Then he sat down beside her. His closeness evoked a peculiar urge in her and made her heart pound like a drum, but she kept a straight face and continued eyeing him coolly.

"You need a plan," he said.

"I got one. I'll go to the punks underneath the rail bridge and make them share their rum with me."

The corner of Jonas's mouth twitched, and his eyes seemed to smile. "How 'bout a better plan?"

"Sorry, but I don't think you can top that."

Now he laughed. The sound of it brought a smile to her lips as well.

"Seriously though ... You changed your mind about leaving this place?"

Alice nodded. Her thoughts flicked back to what had happened on Christmas and on the days that had followed. Her tongue automatically found the hole where her tooth had been and played with the loosened tooth beside it. Her expression got serious. "He'll never change."

Jonas's smile vanished as well. "I was hoping you'd eventually come to that conclusion."

Images of her own reflection in the bathroom mirror appeared on her mind. Her throat tightened and she felt nauseated. She scooted backward on Jonas's bed, ignoring the fact that she was still wearing shoes, until she was able to lean her back against the wall. Shivering, she grabbed the blanket and buried her face in it.

"Alice?" Jonas's voice sounded muffled through the blanket, but she heard the concern in it.

"I did," she said, replying to what he'd previously said.

"I'm sorry," he said softly. "I'm getting you out of here, I promise. I got a plan."

Alice looked up at his words. "You planned my escape even though I told you not to?"

Jonas looked trapped. "I know I said I wouldn't tell you what to do anymore ... But I can't let you rot in here either."

"So ... you decided to break your promise."

He nodded. "Sorry. But I decided to get you out of here, no matter what. Even if I have to drag you and lock you in the boot of my car."

"That won't be necessary."

"Good. 'cause I'm getting you a plane ticket."

"I'm going to leave the country?"

He nodded.

"Is that necessary?"

"Better safe than sorry."

Alice shifted uncomfortably. She felt really cold all of a sudden and pulled the blanket up to her chest. "Where to?" she asked.

Jonas's eyes rested on her, unmoving. "Can you keep it from him?"

Hurt by that question, she scowled at him. "Of course, I can. There are certain *other* things I kept from him as well, you know."

To her satisfaction, a faint blush appeared on his cheeks and his gaze dropped, though only for a second.

"Italy," he said.

"Italy? Why?"

"I have family there. They'll hide you."

"You want to send me to your family?"

"I haven't kept in touch with them in a long time and Danny doesn't even know they exist. He'd never expect you to be there."

Alice met his gaze and it brought goose bumps to her skin. What was that between them and why would Jonas want to hide her with his family? Did he want to keep her close?

Again, he seemed to read her mind. "I won't be around if you don't want me to. Like I said, I'm not that close to them and I don't want to be. Just want to make sure you're in good hands."

"What would I be doing there?" she asked, unconvinced.

"Whatever you like. You'll be a guest."

"What makes you think they'd want me there? You said you haven't talked to them in a while."

"I talked to them last week. They were very ... glad to hear from me and they'd love to help."

"Why ... why don't you keep in touch if they're as nice as you say?"

"It's complicated," Jonas said curtly, almost harshly.

Alice flinched at the sudden shift of his tone and eyed him suspiciously. "Why don't you ever talk to me? You know everything about me and I don't know anything about *you*."

His eyes wandered away from her and she knew that he was avoiding her gaze, but then he sighed and gave in. "I grew up in England," he told her, eyes on the picture on his desk. "We visited my family in Italy quite frequently during my childhood. We moved here when I was fourteen. Afterward, things got complicated." He trailed off and Alice knew she had to keep digging to make him talk. *Afterward*, he had said. Did he mean after moving … or after his sister's death?

"Why?" she asked.

He sighed, irritated by her persistence. His stare was back on her and it was sharp and cold, and she felt something cold trickle down her spine at the sight of him.

"We had … *issues* and my grandparents tried to intervene, and they still do."

Alice bit her lip, not sure if she could leave it at that or not. The curiosity won. "Jonas … if you want me to trust you and your family, you're gonna have to be more specific."

His eyes narrowed and he gave her an annoyed look.

He's trying to intimidate me to silence me … He'll have to try harder than this.

"Just tell me," she urged. "Please?"

He took a deep breath and combed his fingers through his tousled hair. Family appeared to be his weak point. Alice had experienced that once before when she had mentioned his sister. He seemed to be unmovable normally, but now, his discomfort was palpable.

"Fine," he snapped in a way that sounded very unlike him. "My father was … an asshole. Like Danny. He snapped when my mum died. Started drinking and … *hurting* my sister. Grandparents tried to take her in, make her move to Italy. Didn't work out." He took another deep breath, as if talking were depriving him of all his energy. His voice was still hard when he continued. "There's too much history. That's why I don't keep in touch."

Alice was lost for words for a moment. Trying to soothe him, she put a hand on his arm, but he shook her off.

"Don't you think … you should talk about things?" she suggested. "I mean, you said they were happy to hear from you."

"They don't know *shit*."

"What do you mean? It sounds like they like you."

"They *love* me. I'm the only one they have left."

"Then why—"

"Because they deserve better, that's why. I don't want to impose myself on them."

Speechless, Alice studied him. His expression had only mildly changed, but he seemed to be radiating with self-loathing.

"But ... why? Is it because of your work? Because you're doing something illegal?"

"It's because I killed her!"

He rose from the bed and Alice thought he was about to storm out of the room, but he remained standing with his back turned toward her. He rubbed his temple with the knuckles of his right hand, as though talking about his past were giving him a headache.

Her throat felt tight and her thoughts spun while she tried to decide whether it was safe to speak.

"Jonas ... don't blame yourself just because you couldn't save her ..."

He spun around and glared at her. "I did not just *not* save her. I condemned her to death with my selfishness!" His eyes were glistening, and he let out an annoyed growl and turned away from her again.

"What happened?" Alice asked, her voice hoarse.

"I'm a fucking prick, that's what happened."

His anger seemed to make the air around him boil and yet, Alice shivered. Seeing Jonas like that made her feel helpless. She wanted to comfort him and calm him down, but she also didn't want to get too close to him when he was acting like that. So, she remained staring at his back until he finally turned to face her. He looked more sad than angry now and she guessed it must be safe to speak.

"Please don't punch the furniture ... it didn't do anything wrong."

To her relief, his features relaxed and he even smirked. Alice smiled too and gestured for him to sit down again. He hesitated, but then he followed her request and dropped down on the mattress beside her.

"Sorry," he muttered.

Alice scooted closer to him and took his hand. It was warm and she gave it an affectionate squeeze. They sat in silence for a while, Jonas staring at the wall, lost in his memories.

"I left her," he said at last, his voice husky. "I was seventeen and eager to leave home. I left, even though she begged me to take her with me." His voice broke and Alice saw tears glistening in his eyes anew. "I left her there, with *him*. Just because I did not feel like babysitting my fifteen-year-old sister, I just left her there."

Alice felt something twist in her guts. Jonas seemed so sad and fragile in that instant, and she felt incredibly sorry for him, yet she could not deny that leaving his younger sister with their abusive father was a horrible thing to do. She now understood why he blamed himself. Another thought began creeping up in her mind, dark and cold, and she tried to fight it off, but it persisted.

What if Jonas is only helping me to clear his conscience? To make up for what happened with his sister?

When she didn't answer, he slowly turned to look at her and at the sight of her expression, hurt flashed in his eyes.

Alice quickly looked away, knowing he was reading her again. His stare made her feel uncomfortable. She tried to think of something to say, but her mind could not come up with an answer. Feeling ashamed, she remained quiet.

"Now you know why I don't keep in touch."

"But," Alice objected weakly, "they don't blame you."

"They don't know what happened." He pulled his hand away from hers. "All they know is that she killed herself."

"You couldn't have known—"

"That she would slit her wrists? No. But she could as well have been killed by him."

"It's not your fault."

The sadness in his eyes almost took her breath away when he gazed at her. "You know it's my fault. I know you do."

"No. You cannot be blamed."

He sighed. "Yes. But let's not argue about that now."

"I don't want to argue. I just don't want you to feel guilty … You don't deserve that."

Affection flared up in his bright green eyes, and Alice felt something jump in her guts and wanted nothing more than to bury her face in his hoodie and inhale his scent. He gave her a weak smile but she knew it was hopeless—he would feel guilty for the rest of his life. And who could blame him?

I'd feel guilty too if I were him.
"Why didn't she go to your grandparents? You said they offered to take her in."
"She would not leave without me," he muttered in a thick voice.
"Oh. You didn't want to live in Italy with your grandparents?"
He shook his head. "Too boring. No liquor stores nearby."
Alice almost smiled when the image of a seventeen-years-old Jonas in a leather jacket appeared on her mind.
"Liquor stores?" she asked. "You?"
"I used to drink ... before ..." He fell silent and angrily wiped a tear away.
Again, Alice felt the urge to hug him and kiss him, but something held her back. She had almost been certain that he had feelings for her, but now, she was not so sure anymore.
If he's only helping me out of guilt, I'm such an idiot to assume otherwise.
"Let's not talk about it anymore," she muttered.
Jonas said nothing. They sat in complete silence for a while and Alice noticed that he hadn't lit a cigarette since she'd walked into his room. Her eyes scanned her surroundings, and she spotted an open pack of Marlboros on the desk next to the picture of his sister. His eyes were on her as she got off the bed to pick it up.
The pack between her fingers, she sat back down beside him and took two cigarettes out of the little box, then she gently stuck one between his lips.
"Lighter?" she asked.
To her relief, he smiled and pulled a box of matches out of the pocket of his jeans. He lit her cigarette before lighting his own.
They smoked silently and when the smoke began to fill the room, Jonas got up to open the balcony door. After he'd sat back down next to her, he laid the blanket around her shoulders. Cold wind blew into the room and made her shiver, but it felt pleasant. She leaned her head against his shoulder and allowed herself to enjoy his closeness.
Jonas lit another cigarette, but when he offered one to her, Alice shook her head wearily.
"Some wine would be nice ... to celebrate the end of yet another awful year."
Jonas gave her a long, intense look, then he lifted her head off his shoulder gently and got off the bed.
"What you doing?"

"I'll get you a bottle of wine."

Alice made a face. "You can't leave me alone in that creepy house."

He chuckled and took a drag on his cigarette. "I won't. There's wine in the kitchen and plenty in the basement as well."

The wind seemed to be whispering to her, and Alice wrapped the blanket tighter around her shoulders and got off the bed. Her feet carried her to the balcony, and she stepped out into the cold December night. The balcony was quite generous, she noticed. Jonas had a small table with a marble surface and two old, metallic chairs standing next to it. Two overflowing ashtrays sat on the table. Alice walked to the balustrade and leaned over it, resting her elbows on the cold iron and letting her hair get caught in the wind. The little lamp that hung next to the back door of the house was illuminated and its soft, orange light reflected in the frost, which covered the grass and the branches of the naked trees. The pool was covered, and the garden furniture had been removed. The forest, that stretched out beyond the wall, seemed endless in the darkness. Alice's eyes wandered across the yard and then up into the sky, and she noticed that the wind had chased the clouds away and, for the first time in weeks, the moon was visible and sent its ghostly silver light down upon the earth. The sound of the wind drowned out everything else, and when Jonas returned and stepped out onto the balcony, she didn't even hear him. He leaned against the balustrade beside her and handed her a bottle of red wine, already opened.

"I assumed you don't need a glass." His voice was barely audible through the wind.

The wine tasted good. It was thick but tender, neither too sour nor too sweet. As it trickled down into her stomach, it filled her guts with warmth.

"Thank you," she said, smiling at him. He returned the smile and tried to light another cigarette, but the wind eliminated the flame and he gave it up after the third match and put the cigarette back in its box. Leaning back onto the balustrade, he too gazed up at the moon. Alice drank from the bottle, savoring every sip, and watched the wind move through Jonas's hair, bending it in waves almost like a wheat field in a warm summer wind.

Feeling her stare, Jonas turned and looked at her, his expression unreadable. His eyes were bright in the darkness and piercing. He reached out and took the bottle from her hand, and Alice watched, perplexed, as he put it to his lips and drank, letting the wine run down his throat as if it were water. Soon enough though, he put the bottle down onto the balustrade and grimaced.

"Bah," he said. "I know why I don't drink."

Chuckling, Alice reached for the bottle, but Jonas held on to it. "You sure you wanna finish this? I don't want you puking on my bed."

She stuck her tongue out at him. "I need it if I have to spend New Year's Eve alone."

"Who says you have to spend it alone?"

It was just a question, but Alice's heartrate accelerated at his words. Somehow, she had expected him to throw her out of his room sooner or later. His room seemed to be his sacred place and she doubted anybody ever visited him in there. She quickly turned her head away from him and looked up at the stars. It evoked memories of that night in February after the concert. Standing on the field, next to him, surrounded by snow. They had looked at the stars then too, though they hadn't been as clearly visible as now.

It was kind of romantic, she thought sadly, *but we haven't come far since then.*

"You're shivering," he observed. "We should go inside."

Alice stumbled back into the room and dropped down onto his mattress. To warm herself, she pulled her knees up to her chest.

"Shoes," Jonas pointed out while closing the balcony door.

"Sorry." She took them off and placed them in front of the bed.

The bed shook when he sat back down next to her, still clutching the bottle of wine. He stared at it, lost in thoughts.

"Why don't you ever feel cold?" Alice asked him. She took the wine out of his hand and sipped at it.

Jonas lit a cigarette and inhaled deeply. "I remember a certain someone saying I don't have feelings."

Shame burned on her cheeks and she dropped her gaze. "Sorry ... I didn't mean ... I didn't want to offend you. I didn't know you back then."

He looked at her defiantly. "Do you *now*?"

"Well ... better than back then. But how am I supposed to when you never talk?"

"I talk more than I like already," he muttered.

"I'm glad you do."

"I wouldn't do that for everybody."

Is he flirting with me? Alice wondered while she watched him lean back against the wall and close his eyes.

"Tired?" she asked him instead.

"No," he moaned and rubbed his forehead. "Just got a lot to do." He gestured to the books on his desk.

"Oh. I get the hint. I'll go."

Jonas put a hand on her arm and held her back. "Stay ... if you want. But I'll do some work if you don't mind."

"Go ahead."

He got off the bed and sat down on his swivel chair. He grabbed a book and opened it, then he turned around and gave her an uncertain look. "Sure you don't mind?"

"It's fine. I'll watch you study. It's more entertainment than I usually get."

He made a face. "Please don't. That's creepy."

Alice chuckled and drank some more wine while Jonas began reading and taking notes. She couldn't help but watch him and realized that he looked kind of sexy with his forehead furrowed in concentration. After a while, he looked up and gave her a stern look.

"I can't concentrate when you look at me like that."

"Sorry ... can't help it. It's just weird."

"Why?"

"I don't know ... I guess you just don't look like a typical student."

"And what does a typical student look like?"

"Don't know ... not like you?"

"And what do I look like?"

Chewing her lower lip, Alice studied him. "Like a guy who robs liquor stores?"

That made him smile. "You should not judge a book by its cover."

"So ... you never robbed liquor stores?"

"Only once," he admitted. "And maybe I looked like a typical student back then."

"Did you?"

"You'll never know." He gave her a crooked smile and went back to studying.

The wine showed its effect soon enough and made Alice's limbs feel heavier with every sip that she took. She knew that drinking alcohol on an empty stomach wasn't a good idea, especially after not having drunk much for a long time, but deep down, in the pit of her stomach, was an uneasy feeling that needed to be drowned. It was a mixture of a deeply rooted sadness, which she usually tried hard to ignore, and an anxious urge to flee. Jonas must be right, it was better to have a plan, and yet, she could not stop picturing herself out in the forest, in the cold wind, probably half-frozen to death, but free at least. Trying to extinguish these thoughts, she took another big mouthful of wine. The constant rustling of a page being turned and the faint sound of a pencil scratching on paper were like a lullaby to her and made her drowsy. Soon, she drifted off into a deep, dreamless sleep.

A hand shook her awake and the strange yet familiar smell of her surroundings filled her nose. Alice blinked and fought against the thick fog in her mind. The room was still illuminated and slowly, she remembered where she was and what had happened. She quickly pushed herself up from the mattress and tried to flatten her hair.

"Sorry," she mumbled.

Jonas grinned. "Don't apologize."

"How long have I been sleeping?"

He shrugged. "A while. I snatched the wine bottle out of your hand when you were about to drop it."

Her cheeks burning with shame, she hid her face in her hands. "I'm so sorry! If I had spilled it on your bed ... Why didn't you wake me before?"

"You slept so peacefully. I didn't want to disturb you."

Alice forced a loose strand of hair back underneath her hairband. "Why did you wake me now? D'you want me to leave?"

Jonas gave her a cheeky smile and checked his phone. "Ten," he said. "Nine ... eight ... seven ..."

She punched his upper arm lightly. "Aah, please don't! Where's the wine?"

He handed her the bottle, and she took a sip, though it didn't taste as good as before her nap.

"Happy New Year," he said, and Alice forced herself to smile, though she didn't feel like it.

"Happy New Year," she replied.

"That didn't sound very convincing."

"Well ... I can only hope this one'll be better than the last."

"I'll keep my fingers crossed."

Grimacing, Alice tried to take another gulp of wine, but Jonas took the bottle out of her hand before it touched her lips. Sighing, he sat back down beside her and placed the wine bottle on the floor next to the bed.

"Only two more weeks," he said softly. "In two weeks, this will all be over."

"And I'll be in Italy ...?"

He nodded. "You'll be in Italy, sipping wine and eating pizza."

"And where will you be?"

His eyes were on her, unblinking, and he hesitated while he thought of an answer. "I don't know yet."

"But ... you won't stay with *him*, right?"

"I will ... at first. I already told you that, last time we talked about it."

"Right ... you'll make sure he doesn't follow me. And then?"

His eyes flickered away from hers and she felt a pang in her guts. Feeling ashamed, she turned her head and stared at the wall. Didn't his discomfort make obvious that he did not intend to spend any more time with her after her escape? His concern for her now must be nothing but a symptom of his guilt, a sign that he felt responsible for her. Once he'd done his duty, he would no longer be obligated to spend time with her. Self-loathing began eating its way through her guts and she wondered how she could have ever thought that he liked her.

"Never mind," she muttered. "You don't know yet, I get it."

For a moment, he was quiet. But then and to her utter surprise, he put an arm around her shoulders and squeezed her gently.

"I like the hairband," he remarked. "Shows more of your face that way."

The unexpected compliment made her blush and left her highly confused.

"He ... he likes the bangs," she stuttered.

"Right."

She felt his mood shift immediately and regretted her words.

"Sorry," she said quickly. "I shouldn't talk about him."

"I should have been there for you." Guilt clung heavily to his voice.

"There's nothing you could have done."

He grimaced. "I just ... Last thing I remember was you telling me that things were better. That he was nicer ... I didn't think—"

"It's okay," she cut him off. "Like I said, what would you have done anyway?"

"Something," he muttered. "How long has he been treating you like this?"

"Since Christmas."

He winced at her answer, and she knew how guilty he must feel.

"I'm such an idiot. I'm normally in control—"

"It's okay," Alice said again. "It was ... the way he talked about the baby ... I'm glad you showed some emotion because I wasn't sure whether you felt anything about it at all."

Jonas sighed. "Of course I do. But it's not only about the ... baby. It's about what he put you through. Even if it had been his, I would have smashed that glass nonetheless." He pulled her even tighter into his embrace and again, Alice failed to understand his demeanor. It felt good to be held by him though.

"Can I ask you something?" It didn't sound at all like him, but she nodded. "You said ... you had a name for ... *her*?"

Feeling herself blush, she hesitated. Talking about the baby made her heart beat furiously against her ribs, as if it were about to burst. She felt the sadness inside of her revolt against the cage she had put around it.

"Jane," she all but whispered.

He flinched slightly when she said the name. Saying it out loud made everything so real and she felt his arm around her tense.

"*Jane*," he repeated with sadness in his voice.

Alice cleared her throat and shifted uncomfortably. "I mean ... I didn't know it was a girl. But that was the name I had in mind."

Jonas took a deep breath but said nothing.

"What would you have called her?" she asked him, to keep him talking. "I mean ... if you had known."

Jonas appeared to be thinking of an answer. His fingers moved up and down her arm, caressing her softly through the sleeve of her pullover. It evoked goose bumps on her skin and butterflies began to dance around in her belly.

"Maybe ..." His voice cracked and he cleared his throat. "I might have named her after my sister."

Alice looked up into his big, sad eyes and felt a rush of affection toward him that made her cheeks burn. "What was her name?"

"Arianna." His voice sounded hollow when he said the name.

"That's a beautiful name ... is it Italian?"

He shrugged. "I think mostly Greek, but it might be a mixture of Greek and Roman."

"You speak Italian, right?"

He nodded.

"Can I hear some?"

"You will, soon."

Jonas chuckled when he saw the disappointment on her face. "What about you and French?"

Feeling ashamed, Alice grimaced and stared at her hands in her lap. "I never learned it. My mom never taught me." She sighed. "I could recite about every French insult there is, but I can't speak it properly. Would be nice to speak other languages though."

He gave her another affectionate squeeze. "You'll learn Italian soon enough. My family doesn't speak English very well."

Frightened by that notion, she began chewing her swollen lip. "I'll embarrass myself."

He smirked and shook his head. "I doubt it. You're smart."

"You could teach me." She looked up at him and met his gaze. "I'd love to learn it from you."

Silence followed her words, and his stare made her blush again, but he wasn't smiling anymore. Still chewing her lip, she wondered what he was thinking, but his expression was unreadable as always. His eyes seemed to swallow her though and she could not break away from his gaze, as if her eyes were glued to his.

"Did I say something wrong?" she whispered anxiously.

Jonas shook his head but kept staring at her as if he was thinking about something to say.

"I mean … you don't have to teach me if you don't want to," she said hastily. His silence made her nervousness increase with every passing second.

"I'd love to teach you," he finally replied, his voice hoarse.

"But …?"

Sighing, he gave her a sad look. "Do you expect me to come with you?"

Alice quickly dropped her gaze and stared at his T-shirt. "No … I don't expect anything from you. But I'd like you to be there … with me."

Was the wine loosening her tongue? Her cheeks were still burning hot with shame and she felt stupid for having told him that. But then again, he had his arm around her while his fingers kept caressing her arm, and he had hugged her before and held her hand … what was she supposed to think? There had to be *something* between them.

"Unless you don't want to," she added.

"I'd love to," he said again.

"But?"

Again, he sighed, and his eyes seemed to bore right into her. "What is it exactly ... that you want from me?" His tone was soft and warm, yet his words were cold as ice and made her shiver.

Her face heated up at once and she seemed to melt under his gaze, but at the same time, the alcohol had loosened her tongue to such an extent, that she was willing to take risks she would normally never take.

"Right now ... a kiss," she admitted while gazing into his eyes. They looked as if molten gold had dripped into a bright green pond. His lips twitched as if he was about to speak, but his expression remained unreadable. Poker face. He returned her gaze though and the warmth in his eyes made her heart pound faster. Slowly, his left hand moved to her cheek and she flinched lightly under his touch. The tips of his fingers softly glided over her skin, evoking goose bumps on her arms. His breath was hot and smelled of tobacco. He buried his fingers in her hair and pulled her head closer to his, and her heart skipped a beat when he bent forward and kissed ... her forehead.

Startled, she stared at him after he had pulled back, and he gave her a warm smile.

"That was ... *brotherly*," she muttered, her face burning red with embarrassment. There it was, the answer she had been waiting for. There was definitely something between them and she was sure that he cared for her, but clearly it was nothing more than that.

He doesn't find me attractive ... I'm just a replacement for the sister he lost.

About to break into tears, she averted her eyes, and then turned her head away from him. To her surprise, he chuckled, and it made her feel humiliated.

"Alice," he said, trying to pull her back into an embrace.

She pushed him away and scowled at him. "Not funny."

He laughed again and cupped her cheek. "I'm sorry, but you look cute, the way you're glaring at me."

When she said nothing, he sighed, and his expression got serious. "I'm sorry."

"It's okay, you don't have to do anything you don't want to. Guess I misread the signs."

"Please look at me," he said, and the genuineness in his voice made her turn her head. There was sincerity in his eyes when he said, "I do want to."

Again, butterflies began dancing around in her belly, but then confusion took their place. Not able to make sense of his behavior, she could do nothing but stare at him.

"Then why—" she began, but then she saw his eyes flick to her lips for a split second, and blushed. She put her fingers on her mouth at once and felt the swelling of her lower lip, where it had hit the sink. The wound began throbbing when she thought back to how Danny had smashed her face into the ceramic.

"It ... feels wrong," he muttered, barely audibly.

No wonder he doesn't want to kiss me.

Tears of shame and desperation clouded her sight, and she tried again to turn away from him, but his hand still cupped her cheek.

"Sorry," she all but whispered. "I haven't looked in a mirror in a while. I understand."

"No, it's not like that, don't say that!" Again, he let his fingers run over her cheek and wiped one of her tears away with his thumb. "It just feels wrong."

"Why?" She forced a sob back down. She didn't want to cry in front of him again.

He frowned and she felt him tense, struggling to find the right words. "I ... after everything he did to you ... I don't want to take advantage of you. It's not right."

Frowning, Alice looked back up at him. "I *asked* you to kiss me."

"I know. But I don't think it's a good idea. You're vulnerable and—"

"Naïve? Unable to make my own decisions?"

He's treating me like a child.

There were tears in her eyes again, she noticed with disdain. Furiously, she wiped them away. It hurt to be treated by him like that, like he didn't respect her. It made her feel patronized.

"I don't think I'm good for you," he admitted quietly, his voice tormented.

"Why don't you let *me* decide that?"

He shook his head sadly. "You can hate me for this, Alice, and I'm really sorry. But after everything that's happened, I really don't think you're in the right state to make reasonable decisions."

His words stung and the butterflies in her stomach were replaced by needles. The stupid tears managed to break free at last and began running down her cheeks. She hated herself for her weakness. It only proved that he was right.

"I really don't want to hurt you." Jonas's voice was thick with affection, and he tried to caress her cheek again, but she wound herself out of his grip and tried to get off the bed.

"Please don't," he said, holding onto her arm lightly.

She shook his hand off, but he pulled her back onto the bed. When she struggled weakly, he leaned in and kissed her cheek right below the eye, brushing a tear away with his lips.

Startled, she froze in his arms, completely petrified. His touch made her tremble.

Quickly, he let go of her, looking worried. Alice exhaled a breath she hadn't known she'd been holding in, and it took her a moment to realize that her eyes were widened and her heart was racing.

"It's just ... complicated," Jonas confessed. "I'm so scared I might hurt you ... and I feel like you're scared of me."

Alice shook her head quickly and opened her mouth to speak, but it was dry and her tongue wouldn't obey. She knew it wasn't true. She was not scared of Jonas. But her body told a different story and it was utterly confusing.

"You're shaking like a leaf," he commented, and there was guilt in his eyes as well as concern.

Shaking her head again, Alice swallowed the lump in her throat. "I'm just c-confused," she stuttered, still out of breath. "You ... startled me."

"I think you need time to heal before ... before you're able to decide what's best for you."

"You're patronizing me ... again." Feeling cold suddenly, she shivered.

Jonas laid the blanket around her shoulders, but then he realized that he'd just proved what she had said. He blushed slightly and looked ashamed.

"Sorry ..." Sighing, he scooted away from her, as if bringing some distance in between them would change anything.

Alice missed his warmth the moment it was gone. She pulled the blanket tighter around her shoulders and stared at the floor, saying nothing.

"I'm sorry," he said again, sounding tortured. "I'm just ... *terrified* of hurting you, but whatever I do, it's wrong."

She saw his eyes glistening moistly and felt bad at once. He was right. She longed for his touch but at the same time, she winced whenever he made a quick movement and his kiss had made her tremble. The memories of what Danny had done to her were too vivid on her mind and she could not deny that sometimes, she expected Jonas to hurt her as if he were Danny. Her brain knew that he would never do that, but something deep down inside of her expected it anyway. And in that moment, it dawned on her that Danny had not only taken away her present, but also her future, and that no matter how far away she ran and no matter how much time might pass, the scars he had left her with would always hurt. She might feel the urge to feel Jonas with every inch of her body, but at the same time, the mere thought of lying underneath him made her feel suffocated.

Chewing her lip, she stared at her feet.

"I'm sorry," she said quietly, almost in a whisper.

"Why are you apologizing?"

"Because you're right ... I'm confused. I don't even know what I want." She blinked away her tears and hid her face behind her hands. "I want to be with you ... but maybe you're right. Maybe it's just because I don't have anyone else."

Suddenly, the deeply rooted sadness managed to break free all at once, and she wanted nothing more than to end her life once and for all. She bit her swollen lip hard, trying not to cry, until the wound burst open again and she tasted blood in her mouth.

Then everything happened in a heartbeat. She wasn't in Jonas's room anymore. She was in her bathroom, in front of the mirror. Her tongue tasted of iron and Danny's grin was right behind her, his face only inches away from hers. Gasping for air, her body told her to run, completely disorientated by the images flashing through her mind.

Alice hadn't even realized she had jumped off the bed and bolted toward the door, when suddenly, Jonas's arms were around her, holding her in place. He muttered words she couldn't understand and held her, until she stopped shaking.

When the panic dissolved, it left her feeling empty and exhausted.

"I'm a wreck," Alice admitted when they were sitting on his bed again, leaning against the wall. He had his arm around her shoulders and she was pressing a paper tissue on her broken lip. His forehead was still furrowed with concern.

"How did he do that?" he asked.
"Smashed my head into the sink."
She heard him suck in air noisily and his arm around her tensed.
"I can't believe he knocked your tooth out."
"Me neither."
"I won't let it happen again."
Her eyes flicked to his face and she saw determination in his features.
"I don't want to lose any more teeth."

That night, Alice slept with her head on his chest, and when faint sunrays began creeping into the room, Jonas shook her awake softly. Confused, she blinked at him. His eyes were full of affection and he brushed a strand of hair out of her face.

"Morning," he said softly.

Reality stirred her awake at once, and fear crept through her bones and seemed to freeze the blood in her veins. Her night with Jonas had come to an end and Danny would soon be back. Or was he already? She cringed at the thought and lifted her head from Jonas's chest.

"Where is he?" she gasped.

"Don't worry, I've been texting him while you slept. He'll be back at around noon. But I still think you should go back to your room before anyone else arrives."

"I don't want to," she admitted in a weak voice. Nevertheless, she nodded. Jonas smiled at her in a reassuring way.

"What about Jean-Pierre?"

Jonas pushed himself up into a sitting position and leaned his back against the wall. Alice snuggled closer to him and buried her face in his hoodie.

"He left without Danny's consent. He'll keep quiet, I'll make sure of that."

They sat in silence for a couple of minutes, until the last remains of sleep had left her and she felt awake enough to move. Slowly and hesitantly, she began to collect her shoes from the floor.

Jonas walked her to the door and when she stopped, he gave her an encouraging smile and squeezed her hand gently.

"I'm scared," she confessed.

"I know. But this will all be over soon. Only two more weeks."

Alice nodded, but something in her guts twisted at the thought. Doubt kept clinging to her, and she couldn't picture her future. Not in Italy, not even outside of these walls. Somehow, it all seemed unreal and impossible.

The corridor was empty, and she turned back to look at Jonas, who was standing in the doorframe of his room, still smiling warmly.

"Thanks ... for being there for me," she muttered quietly.

Sadness flickered over his face and he put a hand on her cheek and kissed her forehead again. This time though, his lips lingered on her skin for a very long moment, and she closed her eyes, enjoying his touch.

When he pulled away, he had tears in his eyes.

"Only two more weeks," he said again. "You can do this."

Again, she nodded. "I'll survive two more weeks."

30

Everything worked out smoothly and Alice was able to sneak back into her room before Anita or Jean-Pierre arrived. As promised, she left the key in the keyhole on the outside of the door.

At around eight o'clock, the maid knocked on her door and when she found Alice sitting on her bed, she seemed utterly relieved.

Jean-Pierre checked on her about two hours later, to make sure she hadn't escaped. He frowned when he saw the untouched food on the tray on her dresser but said nothing.

Alice had showered to wash off the betraying smell of smoke and she'd climbed into her bed, but sleep wouldn't come.

When Danny stepped into her room at around noon, she was still lying on the mattress, motionless, staring at the ceiling.

He looked tired and worn-out, as if he'd had a rough night. Dark shadows framed his eyes and his hair was a mess. His eyes looked a bit red and swollen, like he was either very tired or had taken drugs. Or maybe both.

For a moment, he stared at her, but then he muttered, "Happy New Year."

Alice said nothing and refrained from looking at him.

"It was a great party," he said with sadness in his voice. "But I think it would have been too loud and crowded for your taste. Maybe it was better that you stayed here."

Her thoughts flashed back to her night with Jonas, and she smiled grimly on the inside, without letting it touch her lips though. It gave her a grim kind of satisfaction to be able to keep secrets from Danny, to know that he couldn't control each and every aspect of her life.

"I would have loved to have you there ... with me. Like old times. We would always kiss when the countdown came."

Unmoving, Alice kept staring at the ceiling. She could feel tears trying to break their way out of her eyes but managed to fight them.

He remained standing in the door for a while, but then he turned without saying another word, and the sound of the door snapping shut echoed in her head long after he had left.

Everybody was busy over the next couple of days. Strangers buzzed around and about in the yard outside, carrying boxes and furniture, tightly wrapped in bubble wrap.

Alice watched the commotion from her window. Often, loud noise and voices in the corridor would wake her up early in the morning.

Danny explained to her one day that he was sending their stuff ahead in a separate plane and that the date of the move had been fixed. They were supposed to leave the country on Monday, the fourteenth of January.

Her own belongings were cleared out as well, at least the things that she wanted (or would have wanted) to take with her. She packed most of her DVDs, her books, and some clothes in the boxes that Danny provided her with, but she kept her diaries and photos hidden underneath the dresser, to take them with her on the day of the escape.

One afternoon, when Danny was busy in the office, Jonas visited her in her room and told her that the flight to Italy would leave late at night on the thirteenth of January, so only hours before the move. That prospect made her anxious, as it seemed as if only a thousand things could go wrong. Alice knew though that it was safer this way since Danny would not have time to look for her and he would also not expect her to be at the airport.

Her passport was ready. It was stowed away in a drawer of Danny's desk, and Jonas was convinced it would not be a problem for him to snatch it before their flight.

When the weather got worse, so did Danny's mood. The first week of January was coming to an end, but no snow had fallen yet. Instead, dark gray rain clouds kept the faint winter sun hidden and made the days look like nights. Thick drops drummed down onto the earth steadily, mercilessly. The lawn, so carefully kept neat and lush by the new gardener, was gone completely. The yard looked like the field of an open-air festival after the last night of wild concerts. Heavy boots on the feet of heavy men carrying heavy loads had turned the ground upside down and created a mud pit.

Alice could only imagine what the living room must look like, since she doubted that any of the men bothered taking off their boots before entering the house. She pitied Helena and Anita, who surely must be working overtime at the moment.

Danny paid her a visit every night to still his needs, and his increasing bad temper made him blow off steam so hard, he left her body covered with bruises.

It was just like it had been the days after Christmas. He was depressed when he was sober, blinded by mad rage when he was drunk, and radiating with cold menace when he was high on cocaine. The way things were going, Alice thought she must have gotten used to his nightly visits and the pain he caused her by now. But something was different. The prospect of leaving him soon had filled her with hope, and the night she'd spent with Jonas had shown her that she was still able to enjoy another person's touch. Now, what Danny did to her felt twice as bad as it had before.

The time dragged and every minute felt like an hour, every hour felt like a day, and every day felt like a week.

She trusted Jonas, but at the same time, she hated having to rely on him. Having to wait for his aid like a princess locked in a tower, guarded by a vicious dragon. Sitting on the windowsill, waiting for her knight in shining armor. Or worn-out leather jacket for that matter. Her impatience grew to an almost unbearable extent and somehow, she could not shake off the feeling that maybe she should have taken matters into her own hands. She wondered where she would be now, had she decided to run instead of stopping at Jonas's door on New Year's Eve.

It didn't matter anyway. The decision had been made and all she could do now was wait.

When the vicious dragon stormed into her room on the evening of an otherwise uneventful Saturday, with nostrils so flared it wouldn't have been surprising if flames had darted from them, Alice pictured smoke coming from his ears and the thought evoked a queer urge in her to laugh out loudly. But the chuckle died in her throat, and she almost choked on it when Danny slammed the door shut behind him and crossed the room with big steps. There was always some reason why he'd be raging, and Alice was used to being his punching bag. But tonight, something was different.

Tall and menacing, he towered over her and when her eyes met his, she froze. The drawing pad, which had been lying on her lap, slid off her thighs and landed on the couch with a soft *thud*. Fear took hold of her, its icy fingers clenched around her throat in an almost painful manner.

He knows.

He took another step toward her and she found herself leaning away, pressing her back against the cold, fogged-up glass of her window. She shivered, not knowing whether it was because of the glass or because of him.

Danny looked like he was ready to kill her, and while dying had seemed like a good idea only a couple of days earlier, it now scared her to the bone. For a moment, it seemed like even her eyes were frozen in their sockets, unable to break off his stare, but when he closed the distance between them and the pungent odor of his cologne hit her nostrils, she finally remembered how to breathe and managed to drop her gaze, escaping the piercing accusation in his big blue eyes.

"Why?" was all he said, pressing the word through clenched teeth. When she didn't answer, he gripped her upper arms with huge sweaty palms and yanked her off the windowsill.

"How?" he asked while his nails dug deeply into her flesh.

The white of his blindingly bleached dress shirt became a blur before her eyes. Somewhere in the back of her head a faint voice appeared, telling her that her silence was treacherous, and that whatever it was he suspected might be allayed by the right choice of words. But her tongue felt heavy and her mind was completely blank.

"How the fuck did you get him on your side?" He shook her, and her head wobbled back and forth like a puppet's. If he killed her by breaking her neck, at least it would not be that painful.

Her silence exasperated him, and he growled—a tortured sound—and shoved her away from him, as if he couldn't stand having to look at her for another fraction of a second.

Surprised by the sudden turn of events, Alice awoke out of her paralysis and lifted an arm to catch her fall, but it was a little too late and the angle was wrong. A faint *crack* filled her ears before a stabbing pain shot through her wrist. Tears blinded her, and she barely saw the door to her room being flung inward with such force that it hit the dresser and bounced back off it. Vaguely, she noticed a pair of big feet in brown leather shoes enter the room.

Dizzied and nauseated by the pain in her arm, she remained curled up on the floor and could only guess who it was.

"You," Danny growled, and she saw him turn, her head on the carpet close to the polished leather of his black shoes. He could step on her head and crush her like a cockroach if he intended to.

Instead, he took a step away from her, and when the person who had entered the room approached her, Danny backed away farther—to her astonishment.

Hands grabbed her and pulled her up from the floor. They held her so she wouldn't fall.

"Did she fuck you too?" Danny spat, contempt in his voice. "Is that why you can't mind your own business?"

Alice's head felt wobbly on her neck and a thick white fog kept clouding her vision, as though she was about to faint.

"What you're doing is wrong," Jean-Pierre said, his voice deep and threatening. "Don't need to fuck nobody to realize that."

"It's none of your goddamned business!" Danny yelled while taking a step toward them, but Jean-Pierre pushed him away with one hand.

To Alice, the world had lost its sense. Once again.

Never, not even in her wildest dreams, would she have thought that Jean-Pierre would step in and defend her against Danny. He'd never shown her any kindness or even looked slightly interested in how she was doing. Now, he made her sit down on the bed before he turned back around to face his boss.

"Beating up your girlfriend? Is that your business?" There was deep disdain in his husky voice.

"I'll fire your ass for this!" Danny snarled.

Alice's eyes flicked to his hands, and she noticed they were balled into fists and shaking. But he didn't fight Jean-Pierre. He didn't even try. Was he afraid of his own bodyguard?

"Not necessary." Jean-Pierre crossed his arms in front of his chest. "I quit. Don't wanna go to Turkey anyway."

Turkey? Alice flinched at that notion. Why would Danny want to move to Turkey? Unless ... her assumptions about the business had been right.

He seemed to be trying to grasp Jean-Pierre's words, shocked by his employee's disobedience. When he finally got a grip however, he hissed, "Then what are you still doing here?"

The big, bearded man took a step toward him and made him back away farther.

"Making sure you don't kill her."

"The fuck you talking about?" Danny's back was almost against the wall next to the window now and his eyes glinted dangerously.

"Know why I took this job?" Jean-Pierre still had his massive arms crossed, and his broad shoulders were like a shield, separating Alice from the threat that was coming from Danny. "I want to pay for my little sister's studies. Never fancied working for a rich prick like you. But I did it for the fucking money. If that means I have to stand here and say nothing while you kill your girlfriend, my sister's gonna have to fry burgers instead. And you *will* kill her."

Jean-Pierre's words kept ringing in Alice's ears long after he'd spoken them, and Danny seemed to feel the same. He was speechless. His eyes lingered on his bodyguard's face for a while, but then they flicked to Alice, and being hit by his stare felt like taking a bullet. Or at least she supposed it did.

For a split second, something soft flickered in his big blues. Was it guilt? Or doubt? But then his stare was back on Jean-Pierre and all softness was gone at once.

"Wanna talk values and morals?" His voice was cold as ice. "What's moral about adultery, huh? She's got you wrapped around her finger, hasn't she? Don't act like you're all saint, I'm not buying it, Jean. I know she's going behind my back with whomever will take her."

Jean-Pierre hissed contemptuously and shook his head. "Fucking paranoid's what you are. The girl's been locked in this room for about as long as I've been here, and I sure as hell haven't done anything but bring her food she won't eat anyway 'cause she'd rather starve than live this life. And who could blame her?"

It was odd to hear the big, bearded man talk so much. Alice had always assumed he barely ever talked, but then she remembered Danny's bodyguards were not allowed to talk to *her*. That didn't mean they didn't talk at all.

"You lying piece of shit," Danny growled though clenched teeth.

"You should go easy on that coke, old friend, 'cause you're fucking hallucinating."

Again, Danny's eyes were on her and he seemed to expect something from her, some reaction or defense maybe? But her right wrist was throbbing violently, and a sharp pain flashed through her arm with every beat of her racing heart. Her gaze dropped under his accusing and expectant stare, and she kept it on the fringed hems of Jean-Pierre's pants instead. She felt oddly safe behind the broad man's back, and the fact that he had stepped in to help her made her feel a warmth in her chest she hadn't felt in a long time. Apparently, Jonas was not the only one who cared.

Danny appeared to consider his options for a moment, but then he turned on his heels and stormed past his bodyguard and toward the door.

"I should have Viktor kill you for this," he threatened on his way out.

Jean-Pierre laughed, a dry and hollow sound. He patted his gun, which was hanging in a holster around his hip, with his left hand. "You're free to try."

He watched his boss leave the room and then turned around and bent down to look at Alice. "You surviving?"

She nodded.

Pleased, he straightened his back, gave her one last look, and then left the room as well, locking the door behind him.

Alice remained sitting on her bed, clutching her throbbing wrist. Her thoughts were spinning and she felt incredibly nauseous. What was going to happen now? Danny surely wouldn't just leave it at that, and Jean-Pierre had quit. She doubted he would linger any longer.

Would she end up wrapped in plastic and buried in the woods after all?

Again, she felt regret for not having left on New Year's Eve. It might have been her only chance.

Jonas appeared sometime later and found her still sitting in the same spot, not having been able to move an inch.

Alice remained staring at the wall opposite her and she barely felt it when he sat down on the mattress beside her. He said something, but the words sounded muffled through the thick fog in her mind. When he took her arm to inspect it though, hot pain flashed through her bone and she gasped.

He gave her a look that made her turn her head away from him. She could feel him radiate with anger, but she didn't need that now and he knew it. So, he said nothing and kept his face blank while he wrapped a thick bandage around her wrist.

When he was done, he kept her bandaged arm in between his hands, and his thumb brushed over her fingers softly. There was nothing enjoyable about his touch though, and she wished he would just leave. She could feel him looking at her but kept her eyes on the window to her left. It was dark and all she could see was the blurred reflection of her and Jonas on the glass.

"Only one more week," he said suddenly and despite its softness, his hoarse voice filled her ears like thunder.

"He knows," she whispered, barely audible.

Jonas's hand around hers tensed. "Alice ... please look at me."

She hesitated, but then she turned her head slowly and stared at the collar of his leather jacket. It was wet, she noticed. Had he been out somewhere?

"*What* does he know?" he asked softly.

Alice said nothing, feeling too tired to respond. She kept her eyes on his jacket.

Jonas took a deep breath and gave her left hand an affectionate squeeze. "When I came home, I found Jean-Pierre guarding your door. He gave me the key and told me Danny's gone mental, and that I should deal with him and keep him away from you."

Alice just stared at him blankly. She didn't know what to say and the throbbing pain in her wrist made it hard to breathe.

"Don't worry," Jonas said, "I'll deal with it. I'll try to talk to him. I *will* get you out of here, I promise."

"War's the business," Alice whispered, still without looking into his eyes.

He frowned and hesitated, but then he nodded.

There it was, the answer she'd dreaded for over a year—and it did nothing to her. Danny had shown her his ugly side more times than she could count already, and nothing surprised her anymore. The pain in her arm was all she could feel.

"I'll deal with him," Jonas said again, his voice sincere. He got up from the bed and gave her a worried look. "And I'll get you painkillers."

The rain stopped the next day and temperatures dropped down to freezing point, leaving the yard covered in frost. Thick white clouds covered the sky. They looked like they were about to burst, but still, no snow fell.

Alice hadn't slept at all and she watched the night turn into day from her windowsill. The painkillers Jonas had given her kept the throbbing in her wrist down to a tolerable level. She knew that her bone was fractured though, and that without a cast it might heal badly. Then again, if Danny killed her, a broken bone would be the least of her worries.

When someone knocked on her door shortly before noon, she flinched, but kept her eyes on the window. There was only one person who knocked before entering her room.

It was quiet for a moment, but then the key clattered in the lock. As soon as the door had been opened, Alice froze. His presence was enough to make the little hairs on her neck stand up, and she quickly turned to look at him, to be prepared for whatever he was about to do.

"I'd like to talk to you," Danny said.

When he stepped into the room, Alice noticed Jonas standing behind him and exhaled the breath she'd been holding in. Still, her eyes were widened in horror and she looked at Jonas for help, but he was wearing his usual poker face and remained standing in the doorframe.

Danny sighed and leaned against the wall next to the window, not more than an arm's length away from her. His presence was utterly intimidating—even with Jonas still there.

"I'm sorry." Danny's voice sounded tormented but also firm, and it was tinged with determination, as if he had made some life-changing decision. "I know that you've heard every apology already and that they mean nothing to you, so I won't waste our time trying to get your forgiveness. I won't get it and I probably don't deserve it. I'm not ready to give you up. To give up on us. But I can't keep doing this either. Jean was right. I'd end up killing you."

Alice let his words wash over her without looking up at him. She was used to his speeches already. Though it was the first time he was willing to let Jonas listen, and she wondered where this was going.

Danny had been staring at her while talking, but now he took his eyes off her to look out of the window, and it felt as if a weight had been lifted.

"Jonas talked to me," he continued. "Managed to hammer some sense into my brain. Didn't think that would still be possible." He paused. "Jean told me yesterday that he doesn't approve of how I treat you and that he'll consider leaving if I don't get a grip. And instead of listening to him, my coke-brain made me assume ridiculous things. I've seen demons everywhere lately and it's been driving me insane. Even Tee and Waldo told me to get a fucking grip and not let my anger out on you. And I thought you'd somehow gotten them on your side by going behind my back, when all they did was what any decent human being would do."

His eyes were back on her now and Alice stared at her hands, which were resting in her lap.

"I don't hate you, Alice. I'm not even mad at you."

That made her look up and she saw that he was staring at her bandaged wrist, a mixture of guilt and disgust in his eyes.

"Know what Jonas told me?" His eyes flicked to hers and she dropped her gaze at once.

"Whenever I look at you, I see my own broken reflection. I see in your eyes what I've become, and I can't stand it. I can't stand to see the fear in your eyes. I still remember how you used to look at me, back when you still loved me. I can't stand to look at what I've become and all I want to do is smash that fucking mirror. But that mirror is you, Alice. I can't keep breaking you. I'm harming you and myself, and I'm harming the business and everybody who's involved. I need to get my anger under control once and for all, and since I'm apparently unable to do so myself, I've decided I need help."

His right hand moved, and Alice flinched, but he only brought it to his head to run his fingers through his hair.

"I need therapy. I need to sober up. Or all of this will have been for nothing." He fell silent, eyes on her.

The silence stretched on and she started chewing her lower lip nervously.

"That's all I have to say to you for now." His voice was soft now and he kept staring at her. Alice felt her heart beat up in her throat and wished intensely for the moment to be over.

When Danny finally sensed that she wasn't going to say anything, he sighed and turned to Jonas.

"Jonas," he said, "I'm giving you your old job back. I'll have a lot of work to do—on myself as well as with relocating the business. I trust you. Don't let anybody harm her. Hear me? *Anybody.*"

With that, he fell quiet and left the room without looking back, like he wanted to escape the uncomfortable situation as fast as possible.

Alice kept staring at the spot where he'd just been, but then she felt Jonas's gaze on her and looked up. The look in his eyes was enough to make her turn her head away from him again. Neither of them said a word. Then an engine was started outside in the yard and tires squealed. Alice looked out the window and saw Danny's new navy-blue Audi speed through the gate so fast, the guard barely had time to open it wide enough. Her gaze lingered on the car and the cloud of dust it left behind, until it was nothing but a dark spot in the distance. She flinched when she felt a hand on her shoulder.

Jonas sat down on the windowsill beside her and took her bandaged arm in his hands while his gaze followed hers.

"Bastard," he muttered under his breath.

His tone made her wince, and she bit her lip, eyes still on the window.

"Sorry. I can't help it. I had to bottle it all up last night. Talking to him for hours. Pretending to be his friend." He closed his eyes and sucked in air. "It's exhausting."

Despite her feeling nothing but emptiness, tears began streaming down Alice's face and she didn't know how to stop them. Jonas scooted closer and she could see that his eyes were shiny as well. He pulled her into an embrace that was well-intended but made her feel suffocated. She buried her head in his hoodie, trying to feel what she had felt on New Year's Eve, but there were only numbness and a strong urge to shake his arms off. Suppressing the urge, she let the embrace continue, feeling his warm breath on her skin.

When Jonas loosened the embrace and leaned back to look at her, she felt like she was about to drown in the green ponds that were his eyes.

"I can't wait to show you all the beautiful places I know in Calabria," he muttered.

Her eyes widened at his words and she opened her mouth for a question that never left her lips. He understood it anyway.

"Yes." He brushed a loose strand of hair back behind her ear. "I'll stay with you. I promise."

It was still early morning on Tuesday, the eighth of January, but Alice had spent yet another night sitting on her windowsill, staring out the window without looking at anything in particular. Low fog covered the land like a thick blanket. There had been no visible sunrise that morning with the seemingly endless layer of thick white and gray clouds that stretched all over the sky. Dawn had come slowly, and it had stayed. The clouds still looked like they might burst, just the way they already had two days ago.

Maybe it will finally snow today.

The outside world looked gray and lifeless and depressing and not at all inviting.

The frost had evoked ice flowers on the glass of her window, and she absent-mindedly traced their patterns with her fingers from the inside. The glass was cold and brought goose bumps to her bare arms. She was wearing her white nightgown, like she did every day. There was no reason to get dressed with being locked in her room all the time.

Alice brushed her overgrown bangs out of her eyes and stared at the beautiful ice flowers, wondering if there were ice flowers in Calabria as well.

The sudden rattling of the key in the lock pulled her out of her thoughts, and she looked at the door just as it was flung open.

Jonas appeared and she stared at him blankly, confused by his unexpected early visit. But when he crossed the room with big steps and pulled her off the windowsill at once, she blinked and finally realized that something was wrong. His stare was dead serious, and his features were hard.

He grabbed her upper arm and dragged her away from the window.

Alice opened her mouth to protest, but he was faster. "No time for explanations," he said curtly. "Don't say a word. Do what I say."

Fear crept through her bones at once and almost paralyzed her, but she did her best to move her feet along while he half led, half dragged her out of her room and into the corridor.

His pace was fast, and she almost had to run to keep up with him. The carpet in the corridor felt soft underneath her bare feet and muffled their footsteps. It was cold though.

At the top of the stairs, he stopped and turned to face her. "Stay here. No sound."

Perplexed, she watched him tiptoe down the steps. He turned his head from side to side, checking whether the living room was empty, and then he beckoned her to follow him.

Alice felt dizzy and dissociated from reality, and she had to grip the banister for support. Her hands kept slipping on the polished wood, but she managed to walk down to him without making any sound.

Again, he grabbed her upper arm and then led her to the basement door. Between her heavy breathing and the pounding of her heart, Alice was able to make out muffled voices coming from Danny's office. She couldn't understand what they were saying, but it sounded like someone was arguing.

Jonas pushed her through the door then followed and closed it behind him. It was dark and he didn't turn on the light, but he took his phone out of the pocket of his jeans and turned on the flashlight before leading her down the steps. There was no heating down here and Alice immediately got goose bumps on her skin, though she barely felt the cold.

The basement was soundproof at least, and Jonas finally dared to speak. "We got a huge problem. Found out this morning."

Alice quietly followed him through the long corridor that led to the men's gym at the other end of the basement.

"Cops are coming. Everything's over."

Her heart seemed to freeze at his words. "What about Italy?" she whispered.

He shook his head and pulled her farther through the corridor. "No time. Not anymore. Cops are already on their way," he spoke hastily, but in a low voice. "Julio's sending his helicopter to fly the others out of here. Road's been blocked."

Alice said nothing, her throat feeling constricted, unable to let neither words nor air pass.

"You'll stay down here and hide from Danny." He pushed open the door to the gym and stowed his phone back into the pocket of his jeans. This room had windows and it was light enough to see where they were going. Alice had only been in here once before, the night with Martin, but there was no time to think about that now.

"You'll hide down here until they're gone, and when the police arrive, you'll tell them everything. You hear me? *Everything!* They won't arrest you, they'll ask questions, but they will let you go. You haven't done anything wrong."

He dragged her to the far-right corner of the room, where a big wooden wardrobe stood near the wall.

"Hide in here," he said while he opened one of its doors.

Alice's heart seemed to drop down into her belly at the sight of the dark wardrobe, opened like a mouth ready to devour her.

"I'm not going to close the door; you'll close it from the inside. You'll be able to free yourself." He grabbed her shoulders with both of his hands and gazed into her eyes. "Alice, *listen* ... there's no time for claustrophobia, no time for fear, do you hear me?"

She nodded slowly, not knowing what else to do.

"Just hide in here until the cops come, promise me that!"

"W-what about you?" she breathed.

He gave her a sad look. "I'll go with the others."

"But ... you said ..."

"I can't. They'd arrest me. I'm not going to prison, Alice, I'm sorry." He sighed and it sounded desperate. "I'm so, so sorry!" Tears were glistening in his bright green eyes and he bent down to kiss her cheek.

"This is not at all how I pictured it." His voice broke and he wiped a tear away from her cheek with his thumb, just like he had done before. Alice just stood there, paralyzed and unable to grasp a clear thought.

"Hide in the wardrobe," he said again. "There's towels in there to keep you warm."

Alice stepped toward the wardrobe hesitantly, but then she turned to look at him.

"We'll see each other again. I promise." Jonas gave her one last sad look, and then he turned and hurried back toward the door.

Before he reached it though, someone opened it from the outside, and the sound of the hinges screaming sent a shiver down Alice's spine. Jonas stopped walking at once and froze in place, and Alice watched, horrified, as Danny stepped into the room.

He jumped when he saw Jonas standing in front of him. "God, you scared me," he exclaimed breathlessly. "I'm looking for my duffel bag. My wallet's in there. I've looked everywhere but I can't find it!"

Apparently, Danny had not spotted her yet. Alice was standing in the shade on the other side of the large room, and she didn't dare move.

"It's not here." Jonas made an attempt to shove Danny out the door, but in that instant, his big blue eyes fell on her and his jaw dropped.

"What's she doing down here?"

Jonas immediately took a step away from him.

"What the fuck, Jonas? We have to go! I told you to get her ready, why would you bring her down here?" He tried to push Jonas aside and walk toward Alice, but Jonas grabbed his shoulders and shoved him back to the door.

"She stays here," he said curtly.

Confusion flickered over Danny's face, but then comprehension trickled in, and his features hardened at once. "Oh. I see."

"Please," Jonas said. "Leave her, let's just get on that bloody helicopter!"

Danny hesitated, eyes on her. His stare made her shiver. Or was it the cold?

"I see," he said again, his voice cold as ice. "I was right all along."

Before Jonas could do anything, Danny rammed his fist into his face—more than once—until he stumbled backward, blinded by the blows. He quickly caught himself though and fought back, and soon, the two of them were on the ground, punching each other furiously.

Alice stood, paralyzed, and watched in horror as the two men rolled around on the ground. She had never seen Danny fight. He'd gotten his muscles from the gym, not from fighting. Jonas was different though. He managed to pin Danny down against a shelf with weights and dumbbells on it. It shuddered under the impact, the weights trembling dangerously.

"Stop that shit," he growled at him, breathless from fighting.

Danny held up one hand defensively. He too was panting heavily.

"Let's just go," Jonas said, his voice almost pleading.

"Never!" Danny's eyes glistened dangerously. "You fucking traitor!"

Jonas put a hand around Danny's throat and dug his fingers deeply into his skin, holding him steady. His head turned to Alice. "Run! Hide somewhere, I'll keep him here!"

Alice felt as if her feet were glued to the cold concrete floor and she stared at him with widened eyes.

"GO!" he yelled, and finally, she managed to move.

Jonas followed her with his eyes as she hurried past him and Danny, and to the door. She had no idea where to go, but there was no time to think.

Once at the door, Alice turned around and found Jonas still looking at her. It was a mistake.

The sadness in his eyes drove all air out of her lungs and his stare paralyzed her, but in that instant, she saw Danny's arm reach out, and grab one of the dumbbells on the shelf to fling it down and let it crash on Jonas's head.

Nausea overcame her at once when she saw him go down.

Danny wasn't done with him though. He climbed on top of his former friend, pinning him down with his knees and flinging his fist at his face again and again in a sickening manner.

"Stop!" she screamed, horrified by the scene in front of her. "Stop it! Danny, please, stop!" She tried to pull him off Jonas, grabbing his shirt with both her hands, but all it did was rip the buttons off and send a sharp pain through her right wrist— and Danny didn't move an inch.

"You're killing him!" she cried out as he grabbed one of the smaller dumbbells to hit Jonas with it.

Alice grasped his arm, ignoring the pain in her wrist, and tried to pull him off, but she was weak and injured, and he was infuriated and aimed at her instead. Hot pain erupted in her shoulder and spread down her arm, and the dumbbell dropped onto the floor, missing her naked toes by an inch. Blinded by the pain, she stumbled backward and tripped over one of the bigger weights on the ground.

Danny continued punching Jonas with his fists, even though his face was already covered in blood and he was lying motionless on the floor.

"Danny please!" Alice cried again. "I'll come with you, I swear, I'm coming with you! Just let go of him, please!" Her voice cracked and she sobbed. "Please," she begged him, "stop it, you're killing him!"

Danny stopped suddenly and turned to look at her. A cold smile parted his lips. "I should have done that long ago." He reached to the shelf and grabbed another dumbbell.

No, no, no! Alice thought desperately. She stumbled back onto her feet and tried once again to pull Danny off Jonas.

Danny dropped the weight and his fingers closed around her throat instead. "Fuck off!" he yelled at her, his face contorted by anger and madness. "You betrayed me! You betrayed me with him, and you will both pay for it!"

In that instant, Alice saw Jonas move. Disorientated by his injuries and the blood on his face, his hand moved slowly, blindly searching until it found the gun holster at his hip and he pulled the weapon from it.

Danny's eyes were still on Alice, and he didn't see it happening. Jonas lifted the gun, his hand shaking, and pointed the muzzle at Danny.

No, she thought, horror-struck, but Danny seemed to notice that her widened eyes were staring at something behind him. At once, he let go of her throat and whirled around. He grabbed the gun with both hands and tried to rip it out of Jonas's weak grip.

They wrestled for the weapon and all Alice could do was watch, until suddenly, a shot fell, and the blast almost tore her eardrums apart. All motion stopped at once.

Even her heart had stopped beating for a moment, and she held her breath, terrified of what had happened. The gun was in Danny's hand now, she saw. He had managed to yank it out of Jonas's grip.

Her knees were trembling violently and her legs felt wobbly underneath her, but her eyes found Jonas's and she realized that he was looking at her, his expression shocked, his eyes wide.

No! she thought desperately.

She looked into his bright green eyes and saw the light in them fade, but then Danny's head turned as well. There was no triumph in his expression. Only shock.

Both of them were staring at her now.

She wanted to speak, but her throat felt tight and her mouth was dry. And then the room began to spin around her.

Suddenly noticing that she was still holding her breath, she quickly inhaled, but instead of air, a horrible pain flashed through her chest, worse than anything she'd ever experienced. When she looked down at herself, she saw that her nightshirt had turned red.

Confused, she looked back at the two men, and then her legs gave in.

Danny caught her before her head hit the ground. The room was still spinning, and she realized that her body was trembling heavily.

Shaking like a leaf, Jonas had said that night when she had been in his room. She didn't know why she was remembering that now.

Her ears were still ringing from the blast of the shot and the pain in her belly made her nauseous. It felt like a fire burning inside her and it made it impossible to breathe.

Danny's arm moved underneath her neck and he shook her lightly. She saw his lips move but his voice seemed far away—too far away to understand.

Her eyes flickered to Jonas, who was still lying in the same spot next to the shelf. He appeared to be struggling for breath, his chest heaving and falling irregularly. His right arm twitched, and pain contorted his features. Blood glistened on his face and his eyes locked with hers. But then his eyelids drooped, and his focus shifted away from her. His body seemed to relax, and Alice stared at him through a veil of tears, until his eyes were shut completely and did not open again.

Slowly, Danny lifted her up into his arms and every movement sent a stab of pain through her body. Breathing was incredibly hard and for a moment, she felt herself panic, thinking she was about to suffocate. But then a tiredness overcame her and wrapped her up like a blanket. She barely noticed the ground growing smaller beneath her when Danny stood up. He kept muttering to her, but his words made no sense.

When he started walking, her left arm dangled loosely at her side. Her bandaged wrist was lying on her belly, and the bandage soaked up blood from her wound and turned red. Her eyelids were heavy, and she felt too drowsy to keep them open. Danny shook her and called her name. He kept moving, first through the darkness, then toward a faint grayish light. Up they went. Up into the light.

The cold hitting her felt like a punch in the face, and everything around her turned a bright white. It blinded her and she closed her eyes.

The cold wind stung like a thousand needles on her skin, but Danny kept moving.

They were out in the yard, she realized. Her eyes flung open, and she saw that Danny had carried her to the backyard. She could see Jonas's balcony from underneath and for a split second, she saw herself standing up there, leaning against the balustrade, with Jonas at her side.

Suddenly, the sound of sirens tore the air apart, and she flinched in Danny's arms.

There was another sound, like the buzzing of a thousand bees, only louder. Much louder. The wind became stronger and threatened to blow them away, and then she heard him scream.

"Noooo! wait for us! waaaiiiit!"

His scream was piercing and when the buzzing sound faded out, she heard him sob.

"No," he kept saying. "No, no, no ..."

The sirens grew louder, and Danny flinched and started moving again. She felt him fumble with something without letting go of her, then a lock clicked, and a door screamed in its hinges.

And then they were out.

The sky was a mixture of shades of gray and white. Little snowflakes were starting to fall. Slowly, dancing lazily through the air. All noise was muffled and seemed far away. Only his heavy breathing close to her ear and her own heartbeat were clearly audible.

Alice knew she had goose bumps on her bare arms, and she felt the icy touch of the flakes landing on her skin, immediately melted by the warmth of her body. Yet she didn't feel that cold.

Her breathing became slower.

With every step he took, he softly rocked her to sleep. Her eyelids got heavier. Her hands and feet felt numb. Was it because of the cold?

Her belly was warm though. There was a fire inside her, but the burning sensation seemed to disappear steadily, fading out like the flames of an unattended fire.

It wasn't hurting anymore.

He was whispering again. She could not understand him. He seemed so distant.

Her eyelids fell shut, but she forced them open quickly, scared of what might come in the darkness.

It was nice to be held by him, facing upward, toward the white sky. Even though the light blinded her, she enjoyed watching the snowflakes dance. They looked so joyful.

She couldn't remember the last time she had looked at snowflakes like that. She could not even remember the last time she had been outside.

The air was so fresh and rich with scents. She could smell trees and earth. Wet soil and fern. Even moss.

Eager, she tried to inhale deeply, but her lungs protested, and the cold air pierced her chest, like tiny icicles stabbing through the membrane of her organs.

Her eyes wandered to his face and she realized he was looking at her. His eyes were shiny and wet, glistening in the faint winter light.

Little droplets of sweat covered his forehead. Strands of his hair stuck to it. His jaw was clenched in agony and anger, so hard it seemed as though it was about to crush.

He looked mad, yet vulnerable.

Desperate.

She felt him move his hand slightly. His thumb began to softly move along the naked skin of her left arm. His fingers were rough against her skin, but not in an unpleasant way.

His hand was warm, but the gun it carried felt cold as ice.

Suddenly, the light disappeared, and Alice couldn't see the sky anymore.

They had gotten deeper into the woods. Dark branches of evergreen trees blocked the snowflakes from falling to the ground. The air felt warmer here. Moister. The ground appeared to be softer too. It was probably still covered in fallen autumn leaves.

She couldn't see them though. She wasn't able to turn her head.

His steps weren't shaking her so hard anymore. The rocking had gotten softer, and the lack of light made her even more tired.

Again, she felt her eyelids close. Her mind protested but was too weak to resist the drowsiness.

The movement stopped suddenly, and she seemed to be falling.

It was only him kneeling on the ground. He shifted her a bit on his lap and began to tap her cheek softly.

"Don't go." His voice was barely more than a whisper. Flat. Toneless. Broken.

Did he mean her? Where would she be going? She could not even move her legs.

She forced her eyes open once again. It cost her more effort than she would have thought.

One of his tears dripped down on her cheek. It felt warm on her skin. He took her left hand, which had been resting on the cold ground, and placed it on her belly.

Her fingers touched something wet and warm.

The blood.

With every drop, her life was running out of her body.

There were voices in the distance. Shouts.

"They're coming," she breathed.

Danny nodded; desperation clearly displayed on his face. He sobbed and the sobbing shook his whole body and hers as well.

"I ... I didn't—" he stammered, his voice shaking. "I didn't want ... I didn't want for this to happen!"

Tears streamed down his face and dripped off his chin, some crashing down on her like hot rain. He wiped them off her cheeks with his sleeve.

"I'm so sorry! I'm so sorry! I'm so, so sorry," he kept saying over and over again, his voice torn by regret and grief. "Don't die, please don't die, Allie! Please don't do this to me!"

She heard his words, but they made no sense. Hadn't he tried to kill her?

Darkness spread before her eyes and lulled her in like a soft and warm blanket.

He shook her, this time harder. "Don't, Allie, please!" His fingers kept caressing her cheek, but feeling the gun against her skin was agitating and made dull panic spread through her. What would dying be like? So far, it was not so bad. The pain was almost gone now. All there was, were the warmth in her belly and the fear of what would come next.

At least she was finally out of the house, outside of those walls that had marked the end of her life for so long. Free at last.

"Stay with me, please ..." He sobbed and buried his face in her hair.

She was barely able to feel his touch anymore. Everything seemed so far away. Apart from the voices in the distance. They were growing louder.

"Stay, Allie, please stay!"

Had he not held on to her long enough? It was finally time for him to let go.

More tears rolled down his cheeks. "I love you; I always have! You know that, right? Please tell me you know that!"

Alice tried to nod, but her head felt as if it weighed a hundred pounds and didn't move an inch.

"I never wanted to hurt you! Please, Allie, you have to believe me! I've always loved you."

I just want to sleep. Just let me sleep, Danny, please.

He shook her vigorously when her eyelids fell shut.

"Don't," he pleaded desperately. "Please don't! Stay with me, please!"

The agony in his voice sent a stab of pain through her chest and out of pity, she forced her eyes open one last time. Only for him. But when she did, she saw shapes emerge from the trees and they appeared to be dancing all around her. Tall, black, grotesque shapes. Panicking, she squirmed in Danny's arms.

Was there a hell after all? The figures had no faces. They were black and shiny from head to toe, and they surrounded her ... and the shouts ... the horrible shouting all around her ...

Fear crept though her bones and the adrenaline woke her up. With it, the pain became stronger as well.

"Monsters," she gasped, trembling in his arms. "Monsters, everywhere!"

Danny squeezed her gently, then he looked up and hatred flickered over his face.

"Drop the gun!" one of the monsters shouted.

Danny's big blue eyes fell back on her face, and he continued caressing her, despite the weapon he was still holding.

"Don't worry, honey," he told her gently. "The monsters won't hurt you."

She saw his hand twitch and he raised the gun. It was only in that instant that she understood the monsters were police officers with black vests and helmets. And they were heavily armed.

"Don't," she gasped, suddenly realizing what was about to happen. "Please, they'll kill you ... don't ... please!" Every word cost her an incredible amount of effort and left her breathless. "Please," she begged him. "Please!"

Hesitating, he looked at her, and the sadness in his eyes was heart-wrenching. But he lowered the gun at last and she saw him toss it away.

"I'm sorry," he whispered and then everything happened quickly.

The monsters leaped at him, grabbing him from all sides, and when they pulled him away from her, she rolled off his lap and onto the moist forest soil. The leaves underneath her were soft like a bed and they didn't even feel cold.

Her back was facing him now, but she heard him scream and curse, and wanted to turn around to look at him, but all strength had drained from her now. The last thing she saw before her eyes fell shut were black leather boots standing on dead, brown leaves.

She heard him calling her name long after she had closed her eyes, and when his voice finally faded out, nothing remained but darkness.

EPILOGUE

He was sitting on a metal bench at one of the tables. The warm summer sun reflected off his hair and gave him a halo.

There was nothing holy about him though.

His hands were resting on the metal table in front of him, chained by handcuffs. His clothes were gray. Gray shirt and gray pants. The shirt was unbuttoned and revealed the white tank top underneath.

He looked up when she approached him, and something flickered in his eyes, some emotion. But it was hard to tell what it was.

She took her place on the bench opposite him and eyed him coldly. He looked older than she remembered. There were scars all over his face. His hair had been cropped short, revealing more scars on the back of his head. His cheeks were hollow and the wrinkles in the corners of his eyes had deepened. So had the ones on his forehead. The worry lines. Had he been worrying too much?

She let her eyes wander across the yard. Who could blame him? There were definitely places less worrisome than this.

The sun burned down on them and she noticed that he'd gotten a tan on his arms already. It made her wonder how often he was allowed to be outside. Then again, he had always gotten a tan quite easily. Unlike her. Her own skin was pale, and she quickly pulled the sleeves of her jacket down over her wrists to keep the sun from burning her and to hide the scars. She hated the sun. It was too hot and bright, and it made people leave their houses. Everything was nicer in the winter. People leave you alone in the winter. They don't mow their lawns or walk around the block with their screaming toddlers. They don't chatter in the streets or expose their naked bodies in their backyards.

Winter was over though.

He was studying her, she noticed. He looked sad, somehow. Had he missed her? Not that she could care less. If he hadn't told her that it was urgent, she would have never come here to visit him. She had thought that it was all behind her at last. All of it. Yet, here she was, sitting at a table with him.

His silence annoyed her. "You gonna talk?"

He winced at the harshness in her voice, but then he nodded.

She tapped her fingers on the metal surface of the table impatiently. Did he think she had all the time in the world?

"How are you?" he asked. His voice sounded hoarse ... tinged with sadness.

"I'm not here for small talk."

"I know. Sorry." He stared at the chains around his wrists sullenly, but then he looked back up at her. "You look different ... blue hair, I like it."

Her hand jerked to her head automatically and she let her fingers run through a strand of hair. The dye had made it dry and frizzy.

"It's already growing out," she muttered.

He nodded. "You cut it. Looks good."

A smile parted his lips, and it made her feel uncomfortable. It evoked old feelings; feelings she had long believed forgotten. She quickly looked away and fished her pack of L&Ms out of the pocket of her denim jacket. She lit one and inhaled the smoke deeply, hoping for it to make her numb inside.

His eyes followed her every movement and she noticed curiosity in them as well as worry. Did he mind her smoking? She sure hoped so.

Her eyes met his and she held his stare coolly while exhaling a cloud of smoke.

Whatever he saw on her face, it appeared to make him uneasy, and he dropped his gaze.

"You didn't get it fixed," he muttered.

"What?"

He looked back up, and there was guilt in his eyes. "The tooth."

Shrugging, she took another drag on her cigarette. "Didn't have the money."

He said nothing, but his eyes seemed glued to her, and he watched her smoke with a hunger in his eyes that made him look dangerous somehow, as if he were a famished lion waiting to attack.

She tossed a cigarette to him, and he took it thankfully and put it between his lips. When she handed him the lighter, he had to lift both hands to light his cigarette since they were chained together.

Seeing him like that made her feel ashamed, but she had to admit that the bad-boy look was kind of sexy. He looked like he belonged in there ... as if it were his natural habitat.

She had wondered whether he would face problems in prison, but he seemed to be a natural.

"Why am I here?" she asked when he didn't talk.

He exhaled a big cloud of smoke, and then he sighed and looked incredibly sad.

"Danny's dead."

The words came out quickly and mercilessly, and for a moment, she forgot to breathe.

Jonas studied her cautiously, concern in his bright green eyes ... though they had lost some of their brightness, she noticed.

Did he expect her to cry?

She brought the cigarette back to her lips and continued smoking, eyes on the high fence to her right. It felt weird, being in here. Surrounded by high fences and walls that were guarded by armed warders. It felt too familiar. Way too familiar. Her throat tightened and she pushed the thought aside. Her life in prison was over, once and for all, and after Jonas had said whatever he wanted to say, she would be able to leave this place and never look back.

"Killed himself," he explained when she didn't answer.

"How many attempts?"

Jonas frowned at the question. A feeling of satisfaction overcame her when she realized she was making him uncomfortable.

"One."

A piece of ash had landed on the black nail polish on her thumb nail, and she blew it off casually.

"Lucky guy."

Hurt flickered in his eyes and he gave her one of those intense, meaningful looks she remembered only too well. It left her cold.

"Could've told me that on the phone," she muttered.

Grimacing, he put his cigarette to his lips and inhaled deeply. "I wanted to see you."

Who said I wanted to see you?

She kept that thought to herself.

"How ... does it make you feel?" he asked carefully.

"What?"

"That he's dead."

Shrugging, she put out her cigarette on the table and crossed her arms in front of her chest. "Am I supposed to cry?"

He shook his head slowly.

"When did he do it?"

"Two days ago."

Surprised, she stared at him. "And it was his first attempt? Wow ... why *now*?"

He shifted on the bench uneasily. "He was ... looking for you. For months. Couldn't find you."

"I'm glad he didn't."

"It's my fault," he confessed.

"Why?"

"He hired someone to find you, and I wanted to make sure he left you alone, so I made the guy tell him you were dead."

Alice let his words sink in for a moment. Her heart had turned to stone luckily, but the thought that Danny had still been alive two days ago made her feel uneasy, nonetheless.

He had killed himself because he'd thought she was dead.

"Charming," she said. "He'll be pissed when he finds I'm not waiting for him at hell's gate."

Again, a look of utter sadness came over Jonas's face, and his eyes seemed to pierce right through her. They couldn't, though. Not anymore.

Nothing was able to break the wall she had built around herself, but it was satisfying to see him try.

"I thought you were dead as well, at first ... you know," he said quietly.

"Right back at you." She lit another cigarette and inhaled deeply.

Again, his eyes looked hungry, and she tossed him another cigarette, like tossing a bone to a dog. He took it eagerly.

"What happened?" he asked carefully. "Tell me, please."

Sighing, she forced herself to think back to that day. The memories had become disconnected and gray. As if they were scenes from an old movie she had watched, rather than from her own life.

The forest, the cops, Danny's arrest. It all seemed to belong to someone else's life.

"Apparently, I was in a coma for about three weeks," she began, before taking another drag on her cigarette.

Jonas's eyes were on her, unblinking.

"Cops were there. They asked questions."

"Did they accuse you of anything?"

She shook her head. "They told me they'd found my diaries. They already knew what happened. They also said that a certain *Mr. Bandiera* had testified in my favor." Her eyes flicked to his face and she saw a faint blush appear on his cheeks.

"*Bandiera* ..." she said again. "You never told me your last name. It sounds nice."

He shrugged. "Danny testified as well, you know. He didn't want you to go to jail. We didn't know whether you were dead or had been arrested ..."

"How generous of him," Alice said sarcastically. "Wasn't your mom Italian?"

"I took her name after ... you know."

"You killed your father."

He looked taken aback. "What? I never–"

"You didn't have to. I figured it out."

His green eyes were widened in shock, but he quickly caught himself and donned a blank expression.

"I'm not stupid, you know," she said.

"I never thought you were," he muttered.

"Do they know?" She nodded toward the guards, but he understood that she meant the cops.

He shook his head. "No one ever found out."

"Lucky you." She took another drag on her cigarette.

He sighed and did the same. "What else happened?"

"Not much." She turned the cigarette over in between her index finger and thumb and pondered. "They kept my diaries for investigational reasons. Bastards."

"Did you get in touch with your friends?"

She shook her head. "Told you I wouldn't, didn't I?"

"I was hoping you'd change your mind."

"Sorry to disappoint you." Her tone made clear that she wasn't.

He heard it too and again, that annoying sad look came over his face.

"You're not ... disappointing me," he said quietly. "I just hoped they'd help you."

"I don't need anyone's help."

Doubt flickered in his eyes and it made her want to slap him.

"You've gone soft. I thought prison would make you harder."

His gaze dropped down to the cigarette between his fingers. "It's you, not prison."

Alice ignored that. "Anyway, I got a job and I'm surviving. Didn't break my promise after all."

Confused, he looked up. "What promise?"

"I told you I'd survive. And I don't break my promises like you do."

He swallowed and the look in his eyes would have made her melt once. But that was long ago, in a different life. Now, she answered his gaze coldly, and hurt flickered over his face.

"I'm glad you did," he said in a hoarse voice.

"I'm not."

He winced at her words.

It's like I'm torturing him. But why don't I care?

"Please don't say that."

"Why? So you don't have to hear it? I'll still think it, though."

"I ... I really hoped you'd be happy." His voice cracked and Alice noticed that the cigarette in his hand had burned down almost unsmoked.

What a waste.

"Yeah, well ..." She put her cigarette out on the table and let her eyes wander across the yard and over the other inmates who had gotten visitors this afternoon. Most of them looked happy to see their loved ones. Some looked sad like Jonas, and some were arguing quietly. There were wives and girlfriends, brothers and sisters, fathers and mothers, and even some children; but the guards were walking up and down, making sure that everyone was safe.

Somewhere deep down, she felt sorry for Jonas.

His eyes were still on her, she noticed.

"You have your freedom back. I thought that would make you happy," he said, his voice pained.

"Freedom is an illusion."

"But–"

"Like I said, sorry to disappoint you."

"This is not about me." His voice was a bit louder now. "You deserve to be happy; you deserve to live a good life. Would you call this a life?"

"I'm a survivor, Jonas. You said it yourself. I'm good at surviving, but I never said I'm good at *living*. Maybe life's not for everyone."

He looked as if she'd slapped him. "Does that mean ... are you still thinking about ...?"

"Killing myself? No. That ship's sailed. Dying doesn't really seem to work and I'm done trying. It's unfair though when you think about it. Isn't it? It took *him* one try. One fucking try, and it worked right away. Makes you wonder, doesn't it?"

He said nothing, but the look on his face said it all.

"Or maybe it's because you weren't there to save his life," she continued. "Or were you?"

He shook his head. "We weren't cell mates."

"Good for you."

He looked as if he was about to cry. Again, Alice felt bad, but the feeling was buried somewhere deep down, in the black hole that had once been her heart, and she couldn't get herself to feel what she was supposed to feel.

"Let me help you," Jonas said suddenly.

She looked up and met his gaze. "I don't need your help."

"It's no shame to get help. Please consider it, let someone help you."

"You? No thanks."

Her words had hurt him again, she saw.

"Why are you like that? Why are you so ... cold?"

Her eyes narrowed at his words and she frowned at him. "I remember somebody telling me I was too emotional."

He winced at that remark and she saw guilt in his eyes. "What about that kid you met ... that night in the Shipwreck. You got his number, don't you?"

Alice frowned. "Aaron? That was over a year ago. Why should I call him?"

"Don't know ... he looked nice. Didn't he? And you need a friend ..."

Anger flared up in her at once and she glared at him. "I don't need a man in my life, if that's what you're implying!"

"But you need men in your bed to pay the rent, don't you?"

His words were like knives, stabbing into her chest and taking her breath away. How did he know that?

She stared at him, speechless, eyes wide.

His expression softened at once and he leaned forward to take her hand, but she quickly pulled back.

"I'm so sorry, Alice! Fuck, I'm sorry, I shouldn't have said that!"

"How ... how do you know about this? Did you have me *watched*?" Her voice was shaking, she noticed, and she hated herself for it. He was making her fall back into old patterns.

"I'm sorry, I really am," he said again, and it was clear that he meant it.

"Answer my question!"

His eyes dropped in shame and he seemed to struggle to find the right words. "No one told us if you were still alive or not. It was ... unbearable not to know how you were doing. So, Danny suggested to pay someone to find you or find out what happened ..." He paused and looked up anxiously. "The guy found you and reported to me."

"And then you told him to tell *him* I'm dead."

He nodded. "I'm sorry."

"So the two of you worked together again. Best buddies like you were before, huh? Like old times, you and him together, making my life hell."

"It wasn't like that," he said desperately.

"You had me *watched*."

For more than a year, she had been locked up in the big English house with its barred windows and walled yard ... with people watching her every step. And now, now that she was finally out of her prison, Danny and Jonas had still had her watched.

The betrayal made her nauseous and she tasted bile on her tongue.

"Sorry," he muttered again.

"I can't believe it ... I can't fucking believe it."

Jonas shifted uncomfortably and his hands jerked forward, but Alice pulled back before he reached her.

"I was worried sick, that's why I did it. I just needed to know how you were doing ... if you were okay or not ..." Tears glistened in his eyes, but they left her cold.

She swallowed the stomach acid back down and winced when it burned in her throat.

"And what's your conclusion?" she asked coldly.

"You ... don't look happy."

"Oh, you're wrong. Some of the men in my bed actually make me *very* happy."

His cheeks turned red and again, he looked as if she had slapped him. "Why do you do it?" he asked in a tortured voice.

"Because the motel where I work doesn't pay well, so sometimes I gotta do some extra hours."

It was none of his business, but she enjoyed watching him blush in shame and anger. He deserved it.

Traitor.

"What's the big deal, Jonas, huh? *He* made me do things I didn't want to all the time, you know. I know how to shut off my mind and let others use me. Only now I get paid for it."

He said nothing for a while, but his hands were clenched into fists and shaking. Was he jealous? Or grossed out?

"Please," he begged. "Let me help you ... financially, I mean. Let me give you some money!"

Alice lit another cigarette and inhaled deeply before asking, "How come you got money?"

"Cops didn't find everything," he explained in a low voice. "There's still accounts ... I can help you."

"I had almost five grand in my savings account before *he* took everything from me. Money I worked for. Money I earned. The cops promised to give me the sum back, along with my diaries."

Jonas snorted disdainfully. "And when did they promise that? Five months ago? They're *cops*, Alice, they're not going to give you anything."

She glared at him. "They have to, and they will."

He shook his head sadly. "Please, just let me help you. You don't need to do ... *these things* ... You don't need to take money from those men."

"How would taking money from *you* be any different?"

Now, he *really* looked hurt. She almost felt sorry for him, but her anger was stronger.

He took a deep breath before answering. "I don't expect anything in return."

Alice scoffed scornfully. "Yeah, well ... First of all, we've already done *that*. Second, I'm pretty sure you *do* want something in return."

"I just want you to be happy."

"Yeah and you want frequent updates concerning my mental status, don't you? Visits? Or would phone calls be adequate?"

He stared down at his hands and Alice noticed that he still had them clenched into fists.

"I don't expect anything from you, Alice. I really just want you to be happy."

Alice put her cigarette to her lips and took a deep drag. Then she blew out the smoke and watched it dissolve in the hot summer air.

"What is that even, *happiness*? Maybe I don't deserve it." she said without looking at him.

Before she could pull away this time, he stretched out his hands over the table and took her left hand in his. She flinched at his touch and tried to wind free, but he kept her hand between his and she couldn't help but look at him.

His eyes were full of affection, just the way they had been five months ago, before they had closed on her, and she had thought they'd never open again.

"Please don't punish yourself. You haven't done anything wrong." His voice sounded thick and heavy, as if talking were really hard for him.

It *was* hard for him, she suddenly remembered. He had never liked to talk much.

"Then why do I feel like I did?" The question was directed at herself, not at him, and she didn't expect him to answer.

The look in his eyes was sad and intense, and she felt the wall crumble after all. *No,* she thought anxiously, *don't let him get to you, not again!*

"Let me help you, *please*," he urged.

A guard walked by and he eyed their hands on the table suspiciously, but Jonas gave him a warning look, and he continued walking.

Alice was amazed. "How did you do that?"

He shrugged. "They respect me."

"You really fit in here."

He frowned at that and looked hurt.

"I mean optically."

His features relaxed and he gave her a weak smile. "Optically? The clothes? The handcuffs?"

"It's hot."

Shocked, Alice bit her tongue and her mouth turned dry at once.

Why did I say that? Why the fuck did I say that?

She didn't want to flirt with him, not anymore. She had gotten over him, she had almost forgotten him even, until he had called her at the motel and begged her to come and visit him. And now she was here with him, and he was making her weak again, just the way he had before.

I'm not weak. Not anymore. I don't need him.

He smiled at what she had said, but when he saw her expression, his smile died.

They said nothing for a while and Alice flicked the cigarette butt away when the embers began to melt the filter.

Jonas kept holding her hand in his and his thumb caressed her skin lightly. She tried to suppress the feelings his touch evoked in her. He was in jail and she didn't want to grow attached to him again.

"So," he said after a while. "Will you let me help you?"

"I don't want money I haven't earned."

He sighed. "We had this conversation before, Alice. I owe it to you. It's yours anyway."

"You don't owe me anything," she objected.

He gave her a meaningful look and squeezed her hand affectionately. "There's at least one thing I owe you."

Confused, Alice stared at him, until comprehension trickled in. "Oh."

She chewed her lip, feeling nervous all of a sudden.

"I love it when you do that," Jonas commented. "Haven't seen it in a while."

"Exactly," she agreed. "Because you've been in here all this time, and as far as I'm concerned, you'll still be here in twenty years."

She put as much indifference in the words as she could, but in the end, they were still tinged with sadness.

"Actually," he said, and his tone made her look up. "That's what I wanted to discuss with you."

Again, he seemed to be struggling to find the right words. "I didn't get a life sentence because I wasn't really part of the business."

The business ... thinking of it made her nauseous again.

The police had told her what Danny and his friends had been doing, and it still made her sick to think about it.

Jonas noticed the change in her expression. "You know now," he said.

"Drones. Selling war like an online game. It's disgusting."

He grimaced at her words. "It made sense. It was meant to fight the terrorists."

"You sold war to people like a game! You let them kill people for their entertainment!"

"*Bad* people," he corrected her.

"There is no good or bad, Jonas. There's no excuse for what you did!" She tried to pull her hand out of his once again, but he held on to it.

"We wanted to help the world ... help kill the enemy."

"No, you wanted to make money and have fun, and to keep your conscience clear, you chose jihadists."

He frowned. "That's not true, Alice. It really isn't. The whole point was to liberate occupied Syrian cities."

"Sure. And how did you do that? How did you know that the people who signed up for the game had the same intentions?"

"There were settings."

Alice scoffed, "That sounds very safe."

"We did have some problems," he confessed.

"You mean when *he* blew up refugees instead of terrorists?"

Jonas's hands tensed around hers and he looked ashamed. "That was the worst thing that ever happened. Nothing like that happened again."

"Does that bring back the dead?"

He shook his head sadly. "I still think we did more good than bad."

Her eyes narrowed and she glared at him. "I can only hope you did."

Sighing, he leaned back a bit without taking his hands from hers, though. "I'm sorry you feel that way."

"I don't even know why I care," she admitted. "It's not like you're a saint anyway, is it?" She lowered her voice a bit. "First you killed your own father and who knows who else, then you shot Martin like other people would kill a mosquito ... and you talked about killing *him* just the same. Why should I even be shocked?"

"I wasn't really a part of it," he said defensively. "And you know Martin and Danny were about saving your life." His voice was toneless now, hollow.

"And your dad? Revenge?"

Suddenly, Jonas's eyes glistened angrily. "Don't do that! Don't dig up the past! It has nothing to do with what's going on here!"

His suddenly harsh tone made her flinch and try to pull her hand back, but still, he held on to it.

He's right. Nothing he ever did matters. Nothing he'll ever do matters.

"Sorry. It's none of my business."

His features softened a bit and his eyes turned sad. There was a long moment of silence before he spoke again.

"I wanted to ask you something."
Alice noticed that he looked a bit nervous, but she said nothing.
"They offered me a deal."
"A deal?"
He nodded. "I could get out of here soon."
Eyebrows raised, she eyed him suspiciously. "You invented a war game that actually kills people; you basically earned money with weapon trade, and you're telling me they wanna let you go?"
"I was never actually part of the business," he said again. "I never ... *played the game*, I didn't help develop it, I didn't even attend any meetings."
"But you still killed people."
"All they know about is Martin, and thanks to what you wrote in your diaries, they don't regard it as murder."
"That's good for you then ... and what's the deal?"
He grimaced and a hard look came over his face. "Maybe you heard that everyone else got away."
Alice thought back to that day when everything had ended, and she remembered the sound of a helicopter above her. "They all got away?"
Jonas nodded. "Cops want names and coordinates. So far, I haven't given them anything."
"Wouldn't be nice to betray your friends," she said coldly.
"They're not my friends. And they turned the whole thing around. They're selling it to everybody now and kill innocent people as well. All they care about is money."
"So ... you think they deserve to be in here more than you do?" she concluded.
"No ... I know I deserve to be in here. But they do too."
"Sounds like a dilemma."
He gave her a meaningful look and his thumb moved lightly over the skin of her hand.
"That's where you come in," he muttered.
"What?"
"We could still go to Italy ... or anywhere else. Or stay here, doesn't matter." His eyes seemed to glow with affection and Alice felt her throat tighten.
"I know a lot has changed, I see it in your eyes," he continued with hurt in his

voice. "But if you ... still want that kiss, I owe you ... or want me in your life as a friend, I'd do it. I'd take the deal."

Speechless, she stared at him, her eyes widened.

He wants me to decide whether or not he deserves freedom ...

"You're making this a bit easy for you, don't you think?" The words were supposed to come out hard and cold, but her voice was higher than usual. He noticed, of course.

"I could help you ... I want you to be happy," he said quietly.

"Last thing I remember is you telling me that you're not good for me. That I only fell for you because I was weak and ... *impressionable*. That I'm better off without you."

His lips twitched and once again, he seemed to have troubles finding the right words. "I may have changed my mind ..."

"Why?"

He sighed. "Because I wasn't there the last five months and you don't look so happy now."

Unbelievable.

"And you think you'd make me happy?"

He squeezed her hand softly. "I could at least try ... Please let me take you away from here, away from this town and its memories. Let's go to Italy or let me at least get you there. I'll still stay away if you don't want me there with you."

Alice opened her mouth to say something, but her tongue felt paralyzed, and she closed it again. The wall was crumbling, she could feel it, and it scared the hell out of her.

"I'm not saying I'd be good for you," he continued. "But I *was* able to make you smile once, remember? Just let me try to ... be there for you."

It almost sounded like a plea when he said it, and he looked at her nervously. He had once been cold and hard and unmovable like a rock, she remembered. He'd been *her* rock. But now, he looked desperate.

Alice swallowed heavily, trying to free her constricted throat, and tried to pull her hand back, but he was still holding it firmly, not letting it go. Not letting *her* go.

Just like when his fingers had locked around her wrists on the day of the move ... Like when he had lifted her up over his shoulder and carried her back to the house through the rain ... like when he had pinned her down on the grass after she'd climbed over the wall. Like when he had brought her back to Danny, each and every time she'd managed to get out. She could still feel his grip, could still feel his weight on her legs.

He always told me what to do, she realized, and for the second time that day, she tasted bile on her tongue. She stared at his hands, bound together with handcuffs. They were large hands, warm and heavy. They could be gentle, she knew that, but then again, Danny's hands had been gentle once too. Until they had grabbed her jaw and pushed her face into the pillow. Until they had closed into a fist and hit her bloody ... more than once. Until they had wandered underneath her clothes and undressed her against her will.

The memories made her shiver and the fence that surrounded the yard seemed to grow taller. Her hand twitched in his and when he saw the fear in her eyes, his expression got worried.

Taking a deep breath, she reminded herself that there was only one wall in her life now, and it was the one she had built herself. The one that was protecting her, rather than keeping her locked up. She would not let it crumble, not even a bit.

"Take the deal or leave it," she said coldly, pleased that her voice was not shaking. "I won't decide about your freedom. I'm not like *you*."

She saw him tense and knew that he dreaded her answer.

"However," she continued. "I'll decide about mine. My answer is no."

He looked as if she had rammed a knife into his chest. The pain was so plainly visible on his face that it made him look like someone else. His poker face had vanished completely.

"I can't just forget all the things you did." Her voice was a bit softer now, but he winced, nonetheless. "Everything that happened ..." She swallowed, her mouth suddenly dry again.

She had seen tears in his eyes before – several times already – but now was the first time she saw them run down his cheeks. The amount of self-loathing in his eyes took her breath away, but it didn't matter. He deserved to hate himself.

Forcing herself to remain hard, she pulled her hand out of his grip, this time with force, but his hands had already gone limp and did not hold her back.

His big green eyes looked glazed, as if he had gone to some place inside his mind. Just like she always had when Danny had touched her.

"Alice ..." His voice sounded torn ... begging.

"I doubt I'll ever want to be with a man again ... But if I do, it won't be a guy like you."

He cringed, and she knew her words were salt in his wounds.

Jonas's eyes followed her every movement when she pushed herself up from the bench, but it didn't look as if he had anything left to say.

Before turning her back to him, she gave him one last look and said, "I'm sorry."

His voice was almost inaudible when he replied.

"Don't apologize."

ABOUT THE AUTHOR

Dominique Simona Binggeli, born 1994 in Bern, Switzerland, has always been passionate about writing. She wrote her first book, an illustrated story about a princess, at six years old.

In 2016, she left everything behind to travel around the world. She started writing Tower Over Me when volunteering on an organic farm in Botswana. Five months and eight countries later, she finished the story in a guesthouse in the Himalayan mountains.

A first version of Tower Over Me was published in 2018. The book has since been rewritten.

Next to writing novels, Dominique works for the biggest union in Switzerland and is politically active for women's rights and animal rights.